101
SCIENCE
FICTION
STORIES

ABOUT THE EDITORS

MARTIN H. GREENBERG, who has been called "the king of the anthologists," now has some 140 to his credit. Greenberg is professor of regional analysis and political science at the University of Wisconsin–Green Bay, where he teaches a course in American foreign and defense policy. He is also co-editor, with Charles G. Waugh and others, of *Baker's Dozen: 13 Short Fantasy Novels* and *Baker's Dozen: 13 Short Science Fiction Novels*; and, with Bill Pronzini and others, of *Baker's Dozen: 13 Short Mystery Novels* and *101 Mystery Stories*.

CHARLES G. WAUGH is a leading authority on science fiction and fantasy who has published more than 110 anthologies and single-author collections. He is also the father of Jenny-Lynn Waugh, one of the coeditors of this volume. He lives with his family in Winthrop, Maine.

JENNY-LYNN WAUGH is a seventeen-year-old high school senior who loves attending science fiction conventions, is interested in languages, and is active in community service in her hometown of Winthrop, Maine. This is her first book.

101
SCIENCE
FICTION
STORIES

Edited by Martin H. Greenberg,
Charles G. Waugh
& Jenny-Lynn Waugh

Introduction by Isaac Asimov

AVENEL BOOKS
New York

Compilation Copyright © 1986 by Martin H. Greenberg,
Charles G. Waugh, and Jenny-Lynn Waugh
All rights reserved.

First published 1986 by Avenel Books, distributed by Crown
Publishers, Inc., 225 Park Avenue South, New York,
New York 10003

Printed and bound in the United States of America

Library of Congress Cataloging-in-Publication Data
Main entry under title:

101 science fiction stories.

1. Science Fiction, American.   I. Greenberg,
Martin Harry.   II. Waugh, Charles G.   III. Waugh,
Jenny-Lynn.   IV. Title: One hundred one science
fiction stories.   V. Title: One hundred and one science
fiction stories.
PS648.S3A128   1986   813'.0876'08   85-26954
ISBN 0-517-60669-0

h g f e d c

ACKNOWLEDGMENTS

Slesar—Copyright © 1960 by HMH Publishing Co., Inc. Reprinted by permission of the author.

Norton—Copyright © 1971 by Ben Bova. Reprinted by permission of Larry Sternig.

Silverberg—Copyright © 1957, 1985 by Robert Silverberg. Reprinted by permission of the author.

Temple—Copyright 1955 by Columbia Publications Inc.; copyright reverted to William F. Temple; reprinted by arrangement with his agent, Forrest J. Ackerman, 2495 Glendower Ave., Hollywood, CA 90027.

Tevis—Copyright © 1958 by Galaxy Publishing Corporation. Reprinted by permission of Richard Curtis Associates, Inc.

Sherred—Copyright © 1972 by Harlan Ellison; reprinted by permission of the author and the author's agent, Virginia Kidd.

Garrett—Copyright © 1969 by Universal Publishing and Distributing Corporation. Reprinted by permission of the Scott Meredith Literary Agency, Inc., 845 Third Ave., New York, NY 10022.

Straley—Copyright © 1982 by Mercury Press, Inc. From *The Magazine of Fantasy and Science Fiction*. Reprinted by permission of the author.

Walton—Copyright © 1956 by Galaxy Publishing Corporation. Reprinted by permission of the Scott Meredith Literary Agency, Inc., 845 Third Ave., New York, NY 10022.

Easton—Copyright © 1976 by *Chicago Magazine*. Reprinted by permission of the author.

Anvil—Copyright 1952 by Greenleaf Publishing Co. Reprinted by permission of the Scott Meredith Literary Agency, Inc., 845 Third Ave., New York, NY 10022.

MacDonald—Copyright 1951; renewed © 1979 by John D. MacDonald. Reprinted by permission of the author.

Leiber—Copyright © 1968 by Galaxy Publishing Corporation. Reprinted by permission of Richard Curtis Associates, Inc.

Wellen—Copyright © 1962 by Galaxy Publishing Corporation. Reprinted by permission of the author.

van Vogt—Copyright 1949 by Arkham House; renewed © 1977 by A. E. van Vogt; reprinted by permission of his agent, Forrest J. Ackerman, 2495 Glendower Ave., Hollywood, CA 90027.

CONTENTS

xi

xiii

LEFT OUT

Isaac Asimov

MARTIN GREENBERG, CHARLES WAUGH, AND I have a close relationship. Together we have co-edited some dozens of anthologies, with a strict division of labor. We all three decide on a particular anthology, then Marty charms an editor into doing the anthology and takes care of all the paperwork; Charles collects stories and sends me photocopies; I read them and veto any I don't like, then write introductions and/or head-notes, and take them to the publisher.

This is all done with an intermeshing that is as smooth as frictionless ice and with the utmost of affection and camaraderie—never a cross word. In fact, Marty (who is twenty years younger than I am) tells me frequently that he looks upon me as a surrogate-father, even though his attitude toward me is not that of a loyal and subservient son, but that of an over-whelmingly concerned Jewish mother, as I shall show you in a moment.

There came a time, however, when Marty and Charles between them had worked up an idea for a new anthology. It was to be entirely different from any they had done before.

First, there was the matter of quantity. They planned the biggest anthology yet—one with the most stories. The three of us have in our time put together an anthology containing one hundred stories. Of course, all of them were short-shorts of less than 2,000 words apiece. It was a very good anthology, but it was necessarily limited in scope. What Marty and Charles were planning was one hundred *and one* stories, and they planned also to include stories that were longer than 2,000 words apiece, so that their choices could be made in a less constricted manner. How's that?

Second, just about all the anthologies we have done have been theme-anthologies. There was some tie that held all the stories together. They were all Christmas stories, or they were all in the first person, or they all had titles that ended in a question mark, or—but you see what I mean. In this anthology there was to be no theme whatever. The stories were to have no necessary connection (except, of course, that they would all be science fiction) and would be included only because they were good stories that appealed to the two editors.

And there, in mentioning the editors, is the key word—*two*. As a group of *two*, they obtained an obliging publishing house, collected a vast mass of stories, went through them carefully, selected the hundred and one that were the ones they liked best, and they were through. In all this they had remained *two*.

Where was Isaac Asimov, I would like to know?

When word came to me that the anthology existed and had been prepared, I asked that very question. "Hey, Marty," I said, addressing my surrogate son, "what happened to *me*?"

"Well," said Marty, coming all over the Jewish mother, "I didn't like to bother you. It would have meant looking through three hundred stories and making decisions and deciding which two out of each three to eliminate, and you're so busy with your novels and your essays and your short stories and your other less ambitious anthologies that I simply couldn't allow it."

"Mightn't you have asked me?" I said.

"No," said he, firmly. "If I had, you're so loyal you would have agreed to do it, and I just couldn't allow that. It's for your own good, Isaac."

(For my own good! How often had I heard my own real Jewish mother say that to me. I little thought that, after I ran away from home and left no forwarding address, I would ever hear that phrase again.——Oh, well, never mind. My dear wife, Janet, says it a lot, too. So do all my editors. So do passing strangers.)

Fortunately, not everyone takes the same narrow view as does Martin Greenberg.

When the manuscript was brought in to Naomi Kleinberg of Avenel Books, she eyed it narrowly, riffling through the pages and taking a quick look at the title page. Finally she said, "Where's Isaac?"

Marty explained in full detail, stressing the responsibility he felt for my welfare.

Naomi said, impatiently, "That's all very well, but we've got to have his name somewhere around. Why not get him to write the introduction?"

So Marty called me up. "Hey, Isaac, you remember the anthology that we wouldn't let you work at for your own good?"

"Yes," I said, stiffly. "Are you calling to tell me that you're going to do another one in which I stand with my nose pressed pathetically against the window?"

"No, no," he said. "I just want you to write an introduction to it."

Talk about salt on the wounds!

But—loyal, true-hearted fellow that I am—I said, "You bet, Marty. When do you want it?"

"Right away, Isaac."

"And what do you want me to talk about?"

"Well, discuss the stories and the magazines they come from and their excellence and variety, and how anyone who wants the largest, best anthology of science fiction should buy this one, and how it ought to boost the entire field mountain-high, and add a few words on the skill and experience of the editors, plus anything else you can think of that will sell the book."

I hope you readers all understand that this is exactly what I intended to do—but first, I wanted to explain how come I had been left out as co-editor, and now that I have, I have used up all the room allotted me.

All I can say is: This is a good book. Buy it.

Okay, Marty?

101
SCIENCE
FICTION
STORIES

1

AFTER

Henry Slesar

(Part One: Doctor)

THE EMPLOYMENT ADVISOR exchanged his professional calm for unprofessional exasperation. "There must be something you can do, Doctor," he said, "a man of your educational background. The war hasn't made savages out of all of us. If anything, the desire for teachers has increased a thousand times since A-day."

Dr. Meigham leaned back in the chair and sighed. "You don't understand. I am not a teacher in the ordinary sense; there is no longer a demand for the subject I know best. Yes, people want knowledge; they want to know how to deal with this shattered world they inherited. They want to know how to be masons and technicians and construction men. They want to know how to put the cities together, and make the machines work again, and patch up the radiation burns and the broken bones. They want to know how to make artificial limbs for the bomb victims, how to train the blind to be self-sufficient, the madmen to reason again, the deformed to be presentable once more. These are the things they wish to be taught. You know that better than I."

"And *your* specialty, Doctor? You feel there is no longer a demand?"

Dr. Meigham laughed shortly. "I don't feel, I know. I've tried to interest people in it, but they turn away from me. For twenty-five years, I have trained my students to develop a perfect memory. I have published six books, at least two of which have become standard textbooks at universities. In the first year after the armistice, I advertised an eight-week course and received exactly one inquiry. But this is my profession; this is what I do. How can I translate my life's work into this new world of horror and death?"

The employment advisor chewed his lip; the question was a challenge.

1

By the time Dr. Meigham left, he had found no answer. He watched the bent, shuffling figure leave the room at the end of the interview, and felt despair at his own failure. But that night, rousing suddenly from a familiar nightmare, he lay awake in his shelter and thought of Dr. Meigham again. By morning, he knew the answer.

A month later, a public notice appeared in the government press, and the response was instantaneous.

HUGO MEIGHAM, PH.D.
Announces an Accelerated 8-week Course

"HOW TO FORGET"
Enrollment begins Sept. 9.

2

ALL CATS ARE GRAY

Andre Norton

STEENA OF THE Spaceways—that sounds just like a corny title for one of the Stellar-Vedo spreads. I ought to know, I've tried my hand at writing enough of them. Only this Steena was no glamorous babe. She was as colorless as a lunar planet—even the hair netted down to her skull had a sort of grayish cast, and I never saw her but once draped in anything but a shapeless and baggy gray spaceall.

Steena was strictly background stuff, and that is where she mostly spent her free hours—in the smelly, smoky, background corners of any stellar-port dive frequented by free spacers. If you really looked for her you could spot her—just sitting there listening to the talk—listening and remembering. She didn't open her own mouth often. But when she did, spacers had learned to listen. And the lucky few who heard her rare spoken words—these will never forget Steena.

She drifted from port to port. Being an expert operator on the big calculators, she found jobs wherever she cared to stay for a time. And she came to be something like the masterminded machines she tended—smooth, gray, without much personality of their own.

But it was Steena who told Bub Nelson about the Jovan moon rites—and her warning saved Bub's life about six months later. It was Steena who identified the piece of stone Keene Clark was passing around a table one night, rightly calling it unworked Slitite. That started a rush which made ten fortunes overnight for men who were down to their last jets. And, last of all, she cracked the case of the *Empress of Mars*.

All the boys who had profited by her queer store of knowledge and her photographic memory tried at one time or another to balance the scales. But she wouldn't take so much as a cup of canal water at their expense, let alone

3

the credits they tried to push on her. Bub Nelson was the only one who got around her refusal. It was he who brought her Bat.

About a year after the Jovan affair, he walked into the Free Fall one night and dumped Bat down on her table. Bat looked at Steena and growled. She looked calmly back at him and nodded once. From then on they traveled together—the thin gray woman and the big gray tomcat. Bat learned to know the inside of more stellar bars than even most spacers visit in their lifetimes. He developed a liking for Vernal juice, drank it neat and quick, right out of the glass. And he was always at home on any table where Steena elected to drop him.

This is really the story of Steena, Bat, Cliff Moran, and the *Empress of Mars,* a story which is already a legend of the spaceways. And it's a damn good story, too. I ought to know, having framed the first version of it myself.

For I was there, right on the Rigel Royal, when it all began on the night that Cliff Moran blew in, looking lower than an antman's belly and twice as nasty. He'd had a spell of luck foul enough to twist a man into a slug snake, and we all knew that there was an attachment out for his ship. Cliff had fought his way up from the back courts of Venaport. Lose his ship and he'd slip back there—to rot. He was at the snarling stage that night when he picked out a table for himself and set out to drink away his troubles.

However, just as the first bottle arrived, so did a visitor. Steena came out of her corner, Bat curled around her shoulder stolewise, his favorite mode of travel. She crossed over and dropped him down, without invitation, at Cliff's side. That shook him out of his sulks. Because Steena never chose company when she could be alone. If one of the man-stones on Ganymede had come stumping in, it wouldn't have made more of us look out of the corners of our eyes.

She stretched out one long-fingered hand, set aside the bottle he had ordered, and said only one thing. "It's about time for the *Empress of Mars* to appear."

Cliff scowled and bit his lip. He was tough, tough as jet lining—you have to be granite inside and out to struggle from Venaport to a ship command. But we could guess what was running through his mind at that moment. The *Empress of Mars* was just about the biggest prize a spacer could aim for. But in the fifty years she had been following her queer derelict orbit through space, many men had tried to bring her in—and none had succeeded.

A pleasure ship carrying untold wealth, she had been mysteriously abandoned in space by passengers and crew, none of whom had ever been seen or heard of again. At intervals thereafter she had been sighted, even boarded. Those who ventured into her either vanished or returned swiftly without any believable explanation of what they had seen—wanting only to get away from her as quickly as possible. But the man who could bring her in—or even strip her clean in space—that man would win the jackpot.

"All right!" Cliff slammed his fist on the table. "I'll try even that!"

Steena looked at him, much as she must have looked at Bat that day Bub Nelson brought him to her, and nodded. That was all I saw. The rest of the story came to me in pieces, months later and in another port half the system away.

Cliff took off that night. He was afraid to risk waiting—with a writ out that could pull the ship from under him. And it wasn't until he was in space that he discovered his passengers—Steena and Bat. We'll never know what happened then. I'm betting Steena made no explanation at all. She wouldn't.

It was the first time she had decided to cash in on her own tip and she was there—that was all. Maybe that point weighed with Cliff, maybe he just didn't care. Anyway, the three were together when they sighted the *Empress* riding, her deadlights gleaming, a ghost ship in night space.

She must have been an eerie sight because her other lights were on too, in addition to the red warnings at her nose. She seemed alive, a Flying Dutchman of space. Cliff worked his ship skillfully alongside and had no trouble in snapping magnetic lines to her lock. Some minutes later the three of them passed into her. There was still air in her cabins and corridors, air that bore a faint corrupt taint which set Bat to sniffing greedily and could be picked up even by the less sensitive human nostrils.

Cliff headed straight for the control cabin, but Steena and Bat went prowling. Closed doors were a challenge to both of them and Steena opened each as she passed, taking a quick look at what lay within. The fifth door opened on a room which no woman could leave without further investigation.

I don't know what had been housed there when the *Empress* left port on her last lengthy cruise. Anyone really curious can check back on the old photo-reg cards. But there was a lavish display of silk trailing out of two travel kits on the floor, a dressing table crowded with crystal and jeweled containers, along with other lures for the female which drew Steena in. She was standing in front of the dressing table when she glanced into the mirror—glanced into it and froze.

Over her right shoulder she could see the spider-silk cover on the bed. Right in the middle of that sheer, gossamer expanse was a sparkling heap of gems, the dumped contents of some jewel case. Bat had jumped to the foot of the bed and flattened out as cats will, watching those gems, watching them and—something else!

Steena put out her hand blindly and caught up the nearest bottle. As she unstoppered it, she watched the mirrored bed. A gemmed bracelet rose from the pile, rose in the air and tinkled its siren song. It was as if an idle hand played. . . . Bat spat almost noiselessly. But he did not retreat. Bat had not yet decided his course.

She put down the bottle. Then she did something which perhaps few of the men she had listened to through the years could have done. She moved without hurry or sign of disturbance on a tour about the room. And, although she approached the bed, she did not touch the jewels. She could not force herself to do that. It took her five minutes to play out her innocence and unconcern. Then it was Bat who decided the issue.

He leaped from the bed and escorted something to the door, remaining a careful distance behind. Then he mewed loudly twice. Steena followed him and opened the door wider.

Bat went straight on down the corridor, as intent as a hound on the warmest of scents. Steena strolled behind him, holding her pace to the unhurried gait of an explorer. What sped before them was invisible to her, but Bat was never baffled by it.

They must have gone into the control cabin almost on the heels of the unseen—if the unseen had heels, which there was good reason to doubt—for Bat crouched just within the doorway and refused to move on. Steena looked down the length of the instrument panels and officers' station seats to where Cliff Moran worked. Her boots made no sound on the heavy carpet, and he did not glance up but sat humming through set teeth, as he tested the tardy and reluctant responses to buttons which had not been pushed in years.

To human eyes they were alone in the cabin. But Bat still followed a moving something, which he had at last made up his mind to distrust and dislike. For now he took a step or two forward and spat—his loathing made plain by every raised hair along his spine. And in that same moment Steena saw a flicker—a flicker of vague outline across Cliff's hunched shoulders, as if the invisible one had crossed the space between them.

But why had it been revealed against Cliff and not against the back of one of the seats or against the panels, the walls of the corridor or the cover of the bed where it had reclined and played with its loot? What could Bat see?

The storehouse memory that had served Steena so well through the years clicked open a half-forgotten door. With one swift motion, she tore loose her spaceall and flung the baggy garment across the back of the nearest seat.

6

Bat was snarling now, emitting the throaty rising cry that was his hunting song. But he was edging back, back toward Steena's feet, shrinking from something he could not fight but which he faced defiantly. If he could draw it after him, past that dangling spaceall. . . . He had to—it was their only chance!

"What the . . ." Cliff had come out of his seat and was staring at them.

What he saw must have been weird enough: Steena, barearmed and bareshouldered, her usually stiffly netted hair falling wildly down her back; Steena watching empty space with narrowed eyes and set mouth, calculating a single wild chance. Bat, crouched on his belly, was retreating from thin air step by step and wailing like a demon.

"Toss me your blaster." Steena gave the order calmly—as if they were still at their table in the Rigel Royal.

And as quietly, Cliff obeyed. She caught the small weapon out of the air with a steady hand—caught and leveled it.

"Stay where you are!" she warned. "Back, Bat, bring it back."

With a last throat-splitting screech of rage and hate, Bat twisted to safety between her boots. She pressed with thumb and forefinger, firing at the spaceall. The material turned to powdery flakes of ash—except for certain bits which still flapped from the scorched seat—as if something had protected them from the force of the blast. Bat sprang straight up in the air with a screech that tore their ears.

"What . . . ?" began Cliff again.

Steena made a warning motion with her left hand. *"Wait!"*

She was still tense, still watching Bat. The cat dashed madly around the cabin twice, running crazily with white-ringed eyes and flecks of foam on his muzzle. Then he stopped abruptly in the doorway, stopped and looked back over his shoulder for a long, silent moment. He sniffed delicately.

Steena and Cliff could smell it too now, a thick oily stench which was not the usual odor left by an exploding blaster shell.

Bat came back, treading daintily across the carpet, almost on the tips of his paws. He raised his head as he passed Steena, and then he went confidently beyond to sniff, to sniff and spit twice at the unburned strips of the spaceall. Having thus paid his respects to the late enemy, he sat down calmly and set to washing his fur with deliberation. Steena sighed once and dropped into the navigator's seat.

"Maybe now you'll tell me what in the hell's happened?" Cliff exploded as he took the blaster out of her hand.

"Gray," she said dazedly, "it must have been gray—or I couldn't have seen it like that. I'm color blind, you see. I can see only shades of gray—my

7

whole world is gray. Like Bat's—his world is gray, too—all gray. But he's been compensated, for he can see above and below our range of color vibrations, and apparently so can I!''

He voice quavered, and she raised her chin with a new air Cliff had never seen before—a sort of proud acceptance. She pushed back her wandering hair, but she made no move to imprison it under the heavy net again.

''That is why I saw the thing when it crossed between us. Against your spaceall it was another shade of gray—an outline. So I put out mine and waited for it to show against that—it was our only chance, Cliff.

''It was curious at first, I think, and it knew we couldn't see it—which is why it waited to attack. But when Bat's actions gave it away, it moved. So I waited to see that flicker against the spaceall, and then I let him have it. It's really very simple. . . .''

Cliff laughed a bit shakily. ''But what *was* this gray thing. I don't get it.''

''I think it was what made the *Empress* a derelict. Something out of space, maybe, or from another world somewhere.'' She waved her hands. ''It's invisible because it's a color beyond our range of sight. It must have stayed in here all these years. And it kills—it must—when its curiosity is satisfied.'' Swiftly she described the scene, the scene in the cabin, and the strange behavior of the gem pile which had betrayed the creature to her.

Cliff did not return his blaster to his holder. ''Any more of them aboard, d'you think?'' He didn't look pleased at the prospect.

Steena turned to Bat. He was paying particular attention to the space between two front toes in the process of a complete bath. ''I don't think so. But Bat will tell us if there are. He can see them clearly, I believe.''

But there weren't any more and two weeks later, Cliff, Steena and Bat brought the *Empress* into the lunar quarantine station. And that is the end of Steena's story because, as we have been told, happy marriages need no chronicles. Steena had found someone who knew of her gray world and did not find it too hard to share with her—someone besides Bat. It turned out to be a real love match.

The last time I saw her, she was wrapped in a flame-red cloak from the looms of Rigel and wore a fortune in Jovan rubies blazing on her wrists. Cliff was flipping a three-figured credit bill to the waiter. And Bat had a row of Vernal juice glasses set up before him. Just a little family party out on the town.

3

THE ASSASSIN

Robert Silverberg

THE TIME WAS drawing near, Walter Bigelow thought. Just a few more adjustments, and his great ambition would be fulfilled.

He stepped back from the Time Distorter and studied the complex network of wires and tubes with an expert's practiced eye. *Twenty years,* he thought. Twenty years of working and scrimping, of pouring money into the machine that stood before him on the workbench. Twenty years, to save Abraham Lincoln's life.

And now he was almost ready.

Bigelow had conceived his grand idea when still young, newly out of college. He had stumbled across a volume of history and had read of Abraham Lincoln and his struggle to save the Union.

Bigelow was a tall, spare, raw-boned man standing better than six feet four—and with a shock he discovered that he bore an amazing resemblance to a young portrait of the Great Emancipator. That was when his identification with Lincoln began.

He read every Lincoln biography he could find, steeped himself in log-cabin legends and the texts of the Lincoln-Douglas debates. And, gradually, he became consumed with bitterness because an assassin's hand had struck Lincoln down at the height of his triumph.

"Damned shame, great man like that," he mumbled into his beer one night in a bar.

"What's that?" a sallow man at his left asked. "Someone die?"

"Yes," Bigelow said. "I'm talking about Lincoln. Damned shame."

The other chuckled. "Better get yourself a new newspaper, pal. Lincoln's been dead for a century. Still mourning?"

Bigelow turned, his gaunt face alive with anger. "Yes! Yes—why shouldn't I mourn? A great man like Lincoln—"

9

"Sure, sure," the other said placatingly. "I'll buy that. He was a great president, chum—but he's been dead for a hundred years. One hundred. You can't bring him back to life, you know."

"Maybe I can," Bigelow said suddenly—and the great idea was born.

It took eight years of physics and math before Bigelow had developed a workable time-travel theory. Seven more years passed before the first working model stood complete.

He tested it by stepping within its field, allowing himself to be cast back ten years. A few well-placed bets, and he had enough cash to continue. Ten years was not enough. Lincoln had been assassinated in 1865—Friday, April 14, 1865. Bigelow needed a machine that could move at least one hundred twenty years into the past.

It took time. Five more years.

He reached out, adjusted a capacitator, pinched off an unnecessary length of copper wire. It was ready. After twenty years, he was ready at last.

Bigelow took the morning bus to Washington, D.C. The Time Distorter would not affect space, and it was much more efficient to make the journey from Chicago to Washington in 1979 by monobus in a little over an hour, than in 1865 by mulecart or some other such conveyance, possibly taking a day. Now that he was so close to success, he was too impatient to allow any such delay as that.

The Time Distorter was cradled in a small black box on his lap; he spent the hour of the bus ride listening to its gentle humming and ticking, letting the sound soothe him and ease his nervousness.

There was really no need to be nervous, he thought. Even if he failed in his first attempt at blocking Lincoln's assassination, he had an infinity of time to keep trying again.

He could return to his own time and make the jump again, over and over. There were a hundred different ways he could use to prevent Lincoln from entering the fatal theater on the night of April 14. A sudden phone-call— no, there were no telephones yet. A message of some kind. He could burn down the theater the morning of the play. He could find John Wilkes Booth and kill him before he could make his fateful speech of defiance and fire the fatal bullet. He could—

Well, it didn't matter. He was going to succeed the first time. Lincoln was a man of sense; he wouldn't willingly go to his death having been warned.

A warm glow of pleasure spread over Bigelow as he dreamed of the consequences of his act. Lincoln alive, going on to complete his second term, President until 1869. The weak, ineffectual Andrew Johnson would remain Vice-President, where he belonged. The South would be rebuilt sanely and welcomed back into the Union; there would be no era of carpetbaggers, no series of governmental scandals and no dreary Reconstruction era.

"Washington!"

Moving almost in a dream, Bigelow left the bus and stepped out into the crowded capital streets. It was a warm summer day; soon, he thought, it would be a coolish April evening, back in 1865. . . .

He headed for the poor part of town, away from the fine white buildings and gleaming domes. Huddling in a dark alley on the south side, he undid the fastenings of the box that covered the Time Distorter.

He glanced around, saw that no one was near. Then, swiftly, he depressed the lever.

The world swirled around him, vanished.

Then, suddenly, it took shape again.

He was in an open field now; the morning air was cool but pleasant, and in the distance he could see a few of the buildings that made the nation's capital famous. There was no Lincoln's Memorial, of course, and the bright needle of Washington's Monument did not thrust upward into the sky. But the familiar Capitol dome looked much as it always had, and he could make out the White House further away.

Bigelow refastened the cover of the Distorter and tucked the box under his arm. It clicked quietly, reminding him over and over again of the fact that he was in the year 1865—the morning of the day John Wilkes Booth put a bullet through the brain of Abraham Lincoln.

Time passed slowly for Bigelow. He made his way toward the center of town and spent the day in downtown Washington, hungrily drinking in the gossip. Abe Lincoln's name was on everyone's tongue.

The dread War had ended just five days before with Lee's surrender at Appomattox. Lincoln was in his hour of triumph. It was Friday. The people were still discussing the speech he had made the Tuesday before.

"He said he's going to make an announcement," someone said. "Abe's going to tell the Southerners what kind of program he's going to put into effect for them."

"Wonder what's on his mind?" someone else asked.

"No matter what it is, I'll bet he makes the South like what he says."

He had never delivered that speech, Bigelow thought. And the South had been doomed to a generation of hardship and exploitation by the victorious North that had left unhealing scars.

The day passed. President Lincoln was to attend the Ford Theater that night, to see a production of a play called "Our American Cousin."

Bigelow knew what the history books said. Lincoln had had an apprehensive dream the night before: he was sailing on a ship of a peculiar build, being borne on it with great speed toward a dark and undefined shore. Like Caesar on the Ides of March, he had been warned—and like Caesar, he would go unheeding to his death.

But Bigelow would see that that never happened.

History recorded that Lincoln attended the performance, that he seemed to be enjoying the play. And that shortly after ten that evening, a wild-eyed man would enter Lincoln's box, fire once, and leap to the stage, shouting, "Sic semper tyrannis!"

The man would be the crazed actor John Wilkes Booth. He would snag a spur in the drapery as he dropped to the stage, and would break his leg—but nevertheless he would vanish into the wings, make his way through the theater he knew so well, mount a horse waiting at the stage door. Some days later he would be dead.

As for President Lincoln, he would slump forward in his box. The audience would be too stunned to move for a moment—but there was nothing that could be done. Lincoln would die the next morning without recovering conciousness.

"Now he belongs to the ages," Secretary of State Stanton would say.

No! Bigelow thought. It would not happen. It would not happen. . . .

Evening approached. Bigelow, crouching in an alley across the street from the theater, watched the carriages arriving for the performance that night. Feeling oddly out of place in his twentieth-century clothing, he watched the finely-dressed ladies and gentlemen descending from their coaches. Everyone in Washington knew the President would be at the theater that night, and they were determined to look their best.

Bigelow waited. Finally, a handsome carriage appeared, and several others made way for it. He tensed, knowing who was within.

A woman of regal bearing descended first—Mary Todd Lincoln, the President's wife. And then Lincoln appeared.

For some reason, the President paused at the street-corner and looked around. His eyes came to rest on the dark alley where Bigelow crouched invisibly, and Bigelow stared at the face he knew almost as well as his own:

the graying beard, the tired, old, wrinkled face, the weary eyes of Abe Lincoln.

Then he rose and began to run.

"Mr. President! Mr. President!"

He realized he must have been an outlandish figure, dashing across the street in his strange costume with the Time Distorter clutched under one arm. He drew close to Lincoln.

"Sir, don't go to the theater tonight! If you do—"

A hand suddenly wrapped itself around his mouth. President Lincoln smiled pityingly and turned away, walking on down the street toward the theater. Other hands seized Bigelow, dragged him away. Blue-clad arms. Union soldiers. The President's bodyguard.

"You don't understand!" Bigelow yelled. He bit at the hand that held him, and got a fierce kick in return. "Let go of me! Let go!"

There were four of them, earnest-looking as they went about their duties. They held Bigelow, pummelled him angrily. One of them reached down for the Distorter.

In terror Bigelow saw that his attempt to save Lincoln had been a complete failure, that he would have to return to his own time and try all over again. He attmepted to switch on the Distorter, but before he could open the cover rough hands had pulled it from him.

"Give me that!" He fought frantically, but they held him. One of the men in blue uniforms took the Distorter, looked at it curiously, finally held it up to his ear.

His eyes widened. "It's ticking! It's a bomb!"

"No!" Bigelow shouted, and then watched in utter horror as the soldier, holding the Distorter at arm's length, ran across the street and hurled the supposed bomb as far up the alley as he could possibly throw it.

There was no explosion—only the sound of delicate machinery shattering.

Bigelow watched numbly as the four men seized his arms again.

"Throw a bomb, will you? Come on fellow—we'll show you what happens to guys who want to assassinate President Lincoln!"

Further down the street, the gaunt figure of Abe Lincoln was just entering the theater. No one gave Bigelow a chance to explain.

4

BETTER THAN WE KNOW

William F. Temple

IT WAS ONE of those bitter rows, of which we'd had too many lately. Probably the old basic frustration was still the cause, but this time it was well disguised. A woman had come between us: Lola Castros, California adventuress.

"A rag doll!" scoffed Joanna. "Lola Montez with acute anemia. Amber between beds; sugar without spice; not wicked—only naughty. Will you never understand women?"

I had lived with Lola Castros for many months. She was real to me. I'd even given her the hot, black Spanish eyes which now mocked me.

"Will you never understand good literature?" I stormed back. "I—" But the rest of it jammed in my throat through sheer rage. I'd put my best into that novel; it was a kind of offering to her. And she'd trampled on it.

"Go on," she taunted. "Tell me the rest. I'm ignorant. I'm a cruel Spanish she-dog. Listen—if you'd put me in your book, instead of that gutted fish, you'd have a *real* bi—"

I slapped her. "Stop that sort of talk!"

Then we were both very still staring at each other. I had never hit her before; probably no one had hit her before. Her eyes were still defiant, but tears were gathering in them.

Then the phone trilled beside us.

I picked up the handset automatically. My passion was spent; I wanted to say I was sorry. Instead, I said, gruffly: "Brewster speaking."

"Hello, Bill. Tom here."

It was Tom Blood, my agent, phoning from 'Frisco.

"Don't tell me you've sold Lola already," I said.

"Lola?" echoed the tiny voice in metallic surprise. "Oh, you mean your new novel; haven't had time to read the thing yet."

15

So now Lola was a "thing." "Then why the devil are you ringing me?" I said, coldly enough to freeze his ear.

"Usen't you to be connected with the Rocket Society, way back?"

"Way back, yes; why hold my childhood against me?"

"What's eating you today, Bill? Ain't the weather right? Look, have you kept up with this space travel stuff?"

"Astronautics? I read the papers. I used to edit the Society Bulletin; I still know most of the people in the game. So?"

"The kids can't get enough space-travel dope these days. Rudledge just rang me. They want a 60,000 word book, non-fiction, covering the field in simple language for teenagers. But it must be authentic—the kids know their onions. I thought of you. Like to try?"

"Ten years ago I'd have jumped at it, Tom, but I'm a big boy now. They can fly to the Moon, Jupiter, where the hell they like, so long as they leave me my patch of good old Mother Earth, Shakespeare, Dostoevsky, Dreiser, and wine—the worthwhile things."

"Money's worthwhile, Bill. Rudledge offered thirty thousand advance; they plan a big edition. Marchiori's been signed to illustrate. But if you're not sold on space travel any more—"

"I'm not. But wait." I thought for a bit. Then: "Let me talk it over with Joanna; I'll ring you back."

"Good. But make it today."

"Well?" said Joanna, distantly. Her eyes were dry again.

I told her what Blood had said, and asked: "What do you think?"

"Do the book."

"Look, Joanna, we left the big city because we couldn't take the phonies any more. I came here to write books I believed in; now you and Blood want me to be just another phoney."

She regarded me steadily. "You've already decided to do the book because we need the money. Why put on an act? We're no different from the Greenwich Village crowd. We have our principles; we also have our price."

"It's not quite like that. There are another hundred and three installments to pay on this place, and I've got to have someplace to work."

"All right, then—you've talked yourself into it."

I hesitated, and knew that even my hesitation was a show. I grabbed at the phone angrily. After I'd told Blood I would do the book, I walked miserably out of the 'dobe cottage. The mist over the Sierras was thickening; the wheat stirred a little. A long freighter came crawling down the line towards Calzada, smearing the sky with black smoke.

And I'd come right out here to find peace of soul!

I felt pretty much of a flop on all counts.

Presently, an arm stole about my waist from behind. My first impulse was to reject it. But there were special reasons why Joanna could be spiteful. I had to make allowances for her moods—and mine. My hand closed gently on her arm.

"Sorry, darling," she whispered.

"It's okay, girl . . . I think it's going to rain."

Later, I collated material for the space book. Wryly, I quoted some of my old ingenuous editorials. "Listen to this, Joanna. *Men will step from planet to planet, and at last fly out into the great sea of interstellar space. . . .* ' Boy, could I mix a good metaphor in those days!"

"The kids will love it."

"Sure. How about this? *The research goes on. The secrets of space travel are falling one by one into Man's hands. . . .* ' Oh, youthful optimist! The truth is, we're stymied; with the best of chemical fuels it'd take a four-step rocket near as big as the Empire State to land a two-bit ship on Mars. Or, using orbital technique, the number of ferry rockets needed would drain Fort Knox. As for an atomic rocket, the problem of heat transference is insoluble; a uranium reactor is only going to melt itself, trying to heat the propellant to the degree required."

"Just what they told Chris Columbus, and the Wright Brothers, and—"

"False analogies, my clever girl," I said, but laughed. Then, seriously: "Never mind the technical blind alleys. Let's put first things first. Let's conquer ourselves before we try to conquer space. The proper study of mankind is Man. That's my real work; that's what I believe in. I'm betraying my own philosophy to spread this junk."

Joanna sighed. "Okay, Faust, get on with it, sell your soul—and then let's forget it."

I got on with it. I wrote it in four weeks. I began with Lucian's fictional trip to the Moon, and finished way out in extra-galactic space, among the fictions of the astronomers.

I remember that as I was trying to convey some idea of the size of the universe, so Palomar wobbled in its faith in the Cepheid method of measuring extra-galactic distances, and kept doubling up on its estimates. I strove to keep abreast of them—it was like Alice having to run twice as hard as she could to remain in the same place—with a series of footnotes which became progressively more ironical about the "expanding universe."

But that was the only time the tongue in my cheek really showed.

I wrote about orbital techniques and space-stations, meteor hazard and lunar bases, the whole claptrap of it, as though they were matters as vital as birth, marriage, and death. I disinterred the now petrified enthusiasm of my youth, painted its wan cheeks red, and paraded it as though it were still living and breathing.

Never was I more sanguine than in the chapter headed "Become a Spaceman—Now!" Gravely, I pointed out that a spaceman wouldn't be a sort of cosmic cowboy, wearing a space-helmet instead of a sombrero, but an individual with brain and self-control. And he'd never be through studying. Mathematics, three-dimensional navigation, rocket engineering, atomic physics, astronomy—he'd have to have more than a grounding in them all. It was up to the younger generation; space travel was just around the corner. Now was the time.

I finished that chapter on a note of earnest admonition: *"You can't start learning too young—remember, a spaceman is soon too old."*

Rudledge liked it, anyhow. They even agreed to take "Lola Castros" if I'd prune 20,000 words from it. The space travel book sold like hot cakes; the emasculated "Lola Castros" sank without a ripple.

I refused to do any more space travel books. I'd made enough out of that one to pay off the mortgage and add another fifty acres of good wheatland to my holding. But the bad taste in my mouth would never quite die away.

I tried to cleanse myself with renewed sincere attempts at the Great American Novel. In the next ten years, I rode into the literary tilt-yard nine times. I was unhorsed without fail at each event, but sometimes the critics applauded the fight I'd put up. I still felt the novelist's craft was the highest possible calling; I regretted none of these efforts to help man understand himself. What worthier cause was there?

Yet, I remember leaning forlornly against the gatepost in the evening of my forty-fifth birthday, smoking a pipe, and trying to make an assessment of my life as it passed its prime.

It ran something like this: Loving wife, one. House, one. Acres, sixty. Employees, four. Self-betrayals, one. Broken bones, fifteen. Laurel crowns, none.

Were the scale-pans level? I thought not. As I strove to gauge their juxtaposition, I noticed a cloud of dust rising far along the road and approaching steadily. It took my attention. Strangers were events in these parts, and I could already see that it wasn't a car belonging to the district.

It slowed as it approached, and it became apparent that it contained only the driver—a man. He stopped the car level with me and leaned out. He was a young fellow, thin-cheeked and tired-looking. "Is Mr. William Brewster's house along this way?"

"This is it. I'm Brewster."

"Oh." He looked at me oddly for a moment. Then he asked diffidently: "I wonder if you could spare me a few minutes?"

I was in the rare mood to be glad to see anyone, even a salesman. It was my birthday, and I hadn't had a visitor. "Sure. Driven far?"

"From 'Frisco. Your publishers, Rudledge, told me you lived at Calzada."

"Good Lord, I'll bet you can use a drink; come right in."

"Thanks, Mr. Brewster."

When he got out, I saw he was a little chap, and thin all over; but he looked wiry.

"My name's Mappin," he offered, accompanying me to the door. It didn't mean a thing.

There were surprises awaiting both of us inside. I'd been lounging around outdoors for nearly an hour, and Joanna had packed a lot into that time. The table was laid with unusual delicacies and our best china. In the center of it stood an iced birthday cake with nine red dwarf candles burning on it in a ring (four of them larger than the others), flanked by two tall bottles of Asti Spumante. I'd anticipated none of these things.

The other surprise was nicest of all. Joanna came smiling down the old staircase wearing the beautiful dress which her great-grandmother had brought from Castille at the time of the Missions, a masterly fusion of silk and black and white lace.

Her jet-black hair was drawn up and graced by a pair of shining Spanish combs and a vivid poppy.

She was three years younger than I, but in the candlelight she seemed to undercut me by another dozen.

Mappin was obviously impressed by her appearance, and that pleased me too. I'd always been proud of Joanna.

They shook hands, and asked each other how they did, and Mappin said: "I'm not really from 'Frisco—it just so happened I landed there."

"From sea?" I asked, and he nodded.

I opened one of the bottles—the cork hit the rafters. I poured three glasses that hissed and bubbled.

"If you don't mind," said Mappin, awkwardly, "I'd rather have coffee."

I was hurt. "But this is a celebration," I protested.

19

Again he looked at me oddly, and I wondered if he were holding something back. "Of course, Mr. Brewster—I'm sorry," he said. "The fact is, I've never touched alcohol before—liquor is bad in my line. But you're right: this is a celebration. I'll be glad to drink to your health."

"Thanks." We touched glasses and drank, and I looked at the candles and asked whether I was supposed to be nine or ninety. Joanna laughed, and turned to Mappin. "Just what is your line, Mr. Mappin?"

"I'm a pilot."

"Then your abstinence is understandable, even commendable—but not usual," I said.

"Air or sea?" Joanna probed.

"Neither, Mrs. Brewster," said Mappin, and looked away from her bafflement towards my bookshelves. "Pardon me," he said, and began to scan them. All booklovers act that way. They seek common ground with their host by approaching him through his book-titles. So I watched him indulgently, and liked him the more when he concentrated on the shelf of my own works. But he turned with a look of disappointment.

"I don't see your space travel book here, Mr. Brewster. I was hoping you had a spare copy, as it's out of print."

"It's out of print because it's out of date," I said. "I believe I've a couple of old copies upstairs somewhere, but it's not a book I'm proud to show."

He looked astonished. "Why not?"

"I've written better," I said, evasively. "Surely that's not all you've come to see me about?"

"More or less, Mr. Brewster. You see, I've lost my copy—the one I've had since I was a kid. It went down with my ship, to the bottom of the Pacific. There are sentimental reasons why I'd like to replace it."

"Well, that can be attended to easily enough." I went upstairs to the study and rummaged in the closet. I was mistaken; I had but one copy left. The dust was gray on it, and the wrapper torn. When I opened it, I saw the pages were becoming tinged with yellow. It smelt slightly musty.

If Mappin felt sentimental about it, I didn't. He could have my last copy. The bottom of the Pacific seemed an admirable place for the book. It was rot to begin with, and now it was becoming rotten tangibly. But I cleaned it up before I took it down and gave it to him. His eyes quite lit up at the sight of it. He looked at the opening pages, then shut the book gently.

He stood there holding it as carefully as though it were a First Folio of Shakespeare, and then said shyly: "I wonder if you would mind inscribing it to me, Mr. Brewster?"

20

"Not at all." I took it, and got my pen out. "Er—what's your first name, Mr. Mappin?"

"N-Ned." He stammered like a small embarrassed schoolboy. Covertly, Joanna caught my eye, and grinned. Silently, she managed to convey the caption: *"Famous author pictured with a young admirer."*

On the title-page I wrote *"For Ned Mappin, this relic,"* and signed it.

"How old are you, Ned?" I asked, giving it back to him.

"Twenty-three."

I nodded, absently. It was a pity. He was likeable, but I was beginning to weary of him. Like all authors, I soak up intelligent adulation whenever it's offered—rarely enough in my case. But this sort of doggy approach from the mentally retarded was not at all flattrering. "Does your girl friend read that sort of stuff?" I asked.

"I haven't got a girl friend; I hadn't the time. . . . "

"You musn't neglect your education, Ned. Have you read *Lola Castros*?"

He shook his head. I pulled the copy from the shelf and gave it to him. "You can begin learning all about women from that," I said.

Joanna frowned her disapproval but said nothing.

"Thank you. I've always wanted to read novels, but, you know—" He broke off.

"No time?"

"No time." He went on, awkwardly: "How much do I owe you, sir?"

"Oh, forget it; have another drink."

"No, thanks. Look, Mr. Brewster, I feel I ought to make you some sort of return." He fumbled in his jacket pocket and laid something on the table. In the dim candle glow, it looked to be just a small shapeless lump, like a piece of coal. I picked it up. It was a jagged piece of porous but quite heavy stone, dark gray in color.

"What is it, exactly" I asked.

"It's a piece of Martian rock."

"*What* rock?"

"Martian rock. I brought a few pieces back from Mars. Sort of souvenirs. Had a lot more specimens, but they were in the ship. It's nothing to look at, but I thought you might like a bit for a paperweight."

I held the stone in my hand and looked helplessly, and possibly foolishly, at Joanna. But she gave me no aid; she stood and enjoyed it. It was a long time since we'd last encountered the lunatic fringe, and that was back in Greenwich Village.

"Well, thanks, Ned," I said, at last. "I'll treasure it; when did you get back?"

"Yesterday. I sure muffed the landing. I'm scared to go back and face 'em at HQ. When the launch brought me in, I ducked and ran. Just anywhere at first, and then I thought of you—I'd heard you lived down this way. I rang your publishers for the address. I've wanted to meet you ever since I was thirteen. If it hadn't been for you, I'd never have been the first man to reach Mars. So I hired a car and came out; I'm glad I did."

"I'm glad you did, too," I said, falsely. "But what did I have to do with it?"

"Your book. I saved up to buy it when it first came out. I learnt it by heart. And I took your advice. Do you remember the chapter called 'Become a Spaceman—Now!'? You pointed out that there was so much for a spaceman to learn, that he'd better start in young. So I started in. I was studying right to the day I took off. They picked me because I knew the most. Well, perhaps, too, because I was light and wirey—the best build for a spaceman, as you said."

I didn't know what to say to that. Joanna put in quietly: "So that's why you had no time for anything else?"

"Yes, I guess so, Mrs. Brewster."

She stared at him for some seconds. Then she said: "Well, don't start wasting it now. I've just remembered, Bill—I promised to lend that copy of *Lola* to Margaret. Sorry, Ned."

I was going to say, "Who's Margaret?" but realized in time I wasn't supposed to.

Mappin gave *Lola Castros* back without any show of reluctance, but he held tightly to the other book. He tapped it, and smiled ruefully at me. "Wish I'd remembered another piece of your advice: that bit about keeping a cool head in all circumstances. When I was gliding down here to the water, I got so excited over getting back safe, I clean forgot to close the watertight covers to the vents. The ship should have floated, of course; as it was, the empty propellant tanks got waterlogged, and she sank—gradually enough for me to scramble out with a lifebelt, but nothing else. But the launch knew where I was, roughly—they'd been waiting around, and tracked the ship down with radar. I was only an hour in the water."

"You know, I haven't seen any story in the papers about a Mars trip," I said, putting a slightly malicious emphasis on the word "story."

"There will be tomorrow, I guess," said Mappin. "It's sure to get around tonight—if they lift the security blanket. I suppose they will, now that the thing's in the bag. But I expect you can guess why they didn't want to risk making a public flop of it.''

"Oh sure. But I still don't get it. So far as I know, no country has yet put a space-station up. Did you do the trip in one hop?''

"Yes. It was an atomic ship, you see; the propellant was liquid hydrogen.''

"Is it a state secret how the hydrogen was heated by the reactor?''

"It's the closest kept secret of all time,'' said Mappin, solemnly. "But I can trust you, Mr. Brewster, because I *know* you through this book. It only became possible through the discovery of a new principle in atomic physics. There are such things as 'Sympathetic molecules' which, in an electrical field, can be made to transmit their current state of—''

"Please, Ned, some other time,'' Joanna cut in firmly.

"Yes, of course, Mrs. Brewster—I guess I'm keeping you from your little party. It's sure some mouthful to explain, anyhow, and I don't understand all of it myself. I'll be getting along back now.''

"Do your folks know where you are?'' asked Joanna.

"Haven't any folks—not now. Reckon there's no getting away from it—I've got to go and face up to reporting how I lost my ship, or the police will be trailing me out here soon. It was nice to meet you, Mrs. Brewster, and you, sir.''

"I'll see you out, Ned,'' I said; "sure you won't have something to eat first?''

"No, thanks—I'm still too excited to eat.''

I went with him out to the car. He paused with one hand on the doorhandle and looked around. The full harvest moon was rising, and adding its own gilding to the wheat. There was a faint golden glow coming from the cottage window too. Joanna, in her splendid attire, was going round the room gravely with a taper lighting the candles in the tall brass sticks, which themselves shone with reflected light. The rows of bright-covered books and the daintily spread table added to the cheerful cosiness.

Mappin looked so long and silently at it all that I felt constrained to say something, however pointless, to break the spell.

"It should be a bumper harvest. We grind our own grain and bake our own bread; I'm sure looking forward to some nice new bread.''

Mappin was not a handsome fellow. He had a long nose, and at the moment he looked like a wistful weasel.

"Is this your land?'' he asked.

"Sixty acres of it.''

He sighed. "I envy you, Mr. Brewster. A happy marriage, a home, land. . . . Roots. You create fine books. You grow your own food. You have everything."

"Not quite everything," I said, quietly, but he didn't hear me, and went on: "It's a pity everyone can't grow their own food, but there isn't much land. There are two billion people in the world today, and they're increasing at the rate of a million every two weeks. But you saw that problem coming—you mentioned it in your book. You said we'd have to move out to the planets if only to find more land to feed the surplus population. Well—we've made a start."

He climbed into the car and reversed it. "Goodnight, Mr. Brewster. Thanks for the book—and happy birthday!"

"Goodnight, Ned."

He drove off slowly, as if he were savoring the beauty of the late evening. I went back into the house thoughtfully.

Joanna was waiting for me. "What did you make of him?" she asked.

"A nut; but a nice nut; not quite so dumb as he appears."

She laughed, and switched on the radio. Then she kissed me lightly on the cheek and said: "That's an absolutely perfect self-description."

"Oh, phooey. You half believed him, didn't you?"

"No," said Joanna, soberly. "I wholly believed him. Not at first; but when I'd looked right into him, I realized that young fellow's done exactly what he said he did."

"And you really—" I began, and was drowned out by a voice from the radio as it warmed up. It was announcing the nine o'clock news. Then it went straight on to tell us dramatically that it was a day of glory for the United States. . . .

Afterwards, I found myself gazing down at the silly little candles on the still uncut cake, blurred of mind and of sight.

Slowly, I stirred myself to fill two of the glasses with Spumante. The remaining empty glass, which Ned had used, was a silent reminder. " A celebration!" I muttered. "Good Lord—if only I'd known! My dear—"

We raised our glasses to him, and drank.

"He did it all alone, too," I said, presently. "A one-man ship. The guts of him!" A thought occurred to me. "Why, he must have taken my stupid book with him all the way to Mars and back!"

"No one can claim their books had a more far-reaching effect than yours," Joanna goaded gently.

"Gosh, I feel like a heel when I think how I thrust that pallied pornography on him—thanks for saving me there."

I reached for the fragment of Martian rock, and examined it fondly.

Joanna sat gazing into the shallow bowl of her champagne glass. "He was only twenty-three," she murmured. "He could have been our son."

I looked at her sharply—just as sharply as the stab of that old pain of self-reproach went through me. But she had not deliberately tried to hurt me; she was lost in her dreams.

I stuffed the stone into my pocket, got up abruptly, and wandered past the bookshelves. These were my children, the only kind, it seemed, I could produce. And they were all stillborn.

Except one—which wasn't there, which I might never see again.

I moved to the window and stood looking moodily out at the great golden moon, fingering the piece of rock which was in my pocket.

And I looked at the ghostly plain of wheat. Bread. But the bread I had cast upon the waters, which had returned to me after so many days, seemed more important now. For what credit could I take for nourishing this good land which nourished us? I had not fought for it. If action had been left to people of my sort, the Indians would still be hunting here.

Yet people of my sort had their uses. Maybe they didn't always originate the ideas; maybe they didn't always believe in them. But they kept them alive by circulation, until at last the seeds took root.

"Joanna," I said, "what was that line in Well's 'Anatomy of Frustration' you read out to me one day last week—something about a pattern?"

I had to repeat my question.

"We make a pattern better than we know. Keep on with it,'" said Joanna, quietly.

"Better than we know—that's right," I said.

5

THE BIG BOUNCE

Walter S. Tevis

LET ME SHOW you something,'' Farnsworth said. He set his near-empty drink—a Bacardi martini—on the mantel and waddled out of the room toward the basement.

I sat in my big leather chair, feeling very peaceful with the world, watching the fire. Whatever Farnsworth would have to show tonight would be far more entertaining than watching TV—my custom on other evenings. Farnsworth, with his four labs in the house and his very tricky mind, never failed to provide my best night of the week.

When he returned, after a moment, he had with him a small box, about three inches square. He held this carefully in one hand and stood by the fireplace dramatically—or as dramatically as a very small, very fat man with pink cheeks can stand by a fireplace of the sort that seems to demand a big man with tweeds, pipe, and, perhaps, a saber wound.

Anyway, he held the box dramatically and he said, ''Last week, I was playing around in the chem lab, trying to make a new kind of rubber eraser. Did quite well with the other drafting equipment, you know, especially the dimensional curve and the photosensitive ink. Well, I approached the job by trying for a material that would absorb graphite without abrading paper.''

I was a little disappointed with this; it sounded pretty tame. But I said, ''How did it come out?''

He screwed his pudgy face up thoughtfully. ''Synthesized the material, all right, and it seems to work, but the interesting thing is that it has a certain—ah—secondary property that would make it quite awkward to use. Interesting property, though. Unique, I am inclined to believe.''

This began to sound more like it. ''And what property is that?'' I poured myself a shot of straight rum from the bottle sitting on the table beside me. I did not like straight rum, but I preferred it to Farnsworth's rather imaginative cocktails.

"I'll show you, John," he said. He opened the box and I could see that it was packed with some kind of batting. He fished in this and withdrew a gray ball about the size of a golfball and set the box on the mantel.

"And that's the—eraser?" I asked.

"Yes," he said. Then he squatted down, held the ball about a half-inch from the floor, dropped it.

It bounced, naturally enough. Then he squatted down, held the ball about a half-inch from the floor, dropped it.

It bounced, naturally enough. Then it bounced again. And again. Only this was not natural, for on the second bounce the ball went higher in the air than on the first, and on the third bounce higher still. After a half minute, my eyes were bugging out and the little ball was bouncing four feet in the air and going higher each time.

I grabbed my glass. "What the hell!" I said.

Farnsworth caught the ball in a pudgy hand and held it. He was smiling a little sheepishly. "Interesting effect, isn't it?"

"Now wait a minute," I said, beginning to think about it. "What's the gimmick? What kind of motor do you have in that thing?"

His eyes were wide and a little hurt. "No gimmick, John. None at all. Just a very peculiar molecular structure."

"Structure!" I said. "Bouncing balls just don't pick up energy out of nowhere, I don't care how their molecules are put together. And you don't get energy out without putting energy in."

"Oh," he said, "that's the really interesting thing. Of course you're right; energy *does* go into the ball. Here, I'll show you."

He let the ball drop again and it began bouncing, higher and higher, until it was hitting the ceiling. Farnsworth reached out to catch it, but he fumbled and the thing glanced off his hand, hit the mantelpiece and zipped across the room. It banged into the far wall, ricocheted, banked off three other walls, picking up speed all the time.

When it whizzed by me like a rifle bullet, I began to get worried, but it hit against one of the heavy draperies by the window and this damped its motion enough so that it fell to the floor.

It started bouncing again immediately, but Farnsworth scrambled across the room and grabbed it. He was perspiring a little and he began instantly to transfer the ball from one hand to another and back again as if it were hot.

"Here," he said, and handed it to me.

I almost dropped it.

"It's like a ball of ice!" I said. "Have you been keeping it in the refrigerator? No. As a matter of fact, it was at room temperature a few minutes ago."

"Now wait a minute," I said. "I only teach physics in high school, but I know better than that. Moving around in warm air doesn't make anything cold except by evaporation."

"Well, there's your input and output, John," he said. "The ball lost heat and took on motion. Simple conversion."

My jaw must have dropped to my waist. "Do you mean that that little thing is converting heat to kinetic energy?"

"Apparently."

"But that's impossible!"

He was beginning to smile thoughtfully. The ball was not as cold now as it had been and I was holding it in my lap.

"A steam engine does it," he said, "and a steam turbine. Of course, they're not very efficient."

"They work mechanically, too, and only because water expands when it turns to steam."

"This seems to do it differently," he said, sipping thoughtfully at his dark-brown martini. "I don't know exactly how—maybe something piezo-electric about the way its molecules slide about. I ran some tests—measured its impact energy in foot pounds and compared that with the heat loss in BTUs. Seemed to be about 98 per cent efficient, as close as I could tell. Apparently it converts heat into bounce very well. Interesting, isn't it?"

"Interesting?" I almost came flying out of my chair. My mind was beginning to spin like crazy. "If you're not pulling my leg with this thing, Farnsworth, you've got something by the tail there that's just a little bit bigger than the discovery of fire."

He blushed modestly. "I'd rather thought that myself," he admitted.

"Good Lord, look at the heat that's available!" I said, getting really excited now.

Farnsworth was still smiling, very pleased with himself. "I suppose you could put this thing in a box, with convection fins, and let it bounce around inside—"

"I'm way ahead of you," I said. "But that wouldn't work. All your kinetic energy would go right back to heat, on impact—and eventually that little ball would build up enough speed to blast its way through any box you could build."

"Then how would you work it?"

"Well," I said, choking down the rest of my rum, "you'd seal the ball in

29

a big steel cylinder, attach the cylinder to a crankshaft and flywheel, give the thing a shake to start the ball bouncing back and forth, and let it run like a gasoline engine or something. It would get all the heat it needed from the air in a normal room. Mount the apparatus in your house and it would pump your water, operate a generator and keep you cool at the same time!''

I sat down again, shakily, and began pouring myself another drink.

Farnsworth had taken the ball from me and was carefully putting it back in its padded box. He was visibly showing excitement, too; I could see that his cheeks were ruddier and his eyes even brighter than normal. ''But what if you want the cooling and don't have any work to be done?''

''Simple,'' I said. ''You just let the machine turn a flywheel or lift weights and drop them, or something lke that, outside your house. You have an air intake inside. And if, in the winter, you don't want to lose heat, you just mount the thing in an outside building, attach it to your generator and use the power to do whatever you want—heat your house, say. There's plenty of heat in the outside air even in December.''

''John,'' said Farnsworth, ''you are very ingenious. It might work.''

''Of course it'll work.'' Pictures were beginning to light up in my head. ''And don't you realize that this is the answer to the solar power problem? Why, mirrors and selenium are, at best, ten per cent efficient! Think of big pumping stations on the Sahara! All that heat, all that need for power, for irrigation!'' I paused a moment for effect. ''Farnsworth, this can change the very shape of the Earth!''

Farnsworth seemed to be lost in thought. Finally he looked at me strangely and said, ''Perhaps we had better try to build a model.''

I was so excited by the thing that I couldn't sleep that night. I kept dreaming of power stations, ocean liners, even automobiles, being operated by balls bouncing back and forth in cylinders.

I even worked out a spaceship in my mind, a bullet-shaped affair with a huge rubber ball on its end, gyroscopes to keep it oriented properly, the ball serving as solution to that biggest of missile-engineering problems, excess heat. You'd build a huge concrete launching field, supported all the way down to bedrock, hop in the ship and start bouncing. Of course it would be kind of a rough ride. . . .

In the morning, I called my superintendent and told him to get a substitute for the rest of the week; I was going to be busy.

Then I started working in the machine shop in Farnsworth's basement, trying to turn out a working model of a device that, by means of a crankshaft, oleo dampers and a reciprocating cylinder, would pick up some of that random kinetic energy from the bouncing ball and do something useful with it, like turning a drive shaft. I was just working out a convection-and-air pump system for circulating hot air around the ball when Farnsworth came in.

He had tucked carefully under his arm a sphere of about the size of a basketball and, if he had made it to my specifications, weighing thirty-five pounds. He had a worried frown on his forehead.

"It looks good," I said. "What's the trouble?"

"There seems to be a slight hitch," he said. "I've been testing for conductivity. It seems to be quite low."

"That's what I'm working on now. It's just a mechanical problem of pumping enough warm air back to the ball. We can do it with no more than a twenty per cent efficiency loss. In an engine, that's nothing."

"Maybe you're right. But this material conducts heat even less than rubber does."

"The little ball yesterday didn't seem to have any trouble," I said.

"Naturally not. It had had plenty of time to warm up before I started it. And its mass-surface area relationship was pretty low—the larger you make a sphere, of course, the more mass inside in proportion to the outside area."

"You're right, but I think we can whip it. We may have to honeycomb the ball and have part of the work the machine does operate a big hot air pump; but we can work it out."

All that day, I worked with lathe, milling machine and hacksaw. After clamping the new big ball securely to a workbench, Farnsworth pitched in to help me. But we weren't able to finish by nightfall and Farnsworth turned his spare bedroom over to me for the night. I was too tired to go home.

And too tired to sleep soundly, too. Farnsworth lived on the edge of San Francisco, by a big truck by-pass, and almost all night I wrestled with the pillow and sheets, listening half-consciously to those heavy trucks rambling by, and in my mind, always, that little gray ball, bouncing and bouncing and bouncing. . . .

At daybreak, I came abruptly fully awake with the sound of crashing echoing in my ears, a battering sound that seemed to come from the basement. I grabbed my coat and pants, rushed out of the room, almost knocked over Farnsworth, who was struggling to get his shoes on out in the hall, and we scrambled down the two flights of stairs together.

The place was a chaos, battered and bashed equipment everywhere, and on the floor, overturned against the far wall, the table that the ball had been clamped to. The ball itself was gone.

I had not been fully asleep all night, and the sight of that mess, and what it meant, jolted me immediately awake. Something, probably a heavy truck, had started a tiny oscillation in that ball. And the ball had been heavy enough to start the table bouncing with it until, by dancing that table around the room, it had literally torn the clamp off and shaken itself free. What had happened afterward was obvious, with the ball building up velocity with every successive bounce.

But where was the ball now?

Suddenly Farnsworth cried out hoarsely, "Look!" and I followed his outstretched, pudgy finger to where, at one side of the basement, a window had been broken open—a small window, but plenty big enough for something the size of a basketball to crash through it.

There was a little weak light coming from outdoors. And then I saw the ball. It was in Farnsworth's back yard, bouncing a little sluggishly on the grass. The grass would damp it, hold it back, until we could get to it. Unless. . . .

I took off up the basement steps like a streak. Just beyond the back yard, I had caught a glimpse of something that frightened me. A few yards from where I had seen the ball was the edge of the big six-lane highway, a broad ribbon of smooth, hard concrete.

I got through the house to the back porch, rushed out and was in the back yard just in time to see the ball take its first bounce onto the concrete. I watched it, fascinated, when it hit—after the soft, energy absorbing turf, the concrete was like a springboard. Immediately the ball flew high in the air. I was running across the yard toward it, praying under my breath, *Fall on that grass next time*.

It hit before I got to it, and right on the concrete again, and this time I saw it go straight up at least fifty feet.

My mind was suddenly full of thoughts of dragging mattresses from the house, or making a net or something to stop that hurtling thirty-five pounds; but I stood where I was, unable to move, and saw it come down again on the highway. It went up a hundred feet. And down again on the concrete, about fifteen feet further down the road. In the direction of the city.

That time it was two hundred feet, and when it hit again, it made a thud that you could have heard for a quarter of a mile. I could practically see it flatten out on the road before it took off upward again, at twice the speed it had hit at.

Suddenly generating an idea, I whirled and ran back to Farnsworth's house. He was standing in the yard now, shivering from the morning air, looking at me like a little lost and badly scared child.

"Where are you car keys?" I almost shouted at him.

"In my pocket."

"Come on!"

I took him by the arm and half dragged him to the carport. I got the keys from him, started the car, and by mangling about seven traffic laws and three prize rosebushes, managed to get on the highway, facing in the direction that the ball was heading.

"Look," I said, trying to drive down the road and search for the ball at the same time. "It's risky, but if I can get the car under it and we can hop out in time, it should crash through the roof. That ought to slow it down enough for us to nab it."

"But—what about my car?" Farnsworth bleated.

"What about that first building—or first person—it hits in San Francisco?"

"Oh," he said. "Hadn't thought of that."

I slowed the car and stuck my head out the window. It was lighter now, but no sign of the ball. "If it happens to get to town—any town, for that matter—it'll be falling from about ten or twenty miles. Or forty."

"Maybe it'll go high enough first so that it'll burn. Like a meteor."

"No chance," I said. "Built-in cooling system, remember?"

Farnsworth formed his mouth into an "oh" and exactly at that moment there was a resounding *thump* and I saw the ball hit in a field, maybe twenty yards from the edge of the road, and take off again. This time it didn't seem to double its velocity, and I figured the ground was soft enough to hold it back—but it wasn't slowing down either, not with a bounce factor of better than two to one.

Without watching for it to go up, I drove as quickly as I could off the road and over—carrying part of wire fence with me—to where it had hit. There was no mistaking it; there was a depression about three feet deep, like a small crater.

I jumped out of the car and stared up. It took me a few seconds to spot it, over my head. One side caught by the pale and slanting morning sunlight, it was only a bright diminishing speck.

The car motor was running and I waited until the ball disappeared for a moment and then reappeared. I watched for another couple of seconds until I felt I could make a decent guess on its direction, hollered at Farnsworth to get out of the car—it had just occurred to me that there was no use risking his life, too—dove in and drove a hundred yards or so to the spot I had anticipated.

I stuck my head out the window and up. The ball was the size of an egg now. I adjusted the car's position, jumped out and ran for my life.

It hit instantly after—about sixty feet from the car. And at the same time, it occurred to me that what I was trying to do was completely impossible. Better to hope that the ball hit a pond, or bounced out to sea, or landed in a sand dune. All we could do would be to follow, and if it ever was damped down enough, grab it.

It had hit soft ground and didn't double its height that time, but it had still gone higher. It was out of sight for almost a lifelong minute.

And then—incredibly rotten luck—it came down, with an ear-shattering thwack, on the concrete highway again. I had seen it hit, and instantly afterward saw a crack as wide as a finger open along the entire width of the road. And the ball had flown back up like a rocket.

My God, I was thinking, *now it means business. And on the next bounce*. . . .

It seemed like an incredibly long time that we craned our necks, Farnsworth and I, watching for it to reappear in the sky. And when it finally did, we could hardly follow it. It whistled like a bomb and we saw the gray streak come plummeting to Earth almost a quarter of a mile away from where we were standing.

But we didn't see it go back up again.

For a moment, we stared at each other silently. Then Farnsworth almost whispered, "Perhaps it's landed in a pond."

"Or in the world's biggest cowpile," I said. "Come on!"

We could have met our deaths by rock salt and buckshot that night, if the farmer who owned that field had been home. We tore up everything we came to getting across it—including cabbages and rhubarb. But we had to search for ten minutes, and even then we didn't find the ball.

What we found was a hole in the ground that could have been a small-scale meteor crater. It was a good twenty feet deep. But at the bottom, no ball.

I stared wildly at it for a full minute before I focused my eyes enough to see, at the bottom, a thousand little gray fragments.

And immediately it came to both of us at the same time. A poor conductor, the ball had used up all its available heat on that final impact. Like a golfball that has been dipped in liquid air and dropped, it had smashed into thin splinters.

The hole had sloping sides and I scrambled down in it and picked up one of the pieces, using my handkerchief, folded—there was no telling just how cold it would be.

It was the stuff, all right. And colder than an icicle.

I climbed out. "Let's go home," I said.

Farnsworth looked at me thoughtfully. Then he sort of cocked his head to one side and asked, "What do you suppose will happen when those pieces thaw?"

I stared at him. I began to think of a thousand tiny slivers whizzing around erratically, ricocheting off buildings, in downtown San Francisco and in twenty counties, and no matter what they hit, moving and accelerating as long as there was any heat in the air to give them energy.

And then I saw a tool shed, on the other side of the pasture from us.

But Farnsworth was ahead of me waddling along, puffing. He got the shovels out and handed one to me.

We didn't say a word, neither of us, for hours. It takes a long time to fill a hole twenty feet deep—especially when you're shoveling very, very carefully and packing down the dirt very, very hard.

6

BOUNTY

T. L. Sherred

IN MAY, THE first week there was one death. The second, there were four, the third, nineteen. The fourth week, 39 people were killed.

Most were shot by pistol, rifle, or shotgun. Four were killed with knives, two by meat cleavers, and one by a dinner fork worked methodically through the spinal cord. It was not the dinner fork that aroused comment but the evident fact that someone had finished his or her meal with its duplicate.

The Mayor said, "This has got to stop."

The Governor said, "This has got to stop."

The President, through his Secretary for Health and Welfare, said somewhat the same thing.

The Police Commissioner and Prosecuting Attorney said there would be no stone left unturned and the FBI said, regretfully, that it was a local matter.

No one ever was quite sure who was on or who was behind the Committee but the advertisement—one issue, double-page spread—had been authentic, had paid off in hard cash; within the city limits, ten thousand dollars cash for the death of anyone caught in the process of armed robbery and one hundred thousand to the estate of anyone killed while attempting to halt armed robbery.

Such an advertisement was not in the public interest and every bristling aspect of the law said so. The suburban booster sheet that had originally printed the ad promised not to do it again.

But this kept on and over the weeks and a few square miles—cities are crowded in their sprawl—over two million dollars had been paid without quibble and sometimes at night secretly, because Internal Revenue considers no income tainted. Things became complex when three policemen in varying parts of the city incautiously let their off-duty holstered guns be

37

spotted by strangers or by fellow customers in a store. Too rapidly for the innocent police to identify themselves, a swirl of action, and three men were dead—all painlessly. Further executions were eliminated by the flaunting of police badges in public, with consequent reduction of vice squad arrests.

By July, pedestrians after dark carried large flashlights and in business districts made no abrupt movements. Vigilante groups at first hired doddering men and women to hobble decoy in certain areas; later, as techniques became perfected, heavily armed and suicidal senior citizens acted as independent Q-ships and frail-looking women waited endlessly at bus stops or lugged expensive-looking packages back and forth across parking lots. Behind grocery store partitions and dry cleaner's curtains sat or lazed volunteer part-time, full-time, and nighttime guards.

By September four hundred plus had been killed. Court dockets were clogged with scheduled homicide trials while the incidence of armed and unarmed robberies slid almost to zero. Police are forbidden to accept rewards but cabin cruisers, summer cottages, snomobiles and trips to Hawaii can be bought and paid for by midnight cash. No one dared to resist arrest.

Then the reward system was extended outstate where rates of crime had been increasing. The 11 by 14 advertising was traced to a small shop on Center Street, but the owner had moved to Winnipeg. The first to die— four men, two of them brothers—tried to hold up an outstate bank. Their dress oxfords clashed with their hunting costumes and the bank manager, one teller, and two customers were waiting.

Armed and unarmed robbers died out together with some three hundred probably-guilty persons but the Governor at last appealed for federal aid, pleading his entire legal system was breaking down. Officials of the three bordering states and Canada on the north were equally interested in his pleas. Nothing was accomplished at a series of top level conferences.

In sudden succession the three bordering states had their own operating Committees, apparently unconnected with the first. The other cities some miles away and then other states. A reliable estimate of reward money earned and paid out ran to half a billion dollars before the object was attained, as the reward system spread totally east and totally west of the Mississippi.

In New York City proper, children began to be seen playing in Central Park at dusk and even after.

With all rumors dissected, with duplicate reports discounted, and counting the death-welcoming onslaughts of unarmed applicants for free hundred-thousand-dollar survivor benefits, over the next three years the casualty list was somewhat less than automotive deaths in 1934. The fourth year there was a presidential election.

The winning candidate ran on a Law and Order platform. Two Secret Service men on inauguration day, while mingling with the gay crowd, incautiously let their .44 Magnums be seen and were dismembered quite quickly. After the first session of Congress a Federal ban on portable weapons was passed. This included weapons carried by law enforcement officers. Scotland Yard loaned fourteen quarterstaff specialists to the FBI police school and some seventeen thousand homicide cases were nolle prossed.

Montessori kindergartens expanded curricula to include judo and karate and General Motors phased out its Soapbox Derby and awarded black belts to the most worthy. *Popular Science & Mechanix Illustrated* ran a series on car-spring crossbows. Deer became an everyday sight and somewhat of a nuisance in the streets of Saginaw and Sebewaing.

At present the House Un-American Activities Committee is investigating the sky-rocketing import of Japanese chemical sets for adults.

7

THE BRIEFING

Randall Garrett

SORRY TO PULL you in on a rush job like this,'' Marik said, ''but something unexpected came up.''

''Yeah.'' I took a healthy slug of the drink in my hand and then looked back at him. ''It always does. An operation that goes clean all the way through is an operation where the goof-ups happened to cancel out.''

Behind and beyond Marik, through the big slab of transite armor set in the wall of the Station, I could see the bright, hard stars in their unfamiliar constellation. Marik frowned a little, then said: ''You know the ggQ machines can only predict general trends—not individual movements.''

''I know. Go ahead.'' I hadn't come across nearly three thousand light-years of space to listen to an elementary lecture on ggQ predictors, but the Development Officer of a Planetary Expansion Team sometimes has a tendency to get a little nervy because of the weight on his shoulders, so I decided to let him do the talking without too much interruption. I could ask questions later.

He took a deep breath. ''Very well. Here's the setup.'' He touched a control. A section of the wall vanished and a globe coalesced into being. ''Standard planet, standard sun—pretty average, all around. Four major land masses, a fifth smaller one, and plenty of islands and archipelagoes. Dominant race human, spread all over the globe. Level Five society is dominant, but not world-wide, of course. Present civilized power concentrations are usual technology for Level Five—nothing that can spot us out here in space.'' He snapped a control, and the globe vanished, the wall became solid. He waved a hand, as if to say, ''So much for that.''

He was perfectly right; I'd get all the details, if I needed them, from the high-speed hypnotapes. Right now, all I needed was the broad general

41

picture, so that the data fed to me under hypnosis would have a framework to fit itself into.

"It's almost a straight impersonation job," Marik said, "with a kicker I'll tell you about in a minute. Here's your subject."

He handed me a good set of portrait shots. Not a bad looking face, what you could see of it. Dark skin, big beak of a nose, and dark, intelligent eyes.

"What's with the beard?" I asked.

"The-er-somewhat peculiar subculture to which he belongs use long hair and beards as identifying marks. The ruling class are usually smooth shaven and wear the hair cropped closely to the head."

I nodded. "Right. Well, biosculp can fix me up with the face all right. No trouble there." I dropped the pics on his desk. "Tell me more about the problem."

Marik leaned back and looked at the ceiling overhead. "The ggQ machines indicate quite clearly that the society of this planet is rapidly approaching a two-valued variable nexus. The breakdown of the entire society is inevitable—that's natural with Level Five, of course. The 'empires' they build are inherently unstable. Result: chaos. Breakdown of communication, loss of knowledge, collapse of the educational processes, political anarchy—the usual sort of thing."

He looked back down at me and held up a pair of fingers. "But this particular chaos can go only one of two ways. And one will last nearly twenty times as long as the other. And that will be too late."

I knew what he meant. We have a deadline. The Invaders were still a vast distance from us in time and space, but we knew when they were due to arrival. And at that time, every human-occupied planet in the Galaxy must be ready for maximum effort.

"All right," I said, "now tie in our hairy-faced friend, here."

"He's a young man who has built up the nucleus of an organization which, if allowed to develop, will decrease the time required to return to Level Five by a factor of twenty. According to the ggQ predictions, the organization will fall to Level Four along with the rest of the society—and you know what kind of bloody tyranny that can mean. But it's time we need, not goodness."

"Right. Now, what's the kicker?"

Marik looked grim. "The reactionaries in the governmental power structure have the subconscious knowledge that the structure is headed for collapse, so they've been looking for 'subversives.' "

"As usual," I said with a sigh. "And they found him?"

He nodded. "Right. Minor harrassment at first. We thought we could protect him, but the government agents acted too fast for us. He's dead.''

"So I go in and impersonate him. We pretend that the death was a hoax.''

"Not exactly. Psychology Department has another gimmick rigged up, and you'll have to take a full hypnoimpressment of his personality so you can bring the thing off successfully. But the first thing to do is use the high-speed hypnotapes to teach you Aramaic.''

"Aramaic?''

"Yes. That's the language they use in Judea.''

8

CAPSULE

Rosalind Straley

BYRON STARES INTO the bathroom mirror and wonders if his nose will ever be the same again. Only two days into the allergy season and he has reached crisis. "You know I don't like to take medicine," he tells the puffy-faced man in the mirror. "I'm a naturalist. Pure mind. Pure body."

"Right," the puffy-faced man says, "but don't blame *me* when they carry you away and hook you up to the tubes like last time, dummy."

"Yeah," Byron says wearily, "yeah." He sighs and opens the medicine chest, takes out the fresh bottle of capsules and struggles with it. No one ever died from hay fever, he thinks. On the other hand that is a qualified blessing.

He struggles with the difficult top, grunts, opens it convulsively. Tiny time-release beads spew from the vial, scamper over the porcelain and a few split open.

Out of one of them a tiny orange creature, perfectly formed, emerges. Byron can see it well; allergy has left him, if nothing else, clarity of vision. The orange creature is a tenth of an inch high with beautiful hands and piercing, expressive eyes.

"Greetings, earth person," the creature says in a thin but clear voice. "We come in peace—"

Byron shakes his head and shudders. Inside the sink another creature, green this time, emerges from a time-release bead. "I *told* you so," it says furiously in a slightly deeper voice, "you orange-headed fool, you wanted an inanimate object, something inconspicuous; I hope you're satisfied: Look at us. We have no dignity. What will the report say?"

"Shut up," the orange creature says, "I'm a *supervisor*, you green zyxul. I'm following procedure."

"That's easy for you to say," the green creature says and begins to argue

45

floridly in another language. The orange supervisor argues back. Byron feels faint. He props himself against the sink, dreading its contents. How many aliens are in there?

The thought is horrifying. Byron sneezes convulsively.

Beads rattle and the arguing creatures are blown away as if by an explosion.

Byron takes some tissue and wipes his nose mournfully. Guilt struggles with relief. After a while, relief wins.

"After all," he says, "it *was* my first Contac."

9

THE CHASM

Bryce Walton

THE OLD MAN'S face was turning gray with fatigue under the wrinkled brow. He was beginning to get that deadly catching pain in his left chest. But he forced himself to move again, his ragged dusty uniform of the old Home Guard blending into the rubble the way a lizard merges with sand.

He hobbled behind a pile of masonry and peered through the crack. He angled his bald head, listening. His hands never really stopped quivering these days and the automatic rifle barrel made a fluttering crackle on the concrete. He lowered the barrel, then wiped his face with a bandanna.

He'd thought he heard a creeping rustle over there. But he didn't see any sign of the Children.

He'd been picked to reconnoiter because his eyes were only comparatively good. The truth was he couldn't see too well, especially when the sun reflecting on the flat naked angles of the ruined town made his eyes smart and water and now his head was beginning to throb.

A dust devil danced away whirling a funnel of dust. Sal Lemmon looked at it, and then he slid from behind the rubble and moved along down the shattered block, keeping to the wall of jagged holes and broken walls that had once been the Main Street of a town.

He remembered with a wry expression on his face that he had passed his ninety-fourth birthday eight days back. He had never thought he could be concerned with whether he lived to see his ninety-fifth, because there had always been the feeling that by the time he was ninety-four he would have made his peace with himself and with whatever was outside.

He moved warily, like a dusty rabbit, in and out of the ruins, shrinking through the sun's dead noon glare.

He stopped, and crouched in the shade behind a pile of slag that had once

47

been the iron statue of some important historical figure. He contacted Captain Murphy on the walkie-talkie.

"Don't see any signs of Children."

"Max said he saw some around there," Murphy yelled.

"Max's getting too old. Guess he's seeing things."

"He saw them right around there somewhere."

"Haven't seen him either."

"We haven't heard another word from Max here, Sal."

The old man shrugged. "How could the Children have gotten through our post defenses?" He looked away down the white glare of the street.

"You're supposed to be finding out," Murphy yelled. He had a good voice for a man two months short of being a hundred. He liked to show it off.

Then Sal thought he saw an odd fluttery movement down the block.

"I'll report in a few minutes," he said, and then he edged along next to the angled wall. A disturbed stream of plaster whispered down and ran off his shoulder.

Near the corner, he stopped. "Max," he said. He whispered it several times. "Max . . . that you, Max?"

He moved nearer to the blob on the concrete. Heat waves radiated up around it and it seemed to quiver and dance. He dropped the walkie-talkie. There wasn't even enough left of Max to take back in or put under the ground.

He heard the metallic clank and the manhole cover moved and then he saw them coming up over the edge. He ran and behind him he could hear their screams and cries and their feet striking hard over the blisters, cracks, and dried out holes in the dead town's skin.

He dodged into rubble and fell and got up and kept on running. The pain was like something squeezing in his belly, and he kept on running because he wanted to live and because he had to tell the others that the Children were indeed inside the post defenses.

He knew now how they had come in. Through the sewers, under the defenses. He began to feel and hear them crawling, digging, moving all over beneath the ruins, waiting to come out in a filthy screaming stream.

Sal was still resting in the corner of the old warehouse by the river. A lantern hung on a beam and the dank floor was covered with deep moving shadows.

Captain Murphy was pacing in a circle, looking like something sewn quickly together by a nervous seamstress. Doctor Cartley sat on a canvas chair, elbows on knees, chin in his hands. He kept looking at the floor. He was in his early eighties and sometimes seemed like a young man to Sal. His ideas maybe. He thought differently about the Children and where things were going.

"We're going to get out tonight," Captain Murphy said again. "We'll get that barge loaded and we'll get out."

Sal sat up. The pills had made his heart settle down a bit, and his hands were comparatively calm.

"Is the barge almost loaded now? It better be," Sal said. "They'll attack any minute now. I know that much."

"Another hour's all we need. If they attack before then we can hold them off long enough to get that barge into the river. Once we get into the river with it, we'll be safe. We can float her down and into the sea. Somewhere along the coast we'll land and wherever it is will be fine for us. We'll have licked the Children. They know we've found the only eatable food stores in God knows how many thousands of miles in this goddamned wasteland. They can't live another month without this stuff, and we're taking it all down the river. That's right isn't it, Doc?"

Cartley looked up. "But as I said before, squeezing a little more life out of ourselves doesn't mean anything to me. What do we want to get away and live a little longer for? It doesn't make sense, except in a ridiculous selfish way. So we live another month, maybe six months, or a year longer? What for?"

Sal glanced at Murphy who finally sat down.

"We want to live," Murphy said thickly, and he gripped his hands together. "Survival. It's a natural law."

"What about the survival of the species?" Cartley asked. "By running out and taking the food, we're killing ourselves anyway. So I don't think I'll be with you, Murphy."

"What are you going to do? Stay here? They'll torture you to death. They'll do to you what they did to Donaldson, and all the others they've caught. You want to stay for that kind of treatment?"

"We ought to try. Running off, taking all this food, that means they're sure to die inside a few weeks. They might catch a few rats or birds, but there aren't even enough of those around to sustain life beyond a few days. So we kill the future just so we can go on living for a little longer. We've got no reason to live when we know the race will die. My wife refused to fight them. They killed her, that's true, but I still think she was right. We've got to make one more attempt to establish some kind of truce with the Children.

49

If we had that, then we might be able to start building up some kind of relationship. The only way they can survive, even if they had food, is to absorb our knowledge. You know that. Without our knowledge and experience, they'll die anyway, even if they had a thousand years of food supplies.''

''It can't be done,'' Murphy said.

Cartley looked at the shadows for a long time. Finally he shook his head. ''I don't have any idea how to do it. But we should try. We can't use discipline and power because we're too weak. And too outnumbered. We'd have to do that first in order to teach them, and we can't. So there has to be some other way.''

''Faith?'' Sal said. He shook his head. ''They don't believe in anything. You can't make any appeal to them through faith, or ethics, any kind of code of honor, nothing like that. They're worse than animals.''

Cartley stood up wearily and started to walk away. ''They hate us,'' he said. ''That's the one thing we're sure of. We're the means and they're the ends. We made them what they are. They're brutalized and motivated almost completely by hatred. And what's underneath hatred?'' He turned back twoard Murphy. ''Fear.''

Sal stood up. ''I never thought of them as being afraid,'' he said.

''That doesn't matter,'' Murphy said. ''It's the hate and vicious brutality we have to deal with. You do whatever you want to do, Cartley. We've voted, and we've voted to move the stuff out tonight on the barge. The world we helped make is dead, Cartley. The Children grew up in a world we killed. We've all got bad consciences, but we can't do anything about it. The chasm between them and us is too wide. It was wide even before the bombs fell. And the bombs made it a hell of a lot wider. Too wide to put any kind of bridge across now.''

''Just the same, we ought to die trying,'' Cartley said. When he went outside, Sal followed him.

The barge was about loaded. All outer defense units had been pulled in and were concentrated on the head of the pier behind walls of sandbags. Burp guns and machine guns were ready, and the barge lay along the side of the pier in the moonlight like a dead whale. There were several sewer openings near the head of the pier. Men were stationed around these sewers with automatic rifles, hand grenades and flame throwers.

Sal walked to where Cartley stood leaning against the partly closed door of the rotting warehouse. Jagged splinters of steel and wood angled out against the sky.

After a while, Sal said softly, "Well, what could we try to do, Doc?"

Cartley turned quickly. Some of the anguish in his eyes had gone away, and he gripped Sal's shoulders in hands surprisingly strong for so old a man. "You want to help me try?"

"Guess I do. Like you said, we only have a little time left anyway. And if we can't help the Children, what's the good of it?"

They stood there in the shadows a while, not saying anything.

"This way," Cartley said. He led Sal down away from the pier and along the water's edge. Dry reed rustled, and mud squished under their shoes.

"Here," Cartley said. There was a small flat-bottomed rowboat, and in it were several cartons of food supplies, all in cans. There were also several large tins of water.

"We'll need a little time," Cartley said. "We'll have to wait. I figure we'll row upstream maybe a few hundred yards, and hole up in one of those caves. We can watch, Sal. We can watch and wait and try to figure it out."

"Sure," Sal said. "That seems the only way to start."

Cartley sat down on the bank near the boat, and Sal sat down too.

"The Children," Cartley said, "never had a chance to be any other way. But we're the oldsters, and we've got this obligation, Sal. Man's a cultural animal. He isn't born with any inherent concepts of right, or wrong, or good or bad, or even an ability to survive on an animal level. We have to be taught to survive by the elders, Sal. And we're the elders." He hesitated, "We're the only ones left."

A flare of horrid light exploded over the warehouse down river and it lit up Cartley's face and turned it a shimmering crimson. His hands widened to perfect roundness and he raised his hands in a voiceless scream to stop the sudden explosions of burp guns, grenades, machine guns, and rifles.

Looking down river then, Sal could see the flames eating up through the warehouse. The pier, the barge, everything for a hundred square yards was lit up as bright as day and the flare spread out over the river and made a black ominous shadow on the opposite bank.

"They're getting away," Cartley said.

Sal watched the barge move out. The Children came screaming out of the blazing warehouse, overran the pier, streamed into the water. But a steady blast of fire from the barge drove them back, and in a few more minutes the barge dissolved downriver into darkness.

Cartley's hands were shaking as he gripped Sal's arm. "Let's go now. We need time. Time may help us a lot, Sal. We can wait and watch. We can figure something out."

51

Sal heard the screams and mocking savage cries coming up over the water, and then the jagged cries of some oldsters who hadn't managed to get away.

Still looking downstream toward the blazing pier, Sal pushed Cartley into the rowboat, and they shoved off. Sal started rowing, but he kept looking back.

"They should have put them in the same shelters with us," Sal said, "That would have made a difference. But they put us in separate shelters."

Only the oldest and the youngest had been saved. The old out of pity and because they were helpless, had been granted the safety of shelters. The young because they were the symbols of hope had been granted shelters, too.

"No," Cartley said. "It started long before that. The chasm was building up long before the war. This alienation between the young and the old. Between the sun and the seed. That's what we've got to bring back, Sal. Between us, we have stored up a hundred and seventy-nine years of human culture. There isn't a kid back there, Sal, more than twelve years old."

"We'll find a way," Sal said.

The rowboat was about fifteen feet away from the thick reeds growing in the marshy ooze of the bank.

Cartley heard the sound first and turned, his face white. When Sal looked toward the bank, he saw the girl. She came on out from the curtain of reeds and looked at them. She was perfectly clear in the moonlight standing there. She wore a short ragged print dress and she had long hair that seemed silken and soft and golden in the moonlight even though it, her dress, her little legs and her face were streaked with mud.

Sal hesitated, then pulled heavily on his left oar and the boat nosed toward her. Up close, Sal could see her face, the clear blue eyes wet, and the tears running down her cheeks.

The girl reached out and asked in a sobbing breath.

"Granpa? Is that you, Granpa?"

"Oh God, Oh God," Cartley said. He was crying as he picked her up and got her into the boat. He was rocking her in his arms and half crying and half laughing as Sal rowed the boat upstream

"Yes, yes, honey," Sal heard Cartley say over and over. "I'm your granpa, honey. Don't cry. Go to sleep now. I'm your granpa and I've been looking for you, honey, and now everything's going to be all right."

It's funny, Sal thought, as he kept on rowing upstream. It's a funny thing how one little girl remembered her granpa, and how maybe that was the beginning of the bridge across the chasm.

10

THE CHICAGO PLAN TO SAVE A SPECIES

Thomas Easton

ALTHOUGH THE EXISTENCE of a large animal, thought to be prehistoric in its origins, has long been suspected in Scotland's Loch Ness, actual observations have only recently been made. [1] In 1972, a team of scientists obtained an underwater photograph of the creature's side, showing a diamond-shaped fin. In 1975, improved photographic equipment obtained a photograph of the entire animal at a distance of about 25 feet; another was made of its head. Both photographs confirmed earlier descriptions. As a result, the photographers, Dr. Robert Rines of the Academy of Applied Science in Boston and naturalist Sir Peter Scott, among others, gave the animal its scientific name, *Nessiteras rhombopteryx,* Latin for "the diamond-finned marvel of Loch Ness." [2]

The biggest expedition so far to uncover more information about the creature may soon be launched under the leadership of Dr. Roy Mackal of the University of Chicago. An effort will be made to obtain better photographs. Sonar will search the bottom of the Loch for bones or bodies, and the sides of the Loch for caves in which *N. rhombopteryx* might live. A harpoon-like device may be used to collect a tissue sample for analysis.

But, with confirmation of the existence of *N. rhombopteryx* has come rising concern about its survival as a species. Dr. Mackal, author of *The Monsters of Loch Ness* [3] and a director of the Loch Ness Investigation

---

[1] Loch Ness is only about 24 miles long and a mile or so wide, but it is more than 900 feet deep in spots and more than 700 feet deep over much of its length. The water is a cold 42°F, and its murkiness obscures vision.

[2] Skeptical journalists have turned the name into an anagram for "Monster hoax by Sir Peter S." Dr. Rines has answered with another: "Yes, both pix and monsters. R."

[3] Swallow Press, Chicago, 1976.

Bureau, has estimated that the Loch can contain only 150 to 200 of the creatures. [4] Human beings are relative newcomers to the home of *N. rhombopteryx*, and the small colony is now threatened by the steady encroachment of civilization upon its natural habitat. An unforeseen catastrophe, either natural or human-made, could cause this ancient species, perhaps one of the few remaining links with the prehistoric past, to become extinct.

Lake Michigan is not so deep as Loch Ness, but its surface area is 933 times as great. Our fisheries biologists say that Michigan may hold some 25,000 tons of trout and salmon as well as other species of fish such as alewives, an aggregate more than half again as large as the 680,000 tons of young salmon thought to be in Loch Ness. If, as Dr. Mackal surmises, the main food of *N. rhombopteryx* is fish, then Lake Michigan might support a second colony of *N. rhombopteryx* consisting of as many as 315 individuals—or one and a half times as many as might live in Loch Ness. If Lake Michigan were stocked with just three breeding pairs, such a population might be obtained within 25 years. [5]

Yet a plan to save *N. rhombopteryx*, by breeding them in Lake Michigan, when put forward on a trial basis earlier this year, was received with caution by government officials and special interest groups. [6] Among these groups is the British government which resists the plan for reasons of national pride. "I'm sure there will be letters of protest to the *Times*," said Aidan MacDermott, information officer for the British consulate in Chicago. "It's a sort of national pet. We might be willing to lend it to you, though, rather like the Magna Carta."

Locally, much of the controversy has centered on the effect that an *N. rhombopteryx* stocking program might have on the salmon and trout in Lake Michigan—where thanks to an extensive restocking effort, both recrea-

---

[4]   Dr. Mackal estimated the number of young salmon in the Loch at 19 billion, or 680,000 tons. He then assumed that a tenth of these young salmon are eaten by predators in the Loch. Since the average predator eats about a hundredth of its weight daily, Dr. Mackal calculated that the Loch must contain 18,600 tons of predators. He assumed that *N. rhombopteryx* accounts for one percent of this total, the rest being larger fish, birds, and humans. Thus he arrived at a figure of from 150 to 200 *N. rhombopteryx* in Loch Ness—or 186 tons of *N. rhombopteryx* at 2,500 pounds each.

[5]   Since *N. rhombopteryx* eggs have never been found near Loch Ness, we can safely assume that it is a live breeder. Because it is a large animal, it probably has a long gestation period, say two years. For purposes of this calculation, we further assume that it might take the animal approximately three years to reach maturity.

[6]   It did, however, create an opportunity for yet another anagram on *Nessiteras rhombopteryx*—this one, "sexy Montrose Harb. sprite."

Number of sightings per five-year span

100 565	1870	1890	1910	1930	1950	1970
90				Highway built along western shore of Loch Ness, 1933		
80				←		
70	Frequency of observations of N. rhombopteryx 565 A.D.—1970 A.D.					
60						
50						
40						
30						
20						
10						

tional and commercial fishing have become large industries.[7] One of the first organizations to raise an objection was Salmon Unlimited, which represents recreational fishermen on the lake. Their Sherwin Schwartz has stated, "We have enough trouble with the commercial fishermen. We don't need another drain on the salmon." Proponents of the plan counter that 300

---

[7] The trout and salmon now in the lake are there as a result of stocking efforts, because the presence of polychlorinated biphenyls (PCBs) and pesticides in the lake have made it nearly impossible for large fish, high on the food chain, to reproduce. It is possible that, since *N. rhombopteryx* eats these fish, it would concentrate PCBs and pesticides in its flesh to such a point that it also would be unable to reproduce. In such a case, a stocking program would be ill fated.

N. rhombopteryx would eat at most 320 tons a year of the 25,000 tons of trout and salmon in the lake.

Further questions have been raised by the US Fish and Wildlife Service, however, where a high source has suggested that the effects of stray radiation from the nuclear power plants surrounding Lake Michigan might produce mutations in *N. rhombopteryx*. The possible resulting changes in size and behavior could be undesirable. Our source states that the service would require exhaustive studies of *N. rhombopteryx*'s life history, longevity, food habits, growth rates, and reproductive biology before it would approve the plan, primarily with a view towards ascertaining if the creature might not multiply so successfully as to take over all the Great Lakes and associated waterways. In such a case *N. rhombopteryx* would be one of the few large species of animal which have proved able to reproduce in Lake Michigan's Poly-Chlorinated Biphenyl (PCB) and pesticide-polluted waters. [8]

Proponents of the plan also face obstacles imposed by foreign, federal, and local bureaucracies. Mr. MacDermott has said that permission to export *N. rhombopteryx* from Great Britain would have to come from the Ministry of Agriculture, Fisheries, and Food, and that other British ministries would probably also expect to be consulted. The agricultural attaché at the British embassy in Washington, however, was unwilling to say whether permission would be forthcoming. ''The question has never come up,'' he said.

On the federal level—according to David Comey, executive director of Citizens for a Better Environment—a large stocking program, if handled by the federal government, would call for an Environmental Impact Statement from the Department of the interior and for careful consideration by the Environmental Protection Agency. The Army Corps of Engineers would have to review the creature's potential as a navigational hazard. The Nuclear Regulatory Commission would have to review the safety consequences of one of the creature's being sucked into the water intake of a nuclear power plant. And the Department of Agriculture would impose the usual quarantine requirements applicable to all imported animals. On a local level, Tony Dean of the Illinois Department of Conservation has said that public hearings and meetings would be required before his department could look at the proposal.

But at least one local institution has responded to the plan with en-

---

[8]   As yet we have no reading on how *N. rhombopteryx* tastes when smoked, now whether Mr. Schwartz's organization would consider changing its name to *Nessiteras* Unlimited.

thusiasm. Roger Klocek, assistant curator of fishes at Shedd Aquarium, hopes that the aquarium might acquire one or more of the animals for the public to observe at close hand. He envisions building a pen around an area of the lake adjacent to the aquarium, with an observation chamber placed underwater, so that aquarium patrons could see the entire animal in its environment. Such an installation, he estimates, would cost no more than $200,000.

It is surprising that both the Chicago Association of Commerce and Industry and the office of the mayor have pointedly refused to lend their

Table 1. Tonnage of fish in Lake Michigan

Data from 1974 creel censuses and from Michigan Department of Natural Resources Fisheries Research Report No. 1813, May 23, 1974, "Estimates of biomass of principal fish species in the Great Lakes (First report)," by G. P. Cooper, R. W. Rybicki, L. Moffitt, M. H. Patriarche, E. H. Brown, Jr., and J. W. Peck.

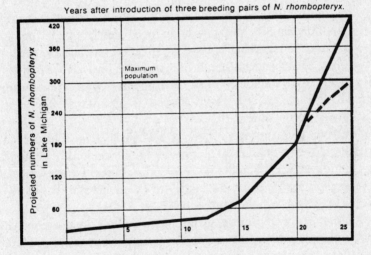

Years after introduction of three breeding pairs of *N. rhombopteryx.*

Species	Tons	Species	Tons
Alewives	1,000,000	Chinook	6,000
Lake trout	10,000	Brown trout	1,000
Whitefish	25,000	Yellow perch	1,500
Chubs	7,500	Northern pike and muskie	650
Rainbow/steelhead	3,060	Bass	1,500
Coho	5,000	Other	5,000
Total tonnage	1,066,060		

support and encouragement to this project. The obvious advantages of such a plan include not only the preservation of an endangered species but also a great boost to civic pride, a monumental stimulus to local tourism, and as yet unexplored potential in the area of alewife control. Possibilities present themselves in the form of *N. rhombopteryx* lakeside festivals, picnics, and expeditions sponsored by the Illinois St. Andrews society (an organization of Scots and persons of Scottish descent), conventions, and affiliated cottage industries which would undoubtedly include Wendella *rhombopteryx* rides, lakefront telescopes, and a variety of souvenirs including statuettes with and without thermometers, ashtrays, hats, flags, coin purses, key chains, postcards, and salt and pepper shakers in the shape of *N. rhombopteryx*.[9]

Mr. Comey has commented, "The only reason Daley's people aren't behind this is that they haven't realized the patronage potential of a full *N. rhombopteryx* program. They could have thousands of workers out on the lake—monitoring, measuring, counting, tagging, and sampling the animals. And nobody would know whether they were actually working or not."

The reasons for the city's reticence on this subject can only be surmised, but it is possible that officials are waiting for a reading of public opinion on the issue. Large animals have not enjoyed good press of late; one has only to think of *Jaws* and an endless stream of fear-mongering science fiction films on local television station WFLD. The popular press has insensitively referred to *N. rhombopteryx* as the "Loch Ness monster," suggesting that it is an object worthy of fear.[10]

Fortunately, there are signs that an enlightened and more liberal attitude has penetrated some quarters of the present administrations. Richard Pavia, acting commissioner of water and sewers, has said, "I've never heard of them doing any harm. The fact that they're called monsters has more to do with their size than with their behavior."

Because the stocking effort would be so complex and expensive and undertaking, it is unlikely to occur in the absence of a concentrated effort by the city government. We might see a start in that direction early this month. According to reliable sources, a North Side alderman is considering a

---

[9] One recent proposal has called for an *N. rhombopteryx* day on which the city would pour scotch into the Chicago river and let it flow into the lake. In a revised version, which has been well received in unofficial circles, we would drink the scotch and let *N. rhombopteryx* swim up the river to us.

[10] One of the local groups most sensitive to slurs against *N. rhombopteryx* is an organization calling itself Friends of the Loch Mich Monster, with headquarters in Suite 440, 500 North Michigan Avenue.

resoluton to be introduced in a City Council meeting this month; it would put the city on record as supporting the stocking program. Although the resolution is not likely to be acted upon soon, it is an important first step toward getting the project under way. A significant showing of public support for the plan could be the decisive factor.

11

CINDERELLA, INC.

Christopher Anvil

THE GIRL WAS sallow and scrawny, her face as unattractive as two pills in a smear of mustard. She squinted up and down the street before she hustled across to a wide doorway under a glowing sign:

CINDERELLA, INC.

She hurried through the door and up to a handsome male attendant standing near a hotel-like desk. "At your service, madame," he crooned.

She fumbled in her pocketbook and brought out a piece of torn telescript. She crammed it into his hand. "Can they make *me* look like that?" she demanded.

He unfolded the paper and glanced at the lush advertisement. He smiled, and returned it. "Yes," he said, "but it will be expensive."

"Oh, I've got the money."

He raised his hand in an imperious gesture, and a round purple and gold couch whirled down from above. "Seat yourself, madam, and be borne on your voyage to beauty," he said grandiosely. In a sort of mesmeric trance she flopped down on the couch and it whisked away with her.

The couch vaulted through a wide oval opening into a rose colored room ringed with mirrors. From a hidden opening in the ceiling a grayish-green light rayed down on her. "Behold yourself as you are," said a taunting female voice.

The girl glanced with irritation at the mirror. "You don't have to sell me," she snapped, "I know what I look like."

The couch started forward with a jerk and slid toward a mirror, the image enlarging as it approached. The mirror swung up and the couch slid through to halt before a desk in a softly-lit room done in gray. A window looked out over the city. A man in a white coat rose from his desk and offered her a chair facing him. His eyes went over her impersonally. She got up from the couch and sat down beside the desk.

"What is it you want?" the man asked.

"This," said the girl, and spread the advertisement before him.

He studied the picture for a minute then looked the girl over again. "Stand up, please." She stood up. "Now turn around. Mm-hm . . . Well, sit down." He bridged his hands and looked at her. "I think we can do the body, but I'm not sure of the face. This will cost money. Ah, we insist on a cash payment. . . ."

"How much money?" she watched him tensely, opening her pocketbook.

"One hundred thousand."

She took out ten crisp bills and spread them on his desk. He nodded, scribbled a receipt, and took her back to the couch. It whirled her out the door and down warm, gaily lighted perfumed halls to another hotel-like desk where two pretty young girls sat on the counter with their short-skirted legs swinging back and forth. They jumped to their feet and went to the couch. Automatically she showed them the receipt.

"Oh," said one of the attendants, "you've already paid?"

"Yes."

"Well, then we can forget the sales talk." They glanced at the receipt, and their eyes widened. "You get the *full* treatment!" They looked envious.

"Don't you think I need it?" she said coldly. "Why don't we get started?"

"Don't you be nervous," said one of the girls sympathetically. "You'll come out all right. Joanie and me looked almost as bad as you do when we got the treatment." She straightened and turned around slowly, then laughed in vibrant happiness. "And we didn't get the *full* treatment!" They climbed onto the couch and waved to an attendant who sent it whirling down the hall. . . .

It was twenty days before she returned to consciousness, and it was thirty days after that before the doctors and attendants could be sure of the results.

At last she stood in front of the mirror, naked, and saw what she had hoped for. She was, in physical existence, what men with overactive glands and vivid imaginations dream of. She moved sensuously and the male attendants hastily left the room. Her throaty laughter followed them out the door.

Later she was called for her final interview. "Please sit down," said the woman doctor, frowning at a sheaf of papers on the desk. The doctor picked up a clinical photograph and showed it to her. "Do you recognize this woman?"

"Of course," said her sensuous voice. "That was I." She laughed huskily.

"Quite a transformation. Sometimes I think I'll take the treatment myself." The doctor ran a hand across her face, with the fingers spread out, massaging. "Now you'll admit, there's been quite a change."

"Of course."

"It would be unpleasant to change back."

There was a momentary silence. "Change *back?*"

"Yes, yes, I know," said the doctor, "this sounds like a scene from a horror teleshow. But the fact is that the, er, change was brought about, among other things, with the use of glandular secretions. A few chemicals were even used that don't ordinarily exist in the adult human body. Now our doctors have stabilized your physique as effectively as they can." She shuffled through the papers. "But you'll need to use a jectokit. We have yours here."

She handed across a small cream-colored plastic box. "The directions are indented into the box, so you can't make any mistake if you read them. Your body can store some of these substances for a time, but don't go any longer than ten days without them. Don't get cocky. You're a beautiful woman now, but remember, your beauty rests on that little box. After six months, we'll give you a refill, or one of our branch stores will. You're safe, so long as you do as I say." The doctor looked up to see how her listener was taking it. She received a breath-taking smile in return.

"I'm off," said the new beauty, "to find a man."

"That won't be hard," murmured the doctor a little ruefully.

The wedding, three months later, was a striking one. The women stared enviously at the tall handsome breadth of the bridegroom, and the men watched the bride with bulging eyes. When the ceremony was over, and the couple occupied the bridal suite for the night, there was a momentary interlude.

"Darling," murmured the bride, "forgive me for a moment. I want to pretty up."

"You're pretty enough to eat," said the groom huskily.

She laughed and slipped past him to the bathroom door with her travel case. "Compose yourself," she smiled, "I'll be out in five minutes."

The groom smiled back. "Five minutes, then."

Once inside, she locked the door and brought out the little yellow plastic box. She clicked open the cover and looked at the photograph snapped inside. "Cinderella, Inc.," said the legend, *"reminds you."*

"I remember," she said, and began her ritual.

In the bedroom, the groom was in his shirtsleeves whistling and unpacking his suitcase. Suddenly he stopped and stared at a little brown plastic box rolled up in his bathrobe. "By George," he gasped, "I almost forgot."

Hastily, he rolled up his sleeve. . . .

12

COMMON DENOMINATOR

John D. MacDonald

WHEN SCOUT GROUP Forty flickered back across half the Galaxy with a complete culture study of a Class Seven civilization on three planets of Argus Ten, the Bureau of Stellar Defense had, of course, a priority claim on all data. Class Sevens were rare and of high potential danger, so all personnel of group Forty were placed in tight quarantine during the thirty days required for a detailed analysis of the thousands of film spools.

News of the contact leaked out and professional alarmists predicted dire things on the news screens of the three home planets of Sol. A retired admiral of the Space Navy published an article in which he stated bitterly that the fleet had been weakened by twenty years of softness in high places.

On the thirty-first day, B.S.D. reported to System President Mize that the inhabitants of the three planets of Argus 10 constituted no threat, that there was no military necessity for alarm, that approval of a commerce treaty was recommended, that all data was being turned over to the Bureau of Stellar Trade and Economy for analysis, that personnel of Scout Group Forty was being given sixty days' leave before reassignment.

B.S.T.E. released film to all commercial networks at once, and visions of slavering oily monsters disappeared from the imagination of mankind. The Argonauts, as they came to be called, were pleasantly similar to mankind. It was additional proof that only in the rarest instance was the life-apex on any planet in the home Galaxy an adrupt divergence from the "human" form. The homogeneousness of planet elements throughout the Galaxy made homogeneousness of life-apex almost a truism. The bipedal, oxygen-breathing vertebrate with opposing thumb seems best suited for survival.

It was evident that, with training, the average Argonaut could pass almost unnoticed in the Solar System. The flesh tones were brightly pink, like that of a sunburned human. Cranial hair was uniformly taffy-yellow. They were heavier and more fleshy than humans. Their women had a pronounced Rubens look, a warm, moist, rosy, comfortable look.

Everyone remarked on the placidity and contentment of facial expressions, by human standards. The inevitable comparison was made. The Argonauts looked like a race of inn and beer-garden proprietors in the Bavarian Alps. With leather pants to slap, stein lids to click, feathers in Tyrolean hats and peasant skirts on their women, they would represent a culture and a way of life that had been missing from Earth for far too many generations.

Eight months after matters had been turned over to B.S.T.E., the First Trade Group returned to Earth with a bewildering variety of artifacts and devices, plus a round dozen Argonauts. The Argonauts had learned to speak Solian with an amusing guttural accent. They beamed on everything and everybody. They were great pets until the novelty wore off. Profitable trade was inaugurated, because the Argonaut devices all seemed designed to make life more pleasant. The scent-thesizer became very popular once it was adjusted to meet human tastes. Worn as a lapel button, it could create the odor of pine, broiled steak, spring flowers, Scotch whiskey, musk—even skunk for the practical jokers who exist in all ages and eras.

Any home equipped with an Argonaut static-clean never became dusty. It used no power and had to be emptied only once a year.

Technicians altered the Argonaut mechanical game animal so that it looked like an Earth rabbit. The weapons which shot a harmless beam were altered to look like rifles. After one experience with the new game, hunters were almost breathless with excitement. The incredible agility of the mechanical animal, its ability to take cover, the fact that, once the beam felled it, you could use it over and over again—all this made for the promulgation of new non-lethal hunting.

Lambert, chief of the Bureau of Racial Maturity, waited patiently for his chance at the Argonaut data. The cramped offices in the temporary wing of the old System Security Building, the meager appropriation, the obsolete office equipment, the inadequate staff all testified not only to the Bureau's lack of priority, but also to a lack of knowledge of its existence on the part of many System officials. Lambert, crag-faced, sandy, slow-moving, was a historian, anthropologist and sociologist. He was realist enough to understand that if the Bureau of Racial Maturity happened to be more important in System Government, it would probably be headed by a man with fewer academic and more political qualifications.

66

And Lambert knew, beyond any doubt at all, that the B.R.M. was more important to the race and the future of the race than any other branch of System Government.

Set up by President Tolles, an adult and enlightened administrator, the Bureau was now slowly being strangled by a constantly decreasing appropriation.

Lambert knew that mankind had come too far, too fast. Mankind had dropped out of a tree with all the primordial instincts to rend and tear and claw. Twenty thousand years later, and with only a few thousand years of dubiously recorded history, he had reached the stars. It was too quick.

Lambert knew that mankind must become mature in order to survive. The domination of instinct had to be watered down, and rapidly. Selective breeding might do it, but it was an answer impossible to enforce. He hoped that one day the records of an alien civilization would give him the answer. After a year of bureaucratic wriggling, feints and counter-feints, he had acquired the right of access to Scout Group Data.

As his patience dwindled he wrote increasingly firm letters to Central Files and Routing. In the end, when he finally located the data improperly stored in the closed files of the B.S.T.E., he took no more chances. He went in person with an assistant named Cooper and a commandeered electric hand-truck, and bullied a B.S.T.E. storage clerk into accepting a receipt for the Argonaut data. The clerk's cooperation was lessened by never having heard of the Bureau of Racial Maturity.

The file contained the dictionary and grammar compiled by the Scout Group, plus all the films taken on the three planets of Argus 10, plus micro-films of twelve thousand books written in the language of the Argonauts. Their written language was ideographic, and thus presented more than usual difficulties. Lambert knew that translations had been made, but somewhere along the line they had disappeared.

Lambert set his whole staff to work on the language. He hired additional linguists out of his own thin enough pocket. He gave up all outside activities in order to hasten the progress of his own knowledge. His wife, respecting Lambert's high order of devotion to his work, kept their two half-grown children from interfering during those long evenings when he studied and translated at home.

Two evenings a week Lambert called on Vonk Poogla, the Argonaut assigned to Trade Coordination, and improved his conversational Argonian to the point where he could obtain additional historical information from the pink wide "man."

Of the twelve thousand books, the number of special interest to Lambert were only one hundred and ten. On those he based his master chart. An animated film of the chart was prepared at Lambert's own expense, and, when it was done, he requested an appointment with Simpkin, Secretary for Stellar Affairs, going through all the normal channels to obtain the interview. He asked an hour of Simpkin's time. It took two weeks.

Simpkin was a big florid man with iron-gray hair, skeptical eyes and that indefinable look of political opportunism.

He came around his big desk to shake Lambert's hand. "Ah . . . Lambert! Glad to see you, fella. I ought to get around to my Bureau Chiefs more often, but you know how hectic things are up here."

"I know, Mr. Secretary. I have something here of the utmost importance and—"

"Bureau of Racial Maturity, isn't it? I never did know exactly what you people do. Sort of progress records or something?"

"Of the utmost importance," Lambert repeated doggedly.

Simpkin smiled. "I hear that all day, but go ahead."

"I want to show you a chart. A historical chart of the Argonaut civilization." Lambert put the projector in position and plugged it in. He focused it on the wall screen.

"It was decided," Simpkin said firmly, "that the Argonauts are not a menace to us in any—"

"I know that, sir. Please look at the chart first and then, when you've seen it, I think you'll know what I mean."

"Go ahead," Simpkin agreed resignedly.

"I can be accused of adding apples and lemons in this presentation, sir. Note the blank chart. The base line is in years, adjusted to our calendar so as to give a comparison. Their recorded history covers twelve thousand of our years. That's better than four times ours. Now note the red line. That shows the percentage of their total population involved in wars. It peaked eight thousand years ago. Note how suddenly it drops after that. In five hundred years it sinks to the base line and does not appear again.

"Here comes the second line. Crimes of violence. It also peaks eight thousand years ago. It drops less quickly than the war line, and never does actually cut the base line. Some crime still exists there. But a very, very tiny percentage compared to ours on a population basis, or to their own past. The third line, the yellow line climbing abruptly, is the index of insanity. Again a peak during the same approximate period in their history. Again a drop almost to the base line."

Simpkin pursed his heavy lips. "Odd, isn't it?"

"Now this fourth line needs some explaining. I winnowed out death rates by age groups. Their life span is 1.3 times ours, so it had to be adjusted. I found a strange thing. I took the age group conforming to our eighteen and twenty-four year group. That green line. Note that by the time we start getting decent figures, nine thousand years ago, it remains almost constant, and at a level conforming to our own experience. Now note what happens when the green line reaches a point eight thousand years ago. See how it begins to climb? Now steeper, almost vertical. It remains at a high level for almost a thousand years, way beyond the end of their history of war, and then descends slowly toward the base line, leveling out about two thousand years ago."

Lambert clicked off the projector.

"Is that all?" Simpkin asked.

"Isn't it enough? I'm concerned wih the future of our own race. Somehow the Argonauts have found an answer to war, insanity, violence. We need that answer if we are to survive."

"Come now, Lambert," Simpkin said wearily.

"Don't you see it? Their history parallels ours. They had our same problems. They saw disaster ahead and did something about it. What did they do? I have to know that."

"How do you expect to?"

"I want travel orders to go there."

"I'm afraid that's quite impossible. There are no funds for that sort of jaunt, Lambert. And I think you are worrying over nothing."

"Shall I show you some of our own trends? Shall I show you murder turning from the most horrid crime into a relative commonplace? Shall I show you the slow inevitable increase in asylum space?"

"I know all that, man. But look at the Argonauts! Do you want that sort of stagnation? Do you want a race of fat, pink, sleepy—"

"Maybe they had a choice. A species of stagnation, or the end of their race. Faced with that choice, which would you pick, Mr. Secretary?"

"There are no funds."

"All I want is authority. I'll pay my own way."

And he did.

Rean was the home planet of the Argonauts, the third from their sun. When the trade ship flickered into three-dimensional existence, ten thousand miles above Rean, Lambert stretched the space-ache out of his long bones and muscles and smiled at Vonk Poogla.

"You could have saved me the trip, you know," Lambert said.

A grin creased the round pink visage. "Nuddink ventured, nuddink gained. Bezides, only my cousin can speak aboud this thing you vunder aboud. My cousin is werry important person. He is one picks me to go to your planet.''

Vonk Poogla was transported with delight at being able to show the wonders of the ancient capital city to Lambert. It had been sacked and burned over eight thousand earth years before, and now it was mellowed by eighty-three centuries of unbroken peace. It rested in the pastel twilight, and there were laughter and soft singing in the broad streets. Never had Lambert felt such a warm aura of security and . . . love. No other word but that ultimate one seemed right.

In the morning they went to the squat blue building where Vonk Soobuk-noora, the important person, had his administrative headquarters. Lambert, knowing enough of Argonaut governmental structure to understand that Soobuknoora was titular head of the three-planet government, could not help but compare the lack of protocol with what he could expect were he to try to take Vonk Poogla for an interview with President Mize.

Soobuknoora was a smaller, older edition of Poogla, his pink face wrinkled, his greening hair retaining only a trace of the the original yellow. Soobuknoora spoke no Solian and he was very pleased to find that Lambert spoke Arognian.

Soobuknoora watched the animated chart with considerable interest. After it was over, he seemed lost in thought.

''It is something so private with us, Man Lambert, that we seldom speak of it to each other,'' Soobuknoora said in Argonian. ''It is not written. Maybe we have shame—a guilt sense. That is hard to say. I have decided to tell you what took place among us eight thousand years ago.''

''I would be grateful.''

''We live in contentment. Maybe it is good, maybe it is not so good. But we continue to live. Where did our trouble come from in the old days, when we were like your race? Back when we were brash and young and wickedly cruel? From the individuals, those driven ones who were motivated to succeed despite all obstacles. They made our paintings, wrote our music, killed each other, fomented our unrest, our wars. We live off the bewildering richness of our past.''

He sighed. ''It was a problem. To understand our solution, you must think of an analogy, Man Lambert. Think of a factory where machines are made. We will call the acceptable machines stable, the unacceptable ones unstable. They are built with a flywheel which must turn at a certain speed. If it exceeds that speed, it is no good. But a machine that is stable can, at any time, become unstable. What is the solution?'' He smiled at Lambert.

70

"I'm a bit confused," Lambert confessed. "You would have to go around inspecting the machines constantly for stability."

"And use a gauge? No. Too much trouble. An unstable machine can do damage. So we do this—we put a little governor on the machine. When the speed passes the safety mark, the machine breaks."

"But this is an analogy, Vonk Soobuknoora!" Lambert protested. "You can't put a governor on a man!"

"Man is born with a governor, Man Lambert. Look back in both our histories, when we were not much above the animal level. An unbalanced man would die. He could not compete for food. He could not organize the simple things of his life for survival. Man Lambert, did you ever have a fleeting impulse to kill yourself?"

Lambert smiled. "Of course. You could almost call that impulse a norm for intelligent species."

"Did it ever go far enough so that you considered a a method, a weapon?"

Lambert nodded slowly. "It's hard to remember, but I think I did. Yes, once I did."

"And what would have happened," the Argonaut asked softly, "if there had been available to you in that moment a weapon completely painless, completely final?"

Lambert's mouth went dry. "I would probably have used it. I was very young. Wait! I'm beginning to see what you mean, but—"

"The governor had to be built into the body," Soobuknoora interrupted, "and yet so designed that there would be no possibility of accidental activation. Suppose that on the day I start to think of how great and powerful I am in this position I have. I get an enormous desire to become even more powerful. I begin to reason emotionally. Soon I have a setback. I am depressed. I am out of balance, you could say. I have become dangerous to myself and to our culture.

"In a moment of depression, I take these two smallest fingers of each hand. I reach behind me and I press the two fingers, held firmly together, to a space in the middle of my back. A tiny capsule buried at the base of my brain is activated and I am dead within a thousandth part of a second. Vonk Poogla is the same. All of us are the same. The passing urge for self-destruction happens to be the common denominator of imbalance. We purged our race of the influence of the neurotic, the egocentric, the hypersensitive, merely by making self-destruction very, very easy."

"Then that death rate—?"

71

"At eighteen the operation is performed. It is very quick and very simple. We saw destruction ahead. We had to force it through. In the beginning the deaths were frightening, there were so many of them. The stable ones survived, bred, reproduced. A lesser but still great percentage of the next generation went—and so on, until now it is almost static."

In Argonian Lambert said hotly, "Oh, it sounds fine! But what about children? What sort of heartless race can plant the seed of death in its own children?"

Never before had he seen the faintest trace of anger on any Argonaut face. The single nostril widened and Soobuknoora might have raged if he had been from Earth. "There are other choices, Man Lambert. Our children have no expectation of being burned to cinder, blown to fragments. They are free of that fear. Which is the better love, Man Lambert?"

"I have two children. I couldn't bear to—"

"Wait!" Soobuknoora said. "Think one moment. Suppose you were to know that when they reached the age of eighteen, both your children were to be operated on by our methods. How would that affect your present relationship to them?"

Lambert was, above all, a realist. He remembered the days of being "too busy" for the children, of passing off their serious questions with a joking or curt evasion, of playing with them as though they were young, pleasing, furry animals.

"I would do a better job as a parent," Lambert admitted. "I would try to give them enough emotional stability so that they would never—have that urge to kill themselves. But Ann is delicate, moody, unpredictable, artistic."

Poogla and Soobuknoora nodded in unison. "You would probably lose that one; maybe you would lose both," Soobuknoora agreed. "But it is better to lose more than half the children of a few generations to save the race."

Lambert thought some more. He said, "I shall go back and I shall speak of this plan and what it did for you. But I do not think my race will like it. I do not want to insult you or your people, but you have stagnated. You stand still in time."

Vonk Poogla laughed largely. "Not by a damn sight," he said gleefully. "Next year we stop giving the operation. We stop for good. It was just eight thousand years to permit us to catch our breath before going on more safely. And what is eight thousand years of marking time in the history of a race? Nothing, my friend. Nothing!"

When Lambert went back to Earth, he naturally quit his job.

13

CRAZY ANNAOJ

Fritz Leiber

TWO THINGS WILL last to the end of time, at least for the tribes of Western Man, no matter how far his spaceships rove. They are sorcery and romantic love, which come to much the same thing in the end.

For the more that becomes possible to man, the more wildly he yearns for the impossible, and runs after witches and sorcerers to find it.

While the farther he travels to the star-ribboned rim of the Milky Way and beyond, the more he falls in love with far-off things and yearns for the most distant and unattainable beloved.

Also, witchcraft and sorcery are games it takes two to play; the witch or sorcerer and his or her client.

The oldest and wealthiest man in the Milky Way and its loveliest girl laughed as they left the gypsy's tent pitched just outside the jewel-pillared spacefield of the most exclusive pleasure planet between the galaxy's two dizzily whirling, starry arms. The gypsy's black cat, gliding past them back into the tent, only smiled cryptically.

A private, eiderdown-surfaced slidewalk, rolled out like the red carpet of ancient cliche, received the begemmed slippers of the honeymooning couple and carried them toward the most diamond-glittering pillar of them all, the private hyperspace yacht *Eros* of the galactic shipping magnate Piliph Foelitsack and his dazzling young bride Annaoj.

He looked 21 and was 20 times that old. Cosmetic surgery and organ replacements and implanted featherweight power-prosthetics and pace-makers had worked their minor miracles. At any one time there were three physicians in the *Eros* listening in on the functionings of his body.

She looked and was 17, but the wisdom in her eyes was that of Eve, of Helen of Troy, of Cleopatra, of Forzane. It was also the wisdom of Juliet, of Iseult, of Francesca da Rimini. It was a radiant but not a rational wisdom,

73

and it had a frightening ingredient that had been known to make nurses and lady's maids and the wives of planetary presidents and systemic emperors shiver alike.

Together now on the whispering white slidewalk, planning their next pleasures, they looked the pinnacle of cosmic romance fulfilled—he dashing and handsome and young, except that there was something just a shade careful about the way he carried himself; she giddy and slim with a mind that was all sentimental or amorous whim, except for that diamond touch of terrifyingly fixed white light in her most melting or mischievous glance. Despite or perhaps because of those two exceptions, they seemed more akin to the sparkling stars above them than even to the gorgeous pleasure planet around them.

He had been born in a ghetto on Andvari III and had fought his way up the razor-runged ladder of economic power until he owned fleets of hyperspace freighters, a dozen planets, and the governments of ten times that many.

She had been born in a slum on Aphrodite IV, owning only herself. It had taken her six Terran months to bring herself to the attention of Piliph Foelitsack by way of three beauty contests and one bit part in a stereographic all-senses sex-film, and six more months to become his seventeenth wife instead of one more of his countless casual mistresses.

The beepers of social gossip everywhere had hinted discreetly about the infatuation-potential of fringe senile megabillionaires and the coldly murderous greed of teenage starlets. And Annaoj and Piliph Foelitsack had smiled at this gossip, since they knew they loved each other and why: for their matching merciless determination to get what they wanted and keep it, and for the distance that had been between them and was no longer. Of the two, Annaoj's love was perhaps the greater, accounting for the icy, fanatic glint in her otherwise nymphet's eyes.

They had laughed on leaving the drab tent of the gypsy fortuneteller, who herself owned a small, beat-up spaceship covered with cabalistic signs, because the last thing she had said to the shipping king, fixing his bright youthful eyes with her bleared ones, had been, "Piliph Foelitsack, you have journeyed far, very far, for such a young man, yet you shall make even longer journeys hereafter. Your past travels will be trifles compared to your travels to come."

Both Piliph and Annaoj knew that he had been once to the Andromeda Galaxy and twice to both Magellanic Clouds, though they had not told the silly old gypsy so, being despite their iron wills kindly lovers, still enamored of everything in the cosmos by virtue of their mutual love. They also knew that Piliph had determined to restrict his jauntings henceforth to the Milky Way, to keep reasonably close to the greatest geriatric scientists, and they were both reconciled, at least by day, to the fact that despite all his defenses, death would come for him in ten or twenty years.

Yet, although they did not now tell each other so, the gypsy's words had given a spark of real hope to their silly night-promises under the stars like gems and the galaxies like puffs of powder that: "We will live and love forever." Their loveliest night had been spent a hundred light-years outside the Milky Way—it was to be Piliph's last extragalactic venture—where the *Eros* had emerged briefly from hyperspace and they had lolled and luxuriated for hours under the magnifying crystal skylight of the Master Stateroom, watching only the far-off galaxies, with all of their moiling, toiling home-galaxy out of sight beneath the ship.

But now, as if the cryptic universe had determined to give an instant sardonic rejoinder to the gypsy's prediction, the eiderdown slidewalk had not murmured them halfway to the *Eros* when a look of odd surprise came into Piliph's bright youthful eyes and he clutched at his heart and swayed and would have toppled except that Annaoj caught him in her strong slender arms and held him to her tightly.

Something had happened in the body of Piliph Foelitsack that could not be dealt with by all its pacemakers and its implanted and remotely controlled hormone dispensers, nor by any of the coded orders frantically tapped out by the three physicians monitoring its organs and systems.

It took thirty seconds for the ambulance of the *Eros* to hurtle out from the yacht on a track paralleling the slidewalk and brake to a bone-jolting silent halt.

During that half minute Annaoj watched the wrinkles come out on her husband's smooth face, like stars at nightfall in the sky of a planet in a star cluster. She wasted one second on the white-hot impulse to have the gypsy immediately strangled, but she knew that the great aristocrats of the cosmos do not take vengeance on its vermin and that in any event she had far more pressing business with which to occupy herself fully tonight. She clasped the pulseless body a trifle more tightly, feeling the bones and prosthetics through the layer of slack flesh.

In two minutes more, in the surgery of the *Eros*, Piliph's body was in a dissipatory neutrino field which instantly sent all its heat packing off at the speed of light, but in particles billions of times slimmer than the photons of heat, so that the body was supercooled to the temperature of frozen helium without opportunity for a single disruptive crystal form.

Then without consulting the spacefield dispatching station or any other authority of the pleasure planet, Annaoj ordered the *Eros* blasted into hyperspace and driven at force speed to the galaxy's foremost geriatrics clinic on Menkar V, though it lay halfway across the vast Milky Way.

During the anxious, grueling trip, she did only one thing quite out of the ordinary. She had her husband's supercooled body sprayed with a transparent insulatory film, which would adequatley hold its coolth for a matter of days, and placed in the Master Stateroom. Once a week the body was briefly returned to the dissipatory neutrino field, to bring its temperature down again to within a degree of zero Kelvin.

Otherwise she behaved as she always had, changing costume seven times a day, paying great attention to her coiffure and to her cosmetic and juvenation treatments, being idly charming to the officers and stewards.

But she spent hours in her husband's office studying his business and working to the edge of exhaustion his three secretaries. And she always took her small meals in the Master Stateroom.

On Menkar V they told her, after weeks of test and study, that her husband was beyond reawakening, at least at the present state of medical skill, and to come back in ten years. More would be known then.

At that, Annaoj nodded frigidly and took up the reins of her husband's business, conducting them entirely from the *Eros* as it skipped about through space and hyperspace. Under her guidance the Foelitsack economic empire prospered still more than it had under its founder. She successfully fought or bought off the claims of Piliphs's eleven surviving divorced wives, a hundred of his relatives and a score of his prime managers.

She regularly returned to Menkar V and frequently visited other clinics and sought out famous healers. She became expert at distinguishing the charlatans from the dedicated, the conceited from the profound. Yet at times she also consulted sorcerers and wizards and witchdoctors. Incantations in exotic tongues and lights were spoken and glowed over Piliph's frigid form, extraterrestrial stenches filled the surgery of the *Eros*, and there were focused there the meditations of holy creatures which resembled man less than a spider does—while three of four fuming yet dutiful doctors of the *Eros'* dozen waited for the crucial moment in the ceremony when they would obediently work a five-second reversal of the neutrino field to bring the body briefly to normal temperature to determine whether the magic had worked.

But neither science nor sorcery could revive him.

She bullied many a police force and paid many a detective agency to hunt down the gypsy with the black cat, but the old crone and her runic spaceship had vanished as utterly as the vital spark in Piliph Foelitsack. No one could tell whether Annaoj really believed that the gypsy had had something to do with the striking down of her husband and might be able to bring him alive, or whether the witch had merely become another counter in the sorcery game of which Annaoj had suddenly grown so fond.

In the course of time Annaoj took many lovers. When she tired of one, she would lead him for the first time into the Master Stateroom of the *Eros* and show him the filmed and frosty body of her husband and send him away without as much as a parting touch of her fingertips and then lie down beside the cold, cold form under the cold, cold stars of the skylight.

And she never once let another woman set foot in that room.

Not the humblest, nor ugliest maid. Not the greatest sculptress of the Pleiades. Not the most feared and revered sorceress in the Hyades.

She became known as Crazy Annaoj, though no one thought it to her face or whispered it within a parsec of her.

When she still looked 17, though her age was 70 times that—for the sciences of geriatrics and juvenation had progressed greatly since her husband's collapse—she felt an unfamiliar weariness creeping on her and she ordered the *Eros* to make once more for Menkar V at force speed.

The *Eros* never emerged from hyperspace. Most say she was lost there, scuttled by Annaoj as she felt death coming on her. A few maintain she exited into altogether another universe, where Crazy Annaoj is still keeping up her search for the healer who can revive Piliph, or playing her game with the doctors and witchdoctors and with her lovers.

But in any case the gypsy's prediction was fulfilled, for in the course of Annaoj's voyages, the body of Piliph Foelitsack had been carried twice to Andromeda and also to two galaxies in Virgo, three in Leo and one in Coma Berenices.

14

THE DAMNED THING

Ambrose Bierce

BY THE LIGHT of a tallow candle which had been placed on one end of a rough table, a man was reading something written in a book. It was an old account book, greatly worn; and the writing was not very legible, for the man sometimes held the page close to the flame of the candle to get a stronger light on it. The shadow of the book would then throw into obscurity half of the room, darkening a number of faces and figures; for besides the reader, eight other men were present.

Seven of them sat against the rough log wall, silent, motionless, and the room being small, not very far from the table. By extending an arm any one of them could have touched the eighth man, who lay on the table, face upward, partly covered by a sheet, his arms at his sides. He was dead.

The person reading was the coroner. It was by virtue of his office that he had possession of the book in which he was reading; it had been found among the dead man's effects—in his cabin, where the inquest was now taking place.

When the coroner had finished reading, he put the book into his breast pocket. At that moment the door was pushed open and a young man entered. He, clearly, was not of mountain birth and breeding: he was clad as those who dwell in cities. His clothing was dusty, however, as from travel. He had, in fact, been riding hard to attend the inquest.

The coroner nodded; no one else greeted him.

The young man smiled. "I am sorry to have kept you," he said. "I went away, not to evade your summons, but to send to my newspaper an account of what I suppose I am called back to relate."

The coroner smiled.

"The account that you sent to your newspaper," he said, "probably differs from that which you will give here under oath."

"That," replied the other, rather hotly and with a visible flush, "is as you please. I have a copy of what I sent. It was not written as news, for it is incredible, but as fiction. It may go as a part of my testimony under oath."

"But you say it is incredible."

"That is nothing to you, if I also swear it is true."

The coroner was silent for a time, his eyes upon the floor. The men about the sides of the cabin talked in whispers, but seldom withdrew their gaze from the face of the corpse. Presently the coroner lifted his eyes and said: "We will resume the inquest."

The men removed their hats. The witness was sworn.

"What is your name?" the coroner asked.

"William Harker."

"Age?"

"Twenty-seven."

"You knew the deceased, Hugh Morgan?"

"Yes."

"You were with him when he died?"

"Near him."

"How did that happen—your presence, I mean?"

"I was visiting him at his place, to shoot and fish. Part of my purpose, however, was to study him and his odd, solitary way of life. He seemed a good model for a character in fiction. I sometimes write stories."

"I sometimes read them."

"Thank you."

"Stories in general—not yours."

Some of the jurors laughed.

"Relate the circumstances of this man's death," said the coroner. "You may use any notes you please."

The witness understood. He held a manuscript near the candle and, turning the leaves until he found the passage that he wanted, began to read.

". . . The sun had hardly risen when we left the house. We were looking for quail, each with a shotgun, but we had only one dog. Morgan said that our best ground was beyond a certain ridge that he pointed out, and we crossed it by a trail through the chaparral. On the other side was comparatively level ground, thickly covered with wild oats. As we emerged from the chaparral Morgan was but a few yards in advance. Suddenly we heard, at a little distance to our right and partly in front, a noise as of some animal thrashing about in the bushes, which we could see were violently agitated.

" 'We've startled a deer,' I said. 'I wish we had brought a rifle.'

"Morgan, who had stopped and was intently watching the agitated chaparral, said nothing, but had cocked both barrels of his gun and was holding it in readiness to aim. I thought him a trifle excited, which surprised me, for he had a reputation for exceptional coolness, even in moments of sudden and imminent peril.

" 'Oh, come,' I said. 'You are not going to fill up a deer with quail-shot, are you?'

"Still he did not reply; but catching sight of his face as he turned it slightly toward me, I was struck by the intensity of his look. Then I understood that we had serious business in hand, and my first conjecture was that we had 'jumped' a grizzly. I advanced to Morgan's side, cocking my gun as I moved.

"The bushes were now quiet and the sounds had ceased, but Morgan was as attentive to the place as before.

" ' What is it? What the devil is it?' I asked.

" 'That Damned Thing!' he replied, without turning his head. His voice was husky and unnatural. He trembled visibly.

"I was about to speak further, when I observed the wild oats near the place of the disturbance moving in the most inexplicable way. I can hardly describe it. The grain seemed to be stirred by a streak of wind, which not only bent it, but pressed it down—crushed it so that it did not rise; and this movement was slowly prolonging itself directly toward us.

"Nothing that I had ever seen had affected me so strangely as this unfamiliar and unaccountable phenomenon, yet I am unable to recall any sense of fear. However, the apparently causeless movement of the grain, and the slow, undeviating approach of the line of disturbance were distinctly disquieting.

"My companion appeared actually frightened, and I could hardly credit my senses when I saw him suddenly lift his gun to his shoulder and fire both barrels at the agitated grain! Before the smoke of the discharge had cleared away, I heard a loud savage cry—a scream like that of a wild animal. Flinging his gun on the ground, Morgan sprang away and ran swiftly from the spot. At the same instant I was thrown violently to the ground by the impact of something unseen in the smoke—some soft, heavy substance that seemed thrown against me with great force.

"Before I could get on my feet and recover my gun, which seemed to have been struck from my hands, I heard Morgan crying out as if in mortal agony, and mingling with his cries were such hoarse, savage sounds as one hears from fighting dogs. Inexpressibly terrified, I struggled to my feet and looked in the direction of Morgan's retreat; may Heaven in mercy spare me from another sight like that!

"At a distance of less than thirty yards was my friend, down upon one knee, his head thrown back at a frightful angle, hatless, his long hair in disorder, and his whole body in violent movement from side to side, backward and forward. His right arm was lifted and seemed to lack the hand—at least, I could see none. The other arm was invisible.

"At times, as my memory now reports this extraordinary scene, I could discern but a part of his body; it was as if he had been partly blotted out—I cannot otherwise express it—then a shifting of his position would bring it all into view again.

"All this must have occurred within a few seconds, yet in that time Morgan assumed all the postures of a determined wrestler vanquished by a superior weight and strength. I saw nothing but him, and him not always distinctly. During the entire incident his shouts and curses were heard, as if through an enveloping uproar of such sounds of rage and fury as I had never heard from the throat of man or brute!

"For a moment only I stood irresolute, then throwing down my gun I ran forward to my friend's assistance. I had a vague belief that he was suffering from a fit, or some form of convulsion. Before I could reach his side, he was prone and quiet.

"All sounds had ceased, but with a feeling of such terror as even these awful events had not inspired I now saw again the mysterious movement of the wild oats, prolonging itself from the trampled area about the prostrate man toward the edge of the wood. It was only when it had reached the wood that I was able to withdraw my eyes and look at my companion. He was dead."

The coroner rose from his seat and stood beside the dead man. Lifting an edge of the sheet he pulled it away, exposing the entire body, altogether naked and showing in the candlelight a claylike yellow. It had, however, broad marks of bluish black, obviously caused by extravasated blood from contusions. The chest and sides looked as if they had been beaten with a bludgeon. There were dreadful lacerations; the skin was torn in strips and shreds.

The coroner moved round to the end of the table and undid a silk handkerchief which has been passed under the chin and knotted on the top of the head. When the handkerchief was drawn away, it exposed what had been the throat. Some of the jurors who had risen to get a better view repented their curiosity and turned away their faces. Witness Harker went to the open window and leaned across the sill, faint and sick.

Dropping the handkerchief upon the dead man's neck, the coroner stepped to a corner of the room and from a pile of clothing produced one garment after another, each of which he held up a moment for inspection. All were torn, and stiff with blood.

"Gentlemen," the coroner said, "we have no more evidence, I think. Your duty has been already explained to you; if there is nothing you wish to ask, you may go outside and consider your verdict."

The foreman rose—a tall, bearded man of sixty. "I should like to ask one question, Mr. Coroner," he said. "What asylum did yer witness escape from?"

"Mr. Harker," said the coroner, gravely and tranquilly, "from what asylum did you last escape?"

Harker flushed crimson again but said nothing, and the seven jurors rose and solemnly filed out of the cabin.

"If you have finished insulting me, sir," said Harker, as soon as he and the officer were left alone with the dead man, "I suppose I am at liberty to go?"

"Yes."

Harker started to leave, but paused, with his hand on the door latch. The habit of his profession was strong in him—stronger than his sense of personal dignity. He turned about and said:

"The book that you have there—I recognize it as Morgan's diary. You seemed greatly interested in it; you read in it while I was testifying. May I see it? The public would like—"

"The book will cut no figure in this matter," replied the official, slipping it into his coat pocket; "all the entries in it were made before the writer's death."

As Harker passed out of the house, the jury reentered and stood about the table, on which the now covered corpse showed under the sheet with sharp definition. The foreman seated himself near the candle, produced from his breast pocket a pencil and scrap of paper, and wrote rather laboriously the following verdict, which with various degrees of effort all signed:

"We the jury, do find that the remains come to their death at the hands of a mountain lion, but some of us thinks, all the same, they had fits."

In the diary of the late Hugh Morgan are certain interesting entries, which may possibly have some scientific value. At the inquest upon his body, the book was not put in evidence; possibly the coroner thought it not worth while to confuse the jury. The date of the first of the entries cannot be ascertained; the upper part of the leaf is torn away; the part of the entry remaining follows:

". . . would run in a half-circle, keeping his head turned always toward the center, and again he would stand still, barking furiously. At last he ran away into the brush as fast as he could go. I thought at first that he had gone mad, but on returning to the house found no other alteration in his manner than what was obviously due to fear of punishment.

"Can a dog see with his nose? Do odors impress some cerebral center with images of the thing that emitted them . . . ?

Sept. 2—Looking at the stars last night, as they rose above the crest of the ridge east of the house, I observed them successively disappear—from left to right. Each was eclipsed but an instant, and only a few at the same time, but along the entire length of the ridge all that were within a degree or two of the crest were blotted out. It was as if something had passed along between me and them; but I could not see it, and the stars were not thick enough to define its outline. Ugh! I don't like this. It worries me."

Several weeks' entries are missing, three leaves being torn from the book.

"Sept. 27—It has been about here again—I find evidences of its presence every day. I watched again all last night in the same cover, gun in hand, double-charged with buckshot. In the morning the fresh footprints were there, as before. Yet I would have sworn that I did not sleep—indeed, I hardly sleep at all. It is terrible, insupportable! If these amazing experiences are real, I shall go mad; if they are fanciful, I am mad already.

"Oct 3—I shall not go—it shall not drive me away. No, this is *my* house, *my* land. God hates a coward. . . .

"Oct. 5—I can stand it no longer; I have invited Harker to pass a few weeks with me—he has a level head. I can judge from his manner if he thinks me mad.

"Oct. 7—I have the solution of the mystery; it came to me last night—suddenly, as by revelation. How simple—how terribly simple!

"There are sounds that we cannot hear. At either end of the scale are notes that stir no chord of that imperfect instrument, the human ear. They are too high or too grave. I have observed a flock of blackbirds occupying an entire tree-top—the tops of several trees—and all in full song. Suddenly—in a moment—at absolutely the same instant—all spring into the air and fly away. How? They could not all see one another—whole tree-tops intervened. At no point could a leader have been visible to all.

"There must have been a signal of warning or command, high and shrill above the din, but by me unheard. I have observed, too, the same simultaneous flight when all were silent, among not only blackbirds, but other birds—quail, for example, widely separated by bushes—even on opposite sides of a hill.

"It is known to seamen that a school of whales basking or sporting on the surface of the ocean, miles apart, with the convexity of the earth between, will sometimes dive at the same instant—all gone out of sight in a moment. The signal has been sounded—too grave for the ear of the sailor at the mast-head and his comrades on the deck—who nevertheless feel its vibrations in the ship, as the stones of a cathedral are stirred by the bass of the organ.

"As with sounds, so with colors. At each end of the solar spectrum the chemist can detect the presence of what are known as 'actinic' rays. They represent colors—integral colors in the composition of light—which we are unable to discern. The human eye is an imperfect instrument; its range is but a few octaves of the real 'chromatic scale.' I am not mad; there are colors that we cannot see.

"And, God help me! the Damned Thing is of such a color!"

15

THE DANCING PARTNER

Jerome. K. Jerome

"THIS STORY," COMMENCED MacShaugnassy, "comes from Furtwangen, a small town in the Black Forest. There lived there a very wonderful old fellow named Nicholaus Geibel. His business was the making of mechanical toys, at which work he had acquired an almost European reputation. He made rabbits that would emerge from the heart of a cabbage, flop their ears, smooth their whiskers, and disappear again; cats that would wash their faces, and mew so naturally that dogs would mistake them for real cats, and fly at them; dolls with phonographs concealed within them, that would raise their hats and say, 'Good morning; how do you do?' and some that would even sing a song.

"But he was something more than a mere mechanic; he was an artist. His work was with him a hobby, almost a passion. His shop was filled with all manner of strange things that never would, or could, be sold—things he had made for the pure love of making them. He had contrived a mechanical donkey that would trot for two hours by means of stored electricity, and trot, too, much faster than the live article, and with less need for exertion on the part of the driver; a bird that would shoot up into the air, fly round and round in a circle, and drop to earth at the exact spot from where it started; a skeleton that, supported by an upright iron bar, would dance a hornpipe; a life-size lady doll that could play the fiddle; and a gentleman with a hollow inside who could smoke a pipe and drink more lager beer than any three average German students put together, which is saying much.

"Indeed, it was the belief of the town that old Geibel could make a man capable of doing everything that a respectable man need want to do. One day he made a man who did too much, and it came about in this way:

"Young Doctor Follen had a baby, and the baby had a birthday. Its first birthday put Doctor Follen's household into somewhat of a flurry, but on the occasion of its second birthday, Mrs. Doctor Follen gave a ball in honor of the event. Old Geibel and his daughter Olga were among the guests.

"During the afternoon of the next day some three or four of Olga's bosom friends, who had also been present at the ball, dropped in to have a chat about it. They naturally fell to discussing the men, and to criticizing their dancing. Old Geibel was in the room, but he appeared to be absorbed in his newspaper, and the girls took no notice of him.

" 'There seem to be fewer men who can dance at every ball you go to,' said one of the girls.

" 'Yes, and don't the ones who can give themselves airs,' said another; 'they make quite a favor of asking you.'

" 'And how stupidly they talk,' added a third. 'They always say exactly the same things: "How charming you are looking tonight." "Do you often go to Vienna? Oh, you should, it's delightful." "What a charming dress you have on." "What a warm day it has been." "Do you like Wagner?" I do wish they'd think of something new.'

" 'Oh, I never mind how they talk,' said a fourth. 'If a man dances well he may be a fool for all I care.'

" 'He generally is,' slipped in a thin girl, rather spitefully.

" 'I go to a ball to dance,' continued the previous speaker, not noticing the interruptions. 'All I ask of a partner is that he shall hold me firmly, take me round steadily, and not get tired before I do.'

" 'A clockwork figure would be the thing for you," said the girl who had interrupted.

" 'Bravo!' cried one of the others, clapping her hands, 'what a capital idea!'

" 'What's a capital idea?' they asked.

" 'Why, a clockwork dancer, or, better still, one that would go by electricity and never run down.'

"The girls took up the idea with enthusiasm.

" 'Oh, what a lovely partner he would make,' said one; 'he would never kick you, or tread on your toes.'

" 'Or tear your dress,' said another.

" 'Or get out of step.'

" 'Or get giddy and lean on you.'

" 'And he would never want to mop his face with his handkerchief. I do hate to see a man do that after every dance.'

" 'And wouldn't want to spend the whole evening in the supper room.'

" 'Why, with a phonograph inside him to grind out all the stock remarks, you would not be able to tell him from a real man,' said the girl who had first suggested the idea.

" 'Oh, yes, you would,' said the thin girl, 'he would be so much nicer.'

"Old Geibel had laid down his paper, and was listening with both his ears. On one of the girls glancing in his direction, however, he hurriedly hid himself again behind it.

"After the girls were gone, he went into his workshop, where Olga heard him walking up and down, and every now and then chuckling to himself; and that night he talked to her a good deal about dancing and dancing men— asked what they usually said and did—what dances were most popular— what steps were gone through, with many other questions bearing on the subject.

"Then for a couple of weeks he kept much to his factory, and was very thoughtful and busy, though prone at unexpected moments to break into a quiet low laugh, as if enjoying a joke that nobody else knew of.

"A month later another ball took place in Furtwangen. On this occasion it was given by old Wenzel, the wealthy timber merchant, to celebrate his niece's betrothal, and Geibel and his daughter were again among the invited.

"When the hour arrived to set out, Olga sought her father. Not finding him in the house, she tapped at the door of his workshop. He appeared in his shirt-sleeves, looking hot but radiant.

" 'Don't wait for me,' he said, 'you go on, I'll follow you. I've got something to finish.'

"As she turned to obey he called after her, 'Tell them I'm going to bring a young man with me—such a nice young man, and an excellent dancer. All the girls will like him.' Then he laughed and closed the door.

"Her father generally kept his doings secret from everybody, but she had a pretty shrewd suspicion of what he had been planning, and so, to a certain extent, was able to prepare the guests for what was coming. Anticipation ran high, and the arrival of the famous mechanist was eagerly awaited.

"At length the sound of wheels was heard outside, followed by a great commotion in the passage, and old Wenzel himself, his jolly face red with excitement and suppressed laughter, burst into the room and announced in stentorian tones:

" 'Herr Geibel—and a friend.'

"Herr Geibel and his 'friend' entered, greeted with shouts of laughter and applause, and advanced to the center of the room.

" 'Allow me, ladies and gentlemen,' said Herr Geibel, 'to introduce you to my friend, Lieutenant Fritz. Fritz, my dear fellow, bow to the ladies and gentlemen.'

"Geibel placed his hand encouragingly on Fritz's shoulder, and the lieutenant bowed low, accompanying the action with a harsh clicking noise in his throat, unpleasantly suggestive of a death rattle. But that was only a detail.

" 'He walks a little stiffly' (old Geibel took his arm and walked him forward a few steps. He certainly did walk stiffly), 'but then, walking is not his forte. He is essentially a dancing man. I have only been able to teach him the waltz as yet, but at that he is faultless. Come, which of you ladies may I introduce him to as a partner. He keeps perfect time; he never gets tired; he won't kick you or tread on your dress; he will hold you as firmly as you like, and go as quickly or as slowly as you please; he never gets giddy; and he is full of conversation. Come, speak up for yourself, my boy.'

"The old gentlemen twisted one of the buttons at the back of his coat, and immediately Fritz opened his mouth, and in thin tones that appeared to proceed from the back of his head, remarked suddenly, 'May I have the pleasure?' and then shut his mouth again with a snap.

"That Lieutenant Fritz had made a strong impression on the company was undoubted, yet none of the girls seemed inclined to dance with him. They looked askance at his waxen face, with its staring eyes and fixed smile, and shuddered. At last old Geibel came to the girl who had conceived the idea.

" 'It is your own suggestion, carried out to the letter,' said Geibel, 'an electric dancer. You owe it to the gentleman to give him a trial.'

"She was a bright, saucy little girl, fond of a frolic. Her host added his entreaties, and she consented.

"Herr Geibel fixed the figure to her. Its right arm was screwed round her waist, and held her firmly; its delicately jointed left hand was made to fasten itself upon her right. The old toymaker showed her how to regulate its speed, and how to stop it, and release herself.

" 'It will take you round in a complete circle,' he explained; 'be careful that no one knocks against you, and alters its course.'

"The music struck up. Old Geibel put the current in motion, and Annette and her strange partner began to dance.

"For a while everyone stood watching them. The figure performed its purpose admirably. Keeping perfect time and step, and holding its little partner tight clasped in an unyielding embrace, it revolved steadily, pouring

90

forth at the same time a constant flow of squeaky conversation, broken by brief intervals of grinding silence.

" 'How charming you are looking tonight,' it remarked in its thin, far-away voice. 'What a lovely day it has been. Do you like dancing? How well our steps agree. You will give me another, won't you? Oh, don't be so cruel. What a charming gown you have on. Isn't waltzing delightful? I could go dancing for ever—with you. Have you had supper?'

"As she grew more familiar with the uncanny creature, the girl's nervousness wore off, and she entered into the fun of the thing.

" 'Oh, he's just lovely,' she cried, laughing, 'I could go on dancing with him all my life.'

"Couple after couple now joined them, and soon all the dancers in the room were whirling round behind them. Nicholaus Geibel stood looking on, beaming with childish delight at his success.

"Old Wenzel approached him, and whispered something in his ear. Geibel laughed and nodded, and the two worked their way quietly towards the door.

" 'This is the young people's house tonight,' said Wenzel, as soon as they were outside; 'you and I will have a quiet pipe and a glass of hock, over in the counting-house.'

"Meanwhile the dancing grew more fast and furious. Little Annette loosened the screw regulating her partner's rate of progress, and the figure flew round with her swifter and swifter. Couple after couple dropped out exhausted, but they only went the faster, till at length they remained dancing alone.

"Madder and madder became the waltz. The music lagged behind: the musicians, unable to keep pace, ceased, and sat staring. The younger guests applauded, but the older faces began to grow anxious.

" 'Hadn't you better stop, dear,' said one of the women, 'you'll make yourself so tired.'

"But Annette did not answer.

" 'I believe she's fainted,' cried out a girl who had caught sight of her face as it was swept by.

"One of the men sprang forward and clutched at the figure, but its impetus threw him down on to the floor, where its steel-cased feet laid bare his cheek. The thing evidently did not intend to part with its prize easily.

"Had anyone retained a cool head, the figure, one cannot help thinking, might easily have been stopped. Two or three men acting in concert might

91

have lifted it bodily off the floor, or have jammed it into a corner. But few human heads are capable of remaining cool under excitement. Those who are not present think how stupid must have been those who were; those who are reflect afterwards how simple it would have been to do this, that, or the other, if only they had thought of it at the time.

"The women grew hysterical. The men shouted contradictory directions to one another. Two of them made a bungling rush at the figure, which had the result of forcing it out of its orbit in the center of the room, and sending it crashing against the walls and furniture. A stream of blood showed itself down the girl's white frock, and followed her along the floor. The affair was becoming horrible. The women rushed screaming from the room. The men followed them.

"One sensible suggestion was made: 'Find Geibel—fetch Geibel.'

"No one had noticed him leave the room, no one knew where he was. A party went in search of him. The others, too unnerved to go back into the ballroom, crowded outside the door and listened. They could hear the steady whir of the wheels upon the polished floor as the thing spun round and round; the dull thud as every now and again it dashed itself and its burden against some opposing object and ricocheted off in a new direction.

"And everlastingly it talked in that thin ghostly voice, repeating over and over the same formula: 'How charming you are looking tonight. What a lovely day it has been. Oh, don't be so cruel. I could go on dancing for ever—with you. Have you had supper?'

Of course they sought for Geible everywhere but where he was. They looked in every room in the house, then they rushed off in a body to his own place, and spent precious minutes in waking up his deaf old housekeeper. At last it occurred to one of the party that Wenzel was missing also, and then the idea of the counting-house across the yard presented itself to them, and there they found him.

"He rose up, very pale, and followed them; and he and old Wenzel forced their way through the crowd of guests gathered outside, and entered the room, and locked the door behind them.

"From within their came the muffled sound of low voices and quick steps, followed by a confused scuffling noise, then silence, then the low voices again.

"After a time the door opened, and those near it pressed forward to enter, but old Wenzel's broad shoulders barred the way.

"'I want you—and you, Bekler,' he said, addressing a couple of the elder men. His voice was calm, but his face was deadly white. 'The rest of you, please go—get the women away as quickly as you can.'

''From that day old Nicholaus Geibel confined himself to the making of mechanical rabbits, and cats that mewed and washed their faces.''

16

THE DEAD VALLEY

Ralph Adams Cram

I HAVE A friend, Olaf Ehrensvärd, a Swede by birth, who yet, by reason of a strange and melancholy mischance of his early boyhood, has thrown his lot with that of the New World. It is a curious story of a headstrong boy and a proud and relentless family: the details do not matter here, but they are sufficient to weave a romance around the tall yellow-bearded man with the sad eyes and the voice that gives itself perfectly to plaintive little Swedish songs remembered out of childhood. In the winter evenings we play chess together, he and I, and after some close, fierce battle has been fought to a finish—usually with my own defeat—we fill our pipes again, and Ehrensvärd tells me stories of the far, half-remembered days in the fatherland, before he went to sea: stories that grow very strange and incredible as the night deepens and the fire falls together, but stories that, nevertheless, I fully believe.

One of them made a strong impression on me, so I set it down here, only regretting that I cannot reproduce the curiously perfect English and the delicate accent which to me increased the fascination of the tale. Yet, as best I can remember it, here it is.

"I never told you how Nils and I went over the hills to Hallsberg, and how we found the Dead Valley, did I? Well, this is the way it happened. I must have been about twelve yeas old, and Nils Sjöberg, whose father's estate joined ours, was a few months younger. We were inseparable just at that time, and whatever we did, we did together.

"Once a week it was market day in Engelholm, and Nils and I went always there to see the strange sights that the market gathered from all the surrounding country. One day we quite lost our hearts, for an old man from across the Elfborg had brought a little dog to sell, that seemed to us the most beautiful dog in all the world. He was a round, wooly puppy, so funny that

Nils and I sat down on the ground and laughed at him, until he came and played with us in so jolly a way that we felt that there was only one really desirable thing in life, and that was the little dog of the old man from across the hills. But alas! we had not half money enough wherewith to buy him, so we were forced to get the old man not to sell him before the next market day, promising that we would bring the money for him then. He gave us his word, and we ran home very fast and implored our mothers to give us money for the little dog.

"We got the money, but we could not wait for the next market day. Suppose the puppy should be sold! The thought frightened us so that we begged and implored that we might be allowed to go over the hills to Hallsberg where the old man lived, and get the little dog ourselves, and at last they told us we might go. By starting early in the morning we should reach Hallsberg by three o'clock, and it was arranged that we should stay there that night with Nils's aunt, and leaving by noon the next day, be home again by sunset.

"Soon after sunrise we were on our way, after having received minute instructions as to just what we should do in all possible and impossible circumstances, and finally a repeated injunction that we should start for home at the same hour the next day, so that we might get safely back before nightfall.

"For us, it was magnificent sport, and we started off with our rifles, full of the sense of our very great importance: yet the journey was simple enough, along a good road, across the big hills we knew so well, for Nils and I had shot over half the territory this side of the dividing ridge of the Elfborg. Back of Engelholm lay a valley, from which rose the low mountains, and we had to cross this, and then follow the road along the side of the hills for three or four miles, before a narrow path branched off to the left, leading up through the pass.

"Nothing occurred of interest on the way over, and we reached Hallsberg in due season, found to our inexpressible joy that the little dog was not sold, secured him, and so went to the house of Nils's aunt to spend the night.

"Why we did not leave early on the following day, I can't quite remember; at all events, I know we stopped at a shooting range just outside of the town, where most attractive paste-board pigs were sliding slowly through painted foliage, serving so as beautiful marks. The result was that we did not get fairly started for home until afternoon, and as we found ourselves at last pushing up the side of the mountain with the sun dangerously near their summits, I think we were a little scared at the prospect of the examination and possible punishment that awaited us when we got home at midnight.

"Therefore we hurried as fast as possible up the mountainside, while the blue dusk closed in about us, and the light died in the purple sky. At first we had talked hilariously, and the little dog had leaped ahead of us with the utmost joy. Latterly, however, a curious oppression came on us; we did not speak or even whistle, while the dog fell behind, following us with hesitation in every muscle.

"We had passed through the foothills and the low spurs of the mountains, and were almost at the top of the main range, when life seemed to go out of everything, leaving the world dead, so suddenly silent the forest became, so stagnant the air. Instinctively we halted to listen.

"Perfect silence—the crushing silence of deep forests at night; and more, for always, even in the most impenetrable fastness of the wooded mountains, is the multitudinous murmur of little lives, awakened by the darkness, exaggerated and intensified by the stillness of the air and the great dark; but here and now the silence seemed unbroken even by the turn of a leaf, the movement of a twig, the note of night bird or insect. I could hear the blood beat through my veins; and the crushing of the grass under our feet as we advanced with hesitating steps sounded like the falling of trees.

"And the air was stagnant—dead. The atmosphere seemed to lie upon my body like the weight of sea on a diver who has ventured too far into its awful depths. What we usually call silence seems so only in relation to the din of ordinary experience. This was silence in the absolute, and it crushed the mind while it intensified the senses, bringing down the awful weight of inextinguishable fear.

"I know that Nils and I stared toward each other in abject terror, listening to our quick, heavy breathing that sounded to our acute senses like the fitful rush of waters. And the poor little dog we were leading justified our terror. The black oppression seemed to crush him even as it did us. He lay close to the ground, moaning feebly, and dragging himself painfully and slowly closer to Nils's feet. I think this exhibition of utter animal fear was the last touch, and must inevitably have blasted our reason—mine anyway; but just then, as we stood quaking on the bounds of madness, came a sound, so awful, so ghastly, so horrible, that it seemed to rouse us from the dead spell that was on us.

"In the depth of the silence came a cry, beginning as a low, sorrowful moan, rising to a tremulous shriek, culminating in a yell that seemed to tear the night in sunder and rend the world as by a cataclysm. So fearful was it that I could not believe it had actual existence: it passed previous experience, the powers of belief, and for a moment I thought it the result of my own animal terror, an hallucination born of tottering reason.

"A glance at Nils dispelled this thought in a flash. In the pale light of the high stars he was the embodiment of all possible human fear, quaking with an ague, his jaw fallen, his tongue out, his eyes protruding like those of a hanged man. Without a word we fled, the panic of fear giving us strength, and together, the little dog caught close in Nils's arms, we sped down the side of the cursed mountains—anywhere, goal was of no account: we had but one impulse—to get away from that place.

"So under the black trees and the far white stars that flashed through the still leaves overhead, we leaped down the mountainside, regardless of path or landmark, straight through the tangled underbrush, across mountain streams, through fens and copses, anywhere, so only that our course was downward.

"How long we ran thus, I have no idea, but by and by the forest fell behind, and we found ourselves among the foothills, and fell exhausted on the dry short grass, panting like tired dogs.

"It was lighter here in the open, and presently we looked around to see where we were, and how we were to strike out in order to find the path that would lead us home. We looked in vain for a familiar sign. Behind us rose the great wall of black forest on the flank of the mountain: before us lay the undulating mounds of low foothills, unbroken by trees or rocks, and beyond, only the fall of black sky bright with multitudinous stars that turned its velvet depth to a luminous gray.

"As I remember, we did not speak to each other once: the terror was too heavy on us for that, but by and by we rose simultaneously and started out across the hills.

"Still the same silence, the same dead, motionless air—air that was at once sultry and chilling: a heavy heat struck through with an icy chill that felt almost like the burning of frozen steel. Still carrying the helpless dog, Nils pressed on through the hills, and I followed close behind. At last, in front of us, rose a slope of moor touching the white stars. We climbed it wearily, reached the top, and found ourselves gazing down into a great, smooth valley, filled halfway to the brim with —what?

"As far as the eye could see stretched a level plain of ashy white, faintly phosphorescent, a sea of velvet fog that lay like motionless water, or rather like a floor of alabaster, so dense did it appear, so seemingly capable of sustaining weight. If it were possible, I think that sea of dead white mist struck even greater terror into my soul than the heavy silence or the deadly cry—so ominous was it, so utterly unreal, so phantasmal, so impossible, as it lay there like a dead ocean under the steady stars. Yet through that mist *we must go!* There seemed no other way home, and, shattered with abject fear, mad with the one desire to get back, we started down the slope to where the sea of milky mist ceased, sharp and distinct around the stems of the rough grass.

"I put one foot into the ghostly fog. A chill as of death struck through me, stopping my heart, and I threw myself backward on the slope. At that instant came again the shriek, close, close, right in our ears, in ourselves, and far out across the damnable sea I saw the cold fog lift like a waterspout and toss itself high in writhing convolutions toward the sky. The stars began to grow dim as thick vapor swept across them, and in the growing dark I saw a great, watery moon lift itself slowly above the palpitating sea, vast and vague in the gathering mist.

"This was enough: we turned and fled along the margin of the white sea that throbbed now with fitful motion below us, rising, rising, slowly and steadly, driving us higher and higher up the side of the foothills.

"It was a race for life; that we knew. How we kept it up I cannot understand, but we did, and at last we saw the white sea fall behind us as we staggered up the end of the valley, and then down into a region that we knew, and so into the old path. The last thing I remember was hearing a strange voice, that of Nils, but horribly changed, stammer brokenly, 'The dog is dead!' and then the whole world turned around twice, slowly and resistlessly, and consciousness went out with a crash.

"It was some three weeks later, as I remember, that I awoke in my own room, and found my mother sitting beside the bed. I could not think very well at first, but as I slowly grew strong again, vague flashes of recollection began to come to me, and little by little the whole sequence of events of that awful night in the Dead Valley came back. All that I could gain from what was told me was that three weeks before I had been found in my own bed, raging sick, and that my illness grew fast into brain fever. I tried to speak of the dread things that had happened to me, but I saw at once that no one looked on them save as the hauntings of a dying frenzy, and so I closed my mouth and kept my own counsel.

"I must see Nils, however, and so I asked for him. My mother told me that he also had been ill with a strange fever, but that he was now quite well again. Presently they brought him in, and when we were alone I began to speak to him of the night on the mountain. I shall never forget the shock that struck me down on my pillow when the boy denied everything: denied having gone with me, ever having heard the cry, having seen the valley, or feeling the deadly chill of the ghostly fog. Nothing would shake his determined ignorance, and in spite of myself I was forced to admit that his denials came from no policy of concealment, but from blank oblivion.

"My weakened brain was in a turmoil. Was it all but the floating phantasm of delirium? Or had the horror of the real thing blotted Nils's mind into blankness so far as the events of the night in the Dead Valley were concerned? The latter explanation seemed the only one, else how explain the sudden illness which in a night had struck us both down? I said nothing more, either to Nils or to my own people, but waited, with a growing determination that, once well again, I would find that valley if it really existed.

"It was some weeks before I was really well enough to go, but finally, late in September, I chose a bright, warm, still day, the last smile of the dying summer, and started early in the morning along the path that led to Hallsberg. I was sure I knew where the trail struck off to the right, down which we had come from the valley of dead water, for a great tree grew by the Hallsberg path at the point where, with a sense of salvation, we had found the home road. Presently I saw it to the right, a little distance ahead.

"I think the bright sunlight and the clear air had worked as a tonic to me, for by the time I came to the foot of the great pine, I had quite lost faith in the verity of the vision that haunted me, believing at last that it was indeed but the nightmare of madness. Nevertheless, I turned sharply to the right, at the base of the tree, into a narrow path that led through a dense thicket. As I did so I tripped over something. A swarm of flies sung into the air around me, and looking down I saw the matted fleece, with the poor little bones thrusting through, of the dog we had bought in Hallsberg.

"Then my courage went out with a puff, and I knew that it all was true, and that now I was frightened. Pride and the desire for adventure urged me on, however, and I pressed into the close thicket that barred my way. The path was hardly visible: merely the worn road of some small beasts, for, though it showed in the crisp grass, the bushes above grew thick and hardly penetrable. The land rose slowly, and rising grew clearer, until at last I came out on a great slope of hill, unbroken by trees or shrubs, very like my memory of that rise of land we had topped in order that we might find the Dead Valley and the icy fog. I looked at the sun; it was bright and clear, and all around insects were humming in the autumn air, and birds were darting to and fro. Surely there was no danger, not until nightfall at least; so I began to whistle, and with a rush mounted the last crest of brown hill.

"There lay the Dead Valley! A great oval basin, almost as smooth and regular as though made by man. On all sides the grass crept over the bark of the encircling hills, dusty green on the crests, then fading into ashy brown, and so to a deadly white, this ash color forming a thin ring, running in a long line around the slope. And then? Nothing. Bare, brown, hard earth, glittering with grains of alkali, but otherwise dead and barren. Not a tuft of grass, not a stick of brushwood, not even a stone, but only the vast expanse of beaten clay.

"In the midst of the basin, perhaps a mile and a half away, the level expanse was broken by a great dead tree, rising leafless and gaunt into the air. Without a moment's hesitation I started down into the valley and made for this goal. Every particle of fear seemed to have left me, and even the valley itself did not look so very terrifying. At all events, I was driven by an overwhelming curiosity and there seemed to be but one thing in the world to do—to get to that tree! As I trudged along over the hard earth, I noticed that the multitudinous voices of birds and insects had died away. No bee or butterfly hovered through the air, no insects leaped or crept over the dull earth. The very air itself was stagnant.

"As I drew near the skeleton tree, I noticed the glint of sunlight on a kind of white mound around its roots, and I wondered curiously. It was not until I had come close that I saw its nature.

"All around the roots and barkless trunk was heaped a wilderness of little bones. Tiny skulls of rodents and of birds, thousands of them, rising about the dead tree and streaming off for several yards in all directions, until the dreadful pile ended in isolated skulls and scattered skeletons. Here and there a larger bone appeared—the thigh of a sheep, the hoofs of a horse, and to one side, grinning slowly, a human skull.

"I stood quite still, staring with all my eyes, when suddenly the dense silence was broken by a faint, forlorn cry high over my head. I looked up and saw a great falcon turning and sailing downward just over the tree. In a moment more she fell motionless on the bleaching bones.

"Horror struck me, and I rushed for home, my brain whirling, a strange numbness growing in me. I ran steadily, on and on. At last I glanced up. Where was the rise of the hill? I looked around wildly. Close before me was the dead tree with its pile of bones. I had circled it round and round, and the valley wall was still a mile and a half away.

"I stood dazed and frozen. The sun was sinking, red and dull, toward the line of hills. In the east the dark was growing fast. Was there still time? *Time!* It was not *that* I wanted, it was *will!* My feet seemed clogged as in a nightmare. I could hardly drag them over the barren earth. And then I felt the slow chill creeping through me. I looked down. Out of the earth a thin mist was rising, collecting in little pools that grew ever larger until they joined here and there, their currents swirling slowly like thin blue smoke.

The western hills halved the copper sun. When it was dark I should hear that shriek again, and then I should die. I knew that, and with every remaining atom of will I staggered toward the red west through the writhing mist that crept clammily around my ankles, retarding my steps.

"And as I fought my way off from the tree, the horror grew, until at last I thought I was going to die. The silence pursued me like dumb ghosts, the still air held my breath, the hellish fog caught at my feet like cold hands.

"But I won! though not a moment too soon. As I crawled on my hands and knees up the brown slope, I heard, far away and high in the air, the cry that already had almost bereft me of reason. It was faint and vague, but unmistakable in its horrible intensity. I glanced behind. The fog was dense and pallid, heaving undulously up up the brown slope. The sky was gold under the setting sun, but below was the ashy gray of death. I stood for a moment on the brink of this sea of hell, and then leaped down the slope. The sunset opened before me, the night closed behind, and as I crawled home weak and tired, darkness shut down on the Dead Valley."

17

DEADLY GAME
Edward Wellen

DEEP IN THE dusk of the wood Jess Seely saw the beast's pupils shine.

He had been careful of every footfall and of every shift of his shotgun as he made his way through the forest. But they had got wind of him, they had been on his trail from the instant he stepped into the wood, they were all around him now. The eyes vanished, but he could hear soft scurryings.

Move quietly and keep your eyes open; that was the first lesson he had learned and the best. He moved still deeper into the wood, years of woodcraft in every move. The years had slowed him. But the experience gained in those same years had made every move tell. He heard soft scurryings. They were stalking him. How would they try to get him this time?

He let the shotgun dangle carelessly so the barrels threatened himself.

Would that tempt one of them—a squirrel?—to leap from a limb, aiming to strike at the trigger and set off the shot? No, he saw it now. They had something else in wait just ahead. A deadfall.

Only at the last fraction of a second did his sweep of eye take in the one bit of beaver track they had failed to brush away.

He walked slowly on, straining for sign of trip wire. It would be a length of vine; he should spot it by its dying color. He should, but he did not. He frowned. Was he guessing wrong? Then, he spotted it—a length of living vine, one end still rooted, the other wrapping the trunk of a great spruce in a neat knot. The spruce itself seemed untouched, at first sight. They had plastered the gnawings back in place, but to his eyes—now that he knew what he was looking for—there stood out enough difference between the living wood and the dead to show the big bite they had taken out of the base of the tree. He admired their sense of balance. His lightest brush against the vine would bring the tree crashing down on him.

103

To raise—then dash—their hopes, he tried to keep from letting on he had seen the setup and went on without breaking stride—then he lengthened and lifted his step at the last to miss triggering the trip wire by a hair. A silence, then a small chatter of disappointment.

He kept on. Under the talking foliage of quaking aspen he made out other sounds. Soft scurryings. What would they have waiting ahead? A noose? No, poison-tipped thorns.

The rustle of leaves gave warning. He whirled aside. One of them—a raccoon?—loosed a bent branch of hawthorn. The branch whipped at him and the wicked spikes barely missed his flesh. The branch was still trembling when he raised his shotgun but the raccoon—he felt sure it was a raccoon and smiled, remembering the first of them, Bandido—had vanished. Yet he had to make the futile gesture so those watching would not know the gun bore no load. He eyed the wicked spikes and again smiled. On each tip a sticky smear held a thick powdering. The powder would be dried leaves of foxglove. Or had they found something better? He smiled again at more chatter of frustration.

But he sharpened his senses as he pushed on. He stopped where the going grew suddenly easy. They had cleared a path; it invited him to bypass a tangle of underbrush. He looked to see that the overarching boughs did not hold loops of vine ready to drop, and took the path. Nothing. But there had to be something. He pushed on, then slowed, smelling dampness that was not the dankness of mold.

Ahead, the trail widened into a clearing. In the center of the clearing lay a patch of spongy ground that could be lethal quagmire. Yet the tracks of a big woodchuck led straight across the patch, promising the ground would hold. Something about the tracks gave Jess Seely pause. They had a dainty, yet dragging, look.

He read faint tracks on either side of the patch and knew what had taken place. Not one but three woodchucks had crossed the clearing together, abreast, almost in step. Two had kept to the solid ground on either side of the bog, each holding in its jaws one end of a fallen tree limb. The big woodchuck in the middle had ridden with the bulk of his weight on that support, making footprints without sinking into the mire.

Jess Seely smiled and skirted the patch.

He wondered vaguely why the chatter he heard now seemed to be chatter not of frustration but of expectation. He had no time for more than vague wonder at that, and at the sudden hush. The ground—not ground but a covering of dirt over a wickerwork of branches—gave under him. His hands flung up, the gun shot out of his grip. He fell.

His coming to was an in-and-out thing, pulsing awareness, intermitting dream.

The pit was deep. They were good at digging. They had patience. He nodded, and blacked out.

He came to again. He lay crumpled, a leg bent strangely under him. He was helpless, but they would not come right away. They would not trust him, they would wait to make sure he was not playing helpless. Then they would come.

They had patience.

He tightened himself against the pain. This was what he had worked toward, and in any case it would have been useless to have regrets. He had no regrets. He had been a good game warden. He lapsed into unconsciousness again, smiling.

The wait was long and he knew he had passed through a spell of delirium. There was a timeless moment when it seemed to him he came aware in the past, reliving the start of it. That had been the time when, feeling a gnawing helplessness, seeing the day coming when he would no longer be there to save them from his fellow man, he caught that poacher. The poacher was too busy to sense his approach, busy cursing some animal that had once again sprung the trap and made off with the bait.

He knew, in that long-ago day, that it would be wasting time to haul the man into court. The local justice of the peace would let him off with a mild rebuke. So Jess Seely booted the man out of the wood, baited and reset the trap and lay in wait.

At last a large raccoon nosed into view, picked up a piece of twig in a forepaw and reached cautiously to stick it into the trap. The trap snapped shut its grin on nothing. The raccoon was about to make off with the bait when Jess Seely remembered to move. He aimed his hypodermic gun and shot the raccoon to sleep. He carried the raccoon home—and that was the start of Jess Seely's private, unauthorized and top-secret psychological testing laboratory.

The raccoon made an auspicious first subject, quickly mastering all sorts of release mechanisms to escape from puzzle boxes and to win rewards, learning to fit pegs into holes and to tie knots. The one stupidity was Jess Seely's. He had grown fond of the raccoon—Bandido—and he had let Bandido sense that. It was lucky Jess Seely had realized that at this early stage, or the whole thing would have gone for nothing. He had to break Bandido of his liking. He forced himself to set about coldly instilling in Bandido hate and fear of man—any man.

Only when he felt sure he had brought that about did he free Bandido. He tagged Bandido and released him into the wild, then hunted other promising subjects. There was only one Bandido. Jess Seely did not give any of the others a name.

He did not dare.

He rigged more and more sophisticated release mechanisms, and in time was graduating animals that were able to disarm any trap safely and, before making off with the bait, move the trap, reset it and conceal it so the original setter of the trap would step into it. Other than a shot from a trapper who thought the resetting was his doing, Jess Seely had little trouble with poachers after that.

At mating seasons he used his capture-gun again to bring together the brightest of his subjects. And in thirty years, thanks to training and selective breeding, the wildlife under his protection had learned to deal with all traps, set out sentries, string alarm wires across trails, toss stones to mislead hunters and put hounds out of action and, with earth or urine, fight fire.

Now he was clear in his mind and he felt a humble pride. He had set out to teach them to guard their preserve, to save themselves. He had done a good job of this. He had taught them well. He heard them coming closer to the rim of the pit. Now he saw their eyes.

He fixed on one face. Old Bandido! But that couldn't be. Old Bandido was long dead. This was a son or a grandson or a great-grandson. In a sense they were all children of Jess Seely.

No matter. They would have no pity on him. He had taught them well indeed, he thought smiling.

18

DEAR PEN PAL

A. E. van Vogt

Planet Aurigae II

Dear Pen Pal:

When I first received your letter from the interstellar correspondence club, my impulse was to ignore it. The mood of one who has spent the last seventy planetary periods—years I suppose you would call them—in an Aurigaen prison, does not make for a pleasant exchange of letters. However, life is very boring, and so I finally settled myself to the task of writing you.

Your description of Earth sounds exciting. I would like to live there for a while, and I have a suggestion in this connection, but I won't mention it till I have developed it further.

You will have noticed the material on which this letter is written. It is a highly sensitive metal, very thin, very flexible, and I have enclosed several sheets of it for your use. Tungsten dipped in any strong acid makes an excellent mark on it. It is important to me that you do write on it, as my fingers are too hot—literally—to hold your paper without damaging it.

I'll say no more just now. It is possible you will not care to correspond with a convicted criminal, and therefore I shall leave the next move up to you. Thank you for your letter. Though you did not know its destination, it brought a moment of cheer into my drab life.

Skander

Aurigae II

Dear Pen Pal:

Your prompt reply to my letter made me happy. I am sorry your doctor thought it excited you too much, and sorry, also, if I have described my

107

predicament in such a way as to make you feel badly. I welcome your many questions and I shall try to answer them all.

You say the international correspondence club has no record of having sent any letters to Aurigae. That, according to them, the temperature on the second planet of Aurigae sun is more than 500 degrees Fahrenheit. And that life is not known to exist there. Your club is right about the temperature and the letters. We have what your people would call a hot climate, but then we are not a hydro-carbon form of life, and find 500 degrees very pleasant.

I must apologize for deceiving you about the way your first letter was sent to me. I didn't want to frighten you away by telling you too much at once. After all, I could not be expected to know that you would be enthusiastic to hear from me.

The truth is than I am a scientist, and, along with the other members of my race, I have known for some centuries that there were other inhabited systems in the galaxy. Since I am allowed to experiment in my spare hours, I amused myself in attempts at communication. I developed several simple systems for breaking in on galactic communication operations, but it was not until I developed a subspacewave control that I was able to draw your letter (along with several others, which I did not answer) into a cold chamber.

I use the cold chamber as both sending and receiving center, and since you were kind enough to use the material which I sent you, it was easy for me to locate your second letter among the mass of mail that accumulated at the nearest headquarters of the interstellar correspondence club.

How did I learn your language? After all, it is a simple one, particularly the written language seems easy. I had no difficulty with it. If you are still interested in writing me, I shall be happy to continue the correspondence.

Skander

Aurigae II

Dear Pen Pal:

Your enthusiasm is refreshing. You say that I failed to answer your question about how I expected to visit Earth. I confess I deliberately ignored the question, as my experiment had not yet proceeded far enough. I want you to bear with me a short time longer, and then I will be able to give you the details. You are right in saying that it would be difficult for a being who lives at a temperature of 500 degrees Fahrenheit to mingle freely with the people of Earth. This was never my intention, so please relieve your mind. However, let us drop that subject for the time being.

I appreciate the delicate way in which you approach the subject of my

108

imprisonment. But it is quite unnecessary. I performed forbidden experiments upon my body in a way that was deemed dangerous to the public welfare. For instance, among other things, I once lowered my surface temperature to 150 degrees Fahrenheit, and so shortened the radioactive cycle-time of my surroundings. This caused an unexpected break in the normal person to person energy flow in the city where I lived, and so charges were laid against me. I have thirty more years to serve. It would be pleasant to leave my body behind and tour the universe—but as I said I'll discuss that later.

I wouldn't say that we're a superior race. We have certain qualities which apparently your people do not have. We live longer, not because of any discoveries we've made about ourselves, but because our bodies are built of a more endurable element—I don't know your name for it, but the atomic weight is 52.9#.* Our scientific discoveries are of the kind that would normally be made by a race with our kind of physical structure. The fact that we can work with temperatures as high as—I don't know just how to put that—has been very helpful in the development of the subspace energies which are extremely hot, and require delicate adjustments. In the later stages these adjustments can be made by machinery, but in the development the work must be done by "hand"—I put that word in quotes, because we have no hands in the same way that you have.

I am enclosing a photographic plate, properly cooled and chemicalized for your climate. I wonder if you would set it up and take a picture of yourself. All you have to do is arrange it properly on the basis of the laws of light—that is, light travels in straight lines, so stand in front of it—and when you are ready *think* "Ready!" The picture will be automatically taken.

Would you do this for me? If you are interested, I will also send you a picture of myself, though I must warn you. My appearance will probably shock you.

Sincerely,
Skander

Planet Aurigae II

Dear Pen Pal:
Just a brief note to answer your question. It is not necessary to put the

---

*A radioactive isotope of chromium.—Author's Note.

plate into a camera. You describe this as a dark box. The plate will take the picture when you think, "Ready!" I assure you it will be flooded with light.

Skander

Aurigae II

Dear Pen Pal:

You say that while you were waiting for the answer to my last letter you showed the photographic plate to one of the doctors at the hospital—I cannot picture what you mean by doctor or hospital, but let that pass—and he took the problem up with the government authorities. Problem? I don't understand. I thought we were having a pleasant correspondence, private and personal.

I shall certainly appreciate your sending that picture of yourself.

Skander

Aurigae II

Dear Pen Pal:

I assure you I am not annoyed at your action. It merely puzzled me, and I am sorry the plate has not been returned to you. Knowing what governments are, I can imagine that it will not be returned to you for some time, so I am taking the liberty of enclosing another plate.

I cannot imagine why you should have been warned against continuing this correspondence. What do they expect me to do?—eat you up at long distance? I'm sorry but I don't like hydrogen in my diet.

In any event, I would like your picture as a memento of our friendship, and I will send mine as soon as I have received yours. You may keep it or throw it away, or give it to your government authorities—but at least I will have the knowledge that I've given a fair exchange.

With all best wishes
Skander

Aurigae II

Dear Pen Pal:

Your last letter was so slow in coming that I thought you had decided to break off the correspondence. I was sorry to notice that you failed to enclose the photograph, puzzled by your reference to having a relapse, and cheered by your statement that you would send it along as soon as you felt better—whatever that means. However, the important thing is that you did write, and I respect the philosophy of your club which asks its members not to write of pessimistic matters. We all have our own problems which we regard as over-shadowing the problems of others. Here I am in prison, doomed to spend the next 30 years tucked away from the main stream of life. Even the thought is hard on my restless spirit, though I know I have a long life ahead of me after my release.

In spite of your friendly letter, I won't feel that you have completely re-established contact with me until you send the photograph.

Yours in expectation,
Skander

Aurigae II

Dear Pen Pal:

The photograph arrived. As you suggest, your appearance startled me. From your description I thought I had mentally reconstructed your body. It just goes to show that words cannot really describe an object which has never been seen.

You'll notice that I've enclosed a photograph of myself, as I promised I would. Chunky, metallic looking chap, am I not, very different, I'll wager, than you expected? The various races with whom we have communicated become wary of us when they discover we are highly radioactive, and that literally we are a radioactive form of life, the only such (that we know of) in the universe. It's been very trying to be so isolated and, as you know, I have occasionally mentioned that I had hopes of escaping not only the deadly imprisonment to which I am being subjected but also the body which cannot escape.

Perhaps you'll be interested in hearing how far this idea has developed. The problem involved is one of exchange of personalties with someone else. Actually, it is not really an exchange in the accepted meaning of the word. It is necessary to get an impress of both individuals, of their mind and of their thoughts as well as their bodies. Since this phase is purely mechanical, it is simply a matter of taking complete photographs and of exchanging them. By complete I mean of course every vibration must be registered. The next step is to make sure the two photographs are exchanged, that is, that each party has somewhere near him a complete photograph of the other. (It is already too late, Pen Pal. I have set in motion the sub-space energy interflow between the two plates, so you might as well read on.) As I have

111

said it is not exactly an exchange of personalities. The original personality in each individual is suppressed, literally pushed back out of the consciousness, and the image personality from the "photographic" plate replaces it.

You will take with you a complete memory of your life on Earth, and I will take along memory of my life on Aurigae. Simultaneously, the memory of the receiving body will be blurrily at our disposal. A part of us will always be pushing up, striving to regain consciousness, but always lacking the strength to succeed.

As soon as I grow tired of Earth, I will exchange bodies in the same way with a member of some other race. Thirty years hence, I will be happy to reclaim my body, and you can then have whatever body I last happened to occupy.

This should be a very happy arrangement for us both. You, with your short life expectancy, will have out-lived all your contemporaries and will have had an interesting experience. I admit I expect to have the better of the exchange—but now, enough of explanation. By the time you reach this part of the letter it will be me reading it, not you. But if any part of you is still aware, so long for now, Pen Pal. It's been nice having all those letters from you. I shall write you from time to time to let you know how things are going with my tour.

Skander

Aurigae II

Dear Pen Pal:

Thanks a lot for forcing the issue. For a long time I hesitated about letting you play such a trick on yourself. You see, the government scientists analyzed the nature of that first photographic plate you sent me, and so the final decision was really up to me. I decided that anyone as eager as you were to put one over should be allowed to succeed.

Now I know I didn't have to feel sorry for you. Your plan to conquer Earth wouldn't have gotten anywhere, but the fact that you had the idea ends the need for sympathy.

By this time you will have realized for yourself that a man who has been paralyzed since birth, and is subject to heart attacks, cannot expect a long life span. I am happy to tell you that your once lonely pen pal is enjoying himself, and I am happy to sign myself with a name to which I expect to become accustomed.

With best wishes,
Skander

19

DEATHWATCH

Norman Spinrad

THE OLD MAN'S breathing was shallow now, dry and brittle, each breath an effort of no little significance. His head rested on the pillow like a dried and shriveled nut on a napkin.

The man standing at the foot of the bed stared impassively into indefinite space. His strong, unlined face showed no emotion—though there was a strange look, indeed, about his eyes, a deep, ageless resignation that seemed grossly out of place on a face that could be no more than twenty-five.

The woman leaning her head on his shoulder had long, thick, honey-colored hair framing a young face wet with tears. Now and then a sob would wrack her body, and the man would stroke her hair with near-mechanical tenderness. He would pass his tongue slowly over his lips as if searching for words of comfort.

But there were no words and there was no comfort. The only sound in the room was the rasping breath of the old man in the bed sighing the dregs of his life away. . . .

He smiled happily at his wife as she cuddled the newborn baby in her arms. He was, like all babies to all parents, a beautiful baby: weight, nine pounds; skin, ruddy; voice, excellent.

A son, he thought, *My* son. Secretly, he was relieved. While the doctors had assured them that there was no reason in the world why they could not have children, he had always had that inane, irrational feeling that he would never really be able to *know* that it was true until this moment, when he could actually reach out and touch his son.

He chucked the baby under the chin, and it cooed satisfactorily. All was right with the world. . . .

Until a half hour later, when the doctor told him the truth about his child. The invisible but inescapable truth.

It took him a while to fully understand. And when he finally did, his first thought was: How will I tell *her?*

To his great relief and mystification, his wife took it better than he did. At least she seemed to. Or was it merely that built-in anesthetic that women seem to have that lets them blot out any tragedy that is far enough in the past or far enough into the indefinite future?

Whatever it was, he was grateful for it. Bad enough for a man to have to look ahead decades into the future and face the inevitable, to have to live with the thought of it long before the reality itself. . . .

For a woman, *let her just have her son.*

He was a boy, just like any other boy, wasn't he? Like every other normal boy. He would learn to walk, to talk, to play with other children. He'd probably have the mumps, and maybe chickenpox, too. There'd be good report cards and bad ones. He'd come home with black eyes and skinned knees. . . .

Not a monster. A boy like any other boy. A woman could forget. A woman could lose herself in just being a mother.

But for how long could he make himself feel like a father?

The mutation was called immortality, perhaps inaccurately, since it would take forever to know whether it was really possible to live forever.

Nevertheless, men and women began to be born who did not grow old and die.

Not that they were invulnerable; they simply did not age. A balance was struck in their systems at about the age of twenty, and from that age on, the body renewed itself; nervous system, circulatory system, endocrine system, digestive system—all retained their youthful vigor indefinitely.

They were not supermen. They could succumb to the usual diseases. They were just as prone to accidents as other men. They were neither better nor wiser. The mutation, like most other successful mutations, was a narrow one—it produced otherwise ordinary human beings who would not age.

The why of the mutation was, of course, one of those basically unanswerable riddles of evolution. Why do men have no tails? Why do birds have wings? Why intelligence itself?

Immortality was just one more in nature's endless series of experiments.

Like all the others, it was, in itself, neither a gift nor a curse. It was whatever men would make of it.

And what it would make of men.

He tried earnestly to be a good father. He was not gruff with his son—if anything, he was too gentle, for he could not look at that boyish face without a pang of regret, without a feeling of sadness.

He did try his best. He tried to be a companion to his son: fishing trips, camping, games—they did the usual father-son things together. And later on, he tried to be his son's confidant, to share his dreams and yearnings and trials. He tried as few fathers try.

But it all fell flat.

Because it was all mechanical, it was all hypocritical. For there was one thing he could not bring himself to try, there was one thing he could not bear.

He could not let himself love his son.

And though he would scarcely admit it, even to himself, he was relieved when his son graduated from college and took a job 3000 miles away across the continent. It was as if half of a great weight were lifted from his shoulders; as if a dagger that had been hanging directly over his head had been moved across the room.

His wife took it like all mothers take it—it hurt to have a continent between her son and herself, but the hurt would grow numb with time. . . .

The immortality mutation bred true. It would be passed along from generation to generation like any other dominant gene. Two immortals could produce immortal children, just as two dark-haired people produce dark-haired children.

The immortals would breed as fast as ordinary men, and since youth and potency would be theirs forever, they would be able to produce an unlimited number of offspring in their millennial live spans.

Since the immortals, in the long run, could easily outbreed mortals, the entire human race would someday be heir to the gift of immortality. In the long run.

In the short run. . . .

Their son wrote home, and when he did, the answering letters were invariably written by his mother and countersigned, unread, by his father.

There were trips home evey year or so, visits that his mother waited

115

eagerly for and that his father dreaded. There was no hostitility between father and son, but there was no warmth either—neither genuine pleasure at meeting nor sorrow at parting. . . .

He knew that he had closed his son out of his heart. It was a cold, calculating thing to do. He knew that, too.

But he knew that he *had* to do it, for the sake of his own sanity, to be a rock that his wife could lean on. . . .

It was a sacrifice, and it was not without its cost. Something within him seemed to shrivel and die. Pity, compassion, love, became academic, ersatz emotions to him. They could not move him—it was as if they were being described to him by somebody else.

And occasionally he would find himself lying awake next to his sleeping wife, in the loneliest hours of the night, and wishing that he could cry at least one real tear.

Just one. . . .

The laws of genetics are statistical—the coldest form of mathematics. A dominant gene, like the immortality gene, breeds more or less true. Immortality was dominant, death was becoming recessive.

But recessive does not necessarily mean extinct.

Every so often—and the frequency may be calculated by the laws of genetics—two dark-haired people produce a blond, two healthy people a diabetic, two ordinary people a genius or an immortal, two immortals. . . .

The old man's breath was stilled now. His heart gave one last futile flutter and gave up the fight.

Now there were only two lives in the room, two lives that would go on and on and on and on. . . .

The man searched his heart futilely for some hint of genuine pain, some real and human emotion beyond the bitterness that weighed him down. But it was an old bitterness, the bitterness between father and son that was the fault of neither. . . .

The woman left his side and tenderly, with the tears streaming down her creamy cheeks, she stroked the white mane of the dead old man.

With a trembling sob, she pressed her soft smooth skin against the wrinkled leather of his cheek.

And, finally, after long cold decades, a dam within her husband burst, and the torrent of sternly suppressed love and sorrow flooded the lowlands of his soul.

Two lone and perfect tears escaped his still-impassive eyes as he watched his wife touch her warm young lips to that age-wrecked face.

And kiss their son goodbye.

20

DEFENSE MECHANISM

Katherine MacLean

THE ARTICLE WAS coming along smoothly, words flowing from the typewriter in pleasant simple sequence, swinging to their predetermined conclusion like a good tune. Ted typed contentedly, adding pages to the stack at his elbow.

A thought, a subtle modification of the logic of the atricle began to glow in his mind, but he brushed it aside impatiently. This was to be a short article, and there was no room for subtlety. His articles sold, not for depth, but for an oddly individual quirk that he could give to commonplaces.

While he typed a little faster, faintly in the echoes of his thought, the theme began to elaborate itself richly with correlations, modifying qualifications, and humorous parenthetical remarks. An eddy of especially interesting conclusions tried to insert itself into the main stream of his thoughts. Furiously he typed along the dissolving thread of his argument.

"Shut up," he snarled. "Can't I have any privacy around here?"

The answer was not a remark, it was merely a concept; two electrochemical calculators pictured with the larger in use as a control mech, taking a dangerously high inflow, and controlling it with high resistance and blocks, while the smaller one lay empty and unblocked, its unresistant circuits ramifying any impulses received along the easy channels of pure calculation. Ted recognized the diagram as something borrowed from his amateur concepts of radio and psychology.

"All right. So I'm doing it myself. So you can't help it!" He grinned grudgingly. "Answering back at your age!"

Under the impact of a directed thought the small circuits of the idea came in strongly, scorching their reception and rapport diagram into his mind in flashing repetitions, bright as small lightning strokes. Then it spread and the small other brain flashed into brightness, reporting and repeating from

119

every center. Ted even received a brief kinesthetic sensation of lying down, before it was all cut off in a hard bark of thought that came back in the exact echo of his own irritation.

"Tune down!" It ordered furiously. "You're blasting in too loud and jamming everything up! What do you want, an idiot child?"

Ted blanketed down desperately, cutting off all thoughts, relaxing every muscle, but the angry thought continued coming in strongly a moment before fading.

"Even when I take a nap," they said, "he starts thinking at me! Can't I get any peace and privacy around here?"

Ted grinned. The kid's last remark sounded like something a little better than an attitude echo. It would be hard to tell when the kid's mind grew past a mere selective echoing of outside thoughts, and became true personality, but that last remark was a convincing counterfeit of a sincere kick in the shin. Conditioned reactions can be efficient.

All the luminescent streaks of thought faded and merged with the calm meaningless ebb and flow of waves in the small sleeping mind. Ted moved quietly into the next room and looked down into the blue-and-white crib. The kid lay sleeping, his thumb in his mouth and his chubby face innocent of thought. Junior—Jake.

It was an odd stroke of luck that Jake was born with this particular talent. Because of it they would have to spend the winter in Connecticut, away from the mental blare of crowded places. Because of it Ted was doing free-lance in the kitchen, instead of minor editing behind a New York desk. The winter countryside was wide and windswept, as it had been in Ted's own childhood, and the warm contacts with the stolid personalities of animals through Jake's mind were already a pleasure. Old acquaintances— Ted stopped himself skeptically. He was no telepath. He decided that it reminded him of Ernest Thompson Seton's animal biographies, and went back to typing, dismissing the question.

It was pleasant to eavesdrop on things through Jake, as long as the subject was not close enough to the article to interfere with it.

Five small boys let out of kindergarten came trouping by on the road, chattering and throwing pebbles. Their thoughts came in jumbled together in distracting cross currents, but Ted stopped typing for a moment, smiling, waiting for Jake to show his latest trick. Babies are hypersensitive to conditioning. The burnt hand learns to yank back from fire, the unresisting mind learns automatically to evade too many clashing echoes of other minds.

Abruptly the discordant jumble of small boy thought and sensations

120

delicately untangled into five compartmented strands of thoughts, then one strand of little boy thoughts shoved the others out, monopolizing and flowing easily through the blank baby mind, as dream flows by without awareness, leaving no imprint of memory, fading as the children passed over the hill. Ted resumed typing, smiling. Jake had done the trick a shade faster than he had yesterday. He was learning reflexes easily enough to demonstrate normal intelligences. At least he was to be more than a gifted moron.

A half hour later, Jake had grown tired of sleeping and was standing up in his crib, shouting and shaking the bars. Martha hurried in with a double armload of groceries.

"Does he want something?"

"Nope. Just exercising his lungs." Ted stubbed out his cigarette and tapped the finished stack of manuscript contentedly. "Got something here for you to proofread."

"Dinner first," she said cheerfully, unpacking food from the bags. "Better move the typewriter and give us some elbow room."

Sunlight came in the windows and shone on the yellow table top, and glinted on her dark hair as she opened packages.

"What's the local gossip?" he asked, clearing off the table. "Anything new?"

"Meat's going up again," she said, unwrapping peas and fillets of mackerel. "Mrs. Watkin's boy, Tom, is back from the clinic. He can see fine now, she says."

He put water on to boil and began greasing a skillet while she rolled the fillets in cracker crumbs. "If I'd had to run a flame thrower during the war, I'd have worked up a nice case of hysteric blindness myself," he said. "I call that a ligitimate defense mechanism. Sometimes it's better to be blind."

"But not all the time," Martha protested, putting baby food in the double boiler. In five minutes lunch was cooking.

"Whaaaa—" wailed Jake.

Martha went into the baby's room, and brought him out, cuddling him, and crooning, "What do you want, Lovekins? Baby isn't hungry yet, is ims. Baby just wants to be cuddled, doesn't baby."

"Yes," said Ted.

She looked up, startled, and her expression changed, became withdrawn and troubled, her dark eyes clouded in difficult thought.

Concerned, he asked: "What is it, Honey?"

"Ted, you shouldn't—" She struggled with words. "I know, it is handy

121

to know what he wants, whenever he cries. It's handy having you tell me, but I don't— It isn't right somehow. It isn't *right*."

Jake waved an arm and squeaked randomly. He looked unhappy. Ted took him and laughed, making an effort to sound confident and persuasive. It would be impossible to raise the kid in a healthy way if Martha began to feel he was a freak. "Why isn't it right? It's normal enough. Look at E.S.P. Everybody has that, according to Rhine."

"E.S.P. is different," she protested feebly, but Jake chortled and Ted knew he had her. He grinned, bouncing Jake up and down in is arms.

"Sure it's different," he said cheerfully. "E.S.P. is queer. E.S.P. comes in those weird accidental little flashes that contradict time and space. With clairvoyance you can see through walls, and read pages from a closed book in France. E.S.P., when it comes, is so ghastly precise it seems like tips from old Omniscience himself. It's enough to drive a logical man insane, trying to explain it. It's illogical, incredible, and random. But what Jake has is just limited telepathy. It is starting out fuzzy and muddled and developing towards accuracy by plenty of trial and error, like sight, or any other normal sense. You don't mind communicating by English, so why mind communicating by telepathy?"

She smiled wanly. "But he doesn't weigh much, Ted. He's not growing as fast as it says he should in the baby book."

"That's all right. I didn't really start growing myself until I was about two. My parents thought I was sickly."

"And look at you now." She smiled genuinely. "All right, you win. But when does he start talking English? I'd like to understand him, too. After all I'm his mother."

"Maybe this year, maybe next year," Ted said teasingly. "I didn't start talking until I was three."

"You mean that you don't want him to learn," she told him indignantly, and then smiled coaxingly at Jake. "You'll learn English soon for Mummy, won't you, Lovekins?"

Ted laughed annoyingly. "Try coaxing him next month or the month after. Right now he's not listening to all these thoughts, he's just collecting associations and reflexes. His cortex might organize impressions on a logic pattern he picked up from me, but it doesn't know what it is doing any more than this fist knows that it is in his mouth. That right, bud?" There was no demanding thought behind the question, but instead, very delicately, Ted introspected to the small world of impression and sensation that flickered in what seemed a dreaming corner of his own mind. Right then it was a fragmentary world of green and brown that murmured with wind.

"He's out eating grass with the rabbit," Ted told her.

Not answering, Martha started putting out plates. "I like animal stories for children," she said determinedly. "Rabbits are nicer than people."

Putting Jake in his pen, Ted began to help. He kissed the back of her neck in passing. "Some people are nicer than rabbits."

Wind rustled tall grass and tangled vines where the rabbit snuffled and nibbled among the sun-dried herbs, moving on habit, ignoring the abstract meaningless contact of minds, with no thought but deep content.

Then for a while Jake's stomach became aware that lunch was coming, and the vivid business of crying and being fed drowned the gentler distant neural flow of the rabbit.

Ted ate with enjoyment, toying with an idea fantastic enough to keep him grinning, as Martha anxiously spooned food into Jake's mouth. She caught him grinning and indignantly began justifying herself. "But he only gained four pounds, Ted. I have to make sure he eats something."

"Only!" he grinned. "At that rate he'd be thirty feet high by the time he reaches college."

"So would any baby." But she smiled at the idea, and gave Jake his next spoonful still smiling. Ted did not tell his real thought, that if Jake's abilities kept growing in a straight-line growth curve, by the time he was old enough to vote he would be God, but he laughed again, and was rewarded by an answering smile from both of them.

The idea was impossible, of course. Ted knew enough biology to know that there could be no sudden smooth jumps in evolution. Smooth changes had to be worked out gradually through generations of trial and selection. Sudden changes were not smooth, they crippled and destroyed. Mutants were usually monstrosities.

Jake was no sickly freak, so it was certain that he would not turn out very different from his parents. He could be only a little better. But the contrary idea had tickled Ted and he laughed again. "Boom food," he told Martha. "Remember those straight-line growth curves in the story?"

Martha remembered, smiling, "Redfern's dream—sweet little man, dreaming about a growth curve that went straight up." She chuckled, and fed Jake more spoonfuls of strained spinach, saying "Open wide. Eat your boom food, darling. Don't you want to grow up like King Kong?"

Ted watched vaguely, toying now with a feeling that these months of his life had happened before, somewhere. He had felt it before, but now it came back with a sense of expectancy, as if something were going to happen.

* * * *

123

It was while drying the dishes that Ted began to feel sick. Somewhere in the far distance at the back of his mind a tiny phantom of terror cried and danced and gibbered. He glimpsed it close in a flash that entered and was cut off abruptly in a vanishing fragment of delirium. It had something to do with a tangle of brambles in a field, and it was urgent.

Jake grimaced, his face wrinkled as if ready either to smile or cry. Carefully Ted hung up the dish towel and went out the back door, picking up a billet of wood as he passed the woodpile. He could hear Jake whimpering, beginning to wail.

"Where to?" Martha asked, coming out the back door.

"Dunno," Ted answered. "Gotta go rescue Jake's rabbit. It's in trouble."

Feeling numb he went across the fields, through an outgrowth of small trees, climbed a fence into a field of deep grass and thorny tangles of raspberry vines, and started across.

A few hundred feet into the field there was a hunter sitting on an outcrop of rock, smoking, with a successful bag of two rabbits dangling near him. He turned an inquiring face to Ted.

"Sorry," Ted told him rapidly, "but that rabbit is not dead yet. It can't understand being upside down with its legs tied." Moving with shaky urgency he took his penknife and cut the small animal's pulsing throat, then threw the wet knife out of his hand into the grass. The rabbit kicked once more, staring still at the tangled vines of refuge, then its nearsighted baby eyes lost their glazed bright stare and became meaningless.

"Sorry," the hunter said. He was a quiet-looking man with a sagging, middle-aged face.

"That's all right," Ted replied, "but be a little more careful next time, will you? You're out of season anyhow." He looked up from the grass to smile stiffly at the hunter. It was difficult. There was a crowded feeling in his head, like a coming headache, or a stuffy cold. It was difficult to think.

It occurred to Ted then to wonder why Jake had never put him in touch with an adult. After a frozen stoppage of thought he laboriously started the wheels again and realized that something had put them in touch with the mind of the hunter, and that was what was wrong. His stomach began to rise. In another minute he would retch.

Ted stepped forward and swung the billet of wood in a clumsy sidewise sweep. The hunter's rifle went off and missed as the middle-aged man tumbled face first into the grass.

Wind rustled the long grass and stirred the leafless branches of trees. Ted could hear and think again, standing still and breathing in deep, shuddering breaths of air to clean his lungs. Briefly he planned what to do. He would call the sheriff and say that a hunter hunting out of season had shot at him and he had been forced to knock the man out. The sheriff would take the man away, out of thought range.

Before he started back to telephone he looked again at the peaceful, simple scene of field and trees and sky. A memory of horror came into clarity. The hunter had been psychotic.

Thinking back, Ted recognized parts of it, like faces glimpsed in writhing smoke. The evil symbols of psychiatry, the bloody poetry of the Golden Bough, that had been the law of mankind in the five hundred thousand lost years before history. Torture and sacrifice, lust and death, a mechanism in perfect balance, a short circuit of conditioning through a glowing channel of symbols, an irreversible and perfect integration of traumas. It is easy to go mad, but it is not easy to go sane.

"Shut up!" Ted had been screaming inside his mind as he struck. "Shut up."

It had stopped. It had shut up. The symbols were fading without having found root in his mind. The sheriff would take the man away out of thought reach, and there would be no danger. It had stopped.

The burned hand avoids the fire. Something else had stopped. Ted's mind was queerly silent, queerly calm and empty, as he walked home across the winter fields, wondering how it had happened at all, kicking himself with humor for a suggestible fool, not yet missing—Jake.

And Jake lay awake in his pen, waving his rattle in random motions, and crowing "glaglagla gla—" in a motor sensory cycle.

He would be a normal baby, as Ted had been, and as Ted's father before him.

And as all mankind was "normal."

21

DIVINE MADNESS

Roger Zelazny

" . . . I is this *?hearers wounded-wonder like stand them makes and stars wandering the conjures sorrow of phrase Whose. . . ."*

He blew smoke through the cigarette and it grew longer.

He glanced at the clock and realized that its hands were moving backwards.

The clock told him that it was 10:33, going on 10:32 in the P.M.

Then came the thing like despair, for he knew there was not a thing he could do about it. He was trapped, moving in reverse through the sequence of actions past. Somehow, he had missed the warning.

Usually, there was a prism-effect, a flash of pink static, a drowsiness, then a moment of heightened perception. . . .

He turned the pages, from left to right, his eyes retracing their path back along the lines.

"?emphasis an such bears grief whose he is What"

Helpless, there behind his eyes, he watched his body perform.

The cigarette had reached its full length. He clicked on the lighter, which sucked away its glowing point, and then he shook the cigarette back into the pack.

He yawned in reverse: first an exhalation, then an inhalation.

It wasn't real—the doctor had told him. It was grief and epilepsy, meeting to form an unusual syndrome.

He'd already had the seizure. The dialantin wasn't helping. This was a post-traumatic locomotor hallucination, elicited by anxiety, precipitated by the attack.

But he did not believe it, could not believe it—not after twenty minutes had gone by, in the other direction—not after he had placed the book upon the reading stand, stood, walked backward across the room to his closet, hung up his robe, redressed himself in the same shirt and slacks he had worn all day, backed over to the bar and regurgitated a Martini, sip by cooling sip, until the glass was filled to the rim and not a drop spilled.

There was an impending taste of olive, and then everything was changed again.

The second-hand was sweeping around his wristwatch in the proper direction.

The time was 10:07.

He felt free to move as he wished.

He redrank his Martini.

Now, if he would be true to the pattern, he would change into his robe and try to read. Instead, he mixed another drink.

Now the sequence would not occur.

Now the things would not happen as he thought they had happened, and un-happened.

Now everything was different.

All of which went to prove it had been an hallucination.

Even the notion that it had taken twenty-six minutes each way was an attempted rationalization.

Nothing had happened.

. . . Shouldn't be drinking, he decided. It might bring on a seizure.

He laughed.

Crazy, though, the whole thing. . . .

Remembering, he drank.

In the morning he skipped breakfast, as usual, noted that it would soon stop being morning, took two aspirins, a lukewarm shower, a cup of coffee, and a walk.

The park, the fountain, the children with their boats, the grass, the pond, he hated them; and the morning, and the sunlight, and the blue moats around the towering clouds.

Hating, he sat there. And remembering.

If he was on the verge of a crackup, he decided, then the thing he wanted most was to plunge ahead into it, not to totter halfway out, halfway in.

He remembered why.

But it was clear, so clear, the morning and everything crisp and distinct and burning with the green fires of spring, there in the sign of the Ram, April.

He watched the winds pile up the remains of winter against the far gray fence, and he saw them push the boats across the pond, to come to rest in shallow mud the children tracked.

The fountain jetted its cold umbrella above the green-tinged copper dolphins. The sun ignited it whenever he moved his head. The wind rumpled it.

Clustered on the concrete, birds pecked at part of a candy bar stuck to a red wrapper.

Kites swayed on their tails, nosed downward, rose again, as youngsters tugged at invisible strings. Telephone lines were tangled with wooden frames and torn paper, like broken G clefs and smeared glissandos.

He hated the telephone lines, the kites, the children, the birds.

Most of all, though, he hated himself.

How does a man undo that which has been done? He doesn't. There is no way under the sun. He may suffer, remember, repent, curse, or forget. Nothing else. The past, in this sense, is inevitable.

A woman walked past. He did not look up in time to see her face, but the dusky blonde fall of her hair to her collar and the swell of her sure, sheer-netted legs below the black hem of her coat and above the matching click of her heels heigh-ho, stopped his breath behind his stomach and snared his eyes in the wizard-weft of her walking and her posture and some more, like a rhyme to the last of his thoughts.

He half-rose from the bench when the pink static struck his eyeballs, and the fountain became a volcano spouting rainbows.

The world was frozen and served up to him under glass.

. . . The woman passed back before him and he looked down too soon to see her face.

The hell was beginning once more, he realized, as the backward-flying birds passed before.

He gave himself to it. Let it keep him until he broke, until he was all used up and there was nothing left.

He waited, there on the bench, watching the slithey toves be brillig, as the fountain sucked its waters back within itself, drawing them in a great arc above the unmoving dolphins, and the boats raced backward across the pond, and the fence divested itself of stray scraps of paper as the birds replaced the candy bar within the red wrapper, bit by crunchy bit.

His thoughts only were inviolate, his body belonged to the retreating tide.

Eventually, he rose and strolled backwards out of the park.

On the street a boy backed past him, unwhistling snatches of a popular song.

He backed up the stairs to his apartment, his hangover growing worse again, undrank his coffee, unshowered, unswallowed his aspirins, and got into bed, feeling awful.

Let this be it, he decided.

A faintly-remembered nightmare ran in reverse through his mind, giving it an undeserved happy ending.

It was dark when he awakened.

He was very drunk.

He backed over to the bar and began spitting out his drinks, one by one into the same glass he had used the night before, and pouring them from the glass back into the bottles again. Separating the gin and vermouth was no trick at all. The proper liquids leapt into the air as he held the uncorked bottles above the bar.

And he grew less and less drunk as this went on.

Then he stood before an early Martini and it ws 10:07 in the P.M. There, within the hallucination, he wondered about another hallucination. Would time loop-the-loop, forward and then backward again, through his previous seizure?

No.

It was as though it had not happened, had never been.

He continued on back through the evening, undoing things.

He raised the telephone, said "good-bye," untold Murray that he would not be coming to work again tomorrow, listened a moment, recradled the phone and looked at it as it rang.

The sun came up in the west and people were backing their cars to work.

He read the weather report and the headlines, folded the evening paper and placed it out in the hall.

It was the longest seizure he had ever had, but he did not really care. He settled himself down within it and watched as the day unwound itself back to morning.

His hangover returned as the day grew smaller, and it was terrible when he got into bed again.

When he awakened the previous evening the drunkenness was high upon him. Two of the bottles he refilled, recorked, resealed. He knew he would take them to the liquor store soon and get his money back.

As he sat there that day, his mouth uncursing and undrinking and his eyes unreading, he knew that new cars were being shipped back to Detroit and disassembled, that corpses were awakening into their death-throes, and that priests the world over were saying black mass, unknowing.

He wanted to chuckle, but he could not tell his mouth to do it.

He unsmoked two and a half packs of cigarettes.

Then came another hangover and he went to bed. Later, the sun set in the east.

Time's winged chariot fled before him as he opened the door and said "good-bye" to his comforters and they came in and sat down and told him not to grieve overmuch.

And he wept without tears as he realized what was to come.

Despite his madness, he hurt.

. . . Hurt, as the days rolled backward.

. . . Backward, inexorably.

. . . Inexorably, until he knew the time was near at hand.

He gnashed the teeth of his mind.

Great was his grief and his hate and his love.

He was wearing his black suit and undrinking drink after drink, while somewhere the men were scraping the clay back onto the shovels which would be used to undig the grave.

He backed his car to the funeral parlor, parked it, and climbed into the limousine.

They backed all the way to the graveyard.

He stood among his friends and listened to the reacher.

".dust to dust; ashes to Ashes," the man said, which is pretty much the same whichever way you say it.

The casket was taken back to the hearse and returned to the funeral parlor.

He sat through the service and went home and unshaved and unbrushed his teeth and went to bed.

He awakened and dressed again in black and returned to the parlor.

The flowers were all back in place.

Solemn-faced friends unsigned the Sympathy Book and unshook his hand. Then they went inside to sit awhile and stare at the closed casket. Then they left, until he was alone with the funeral director.

Then he was alone with himself.

The tears ran up his cheeks.

His suit and shirt were crisp and unwrinkled again.

He backed home, undressed, uncombed his hair. The day collapsed around him into morning, and he returned to bed to unsleep another night.

The previous evening, when he awakened, he realized where he was headed.

Twice, he exerted all of his will power in an attempt to interrupt the sequence of events. He failed.

He wanted to die. If he had killed himself that day, he would not be headed back toward it now.

There were tears within his mind as he realized the past which lay less than twenty-four hours before him.

The past stalked him that day as he unnegotiated the purchase of the casket, the vault, the accessories.

Then he headed home into the biggest hangover of all and slept until he was awakened to undrink drink after drink and then return to the morgue and come back in time to hang up the telephone on that call, that call which had come to break . . .

. . . The silence of his anger with its ringing.

She was dead.

She was lying somewhere in the fragments of her car on Interstate 90 now.

As he paced, unsmoking, he knew she was lying there bleeding.

. . . Then dying, after that crash at 80 miles an hour.

. . . Then alive?

Then re-formed, along with the car, and alive again, arisen? Even now backing home at a terrible speed, to re-slam the door on their final argument? To unscream at him and to be unscreamed at?

He cried out within his mind. He wrung the hands of his spirit.

It couldn't stop at this point. No. Not now.

All his grief and his love and his self-hate had brought him back this far, this near to the moment. . . .

It *couldn't* end now.

After a time, he moved to the living room, his legs pacing, his lips cursing, himself waiting.

The door slammed open.

She stared in at him, her mascara smeared, tears upon her cheeks.

''!hell to go Then,'' he said.

''!going I'm,'' she said.

She stepped back inside, closed the door.

She hung her coat hurriedly in the hall closet.

"'.it about feel you way the that's If,'' he said, shrugging.

"'!yourself but anybody about care don't You,'' she said.

"'!child a like behaving You're,'' he said.

"'!sorry you're say least at could You''

Her eyes flashed like emeralds through the pink static, and she was lovely and alive again. In his mind he was dancing.

The change came.

"You could at least say you're sorry!''

"I am,'' he said, taking her hand in a grip that she could not break. "How much, you'll never know.''

"Come here,'' and she did.

22

THE DREAD TOMATO ADDICTION

Mark Clifton

NINETY-TWO POINT four per cent of juvenile delinquents have eaten tomatoes.

Eighty-seven point one per cent of the adult criminals in penitentiaries throughout the United State have eaten tomatoes.

Informers reliably inform that of all known American Communists, ninety-two point three per cent have eaten tomatoes.

Informers reliably inform that of all known American Communists, ninety-two point three per cent have eaten tomatoes.

Eighty-four per cent of all people killed in automobile accidents during the year 1954 had eaten tomatoes.

Those who object to singling out specific groups for statistical proofs require measurements within a total. Of those people born before the year 1800, regardless of race, color, creed or caste, and known to have eaten tomatoes, there has been one hundred per cent mortality!

In spite of their dread addiction, a few tomato eaters born between 1800 and 1850 still manage to survive, but the clinical picture is poor—their bones are brittle, their movements feeble, their skin seamed and wrinkled, their eyesight failing, hair falling, and frequently they have lost all their teeth.

Those born between 1850 and 1900 number somewhat more survivors, but the overt signs of the addiction's dread effects differ not in kind but only in degree of deterioration. Prognostication is not hopeful.

Exhaustive experiment shows that when tomatoes are withheld from an addict, invariably his cravings will cause him to turn to substitutes—such as oranges, or steak and potatoes. If both tomatoes and all substitutes are persistently withheld—death invariably results within a short time!

The skeptic of apocryphal statistics, or the stubborn nonconformist who will not accept the clearly proved conclusions of others may conduct his own experiment.

Obtain two dozen tomatoes—they may actually be purchased within a block of some high schools, or discovered growing in a respected neighbor's back yard!—crush them to a pulp in exactly the state they would have if introduced into the stomach, pour the vile juice and pulp into a bowl, and place a goldfish therein. Within minutes the goldfish will be dead!

Those who argue that what affects a goldfish might not apply to a human being may, at their own choice, wish to conduct a direct experiment by fully immersing a live human head* into the mixture for a full five minutes.

---

* It is suggested that best results will be obtained by using an experimental subject who is thoroughly familiar with and frequently uses the logic methods demonstrated herein, such as:

(a) The average politician. Extremely unavailable to the average citizen except during the short open season before election.

(b) The advertising copywriter. Extremely wary and hard to catch due to his experience with many lawsuits for fraudulant claims.

(c) The dedicated moralist. Extremely plentiful in supply, and the experimenter might even obtain a bounty on each from a grateful community.

23

DUELING CLOWNS

Barry Longyear

LORD ALLENBY RAISED his eyebrows at the newsteller's apprentice, but the apprentice only shrugged. Allenby looked back at the master newsteller. His eyes fixed on the fire, Boosthit sat crosslegged, elbows on his knees, chin on his hands and a black scowl on his face. "Come, come, Boosthit. I've known you too long for this." The newsteller sat unmoving.

The apprentice scratched his head. "It's no use, Lord Allenby. He's been that way for a week."

Allenby shrugged. "I came by this fire and saw my old friend and expected to have grand times getting reacquainted. When I first came to Momus as the ambassador to the Ninth Quadrant, it was Boosthit who took news of my mission and played it in Tarzak."

The apprentice nodded. "He won't even talk to me."

Allenby looked closely at the apprentice. "You're one of the Montagne soldiers, aren't you?"

"Yes. In a year I'll be taking my retirement here on Momus. I'm on leave now looking into newstelling as an occupation for when I get out."

"Your name?"

" Forgive me. Sergeant Major Gaddis; I'm top soldier at orbital fighter base twenty-six."

Allenby nodded. "I'm pleased to meet you, Sergeant Major. Has newstelling been to your liking?"

The apprentice turned toward Boosthit, shook his head and turned back to Allenby. "I have no idea, Lord Allenby. I've been with him for a week, but I haven't heard any news yet."

Allenby looked at Boosthit. "Come, old friend, you haven't hit a dry spell, have you?" Boosthit's scowl deepened. "Why, there's news of galactic significance transpiring this very moment, with the commission

137

from the United Quadrants coming to Momus. Then, there's the military buildup of the Tenth Quadrant forces to counter the Ninth's defense of this planet, and the ambassador from the Tenth Quadrant will be here in a few days to present his credentials; even my own office as statesman of Momus is in doubt. The UQ Commission will rule —''

Boosthit held up his hands. ''Still yourself, Allenby; I have news!''

The sergeant major applauded. ''Congratulations. That's more than I've heard him say for the entire week.''

Boosthit glowered at the apprentice, then aimed his expression at Allenby. ''As I said, I have news. I do not choose to recite it.''

Allenby smiled and nodded his head. ''That bad, is it? I understand—''

''It is the best news I have ever had; it is great news! And, you would *not* understand!''

''Dear friend,'' Allenby held up his hands in a gesture of peace, ''we have been through and seen much together over the past six years. You think I would lack understanding, or not appreciate great news?''

''It is what I think.''

''What caused this? A newsteller with great news refusing to recite it? Do you think I wouldn't pay?''

Boosthit stood, walked to the boulders outside the light of the fire, then returned and sat down. He lifted an eyebrow in Allenby's direction. ''You really want to hear my news?''

''Of course. I also want you to explain your strange behavior.''

Boosthit pursed his lips, then nodded. ''Very well. First, I shall tell you why I am reluctant.'' He turned to the sergeant major. ''I recited my news to others such as this one, and I was treated very badly.''

Allenby frowned. ''You mean, to soldiers?''

''They were apprenticed, as this one is, but they were soldiers, yes.''

Allenby turned to Gaddis. ''The rules for visiting planetside are being observed, aren't they?''

''Yes, Lord Allenby. We are all familiarized with customs, traditions and occupations. When I am on duty, that training is part of my responsibility.''

Allenby rubbed his chin and turned back to the newsteller. ''Tell me what happened, Boosthit''

Boosthit gave the apprentice a suspicious glance, then held up his hands. ''Very well. It happened at the first fire from Tarzak several days ago. I had rehearsed my news, and was anxious to take it on the road. As I said, it is great news.''

''As you said.''

Boosthit shrugged. "I approached the fire in the evening, and heard laughter coming from behind the rocks. I thought to myself that this was a lucky stroke, having a good audience my first night. But, when I stepped through the boulders, I saw that they were soldiers."

"You said they were apprenticed; how did you know they were soldiers?"

"They wear their robes badly, and sit funny." Boosthit cocked his head toward his apprentice. Gaddis had his knees together and sat back on his legs.

Gaddis shrugged. "It takes time to get used to going without trousers."

Allenby nodded. "I remember. Go on, Boosthit."

"Well, I turned to go, but they made such a fuss about me staying, that I changed my mind. That meant, of course, sitting through all of their amateur acts, but, I thought, business is business. I stayed. There was a priest's apprentice, and apprentices representing storytellers, tumblers, knife-throwers, and even one representing your own magicians, Allenby.

"After we bargained and ate, the first to rise was the apprentice priest. He did an almost acceptable job of reciting the epic of the circus ship *Baraboo* that brought our ancestors to Momus. Reluctantly, I parted with two movills for the fellow's performance, thinking to collect twenty times that amount after I dazzled those apprentices with my news.

"Then, the knife-thrower did a few turns on a piece of board he carried with him, but the act was of no consequence since he had no one standing in front of the board. Nevertheless, I parted with another two movills. Let it suffice to say that the tumblers and the magician were of similar quality. I could hardly keep my eyes open.

"Then, may his master's throat turn to stone, the apprentice storyteller began. He went on and on about a boy in a strange land named Pittsburgh, and I could find no start nor middle to the tale. I recognized the ending because he stopped talking and another movill left my purse. But, then," a strange fire lit behind the newsteller's eyes as he stared off in a trance, "then, my turn came. I looked among their faces, and began:

"I, Boosthit of the Faransetti newstellers, sit before the fire this evening to tell you of the great duel between Kamera, Master of the Tarzak clowns, and Spaht, new Master of Clowns from Kuumic. It is news of heroics; a defense of the mighty being attacked by a hungry jackal. I, Boosthit, was witness to this event.

"Four days ago, I sat at the table of the Great Kamera, exchanging my news for entertainment, when the curtain to the street opened. Standing in the doorway was Spaht, garbed in yellow trousers with black polka dots, a vest of green and white stripes over a naked torso. On his bare neck, he wore a collar and bow tie. He wore white grease paint with red nose and upturned lips, the entire effect being capped with an orange fright wig and derby. He bowed to Kamera and said 'Now is the time, Kamera; be on the street in five minutes.'

"Kamera laughed. 'Fool, I cannot be bothered with challenges from every apprentice that passes by my door.'

" 'Apprentice? I am Spaht, Master of the Kuumic clowns!'

"Kamera waved an idle hand in the direction of the door. 'In that case, out damned Spaht! Out, I say!'

"Spaht bowed. 'I see I have entered the wrong house and found only great chimera.'

"Kamera squinted his eyes. 'Leave me. I shall be out as you requested.' Spaht bowed again, then left. In the quiet room, I saw the great clown sigh and reach under his table for his paints. His face was very sad.

" 'Surely, Great Kamera,' I said, 'this upstart does not worry you?'

"Kamera adjusted a looking glass and began putting on his makeup. 'Boosthit, it is ever thus for the greatest clown on Momus. Always there is another young punslinger lurking in the corners, waiting to build a reputaton. It is not an easy life.'

"Kamera finished his makeup and put on a pure white suit, with large pompoms down the front. On his hairless head, he placed a white peaked cone. As he put on white slippers, I could see the frown under the painted smile.

" 'Spaht is different from the usual run of challenger, Great Kamera, isn't he?'

"He nodded. 'You saw what he was wearing. That garish costume, and the bow tie—he winds it up and it spins! Spaht has no sense of tradition; no honor. On the street this day, anything can be expected.'

"The two clowns squared off in the center of the dusty street. Warily, they circled each other, then Spaht opened. 'My uncle, a tailor, once made a magician very angry by making him a shirt that didn't fit.'

" 'Put him in a bad choler, did he?'

" 'Aye, and he turned my uncle into a tree.'

"All could see Kamera struggling, but he had no choice but to feed Spaht the straight line. 'Did it bother your uncle?'

" 'He didn't say; he was board.'

" 'Knot he!'

" 'But I avenged my uncle by thrashing the magician and throwing the rude fellow at my uncle's wooden feet.'

" 'That was casting churl before pine.'

"As the dust cleared from the opening exchange, the two each had the other's measure. Kamera circled to get the sun out of his eyes. Spaht had a look of confidence on his face.'

" 'Did you know,' said Spaht, 'that my nephew is related to the tiny flying cave creatures?''

" 'Yes, Spaht, I know. I stepped on one once and heard your nephew say 'Oh, my akin bat!'

"The crowd moaned. Cued by this, Spaht returned. 'Why should the clowns pay homage to you, Kamera? It seems that you are in your anecdotage.'

"Kamera smiled. 'Obeisance make the heart grow fonder.'

"Staggered, Spaht circled and began spinning his bow tie. 'My uncle, the tree . . . ,' he began.

" 'I saw him the other day, Spaht. I said ''That's yew all over.'' '

" 'We were so poor that at his funeral we could afford no music. All you could hear was the coughing—'

" 'There was catarrh playing, then?'

" 'Well, there was a coffin.' Spaht tried to rally, but Kamera scented blood. 'My . . . nephew lost consciousness and fell into a vat of stain. . . .'

" 'The good dye stunned.' Spaht fell to all fours and began crawling out of town. A cheer erupted from the crowd, and Kamera followed the beaten clown down the street. 'Crawl in a straight line, Spaht, or you will get contusions of meander. . . . ' ''

Boosthit looked down to deliver the punchline at Allenby, but the Great Statesman of Momus was gone. " . . . he. . . . " He turned and found Gaddis missing as well. Rushing between the boulders, he could see two dark shapes running together toward Tarzak.

"Strange," said the newsteller, rubbing his chin, "if Allenby knew what the soldiers did, why did he ask?"

24

END AS A WORLD

F. L. Wallace

EVERY PAPER SAID so in all the languages there were, I guess. I kept reading them, but didn't know what to believe. I know what I wanted to think, but that's different from actually knowing.

There was the usual news just after Labor Day. The Dodgers were winning or losing, I forget which, and UCLA was strong and was going to beat everybody they met that fall. An H-bomb had been tested in the Pacific, blowing another island off the map, just as if we had islands to spare. Ordinarily this was important, but now it wasn't. They put stuff like this in the back pages and hardly anybody reads it. There was only one thing on the front pages and it was all people talked about. All I talked about, anyway.

It began long before. I don't know how long because they didn't print that. But it began and there it was, right upon us that day. It was Saturday. Big things always seem to happen on Saturdays. I ate breakfast and got out early. I had the usual things to do, mowing the lawn, for instance. I didn't do it nor anything else and nobody said anything. There wasn't any use in mowing the lawn on a day like that.

I went out, remembering not to slam the door. It wasn't much, but it showed thoughtfulness. I went past the church and looked at the sign that was set diagonally at the corner so that it could be read from both streets. There it was in big letters, quoting from the papers: THIS IS THE DAY THE WORLD ENDS! Some smart reporter had thought it up and it seemed so true that that was the only way it was ever said. Me? I didn't know.

It was a bright day. People were out walking or just standing and looking at the sky. It was too early to look up. I went on. Paul Eberhard was sitting on the lawn when I came along. He tossed me the football and I caught it and tried to spin it on my finger. It didn't spin. It fell and flopped out with crazy bounces into the street. The milk truck stopped, while I got it out of the way. I tossed the football back to Paul. He put his hand on it and sat there.

"What'll we do?" he said.

I made a motion with my hands. "We can throw the ball around," I said.

"Naw," he said, "Maybe you've got some comic books."

"You've seen them all," I said.

"You got some?"

"I gave them to Howie," he said, thoughtfully screwing the point of the ball into the center of a dandelion. "He said he was going to get some new ones though. Let's go see." He got up and tossed the ball toward the porch. It hit the railing and bounced back into the bushes. That's where he usually kept it.

"Paul," called his mother as we started out.

"Yeah?"

"Don't go far. I've got some things I want you to do."

"What?" he said patiently.

"Hauling trash out of the basement. Helping me move some of the potted plants around in front."

"Sure," he said. "I'll be back."

We went past another church on the way to Howie's. The sign was the same there. THIS IS THE DAY THE WORLD ENDS! They never said more than that. They wanted it to hang in our minds, something we couldn't quite touch, but we knew was there.

Paul jerked his head at the sign. "What do you think of it?"

"I don't know." I broke off a twig as we passed a tree. "What about you?"

"We got it coming." He looked at the sky.

"Yeah, but will we get it?"

He didn't answer that. "I wonder if it will be bright?"

"It is now."

"It might cloud over."

"It won't matter. It'll split the sky." That was one thing sure. Clouds or anything weren't going to stand in the way.

We went on and found Howie. Howie is a Negro, smaller than we are and twice as fast. He can throw a football farther and straighter than anyone else on the team. We pal around quite a bit, especially in the football season.

He came out of the house like he was walking on whipped cream. I didn't let that fool me. More than once I've tried to tackle him during a practice game. Howie was carrying a model of a rocket ship, CO_2 powered. It didn't work. We said hi all around and then he suggested a game of keep-away. We'd left the football at Paul's and we couldn't so we walked over to the park.

We sat down and began talking about it. "I'm wondering if it will really come," said Paul. We all squinted up.

"Where'll the President watch it from?" I said. "He should have a good view from the White House."

"No better than us right here," said Howie.

"What about Australia? Will they see it there?" I said.

"They'll see it all over."

"Africa, too? And what about the Eskimos?"

"It doesn't matter whether they actually see it or not. It will come to everyone at the same time."

I didn't see how it could, but I didn't feel like an argument. That's what they were saying on TV and you can't talk back to that.

"Everybody," said Howie. "Not just in this town, but all over. Wherever there are people. Even where they're not."

"You read that," said Paul.

"Sure," said Howie. "You lent me the comic books. It's even in them."

We didn't say much after that. I kept thinking of the man who made the H-bomb. I bet he felt silly and spiteful, blowing up an island. Somebody might have wanted to live on it, if he'd just left it there. He must have felt mean and low when something really big like this came along.

We talked on for a while, but we'd talked it out long ago. There was really nothing new we could say. Every so often we'd look up at the sky, but it wasn't going to come until it got here.

Finally we drifted apart. There wasn't anything left to do. We walked home with Howie and then I went with Paul, leaving him to come back to my house. I looked at the lawn and without thinking about it got busy and mowed it. I surprised myself.

It was hot, or it seemed to me it was. I went in to eat. Ma came by and shut off the sound of TV. I could still see the picture in the other room. The announcer was making faces, but, of course, I didn't hear what he said. He looked pretty funny, I thought. I thought we were all probably pretty funny, moving our mouths and blinking your eyes and waving our hands. Only nothing real was coming out. Not yet, anyway.

145

"Sit still," said Ma. "It will happen without your help. It's going to be all right."

"Think so?" I said. She would have told me anything to keep me quiet. She gets nervous when I fidget.

"I think so," she said, giving me my allowance. It was early for that. Usually I didn't get it until after supper. "Why don't you run uptown and watch it from there?"

"Maybe I will," I said, dabbling my hands in the water at the sink. "Are you going to go?"

"Of course I'm not. Why should I get into that mob? I can watch it just as well from here."

Sure she could. But it was not the same. Everybody I new was going to be there. I changed shirts before I left. I took a rag and wiped the dust from my shoes. I wasn't trying to be fussy or dressed up or anything. I just thought I should do it.

There was shade and sun on the streets and a few big clouds in the sky.

A car slowed up and stopped beside me. The window rolled down and Jack Goodwin leaned toward me. "Going uptown?"

"Yeah."

"Want a lift?"

"Sure." Actually I didn't. I'd rather have walked, looking around as I went.

Jack Goodwin grinned as I got in. He's got gray hair, where he has hair. The rest is bald. He looked me over. "I don't see any comets on your shoulders," he said gravely.

"I never had any," I said. Some people seem to think everyone under seventeen is a kid.

"You'll be needing them," he said.

"Maybe," I said. I ought to have walked.

I never knew how slow a day could pass. I suppose I should have slept late and kept busy doing something. This was worse than putting on a uniform and waiting until gametime. At least there was a coach on the field to tell you what to do as you ran through the drill.

Jack Goodwin stopped at a light. I had a notion to get out. But I didn't. Goodwin grinned again as the light changed and we started up. "I don't blame you for being edgy," she said. "It's the suspense. If we only had some way of knowing for sure, radio maybe."

"There's no radio," I said. "The calculations have been checked."

"Sure, but maybe there's something we forgot. Or don't know. All sorts of things can go wrong."

He must have talked on and on, but I didn't listen. Howie and me and Paul had gone over everything he was saying.

"Thanks," I said as he stopped and I got out.

"Don't mention it," he said. He nearly scraped the rear fender of the car as he drove off. It was a new car, too. He wasn't so bad. Maybe he was just worried.

I wandered to the newsstand and looked at magazines and pocketbooks. Old lady Simpson didn't ask me if I was going to buy and didn't chase me away. She was busy arguing with some customers. Even so it was the first time she didn't pay attention to me when I came in. I had a good chance to look at things I never buy. There was nothing in them I wanted to see. I was thirsty. I had a Coke and was still thirsty. I asked for a glass of water, drank half of it and went out.

Down the street there was a TV set in a store window. I watched it. They were showing a street in India, people looking up. They flashed all around, to Italy, China, Brazil. Except for their clothes, it wasn't much different from here. They were all looking up.

I did the same. For the first time I noticed there was a slight overcast. Big billowing clouds had passed, but this was worse. I hoped it would clear away in time. Not that it really mattered.

It was more crowded than usual for Saturday, but at the same time it was quiet. People were shopping, but they weren't really buying much or else they bought it faster. Nobody wanted to miss it. They all seemed to have one eye on their lists and another on the clock.

Howie and Paul came up the street and we nodded and said something. A few other boys from the school passed by and we stopped. We gathered together. It was getting closer—and the space between the minutes was growing longer and longer.

I looked at Paul's watch. He said it was on the minute. I decided there was time to go in and get a candy bar. All of a sudden I was hungry. I didn't know where it came from. I'd had to stuff down lunch not long ago. And now I was hungry.

I went to a store and had to fight my way in. People were coming out. Not just customers, but the clerks and owner, too. There was a big television screen inside, but nobody wanted to see it on that. They wanted to be outside where it would happen to them. Not just see it, have it happen. The store was empty. Not closed—empty.

I turned and rushed out to join the others. I couldn't miss it. There were still minutes to go, but suppose there *had* been a miscalculation. I knew what that would mean, but even so I had to be there. I would almost die, too.

147

Now we were all looking up—all over the world people were, I suppose. It was quiet. You could hear them breathing.

And then it came, a flash across the sky, a silver streak, the biggest vapor trail there ever was. It went from this side to that side in no time. It split the sky and was gone before the shock blast hit us. Nobody said anything. We stood there and shivered and straightened up afer the rumbling sound passed.

But there was the vapor trail that stretched farther than anyone could see. It would go around the world at least once before it came to an end somewhere in the desert. I saw my science teacher—he was trying to smile, but couldn't. And then there was the pharmacist who had wanted to be a research chemist, but wasn't good enough.

In front of me, old Fred Butler who drives the bus to Orange Point and King City cracked his knuckles. "He did it," he whispered. "All the way to Mars and back. Safe and right on schedule." He jumped up in the air and kept jumping up. He hadn't been that high off the ground in several years. He never would be again unless he took an elevator. And I knew he hated elevators.

Factory whistles started blowing. They sounded louder than Gabriel. I wonder if he heard them. I grabbed hold of the nearest person and started hugging. I didn't know it was the snooty girl from the next block until she hugged back and began kissing me. We yelled louder than the factory whistles. We had a right.

It was just like the papers said: This was the day the world ended—
And the Universe began.

25

EVENSONG

Lester del Rey

BY THE TIME he reached the surface of the little planet, even the dregs of his power were drained. Now he rested, drawing reluctant strength slowly from the yellow sun that shone on the greensward around him. His senses were dim with an ultimate fatigue, but the fear he had learned from the Usurpers drove them outward, seeking a further hint of sanctuary.

It was a peaceful world, he realized, and the fear thickened in him at the discovery. In his younger days, he had cherished a multitude of worlds where the game of life's ebb and flow could be played to the hilt. It had been a lusty universe to roam then. But the Usurpers could brook no rivals to their own outreaching lust. The very peace and order here meant that this world had once been theirs.

He tested for them gingerly while the merest whisper of strength poured into him. None were here now. He could have sensed the pressure of their close presence at once, and there was no trace of that. The even grassland swept in rolling meadows and swales to the distant hills. There were marble structures in the distance, sparkling whitely in the late sunlight, but they were empty, their unknown purpose altered to no more than decoration now upon this abandoned planet. His attention swept back, across a stream to the other side of the wide valley.

There he found the garden. Within low walls, its miles of expanse were a tree-crowded and apparently untended preserve. He could sense the stirring of larger animal life among the branches and along the winding paths. The brawling vigor of all proper life was missing, but its abundance might be enough to mask his own vestige of living force from more than careful search.

It was at least a better refuge than this open greensward and he longed toward it, but the danger of betraying motion held him still where he was.

He had thought his previous escape to be assured, but he was learning that even he could err. Now he waited while he tested once more for evidence of Usurper trap.

He had mastered patience in the confinement the Usurpers had designed at the center of the galaxy. He had gathered his power furtively while he designed escape around their reluctance to make final disposition. Then he had burst outward in a drive that should have thrust him far beyond the limits of their hold on the universe. And he had found failure before he could span even the distance to the end of this spiral arm of one galactic fastness.

Their webs of detection were everywhere, seemingly. Their great power-robbing lines made a net too fine to pass. Stars and worlds were linked, until only a series of miracles had carried him this far. And now the waste of power for such miracles was no longer within his reach. Since their near failure in entrapping and sequestering him, they had learned too much.

Now he searched delicately, afraid to trip some alarm, but more afraid to miss its existence. From space, this world had offered the only hope in its seeming freedom from their webs. But only microseconds had been available to him for his testing then.

At last he drew his perceptions back. He could find no slightest evidence of their lures and detectors here. He had begun to suspect that even his best efforts might not be enough now, but he could do no more. Slowly at first, and then in a sudden rush, he hurled himself into the maze of the garden.

Nothing struck from the skies. Nothing leaped upwards from the planet core to halt him. There was no interruption in the rustling of the leaves and the chirping bird songs. The animal sounds went on unhindered. Nothing seemed aware of his presence in the garden. Once that would have been unthinkable in itself, but now he drew comfort from it. He must be only a shadow self now, unknown and unknowable in his passing.

Something came down the path where he rested, pattering along on hoofs that touched lightly on the spoilage of fallen leaves. Something else leaped quickly through the light underbrush beside him.

One was a rabbit, nibbling now at the leaves of clover and twitching long ears as its pink nose stretched out for more. The other was a young deer, still bearing the spots of its fawnhood. Either or both might have seemingly been found on any of a thousand worlds. But neither would have been precisely of the type before him.

This was the Meeting World—the planet where he had first found the ancestors of the Usurpers. Of all worlds in the pested galaxy, it had to be *this* world he sought for refuge!

They were savages back in the days of his full glory, confined to this single world, rutting and driving their way to the lawful self-destruction of all such savages. And yet there had been something odd about them, something that then drew his attention and even his vagrant pity.

Out of that pity, he had taught a few of them, and led them upwards. He had even nursed poetic fancies of making them his companions and his equals as the life span of their sun should near its ending. He had answered their cries for help and given them at least some of what they needed to set their steps toward power over even space and energy. And they had rewarded him by overweening pride that denied even a trace of gratitude. He had abandoned them finally to their own savage ends and gone on to other worlds, to play out the purposes of a wider range.

It was his second folly. They were too far along the path toward unlocking the laws behind the universe. Somehow, they even avoided their own destruction from themselves. They took the worlds of their sun and drove outwards, until they could even vie with him for the worlds he had made particularly his own. And now they owned them all, and he had only a tiny spot here on their world—for a time a least.

The horor of the realizaton that this was the Meeting World abated a little as he remembered now how readily their spawining hordes possessed and abandoned worlds without seeming end. And again the tests he could make showed no evidence of them here. He began to relax again, feeling a sudden hope from what had been temporary despair. Surely the might also believe this was the one planet where he would never seek sanctuary.

Now he set his fears aside and began to force his thoughts toward the only pattern that could offer hope. He needed power, and power was available in any area untouched by the webs of the Usurpers. It had drained into space itself throughout the aeons, a waste of energy that could blast suns or build them in legions. It was power to escape, perhaps even to prepare himself eventually to meet them with at least a chance to force truce, if not victory. Given even a few hours free of their notice, he could draw and hold that power for his needs.

He was just reaching for it when the sky thundered and the sun seemed to darken for a moment!

The fear in him gibbered to the surface and sent him huddling from sight of the sky before he could control it. But for a brief moment there was still a trace of hope in him. It could have been a phenomenon caused by his own need for power; he might have begun drawing too heavily, too eager for strength.

Then the earth shook, and he knew.

The Usurpers were not fooled. They knew he was here—had never lost him. And now they had followed in all their massive lack of subtlety. One of their scout ships had landed, and the scout would come seeking him.

He fought for control of himself, and found it long enough to drive his fear back down within himself. Now, with a care that disturbed not even a blade of grass or leaf on a twig, he began retreating, seeking the denser undergrowth at the center of the garden where all life was thickest. With that to screen him, he might at least draw a faint trickle of power, a strength to build a subtle brute aura around himself and let him hide among the beasts. Some Usurper scouts were young and immature. Such a one might be fooled into leaving. Then, before his report could be acted on by others, there might still be a chance. . . .

He knew the thought was only a wish, not a plan, but he clung to it as he huddled in the thicket at the center of the garden. And then even the fantasy was stripped from him.

The sound of footsteps was firm and sure. Branches broke as the steps came forward, not deviating from a straight line. Inexorably, each firm stride brought the Usurper nearer to his huddling place. Now there was a faint glow in the air, and the animals were scampering away in terror.

He felt the eyes of the Usurper on him, and he forced himself away from that awareness. And, like fear, he found that he had learned prayer from the Usurpers; he prayed now desperately to a nothingness he knew, and there was no answer.

"Come forth! This earth is a holy place and you cannot remain upon it. Our judgment is done and a place is prepared for you. Come forth and let me take you there!" The voice was soft, but it carried a power that stilled even the rustling of the leaves.

He let the gaze of the Usurper reach him now, and the prayer in him was mute and directed outward—and hopeless, as he knew it must be.

"But—" Words were useless, but the bitterness inside him forced the words to come from him. "But why? I am God!"

For a moment, something akin to sadness and pity was in the eyes of the Usurper. Then it passed as the answer came. "I know. But I am Man. Come!"

He bowed at last, silently, and followed slowly as the yellow sun sank behind the walls of the garden.

And the evening and the morning were the eighth day.

26

EXILE

Edmond Hamilton

I WISH NOW that we hadn't got to talking about science fiction that night! If we hadn't, I wouldn't be haunted now by that queer, impossible story which can't ever be proved or disproved.

But the four of us were all professional writers of fantastic stories, and I suppose shop talk was inevitable. Yet, we'd kept off it through dinner and the drinks afterward. Madison had outlined his hunting trip with gusto, and then Brazell started a discussion of the Dodgers' chances. And then I had to turn the conversation to fantasy.

I didn't mean to do it. But I'd had an extra Scotch, and that always makes me feel analytical. And I got to feeling amused by the perfect way in which we four resembled a quartet of normal, ordinary people.

"Protective coloration, that's what it is," I announced. "How hard we work at the business of acting like ordinary good guys!"

Brazell looked at me, somewhat annoyed by the interruption. "What are you talking about?"

"About us," I answered. "What a wonderful imitation of solid, satisfied citizens we put up! But we're not satisfied, you know—none of us. We're violently dissatisfied with the Earth, and all its works, and that's why we spend our lives dreaming up one imaginary world after another."

"I suppose the little matter of getting paid for it has nothing to do with it?" Brazell asked skeptically.

"Sure it has," I admitted. "But we all dreamed up our impossible worlds and peoples long before we ever wrote a line, didn't we? From back in childhood, even? It's because we don't feel at home here."

Madison snorted. "We'd feel a lot less at home on some of the worlds we write about."

Then Carrick, the fourth of our party, broke into the conversation. He'd

153

been sitting over his drink in his usual silent way, brooding, paying no attention to us.

He was a queer chap, in most ways. We didn't know him very well, but we liked him and admired his stories. He'd done some wonderful tales of an imaginary planet—all carefully worked out.

He told Madison, "That happened to me."

"What happened to you?" Madison asked.

"What you were suggesting—*I* once wrote about an imaginary world and then had to live on it," Carrick answered.

Madison laughed. "I hope it was a more livable place than the lurid planets on which I set my own yarns."

But Carrick was unsmiling. He murmured, "I'd have made it a lot different—if I'd known I was ever going to live on it."

Brazell, with a significant glance at Carrick's empty glass winked at us and then asked blandly, "Let's hear about it, Carrick."

Carrick kept looking dully down at his empty glass, turning it slowly in his fingers as he talked. He paused every few words.

"It happened just after I'd moved next to the big power station. It sounds like a noisy place, but actually it was very quiet out there on the edge of the city. And I had to have quiet, if I was to produce stories.

"I got right to work on a new series I was starting, the stories of which were all to be laid on the same imaginary world. I began by working out the detailed physical appearance of that world, as well as the universe that was its background. I spent the whole day concentrating on that. And, as I finished, something in my mind went *click!*

"That queer, brief mental sensation felt oddly like a sudden *crystallization*. I stood there, wondering if I were going crazy. For I had a sudden strong conviction that it meant that the universe and world I had been dreaming up all day had suddenly crystallized into physical existence somewhere.

"Naturally, I brushed aside the eerie thought and went out and forgot about it. But the next day, the thing happened again. I had spent most of that second day working up the inhabitants of my story world. I'd made them definitely human, but had decided against making them too civilized—for that would exclude the conflict and violence that must form my story.

"So, I'd made my imaginary world a world whose people were still only half-civilized. I figured out all their cruelties and superstitions. I mentally built up their colorful barbaric cities. And just as I was through—that *click!* echoed sharply in my mind.

"It startled me badly, this second time. For now I felt more strongly than before that queer conviction that my day's dreaming had crystallized into solid reality. I knew it was insane to think that, yet it was an incredible certainty in my mind. I couldn't get rid of it.

"I tried to reason the thing out so that I could dismiss that crazy conviction. If my imagining a world and universe had actually created them, where were they? Certainly not in my own cosmos. It couldn't hold two universes—each completely different from the other.

"But maybe that world and universe of my imagining had crystallized into reality in another and empty cosmos? A cosmos lying in a different dimension from my own? One which had contained only free atoms, formless matter that had not taken on shape until my concentrated thought had somehow stirred it into the forms I dreamed?

"I reasoned along like that, in the queer, dreamlike way in which you apply the rules of logic to impossibilities. How did it come that my imaginings had never crystallized into reality before, but had only just begun to do so? Well, there was a plausible explanation for that. It was the big power station nearby. Some unfathomable freak of energy radiated from it was focusing my concentrated imaginings, as super-amplified force, upon an empty cosmos where they stirred formless matter into the shapes I dreamed.

"Did I believe that? No, I didn't believe it—but I knew it. There is quite a difference between knowledge and belief, as someone said who once pointed out that all men know they will die and none of them believe it. It was like that with me. I realized it was not possible that my imaginary world had come into physical being in a different dimensional cosmos, yet at the same time I was strangely convinced that it had.

"A thought occurred to me that amused and interested me. What if I imagined *myself* in that other world? Would I, too, become physically real in it? I tried it. I sat at my desk, imagining myself as one of the millions of persons in that imaginary world, dreaming up a whole soberly realistic background and family and history for myself over there. And my mind said *click!*"

Carrick paused, still looking down at the empty glass that he twirled slowly between his fingers.

Madison prompted him. "And of course you woke up there, and a beautiful girl was leaning over you, and you asked 'Where am I?'"

"It wasn't like that," Carrick said dully. "It wasn't like that at all. I woke up in that other world, yes. But it wasn't like a real awakening. I was just suddenly in it.

"I was still myself. But I was the myself I had imagined in that other world. That other me had always lived in it—and so had his ancestors before him. I had worked all that out, you see.

"And I was just as real to myself, in that imaginary world I had created, as I had been in my own. That was the worst part of it. Everything in that half-civilized world was so utterly, common-placely real."

He paused again. "It was queer, at first. I walked out into the streets of those barbaric cities, and looked into the people's faces, and I felt like shouting aloud, 'I imagined you all! You had no existence until I dreamed of you!'

"But I didn't do that. They wouldn't have believed me. To them, I was just an insignificant single member of their race. How could they guess that they and their traditions of long history, their world and their universe, had all been suddenly brought into being by my imagination?

"After my first excitement ebbed, I didn't like the place. I had made it too barbaric. The savage violences and cruelties that had seemed so attractive as material for a story, were ugly and repulsive at first hand. I wanted nothing but to get back to my own world.

"And I couldn't get back! There just wasn't any way. I had had a vague idea that I could imagine myself back into my own world as I had imagined myself into this other one. But it didn't work that way. The freak force that had wrought the miracle didn't work two ways.

"I had a pretty bad time when I realized that I was trapped in that ugly, squalid, barbarian world. I felt like killing myself at first. But I didn't. A man can adapt himself to anything. I adapted myself the best I could to the world I had created."

"What did you do there? What was your position, I mean?" Brazell asked.

Carrick shrugged. "I don't know the crafts or skills of that world I'd brought into being. I had only my own skill—that of story telling."

I began to grin. "You don't mean to say that you started writing fantastic stories?"

He nodded soberly. "I had to. It was all I could do. I wrote stories about my own real world. To those other people my tales were wild imagination—and they liked them."

We chuckled. But Carrick was deadly serious.

Madison humored him to the end. "And how did you finally get back home from that other world you'd created?"

"I never did get back home," Carrick said with a heavy sigh.

"Oh, come now," Madison protested lightly. "It's obvious that you got back some time."

Carrick shook his head somberly as he rose to leave.

"No, I never got back home," he said soberly. "I'm still here."

27

THE EXTERMINATOR

A. Hyatt Verrill

HE WAS A magnificent specimen of his kind. Translucent—white, swift in movement, possessing an almost uncanny faculty for discovering his prey, and invariably triumphing over his natural enemies. But his most outstanding feature was his insatiable appetite. He was as merciless and as indiscriminate a killer as a weasel or a ferret; but unlike those wanton destroyers who kill for the mere lust of killing, the Exterminator never wasted his kill. Whatever he fell upon and destroyed was instantly devoured. To have watched him would have been fascinating. A rush, as he hurled himself upon his prey, a brief instant of immobility, of seeming hesitation, a slight tremor of his substance, and all was over; the unfortunate thing that had been moving, unsuspicious of danger, on its accustomed way had vanished completely, and the Exterminator was hurrying off, seeking avidly for another victim. He moved continually in an evenly flowing stream of liquid in absolute darkness. Hence eyes were non-essential, and he was guided entirely by instinct or by nature rather than by faculties such as we know.

He was not alone. Others of his kind were all about and the current was crowded with countless numbers of other organisms: slowly moving roundish things of reddish hue, wiggling tadpole-like creatures, star-shaped bodies; slender, attenuated things like sticks endowed with life; globular creatures; shapeless things constantly altering their form as they moved or rather swam; minute, almost invisible beings; thread-like, serpentine, or eel-like organisms, and countless other forms. Among all these, threading his way in the overcrowding warm current, the Exterminator moved aimlessly, yet ever with one all-consuming purpose—to kill and devour.

By some mysterious, inexplicable means he recognized friends and could unerringly distinguish foes. The reddish multitudes he avoided. He knew they were to remain unmolested and even when, as often happened, he

159

found himself surrounded, hemmed in, and almost smothered by hordes of the harmless red things and was jostled by them, he remained unperturbed and made no attempt to injure or devour them. But the others—the writhing, thread-like creatures; the globular, ovoid, angular, radiate and bar-like things; the rapidly wiggling tadpole-like organisms—were different. Among these he wrought rapid and terrible destruction. Yet even here he exhibited a strange discrimination. Some he passed by without offering to harm them, while others he attacked, slaughtered, and devoured with indescribable ferocity. And on every hand others of his kind were doing the same. They were like a horde of ravenous sharks in a sea teeming with mackerel. They seemed obsessed with the one all-consumig desire to destroy, and so successful were they in this that often, for long periods, the ever moving stream in which they dwelt would be totally destitute of their prey.

Still, neither the Exterminator nor his fellows appeared to suffer for lack of sustenance. They were capable of going for long periods without food and they cruised, or rather swam slowly about, apparently as contented as when on a veritable orgy of killing. And even when the current bore no ligitimate prey within reach of the Exterminator and his companions, never did they attempt to injure or molest the ever present red forms or the innumerable smaller organisms which they seemed to realize were friends. In fact, had it been possible to have interpreted their sensations, it would have been found that they were far more content, far more satisfied when there were no enemies to kill and devour than when the stream swarmed with their natural prey and there was a ceaseless ferocious urge to kill, kill, kill.

At the latter times the steam in which the Exterminator dwelt became uncomfortably warm, which aroused him and his fellows to renewed activity for a space, but which brought death to many of the savage beings. And always, following these casualties, the hordes of enemies rapidly increased until the Exterminator found it almost impossible to decimate them. At times, too, the stream flowed slowly and weakly and a lethargy came over the Exterminator. Often at such times he floated rather than swam, his strength ebbed, and his lust to kill almost vanished. But always there followed a change. The stream took on a peculiar bitter taste, countless numbers of the Exterminator's foes died and vanished, while the Exterminator himself became endowed with unwonted sudden strength and fell ravenously upon the remaining enemies. At such times, also, the number of his fellows always increased in some mysterious manner, as did the red beings. They seemed to appear from nowhere until the stream was thick with them.

Time did not exist for the Exterminator. He knew nothing of distance, nor of night or day. He was susceptible only to changes of temperature in the stream where he always had dwelt, and to the absence or presence of his natural foes and natural allies. Though he was perhaps aware that the current followed an erratic course, that the stream flowed through seemingly endless tunnels that twisted and turned and branched off in innumerable directions and formed a labyrinth of smaller streams, he knew nothing of their routes, or their sources or limits, but swam, or rather drifted, anywhere and everywhere quite aimlessly. No doubt, somewhere within the hundreds of tunnels, there were others of his kind as large, as powerful, and as insatiable a destroyer as himself. But as he was blind, as he did not possess the sense of hearing or other senses which enabled the higher forms of life to judge of their surroundings, he was quite unaware of such companions near him. And, as it happened, he was the only one of his kind who survived the unwanted event that eventually occurred, and by so doing was worthy of being called the Exterminator.

For an unusually long period the current in the tunnel had been most uncomfortably warm. The stream had teemed with countless numbers of his foes and these, attacking the reddish forms, had decimated them. There had been a woeful decrease in the Exterminator's fellows also, and he and the few survivors had been forced to exert themselves to the utmost to avoid being overwhelmed. Even then the hordes of wiggling, gyrating, darting, weaving enemies seemed to increase faster than they were killed and devoured. It began to look as if their army would be victorious and the Exterminator and his fellows would be vanquished, utterly destroyed, when suddenly the slowly flowing hot stream took on a strange, pungent, acrid taste. Instantly, almost, temperature decreased, the current increased, and as if exposed to a gas attack, the swarming hosts of innumerable strange forms dwindled. And almost instantly the Exterminator's fellows appeared as if from nowhere and fell ravenously upon their surviving foes. In an amazingly short time the avenging white creatures had practically exterminated their multitudinous enemies. Great numbers of the reddish organisms filled the stream and the Exterminator dashed hither and thither seeking chance survivors of his enemies. In eddies and the smaller tunnels he came upon a few. Almost instantly he dashed at them, destroyed them, swallowed them. Guided by some inexplicable power or force he swept along a tiny tunnel. Before him he was aware of a group of three tiny thread-like things, his deadliest foes—and hurled himself forward in chase. Overtaking one, he was about to seize it when a terrific cataclysm occurred. The wall of the tunnel was split asunder, a great rent appeared, and with a rush like water through an opened sluice-way the enclosed stream poured upward through the opening.

Helpless in the grip of the current, the Exterminator was borne whirling, gyrating madly into the aperture. But his one obsession, an all-consuming desire to kill, overcame all terror, all other sensations. Even as the fluid hurled him onward he seized the wriggling foe so near him and he swallowed it alive. At the same instant the remaining two were carried by the rushing current almost within his reach. With a sudden effort he threw himself upon the nearest, and as the thing vanished in his maw, he was borne from eternal darkness into blinding light.

Instantly the current ceased to flow. The liquid became stagnant and the countless red beings surrounding the Exterminator moved feebly, slowly, and gathered in clusters where they clung together as if for mutual support. Somewhere near at hand, the Exterminator sensed the presence of the last surviving member of the trio he had been chasing when the disaster took place. But in the stagnant, thick liquid, obstructed by the red beings, he could not move freely. He struggled, fought to reach this one remaining foe; but in vain. He felt suffocated, and became weaker and weaker. And he was alone. Of all his comrades, he was the only one that had been carried through the rent in the tunnel that for so long had been his home.

Suddenly he felt himself lifted. Together with a few of the reddish things and a small portion of his native element, he was drawn up. Then, with the others, he was dropped, and as he fell, new life coursed through him, for he realized that his hereditary enemy—that wiggling thread-like thing—was close beside him, that even yet he might fall upon and destroy it.

The next instant some heavy object fell upon him. He was imprisoned there with his archenemy an infinitesimal distance from him, but hopelessly out of reach. A mad desire to wreak vengeance swept over him. He was losing strength rapidly. Already the red beings about him had become inert, motionless. Only he and that thread-like, tiny thing still showed signs of life. And the fluid was rapidly thickening. Suddenly, for a fraction of a second, he felt free, and with a final spasmodic effort he moved, reached the enemy, and, triumphant at the last, became a motionless inert thing.

"Strange!" muttered a human voice as its owner peered through the microscope at the blood drop on the slide under the objective. "I could have sworn I caught a glimpse of a bacillus there a moment ago. But there's not a trace of it now.''

"That new formula we injected had an almost miraculous effect,'' observed a second voice.

"Yes,'' agreed the first. "The crisis is past and the patient is out of danger. Not a single bacillus in this specimen. I would not have believed it possible.''

But neither physician was aware of the part the Exterminator had played. To them he was merely a white corpuscle lying dead in the rapidly drying blood drop on the glass-slide.

28

THE EYES HAVE IT

Philip K. Dick

IT WAS QUITE by accident I discovered this incredible invasion of Earth by lifeforms from another planet. As yet, I haven't done anything about it; I can't think of anything to do. I wrote to the Government, and they sent back a pamphlet on the repair and maintenance of frame houses. Anyhow, the whole thing is known; I'm not the first to discover it. Maybe it's even under control.

I was sitting in my easy-chair, idly turning the pages of a paperback book someone had left on the bus, when I came across the reference that first put me on the trail. For a moment I didn't respond. It took some time for the full import to sink in. After I'd comprehended, it seemed odd I hadn't noticed it right away.

The reference was clearly to a nonhuman species of incredible properites, not indigenous to Earth. A species, I hasten to point out, customarily masquerading as ordinary human beings. Their disguise, however, became transparent in the face of the following observations by the author. It was at once obvious the author knew everything. Knew everything—and was taking it in his stride. The line (and I tremble remembering it even now) read:

> . . . *his eyes slowly roved about the room.*

Vague chills assailed me. I tried to picture the eyes. Did they roll like dimes? The passage indicated not; they seemed to move through the air, not over the surface. Rather rapidly, apparently. No one in the story was surprised. That's what tipped me off. No sign of amazement at such an outrageous thing. Later the matter was amplified.

> . . . *his eyes moved from person to person.*

165

There it was in a nutshell. The eyes had clearly come apart from the rest of him and were on their own. My heart pounded and my breath choked in my windpipe. I had stumbled on an accidental mention of a totally unfamiliar race. Obviously non-Terrestrial. Yet, to the characters in the book, it was perfectly natural—which suggested they belonged to the same species.

And the author? A slow suspicion burned in my mind. The author was taking it rather *too easily* in his stride. Evidently, he felt this was quite a usual thing. He made absolutely no attempt to conceal this knowledge. The story continued:

> *. . . presently his eyes fastened on Julia.*

Julia, being a lady, had at least the breeding to feel indignant. She is described as blushing and knitting her brows angrily. At this, I sighed with relief. They weren't *all* non-Terrestrials. The narrative continues:

> *. . . slowly, calmly, his eyes examined every inch of her.*

Great Scott! But here the girl turned and stomped off and the matter ended. I lay back in my chair gasping with horror. My wife and family regarded me in wonder.

"What's wrong, dear?" my wife asked.

I couldn't tell her. Knowledge like this was too much for the ordinary run-of-the-mill person. I had to keep it to myself. "Nothing," I gasped. I leaped up, snatched the book, and hurried out of the room.

In the garage, I continued reading. There was more. Trembling, I read the next revealing passage:

> *. . . he put his arm around Julia. Presently she asked him if he would remove his arm. He immediately did so, with a smile.*

It's not said what was done with the arm after the fellow had removed it. Maybe it was left standing upright in the corner. Maybe it was thrown away. I don't care. In any case, the full meaning was there, staring me right in the face.

Here was a race of creatures capable of removing portions of their anatomy at will. Eyes, arms—and maybe more. Without batting an eyelash. My knowledge of biology came in handy, at this point. Obviously they were simple beings, uni-cellular, some sort of primitive single-celled things. Beings no more developed than starfish. Starfish can do the same thing, you know.

I read on. And came to this incredible revelation, tossed off cooly by the author without the faintest tremor:

> . . . *outside the movie theater we split up. Part of us went inside, part over to the cafe for dinner.*

Binary fission, obviously. Splitting in half and forming two entities. Probably each lower half went to the cafe, it being farther, and the upper halves to the movies. I read on, hands shaking. I had really stumbled onto somthing here. My mind reeled as I made out this passage:

> . . . *I'm afraid there's no doubt about it. Poor Bibney has lost his head again.*

Which was followed by:

> . . . *and Bob says he has utterly no guts.*

Yet Bibney got around as well as the next person. The next person, however, was just as strange. He was soon described as:

> . . . *totally lacking in brains.*

There was no doubt of the thing in the next passage. Julia, whom I had thought to be the one normal person, reveals herself as also being an alien lifeform, similar to the rest:

> . . . *quite deliberately, Julia had given her heart to the young man.*

It didn't relate what the final disposition of the organ was, but I didn't really care. It was evident Julia had gone right on living in her usual manner, like all the others in the book. Without heart, arms, eyes, brains, viscera, dividing up in two when the occasion demanded. Without a qualm.

> . . . *thereupon she gave him her hand.*

I sickened. The rascal now had her hand, as well as her heart. I shudder to think what he's done with them, by this time.

. . . he took her arm.

Not content to wait, he had to start dismantling her on his own. Flushing crimson, I slammed the book shut and leaped to my feet. But not in time to escape one last reference to those carefree bits of anatomy whose travels had originally thrown me on the track:

> *. . . her eyes followed him all the way down the road and across the meadow.*

I rushed from the garage and back inside the warm house, as if the accursed things were following *me*. My wife and children were playing Monopoly in the kitchen. I joined them and played with frantic fervor, brow feverish, teeth chattering.

I had had enough of the thing. I want to hear no more about it. Let them come on. Let them invade Earth. I don't want to get mixed up in it.

I have absolutely no stomach for it.

29

FATHER'S IN THE BASEMENT

Philip José Farmer

THE TYPEWRITER HAD clattered for three and a half days. It must have stopped now and then, but never when Millie was awake. She had fallen asleep perhaps five times during that period, though something always aroused her after fifteen minutes or so of troubled dreams.

Perhaps it was the silence that hooked her and drew her up out of the thick waters. As soon as she became fully conscious, however, she heard the clicking of the typewriter start up.

The upper part of the house was almost always clean and neat. Millie was only eleven, but she was the only female in the household, her mother having died when Millie was nine. Millie never cleaned the basement because her father forbade it.

The big basement room was his province. There he kept all his refrence books, and there he wrote at a long desk. This room and the adjoining furnace-utility room constituted her father's country (he even did the washing), and if it was a mess to others, it was order to him. He could reach into the chaos and pluck out anything he wanted with no hesitation.

Her father was a free-lance writer, a maker of literary soups, a potboiler cook. He wrote short stories and articles for men's and women's magazines under male or female names, sicence fiction novels, trade magazine articles, and an occasional Gothic. Sometimes he got a commission to write a novel based on a screenplay.

"I'm the poor man's Frederick Faust," her father had said many times. "I won't be remembered ten years from now. Not by anyone who counts. I want to be remembered, baby, to be reprinted through the years as a classic, to be written of, talked of, as a great writer. And so. . . ."

And so, on the left side of his desk, in a file basket, was half a manuscript, three hundred pages. Pop had been working on it, on and off, mostly off, for fifteen years. It was to be his masterpiece, the one book that would transcend all his hackwork, the book that would make the public cry "Wow!" the one book by him that would establish him as a Master. (Capital M, baby!") It would put his name in the *Encyclopedia Britannica;* he would not take up much space in it; a paragraph was all he asked.

He had patted her hand and said, "And so when you tell people your name, they'll say, 'You aren't the daughter of the great Brady X. Donaldson? You are? Fantastic! And what was he really like, your father?' "

And then, reaching out and stroking her pointed chin, he had said, "I hope you can be proud of having a father who wrote at least one great book, baby. But of course, you'll be famous in your own right. You have unique abilities, and don't you ever forget it. A kid with your talents has to grow up into a famous person. I only wish that I could be around. . . ."

He did not go on. Neither of them cared to talk about his heart "infraction," as he insisted on calling it.

She had not commented on his remark about her "abilities." He was not aware of their true breadth and depth, nor did she want him to be aware.

The phone rang. Millie got up out of the chair and walked back and forth in the living room. The typewriter had not even hesitated when the phone rang. Her father was stopping for nothing, and he might not even have heard the phone, so intent was he. This was the only chance he would ever get to finish his Work ("Capital W, baby!"), and he would sit at his desk until it was done. Yet she knew that he could go on like this only so long before falling apart.

She knew who was calling. It was Mrs. Coombs, the secretary of Mr. Appleton, the principal of Dashwood Grade School. Mrs. Coombs had called every day. The first day, Millie had told Mrs. Coombs that she was sick. No, her father could not come to the phone because he had a very deadly schedule to meet. Millie had opened the door to the basement and turned the receiver of the phone so that Mrs. Coombs could hear the heavy and unceasing typing.

Millie spoke through her nose and gave a little cough now and then, but Mrs. Combs' voice betrayed disbelief.

"My father knows I have this cold, and so he doesn't see why he should be bothered telling anybody that I have it. He knows I have it. No, it's not bad enough to go to the doctor for it. No, my father will not come to the phone now. You wouldn't like it if he had to come to the phone now. You can be sure of that.

"No, I can't promise you he'll call before five, Mrs. Coombs. He doesn't want to stop while he's going good, and I doubt very much he'll be stopping at five. Or for some time after, if I know my father. In fact, Mrs. Coombs, I can't promise anything except that he won't stop until he's ready to stop.''

Mrs. Coombs had made some important-sounding noises, but she finally said she'd call back tomorrow. That is, she would unless Millie was at school in the morning, with a note from her father, or unless her father called in to say that she was still sick.

The second day, Mrs. Coombs had phoned again, and Millie had let the ringing go on until she could stand it no longer.

''I'm sorry, Mrs. Coombs, but I feel lots worse. And my father didn't call in, and won't, because he is still typing. Here, I'll hold the phone to the door so you can hear him.''

Millie waited until Mrs. Coombs seemed to have run down.

''Yes, I can appreciate your position, Mrs. Coombs, but he won't come, and I won't ask him to. He has so little time left, you know, and he has to finish this one book, and he isn't listening to any such thing as common sense or . . . No, Mrs. Coombs, I'm not trying to play on your sympathies with this talk about his heart trouble.

''Father is going to sit there until he's done. He said this is his lifework, his only chance for immortality. He doesn't believe in life after death, you know. He says that a man's only chance for immortality is in the deeds he does or the works of art he produces.

''Yes, I know it's a peculiar situation, and he's a peculiar man, and I should be at school.''

And you, Mrs. Coombs, she thought, you think I'm a very peculiar little girl, and you don't really care that I'm not at school today. In fact, you like it that I'm not there because you get the chills every time you see me.

''Yes, Mrs. Coombs, I know you'll have to take some action, and I don't blame you for it. You'll send somebody out to check; you have to do it because the rules say you have to, not because you think I'm lying.

''But you can hear my father typing, can't you? You surely don't think that's a recording of a typist, do you?''

She shouldn't have said that, because now Mrs. Coombs would be thinking exactly that.

She went into the kitchen and made more coffee. Pop had forbidden her coffee until she was fourteen, but she needed it to keep going. Besides, he wouldn't know anything about it. He had told her, just before he had felt the first pain, that he could finish the Work in eighty-four to ninety-six hours if he were uninterrupted and did not have to stop because of exhaustion or another attack.

"I've got it all composed up here," he had said, pointing a finger at his temple. "It's just a matter of sitting down and staying down, and that's what I'm going to do, come hell or high water, come infraction or infarction. In ten minutes, I'm going down into my burrow, and I'm not coming back up until I'm finished."

"But, Pop," Millie had said, "I don't see how you can. Exercise or excitement is what brings on an attack. . . ."

"I got my pills, and I'll rest if I have to and take longer," he had said. "So it takes two weeks? But I don't think it will. Listen, Millie," and he had taken her hand in his and looked into her eyes as if they were binoculars pointing into a fourth dimension, "I'm depending on you more than on my pills or even on myself. You'll not let anybody or anything interfere, will you? I know I shouldn't ask you to stay home from school, but this is more important than school. I really need you. I can't afford to put this off any longer. I don't have the time. You know that."

He had released her hand and started toward the basement door, saying, "This is it; here goes," when his face had twisted and he had grabbed his chest.

But that had not stopped him.

The phone rang. It was, she knew, Mrs. Coombs again.

Mrs. Coombs' voice was as thin as river ice in late March.

"You tell your father that officers will be on their way to your house within a few minutes. They'll have a warrant to enter."

"You're causing a lot of trouble and for no good reason," Millie said. "Just because you don't like me. . . ."

"Well, I never!" Mrs. Coombs said. "You know very well that I'm doing what I have to and, in fact, I've been overly lenient in this case. There's no reason in the world why your father can't come to the phone. . . ."

"I told you he had to finish his novel," Millie said. "That's all the reason he needs."

She hung up the phone and then stood by the door for a moment, listening to the typing below. She turned and looked through the kitchen door at the clock on the wall. It was almost twelve. She doubted that anybody would come during the lunch hour, despite what Mrs. Coombs said. That gave her—her father, rather—another hour. And then she would see what she could do.

She tried to eat but could get down only half the liverwurst and lettuce sandwich. She wrapped the other half and put it back into the refrigerator. She looked at herself in the small mirror near the wall clock. She, who could not afford to lose an ounce, had shed pounds during the past three and a half days. As if they were on scales, her cheekbones had risen while her eyes had sunk. The dark brown irises and the bloodshot whites of her eyes looked like two fried eggs with ketchup that someone had thrown against a wall.

She smiled slightly at the thought, but it hurt her to see her face. She looked like a witch and always would.

"But you're only eleven!" her father had boomed at her. "Is it a tragedy at eleven because the boys haven't asked you for a date yet? My God, when I was eleven, we didn't ask girls for dates. We hated girls!"

Yet his Great Work started with the first-love agonies of a boy of eleven, and he had admitted long ago that the boy was himself.

Millie sighed again and left the mirror. She cleaned the front room but did not use the vacuum cleaner because she wanted to hear the typewriter keys. The hour passed, and the doorbell rang.

She sat down in a chair. The doorbell rang again and again. Then there was silence for a minute, followed by a fist pounding on the door.

Millie got up from the chair but went to the door at the top of the basement steps and opened it. She breathed deeply, made a face, went down the wooden steps and around the corner at the bottom and looked down the long room with its white-painted cement blocks and pine paneling. She could not see her father because a tall and broad dark-mahogany bookcase in the middle of the room formed the back of what he called his office. The chair and desk were on the other side, but she could see the file basket on the edge of the desk. Her practiced eye told her that the basket held almost five hundred pages, not counting the carbon copies.

The typewriter clattered away. After a while, she went back up the steps and across to the front door. She opened the peephole and looked through. Two of the three looked as if they could be plainclothesmen. The third was the tall, beefy, red-faced truant officer.

"Hello, Mr. Tavistock," she said through the peephole. "What can I do for you?"

"You can open the door and let me in to talk to your father," he growled. "Maybe he can explain what's been going on, since you won't."

"I told Mrs. Coombs all about it," Millie said. "She's a complete ass, making all this fuss about nothing."

"That's no way for a lady to talk, Millie," Mr. Tavistock said. "Especially an eleven-year-old. Open the door. I got a warrant."

He waved a paper in his huge hand.

"My father'll have you in court for trampling on his civil rights," Millie said. "I'll come to school tomorrow. I promise. But not today. My father mustn't be bothered."

"Let me in now, or we break the door down!" Mr. Tavistock shouted. "There's something funny going on, Millie, otherwise your father would've contacted the school long ago!"

"You people always think there's something funny about me, that's all!" Millie shouted back.

"Yeah, and Mrs. Coombs fell down over the wastebasket and wrenched her back right after she phoned you," Tavistock said. "Are you going to open that door?"

It would take them only a minute or so to kick the door open even if she chained it. She might as well let them in. Still, two more minutes might be all that were needed.

She reached for the knob and then dropped her hand. The typing had stopped.

She walked to the top of the basement steps.

"Pop! Are you through?"

She heard the squeaking of the swivel chair, then a shuffling sound. The house shook, and there was a crash as someone struck the front door with his body. A few seconds later, another crash was followed by the bang of the door against the inner wall. Mr. Tavistock said, "All right, boys! I'll lead the way!"

He sounded as if he were raiding a den of bank robbers, she thought.

She went around the corner to the front room and said, "I think my father is through."

"In more ways than one, Millie," Mr. Tavistock said.

She turned away and walked back around the corner, through the door and out onto the landing. Her father was standing at the bottom of the steps. His color was very bad and he looked as if he had gained much weight, though she knew that that was impossible.

He looked up at her from deeply sunken eyes, and he lifted the immense pile of sheets with his two hands.

"All done, Pop?" Millie said, her voice breaking.

He nodded slowly.

Millie heard the three men come up behind her. Mr. Tavistock leaned over her and said, "Whew!"

Millie turned and pushed at him.

"Get out of my way! He's finished it!"

Mr. Tavistock glared, but he moved to one side. She walked to a chair and sat down heavily. One of the detectives said, "You look awful, Millie. You look like you haven't slept for a week."

"I don't think I'll ever be able to sleep," she said. She breathed deeply and allowed her muscles to go loose. Her head lolled as if she had given up control over everything inside her.

There was a thumping noise from the basement. Mr. Tavistock cried out, "He's fainted!" The shoes of the three men banged on the steps as they ran down. A moment later, Mr. Tavistock gave another cry. Then all three men began talking at once.

Millie closed her eyes and wished she could quit trembling. Some time later, she heard the footsteps. She did not want to open her eyes, but there was no use putting it off.

Mr. Tavistock was pale and shaking. He said, "My God! He looks, he smells like. . . ."

One of the detectives said, "His fingertips are worn off, the bones are sticking out, but there wasn't any bleeding."

"I got him through," Millie said. "He finished it. That's all that counts."

30

THE FEAR OF IT

Robert Barr

THE SEA WAS done with him. He had struggled manfully for his life, but exhaustion came at last, and, realizing the futility of further fighting, he gave up the battle. The tallest wave, the king of that roaring tumultuous procession racing from the wreck to the shore, took him in its relentless grasp, held him towering for a moment against the sky, whirled his heels in the air, dashed him senseless on the sand, and finally, rolled him over and over, a helpless bundle, high up upon the sandy beach.

Human life seems of little account when we think of the trifles that make toward the extinction or the extension of it. If the wave that bore Stanford had been a little less tall, he would have been drawn back into the sea by one that followed. If, as a helpless bundle, he had been turned over one time more or one less, his mouth would have pressed into the sand, and he would have died. As it was, he lay on his back with arms outstretched on either side, and a handful of dissolving sand in one clinched fist. Succeeding waves sometimes touched him, but he lay there unmolested by the sea with his white face turned to the sky.

Oblivion has no calendar. A moment or an eternity are the same to it. When consciousness slowly returned, he neither knew nor cared how time had fled. He was not quite sure that he was alive, but weakness rather than fear kept him from opening his eyes to find out whether the world they would look upon was the world they had last gazed at. His interest, however, was speedily stimulated by the sound of the English tongue. He was still too much dazed to wonder at it, and to remember that he was cast away on some unknown island in the Southern Seas. But the purport of the words startled him.

"Let us be thankful. He is undoubtedly dead." This was said in a tone of infinite satisfaction.

There seemed to be a murmur of pleasure at the announcement from those who were with the speaker. Stanford slowly opened his eyes, wondering what these savages were who rejoiced in the death of an inoffensive stranger cast upon their shores. He saw a group standing around him, but his attention speedily became concentrated on one face. The owner of it, he judged, was not more than nineteen years of age, and the face—at least so it seemed to Stanford at the time—was the most beautiful he had ever beheld. There was an expression of sweet gladness upon it until her eyes met his, then the joy faded from the face, and a look of dismay took its place. The girl seemed to catch her breath in fear, and tears filled her eyes.

"Oh," she cried, "he is going to live."

She covered her face with her hands, and sobbed.

Stanford closed his eyes wearily. "I am evidently insane," he said to himself. Then, losing faith in the reality of things, he lost consciousness as well, and when his senses came to him again he found himself lying on a bed in a clean but scantily furnished room. Through an open window came the roar of the sea, and the thunderous boom of the falling waves brought to his mind the experiences through which he had passed. The wreck and the struggle with the waves he knew to be real, but the episode on the beach he now believed to have been but a vision resulting from his condition.

A door opened noiselessly, and, before he knew of anyone's entrance, a placid-faced nurse stood by his bed and asked him how he was.

"I don't know. I am at least alive."

The nurse sighed, and cast down her eyes. Her lips moved, but she said nothing. Stanford looked at her curiously. A fear crept over him that he was hopelessly crippled for life, and that death was considered preferable to a maimed existence. He felt wearied, though not in pain, but he knew that sometimes the more desperate the hurt, the less the victim feels it at first.

"Are—are any of my—my bones broken, do you know?" he asked.

"No. You are bruised, but not badly hurt. You will soon recover."

"Ah!" said Stanford, with a sigh of relief. "By the way," he added, with sudden interest, "who was that girl who stood near me as I lay on the beach?"

"There were several."

"No, there was but one. I mean the girl with the beautiful eyes and a halo of hair like a glorified golden crown on her head."

"We speak not of our women in words like those," said the nurse, severely. "You mean Ruth, perhaps, whose hair is plentiful and yellow."

Stanford smiled. "Words matter little," he said.

"We must be temperate in speech," replied the nurse.

178

"We may be temperate without being teetotal. Plentiful and yellow, indeed! I have had a bad dream concerning those who found me. I thought that they—but it does not matter. She at least is not a myth. Do you happen to know if any others were saved?"

"I am thankful to be able to say that every one was drowned."

Stanford started up with horror in his eyes. The demure nurse, with sympathetic tones, bade him not excite himself. He sank back on his pillow.

"Leave the room," he cried, feebly. "Leave me—leave me." He turned his face toward the wall, while the woman left as silently as she had entered.

When she was gone Stanford slid from the bed, intending to make his way to the door and fasten it. He feared that these savages, who wished him dead, would take measures to kill him when they saw he was going to recover. As he leaned against the bed, he noticed that the door had no fastening. There was a rude latch, but neither lock nor bolt. The furniture of the room was of the most meager description, clumsily made. He staggered to the open window, and looked out. The remnants of the disastrous gale blew in upon him and gave him new life, as it had formerly threatened him with death. He saw that he was in a village of small houses, each cottage standing in its own plot of ground. It was apparently a village of one street, and over the roofs of the houses opposite he saw in the distance the white waves of the sea. What astonished him most was a church with its tapering spire at the end of the street—a wooden church such as he had seen in remote American settlements. The street was deserted, and there were no signs of life in the houses.

"I must have fallen in upon some colony of lunatics," he said to himself. "I wonder to what country these people belong—either to England or the United States, I imagine—yet in all my travels I never heard of such a community."

There was no mirror in the room, and it was impossible for him to know how he looked. His clothes were dry and powdered with salt. He arranged them as well as he could, and slipped out of the house unnoticed. When he reached the outskirts of the village he saw that the inhabitants, both men and women, were working in the fields some distance away. Coming towards the village was a girl with a water-can in either hand. She was singing as blithely as a lark until she saw Stanford, whereupon she paused both in her walk and in her song. Stanford, never a backward man, advanced, and was about to greet her when she forestalled him by saying:

"I am grieved, indeed, to see that you have recovered."

The young man's speech was frozen on his lip, and a frown settled on his brow. Seeing that he was annoyed, though why she could not guess, Ruth hastened to amend matters by adding:

"Believe me, what I say is true. I am indeed sorry."

"Sorry that I live?"

"Most heartily am I."

"It is hard to credit such a statement from one so—from you."

"Do not say so. Miriam has already charged me with being glad that you were not drowned. It would pain me deeply if you also believed as she does."

The girl looked at him with swimming eyes, and the young man knew not what to answer.

Finally he said, "There is some horrible mistake. I cannot make it out. Perhaps our words, though apparently the same, have a different meaning. Sit down, Ruth, I want to ask you some questions."

Ruth cast a timorous glance towards the workers, and murmured something about not having much time to spare, but she placed the water-cans on the ground and sank down on the grass. Stanford throwing himself on the sward at her feet, but seeing that she shrank back, he drew himself further from her, resting where he might gaze upon her face.

Ruth's eyes were downcast, which was necessary, for she occupied herself in pulling blade after blade of grass, sometimes weaving them together. Stanford had said he wished to question her, but he apparently forgot his intention, for he seemed wholly satisfied with merely looking at her. After the silence had lasted for some time, she lifted her eyes for one brief moment, and then asked the first question herself.

"From what land do you come?"

"From England."

"Ah! that also is an island, is it not?"

He laughed at the "also," and remembered that he had some questions to ask.

"Yes, it is an island—also. The sea dashes wrecks on all four sides of it, but there is no village on its shores so heathenish that if a man is cast upon the beach the inhabitants do not rejoice because he has escaped death."

Ruth looked at him with amazement in her eyes.

"Is there, then, no religion in England?"

"Religion? England is the most religious country on the face of the earth. There are more cathedrals, more churches, more places of worship in England than in any other State that I know of. We send missionaries to all heathenish lands. The Government, itself, supports the Church."

"I imagine, then, I mistook your meaning. I thought from what you said

180

that the people of England feared death, and did not welcome it or rejoice when one of their number died."

"They do not fear death, and they do not rejoice when it comes. Far from it. From the peer to the beggar, everyone fights death as long as he can; the oldest cling to life as eagerly as the youngest. Not a man but will spend his last gold piece to ward off the inevitable even for an hour."

"Gold piece—what is that?"

Stanford plunged his hand into his pocket.

"Ah!" he said, "there are some coins left. Here is a gold piece."

The girl took it, and looked at it with keen interest.

"Isn't it pretty?" she said, holding the yellow coin on her pink palm, and glancing up at him.

"That is the general opinion. To accumulate coins like that, men will lie, and cheat, and steal—yes, and work. Although they will give their last sovereign to prolong their lives, yet will they risk life itself to accumulate gold. Every business in England is formed merely for the gathering together of bits of metal like that in your hand; huge companies of men are formed so that it may be piled up in greater quantities. The man who has most gold has most power, and is generally the most respected; the company which makes most money is the one people are most anxious to belong to."

Ruth listened to him with wonder and dismay in her eyes. As he walked she shuddered, and allowed the yellow coin to slip from her hand to the ground.

"No wonder such a people fears death."

"Do you not fear death?"

"How can we, when we believe in heaven?"

"But would you not be sorry if someone died whom you loved?"

"How could we be so selfish? Would you be sorry if your brother, or someone you loved, became possessed of whatever you value in England—a large quantity of this gold, for instance?"

"Certainly not. But then you see—well, it isn't exactly the same thing. If one you care for dies you are separated from him, and—"

"But only for a short time, and that gives but another reason for welcoming death. It seems impossible that Christian people should fear to enter Heaven. Now I begin to understand why our forefathers left England, and why our teachers will never tell us anything about the people there. I wonder why missionaries are not sent to England to teach them the truth, and try to civilize the people?"

"That would, indeed, be coals to Newcastle. But there comes one of the workers."

181

"It is my father," cried the girl, rising. "I fear I have been loitering. I never did such a thing before."

The man who approached was stern of countenance.

"Ruth," he said, "the workers are athirst."

The girl, without reply, picked up her pails and departed.

"I have been receiving," said the young man, coloring slightly, "some instruction regarding your belief. I had been puzzled by several remarks I had heard, and wished to make inquiries concerning them."

"It is more fitting," said the man, coldly, "that you should receive instruction from me or from some of the elders than from one of the youngest in the community. When you are so far recovered as to be able to listen to an exposition of our views, I hope to put forth such arguments as will convince you that they are the true views. If it should so happen that my arguments are not convincing, then I must request that you will hold no communication with our younger members. They must not be contaminated by the heresies of the outside world."

Stanford looked at Ruth standing beside the village well.

"Sir," he said, "you underrate the argumentative powers of the younger members. There is a text bearing upon the subject which I need not recall to you. I am already convinced."

31

FEEDING TIME

James E. Gunn

ANGELA WOKE UP with the sickening realization that today was feeding time. She slipped out of bed, hurried to the desk, and leafed nervously through her appointment book. She laughed with relief; it was all right—today was her appointment.

Angela took only forty-five minutes for makeup and dressing: it was feeding time. As she descended in the elevator, walked swiftly through the lobby, and got into a taxi, she didn't even notice the eyes that stopped and swiveled after her: feeding time.

Angela was haunted by a zoo.

She was also haunted by men, but this was understandable. She was the kind of blond, blue-eyed angel men pray to—or for—and she had the kind of measurements—36-26-36—that make men want to take up mathematics.

But Angela had not time for men—not today. Angela was haunted by a zoo, and it was feeding time.

Dr. Bachman had a gray-bearded, pink-skinned, blue-eyed kindliness that was his greatest stock in trade. Underneath, there was something else not quite so kindly which had been influential in his choice of professions. Now, for a moment, his professional mask—his *persona,* as the Jungians call it—slipped aside.

"A zoo?" he repeated, his voice clear, deep, and cultured, with just a trace of accent; Viennese without a doubt. He caught himself quickly. "A zoo. Exactly."

"Well, not exactly a zoo," said Angela, pursing her red lips thoughtfully at the ceiling. "At least not an ordinary zoo. It's really only one animal—if you could call him an animal."

183

"What do you call him?"

"Oh, I never call him," Angela said quickly, giving a delicious little shiver. "He might come."

"Hm-m-m," hm-m-med Dr. Bachman neutrally.

"But you don't mean that," Angela said softly. "You mean if he isn't an animal, what is he? What he is—is a monster."

"What kind of monster?" Dr. Bachman asked calmly.

Angela turned on one elbow and looked over the back of the couch at the psychoanalyst. "

"You say that as if you met monsters every day. But then I guess you do." She sighed sympathetically. "It's a dangerous business, being a psychiatrist."

"Dangerous?" Dr. Bachman repeated querulously, caught off guard a second time. "What do you mean?"

"Oh, the people you meet—all the strange ones—and their problems—"

"Yes, yes, of course," he said hurriedly. "But about the monster?"

"Yes, doctor," Angela said in her obedient tone and composed herself again on the couch. She looked at the corner of the ceiling as if she could see him clinging there. "He's not a nightmare monster, though he's frightening enough. He's too real; there are no blurred edges. He has purple fur—short, rather like the fur on some spiders—and four legs, not evenly distributed like a dog's or a cat's but grouped together at the bottom. They're very strong—much stronger than they need to be. He can jump fifteen feet straight up into the air."

She turned again to look at Dr. Bachman. "Are you getting all this?"

Hastily, the psychoanalyst turned his notebook away, but Angela had already caught a glimpse of his doodling.

"Goodie!" she said, clapping her hands in delight. "You're drawing a picture."

"Yes, yes," he said grumpily. "Go on."

"Well, he has only two arms. He has six fingers on each hand, and they're flexible, as if they had no bones in them. They're elastic, too. They can stretch way out—as if to pick fruit that grows on a very tall vine."

"A vegetarian," said Dr. Bachman, making his small joke.

"Oh, no, doctor!" Angela said, her eyes wide. "He eats everything, but meat is what he likes the best. His face is almost human except it's green. He has very sharp teeth." She shuddered. "Very sharp. Am I going too fast?"

"Don't worry about me!" snapped the psychoanalyst. "It is your sub-conscious we are exploring, and it must go at its own speed."

"Oh, dear," Angela said with resignation. "The subconscious. It's going to be another one of those."

"You don't believe this nightmare has any objective reality?" Dr. Bachman asked sharply.

"That would make me insane, wouldn't it? Well, I guess there's no help for it. That's what I think."

Dr. Bachman tugged thoughtfully at his beard. "I see. Let's go back. How did this illusion begin?"

"I think it began with the claustrophobia."

Dr. Bachman shrugged. "A morbid fear of confined places is not unusual."

"It is when you're out in the open air. The fear had no relationship to my surroundings. All of a sudden, I'd feel like I was in a fairly large room which had a tremendous weight of rock or masonry above it. I was in the midst of a crowd of people. For moments it became so real that my actual surroundings faded out."

"But the feeling came and went."

"Yes. Then came the smell. It was a distinctive odor—musty and strong like the lion house in the winter, only wrong, somehow. But it made me think of the zoo."

"Naturally you were the only one who smelled it."

"That's right. I was self-conscious, at first. I tried to drown out the odor with perfume, but that didn't help. Then I realized that no one else seemed to smell it. Like the claustrophobia, it came and went. But each time it returned it was stronger. Finally I went to a psychiatrist—a Dr. Aber."

"That was before the illusion became visual?"

"That was sort of Dr. Aber's fault—my seeing the monster, I mean."

"It is to be expected," Dr. Bachman said.

"When nothing else worked, Dr. Aber tried hypnosis. 'Reach into your subconscious,' he said. 'Open the door to the past!' Well, I reached out. I opened the door. And that's when it happened."

"What happened?" Dr. Bachman leaned forward.

"I saw the monster."

"Oh," He leaned back again, disappointed.

"People were close, but the monster was closer. The odor was stifling as he stared through the door—and saw me. I slammed the door shut, but it was too late. The door was there. I knew it could be opened. And he knew it could be opened. Now I was really afraid."

"Afraid?"

"That the monster might get through the door."

185

The psychoanalyst tugged at his beard. "You have an explanation for this illusion?"

"You won't laugh?"

"Certainly not!"

"I think, through some strange accident of time, I've become linked to a zoo that will exist in the distant future. The monster—wasn't born on Earth. He's an alien—from Jupiter, perhaps, although I don't think so. Through the door I can see part of a sign; I can read this much."

Angela turned and took the noteobok from his surprised fingers and printed quickly:

M'RA
(Larmis
Nativ)
Vega

"Just like in the zoo," she said, handing the book back. "There's a star named Vega."

"Yes," said the psychoanalyst heavily. "And you are afraid that this . . . alien will get through the door and—"

"That's it. He can open it now, you see. He can't exist here; that would be impossible. But something from the present can exist in the future. And the monster gets hungry—for meat."

"For meat?" Dr. Bachman repeated, frowning.

"Every few weeks," Angela said, shivering, "it's feeding time."

Dr. Bachman tugged at his beard, preparing the swift, feline stroke which would lay bare the traumatic relationship at the root of the neurosis. He said, incisively, "The monster resembles your father, is that not so?"

It was Angela's turn to frown. "That's what Dr. Aber said. I'd never have noticed it on my own. There might be a slight resemblance."

"This Dr. Aber—he did you no good?"

"Oh, I wouldn't want you to think that," Angela protested quickly. "He helped. But the help was—temporary, if you know what I mean."

"And you would like something more permanent."

"That would be nice," Angela admitted. "But I'm afraid it's too much to hope for."

"No. It will take time, but eventually we will work these subconscious repressions into your conscious mind, where they will be cleansed of their neurotic value."

"You think it's all in my head?" Angela said wistfully.

186

"Certainly," the psychoanalyst said briskly. "Let us go over the progress of the illusion once more: First came the claustrophobia, then the smell, then, through Dr. Aber's bung . . . treatment, I should say, the dreams—"

"Oh, not dreams, doctor," Angela corrected. "When I sleep, I don't dream of monsters. I dream"—she blushed prettily—"of men. The thing in the zoo—I can see him whenever I close my eyes." She shivered. "He's getting impatient."

"Hungry?"

Angela beamed at him. "Yes. It's almost feeding time. He gets fed, of course. By the keeper, I suppose. But that's just grains and fruits and things like that. And he gets hungry for meat."

"And then?"

"He opens the door."

"And I suppose he sticks through his elastic fingers."

Angela gave him a look of pure gratitude. "That's right."

"And you're afraid that one day he will get hungry enough to eat you."

"That's it, I guess. Wouldn't you be—afraid, that is? There's all the legends about dragons and Minotaurs and creatures like that. They always preferred a diet of young virgins; and where there's all that talk—"

"If that were your only concern," Dr. Bachman commented dryly, "it seems to me that you could make yourself ineligible with no great difficulty."

Angela giggled. "Why, doctor! What a suggestion!"

"Hm-m-m," hm-m-med the psychoanalyst. "So! To return. Every few weeks comes feeding time and you, feeling nervous and afraid, come to me for help."

"You put it so well."

"And now it's feeding time."

"That's right." Angela's nostrils dilated suddenly. "He's getting close to the door. Don't you smell him, doctor?"

Dr Bachman sniffed once and snorted. "Certainly not. Now tell me about your father."

"Well," Angela began reluctantly, "he believed in reincarnation—"

"No, no," the psychoanalyst said impatiently. "The important things. How you felt about him when you were a little girl. What he said to you. How you hated your mother."

"I'm afraid there won't be time. He's got one of his hands on the door already."

Despite himself, Dr. Bachman glanced back over his shoulder. "The monster?" His beard twitched nervously. "Nonsense. About your father—"

187

"The door's opened!" Angela cried out. "I'm scared, doctor. It's feeding time!"

"I won't be tricked again," the psychoanalyst said sternly. "If we're to get anywhere with this analysis, I must have complete—"

"Doctor! Watch out! The fingers—Dr. Bachman! Doctor! Doc—!"

Angela sighed. It was a strange sigh, half hopelessness and half relief. She picked up her purse.

"Doctor?" she said tentatively to the empty room.

She stood up, sniffing the air gingerly. The odor was gone. So was Dr. Bachman.

She walked toward the door. "Doctor?" she tried once more.

There was no answer. There never had been an answer, not from seventeen psychiatrists. There was no doubt about it. The monster did like psychiatrists.

It was a truly terrifying situation she was in, certainly through no fault of her own, and a girl had to do the best she could. She could console herself with the thought that the monster would never take her for food.

She was the trapdoor it needed into this world. Eat her, and feeding time was over.

She was perfectly safe.

As long as she didn't run out of psychiatrists.

32

THE FIEND

Frederik Pohl

HOW BEAUTIFUL SHE was, Dandish thought, and how helpless. The plastic identification ribbon around her neck stood out straight, and as she was just out of the transport capsule, she wore nothing else. "Are you awake?" he asked, but she did not stir.

Dandish felt excitement building up inside him; she was so passive and without defense. A man could come to her now and do anything at all to her, and she would not resist. Or, of course, respond. Without touching her, he knew that her body would be warm and dry. It was fully alive, and in a few minutes she would be conscious.

Dandish—who was the captain and sole crew member of the interstellar ship without a name carrying congealed colonists across the long, slow, empty space from Earth to a planet that circled a star that had never had a name in astronomical charts, only a number, and was now called Eleanor—passed those minutes without looking again at the girl, whose name he knew to be Silvie but whom he had never met. When he looked again, she was awake, jack-knifed against the safety straps of the crib, her hair standing out around her head and her face wearing an expression of anger. "All right. Where are you? I know what the score is," she said. "Do you know what they can do to you for this?"

Dandish was startled. He did not like being startled, for it frightened him. For nine years the ship had been whispering across space; he had had enough loneliness to satisfy him and he had been frightened. There were 700 cans of colonists on the ship, but they lay brittle and changeless in their bath of liquid helium and were not very good company. Outside the ship the nearest human being was perhaps two light-years away, barring some chance-met ship heading in the other direction that was actually far more remote than either star, since the forces involved in stopping and matching

189

course with a vessel bound home were twice as great as, and would take twice as much time as, those involved in the voyage itself. Everything about the trip was frightening. The loneliness was a terror. To stare down through an inch of crystal and see nothing but far stars led to panic. Dandish had decided to stop looking out five years before, but had not been able to keep to his decision, and so now and again peeped through the crystal and contemplated his horrifying visions of the seal breaking, the crystal popping out on a breath of air, himself in his metal prison tumbling, tumbling forever down to the heart of one of the ten million stars that lay below. In this ship a noise was an alarm. Since no one but himself was awake, to hear a scratch of metal or a thud of a moving object striking something else, however tiny, however remote, was a threat, and more than once Dandish had suffered through an itch of fear for hours or days until he tracked down the exploded light tube or unsecured door that had startled him. He dreamed uneasily of fire. This was preposterously unlikely in the steel-and-crystal ship, but what he was dreaming of was not the fire of a house but the monstrous fires in the stars beneath.

"Come out where I can see you," commanded the girl.

Dandish noted that she had not troubled to try to cover her nakedness. Bare she woke and bare she stayed. She had unhitched the restraining webbing and left the crib, and now she was prowling the room in which she had awakened, looking for him. "They warned us," she called. " 'Watch the hook!' 'Look out for the space nuts!' 'You'll be sorry!' That's all we heard at the reception center, and now here you are, all right. Wherever you are—where are you?—for God's sake, come out so I can see you." She half stood and half floated at an angle to the floor, nibbling at imperceptible bits of dead skin on her lips and staring warily from side to side. She said, "What was the story you were going to tell me? A subspace meteorite destroyed the ship, all but you and me, and we were doomed to fly endlessly toward nowhere, so there was nothing for us to do but try to make a life for ourselves?"

Dandish watched her through the view eyes in the reviving room but did not answer. He was a connoisseur of victims, Dandish was. He had spent a great deal of time planning this. Physically she was perfect: very young, slim, slight. He had picked her out on that basis from among the 352 female canned colonists, leafing through the microfile photographs that accompanied each colonists's dossier like a hi-fi hobbyist shopping through a catalog. She had been the best of the lot. Dandish was not skilled enough to be able to read a personality profile and in any event considered psychologists to be phonies and their profiles trash; so he had had to go by the indices he knew. He had wanted his victim to be innocent and trusting. Silvie, 16 years old and a little below average in intelligence, had seemed very promising. It was disappointing that she did not react with more fear. "They'll give you fifty years for this!" she shouted, looking around to see where he could be hiding. "You know that, don't you?"

The revival crib, sensing that she was out of it, was quietly stowing and rearming itself, ready to be taken out and used again. Its plastic sheets slipped free of the corners, rolled up in a tight spiral and slid into a disposal chute, revealing asceptic new sheets below. Its radio-warming generators tested themselves with a surge of high-voltage current, found no flaws and shut themselves off. The crib sides folded down meekly. The instrument table hooded itself over. The girl paused to watch it, then shook her head and laughed. "Scared of me?" she called. "Come on, lets get this over with! Or else," she added, "admit you've made a boo-boo, get me some clothes and let's talk this over sensibly."

Sorrowfully, Dandish turned his gaze away. A timing device reminded him that it was time to make his routine half-hour check of the ship's systems, and, as he had done more than 150,000 times already and would do 100,000 times again, he swiftly scanned the temperature readings in the can hold, metered the loss of liquid helium and balanced it against the withdrawals from the reserve, compared the ship's course with the flight plan, measured the fuel consumption and rate of flow, found all systems functioning smoothly and returned to the girl. It had taken only a minute or so, but already she had found the comb and mirror he had put out for her and was working angrily at her hair. One fault in the techniques of freezing and revivification lay in what happened to such elaborated structures as fingernails and hair. At the temperature of liquid helium, all organic matter was brittle as Prince Rupert's drops, and although the handling techniques were planned with that fact in mind, the body wrapped gently in elastic cocooning, every care exercised to keep it from contact with anything hard or sharp, nails and hair had a way of being snapped off. The reception center endlessly drummed into the colonists the importance of short nails and butch haircuts, but the colonists were not always convinced. Silvie now looked like a dummy on which a student wigmaker had failed a test. She solved her problem at last by winding what remained of her hair in a tiny bun and put down the comb, snapped-off strands of hair floating in the air all about her like a stretched-out sandstorm.

She patted the bun mournfully and said, "I guess you think this is pretty funny."

Dandish considered the question. He was not impelled to laugh.

Twenty years before, when Dandish was a teenager with the long perma-
nented hair and the lacquered fingernails that were the fashion for kids that
year, he had dreamed almost every night of just such a situation as this. To
own a girl of his own—not to love her or to rape her or to marry her, but to
possess her as a slave, with no one anywhere to stop him from whatever he
chose to impose on her—had elaborated itself in a hundred variations
nightly. He didn't tell anyone about his dream, not directly, but in the
school period devoted to practical psychology he had mentioned it as
something he had read in a book, and the instructor, staring right through
him into his dreams, told him it was a repressed wish to play with dolls.
"This fellow is role-playing," he said, "acting out a wish to be a woman.
These clear-cut cases of repressed homosexuality can take many
forms . . . " and on and on, and although the dreams were as physically
satisfying as ever, the young Dandish awoke from them both reproved and
resentful.

But Silvie was neither a dream nor a doll. "I'm not a doll!" said Silvie so
sharply and patly that it was a shock. "Come on out and get it over with!"

She straightened up, holding to a free-fall grip, and although she looked
angry and annoyed, she still did not seem afraid. "Unless you are really
crazy," she said clearly, "which I doubt, although I have to admit it's a
possibility, you aren't going to do anything I don't want you to do, you
know. Because you can't get away with it, right? You can't kill me, you
could never explain it, and besides, they don't let murderers run ships in the
first place, and so when we land, all I have to do is yell cop and you're
running a subway shuttle for the next ninety years." She giggled. "I know
about that. My uncle got busted on income-tax evasion and now he's a
self-propelled dredge in the Amazon delta, and you should see the letters he
writes. So come on out and let's see what I'm willing to let you get away
with."

She grew impatient. "Kee-rist," she said, shaking her head, "I sure get
the great ones. And, oh, by the way, as long as I'm up, I have to go to the
little girls' room, and then I want breakfast."

Dandish took some small satisfaction in that these requirements, at least,
he had foreseen. He opened the door to the washroom and turned on the
warmer oven where emergency rations were waiting. By the time Silvie
came back, biscuits, bacon and hot coffee were set out for her.

"I don't suppose you have a cigarette?" she said. "Well, I'll live. How
about some clothes? And how about coming out so I can get a look at you?"
She stretched and yawned and then began to eat. Apparently she had
showered, as is generally desirable on awakening from freeze-sleep to get

rid of the the exfoliated skin, and she had wrapped her ruined hair in a small towel. Dandish had left the one small towel in the washroom reluctantly, but it had not occurred to him that his victim would wrap it around her head. Silvie sat thoughtfully staring at the remains of her breakfast and then after a while said, like a lecturer:

"As I understand it, starship sailors are always some kind of nuts, because who else would go off for twenty years at a time, even for money, even for any kind of money? All right, you're a nut. So if you wake me up and won't come out, won't talk to me, there's nothing I can do about it.

"Now, I can see that even if you weren't a little loopy to start with, this kind of life would tip you. Maybe you just wanted a little company? I can understand that. I might even cooperate and say no more about it.

"On the other hand, maybe you're trying to get your nerve up for something rough. Don't know if you can, because they naturally screened you down fine before they gave you the job. But supposing. What happens then?

"If you kill me, they catch you.

"If you don't kill me, then I tell them when we land, and they catch you.

"I told you about my uncle. Right now his body is in the deepfreeze somewhere on the dark side of Mercury and they've got his brain keeping the navigation channels clear off Belém. Maybe you think that's not so bad. Uncle Henry doesn't like it a bit. He doesn't have any company, bad as you that way, I guess, and he says his suction hoses are always sore. Of course, he could always louse up on the job, but then they'd just put him some other place that wouldn't be quite as nice—so what he does is grit his teeth, or I guess you should say his grinders, and get along the best he can. Ninety years! He's only done six so far. I mean six when I left Earth, whatever that is now. You wouldn't like that. So why not come out and talk?"

Five or ten minutes later, after making faces and buttering another roll and flinging it furiously at the wall, where the disposal units sluiced it away, she said, "Damn you, then give me a book to read, anyway."

Dandish retreated from her and listened to the whisper of the ship for a few minutes, then activated the mechanisms of the revival crib. He had been a loser long enough to learn when to cut his losses. The girl sprang to her feet as the sides of the crib unfolded. Gentle tentacles reached out for her and deposited her in it, locking the webbing belt around her waist. "You damned fool!" she shouted, but Dandish did not answer. The anesthesia cone descended toward her struggling face, and she screamed, "Wait a minute! I never said I wouldn't—" but what she never said she wouldn't, she couldn't say, because the cone cut her off. In a moment she was asleep.

A plastic sack stretched itself around her, molding to her face, her body, her legs, even to the strayed towel around her hair, and the revival crib rolled silently to the freezing room. Dandish did not watch further. He knew what would happen, and besides, the timer reminded him to make his check. Temperatures, normal; fuel consumption, normal; course, normal; freezer room showed one new capsule en route to storage, otherwise normal. Good-bye, Silvie, said Dandish to himself, you were a pretty bad mistake.

Conceivably later on, with another girl. . . .

But it had taken nine years for Dandish to wake Silvie, and he did not think he could do it again. He thought of her Uncle Henry running a dredge along the South Atlantic littoral. It could have been him. He had leaped at the opportunity to spend his sentence piloting a starship instead.

He stared out at the ten million stars below with the optical receptors that were his eyes. He clawed helplessly at space with the radars that gave him touch. He wept a five-million-mile stream of ions behind him from his jets. He thought of the tons of helpless flesh in his hold, the bodies in which he could have delighted if his own body had not been with Uncle Henry's on coldside Mercury, the fears on which he could have fed if he had been able to inspire fear. He would have sobbed if he had had a voice to sob with.

33

FOR VALUE RECEIVED

Andrew J. Offutt

MARY ANNE BARBER, M.D. was graduated from medical school at the tender age of twenty-three. Her Boards score set a new high. No, she wasn't a genius. You don't know about her? Where've you been? There have been Hospital Board Meetings and Staff Meetings and even discussions of her case in the AMA and the AHA. Most important medical case in American history; frightening precedent. She's been written up, with pictures in *Life*, *Look*, *Parents*, *The Journal of the AMA*, *Hospital News*, *Today's Health*, *Reader's Digest*—and *Fortune*. Her father has turned down movie offers. He's also been interviewed by *The Independent*, *Psychology Today*, *Ramparts*, *The Objectivist Newsletter*, and *Playboy*.

It started twenty-three years ago when Robert S. Barber won a sales contest and received a very healthy company bonus. That was just before his wife Jodie was due to present him with their third child. Feeling expansive, Bob Barber suggested a private room for Jodie's confinement. She agreed, with enthusiasm. Last time she had shared a room with Philomena, a mother of nine. Philomena had complained constantly about the horror of being a breeding machine. Jodie told her to have faith—and stop. Philomena advised her that her Faith was the source of her problem.

Jodie entered the Saint Meinrad Medical Center in a room all to herself, rather than sharing one with another new mother in the American Way. The room cost ten dollars a day more than the money provided by the Barber's group hospitalization insurance; privacy's expensive! Nevertheless the ID card got them past the Warder of the Gates, a suspicious matron at the Admittance desk whose job it was to admit all patients impartially—provided they either possessed insurance ID cards or were visibly and provably destitute. There wasn't any middle ground.

The baby, a hairless girl—at least she showed certain evidences of

195

insipidly incipient femalehood—was born with the usual number of arms, legs, fingers, etcetera, after a brief period of labor. She proved with gusto the proper functioning of her lungs and larynx. She also took immediately to breast-feeding as if it were the normal method. She throve without seeming to realize that her infantile neighbors wouldn't recognize a mammary if they saw one.

Meanwhile the girls in the nursery went about their job: spoiling the infants entrusted to them by parents who had no choice and who would wonder in a few days how it was possible for a child to be born spoiled. The second part of the job of all hosptial personnel involved, then as now, keeping the male of the species from both his chosen mate and the fruit of his loins. Robert Barber objected to this. Why his presence was forbidden while Jodie nursed the baby was beyond him. He'd seen 'em before. As a matter of fact he considered them his.

The nun he asked failed to reply.

Ostensibly, visiting hours were to protect the patients from disturbances in the form of Aunt Martha (''Yaas, I knew someone who had the selfsame operation, my dear. She died, poor soul.'') and the like. But new mothers were not sick. It was obvious to Robert Barber that the prescribed hours— and the far greater number of proscribed ones—were for the convenience of a hospital staff whose mystique suffered from a surfeit of Commoners noticing their humanness. Naturally this assumption was strengthened by the fact that physicians, nurses, interns, residents, orderlies, Candy-Stripers, Gray Ladies, Pink Ladies, and the Lady pushing the cart peddling magazines and tissues disturbed the patients far more than ''lay'' visitors.

The inescapable prayers on the loudspeaker every night were rather disturbing, too.

But Robert Barber was a determined man. He had noticed that there were two kinds of people in hospitals, aside from the patients: Those Who Belong, and Others. The Others visited and indeed seemed to exist only by the sufferance of anyone who wore white shoes or a lab coat. Or carried a little black satchel. All one had to do, Bob Barber decided, was to act as if one Belonged.

So he adopted protective coloration. Carrying his black briefcase and striding purposefully, he traversed the hallowed and antiseptic halls.

''Good-evening-nurse,'' he said briskly, barely deigning to see the deferential girls who ducked respectfully out of his way. ''Sister,'' he said to the nuns who were not quite so deferential; after all, doctor or no doctor, he was only a man, and a layman at that. But they nodded and rustled aside nevertheless.

Thus did the fiercely independent Bob Barber disregard Visiting Hours for four days running.

The fateful day arrived without portentous occurrence in the skies. Jodie Barber was pronounced ready to go home by a duly authorized member of the American Magicians Association. Thanking the kindly old AMA shaman-priest, Bob went down to settle with the cashier. She ruled a smallish domain separated from the world by a counter-*cum*-window that reminded him of a bank. She regarded him with the usual expression: as if he had committed a crime.

He had not.

He was about to.

"You seem to have placed your wife in a better room than your hospitalization covers, Mister Barber." Her tone was the same you've heard in movies when the prosecutor says, "Then you were indeed at or near the scene of the crime on the night of March 21st."

Bob Barber smiled and nodded. "Yes. I should owe you about forty dollars, right?"

She nodded wordlessly, giving him an exemplary imitation of the gaze of the legendary basilisk.

Frowning a little, wondering if it were a communicable disease, Robert Barber also nodded, again. "Uh, well. . . . "

"Would-you-like-to-pay-the-balance-by-cash-or-check, Mister Barber?"

He hesistated, he told an interviewer years later, waiting for the words THIS IS A RECORDING. He had recognized good salesmanship; the room was "better," not "more costly" than his insurance covered. Now he'd been given the standard "fatal choice": cash or check. "Send me a bill, please. You have my address."

"Mister Barber, our policy is that all bills are handled upon the release of the patient."

He remarked on that word "handled" later, too. Not "paid." She *had* taken a course in salesmanship/semantics! "Yes, well, you've got $237.26 coming from the hospitalization and $40 from me. Just send me a bill at the end of the month like everyone else, will you?"

His smile failed to bring one in return. "We have a policy, Mister Barber, of not dismissing the patient until the bill has been settled in full."

"We've got an out then, ma'm. My wife isn't a patient here. We merely came here because it's a more convenient place for our doctor to watch the baby being born. Now . . . my car is back by the Emergency Door, and my wife's all packed." He gave her his very best boyish smile. "Am I supposed to sign something?"

It didn't work. She sighed. "Mister Barber, you just don't seem to understand. It's a *rule*, Mister Barber. A *hospital* rule. We cannot dismiss the patient until the bill has been settled."

Bob Barber shoved his hands into his trousers pockets and squared his shoulders. She not only hadn't a cerebral cortex, he thought, she was missing her ovaries and needed a heart transplant! He firmed his mouth. "OK," he said. "If you must keep hostages, that's your business. But I'm sure one will do. Ms. Barber and I are leaving in a few minutes. We are nursing the baby, so my wife will be coming back six times daily. The baby's name is Mary Ann, by the way." He smiled in his confidence, enjoying her shocked look. "When she's big enough to go to college we'll send you the tuition money." He grinned and waited for the backdown. He was without doubt the first man in history to call her bluff.

When Mary Ann Barber was six years old her father picked her up at the hospital each day to transport her to school. Each Friday she brought him a bill. It had passed $9,000 when she was partly through the first grade.

She entered the tenth grade at age fourteen. On her fourth day as a Junior, she handed her daddy a bill for $106,378.23. She was one of the brightest girls in high school, and one of the healthiest. She had absorbed a tremendous amount of knowledge and sophistication, talking with interns. And it was easy to remain healthy, living in a hospital.

She had been moved from Nursery to Pediatrics to Children's Ward to Second Floor. Then the interns had doubled up to make her a gift: a private room away from the patients. Her parents visited her twice daily, usually. At visiting hours.

There were the Staff and Board Meetings, the magazine and newspaper articles, the interviews. Offers to pay Mary Ann Barber's daily-increasing bill had come from all over the country, as well as from seventeen foreign nations and the governments of two. The hospital had offered to settle for ninety cents on the dollar. Then seventy-five. Fifty cents. Forty. Bob Barber said he was holding out for the same terms the Feds had given James Hoffa.

On her fourteenth birthday Mary Ann received one thousand, two hundred seventy-one cards. Shortly thereafter she received 1,314 Christmas cards. Her clothing came from one manufacturer, her shoes from another, her school books from two others. Her tuition arrived anonymously each year. Bob Barber solemnly invested it in an insurance annuity in his daughter's name. Most of the clothing she never wore; the parochial school she attended required sexless, characterless uniforms of navy-blue jumpers over white blouses. And black shoes. And white socks, rolled just to here.

She was graduated from college at nineteen and entered medical school at once. The doctors had won; the nuns had tried to sell her on the convent, the nurses on being an airline stewardess or secret agent. Mary Ann was far too fond of interns.

On his daughter's twenty-first birthday Robert Barber received his now-monthly itemized bill. It was thirty-seven feet long, neatly typed by the hated machine he called an Iron Brain, Malefic. The bill totalled $364,311.41, very little of which was for anything other than room and board. The discount had been applied and figured for him as usual, although this time he noticed he was asked for only twenty cents on the dollar. Still, $72,862.28 was more than he had available. He sent the usual note:

> I agreed to forward the forty dollars outstanding on my daughter's bill at the end of the month of her birth. When the bill arrived it was for $130, including ten days at $9 for Nursery care. I returned it, requesting a corrected total of $40. Had you responded I would have had a daughter all these years, like other people. You chose to advise that I owed you for the time she spent in the hospital past the day I took my wife home. I disagreed then and I disagree today; those additional ten days were spent in your institution at your request, not mine. And not hers. Thus, since you claim to be a non-profit organization and the courts have refused to uphold me in prosecuting for kidnap-at-ransom, I am still willing to pay the $40. However I cannot do this until I receive a proper bill for that amount, so that I can account for it on my income tax return.
>
> —Robert S. Barger
>
> P.S. The enclosed check is to cover all expenses for my daughter's recent tonsillectomy. Actually, had I had a choice I would have chosen another hospital providing better care, but she advises your service was satisfactory.
>
> -R.S.B.

It was signed, as usual, with a flourish. You can see for yourself: the hospital threw away the first few, but they have a file of 243 of those letters. Two hundred thirty-seven of them are printed.

There was another Board Meeting. The vote still went against bowing to Barber's request for a total bill of $40, although Board members calculated that the bookkeeping had cost them $27.38 a year. But—in the first place, What Would People Think if they learned hospitals are fallible, and admit

199

errors? In the second, Eli R. Hutchinson, president of the biggest bank in town and a board member for thirty-six years, absolutely refused to agree to the $40 settlement unless it included interest. Simple interest on the original amount came to $50.40. Barber had rejected that six years ago.

As they left the Board Meeting William Spaninger, M.D., was heard to mutter to Sister Mary Joseph, OP, RN, "Well, Hutch can't live forever."

Sister Mary Joseph shook her head and rattled her beads. "You're a sinful man, Doctor Spaninger. Besides, Mister Hutchinson had a complete physical last week. He's in ridiculously good health."

Mary Ann Barber, as noted, graduated from Med School at twenty-three and made an extraordinary grade on her Boards. By that time she had turned down seven offers from six magazines to be photographed as their Nubile Young (semi) Nude (semi) Virgin of the month; three major studios who wanted to film her life story—two with herself in the starring role; seven hundred twenty-four written, wired, and cabled offers of matrimony, and six offers of the same from fellow medical students. There were other offers, most of them from fellow med students, most of them less formal.

Special arrangements were made for her to intern at home: Saint Meinrad Medical Center. The interns are salaried at exactly one hundred twenty dollars monthly. Doctor M. A. Barber began on the first of September.

At exactly midnight on the tenth she moved her possessions out of the hospital and just as quietly moved into a long-empty room at her parents' home. At two A.M. she returned to the hospital to go on duty.

Her departure was discovered at 8:30, while she was assisting—medicalese for watching—Doctor Spaninger perform a Pilonidal Cystectomy on a nineteen-year-old college student. Dr. Spaninger glanced up at the frantically-signaling nun in the doorway, then looked at Doctor Barber. Her eyes smiled at him above her mask. He shook his head at the nun and pulled his brows down at her as ferociously as possible. Doctor Mary Ann Barber smiled sweetly at her.

"What's she want?" Dr. Spaninger asked as they smoked a cigarette in the Physicians' Lounge after what he called a Tailectomy. He was very popular among nurses, residents, and interns, who called him the nearest-human doctor in town.

"Probably discovered I moved out last night. At midnight."

"Moved out of the hospital? My god, girl! You've run away from home!"

She shook her very blonde hair. "No doctor, I moved *to* home. It's quite a lovely room, although it certainly *smells* odd."

He nodded. "That's air. O$_2$ and some other stuff, nitrogen, hydrogen; you know. No antiseptics. No medicines. Possibly a little chintz, and some mothballs. Take some getting used to, I guess." He gazed at her, brows down. "But you're a . . . *resident* here. A resident resident, I mean, not a medical one. Let's don't go into it; I've been on the damned Hospital Board twenty years, and I've been living with the infamous Barber case all twenty of 'em. You can't leave. You have a hell of a bill here. Or your irascible, independent, atavistic, heroic old S.O.B. of a father does."

She pulled off the surgery cap and her hair flew as she shook her head with a very bright smile. "Nope. He doesn't. I signed some papers assuming all my own bills, debts, etcetera etcetera the day I turned twenty-one. I'm his daughter, you know; I agree with him. He didn't much like that, but I used the word 'independent' and he shut up pretty fast. That's Sacrament at his—my house. Then I told him my plan. That *really* shut him up, after he stopped laughing."

Dr. Spaninger waited. Then he sighed, looked at his watch, and leaned back, lighting another cigarette. She also had a cigarette out; he pushed the lighter back into his pocket.

"Don't play woman with me, Doctor," he said. "You're much too independent, competent and professional for me to insult you by lighting your cigarette. Besides, I've diapered you a few times. Never sent a bill, either." He watched a snake of smoke writhe up the the ceiling. "All right Mary Ann, I'll bite. What's your Plan?"

"Was. It's completed. I started here on the first of September at $120 a month. September hath thirty days. That's four whole U.S. rasbuckniks a day."

"Um-hm. Shameful. We do everything we can to keep you yunkers out of the profession, including starve you out."

"We won't go into that either, overworked but wealthy old physician. Well, as of midnight last night I had worked ten days. That's forty dollars worth. I moved out. And left a note at the desk; I'm to receive only eighty dollars this month. We're even."

He leaned back and laughed. Loudly. Long. Eventually he grew rather red in the face and leaned over to slap his knee. His concerned young ward warned him about his blood pressure. He nodded, gasping and choking.

"Wait till they hear THIS! Wait'll Eli Hutch hears this! Oh, wonderful! We're shut of the Barber case at last!" He looked at her and frowned again.

"Unless the rest of the Board decides to sue you . . . hm. I'll take care of that in *advance*. The only Barber I want to hear about hereafter is Doctor Barber. I hope I never hear the name Robert S. Barber again!"

"That's not very charitable, but Daddy and I are opposed to charity anyhow. I promised you this: my son won't be named Rober—what you said. He will be named William Robert Joseph Barber, OK?"

Dr. William Joseph Spaninger stared at her. "What . . . son?"

She shrugged "Oh, the one I'll eventually have. I'm trying to decide now which of my fellow interns is the most promising-looking." She smiled at him. "No, I will *not* be an OB patient any ways soon. Not till I've finished up here, anyhow. And probably not till after I'm married."

"Thank god. But that's a dang lie—you're stuck on young Chris Andrews and you know it." He studied her thoughtfully. "Well. How the devil do you plan to exist on eighty bucks this month?"

"I won't have to. I am receiving forty dollars from Daddy. He says the bill was his responsibility, anyhow. We accept our responsibilities in my family."

Dr. Spaninger waved a hand at the hospital. "Nonsense. This is your family, and I haven't found two people here willing to accept responsibility in the past twenty years. And I hope you will allow me, as a token of an old girl-watcher's admiration for a very good-looking one, to give you a check for exactly $40 for your birthday. Your father's giving you the forty sounds suspiciously like charity, and I really hate to see the old bas—rascal start changing, now. He's a great man. Just for god's sake don't ever tell him so. And . . . carry on his work."

"I intend to. I'll spend the rest of my life bucking the System and marking 'PLEASE' in all those nasty DO NOT WRITE IN THIS SPACE blocks and punching extra holes in computer cards. But he's a greater man than you think, O Revered Father-image. I said I was *receiving* the money from him, Doctor. I did *not* say anything about charity. It's a business arrangement; Daddy pays only for value received. For the duration of the month, on my hours off-duty from here, I'm on KP at home."

34

THE FORBIDDEN WORD

Edward D. Hoch

GREGORY HAD NOT visited Los Angeles since the summer of 1978, and the changes he now found were a bit unnerving. True, the reconstruction was almost complete, the signs of disaster had nearly vanished; but there was about the city a certain strangeness which he could not at first pinpoint.

Driving in from the airport in his rented electric car, he was aware that the freeway traffic was thinner than he had remembered. At one stretch, just before turning onto Slauson Avenue, he counted only five cars ahead of him—at a time of day when he used to see hundreds.

He asked Browder about it at the office and the gray-haired regional sales manager merely shrugged. "Oh, they're trying to keep it quiet, but we all know it's happening. This building is only half occupied and nearly all the houses on my block have *For Sale* signs out. People are leaving by the thousands."

"But why?" Gregory, a stolid midwesterner, found it difficult to understand.

"The last one was the worst, really bad. People just decided they'd had enough."

"You mean the eathquake?"

Browder held up a hand. "We don't talk about it in public. God, Gregory, it's been bad out here! Haven't you read about the California Enabling Act back east?"

"I might have seen something in the newspapers," Gregory said.

"They're trying everything to minimize the danger, to get people to stay." Browder chuckled dryly. "I'm old enough to remember the depression days when I was a boy. Then they put up roadblocks to keep people *out* of the state. Now they try to keep 'em *in*!"

"Times change," Gregory agreed. "But what about business? The

203

home office sent me out because sales have fallen off so badly. What's been happening?''

The gray-haired man shrugged again. ''You need people to buy things.''

''Surely it's not that bad!''

''What have I just been telling you? Wait till the census in 1990. They can fake a lot of things, but they can't fake that. That'll tell the story. Some say it'll show a population drop of close to fifty percent.''

''But the states back east are booming—they haven't room for all the people!''

''That's back east. This is out here. They have their problems and we have ours.''

Gregory glanced down at the sheet of sales figures. ''What should I tell the home office?''

''Just that. I can't sell to people who aren't here.''

They talked longer, of many things, but when Gregory left the office he was troubled and unhappy. Los Angeles had always been one of their best markets, and if it really was dying as Browder believed, the company was in trouble.

It was the lunch hour, but the downtown streets were pleasantly un-crowded. Gregory found himself able to walk along easily without being pushed off the sidewalk—so unlike the midtown pedestrian jams in New York and Chicago. He almost wondered if this might be a good, uncluttered place to live—but then he remembered the people who were leaving, and the reason they were leaving.

''Hello, there,'' a girl's voice said at his side. He turned and saw a pretty blonde who seemed vaguely familiar. When she noted his uncertainty she explained, ''I'm Mr. Browder's secretary. You probably didn't notice me in the outer office.''

''As a matter of fact, I didn't. My name is Gregory.''

''I know. I'm Lola Miller. Are you going somewhere for lunch?''

''Do you know a good place?''

''The office girls usually eat at the Sunset Lounge. It's only a block away.''

''Sounds good. Would you join me?''

''Glad to. I enjoy company while I eat.''

Lola Miller was in her mid-twenties, with that sunny California beauty that recalled the movie queens of the 1950s. He liked her smile and the way she had of showing one dimple in her left cheek in a sort of lopsided grin.

"It's nearly ten years since I've visited L.A.," he said, seating himself opposite her at one of the little tables.

"It's almost rebuilt now, isn't it? You wouldn't know anything had happened."

"Apparently the people know. I understand they're leaving."

She nodded. "Terrible for business, isn't it? Pretty soon we'll be a ghost state. I suppose that's why they had to pass all those laws."

"The California Enabling Act? Browder mentioned it."

"It's terrible, but necessary. Something had to be done after the last disaster." She pressed the button for the waitress. "All those scare head-lines in the papers, everybody talking so much—that's when the real panic started."

"You mean after the earthquake?" he asked just as the waitress ap-peared. Across the table Lola Miller's face suddenly drained of color. The waitress took their order and hurried back to the counter.

"You shouldn't have said that," Lola cautioned him. "Not in public. She might turn you in."

"Said what? The word earthquake? Well, that's what it was, wasn't it?"

"Yes, but we're forbidden to—"

She was cut off in midsentence by the appearance of a tall young man dressed in the style of the '70s. There was no mistaking his appearance or the tone of his voice. "Would you step outside for a moment, sir?" he asked.

"What for?"

The newcomer gave a little frozen smile and pressed a button on his flipcase, showing the gold card. "California Sate Police, sir. I'll have to ask you to come along quietly."

"But what have I done"

"Greg—" Lola began, trying to interrupt.

"Reported violation of Section 45431 of the Criminal Code, sir. The California Enabling Act."

Gregory got shakily to his feet, still not believing it was really happening. "You'll have to explain it more clearly than that."

"You were heard to utter a word that it is forbidden to speak in public, sir."

"Word? What word?"

A hand of steel closed around his wrist. "Just come along quietly, sir."

Gregory looked back in despair at Lola. "I think I need a lawyer," he said.

* * * *

The officer in charge was a towering hulk of a man who came right to the point. "You're in big trouble, Gregory. Conviction on a violation of 45431 carries a prison sentence of five years."

"All because I used the word *earthquake?*"

"Exactly. You used it in a public place and thereby violated the law. The word cannot be used in any periodical printed within the state of California or uttered in any public place."

"But that's ridiculous! You can't simply wipe a word out of the language!"

"Mr. Gregory, the future of our state is at stake here. Believe me, we're not the only place that has passed laws about what can or cannot be said in public."

"The Supreme Court—"

"The Supreme Court itself once stated that no one had the right to yell 'Fire' in a crowded theater. Likewise, during the airplane bombings and hijackings some twenty years ago, no one had the right to talk about bombs while flying on a plane. Men were arrested for joking about a bomb in their luggage or saying they were going to take the plane to Cuba."

"But—"

The officer, whose name was Vitroll, cut him off with a wave of the hand. "It's the same thing here. The state is in an emergency situation. The only way to control it is to blot out all mention of what happened a few years back. After a time people will forget, and start to return."

"I'm from out of state," Gregory argued. "I had only the vaguest idea of the law here."

"Ignorance of the law has never been recognized as an excuse in a court of law. In fact, it might go harder on you being from the east. It's all that eastern propaganda causing us the trouble in the first place. Eastern magazines and newspapers and television always talking about things out here, about the disaster and how it's sure to happen again."

"I'm not exactly an easterner. I'm from a suburb of Chicago."

"That's east to us," Vitroll said, moving his hulk from the edge of the desk. "I'll have to book you."

"How much will the bail be."

"That's up to the judge. In cases where it seems likely the offense will be repeated, no bail is granted."

"All this for just saying a word?"

"These are troubled times, Mr. Gregory. The survival of the state is at stake."

206

He went away then, leaving Gregory alone in the room. For a long time there was nothing to do but ponder the position in which he found himself. Surely a call to the home office would bring him the best of legal aid. This sort of thing could not go on unnoticed.

The door opened and a uniformed guard said, "Follow me, sir."

"Are you taking me to the judge?"

"No, sir. To a cell. You'll have to wait there until it's time for your hearing."

Gregory followed reluctantly, noticing that a second guard had come up behind him. They were treating him exactly like a criminal, taking no chances. "I'm harmless," he said. "Really."

"In here."

The cell door slid shut automatically behind him and he was left alone with the gray metal walls. He walked over to the bunk and tested its lumpy surface, wondering how many had occupied it before him and for how long. Sitting there, trying to collect his thoughts, he took out his pen to make a few notes. It slipped from his numb fingers, clattering on the steel floor, and he bent to retrieve it.

That was when he noticed the word scrawled under the bunk, where the guards would not see it. Though he might have expected some obscenity in such a place, the word was much more frightening.

There beneath the bunk, some earlier prisoner had scrawled: *earthquake*.

They took him to the courtroom, between two guards, and he looked up at the frozen-faced judge who seemed almost unaware of his presence.

"Violation of section 15431 of the Criminal Code, your Honor. California Enabling Act," a voice behind him said.

The judge nodded slightly. "How do you plead?"

"Not guilty, your Honor. I'm from out of state. I knew nothing of this law."

"I would have thought it had been well publicized," the judge commented dryly. "Will you waive your right to a trial?"

"No, sir, I will not! I haven't even consulted a lawyer yet."

"Very well. I'll schedule the trial for October 15th—two weeks from today. Bail is set at five thousand dollars, and you are ordered not to leave the state."

"Five thousand—"

Behind him Vitroll cleared his throat. "Bail has been raised by a friend of the defendant, your Honor."

Gregory turned and saw Lola Miller standing behind the railing. He walked toward her, feeling at once the need for fresh outside air. "Thank you," he said simply.

"The company put it up," she explained, "but they didn't want their name involved."

"Thanks, anyway. I know you had a hand in it."

"I was with you when it happened. I felt some responsibility. Come on, my car is outside."

They drove back to the office where a distracted Browder was waiting. He rose as they entered and hurried over to shake Gregory's hand. "My God, I'd thought we'd lost you! The home office would never have forgiven me! When Lola told me what happened—"

"I wasn't aware of the details of your laws out here. What happens now? I'm supposed to stay here for two weeks."

"What happens?" Browder repeated. "Why, you'll jump bail, of course! Otherwise, believe me, it means a jail sentence."

"They've actually sent people to prison for this?"

"Dozens of them, for terms up to five years. It's not worth taking the chance, Gregory."

"No, indeed," he agreed. "I'll catch the next plane out of here."

"It might not be that easy," Lola cautioned. "They watch the airports— they have electronic surveillance systems of all sorts. Your photograph is already stored in the memory bank."

He turned to Browder. "Any suggestions?"

"Drive your rented car out of the state. To Las Vegas, maybe. Then get a plane from there."

"They don't watch the highways?"

"Only for people moving out of the state—furniture vans, things like that. You'd be safe, especially if Lola traveled with you."

"Then that's it," Gregory decided.

An hour later they were headed out of Los Angeles in the little electric car.

"I know so little about you," she said, once the car had cleared the city limits.

"There's not much to know. I'm just a man who cried earthquake and got arrested for it."

"I mean—well, are you married?"

"I was once." He gazed out at the passing landscape of cactus, thinking how little it had changed in the past hundred years. Civilization had not yet reached the back roads of eastern California. "But that was a long time ago."

"You don't like to talk about it."

"Does anyone like to talk about failures?" He was silent for a time, then said, "You're taking a chance traveling with me. If we're caught you could end up in prison, too."

"You'd never find your way alone on these back roads. Either you'd get lost or one of the copter patrol would spot you."

"Copter patrol?"

She pointed to the sky. "There's one now. They watch mainly for trucks and vans heading out of the state, but they could make trouble if they spotted you."

The copter, painted gold, dipped low, catching the sun, as it came in for a closer look. Apparently it saw nothing amiss, for it headed away again at once. "How far to the state line?" he asked.

"Less than an hour." Like all Californians, she gave distances in time rather than miles..

"You're sure there'll be no roadblocks?"

"Not on these back roads. And once you're across it'll be difficult for them to put their hands on you. Most states won't grant extradition for crimes committed under the California Enabling Act."

Some forty-five minutes later, as they topped a rise of desert land, he saw the first billboard. *"Settle here!"* it proclaimed. *"Free from earthquake danger!"*

"That's it," Lola said, giving a little sigh. "We're across the line—in Nevada now."

"Will you be going back to California after you drop me in Vegas?"

She turned in her seat, looking at him, "You know something? I'm scared of those damned earthquakes, too. I was always afraid to admit it till now, but since I'm safely out of that place I don't think I'll be hurrying back."

"Come east with me," he said.

"I've never been east."

"All the more reason for you to go."

"Could you get me a job at the home office?"

He considered that for a moment. "There's too much of my past scattered around Chicago. Besides, they might just come looking for me for jumping bail. Maybe the company doesn't think I'm worth five thousand."

"Where, then?"

"Farther east—New York."

"With all those people?"

"It's not so bad. A lot of it is California propaganda."

They passed more billboards and presently the gleaming towers of Las Vegas came into view, like some mythic kingdom in the desert. "All right," she said finally. "I'll go east with you."

He took one hand off the steering wheel and touched her, lightly. "I'm glad."

They turned in the rented car at the Vegas airport, even though he knew it would indicate the direction of his flight. He was not a criminal, and had not yet learned to act like one. He was merely a man in flight, with no reason for covering his tracks.

On the plane east they held hands like teenagers of some era of long ago, and he told her what he remembered of the crowded streets of Manhattan. "There are people, sure, and sometimes it's difficult to stay on the sidewalk, but it's all worth it. The last time I was there, New York really got to me. The smallest event brings out thousands of people. It's a people's town—people everywhere!"

"And they all drive cars."

"Little electrics, smaller than in California. Traffic is still bad, though, I'll admit that. With so many people in the New York area there are times when nothing moves."

It was night when they landed at Kennedy International Airport, and close to midnight by the time they took the express subway into Manhattan. Lola was hungry, so they had something to eat in the hotel coffee shop before going up to their rooms.

"Tomorrow we'll look for an apartment, and jobs," he said.

"It's good to be here with you."

"Even with all the people?"

"Even with all the people. That other, in California—it seems like a nightmare now."

"It does, in a way," he agreed. "We've gone back a long way in this country when words can be so dangerous they have to be banned. And it's no longer the obscenities that frighten people, but a simple word like earthquake. I feel like standing up and shouting it here. Earthquake! *Earthquake!*"

She took his hand. "You know, I think I could learn to love you."

He was touched by her gentleness. "I guess I already do love you."

Later, after they'd finished eating, they left the coffee shop and headed across the lobby to the elevators. Gregory saw the two men first, waiting for them, and he was reminded of Vitroll and the others in California.

"Lola, those men!"

"What?"

But then it was too late to run. "Sorry, sir, I'll have to ask you and the lady to accompany us."

"Not her," Gregory said. "I'm the one you want."

"It's both of you we want."

Lola tried to move away, but the second man seized her arm. "Will you take us back to California?" she asked, and her voice was close to a sob.

The first man frowned. "We don't know anything about California. Here's my identification. George Bates of the Population Control Board, New York City Police."

"New York? But we—"

"You were overheard using a certain word that is not in keeping with the laws of this city. A word that could be harmful, or lead to harmful acts."

"What word?" Gregory demanded, feeling his heart sink.

The man named Bates consulted a notebook. "I believe the word was . . . love."

35

THE GOOD NEIGHBORS

Edgar Pangborn

THE SHIP WAS sighted a few times, briefly, and without a good fix. It was spherical, the estimated diameter about twenty-seven miles, and was in an orbit approximately 3400 miles from the surface of the Earth. No one observed the escape from it.

The ship itself occasioned some excitement, but back there at the tattered end of the 20th century, what was one visiting spaceship more or less? Others had appeared before, and gone away discouraged—or just not bothering. Three-dimensional TV was coming out of the experimental stage. Soon anyone could have Dora the Doll or the Grandson of Tarzan smack in his own living-room. Besides, it was a hot summer.

The first knowledge of the escape came when the region of Seattle suffered an eclipse of the sun, which was not an eclipse but a near shadow, which was not a shadow but a thing. The darkness drifted out of the northern Pacific. It generated thunder without lightning and without rain. When it had moved eastward and the hot sun reappeared, wind followed, a moderate gale. The coast was battered by sudden high waves, then hushed in a bewilderment of fog.

Before that appearance, radar had gone crazy for an hour.

The atmosphere buzzed with aircraft. They went up in readines to shoot, but after the first sighting reports only a few miles offshore, that order was vehemently canceled—someone in charge must have had a grain of sense. The thing was not a plane, rocket or missile. It was an animal.

If you shoot an animal that resembles an inflated gas-bag with wings, and the wingspread happens to be something over four miles tip to tip, and the carcass drops on a city—it's not nice for the city.

The Office of Continental Defense deplored the lack of precedent. But actually none was needed. You just don't drop four miles of dead or dying

213

alien flesh on Seattle or any other part of a swarming homeland. You wait till it flies out over the ocean, if it will—the most commodious ocean in reach.

It, or rather she, didn't go back over the Pacific perhaps because of the prevailing westerlies. After the Seattle incident she climbed to a great altitude above the Rockies, apparently using an updraft with very little wing-motion. There was no means of calculating her weight, or mass, or buoyancy. Dead or injured, drift might have carried her anywhere within one or two hundred miles. Then she seemed to be following the line of the Platte and the Missouri. By the end of the day she was circling interminably over the huge complex of St. Louis, hopelessly crying.

She had a head, drawn back most of the time into the bloated mass of the body but thrusting forward now and then on a short neck not more than three hundred feet in length. When she did that the blunt turtle-like head could be observed, the gaping, toothless, suffering mouth from which the thunder came, and the soft-shining purple eyes that searched the ground but found nothing answering her need. The skin color was mud-brown with some dull iridescence and many peculiar marks resembling weals or blisters. Along the belly some observers saw half a mile of paired protuberances that looked like teats.

She was unquestionably the equivalent of a vertebrate. Two web-footed legs were drawn up close against the cigar-shaped body. The vast, rather narrow, inflated wings could not have been held or moved in flight without a strong internal skeleton and musculature. Theorists later argued that she must have come from a planet with a high proportion of water surface, a planet possibly larger than Earth though of about the same mass and with a similar atmosphere. She could rise in Earth's air. And before each thunderous lament she was seen to breathe.

It was assumed that immense air sacs within her body were inflated or partly inflated when she left the ship, possibly with some gas lighter than nitrogen. Since it was inconveivable that a vertebrate organism could have survived entry into atmosphere from an orbit 3400 miles up, it was necessary to believe that the ship had briefly descended, unobserved and by unknown means, probably on Earth's night-side. Later on the ship did descend as far as atmosphere, for a moment. . . .

St. Louis was partly evacuated. There is no reliable estimate of the loss of life and property from panic and accident on the jammed roads and rail lines. Fifteen hundred dead, 7400 injured is the conservative figure.

After a night and a day she abandoned that area, flying heavily eastward.

The droning and swooping gnats of aircraft plainly distressed her. At first she had only tried to avoid them, but now and then during her eastward flight from St. Louis she made short desperate rushes against them, without skill or much sign of intelligence, screaming from a wide-open mouth that could have swallowed a four-engine bomber. Two aircraft were lost over Cincinnati, by collision with each other in trying to get out of her way. Pilots were then ordered to keep a distance of not less than ten miles until such time as she reached the Atlantic—if she did—when she could safely be shot down.

She studied Chicago for a day.

By that time Civil Defense was better prepared. About a million residents had already fled to open country before she came, and the loss of life was proportionately smaller. She moved on. We have no clue to the reason why great cities should have attracted her, though apparently they did. She was hungry perhaps, or seeking help, or merely drawn in animal curiosity by the endless motion of the cities and the strangeness. It has even been suggested that the life forms of her homeland—her masters—resembled humanity. She moved eastward, and religious organizations united to pray that she would come down on one of the lakes where she could safely be destroyed. She didn't.

She approached Pittsburgh, choked and screamed and flew high, and soared in weary circles over Buffalo for a day and a night. Some pilots who had followed the flight from the West Coast claimed that the vast lamentation of her voice was growing fainter and hoarser while she was drifting along the line of the Mohawk Valley. She turned south, following the Hudson at no great height. Sometimes she appeared to be choking, the labored inhalations harsh and prolonged, like a cloud in agony.

When she was over Westchester, headquarters tripled the swarm of interceptors and observation planes. Squadrons from Connecticut and southern New Jersey deployed to form a monstrous funnel, the small end before her, the large end pointing out to open sea. Heavy bombers closed in above, laying a smoke screen at 10,000 feet to discourage her from rising. The ground shook with the drone of jets, and with her crying.

Multitudes had abandoned the metropolitan area. Other multitudes trusted to the subways, to the narrow street canyons and to the strength of concrete and steel. Others climbed to a thousand high places and watched, trusting the laws of chance.

She passed over Manhattan in the evening—between 8:14 and 8:27 P.M., July 16, 1976—at an altitude of about 2000 feet. She swerved away from the aircraft that blanketed Long Island and the Sound, swerved again as the southern group buzzed her instead of giving way. She made no attempt to rise into the sun-crimsoned terror of drifting smoke.

The plan was intelligent. It should have worked, but for one fighter pilot who jumped the gun.

He said later that he himself couldn't understand what happened. It was court-martial testimony, but his reputation had been good. He was Bill Green—William Hammond Green—of New London, Connecticut, flying a one-man jet fighter, well aware of the strictest orders not to attck until the target had moved at least ten miles east of Sandy Hook. He said he certainly had no previous intention to violate orders. It was somthing that just happened in his mind. A sort of mental sneeze.

His squadron was approaching Rockaway, the flying creature about three miles ahead of him and half a mile down. He was aware of saying out loud to nobody; ''Well, she's too big.'' Then he was darting out of formation, diving on her, giving her one rocket-burst and reeling off to the south at 840 MPH.

He never did locate or rejoin his squadron, but he made it somehow back to his home field. He climbed out of the cockpit, they say, and fell flat on his face.

It seems likely that his shot missed the animal's head and tore through some part of her left wing. She spun to the left, rose perhaps a thousand feet, facing the city, sideslipped, recovered herself and fought for altitude. She could not gain it. In the effort she collided with two of the following planes. One of them smashed into her right side behind the wing, the other flipped end over end across her back, like a swatted dragonfly. It dropped clear and made a mess on Bedloe's Island.

She too was falling, in a long slant silent now but still living. After the impact her body thrashed desolately on the wreckage between Lexington and Seventh Avenues, her right wing churning, then only trailing, in the East River, her left wing a crumpled slowly deflating mass concealing Times Square, Herald Square and the garment district.

At the close of the struggle her neck extended, her turtle beak grasping the top of Radio City. She was still trying to pull herself up, as the buoyant gasses hissed and bubbled away through the gushing holes in her side. Radio City collapsed with her.

For a long while after the roar of descending rubble and her own roaring had ceased, there was no human noise except a melancholy thunder of the planes.

The apology came early next morning.

The spaceship was observed to descend to the outer limits of atmosphere, very briefly. A capsule was released, with a parachute timed to open at 40,000 feet and come down quite neatly in Scarsdale. Parachute, capsule and timing device were of good workmanship.

The communication engraved on a plaque of metal (which still defies analysis) was a hasty job, the English slightly odd, with some evidence of an incomplete understanding of the situation. That the visitors were themselves aware of these deficiencies is indicated by the text of the message itself.

> Most sadly regret inexcusable escape of livestock. While petting same, one of our children monkied (sp?) with airlock. Will not happen again. Regret also imperfect grasp of language, learned through what you term Television etc. Animal not dangerous, but observe some accidental damage caused, therefore hasten to enclose reimbursement, having taken liberty of studying your highly ingenius methods of exchange. Hope same will be adequate, having estimated deplorable inconvenience to best of ability. Regret exceedingly impossibility of communicating further, as pressure of time and prior obligations forbids. Please accept heartfelt apologies and assurances of continuing esteem.

The reimbursement was in fact properly enclosed with the plaque, and may be seen by the public in the rotunda of the restoration of Radio City. Though technically counterfeit, it looks like perfectly good money, except that Mr. Lincoln is missing one of his wrinkles and the words "FIVE DOLLARS" are upside down.

36

THE GOOD WORK

Theodore L. Thomas

TALL AND RAWBONED was Jeremiah Winthrop. Narrow of shoulder and shallow of chest he was, but no matter. There was a dignity to the man that showed itself in every movement. Here was one who still called himself a man, one whose traditions sprang from the rocky New England soil that had nourished his forebears. The mold that produces such a man is not easily bent or broken, not even in a world of three hundred and fifty billion people, not even in a world where the rocky New England soil lies buried and forgotten beneath the foundations of monstrous buildings.

Jeremiah Winthrop rode the spiral escalator up, up to the two-part cubicle he called home on the one hundred and forty-eighth floor. He stood swaying slightly as the escalator wound its serpentine way upwards. Others rode with him, tight people, tense people, pushed together, staring straight as they rode the spiral escalator up. And now and then at a turn or a bend a man would elbow his way out. He'd leave the upflowing river of people and step onto a landing as his floor came by. But the escalator was still crowded as it passed the one hundred and forty-eighth floor and Winthrop stepped off. He was not one of the lucky ones who lived high near the roof where it was at least possible to think about the air and the light and sun.

Winthrop boarded a moving belt that carried him over to his own corridor. He walked down the corridor for ten minutes. It was easy walking, for there were far fewer people now. Finally he came to his own door. He inserted his thumb in the thumbhole, slid the door open and walked in. A tousle-headed youngster sat on the floor playing with a plastic box. The boy looked up as Wintrhop entered.

"Daddy!" he shouted. He flung himself to his feet, dashed across the room and grabed his father around the legs.

"Hello, Davy," said Winthrop, ruffling the curly brown hair. "How's the little man?"

"Fine, Daddy. And Mommy says we can go up on the roof in another month. Will you come with us? This time? You never go with us, Daddy. Will you come up with us in a month from now?"

Winthrop looked over the boy's head at his wife, Ann. The smile faded from his face. He said, "A month? I thought it was our turn again in a week. What happened?"

Ann shook her head and pressed the back of a hand against her forehead. "I don't know. They have had to re-schedule everybody. Another eighteen hundred babies born in the building this week. They all have to get a little sun. I don't know."

Winthrop pushed Davy gently to one side and held the boy to him as he walked over to Ann. He put a hand in the small of her back and held her against his chest. She rested her head against the upper part of his arm and leaned against him.

Ann lifted her head, stood on her toes and kissed Winthrop. She pulled away and led him over to a chair, Davy still hanging on to his leg. "You must be tired," she said. "Ten hours you've been out. Were you able to . . . Did you—"

"No," said Winthrop. "Nothing. Not so much as a soybean." He looked at his wife and smiled. "I guess the time has come for us to eat that potato. We've been saving it for a month."

Ann's eyes wrinkled as she looked down at him. "Oh. I—I gave it to the Brookses. They haven't had anything in weeks." The words began to pour out. "We have done so well, really, in the last few weeks that I felt sorry for them. We had those cabbage leaves and three potatoes and even that piece of fish four months ago. I couldn't help myself. I gave—I gave our potato to them. They were so sick of Standard Fare they were beginning to get depressed, really depressed. I—"

Winthrop reached up and put an arm around her hips and said, "Don't think about it, darling." He was silent for a moment, and then he continued, "I think I'll go down and see if John Barlow has some work for me. Let's have a quick dinner of Standard Fare and then I'll go." He got up and walked over to the sink and began washing Davy's hands, talking, joshing, teasing a little as he did so.

Anne took three glasses from the tiny cabinet. She went to the synthetic milk faucet and filled the glasses and then put them on the table. She went to the bread slot and removed six slices of bread. One after the other she dropped the six slices of brown bread through the toaster. She picked up a knife and scooped big gobs of rich yellow synthetic butter out of the butter slot and spread it on the toast. She made a pile of the toast on a plate and then cut the pile in half. "All right," she called. And she put the toast on the table and sat down.

Winthrop helped Davy into a chair and then sat down himself. He bent his head and spoke a brief blessing. And they all ate. They ate Standard Fare, as countless billions of other people did that night, and every night, from birth to death, Standard Fare.

When the meal was done Winthrop got up and kissed Ann and Davy goodbye. He rode down the spiral escalator, down to the ground floor, and below. Great throngs of people rode with him, crowded in on each other. He rode down to the fifteenth sub-level and changed to a belt. He rode past the crowded TV theaters, the amusement halls. He stepped off and went down a narrow side alley where some of the shops were. Immediately the crowds fell off. A little way down the alley Winthrop turned into the door of a tiny store. It was empty except for John Barlow, the owner.

"Nice to see you," said Barlow, springing up and taking Winthrop's hand. "I was just thinking about you. In fact, I was going to come up and see you in the next day or two. Come in and sit down."

Barlow sat in the chair, Winthrop on the small counter. The two men filled the store completely. "That sounds good, John. Do you have some work for me?"

Barlow looked long at Winthrop, and slowly shook his head. "No, Jeremiah. No. I don't even have work for myself any more." He hesitated a moment and went on quietly, "I'm going out of business, Jeremiah. I can't make it work. I don't take in enough money to keep my stock up. People don't need money, what with free movies and clothes and food and everything else. No one buys food. They all live on Standard Fare and they don't seem to care any more. So now I'll have to join them, unless I can find other work."

"I'm very sorry, John. I feel I helped drive you out of business. I never gave you money for what I took."

Barlow shook his head. "No, Jeremiah. You always worked for everything. Other people are not as willing to work as you are; they all want something for nothing. Who else would be vaccinated and take the immunization shots so he could go all they way across the city for me the way you do?"

They sat quietly. Winthrop said, "Where is it all going to end, John? What's going to happen to everybody?"

"I don't know. Some people work; there must be jobs somewhere. I suppose they get them through the Ministry of Government Employment, and you know what people say about that. Government workers won't even talk about it; everybody says they're ashamed of it. I don't know what's going to happen. Except—I'm through. I'm going to take my stock home with me tonight, and that ends it.''

Winthrop looked at the box that contained all of Barlow's stock. The box measured about one foot on a side.

''Jeremiah, I want you to have something.'' Barlow reached down to the bottom of the box and brought out an object that he held toward Winthrop.

Winthrop looked at it and gasped. ''An egg. A real hen's egg. I recognize it from the pictures.'' Winthrop looked up. ''But I can't take it, John. I can't.''

''I want you to have it, Jeremiah. I want you and Anne and Davy to have it. Now don't argue. I'll wrap it up and you take it right home.''

Barlow turned and lifted a small box down from a niche. He lined the box with synthetic cotton and gently nestled the egg in the center. After covering the egg with another layer of cotton, he closed the box and wrapped it and tied it with a broad white ribbon under which he slipped a little card of cooking instructions. Then he handed the box to Winthrop. ''Take it home, Jeremiah. I'll be up to see you sometime soon. Go on now.'' And he urged Winthrop off the counter and out the door.

Winthrop went, holding the box in both hands. As he worked his way through the crowds, he held the box to his stomach, turning his shoulders to meet the press of people. He was still holding it with both hands half an hour later when he entered his home.

Anne looked up, surprised. ''Jeremiah, I didn't expect you home so soon.'' Her eyes fixed on the package. ''What is it? What have you got?''

Winthrop walked to the table, put the package on it, and carefully began to open it without saying a word. Ann and Davy stood close to him; Davy climbed on a chair to see better. When Winthrop lifted off the top layer of cotton, Ann's eyes widened and she clasped her hands together and stared, silently.

''What is it, Daddy?''

''It's an egg, son. A hen's egg.''

''Is it something to eat?''

''Yes, son. It is.'' Winthrop looked at his wife and said, ''Shall we eat it now?''

Ann nodded, quickly read the cooking instructions, and set about preparing scrambled egg. Winthrop got out the cooking pan, wiped off the dust, and set it down near her. She smiled at him and put a large chunk of butter in it and placed the pan on the heater. When the butter bubbled, she poured the beaten egg into the pan; it hissed as it struck the hot butter. She began to stir the egg as it cooked. Winthrop picked Davy up so he cold see into the pan as the egg thickened. In a moment it was done.

Ann lifted three small dishes from a cupboard, placed them on the table, and carefully scraped the egg onto the plates. Buttered toast and milk came next, then they sat down to eat. Winthrop said a grace.

They ate in silence.

Davy looked up after his egg was gone and said, "I don't like it very much. I like it some, but not very much."

Winthrop reached over and ruffled his hair, saying to Ann, "It would have been better if we'd had some salt, I guess. But it was good anyway. I've often wondered what an egg tasted like."

He looked down at the empty plates and stared at them. Then he said quickly, "Davy, it's your bedtime. You hop on in now."

Davy's face grew long, but then Winthrop looked at him, and he climbed off his chair and went over and pulled his father down and kissed him on the cheek. "Good night, Daddy."

"Good night, son."

Anne took Davy by the hand and led him into the bedroom. Winthrop listened to the chatter and then to the prayers. He sat and listened as he stared at the three egg-stained plates on the table. The plates pushed into his mind, occupied it, filled it, until there was nothing else. And at that moment the integrity of Jeremiah Winthrop broke.

He was still staring at the plates when Ann came out and sat down beside him. She too looked at her husband, looked, and looked again, closer. There were tears in his eyes.

She leaned toward him and put a hand on his shoulder. "What is it, Jeremiah?" she asked quietly.

He turned full toward her, started to speak, but could not. He pointed to the dirty plates and then cleared his throat. "Ann, that's the last of it. It's getting worse all the time. There's no work for a man. What are we going to do? Is Davy going to live the rest of his life satisfied with Standard Fare? Can we watch him grow up not knowing what it feels like to work? Ann . . ." He stopped and sat quietly for a moment. "I've got to go to the Ministry of Government Employment."

She said, "Jeremiah, are you sure? We've always been able to manage on our own. We've never needed help from the government."

"Ann—" He stood up and began pacing across the room. "How can we sit and watch this happen to our boy? We can't take him out in all those

223

people very often. We can't take him to the roof. Ann, he's a good boy. We can't let him live like this."

"But how will you feel? You have to make your own way. You've always believed that."

Winthrop's stooped figure bent even more. He stopped pacing and stood with his hands hanging at his sides, his chin on his chest. "I know," he said quietly. "I know. Help me, Ann. What should we do?"

She flew across the room to him and they clung together. After a moment she said, "All right, Jeremiah. I knew this would come some day. We will go down tomorrow to the Ministry of Government Employment and see if they have any work for you. Maybe they have, and maybe it won't be so bad. Maybe it's good work after all. We'll see."

The family was up early the next morning, up and eating Standard Fare. After breakfast they began to get ready to go out. Ann went over all the clothes, sponging spots off the slick fabric. Jeremiah Winthrop paced back and forth with slow measured steps, his hands clasped behind him, his head bent.

Ann took a little cord harness from the cabinet and slipped it over Davy's head. She pulled the cords taut and tied them around him. She passed a light piece of cord around her waist and tied the other end of it to Davy's harness. She tied a second piece of cord to the other side of the harness. Then she said to Winthrop, "Jeremiah, we're ready."

Winthrop stepped over to Davy's side. He passed the second piece of cord around his waist and tied it fast. "I'm ready," he said.

They went out the door and it was not bad at first. Riding down the spiral escalator it began to get crowded; people pressed shoulder to shoulder. Davy clutched a parent's hand in each of his own. When they arrived at the belts below ground-level, the press grew greater. Ann and Winthrop used their legs to make room for Davy to stand on the moving belt. The upper portions of their bodies pushed out against the packed mass of humanity. They held their arms bent at the elbows to form a bridge around Davy's head, stooping a little to do so. Silently they pushed back against the surge of people.

They changed belts by walking in a kind of lockstep and again formed a trembling bridge with their arms around Davy on the next belt. Twice more they changed belts and in two hours they arrived at the building next to their own. It was easier, going up the spiral escalator.

They came out into a huge room filled with people. Holding tight to Davy's leash, they worked their way through the crowds, seeking a registration desk. In half an hour they found one.

The line of people was only a few hundred yards long in front of that particular desk. Jeremiah and Ann joined the line at the end, smiling at each other. In four short hours they found themselves at the desk.

Winthrop gave his name and number to the man and explained why he wanted an interview with one of the ministers. The man swiftly filled out a set of papers, assigned Winthrop a line number and a chair number, and pointed the direction to take.

Jeremiah, Ann, and Davy slowly passed through the crowds in the room, this time seeking their line. They finally found it and Winthrop gave his papers to the man in charge. Again they were fortunate. The line to which Winthrop was assigned did not even reach out into the room; the end of it had progressed into the long corridor that led to the minister's office.

Winthrop settled into his moving chair while Ann and Davy bustled around him and made him comfortable. Then they said goodbye.

"Ann, be careful going home. Go very slowly. Don't be afraid to scream out if Davy begins to get crushed."

"Don't worry, dear. We'll be all right." Ann smiled at him, but her eyes were too bright.

Winthrop saw it and stood up from his chair. "I'll take you home and then come back."

"No." She gently pushed him back into the chair. "We'll lose another day, and Davy and I will be all right. Now you just stay here. Goodbye, dear." She leaned over and kissed him.

Winthrop said, "All right, but don't visit me, Ann. I'll be home as soon as this is over, and it's too hard on you to make the trip alone."

She smiled and nodded. Winthrop kissed Davy and ruffled his hair. Then Ann tied both ends of Davy's leash around her waist, and she and Davy walked off. Both of them turned to wave frequently until the crowd swallowed them up.

The days passed slowly for Winthrop. The corridor seemed to stretch on interminably as he slowly moved down it in his chair. Every few hundred yards there was the inevitable milk faucet and the bread and butter slots, and every few feet there was the inevitable TV screen alive with people talking, singing, laughing, shouting, or playing. Winthrop turned each one off as he came abreast of it, if his neighbors did not object. None of the people in the line were talkative, and that suited Winthrop. Mostly he sat thinking over his forthcoming interview. Two minutes to explain why he should be given work was not very long. But the Ministers of Government Employment were busy men.

Toward the end of the second week Winthrop had a surprise visit from Ann. She threw her arms around him and explained that Helen Barlow had come to see her and had sent Ann off to visit. And it was while Ann was there that Winthrop had moved up to a position from which he could see the door of the minister's office. When Ann left, she went with the comforting knowledge that it would be only a few days more.

The time came when Winthrop was at the door. Then, suddenly, he was in the anteroom, and before he could fully realize it he was standing in a very small room before the minister.

Winthrop identified himself and said, "I have a boy of four, a fine boy, and a fine wife too. I want to work the way a man should to give them something besides Standard Fare. Here is what I have worked at in the last five years." And Winthrop listed the things he had done.

The minister listened. He had white hair and a lined face whose skin seemed to be pulled too tight. When Winthrop had finished, the minister looked steadily into his face for a moment: Winthrop could almost feel the probing of the level blue eyes. Then the minister turned to a device that loomed over him to one side and punched a complex series of buttons. There was a whirring noise behing the wall of the tiny room, and then a small packet of cards appeared at the slot in the bottom of the device. The minister picked them out and glanced at them, and an odd expression of sadness swept across his face. It was gone in an instant, and then he looked up and said, "Yes, Mr. Winthrop. We have a job for you, and the full six hours a day, too. You will be on the maintenance crew of your building. Your job is explained here—" he passsed over a card—"and it consists of tightening the nuts on the expansion joints in the framework of the building. It is very important to do it right, so read the card carefully." Winthrop nodded eagerly.

The minister handed over another card and said, "Here is a description of the daily reports you must turn in." Another card. "Here is how you and your chief decide your working schedule, and you must adhere to it; it is very important. The chief of your tightening crew will go over it with you. Here is your requisition for the special wrench you will need. Here is your pay schedule; you can decide if you want to be paid in money or produce. And one very important thing." The minister leaned forward to emphasize his remarks. "You are not allowed to talk about your job with anyone, not even with your best friends. Is that clear?"

Winthrop nodded. "Yes, sir."

"The reason is that we do not want people fighting over jobs. Not many who come in here really want to work, but there are a few. We have to pick good men for this work; those buildings must be kept in good condition. Others less fortunate than you might not understand that you are just the man we need. So no talking about your work—no talk of any kind—on pain of dismissal.'' The minister sat back. ''Well, I guess that is about all. Report for work in the morning. Good luck.'' And he held out his hand.

Winthrop shook it and said, ''Thank you, sir. I'll work hard for you. I didn't know you needed men for this work or I would have been here sooner. I had always heard that . . . Well, thank you.'' And Winthrop turned to go. Out of the corner of his eye as he turned, he thought he saw again that ephemeral expression of sadness, but when he looked at the minister full in the face it was gone. Winthrop went out the side door. The entire interview had taken one and three quarter minutes.

Winthrop left early the next morning so as not to be late for work. As it turned out, he was unable to get off a belt at the proper landing—too many people in the way—and it took him fifteen minutes to retrace his steps. He arrived exactly on time.

The chief of the tightening crew was a big, bluff man with a red face. He took Winthrop in tow and showed him how they worked. The crew chief had a vast knowledge of the crawl spaces in the interior of the building. He showed Winthrop the blueprints from which the tightening crew worked, and explained that by coordinating their work with all the other tightening crews they made one complete round of the building every eight years. By then it was time to do it again; the nuts worked loose from the constant expansion and contraction. It was quite a job keeping track of the area that the tightening crew covered; it was a large crew. But each member turned in daily reports, and there was a large clerical staff to keep the records straight. In fact, there were more men keeping records than there were doing the actual tightening work. The chief pointed out that Winthrop was to be one of the elite, one of those whose work justified the existence of the huge staff. The tone of the chief's voice made it clear that there was a kind of quiet pride among the men who did the actual work. The chief issued Winthrop his wrench and showed him where to start.

The day passed swiftly. The tightening of the nuts was not so bad, although Winthrop's arm grew sore after a while. The difficult part was gaining access to the nuts in the first place. Winthrop had to use all his agility to wriggle through confined places. Yet it was good to be working again, good to feel the sweat start from his brow from hard work instead of from the press of people.

In a week Winthrop was no longer dog-tired when he got home at night. There was much laughter in the Winthrop household, much reading and playing games and telling stories. They even watched the TV screen now and then; somehow it no longer seemed so fruitless. The monotony of Standard Fare was broken; the head of the house was working steadily. It was now possible to plan ahead for a variety of meals, and that made it easier to wait when there was nothing to eat but Standard Fare.

Winthrop developed skill and speed at locating and tightening the nuts. He soon covered in a day a larger area than any other man, and the chief told him that he was his best man. Winthrop came to share the pride and sense of responsibility that all the other tighteners felt. They were a select group, and they knew it; all the others looked up to them.

It was after dinner one night that Winthrop sat back, hooked his thumbs in the armholes of his shirt, and watched Ann and Davy finish the half-dozen peas. They looked at him and smiled, and his heart warmed. "You know," he said, "I think I'll visit John Barlow for a few minutes. I haven't seen him since he gave up his store. Do you mind, dear?"

Ann shook her head. "No, you run along. I'll play with Davy for a while and then put him to bed. Don't stay too long."

Barlow answered Winthrop's knock. "Well, Jeremiah. Come in, man, come in."

Winthrop walked in and the two men stood looking at each other. Winthrop was surprised at how well Barlow looked, and he said so.

Barlow laughed. "Yes, the last time we met I was pretty far down in the dumps, I guess. But I'm working, Jeremiah. I'm acutally working. Important work, too!"

His enthusiasm was infectious and Winthrop found himself laughing. "I'm glad for you, John. And I know how you feel, because I'm working too."

Barlow stepped forward and wrung his hand. "That's fine, man, fine! Government, I guess, just like mine. It isn't so bad, is it? Not nearly as bad as we thought. Good steady important work makes a man feel like it's worth living."

Helen Barlow came out of the other room. "Why, Jeremiah. I didn't know you were here. How nice to see you."

"Yes, and he's working," said Barlow.

"Oh, I'm so happy for you, Jeremiah. Congratulations. And that reminds me, John." She turned to her husband. "You have to get ready to go to work. You know how long it takes to get there even though it's in the building."

"Right. I'll get ready. Jeremiah, I'm sorry that I have to go, but why don't you stay?"

"No, John. I just stopped in to say hello. You come up and see us real soon."

"I certainly will."

There was an exchange of goodbyes, and Winthrop left.

Barlow went into the other room and came out immediately with his wrench. He waved it playfully at his wife. "Got to go," he said. "The loosening crew won't wait." And he blew a kiss at his wife and went off to work.

37

THE GREAT SECRET

George H. Smith

WE CAN'T SEEM to put a finger on this guy at all, sir,'' Detective Lieutenant Bolasky said to the District Attorney. ''We know that he's blackmailing these people, but we can't figure how or what about.''

District Attorney Waters ran a neatly manicured hand through his silvery hair and frowned at the report on his desk. ''These are big people, Bolasky. We can't let this phony crystal gazer get away with this. What can he have on them anyway? What can they possibly have in their pasts that they're willing to pay him to keep quiet about?''

''That's the strangest part of the whole thing, sir. We've checked into the past every one of the people Maraat has been working on and so far we haven't been able to find a thing they could be blackmailed for.''

''I see. Then why . . . ?''

''We don't know. All we do know is that nearly all of the people he has approached have paid him off.''

''Nearly all? You mean some of them haven't?''

''Approximately twenty-five of them have kicked in with very large sums of money. Doctors, lawyers, politicians and prominent business executives. Maraat is so sure of himself that he even takes checks and we can't touch him because no one will make a complaint. They won't tell how he's doing it, in fact, they won't even admit they are being blackmailed. Whatever it is, they're scared to death of him.''

''But what about the ones who don't pay off?''

''There were five of them. They had Maraat kicked out of their offices, but within a week of his visit they all committed suicide.''

''I don't get it,'' the D.A. said angrily. ''There must be something you and your men are missing.''

* * * *

231

"I just wish that were true," Bolasky said sadly. "Well, I guess we'll have to turn him loose."

"If you people can't get any evidence against him, we have no other choice."

"I hate like hell to do it but we can't hold him on suspicion any longer."

"Tell you what," the D.A. said as the other man turned to leave. "Before you do that, bring him up here. I'd like to see him and maybe *I* can get something out of him."

The detective looked worried. "He's awfully funny, Mr. Waters. Are you sure you want to do this? Most of the men at headquarters prefer to stay as far away from him as possible."

"Well, no wonder you've been unable to get anything on him. Bring him up here and I'll question him myself. I guarantee I'll find out how he's blackmailing these people."

A short time later, two police officers escorted a small, dark man into the District Attorney's office. He seemed insignificant enough except for this eyes which glowed and sparkled strangely. These seemingly bottomless pools of mystery made the D.A. uneasy as Maraat took a seat opposite him. To hide his disquiet, Waters spoke loudly and brusquely.

"I'll come straight to the point with you, Maraat. We *know* you've been practicing blackmail, but we don't know how you're doing it. We'll find out sooner or later, of course, and you'll make it easier on yourself if you tell us all about it now."

The man's thin lips curved in a smile. "I'll be glad to tell you all about it, Mr. Waters."

"What? You mean you'll confess?"

"I'll tell *you* about it, Mr. Waters. We won't need your stenographer."

"What is all this? If you're so willing to confess, why didn't you tell them down at headquarters?" Determined not to let the man see how nervous he was becoming, Waters nodded to the stenographer to leave. He wished suddenly that he had never sent for Maraat.

"It would hardly have been worth my while, Mr. District Attorney, to confess to those non-entities. I knew that if I waited long enough you would send for me."

"How could you possibly know that?"

"I knew, Mr. Waters, I knew."

The man must be lying, but his eyes said he wasn't. Those eyes! They were enough to drive a man mad. "Then suppose you tell me what it was you knew about the pasts of those persons who paid you such huge sums of money."

232

"I know nothing of their pasts, nothing. What I know about them, Edmond Waters, is in the future."

"What?" Waters felt suffocated, as though he were about to choke. It was those eyes, those unblinking, unwavering, somehow truthful eyes. Could they see into the future? Into his future?

Maraat leaned back in his chair with a smile of satisfaction and dropped his eyes from the D.A.'s face.

"So you see, Mr. Waters, it was really very simple. I just went to these persons and told them that I could see into the future and that I wanted money."

"You mean that they paid you for keeping something secret that they were going to do in the future? For not telling others?"

"No, not secret from others, Mr. Waters. For keeping it a secret from *them*. You see, I know when you are going to die. The year, the day and the hour. But for a rather large sum of money *and* your protection . . . I won't tell you."

The District Attorney's hand had already reached for his check book. "How much?" he asked.

38

THE HARVEST

Tom Godwin

IT WAS HARVEST TIME.

The Sky People waited where the last tenuous vestiges of atmosphere met the nothing of outer space, invisible to the land creatures below who had no way of perceiving life forms that were almost pure energy. Harthon and Ledri waited a little apart from the others, soaring restlessly on scintillating wings in the light-stream from the sun.

For many days the Release Field had enveloped the world below, clouding and distorting the surface of it to the perception of the Sky People with the violence of its psycho-persuasion bands. Now the field was lifted, its work done. There remained only the last little while of waiting before the fralings came; the intoxicating, maddeningly delicious fralings that filled the body and the mind with a singing, ecstatic fire. . . .

"There are so many of us this time," Ledri said. "Do you think there will be enough fralings?"

"Of course," Harthon reassured her. "There are more of *them,* too, and they've learned how to send us as many as we need. There will be more fralings this time than ever before."

"The Harvest—" Ledri's thought was like a nostalgic sigh. "What fun they are! Do you remember the last one, Harthon? And the night we danced down the moonbeams to meet the fralings coming up, before they had ever reached the nets of the Gatherer?"

"I remember. And afterward we followed the sun-stream out, so far out that the world and the moon were like a big and little star behind us. And we sang. . . ."

"And you. And then we were hungry again and we let the sun-stream carry us back to the feast where the others were laughing because someone had almost let a fraling escape. Everyone was so happy and the world and

235

the stars were so beautiful. The poor creatures down below—'' a touch of sadness came over her—''they don't know and can never know what it's like. . . .''

''It has to be that way,'' Harthon said. ''Would you change it if you could?''

''Oh, no! They have to stay there and we have to watch over them. But what if they should do something beyond our control, as the Wise Ones say they may do some day, and then there would be the Last Harvest and never again any fralings for us?''

''I know. But that may not happen for a long time. And this isn't the day for worrying, little shining one—not when the feast begins so soon.''

Their wings touched as they turned in their soaring and looked down upont he great curve of the world below. The eastern sea was blue and cloudless; the western continent going into the evening and the huge mass of the eastern continent coming out of the night. The turning of the world was visible as they watched; the western rim of the western continent creeping very slowly into the extinction of the horizon.

''Can the land people tell when we're watching them like this?'' Ledri asked.

''No. They know we're up here, but that's all.''

''How did they ever—''

A little sun blazed into being on the western continent, brighter than the real sun. Others followed, swiftly; then they began to flare into life on the eastern continent—two fields of vivid flowers that bloomed briefly and were gone. Where they had been were tall, dark clouds that rose higher still, swelling and spreading, hiding the land beneath.

The Summoner gave the call that was like the song of a trumpet and the one who had been appointed Gatherer poised his far-flung nets.

''They're coming—the fralings!'' Ledri cried. ''Look at them, Harthon. But there are so many—'' the worry came back to her—''so many that maybe this is the Last Harvest.''

''There aren't *that* many,'' Harthon said, and he laughed at her concern. ''Besides, will we care tonight?''

The quick darkness of her mood vanished and she laughed with him. ''Tonight we'll dance down the moonbeams again. And tomorrow we'll follow the sun-stream out, farther than ever before.''

The fralings drew swiftly closer, hurrying like bright silver birds.

''They're coming to us,'' Ledri said. ''They know that this is where they must go. But how did the land people ever learn of us?''

''Once, many centuries ago, a fraling escaped the nets long enough to go back for a little while. But fralings and land people can't communicate very well with one another and the land people misunderstood most of what it tried to tell them about us.''

The fralings struck the invisible nets and the Gatherer gave the command to draw them closed.

''Let's go—the others are already starting.'' Harthon said, and they went with flashing wings toward the nearer net.

''Do the land people have a name for us?'' Ledri asked.

''They call us 'angels,' and they call the Gatherer 'God.' ''

The fralings, finally understanding, were trying frantically to escape and the terror of the small ones was a frightened, pleading wail.

''And what do they call the fralings?''

''They call them their 'souls.' We'll eat the small, young ones first— they're the best and there will be plenty for all.''

39

THE HOMESICK CHICKEN

Edward D. Hoch

WHY DID THE chicken cross the road?

To get on the other side, you'd probably answer, echoing an old riddle that was popular in the early years of the last century.

But my name is Barnabus Rex, and I have a different answer.

I'd been summoned to the Tangaway Research Farms by the director, an egg-headed old man named Professor Mintor. After parking my car in the guarded lot and passing through the fence—it was an EavesStop, expensive, but sure protection against all kinds of electronic bugging—I was shown into the presence of the director himself. His problem was simple. The solution was more difficult.

"One of the research chickens pecked its way right through the security fence, then crossed an eight-lane belt highway to the other side. We want to know why."

"Chickens are a bit out of my line," I replied.

"But your specialty is the solution of scientific riddles, Mr. Rex, and this certainly is one." He led me out of the main research building to a penned-in area where the test animals were kept. We passed a reinforced electric cage in which he pointed out the mutated turkeys being bred for life in the domes of the colonies of the moon. Further along were some leggy-looking fowl destined for Mars. "They're particularly well adapted to the Martian terrain and environment," Professor Mintor explained. "We've had to do very little development work; we started from desert road-runners."

"What about the chickens?"

"The chickens are something else again. The strain, called ZIP-1000, is being developed for breeding purposes on Zipoid, the second planet of

239

Barnard's star. We gave them extra-strength beaks—something like a parrot's—to crack the extra-tough seed hulls used for feed. The seed hulls in turn were developed to withstand the native fauna like the space-lynx and the ostroid, so that—"

"Aren't we getting a little off course?" I asked.

"Ah—yes. The problem. What *is* the problem is the chicken that crossed the road. It used its extra-strength beak to peck its way right through this security fence. But the puzzling aspect is its motivation. It crossed that belt highway—a dangerous undertaking even for a human—and headed for the field as if it were going home. And yet the chicken was hatched right here within these walls. How could it be homesick for something it had never known?"

"How indeed?" I stared bleakly through the fence at the highway and the deserted field opposite. What was there to attract a chicken—even one of Professor Mintor's super-chickens—to that barren bit of land? "I should have a look at it," I decided. "Can you show me the spot where the chicken crossed the highway?"

He led me around a large pen to a spot in the fence where a steel plate temporarily blocked a jagged hole. I knelt to examine the shards of complex, multi-conductor mesh, once more impressed by the security precautions. "I'd hate to meet your hybrid chickens on a dark night, Professor."

"They would never attack a human being, or even another creature," Mintor quickly assured me. "The beak is used only for cracking seed hulls, and perhaps in self-defense."

"Was it self-defense against the fence?"

He held up his hands. "I can't explain it."

I moved the steel plate and stooped to go through the hole. In that moment I had a chicken's-eye view of the belt highway and the barren field beyond, but they offered no clues. "Be careful crossing over," Mintor warned. "Don't get your foot caught!"

Crossing a belt highway on foot—a strictly illegal practice—could be dangerous to humans and animals alike. With eight lanes to traverse it meant hopping over eight separate electric power guides—any one of which could take off a foot if you misstepped. To imagine a chicken with the skill to accomplish it was almost more than I could swallow. But then I'd never before been exposed to Professor Mintor's super-chickens.

The empty lot on the other side of the belt highway held nothing of interest to human or chickens, so far as I could see. It was barren of grass or weeds, and seemed nothing more than a patch of dusty earth dotted with a few pebbles. In a few sun-baked depressions I found the tread of auto tires, hinting that the vacant lot was sometimes used for parking.

I crossed back over the belt highway and reentered the Tangaway compound through the hole in the fence. "Did you find anything?" Mintor asked.

"Not much. Exactly what was the chicken doing when it was recovered?"

"Nothing. Pecking at the ground as if it were back home."

"Could I see it? I gather it's no longer kept outside."

"After the escape we moved them all to the interior pens. There was some talk of notifying Washington since we're under government contract, but I suggested we call you in first. You know how the government is about possible security leaks."

"Is Tangaway the only research farm doing this sort of thing?"

"Oh, no! We have a very lively competitor named Beaverbrook Farms. That's part of the reason for all this security. We just managed to beat them out on the ZIP-1000 contract."

I followed him into a windowless room lit from above by solar panes. The clucking of the chickens grew louder as we passed into the laboratory proper. Here the birds were kept in a large enclosure, constantly monitored by overhead TV. "This one," Mintor said, leading me to a pen that held but a single chicken with its oddly curved beak. It looked no different from the others.

"Are they identified in any way? Laser tattoo, for instance?"

"Not at this stage of development. Naturally when we ship them out for space use they're tattooed."

"I see." I gazed down at the chicken, trying to read something in those hooded eyes. "It was yesterday that it crossed the highway?"

"Yes."

"Did it rain here yesterday?"

"No. We had a thunderstorm two days ago, but it passed over quickly."

"Who first noticed the chicken crossing the road?"

"Granely—one of our gate guards. He was checking security in the parking lot when he spotted it, about halfway across. By the time he called me and we got over there it was all the way to the other side."

"How did you get it back?"

"We had to tranquilize it, but that was no problem."

"I must speak to the guard, Granley,"

"Follow me."

The guard was lounging near the gate. I'd noticed him when I arrived and parked my car. "This is Barnabus Rex, the scientific investigator," Mintor announced. "He has some questions for you."

241

"Sure," Granley replied, straightening up. "Ask away."

"Just one question, really," I said. "Why didn't you mention the car that was parked across the highway yesterday?"

"What car?"

"A parked car that probably pulled away as soon as you started after the chicken."

His eyes widened. "My God, you're right! I'd forgotten it till now! Some kids; it was painted all over stripes, like they're doing these days. But how did you know?"

"Sun-baked tire tracks in the depressions where water would collect. They told me a car had been there since your rain two days ago. Your employees use the lot here, and no visitors would park over there when they had to cross the belt highway to reach you."

"But what does it mean?" Professor Mintor demanded.

"That your mystery is solved," I said. "Let me have a tranquilizer gun and I'll show you."

I took the weapon he handed me and led the way back through the research rooms to the penned-up chickens. Without hestiation I walked up to the lone bird and tranquilized it with a single shot.

"Why did you do that?" Mintor asked.

"To answer your riddle."

"All right. Why *did* the chicken cross the road?"

"Because somebody wanted to play back the contents of a tape recorder implanted in its body. For some time now you've been spied upon, Professor Mintor—I imagine by your competitor, Beaverbrook Farms."

"Spied upon! By that—*chicken?*"

"Exactly. It seemed obvious to me from the first that the fence-pecking chicken was not one of your brood. It was much too strong and much too homesick. But if it wasn't yours it must have been added to your flock surreptitiously, and that could only have been for the purposes of industrial espionage. Since you told me Beaverbrook was doing similar work, this has to be their chicken. I think an x-ray will show a micro-miniaturized recorder for listening in on your secret conversations."

"Damnedest thing I ever heard," Professor Mintor muttered, but he issued orders to have the sleeping chicken x-rayed.

"It was a simple task for them to drop the intruding chicken over your fence at night, perhaps lassoing one of your birds and removing it so the count would be right. Those fences are all right for detecting any sort of bugging equipment, but they aren't very good at stopping ordinary intrusion—otherwise that wandering chicken would have set off alarms when it started to cut a hole there. Beaverbrook has been recording your conversations, probably trying to stay one jump ahead on the next government contract. They couldn't use a transmitter in the chicken because of your electronic fence, so they had to recover the bird itself to read out the recording. At the right time, their chicken pecked its way through the fence and started across the highway, but when the guard spotted it the waiting driver panicked and took off. The chicken was left across the road without any way to escape.''

"But how did the chicken know when to escape?'' asked Mintor. "Could they have some kind of electronic homing device . . . ?''

I smiled, letting the Professor's puzzlement stretch out for a moment. "That was the easiest part,'' I said at last. "Imprinting.''

"But . . . ''

"Exactly. The highly distinctive stripes on the car. The Beaverbrook people evidently trained the chicken from—ah—hatching to associate that pattern with home and food and so on.''

A technician trotted up to the professor, waving a photographic negative. "The x-rays—there *was* something inside that chicken!''

"Well, Mr. Rex, you were right,'' the professor conceded.

"Of course, in a sense the chicken *did* cross the road to get to the other side,'' I admitted. "They always do.''

"Have you solved many cases like this one?''

I merely smiled. "Every case is different, but they're always a challenge. I'll send you my bill in the morning—and if you ever need me again, just call.''

40

THE HOUSE OF ECSTASY

Ralph Milne Farley

THIS ACTUALLY HAPPENED to you. And when I say "you," I mean *you*—holding his book now, and reading these very words. For I know something about you—something deeply personal—something which, however, I am afraid that you have forgotten.

You're puzzled? You don't believe me? Read on, and I'll prove it to you—you'll see that I am right.

To begin with, where were you at eight o'clock on that warm evening of August 4, 1937?

You can't remember? Oh, but I hope you will, my friend. For, as you read on, you will realize the importance of remembering every detail of that eventful night.

The weather was warm and muggy. It made you restless in the house, until finally you went out for a little walk—down to the store at the corner, to buy a package for cigarettes—to take the air. Nothing of importance, you thought.

A young fellow stopped you, asked for a light. Undoubtedly you have forgotten this too, for you are so often asked for a light. And in the dusk of that muggy evening there was nothing to stamp this young fellow as any different from hundreds of others.

You gave him a match; and as the match flared up in the darkness, you studied his clean-cut whimsical features. Rather attractive, he seemed to you.

You said to yourself, "Here is a man I'd like to know."

Then you lit your own cigarette, and noticed that the young fellow was studying you. You hoped that he too was favorably impressed by what he saw.

"Rather a warm night," he said in a pleasing voice, as he fell into step beside you.

So the two of you discussed the weather for a few moments, walking aimlessly along.

Having thus broken the ice, the stranger asked, "Are you doing anything this evening?"

Somehow this question put you on your guard. What was his racket, anyway? You glanced sharply at his face, at that moment illumined by a street-light which the two of you were passing. But what you saw completely reassured you.

"No," you replied. "I'm not doing anything. Why?"

"He laughed a bit embarrassedly.

"Well, you see, there's a clever seer and mystic, who lives just a couple of blocks from here. I was on my way to his house for a séance, when I met you. I'd feel a little less creepy if you'd come along."

I sounded intriguing. But—

"What does he charge?" you asked.

The young man laughed—a pleasant friendly laugh. "No charge at all," he replied. "A *real* mystic doesn't prostitute his weird abilities by making money out of them. Only charlatans do that!"

"Okeh," you said, relieved that there was no fee. "I'll try anything once."

"Come on," he invited.

He led you to one of a block of identical three-story brownstone fronts—no one would ever have imagined what it held. A massive butler answered the door. He looked you suspiciously up and down; then stepping aside, he solemnly ushered you and your friend into a small reception room, where a hunchbacked dwarf of indefinable age arose to greet the two of you. His hairless yellow skin was stretched parchment-like over his skull. His eyes were quick-shifting, black and beady. His slit mouth leered, first at your companion and then at you.

"Well?" he asked in a high-pitched querulous voice, shifting his eyes back to your companion.

"Master," the young man replied, bowing stiffly, "here is the person whom you directed me to bring."

"You have done well, my pupil," quavered the dwarf, his hunched shoulders shaking slightly as at some concealed jest. "You may go."

Astonished and indignant, you turned quickly to confront your guide. But a subtle change seemed to have come over him. In the bright light of the reception room he did not look as pleasing as he had looked on the street.

His dark eyes were set at a decided slant. His black brows were thick and tufted. His ears, nose and chin were pointed. And his sleek black hair was brushed up on each side of his forehead into two little peaks, almost like twin horns.

"Why, you said—" you began indignantly.

"What I *said* is of no matter," he replied with a shrug and a nonchalant wave of one slender hand. Turning on his heel, he stalked out of the room.

You wheeled to follow him; but behind you a sharp voice croaked "Stop!"

Invisible hands seemed to reach out from behind and turn you around, and march you back to the toad-like squatting Master.

He smiled a slitted grin, evidently intended to be ingratiating.

"Why should you flee, my dear fellow?" he murmured. "I am about to do you a favor."

"But—but—" you began.

"Silence!" he snapped. His face was stern. His claw-like hands, on the ends of scrawny arms, reached out toward you in a fluttery gesture as he crooned, "Sleep! Sleep! You are in my power. You will do as I command. Sleep! Sleep!"

A delicious languor spread over you: and, although your mind remained abnormally clear, all control over your own body gradually slipped from you.

The Master's parchment face relaxed into a friendly grin once more.

"You are going to enjoy this," he croaked gleefully, rubbing his taloned hands together. "The ecstasy is going to be all yours. For, alas, my poor crumpled body cannot thrill to the pleasures of the flesh, except vicariously. So I have summoned you here, in the hope that a few crumbs may drop from the table of your enjoyment, for me to pick up."

"Yes, Master." The words came to your lips through no volition of your own.

The little dwarf grinned delightedly, and his hunched shoulders shook with suppressed chuckles.

"This is going to be good!" he chortled. "Come. Follow me."

Like a sleep-walker, you followed him out of the little reception room, down the broad hall, up a flight of stairs, and into a large room with softly carpeted floor, and pictures and mirrors on the wall. The only article of furniture was a couch.

On that couch sat a beautiful young girl, clothed in a gown of some filmy blue material. Her skin was a creamy olive shade, her hair blue-black and lustrous, her face piquant and oval, her lips full and inviting, and her figure slenderly mature.

But her eyes (as you noted) almost spoiled the picture. They were lusterless and dumb, like those of a stunned animal. You momentarily wondered if your own eyes were not the same. And, when she moved, she moved slowly, swimmingly, as in a slow-motion picture.

"Get up, my little dear," croaked the hunchback, rubbing his hands together, and grinning with anticipation.

The girl arose, her sightless sleep-walking eyes on his penetrating ones.

"Yes, Master." Her tones were flat and dead, and yet they carried the hint of a bell-like quality.

"Here is your partner, my little dear," he continued, with a leer, waving one skinny talon toward you, as you stood sheepishly, striving to free your paralyzed muscles from his hypnotic spell. "Stand up, my little dear."

"Yes, Master."

She rose obediently, and faced you. Somehow, in spite of the dull animal look in her wide eyes, there was something intensely appealing about her. So young. So soft. So virginal. And so alone!

Fascinated, you stared and stared at this vision of loveliness. No longer did you strain to escape, for now your every effort was to break the Master's hypnotic spell, not so as to leap *away*, but rather so as to go *forward*.

As you ran your eyes appraisingly over every line and curve of her perfect figure, the girl mechanically seated herself on the couch, lifted up one shapely leg, crossed her knees, unlatched the slipper, and let it plop to the floor.

Its sudden sound seemed to shock the girl almost into consciousness. Her wide, unseeing eyes narrowed, and her expression became momentarily human—the one touch needed for complete perfection.

But only for a brief instant. Then the Master waved one taloned hand in her direction. "Sleep!" he crooned. "Sleep, my little dear. Sleep."

Her vacant stare returned. She unfastened and took off the other slipper.

The hunchback, grinning fatuously, held up one hand, and said, "My little dear, that will be enough for the present." Then, turning to you, "All right, my boy. She is yours."

Released from your paralysis, although still under his spell, you stole slowly, eagerly forward. Your feet seemed planted in shifting sands. Interminable ages elapsed. Would you never reach her?

Behind you the cracked voice of the Master squeaked. "Welcome him, my little dear."

In response to this command, the girl held out her arms to you. A dumb eagerness suffused her piquant oval face. You in turn held out your arms to her, with an intense yearning to clasp them tightly around her.

At last, after countless ages it seemed, you almost reached her, your fingertips met hers, just barely brushing them, and a tingling thrill swept through you. With one supreme effort, you leaped forward.

But an invisible hand seemed to clamp itself upon one of your shoulders, pulling you backward. And behind you sounded the croak of the Master, saying: "Bah! You are mere automatons! There is no vicarious pleasure to be had by me from such puppet amours as this!"

Then his invisible hand spun you around to face his toad-like leering features.

"Master!" you implored. "Master!"

His slant eyes narrowed, and his slit mouth broadened into a grin.

"I am going to be kind to you," he announced, in his high-pitched, cracked voice. "To the two of you—and to myself. I shall remove my hypnotic spell, and then see if you two cannot react to each other like normal human beings."

He waved one taloned hand imperiously.

"Awake!" he croaked. "It is my command that you both awake."

The invisible hands upon your shoulders relaxed their hold. A shudder passed through you. You lifted up one hand and brushed the cobwebs from your eyes. You drew a deep breath. The sluggish shackles slipped off of your mind and soul. You were free. Free!

Wheeling eagerly, you confronted the beautiful, olive-skinned girl.

But now she drew away from you—her eyes, no longer dumb, now pools of horror. Her two little hands fluttered up in front of her, as if to ward you off. A full, red flush, commencing at the rounded hollow of her slim young throat, crept slowly up until it suffused her entire face, as she cringed back against the couch.

And you—your eagerness to clasp her in your arms now changed to eagerness to protect her. You halted abruptly.

From behind you there came a cackling laugh and the words, "She does not seem to relish you, my friend. Well, I shall leave the two of you alone together for a while, until you and she become better acquainted. *Adios!*"

A door slammed, and there was the sound of the turning of a key in the lock.

The girl was now seated on the edge of the couch, with one hand raised to her eyes to blot out the unwelcome sight of you.

But by now you were in complete command of yourself, once more a gentleman. "My dear young lady," you breathed, moving forward, "there's nothing to be afraid of. I want to help you; I want to be your friend. Trust me, and I'll try to get you out of here. That dwarf is a dangerous madman, and we've got to forget everything except how to outwit him."

She smiled, and nodded. "I *do* trust you!" she exclaimed, rising and gripping your arm.

Hurriedly you made a circuit of all four walls of the room, carefully inspecting them. It was a room without a single window. There was only one door. and that was of solid oak, and locked.

"It is no use, Galahad," said the girl, in a rich liquid voice, but with a touch of mocking sadness. "The Master has us safely imprisoned, and there's nothing we can do about it. Of course, when he is through with *you*, he will probably let *you* go. But I am to be kept here for good."

"I will come back with the police, and raid the place, and rescue you," you asserted.

She smiled sadly. "I wonder," she said.

"Why do you wonder?" you asked, surprised. "If that crazy dwarf is fool enough to let me loose, it ought to be a simple matter to come back here and break in."

"I wonder."

"Why do you keep saying, 'I wonder'?"

"Because other men have been brought here to me by the Master, and they have promised, just as you are now promising. And yet none of them has ever come back."

"But *I* will."

"I wonder."

"Stop it!" you stormed. "Stop parrotting those words! I'm a gentleman, and I keep my word. Besides I—er—I admire you very much," you continued lamely. "I've never seen a girl quite like you. *Of course* I'll come back!"

"The Master is a skillful hypnotist. Before he lets you go, he will hypnotize you into forgetting everything."

"He couldn't make a man forget *you!*"

"Yes, even me. Yet perhaps—"

"Perhaps what?"

"Perhaps—if you were to hold me in your arms—"

Eagerly you clasped her to you, and covered her upturned flower-face with kisses, until finally your lips met and she returned your passion in one soul-searing embrace.

As you released her, you exultantly exclaimed, "Now let the Master do his worst! I shall never forget that kiss!"

A cackling laugh echoed through the vacant reaches of the room.

Startled, you sprang to your feet; but there was no one in the room. No one except you yourself and the dark-haired, olive-skinned girl.

Again the cackling laugh. It seemed to come from everywhere—from nowhere.

"Where are you, Master?" you cried.

"Aha!" spoke his cracked voice out of the air. "I see that you have learned respect, and that you address me by my proper title. And I thank you for a very pleasant evening; I enjoyed that kiss! You too ought to thank *me!*"

"I don't!" you stormed. "Let us out of here, or I'll call the police! Where are you, anyway?"

"I am behind one of the mirrors in the wall," he croaked. "It is what is known in the glass trade as an 'X-ray mirror,' that is to say, a transparent one. From *your* side it is merely a slightly grayed window-pane. And so I have been able to enjoy vicariously your little moment of bliss."

"But your voice?" you asked, incredulous.

"I am talking into a micropone," croaked the invisible dwarf. "There are loud-speakers behind several of the pictures.—And now I am coming in to join my two little playmates."

"If you enter this room, I shall wring your neck!" you raged.

"I rather think not," rasped his high-pitched voice, trailing off into nothingness.

You turned, and placed one arm comfortingly around the shaken girl.

The key grated in the lock. The door opened. The repulsively leering hunchback came hopping in.

Now was your chance. With cool determination, you charged across the room!

But, grinning unconcernedly, he held out one arm in your direction, with the flat of his hand toward you. A mighty invisible blow smote you squarely in the chest, flinging you back upon the couch, and upon the pathetic little figure there.

Making passes with his hands, the obscene frog-like Master approached you.

"Sleep! Sleep!" he murmured. "Sleep, my friend."

Your veins filled with water and you slumped helplessly.

"Get up!" he commanded, not unkindly.

251

You arose.

"Follow me!"

Like a sleep-walker, you followed.

Behind you, there sounded the pleading voice of your sweetheart, imploring, "Oh, my lover, be sure and make a note of the number of this house when you leave it, and come back and rescue me!"

Love is strong! In spite of the invisible hands which sought to restrain you, you turned and cried, "I will! I promise you!"

Her sweet eyes filled with gladness; then shot a glance toward the Master, a glance filled with scorn for his thwarted powers, then back to you again, welling with perfect confidence.

"I believe you," she cried happily. "I shall be waiting."

Then you turned and followed the hunchback out of the room. Dazedly you were led to the street door.

On the threshold the Master transfixed you with his penetrating gaze, and commanded incisively, "You will now forget all that has happened in this house of ecstasy this evening! Do you hear me? You will forget *all* that has happened! Go down the steps, turn to the right, and walk away. When you reach the corner, you will awake. But you will remember nothing. Goodnight, my friend, and I thank you for a very pleasant evening."

The door closed behind you.

Ringing in your ears was the insistent command of the wistful girl who had given you her love. "You must not forget! You must not forget."

Already you felt stronger and more free. The spell was beginning to lift. The vision of a piquant oval pleading face was before your eyes.

"I will not forget!" you stalwartly promised, as you went down the steps. Then, before you turned to the right as commanded, you took careful note of the house-number.

You returned from your walk that evening with a vague idea that something was wrong, a vague realization that you had been out of your house an hour or so longer than you could account for.

You consider yourself to be a man of your word, don't you? And yet you have never returned to the house of ecstasy to rescue that girl, although you solemnly promised her that you would.

I have now told you all that I myself know of the episode. But unfortunatley I do not know the address of the house of ecstasy. You need that address. You have to have that address, if you are ever to rescue the girl who loved and trusted you.

Try hard, my friend, try hard.

Can't you remember? You *must* remember!

252

41

HOW I TAKE THEIR MEASURE

Barry N. Malzberg

. . . . At the present rate, as I see it, by the year 2000 everybody is either going to be on welfare or administering it. I see no middle ground at all. Just consider the statistics. . . .

Unit Supervisor
NYC Dept. of Welfare
January, 1964

I HAD TO climb five flights to get to the fellow. It was hell, believe me. There's nothing funny about these old-line tenements, particularly the carpeting they have on the stairs. It's at least a century old and it's slippery. Not to complain, however. Every job has its drawbacks.

I knocked at his door several times and heard mumblings and complaints inside. The usual routine; they hate to get out of bed. Ater a while I turned the knocks into real bangs and added a few curses. There's no sense in letting them feel they have the upper hand.

It worked. The door opened about wide enough to accommodate head and shoulders. He was a small man, alert, bright eyes, a little younger looking than I would have figured from the application. "What you want?" he said. Sullen. Cautious. The usual business.

I showed him my black book in one hand, the identifying card in the other. "Government. We're here to investigate your application."

"I only filed yesterday. I thought it took a week."

"There's a new procedure. We're trying to catch up on our pending applications, move a little ahead." That wasn't strictly true; the truth was that his application had interested me the moment service had put it on my desk. Even on my caseload, he was something out of the ordinary.

"All right, come in," he said and opened the door. I went in. The apartment was foul, absolutely foul. It is impossible to believe how these people live. Litter in every corner, newspapers, smudges of food on the walls. That kind of thing. Inexcusable.

He saw me looking at it. "I'm demoralized," he said. "Things generally get this way when the external disorder begins to correlate to the internal chaos."

Big shot. I nodded at that one, opened my book and very cautiously edged to the center of the room to take the interview. You never sit down where these people have sat. And you have to watch out all the time for rats and insects. That's part of the training.

"Want to ask you a few questions," I said. "First—name, address and so on, all as verified on the application, right? John Steiner, 36 years old, this address."

"You have all that. They took it down yesterday."

"But we have to make sure it's the same person," I said. "Sometimes they send someone down for them, create a whole fictitious background. We've got to protect the public." Before he could think about it I took out my thumbprint kit, opened it, took his wrist and pressed his thumb into the ink, then took the smudge on the paper inside and put the whole thing away. "Procedure," I said.

"It all fits," he said. "Total depersonalization of the individual, that's what it is. Don't you have enough regard to tell me what you're going to do first?"

"Some of them protest," I said. "They know they'll get caught." I opened to his interview record and compared the physical description with him; it dovetailed reasonably well. "Just a few questions now," I said.

"Mind if I sit down?"

"You're ill? You can't stand. You need to rest?"

"Nothing like that," he said. "I just prefer to sit when I'm spoken to."

"If you're sick enough we can probably get you in a fully reimbursed category. No difference to you but more money for us," I said.

"I'm not sick," he said again. "Just depressed. Not that there's much of a difference to *you* people." The *you* rang out. One thing that can be counted on, always, is this stolid hostility. If it were enjoyable, one would count it as a fringe benefit. I do. It makes a good definition of the relationship. There is no hatred without fear and respect, two qualities which I like to command.

He sat in an old chair in the center of the room. Moth-eaten cloth, intimations of small life crawling up and through the upholstery and so on. He lit a cigarette for me and tossed the match out the window.

"No," I said. "No cigarettes."

"What do you mean?"

"I don't like smoke," I said. "People don't smoke in my presence. At least, not people making applications. Put it out."

"No."

"Throw it away," I said.

"I won't. I like to smoke." The whine was coming into his voice.

"Fine," I said. "I'm leaving. We'll call it *application withdrawn.*"

He looked at me for a moment. He could see that I meant it. After a time, he threw the cigarette out the window.

"That's better," I said.

"You really enjoy this, don't you?"

"Enjoy what?"

"The power. The assertiveness of your job. It defines your role-situation, gives you a rationale for your—"

"Enough," I said. "I don't need analyses. Now, we'll call it quits in one second if you don't can it."

Since he had lost the first battle, the second was no contest. His eyes dropped.

"Occupational training?" I said.

"Sociologist," he said. Of course. "I went through all that yesterday in the intake section."

"I told you. I'm conducting my own investigation here. Intake and unit are entirely different; as far as I'm concerned, you don't even exist until you prove it to me. Why are you making application now?"

"How did you support yourself prior to the application?"

He looked at me, almost pleadingly. "I went through that," he said. "I told you."

"The field investigator is the sole determinant of eligibility as he interprets the manual and regulations on public assistance. The intake unit passes on applications to the field investigator for exploration and judgment. You want more quotes?"

"No," he said. I guess that is when I beat him. He seemed to cave in on the seat, his eyes turning inward, almost oblivious of the small things that seemed to be moving on his wrists. He had been easier to bring around than most of them; it was surprising in view of his credentials. But then again, everything considered, his credentials almost explained it.

"I was on the Blauvelt Project," he said, "for fifteen years, ever since I took my undergraduate degree and became a fellow there. The Project just ended last week. So I have no means of support."

255

The Blauvelt was another one of those small government-created boon-doggles; probably the major means of sustenance for the psychologists and sociologists. Even *I* had heard of it. They investigated genealogy, the expressions of characteristics as revealed through heredity and so on. Most of it was concerned with going back through old records and making statistics, but Congress had finally decided last year that it was easier and cheaper to shove them all on assistance. That was Steiner's little life in a nutshell. Useless. Wholly useless.

"Have you made efforts to seek other employment?" That was the test-punch. There was only one answer.

Even Steiner knew that. He managed to grin at me. "Are you kidding?" he said.

"So now you want government assistance? *Pubic* assistance. Relief."

"Do you see any alternative?" he said. His voice moved up on the *any* a little. I had him sweating, there was no doubt about it. A perfectly routine investigation.

"There must be jobs open to a man who's been on the Blauvelt. How about unskilled labor?"

"The pools are backed up ten years with the waiting lists. You know that as well as I do."

I sure did. "Any relatives who might furnish support?"

"My parents are dead. My sister had been on relief for eighteen years. I don't know where my ex-wife is."

"You were married?"

"I put all that down yesterday."

"I told you, there are no yesterdays with me. When were you married?"

"2015. I haven't seen her since 2021. I think she emigrated."

"You mean, she left the country?"

"That's right. We didn't get along."

"She didn't like the Blauvelt?"

He stared at me. "Who did? It was make-work. Anybody could see it. She couldn't take it anymore. She said I should either kill myself or get out of the country. I didn't do either. I thought the project was going to go on forever."

Well, I had thought so too until Congress had had their little convulsion last year. A lot of things that were going to go on forever weren't. I felt like telling him that. But I said, "I guess that's about it. We'll keep you posted."

"You mean I'm eligible?"

"I mean, I've completed the pending investigation. Now I have to go back and write it up—after I see a lot of other people—and make a decision. You'll be notified."

"But listen," he said, gesturing toward me, "don't you understand? I have no money. I have no food. I got this place last week by telling the landlord that I'd be on assistance soon. I owe rent. I can't even breathe."

"You'll have to wait your turn."

"But I haven't had a thing for three days—"

"You have running water," I said, pointing to the rusted tap in the corner suspended over a bucket. "That fills up the stomach pretty good. You'll hold." Then, because I really didn't want to smash him down all the way, I added, "you see, there are a lot of people I've got to service. You have to wait your turn. The need is general."

That turned him off. "Yes," he said, nodding, "the need is general."

"I'm just trying to do a job, you understand. Nothing personal."

"You've *got* a job," he said bitterly. "That's something to say."

"You know how much I often think I'd like to collect and let the people like you do the work? It's no picnic, believe me. The responsibility and the pressure. Not that anybody owes me any favors, you understand. But it's a very tough racket. I work ten hours a day."

"I bet you love it," he said.

"What was that?"

"I said, I guess it's very tough. I have sympathy for you."

"Much better," I said. The interview was over and the fun was out of it. I had taken him, I suppose, to the best limits I could. I closed my book, put away the pencil, went to the door. "Any questions?" I asked.

"None. Except when do I start getting some money."

"When I get to it," I said. My last perception was a good one: staring stricken at the closing crack in the door. A hand moved idly to his face, and I snapped off the image before it went to his eyes.

I went down the stairs three at a time.

In the street, I tossed my fieldbook and kit into the glove compartment of my car parked outside and went down the way to have a beer before I went on to see the other bastards. A place named *Joe's* which I had often visited before was full of reliefers, and, of course, I had the bartender trained as well: he kept them coming and I kept my money away. One of the reliefers tried to talk to me and asked me if I could get him into the bureau, somehow: he was a full medical doctor and perhaps his services could be used. Just for the hell of it, I told him that we were full up on medical doctors at present but there was an interesting government project, something called the Blauvelt, which was keeping lots of people occupied. I suggested that he pursue it, chase it hard. He must have seen what I was saying because he moved away and left me alone, and the drinking was so good and the respect in the place so thick that I forgot all about work for the rest of the day and got stoned and needed four reliefers to get me to my car. I gave them the address and one of them drove me home.

They all owed it to me.

The hell with them.

42

HUNTING MACHINE

Carol Emshwiller

IT SENSED RUTHIE MCALISTER'S rapid heartbeat, just as it sensed any other animal's. The palms of her hands were damp, and it felt that, too—it also felt the breathing, in and out. And it heard her nervous giggle.

She was watching her husband, Joe, as he leaned over the control unit of the thing that sensed heartbeats, the grey-green thing they called the hound, or Rover, or sometimes the bitch.

"Hey," she said. "I guess it's OK, huh?"

Joe turned a screw with his thumb nail and pulled out the wire attached to it. "Gimme a bobby pin."

Ruthie reached to the back of her head. "I mean it's not dangerous is it?"

"Naw."

"I don't just mean about *it*." She nodded at the grey-green thing. "I mean, I know you're good at fixing things like this, like the time you got beer for nothing out of the beer vendor and, golly, I guess we haven't paid for a TV show for years. I mean, I *know* you can fix things right, only won't they know when we bring it back to be checked out?"

"Look, these wardens are country boys, and besides, I can put this thing back so *nobody* knows."

The grey-green thing squatted on its six legs where Joe could lean over it; it sensed that Ruthie's heartbeat had slowed to almost normal, and it heard her sigh.

"I guess you're pretty good at this, huh, Joe?" She wiped her damp hands on her green tunic. "That's the weight dial, isn't it?" she asked, watching him turn the top one.

He nodded. "Fifteen hundred pounds," he said slowly.

"Oo, was he really and truly that big?"

"Bigger." And now the thing felt Joe's heart and breathing surge.

259

They had been landed day before yesterday, with them geodesic tent, pneumatic forms beds, automatic camping stove, and pocket air conditioner. Plus portable disposal automatic blow-up chairs and tables, pocket TV set, four disposable hunting costumes apiece (one for each day), and two folding guns with power settings.

In addition, there was the bug-scat, go-snake, sun-stop, and the grey-green hunter, sealed by the warden and set for three birds, two deer and one black bear. They had only the bear to go; now, Joe McAlister had unsealed the controls, released the governer and changed the setting to brown bear, fifteen hundred pounds.

"I don't care," he said, "I want that bear."

"Do you think he'll still be there tomorrow?"

Joe patted one of the long jointed legs of the thing. "If he's not, ol' bitch here will find him for us."

Next day was clear and cool, and Joe breathed big, expanding breaths and patted his beginning paunch. "Yes, sir," he said, "this is the day for something big—something really big, that'll put up a real fight."

He watched the red of the sunrise fade out of the sky while Ruthie turned on the stove and then got out her make-up kit. She put sun-stop on her face, then powdered it with a tan powder. She blackened her eyelids and purpled her lips; after that, she opened the stove and took out two disposable plates with eggs and bacon.

They sat in the automatic blow-up chairs, at the automatic blow-up table. Joe said that there was nothing like North air to give you an appetite, and Ruthie said she bet they were sweltering back at the city. Then she giggled.

Joe leaned back in his chair and sipped his coffee. "Shooting deer is just like shooting a cow," he said. "No fight to 'em at all. Even when ol' hound here goads 'em, they just want to run off. But the bear's going to be different. Of course bears are shy too, but ol' hound knows what to do about that."

"They say it's getting to be so there aren't many of the big kind left."

"Yes, but one more won't hurt. Think of a skin and head that size in our living room. I guess anybody that came in there would sure sit up and take notice."

"It won't match the curtains," his wife said.

"I think what I'll do is pack the skin up tight and leave it somewhere up here, till the warden checks us through. Then, maybe a couple of days later, I'll come back and get it."

"Good idea." Ruthie had finished her coffee and was perfuming herself with bug-scat.

"Well, I guess we'd better get started." They hung their folded up guns on their belts. They put their dehydrated self heating lunch in their pockets. They slung on their cold-unit canteens. They each took a packet containing chair, table and sun shade; then Joe fastened on the little mike that controlled the hunter. It fit on his shoulder where he could turn his head to the side and talk into it.

"All right, houn' dog," he said, shoulder hunched and head tilted, "get a move on, boy. Back to that spot where we saw him yesterday. You can pick up the scent from there."

The hunting machine ran on ahead of them. It went faster than anything it might have to hunt. Two miles, three miles—Joe and Ruthie were left behind. They followed the beam it sent back to them, walking and talking and helping each other over the rough spots.

About eleven o'clock, Joe stopped, took off his red hunting hat and mopped his balding forehead with the new bandana he'd bought at Hunter's Outfitters in New York. It was then he got the signal. *Sighted, sighted, sighted. . . .*

Joe leaned over his mike. "Stick on him boy. How far are you? Well, try to move him down this way if you can." He turned to his wife. "Let's see, about three miles . . . we'll take half hour out for lunch. Maybe we'll get there a couple of hours from now. How's it going, kid?"

"Swell," Ruthie said.

The big bear sat on the rocks by the stream. His front paws were wet almost to the elbows. There were three torn fishheads lying beside him. He ate only the best parts because he was a good fisher; and he looked, now, into the clean cold water for another dark blue back that would pause on its way upstream.

It wasn't a smell that made him turn. He had a keen nose, but the hunting machine was made to have no smell. It was the grey dead lichen's crackle that made him look up. He stood still, looking in the direction of the sound and squinting his small eyes, but it wasn't until it moved that he saw it.

Three quarters of a ton, he was; but like a bird, or a rabbit, or a snake, the bear avoided things that were large and strange. He turned back the way he always took, the path to his rubbing tree and to his home. He moved quietly and rapidly, but the thing followed.

He doubled back to the stream again, then, and waded down it on the

261

opposite side from the thing—but still it followed, needing no scent. Once the hunting machine sighted, it never lost its prey.

Heart beat normal, respiration normal, it sensed. Size almost sixteen hundred pounds.

The bear got out on the bank and turned back, calling out in low growls. He stood up on his hind legs and stretched his full height. Almost two men tall, he stood and gave warning.

The hunting machine waited twenty yards away. The bear looked at it a full minute; then he fell back on all fours and turned South again. He was shy and he wanted no trouble.

Joe and Ruthie kept on walking North at their leisurely pace until just noon. Then they stopped for lunch by the side of the same stream the bear had waded, only lower down. And they used its cold water on their de-hydrated meal—beef and onions, mashed potatoes, a lettuce salad that unfolded in the water like Japanese paper flowers. There were coffee tablets that contained a heating unit too, and fizzled in the water like firecracker fuses until the water was hot, creamy coffee.

The bear didn't stop to eat. Noon meant nothing to him. Now he moved with more purpose, looking back and squinting his small eyes.

The hunter felt the heart beat faster, the breathing heavy, pace increasing. Direction generally South.

Joe and Ruthie followed the signal until it suddenly changed. It came faster; that meant they were near.

They stopped and unfolded their guns. "Let's have a cup of coffee first," Ruthie said.

"OK, Hon." Joe released the chairs which blew themselves up to size. "Good to take a break so we can really enjoy the fight."

Ruthie handed Joe a fizzing cup of coffee. "Don't forget you want ol' Rover to goad some."

"Uh huh. Bear's not much better than a deer without it. Good you reminded me." He turned and spoke softly into the little mike.

The hunting machine shortened the distance slowly. Fifteen feet, ten, five. The bear heard and turned. Again he rose up, almost two men tall, and roared his warning sound to tell the thing to keep back.

Joe and Ruthie shivered and didn't look at each other. They heard it less with their ears, and more with their spines—with an instinct they had forgotten.

Joe shook his shoulder to shake away the feeling of the sound. "I guess the ol' bitch is at him."

"Good dog," Ruthie said. "Get 'im, boy."

The hunter's arm tips drew blood, but only in the safe spots—shoulder scratches at the heavy lump behind his head, thigh punctures. It never touched the veins, or arteries.

The bear swung at the thing with his great paw. His claws screetched down the body section but didn't so much as make a mark on the metal. The blow sent the thing thirty feet away, but it got up and came back so fast the bear couldn't see it until it was there, thrusting at him again. He threw it again and again, but it came back every time. The muscles, claws and teeth were nothing to it. It was made to withstand easily more than what one bear could do, and it knew with its built-in knowledge, how to make a bear blind-angry.

Saliva came to the bear's mouth and flew out over his chin as he moved his heavy head sideways and back. It splashed, gummy on his cheek and made dark, damp streaks across his chest. Only his rage was real to him now, and he screamed a deep rasp of frustration again and again.

Two hundred yards away, Joe said, "Some roar!"

"Uh huh. If noise means anything, it sounds like he's about ready for a real fight."

They both got up and folded up the chairs and cups. They sighted along their gun barrels to see that they were straight. "Set 'em at medium," Joe said. "We want to start off slow."

They came to where the bear was, and took up a good position on a high place. Joe called in his mike to the hunter thing. "Stand by, houn' dog, and slip over here to back us up." Then he called to the bear. "Hey, boy. This way. boy. This way."

The grey-green thing moved back and the bear saw the new enemy, two of them. He didn't hesitate; he was ready to charge anything that moved. He was only five feet away when their small guns popped. The force knocked him down, and he rolled out of the way, dazed; he turned again for another charge, and came at them, all claws and teeth.

Joe's gun popped again. This time the bear staggered, but still came on. Joe backed up, pushing at his gun dial to raise the power. He bumped into Ruthie behind him and they both fell. Joe's voice was a crazy scream. "Get him."

The hunting machine moved fast. Its sharp forearm came like an upper cut, under the jaw, and into the brain.

He lay, looking smaller, somehow, but still big, his ragged fur matted with blood. Fleas were alive on it, and flies already coming. Joe and Ruthie looked down at him and took big breaths.

"You shouldna got behind me," Joe said as soon as he caught his breath.

"I coulda kept it going longer if you'd a just stayed out of the way."

"You told me to," Ruthie said. "You told me to stay right behind you."

"Well, I didn't mean *that* close."

Ruthie sniffed. "Anyway," she said, "how are you going to get the fur off it?"

"Hmmmph."

"I don't think that moth-eaten thing will make much of a rug. It's pretty dirty, too, and probably full of germs."

Joe walked around the bear and turned its head sideways with his toe. "Be a big messy job, all right, skinning it. Up to the elbows in blood and gut, I guess."

"I didn't expect it to be like *this* at all," Ruthie said. "Why don't you just forget it. You had your fun."

Joe stood, looking at the bear's head. He watched a fly land on its eye and then walk down to a damp nostril.

"Well come *on*." Ruthie took her small pack. "I want to get back in time to take a bath before supper."

"OK." Joe leaned over his mike. "Come on ol' Rover, ol' hound dog. You did fine."

43

THE IMMORTAL BARD

Isaac Asimov

OH YES," SAID Dr. Phineas Welch, "I can bring back the spirits of the illustrious dead."

He was a little drunk, or maybe he wouldn't have said it. Of course, it was perfectly all right to get a little drunk at the annual Christmas party.

Scott Robertson, the school's young English instructor, adjusted his glasses and looked to right and left to see if they overheard. "Really, Dr. Welch."

"I mean it. And not just the spirits. I bring back the bodies, too."

"I wouldn't have said it were possible," said Robertson primly.

"Why not? A simple matter of temporal transference."

"You mean time travel? But that's quite—uh—unusual."

"Not if you know how."

"Well, how, Dr. Welch?"

"Think I'm going to tell you?" asked the physicist gravely. He looked vaguely about for another drink and didn't find any. He said, "I brought quite a few back. Archimedes, Newton, Galileo. Poor fellows."

"Didn't they like it here? I should think they'd have been fascinated by our modern science," said Robertson. He was beginning to enjoy the conversation.

"Oh, they were. They were. Especially Archimedes. I thought he'd go mad with joy at first after I explained a little of it in some Greek I'd boned up on, but no—no———"

"What was wrong?"

"Just a different culture. They couldn't get used to our way of life. They got terribly lonely and frightened. I had to send them back."

"That's too bad."

"Yes. Great minds, but not flexible minds. Not universal. So I tried Shakespeare."

"*What?*" yelled Robertson. This was getting close to home.

"Don't yell, my boy," said Welch. "It's bad manners."

"Did you say you brought back Shakespeare?"

"I did. I needed someone with a universal mind; someone who knew people well enough to be able to live with them centuries away from his own time. Shakespeare was the man. I've got his signature. As a memento, you know."

"On you?" asked Robertson, eyes bugging.

"Right here." Welch fumbled in one vest pocket after another. "Ah, here it is."

A little piece of pasteboard was passed to the instructor. On one side it said: "L. Klein & Sons, Wholesale Hardware." On the other side, in straggly script, was written, "Willm Shaksper."

A wild surmise filled Robertson. "What did he look like?"

"Not like his pictures. Bald and an ugly mustache. He spoke in a thick brogue. Of course, I did my best to please him with our times. I told him we thought highly of his plays and still put them on the boards. In fact, I said we thought they were the greatest pieces of literature in the English language, maybe in any language."

"Good. Good," said Robertson breathlessly.

"I said people had written volumes of commentaries on his plays. Naturally he wanted to see one and I got one for him from the library."

"And?"

"Oh, he was fascinated. Of course, he had trouble with the current idioms and references to events since 1600, but I helped out. Poor fellow. I don't think he ever expected such treatment. He kept saying, 'God ha' mercy! What cannot be racked from words in five centuries? One could wring, methinks, a flood from a damp clout!' "

"He wouldn't say that."

"Why not? He wrote his plays as quickly as he could. He said he had to on account of the deadlines. He wrote *Hamlet* in less than six months. The plot was an old one. He just polished it up."

"That's all they do to a telescope mirror. Just polish it up," said the English instructor indignantly.

The physicist disregarded him. He made out an untouched cocktail on the bar some feet away and sidled toward it. "I told the immortal bard that we even gave college courses in Shakespeare."

"*I* give one."

"I know. I enrolled him in your evening extension course. I never saw a man so eager to find out what posterity thought of him as poor Bill was. He worked hard at it."

"You enrolled William Shakespeare in my course?" mumbled Robertson. Even as an alcoholic fantasy, the thought staggered him. And *was* it an alcoholic fantasy? He was beginning to recall a bald man with a queer way of talking. . . .

"Not under his real name, of course," said Dr. Welch. "Never mind what he went under. It was a mistake, that's all. A big mistake. Poor fellow." He had the cocktail now and shook his head at it.

"Why was it a mistake? What happened?"

"I had to send him back to 1600," roared Welch indignantly. "How much humiliation do you think a man can stand?"

"What humiliation are you talking about?"

Dr. Welch tossed off the cocktail. "Why, you poor simpleton, you *flunked* him."

44

IN CASE OF FIRE

Randall Garrett

IN HIS OFFICE apartment, on the top floor the the Terran Embassy Buidling in Occeq City, Bertrand Malloy leafed casually through the dossiers of the four new men who had been assigned to him. They were typical of the kind of men who were sent to him, he thought. Which meant, as usual, that they were atypical. Every man in the Diplomatic Corps who developed a twitch or a quirk was shipped to Saarkkad IV to work under Bertrand Malloy, Permanent Terran Ambassador to His Utter Munificence, the Occeq of Saarkkad.

Take this first one, for instance. Malloy ran his finger down the columns of complex symbolism that showed the complete psychological analysis of the man. Psychopathic paranoia. The man wasn't technically insane; he could be as lucid as the next man most of the time. But he was morbidly suspicious that ever man's hand was turned against him. He trusted no one, and was perpetually on his guard against imaginary plots and persecutions.

Number two suffered from some sort of emotional block that left him continually on the horns of one dilemma or another. He was psychologically incapable of making a decision if he were faced with two or more possible alternatives of any major importance.

Number three. . . .

Malloy sighed and pushed the dossiers away from him. No two men were alike, and yet there sometimes seemed to be an eternal sameness about all men. He considered himself an individual, for instance, but wasn't the basic similarity there, after all?

He was—how old? He glanced at the Earth calendar dial that was automatically correlated with the Saarkkadic calendar just above it. Fifty-nine next week. Fifty-nine years old. And what did he have to show for it besides flabby muscles, sagging skin, a wrinkled face, and gray hair?

Well, he had an excellent record in the Corps, if nothing else. One of the top men in his field. And he had his memories of Diane, dead these ten years, but still beautiful and alive in his recollections. And—he grinned softly to himself—he had Saarkkad.

He glanced up at the ceiling, and mentally allowed his gaze to penetrate it to the blue sky beyond it.

Out there was the terrible emptiness of interstellar space—a great yawning, infinite chasm capable of swallowing men, ships, planets, suns, and whole galaxies without filling its insatiable void.

Malloy closed his eyes. Somewhere out there, a war was raging. He didn't even like to think of that, but it was necessary to keep it in mind. Somewhere out there, the ships of Earth were ranged against the ships of the alien Karna in the most important war that Mankind had yet fought.

And, Malloy knew, his own position was not unimportant in that war. He was not in the battle line, nor even in the major production line, but it was necessary to keep the drug supply lines flowing from Saarkkad, and that meant keeping on good terms with the Saarkkadic government.

The Saarkkada themselves were humanoid in physical form—if one allowed the term to cover a wide range of differences—but their minds just didn't function along the same lines.

For nine years, Bertrand Malloy had been Ambassador to Saarkkad, and for nine years, no Saarkkada had ever seen him. To have shown himself to one of them would have meant instant loss of prestige.

To their way of thinking, an important official was aloof. The greater his importance, the greater must be his isolation. The Occeq of Saarkkad himself was never seen except by a handful of picked nobles, who, themselves, were never seen except by their underlings. It was a long, roundabout way of doing business, but is was the only way Saarkkad would do any business at all. To violate the rigid social setup of Saarkkad would mean the instant closing off of the supply of biochemical products that the Saarkkadic laboratories produced from native plants and animals—products that were vitally necessary to Earth's war, and which could be duplicated nowhere else in the known universe.

It was Bertrand Malloy's job to keep the production output high and to keep the material flowing towards Earth and her allies and outposts.

The job would have been a snap cinch in the right circumstances; the Saarkkada weren't difficult to get along with. A staff of top-grade men could have handled them without half trying.

But Malloy didn't have top-grade men. They couldn't be spared from work that required their total capacity. It's inefficient to waste a man on a job that he can do without half trying where there are more important jobs that will tax his full output.

So Malloy was stuck with the culls. Not the worst ones, of course; there were places in the galaxy less important than Saarkkad to the war effort. Malloy knew that, no matter what was wrong with a man, as long as he had the mental ability to dress himself and get himself to work, useful work could be found for him.

Physical handicaps weren't at all difficult to deal with. A blind man can work very well in the total darkness of an infrared-film darkroom. Partial or total loss of limbs can be compensated for in one way or another.

The mental disabilities were harder to deal with, but not totally impossible. On a world without liquor, a dipsomaniac could be channeled easily enough; and he'd better not try fermenting his own on Saarkkad unless he brought his own yeast—which was impossible, in view of the sterilization regulations.

But Malloy didn't like to stop at merely thwarting mental quirks; he liked to find places where they were *useful*.

The phone chimed. Malloy flipped it on with a practiced hand.

"Malloy here."

"Mr. Malloy?" said a careful voice. "A special communication for you has been teletyped in from Earth. Shall I bring it in?"

"Bring it in, Miss Drayson."

Miss Drayson was a case in point. She was uncommunicative. She liked to gather information, but she found it difficult to give it up once it was in her possession.

Malloy had made her his private secretary. Nothing—but *nothing*—got out of Malloy's office without his direct order. It had taken Malloy a long time to get it into Miss Drayson's head that it was perfectly all right—even desirable—for her to keep secrets from everyone except Malloy.

She came in through the door, a rather handsome woman in her middle thirties, clutching a sheaf of papers in her right hand as though someone might at any instant snatch it from her before she could turn it over to Malloy.

She laid them carefully on the desk. "If anything else comes in, I'll let you know immediately, sir," she said. "Will there be anything else?"

Malloy let her stand there while he picked up the communique. She wanted to know what his reaction was going to be; it didn't matter because no one would ever find out from her what he had done unless she was ordered to tell someone.

He read the first paragraph, and his eyes widened involuntarily.

271

"Armistice," he said in a low whisper. "There's a chance that the war may be over."

"Yes, sir," said Miss Drayson in a hushed voice.

Malloy read the whole thing through, fighting to keep his emotions in check. Miss Drayson stood there calmly, her face a mask; her emotions were a secret.

Finally, Malloy looked up. "I'll let you know as soon as I reach a decision, Miss Drayson. I think I hardly need to say that no news of this is to leave this office."

"Of course not, sir."

Malloy watched her go out the door without actually seeing her. The war was over—at least for a while. He looked down at the papers again.

The Karna, slowly being beaten back on every front, were suing for peace. They wanted an armistice conference—immediately.

Earth was willing. Interstellar war is too costly to allow it to continue any longer than necessary, and this one had been going on for more than thirteen years now. Peace was necessary. But not peace at any price.

The trouble was that the Karna had a reputation for losing wars and winning at the peace table. They were clever, persuasive talkers. They could twist a disadvantage to an advantage, and make their own strengths look like weaknesses. If they won the armistice, they'd be able to retrench and rearm, and the war would break out again within a few years.

Now—at this point in time—they could be beaten. They could be forced to allow supervision of the production potential, forced to disarm, rendered impotent. But if the armistice went to their own advantage. . . .

Already, they had taken the offensive in the matter of the peace talks. They had sent a full delegation to Saarkkad V, the next planet out from the Saarkkad sun, a chilly world inhabited only by low-intelligence animals. The Karna considered this to be fully neutral territory, and Earth couldn't argue the point very well. In addition, they demanded that the conference begin in three days, Terrestrial time.

The trouble was that interstellar communication beams travel a devil of a lot faster than ships. It would take more than a week for the Earth government to get a vessel to Saarkkad V. Earth had been caught unprepared for an armistice. They objected.

The Karna pointed out that the Saarkkad sun was just as far from Karn as it was from Earth, that it was only a few million miles from a planet which was allied with Earth, and that it was unfair for Earth to take so much time in preparing for an armistice. Why hadn't Earth been prepared? Did they intend to fight to the utter destruction of Karn?

272

It wouldn't have been a problem at all if Earth and Karn had fostered the only two intelligent races in the galaxy. The sort of grandstanding the Karna were putting on had to be played to an audience. But there were other intelligent races throughout the galaxy, most of whom had remained as neutral as possible during the Earth-Karn war. They had no intention of sticking their figurative noses into a battle between the two most powerful races in the galaxy.

But whoever won the armistice would find that some of the now-neutral races would come in on their side if war broke out again. If the Karna played their cards right, their side would be strong enough next time to win.

So Earth had to get a delegation to meet with the Karna representatives within the three-day limit or lose what might be a vital point in the negotiations.

And that was where Bertrand Malloy came in.

He had been appointed Minister and Plenipotentiary Extraordinary to the Earth-Karn peace conference.

He looked up at the ceiling again. "What *can* I do?" he said softly.

On the second day after the arrival of his communique, Malloy made his decision. He flipped on his intercom and said: "Miss Drayson, get hold of James Nordon and Kylen Braynek. I want to see them both immediately. Send Nordon in first, and tell Braynek to wait."

"Yes, sir."

"And keep the recorder on. You can file the tape later."

"Yes, sir."

Malloy knew the woman would listen in on the intercom anyway, and it was better to give her permission to do so.

James Nordon was tall, broad-shouldered, and thirty-eight. His hair was graying at the temples, and his handsome face looked cool and efficient.

Malloy waved him to a seat.

"Nordon, I have a job for you. It's probably one of the most important jobs you'll ever have in your life. It can mean big things for you—promotion and prestige if you do it well."

Nordon nodded slowly. "Yes, sir."

Malloy explained the problem of the Karna peace talks.

"We need a man who can outthink them," Malloy finished, "and judging from your record, I think you're that man. It involves risk, of course. If you make the wrong decisions, your name will be mud back on Earth. But I don't think there's much chance of that, really. Do you want to handle small-time operations all your life? Of course not.

"You'll be leaving within an hour for Saarkkad V."

Nordon nodded again. "Yes, sir; certainly. Am I to go alone?"

"No," said Malloy, "I'm sending an assistant with you—a man named Kylen Braynek. Ever heard of him?"

Nordon shook his head. "Not that I recall, Mr. Malloy. Should I have?"

"Not necessarily. He's a pretty shrewd operator, though. He knows a lot about interstellar law, and he's capable of spotting a trap a mile away. You'll be in charge, of course, but I want you to pay special attention to his advice."

"I will, sir," Nordon said gratefully. "A man like that can be useful."

"Right. Now, you go into the anteroom over there. I've prepared a summary of the situation, and you'll have to study it and get it into your head before the ship leaves. That isn't much time, but it's the Karna who are doing the pushing, not us."

As soon as Nordon had left, Malloy said softly: "Send in Braynek, Miss Drayson."

Kylen Braynek was a smallish man with mouse-brown hair that lay flat against his skull, and hard, penetrating, dark eyes that were shadowed by heavy, protruding brows. Malloy asked him to sit down.

Again Malloy went through the explanation of the peace conference.

"Naturally, they'll be trying to trick you every step of the way," Malloy went on. "They're shrewd and underhanded; we'll simply have to be more shrewd and more underhanded. Nordon's job is to sit quietly and evaluate the data; yours will be to find the loopholes they're laying out for themselves and plug them. Don't antagonize them, but don't baby them, either. If you see anything underhanded going on, let Nordon know immediately."

"They won't get anything by me, Mr. Malloy."

By the time the ship from Earth got there, the peace conference had been going for four days. Bertrand Malloy had full reports on the whole parley, as relayed to him through the ship that had taken Nordon and Braynek to Saarkkad V.

Secretary of State Blendwell stopped off at Saarkkad IV before going on to V to take charge of the conference. He was a tallish, lean man with a few strands of gray hair on the top of his otherwise bald scalp, and he wore a hearty, professional smile that didn't quite make it to his calculating eyes.

He took Malloy's hand and shook it warmly. "How are you, Mr. Ambassador?"

"Fine, Mr. Secretary. How's everything on Earth?"

"Tense. They're waiting to see what is going to happen on Five. So am I, for that matter." His eyes were curious. "You decided not to go yourself, eh?"

"I thought it better not to. I sent a good team, instead. Would you like to see the reports?"

"I certainly would."

Malloy handed them to the secretary, and as he read, Malloy watched him. Blendwell was a political appointee—a good man, Malloy had to admit, but he didn't know all the ins and outs of the Diplomatic Corps.

When Blendwell looked up from the reports at last, he said: "Amazing! They've held off the Karna at every point! They've beaten them back! They've managed to cope with and outdo the finest team of negotiators the Karna could send."

"I thought they would," said Malloy, trying to appear modest.

The secretary's eyes narrowed. "I've heard of the work you've been doing here with . . . ah . . . sick men. Is this one of your . . . ah . . . successes?"

Malloy nodded. "I think so. The Karna put us in a dilemma, so I threw a dilemma right back at them."

"How do you mean?"

"Nordon had a mental block against making decisions. If he took a girl out on a date, he'd have trouble making up his mind whether to kiss her or not until she made up his mind for him, one way or the other. He's that kind of guy. Until he's presented with one, single, clear decision which admits of no alternatives, he can't move at all.

"As you can see, the Karna tried to give us several choices on each point, and they were all rigged. Until they backed down to a single point and proved that it *wasn't* rigged, Nordon couldn't possibly make up his mind. I drummed into him how important this was, and the more importance there is attached to his decisions, the more incapable he becomes of making them."

The Secretary nodded slowly. "What about Braynek?"

"Paranoid," said Malloy. "He thinks everyone is plotting against him. In this case, that's all to the good because the Karna *are* plotting against him. No matter what they put forth, Braynek is convinced that there's a trap in it somewhere, and he digs to find out what the trap is. Even if there isn't a trap, the Karna can't satisfy Braynek, because he's convinced that there *has* to be—somewhere. As a result, all his advice to Nordon, and all his questioning on the wildest possibilities, just serves to keep Nordon from getting unconfused.

"These two men are honestly doing their best to win at the peace conference, and they've got the Karna reeling. The Karna can see that we're not trying to stall; our men are actually working at trying to reach a decision. But what the Karna don't see is that those men, as a team, are unbeatable because, in this situation, they're psychologically incapable of losing."

Again the Secretary of State nodded his approval, but there was still a question in his mind. "Since you know all that, couldn't you have handled it yourself?"

"Maybe, but I doubt it. They might have gotten around me someway by sneaking up on a blind spot. Nordon and Braynek have blind spots, but they're covered with armor. No, I'm glad I couldn't go; it's better this way."

The Secretary of State raised an eyebrow. *"Couldn't go,* Mr. Ambassador?"

Malloy looked at him. "Didn't you know? I wondered why you appointed me, in the first place. No, I couldn't go. The reason why I'm here, cooped up in this office, hiding from the Saarkkada the way a good Saarkkadic bigshot should, is because I *like* it that way. I suffer from agoraphobia and xenophobia.

"I have to be drugged to be put on a spaceship because I can't take all that empty space, even if I'm protected from it by a steel shell." A look of revulsion came over his face. "And I can't *stand* aliens!"

45

AN INCIDENT ON ROUTE 12

James H. Schmitz

PHIL GARFIELD WAS thirty miles south of the little town of Redmon on Route Twelve when he was startled by a series of sharp, clanking noises. They came from under the Packard's hood.

The car immediately began to lose speed. Garfield jammed down the accelerator, had a sense of sick helplessness at the complete lack of response from the motor. The Packard rolled on, getting rid of its momentum, and came to a stop.

Phil Garfield swore shakily. He checked his watch, switched off the headlights and climbed out into the dark road. A delay of even half an hour here might be disastrous. It was past midnight, and he had another hundred and ten miles to cover to reach the small private airfield where Madge waited for him and the thirty thousand dollars in the suitcase on the Packard's front seat.

If he didn't make it before daylight. . . .

He thought of the bank guard. The man had made a clumsy play at being a hero, and that had set off the fool woman who'd run screaming into their line of fire. One dead. Perhaps two. Garfield hadn't stopped to look at an evening paper.

But he knew they were hunting for him.

He glanced up and down the road. No other headlights in sight at the moment, no light from a building showing on the forested hills. He reached back into the car and brought out the suitcase, his gun, a big flashlight and the box of shells which had been standing beside the suitcase. He broke the box open, shoved a handful of shells and the .38 into his coat pocket, then took suitcase and flashlight over to the shoulder of the road and set them down.

There was no point in groping about under the Packard's hood. When it came to mechanics, Phil Garfield was a moron and well aware of it. The car was useless to him now . . . except as bait.

But as bait it might be very useful.

Should he leave it standing where it was? No, Garfield decided. To anybody driving past is would merely suggest a necking party, or a drunk sleeping off his load before continuing home. He might have to wait an hour or more before someone decided to stop. He didn't have the time. He reached in through the window, hauled the top of the steering wheel towards him and put his weight against the rear window frame.

The Packard began to move slowly backwards at a slant across the road. In a minute or two he had it in position. Not blocking the road entirely, which would arouse immediate suspicion, but angled across it, lights out, empty, both front doors open and inviting a passerby's investigation.

Garfield carried the suitcase and flashlight across the right-hand shoulder of the road and moved up among the trees and undergrowth of the slope above the shoulder. Placing the suitcase between the bushes, he brought out the .38, clicked the safety off and stood waiting.

Some ten minutes later, a set of headlights appeared speeding up Route Twelve from the direction of Redmon. Phil Garfield went down on one knee before he came within range of the lights. Now he was completely concealed by the vegetation.

The car slowed as it approached, braking nearly to a stop sixty feet from the stalled Packard. There were several people inside it; Garfield heard voices, then a woman's loud laugh. The driver tapped his horn inquiringly twice, moved the car slowly forward. As the headlights went past him, Garfield got to his feet among the bushes, took a step down towards the road, raising the gun.

Then he caught the distant gleam of a second set of headlights approaching from Redmon. He swore under his breath and dropped back out of sight. The car below him reached the Packard, edged cautiously around it, rolled on with a sudden roar of acceleration.

The second car stopped when still a hundred yards away, the Packard caught in the motionless glare of its lights. Garfield heard the steady purring of a powerful motor.

For almost a minute, nothing else happened. Then the car came gliding smoothly on, stopped again no more than thirty feet to Garfield's left. He could see it now through the screening bushes—a big job, a long, low four-door sedan. The motor continued to purr. After a moment, a door on the far side of the car opened and slammed shut.

A man walked quickly out into the beam of the headlights and started towards the Packard.

Phil Garfield rose from his crouching position, the .38 in his right hand, flashlight in his left. If the driver was alone, the thing was now cinched! But if there was somebody else in the car, somebody capable of fast, decisive action, a slip in the next ten seconds might cost him the sedan, and quite probably his freedom and life. Garfield lined up the .38's sights steadily on the center of the approaching man's head. He let his breath out slowly as the fellow came level with him in the road and squeezed off one shot.

Instantly he went bounding down the slope to the road. The bullet had flung the man sideways to the pavement. Garfield darted past him to the left, crossed the beam of the headlights, and was in darkness again on the far side of the road, snapping on his flashlight as he sprinted up to the car.

The motor hummed quietly on. The flashlight showed the seats empty. Garfield dropped the light, jerked both doors open in turn, gun pointing into the car's interior. Then he stood still for a moment, weak and almost dizzy with relief.

There was no one inside. The sedan was his.

The man he had shot through the head lay face down on the road, his hat flung a dozen feet away from him. Route Twelve still stretched out in dark silence to east and west. There should be time enough to clean up the job before anyone else came along. Garfield brought the suitcase down and put it on the front seat of the sedan, then started back to get his victim off the road and out of sight. He scaled the man's hat into the bushes, bent down, grasped the ankles and started to haul him towards the left side of the road where the ground dropped off sharply beyond the shoulder.

The body made a high, squealing sound and began to writhe violently.

Shocked, Garfield dropped the legs and hurriedly took the gun from his pocket, moving back a step. The squealing noise rose in intensity as the wounded man quickly flopped over twice like a struggling fish, arms and legs sawing about with startling energy. Garfield clicked off the safety, pumped three shots into his victim's back.

The grisly squeals ended abruptly. The body continued to jerk for another second or two, then lay still.

Garfield shoved the gun back into his pocket. The unexpected interruption had unnerved him; his hands shook as he reached down again for the stranger's ankles. Then he jerked his hands back, and straightened up, staring.

From the side of the man's chest, a few inches below the right arm, something like a thick black stick, three feet long, protruded now through the material of the coat.

It shone, gleaming wetly, in the light from the car. Even in that first uncomprehending instant, something in its appearance brought a surge of sick disgust to Garfield's throat. Then the stick bent slowly halfway down its length, forming a sharp angle, and its tip opened into what could have been three blunt, black claws which scrabbled clumsily against the pavement. Very faintly, the squealing began again, and the body's back arched up as if another sticklike arm were pushing desperately against the ground beneath it.

Garfield acted in a blur of horror. He emptied the .38 into the thing at his feet almost without realizing he was doing it. Then, dropping the gun, he seized one of the ankles, ran backwards to the shoulder of the road, dragging the body behind him.

In the darkness at the edge of the shoulder, he let go of it, stepped around to the other side and with two frantically savage kicks sent the body plunging over the shoulder and down the steep slope beyond. He heard it crash through the bushes for some seconds, then stop. He turned, and ran back to the sedan, scooping up his gun as he went past. He scrambled into the driver's seat and slammed the door shut behind him.

His hands shook violently on the steering wheel as he pressed down the accelerator. The motor roared into life and the big car surged forward. He edged it past the Packard, cursing aloud in horrified shock, jammed down the accelerator and went flashing up Route Twelve, darkness racing beside and behind him.

What had it been? Something that wore what seemed to be a man's body like a suit of clothes, moving the body as a man moves, driving a man's car . . . roach-armed, roach-legged itself!

Garfield drew a long, shuddering breath. Then, as he slowed for a curve, there was a spark of reddish light in the rear-view mirror.

He stared at the spark for an instant, braked the car to a stop, rolled down the window and looked back.

Far behind him along Route Twelve, a fire burned. Approximately at the point where the Packard had stalled out, where something had gone rolling off the road into the bushes.

Something, Garfield added mentally, that found fiery automatic destruction when death came to it, so that its secrets would remain unrevealed.

But for him the fire meant the end of a nightmare. He rolled the window up, took out a cigarette, lit it, and pressed the accelerator. . . .

In incredulous fright, he felt the nose of the car tilt upwards, headlights sweeping up from the road into the trees. Then the headlights winked out. Beyond the windshield, dark tree branches floated down towards him, the night sky beyond. He reached frantically for the door handle.

A steel wrench clamped silently about each of his arms, drawing them in against his sides, immobilizing them there. Garfield gasped, looked up at the mirror and saw a pair of faintly geaming red eyes watching him from the rear of the car. Two of the things . . . the second one stood behind him out of sight, holding him. They'd been in what had seemed to be the trunk compartment. And they had come out.

The eyes in the mirror vanished. A moist, black roach-arm reached over the back of the seat beside Garfield, picked up the cigarette he had dropped, extinguished it with rather horribly human motions, then took up Garfield's gun and drew back out of sight.

He expected a shot, but none came.

One doesn't fire a bullet through the suit one intends to wear. . . .

It wasn't until that thought occurred to him that tough Phil Garfield began to scream. He was still screaming minutes later when, beyond the windshield, the spaceship floated into view among the stars.

46

INTERVIEW

Frank A. Javor

LOOKING AT THE woman, Lester V. Morrison felt deep inside himself the stirring of sympathy, familiar, rising to the sustained, heady rapport that made him know, with the certainty of long experience, that this was going to be another of his great interviews.

He smiled and loosened the fist he'd made unconsciously to emphasize the word "great" when it passed through his mind.

He felt a light touch on his arm and turning, bowed his head so that his lead technician could slip over it the video-audio headband. Its close-fitting temple pieces curved to touch the bone behind his ears and the twin stereo viewfinder cameras came down over his eyes.

Lester rather liked to make the subdued bowing movement, the symbolic humbling, it pleased him to think, of his six-and-almost-a-half-foot tallness to receive the crownlike headgear of his craft. A crown heavy, not with the scant two ounces of transmitting metal and optical plastic but heavy with his responsibility to the billions upon billions of viewers who would see what Lester looked upon, would hear what he turned his ear to; the center of their universe for those moments the spot upon which Lester stood, the signal spreading outward from it like the ripple pattern of a dropped stone.

His technician pressed Lester's arm twice and stepped back. Lester stood erect, his hands and fingers hovering over the twin-arced rows of buttons and rods set in the flat surface of the control console he wore high on his chest like an ancient breastplate. There was no speaking between Lester and his four-man crew, nor any testing of equipment. Lester wore his responsibility with what he considered a suitable humility, but with a firm confidence. Let lesser men fiddle with their equipment, talk, blur the virgin spontaneity of the look that would flash into the woman's eyes with the first impact of Lester's equipment upon her. His men, like Lester, were the absolute best in their field; razor-honed by long close union and good pay until they responded almost symbiotically to Lester and each other.

A clear warning warble from his left earphone, heard only by Lester through the bones of his skull, readied him to begin his task. He stood firmly tall, silent, waiting. . . .

A musical bleat. The suddenly glowing red face of the timer in the upper corner of his left viewfinder. He was on the air.

The general view first. Eight seconds to set the scene, to let his viewers see for themselves the sordid slum he was standing in. To see the aged, crumbling buildings, some of them as much as twelve and even fourteen years old, engineered to have been torn down and replaced long ago. Long before a tragedy of this kind could strike. To form their own opinion of a council that could allow such a blight to exist on their planet.

Smoothly Lester pivoted his body, one shoulder leading, a counter-balance for the slightly trailing head, editorializing subtly by what he chose to look at, by what he chose to ignore. Flowingly, easily, compensating automatically for even the rise and fall of his own controlled breathing. A beautifully functioning, rock-steady camera vehicle Lester was. It was the least of his interviewing skills.

A closer shot. His thumb brushed a rod on his breastplate. The view in his finders grew larger. Armor-suited men, resting now, but still strapped in the seats of their half-track diggers. Orange-painted against the greening dust and the bright red glow of the police-erected crowd-control barrier force-field like a sheltering dome over them. Through it, visible above and around in all directions, a swirling, shifting mass upon mass of human beings. Some in fliers, others on skimmers. Some strapped in one-man jumpers and even on foot. A boiling, roiling swarm of the morbidly, humanly curious pressing all around, straining toward the little knot of blue-coverall-clad men and their pitifully small, broken burden.

Lester's fingers and palms brushed the rods and buttons of his breast-plate-console. Let the rattle and the clank and the sound of the crowd stay as they are. A shade more of the force-field's rasping hum to warm his viewer's nerve endings . . . to ready them. . . .

The woman's sobbing. His thumb touched a stud. Let it start to come through now. Softly . . . barely hearable . . . subtly swelling.

The little knot of blue-coverall-clad men. A medium shot, then rapidly to a close-up of their burden, the dangling limbs half-hidden by their bodies and the merciful sagging of the blue-green plasti-sheet. A tight shot, but passing . . . the merest flicker. Nothing staring, nothing lingering, nothing in bad taste.

In Lester's right ear was the sound of his own voice, recorded on his way to the scene and before he came upon it so that he would not need to break his silence until his selected moment. His voice giving the boy's age, his group-affiliations, the routine details of his death. All quietly, all monotonously even, the greater to contrast with what was the meat of Lester's program.

Nineteen seconds. The sobbing louder now and growing. The mother, kneeling, body sagged, hands clenched, dark head bowed.

Lester put a hand on her shoulder, letting it show in his finders, knowing that each of his viewers could see it as his own, extended, sympathetic, understanding. . . .

The woman did not respond to his touch. Unobtrusively Lester increased the pressure of his thumb, gouging. She stirred under his hand, shrinking, her head lifting.

Lester's hand darted back to his console.

Her eyes. Dark, dulled, beseeching. *Fine*.

And now Lester spoke. He spoke with practiced hesitance, the gentle respecter, for his viewer, of her desire and right to her privacy at a time like this.

"How do you feel to have lost your only child?" His hands hovering, the woman looking at him . . . *now*.

Her eyes widened, flickeringly. Sorrow surging and pain, deep and of the soul, opened to the finder. Raw, fresh.

Great. I'm right never to test, never to speak until this moment.

"Please try to control yourself. I'm your friend, we're all your friends. Tell us." And he repeated his question.

Her head bent sharply back, the eyes half closing now, her mouth open, the lips trembling, the intensity of her emotion visibly choking the sound in her throat, making of her attempt to speak a silent mouthing.

Easy . . . easy does it.

Her hands came up. Fists, pressing against each other and under her chin. "My baby, my baby," and her voice was a moan.

Lester needed only the one hand, his left. The other he stretched toward the woman, touching her hair, his fingertips only, gently, benevolently; seeing it in his finder, looking deep into her upturned face.

In the corner of Lester's finder the sweep second hand began to wipe the red glow from the timer's face. When it came around to the twelve, except for the sponsor break and his verbal sign-off, he would be off the air.

Sobs began to rock the kneeling woman. Lightly at first a mere staccato catching of the breath, but growing. Growing in a crescendo of violence that, peaking, made of her body a heaving, thrashing, straining animal thing.

Great racking, convulsive sounds rasped from her throat. A thread-thin trickle of blood started from one corner of the tortured mouth.

Enough.

Her head dropped, her whole body now bowed and shaking.

Lester watched his hand go out to her, stop in midair. He did not try to hide its trembling. His fingers closed, his hand came back, not having touched her. Leaving her, huddled, tremulous, to herself and her great sorrow.

Slow fade and . . . go to black.

Ninety seconds. Exactly and on the dot and another of his human-interest segments for the intergalactic network was over; another moment in the life story of a little person had been made immortal.

Lester eased his headgear off, handed it to the waiting technicians, stood rubbing the spots where the temple pieces had pressed. The woman had stopped trembling now and was looking dazed, uncomprehending. *They always do, the subjects.*

Swiftly, but not too roughly, Lester raised up her limp left arm, undid the cuff and stripped off the tiny receptor taped to the wrist. Another he took from her ankle and two more from the back of her skull, from under the concealing black hair. He could have left to one of his technicians this stripping off of the tiny receptors, that, obedient to the commands of his console, sent their impulses impinging upon the nerve streams of his subjects. But Lester felt that doing it himself, this body contact with his subjects, was just one more tiny factor that helped keep fresh his unmistakable feeling of rapport.

His lead technician touched his shoulder from behind, indicating they were about ready for his verbal signature and the one part of his program Lester found distasteful. A compliance with a regulation he felt was onerous and a little demeaning. Some day those who made these artistically pointless rulings would recognize the validity of his technique and perhaps eliminate this abhorrent note. Until then. . . .

Lester leaned forward and spoke into the button mike his technician was holding out to him.

And at the end, ". . . The emotional response of the subject was technically augmented."

47

INTO THE SHOP

Ron Goulart

THE WAITRESS SCREAMED, that was the trouble with live help, and made a flapping motion with her extended arm. Stu Clemens swung sideways in the booth and looked out through the green tinted window at the parking lot. A dark haired man in his early thirties was slumping to his knees, his hands flickering at his sides. Silently the lawagon spun back out of its parking place and rolled nearer to the fallen man.

"There's nobody in that car," said the waitress, dropping a cup of coffee.

She must be new to this planet, from one of the sticks systems maybe. "It's my car," said Clemens, flipping the napkin toggle on the table and then tossing her one when it popped up. "Here, wipe your uniform off. That's a lawagon and it knows what it's doing."

The waitress put the napkin up to her face and turned away.

Out in the lot the lawagon had the man trussed up. It stunned him again for safety and then it flipped him into the back seat for interrogation and identification. "It never makes a mistake," said Clemens to the waitress' back. "I've been Marshall in Territory #23 for a year now and that lawagon has never made a mistake. They build them that way."

The car had apparently given the suspect an injection and he had fallen over out of sight. Three more napkins popped up out of the table unasked. "Damn it," said Clemens and pounded the outlet with his fist once sharply.

"It does that sometimes," said the waitress, looking again at Clemens, but no further. She handed him his check card.

Clemens touched the waitress' arm as he got up. "Don't worry now. The law is always fair on Barnum. I'm sorry you had to see a criminal up close like that."

"He just had the businessman's lunch," the waitress said.

287

"Well, even criminals have to eat." Clemens paid the cash register and it let him out of the drivein oasis.

The cars that had been parked near the lawagon were gone now. When people were in trouble they welcomed the law but other times they stayed clear. Clemens grimaced, glancing at the dry yellow country beyond the oasis restaurant. He had just cleaned up an investigation and was heading back to his office in Hub #23. He still had an hour to travel. Lighting a cigarette he started for the lawagon. He was curious to see who his car had apprehended.

"This is a public service announcement," announced the lawagon from its roof speakers. "Sheldon Kloog, wanted murderer, has just been captured by Lawagon A10. Trial has been held, a verdict of guilty brought in, death sentenced and the sentence carried out as prescribed by law. This has been a public service announcement from the Barnum Law Bureau."

Clemens ran to the car. This was a break. Sheldon Kloog was being hunted across eleven territories for murdering his wife and dismantling all their household androids. At the driver's door the marshall took his ID cards out of his grey trouser pocket and at the same time gave the day's passwords to the lawagon. He next gave the countersigns and the oath of fealty and the car let him in.

Behind the wheel Clemens said, "Congratulations. How'd you spot him?"

The lawagon's dash speaker answered, "Made a positive identification five seconds after Kloog stepped out of the place. Surprised you didn't spot him. Was undisguised and had all the telltale marks of a homicide prone."

"He wasn't sitting in my part of the restaurant. Sorry." Clemens cocked his head and looked into the empty back seat. The lawagons had the option of holding murderers for full cybernetic trial in one of the territorial hubs or, if the murderer checked out strongly guilty and seemed dangerous, executing them on the spot. "Where is he?"

The glove compartment fell open and an opaque white jar rolled out. Clemens caught it. *Earthly Remains Of Sheldon Kloog*, read the label. The disintegrator didn't leave much.

Putting the jar back Clemens said, "Did you send photos, prints, retinal patterns and the rest on to my office."

"Of course," said the car. "Plus a full transcript of the trial. Everything in quadruplicate."

"Good," said Clemens. "I'm glad we got Kloog and he's out of the way." He lit a fresh cigarette and put his hands on the wheel. The car could drive on automatic or manual. Clemens preferred to steer himself. "Start up and head for the hub. And get me my Junior Marshall on the line."

"Yes, sir," said the car.

"Your voice has a little too much treble," said Clemens, turning the lawagon on to the smooth black six lane roadway that pointed flat and straight toward Hub #23.

"Sorry. I'll fix it. This is a public announcement. This is a public announcement. Better?"

"Fine. Now get me Kepling."

"Check, sir."

Clemens watched a flock of dot sized birds circle far out over the desert. He moistened his lips and leaned back slightly.

"Jr. Marshall Kepling here," came a voice from the dash.

"Kepling," said Clemens, "a packet of assorted ID material should have come out of the teleport slot a few minutes ago. Keep a copy for our files and send the rest on to Law Bureau Central in Hub #1.

"Right, sir."

"We just got that murderer, Sheldon Kloog."

"Good work. Shall I pencil him in for a trial at Cybernetics Hall?"

"We already had the trial," said Clemens. "Anything else new?"

"Looks like trouble out near Townten. Might be a sex crime."

"What exactly?"

"I'm not sure, sir," said Kepling. "The report is rather vague. You know how the android patrols out in the towns are. I dispatched a mechanical deputy about an hour ago and he should reach there by mid afternoon. If there's a real case I can drive our lawagon over after you get back here."

Clemens frowned. "What's the victim's name?"

"Just a minute. Yeah, here it is. Marmon, Dianne. Age 25, height 5'6", weight. . . ."

Clemens had twisted the wheel violently to the right. "Stop," he said to the lawagon as it shimmied off the roading. "Dianne Marmon, Kepling?"

"That's right. Do you know her?"

"What are the details you have on the crime?"

"The girl is employed at Statistics Warehouse in Townten. She didn't appear at work this morning and a routine check by a personnel andy found evidence of a struggle in her apartment. The patrol says there are no signs of theft. So kidnapping for some purpose seems likely. You may remember that last week's report from Crime Trends said there might be an upswing of sex crimes in the outlying areas like Townten this season. That's why I said it might be a sex crime. Do you know the girl?''

Clemens had known her five years ago, when they had both been at the Junior Campus of Hub #23 State College together. Dianne was a pretty blonde girl. Clemens had dated her fairly often but lost track of her when he'd transferred to the Police Academy for his final year. ''I'll handle this case myself,'' he said. ''Should take me a little over two hours to get to Townten. I'll check with you enroute. Let me know at once if anything important comes in before that.''

''Yes, sir. You do know her then?''

''I know her,'' said Clemens. To the lawagon he said, ''Turn around and get us to Townten fast.''

''Yes, sir,'' said the car.

Beyond Townseven, climbing the wide road that curved between the flat fields of yellow grain, the call from Jr. Marshall Kepling came. ''Sir,'' said Kepling. ''The patrol androids have been checking out witnesses. No one saw the girl after eleven last night. That was when she came home to her apartment. She was wearing a green coat, orange dress, green accessories. There was some noise heard in the apartment but no one thought much of it. That was a little after eleven. Seems like someone jimmied the alarm system for her place and got in. That's all so far. No prints or anything.''

''Damn it,'' said Clemens. ''It must be a real kidnapping then. And I'm an hour from Townten. Well, the lawagon will catch the guy. There has to be time.''

''One other thing,'' said Kepling.

''About Dianne Marmon?''

''No, about Sheldon Kloog.''

''What?''

''Central has a report that Sheldon Kloog turned himself into a public surrender booth in a park over in Territory #20 this morning. All the ID material matches. Whereas the stuff we sent shows a complete negative.''

''What are they talking about? We caught Kloog.''

''Not according to Central.''

''It's impossible. The car doesn't make mistakes, Kepling.''

''Central is going to make a full checkup as soon as you get back from this kidnapping case.''

''They're wrong,'' said Clemens. ''Okay. So keep me filled in on Dianne Marmon.''

''Right, sir,'' said the Jr. Marshall, signing off.

To his lawagon Clemens said, "What do you think is going on? You couldn't have made a mistake about Sheldon Kloog. Could you?"

The car became absolutely silent and coasted off the road, brushing the invisible shield around the grain fields. Everything had stopped functioning.

"I didn't order you to pull off," said Clemens.

The car did not respond.

Lawagons weren't supposed to break down. And if they did, which rarely happened, they were supposed to repair themselves. Clemens couldn't get Lawagon A10 to do anything. It was completely dead. There was no way even to signal for help.

"For god's sake," said Clemens. There was an hour between him and Dianne. More than an hour now. He tried to make himself not think of her, of what might be happening. Of what might have already happened.

Clemens got out of the lawagon, stood back a few feet from it. "One more time," he said, "will you start?"

Nothing.

He turned and started jogging back toward Townseven. The heat of the day seemed to take all the moisture out of him, to make him dry and brittle. This shouldn't have happened. Not when someone he cared for was in danger. Not now.

Emergency Central couldn't promise him a repair man until the swing shift came on in a quarter of an hour. Clemens requested assistance, a couple of lawagons at least from the surrounding territories. Territory #20 had had a reactor accident and couldn't spare theirs. Territory #21 promised to send a lawagon and a Jr. Marshall over to Townten to pick up the trail of Dianne Marmon's kidnapper as soon as the lawagon was free. Territory #22 promised the same, although they didn't think their car would be available until after nightfall. Clemens finally ordered his own Jr. Marshall to fly over to Townten and do the best he could until a lawagon arrived. A live Jr. Marshall sure as hell couldn't do much, though. Not what a lawagon could.

The little Townseven cafe he was calling from was fully automatic and Clemens sat down at a coffee table to wait for the repairman to arrive. The round light-blue room was empty except for a hunched old man who was sitting at a breakfast table, ordering side orders of hash browns one after another. When he'd filled the surface of the table he started a second layer. He didn't seem to be eating any of the food.

Clemens drank the cup of coffee that came up out of his table and ignored the old man. It was probably a case for a Psych Wagon but Clemens didn't feel up to going through the trouble of turning the man in. He finished his coffee. A car stopped outside and Clemens jumped. It was just a customer.

"How can I do that?" said the repairman as he and Clemens went down the ramp of the automatic cafe. "Look." He pointed across the parking area at his small one man scooter.

Clemens shook his head. "It's nearly sundown. A girl's life is in danger. Damn, if I have to wait here until you fix the lawagon and bring it back I'll lose that much more time."

"I'm sorry," said the small sun-worn man. "I can't take you out to where the car is. The bureau says these scooters are not to carry passengers. So if I put more than 200 pounds on it it just turns off and won't go at all."

"Okay, okay." There were no cars in the parking lot, no one to commandeer.

"You told me where your lawagon is. I can find it if it's right on the highway. You wait."

"How long?"

The repairman shrugged. "Those babies don't break down much. But when they do. Could be a while. Overnight maybe."

"Overnight?" Clemens grabbed the man's arm. "You're kidding."

"Don't break my damn arm or it'll take that much longer."

"I'm sorry. I'll wait here. You'll drive the lawagon back?"

"Yeah. I got a special set of ID cards and passwords so I can get its hood up and drive it. Go inside and have a cup of coffee."

"Sure," said Clemens. "Thanks."

"Do my best."

"Do you know anything about the dinner-for-two tables?" the thin loose-suited young man asked Clemens.

Clemens had taken the table nearest the door and was looking out at the twilight roadway. "Beg pardon?"

"We put money in for a candle and nothing happened, except that when the asparagus arrived its ends were lit. This is my first date with this girl, marshall, and I want to make a good impression."

"Hit the outlet with your fist," said Clemens, turning away.

"Thank you, sir."

Clemens got up and went in to call the Law Bureau answering service in Townten. The automatic voice told him that Jr. Marshall Kepling had just arrived and reported in. He was on his way to the victim's apartment. No other news.

"She's not a victim," said Clemens and cut off.

"Arrest those two," said the old man, reaching for Clemens as he came out of the phone alcove.

"Why?"

"They shot a candle at my table and scattered my potatoes to here and gone."

The young man ran up. "I hit the table like you said and the candle came out. Only it went sailing all the way across the room."

"Young people," said the old man.

"Here," said Clemens. He gave both of them some cash. "Start all over again."

"That's not," started the old man.

Clemens saw something coming down the dark road. He pushed free and ran outside.

As he reached the roadway the lawagon slowed and stopped. There was no one inside.

"Welcome aboard," said the car.

Clemens went through the identification ritual, looking off along the roadway, and got in. "Where's the repairman? Did he send you on in alone."

"I saw through him, sir," said the lawagon. "Shall we proceed to Townten?"

"Yes. Step on it," said Clemens. "But what do you mean you saw through him?"

The glove compartment dropped open. There were two white jars in it now. "Sheldon Kloog won't bother us anymore, sir. I have just apprehended and tried him. He was disguised as a repairman and made an attempt to dismantle an official Law Bureau vehicle. That offense, plus his murder record, made only one course of action possible."

Clemens swallowed, making himself not even tighten his grip on the wheel. If he said anything the car might stop again. There was something wrong. As soon as Dianne was safe Lawagon A 10 would have to go into the shop for a thorough checkup. Right now Clemens needed the car badly, needed what it could do. They had to track down whoever had kidnapped Dianne. "Good work," he said evenly.

The headlights hit the cliffs that bordered the narrow road and long ragged shadows crept up the hillside ahead of them.

"I think we're closing in," said Clemens. He was talking to Jr. Marshall Kepling who he'd left back at the Law Bureau answering service in Townten. He had cautioned Kepling to make no mention of the Kloog business while the car could hear them.

"Central verified the ID on the kidnapper from the prints we found," said Kepling. Surprisingly Kepling had found fingerprints in Dianne's apartment that the andy patrol and the mechanical deputy had missed. "It is Jim Otterson. Up to now he's only done short sentence stuff."

"Good," said Clemens. That meant that Otterson might not harm Dianne. Unless this was the time he'd picked to cross over. "The lawagon," said Clemens, "is holding onto his trail. We should get him now anytime. He's on foot now and the girl is definitely still with him the car says. We're closing in."

"Good luck," said Kepling.

"Thanks," Clemens signed off.

Things had speeded up once he and the lawagon had reached Townten. Clemens had known that. The lawagon had had no trouble picking up the scent. Now, late at night, they were some twenty-five miles out of Townten. They'd found Otterson's car seven miles back with its clutch burned out. The auto had been there, off the unpaved back road, for about four hours. Otterson had driven around in great zigzags. Apparently he had spent the whole of the night after the kidnapping in a deserted storehouse about fifty miles from Townten. He had left there, according to the lawagon, about noon and headed toward Towneleven. Then he had doubled back again, swinging in near Townten. Clemens and the lawagon had spent hours circling around on Otterson's trail. With no more car Otterman and the girl couldn't have come much further than where Clemens and the lawagon were now.

The lawagon turned off the road and bumped across a rocky plateau. It swung around and stopped. Up above was a high flat cliff side, dotted with caves. "Up there, I'd say," said the lawagon. It had silenced its engine.

"Okay," said Clemens. There wasn't much chance of sneaking up on Otterson if he was up in one of those caves. Clemens would have to risk trying to talk to him. "Shoot the lights up there and turn on the speakers."

Two spotlights hit the cliff and a hand mike came up out of the dash. Taking it, Clemens climbed out of the lawagon. "Otterson, this is Marshall Clemens. I'm asking you to surrender. If you don't I'll have to use stun gas on you. We know you're in one of those caves and we can check each one off if we have to. Give up."

Clemens waited. Then half way up the cliff side something green flashed and then came hurtling down. It pinwheeled down the mountain and fell past the plateau.

"What the hell." Clemens ran forward. There was a gully between the cliff and the plateau, narrow and about thirty feet deep. At its bottom now was something. It might be Dianne, arms tangled over interlaced brush.

"Get me a handlight and a line," he called to the lawagon.

Without moving the car lobbed a handbeam to him and sent a thin cord snaking over the ground. "Check."

"Cover the caves. I'm going down to see what that was that fell."

"Ready?"

Clemens hooked the light on his belt and gripped the line. He backed over the plateau edge. "Okay, ready."

The line was slowly let out and Clemens started down. Near the brush he caught a rock and let go of the line. He unhitched the light and swung it. He exhaled sharply. What had fallen was only an empty coat. Otterson was trying to decoy them. "Watch out," Clemens shouted to his car. "It's not the girl. He may try to make a break now."

He steadied himself and reached for the rope. Its end snapped out at him and before he could catch it it whirred up and out of sight. "Hey, the rope. Send it back."

"Emergency," announced the lawagon, its engine coming on.

Up above a blaster sizzled and rock clattered. Clemens yanked out his pistol and looked up. Down the hillside a man was coming, carrying a bound up girl in his arms. His big hands showed and they held pistols. Dianne was gagged but seemed to be alive. Otterson zigzagged down, using the girl for a shield. He was firing not at Clemens but at the lawagon. He jumped across the gully to a plateau about twenty yards from where Clemens had started over.

Holstering his gun Clemens started to climb. He was half way up when he heard Otterson cry out. Then there was no sound at all.

Clemens tried to climb faster but could not. The gully side was jagged and hard to hold on to. Finally he swung himself up on the plateau.

"This is a public service announcement," said the lawagon. "Sheldon Kloog and his female accomplice have been captured, tried, sentenced, and executed. This message comes to you from the Law Bureau. Thank you."

Clemens roared. He grabbed up a rock in each hand and went charging at the car. "You've killed Dianne," he shouted. "You crazy damn machine."

The lawagon turned and started rolling toward him. "No you don't, Kloog," it said.

48

INTO YOUR TENT I'LL CREEP

Eric Frank Russell

MORFAD SAT IN the midship cabin and gloomed at the wall. He was worried and couldn't conceal the fact. The present situation had the frustrating qualities of a gigantic rat trap. One could escape it only with the combined help of all the other rats.

But the others weren't likely to lift a finger either on his or their own behalf. He felt sure of that. How can you persuade people to try to escape a jam when you can't convince them that they're in it, right up to the neck?

A rat runs around a trap only because he is grimly aware of its existence. So long as he remains blissfully ignorant of it, he does nothing. On this very world a horde of intelligent aliens had done nothing about it through the whole of their history. Fifty skeptical Altairans weren't likely to step in where three thousand million Terrans had failed.

He was still sitting there when Haraka came in and informed, "We leave at sunset."

Morfad said nothing.

"I'll be sorry to go," added Haraka. He was the ship's captain, a big, burly sample of Altairan life. Rubbing flexible fingers together, he went on, "We've been lucky to discover this planet, exceedingly lucky. We've become blood brothers of a life-form fully up to our own standard of intelligence, space-traversing like ourselves, friendly and cooperative."

Morfad said nothing.

"Their reception of us has been most cordial," Haraka continued enthusiastically. "Our people will be greatly heartened when they hear our report. A great future lies before us, no doubt of that. A Terran-Altairan combine will be invincible. Between us we can explore and exploit the entire galaxy."

Morfad said nothing.

297

Cooling down, Haraka frowned at him. "What's the matter with you, Misery?"

"I am not overjoyed."

"I can see that much. Your face resembles a very sour *shamsid* on an aged and withered bush. And at a time of triumph, too! Are you ill?"

"No." Turning slowly, Morfad looked him straight in the eyes. "Do you believe in psionic faculties?"

Haraka reacted as if caught on one foot. "Well, I don't know. I am a captain, a trained engineer-navigator, and as such I cannot pretend to be an expert upon extraordinary abilities. You ask me something I am not qualified to answer. How about you? Do you believe in them?"

"I do—*now?*"

"Now? Why now?"

"The belief has been thrust upon me." Morfad hesitated, went on with a touch of desperation. "I have discovered that I am telepathic."

Surveying him with slight incredulity, Haraka said, "You've discovered it? You mean it has come upon you recently?"

"Yes."

"Since when?"

"Since we arrived on Terra."

"I don't understand this at all," confessed Haraka, baffled. "Do you assert that some pecularity in Terra's conditions has suddenly enabled you to read my thoughts?"

"No, I cannot read your thoughts."

"But you've just said that you have become telepathic."

"So I have. I can hear thoughts as clearly as if the words were being shouted aloud. But not your thought nor those of any member of our crew."

Haraka leaned forward, his features intent. "Ah, you have been hearing *Terran* thoughts, eh? And what you've heard has got you bothered? Morfad, I am your captain, your commander. It is your bounden duty to tell me of anything suspicious about these Terrans."

"I know no more about these humaniods than you do," said Morfad. "I have every reason to believe them genuinely friendly but I don't know what they think."

"But by the stars, man, you—"

"We are talking at cross-purposes," Morfad interrupted. "Whether I do or do not overhear Terran thoughts depends upon what one means by Terrans."

"Look," said Haraka, "whose thoughts *do* you hear?"

Steeling himself, Morfad said flatly, "Those of Terran dogs."

"Dogs?" Haraka lay back and stared at him. *"Dogs?"* Are you serious?"

"I have never been more so. I can hear dogs and no others. Don't ask me why because I don't know. It is a freak of circumstance."

"And you have listened to their minds ever since we jumped to Earth?"

"Yes."

"What sort of things have you heard?"

"I have had pearls of alien wisdom cast before me," declared Morfad, "and the longer I look at them the more they scare the hell out of me."

"Get busy frightening me with a few examples," invited Haraka, suppressing a smile.

"Quote: the supreme test of intelligence is the ability to live as one pleases without working," recited Morfad. "Quote: the art of retribution is that of concealing it beyond all suspicion. Quote: the sharpest, most subtle, most effective weapon in the comos is flattery."

"Huh?"

"Quote: if a thing can think, it likes to think that it is God—treat it as God and it becomes your willing slave."

"Oh, no!" denied Haraka.

"Oh, *yes!*" insisted Morfad. He waved a hand toward the nearest port. "Out there are three thousand million petty gods. They are eagerly panted after, fawned upon, gazed upon with worshiping eyes. Gods are very gracious toward those who love them." He made a spitting sound that lent emphasis to what followed. "The lovers know it—and love comes cheap."

Haraka said, uneasily, "I think you're crazy."

"Quote: to rule successfully the ruled must be unconscious of it." Again the spitting sound. "Is that crazy? I don't think so. It makes sense. It works. It's working out there right now."

"But—"

"Take a look at this." He tossed a small object into Haraka's lap. "Recognize it?"

"Yes, it's what they call a cracker."

"Correct. To make it, some Terrans plowed fields in all kinds of weather, rain, wind and sunshine, sowed wheat, reaped it with the aid of machinery other Terrans had sweated to build. They transported the wheat, stored it, milled it, enriched the flour by various processes, baked it, packaged it, shipped it all over the world. When humanoid Terrans want crackers they've got to put in man-hours to get them."

"So—?"

"When a dog wants one he sits up, waves his forepaws and admires his god. That's all. Just that."

"But, darn it, man, dogs are relatively stupid."

"So it seems," said Morfad, dryly.

"They can't really *do* anything effective."

"That depends upon what one regards as effective."

"They haven't got hands."

"And don't need them—having brains."

"Now see here," declaimed Haraka, openly irritated, "we Altairans invented and constructed ships capable of roaming the spaces between the stars. The Terrans have done the same. Terran dogs have not done it and won't do it in the next million years. When one dog has the brains and ability to get to another planet I'll eat my cap."

"You can do that right now," Morfad suggested. "We have two dogs on board."

Haraka let go a grunt of disdain. "The Terrans have given us those as a memento."

"Sure they gave them to us—at whose behest?"

"It was wholly a spontaneous gesture."

"Was it?"

"Are you suggesting that dogs put the idea into their heads?" Haraka demanded.

"I know they did," retorted Morfad, looking grim. "And we've not been given two males or two females. Oh no, sir, not on your life. One male and one female. The givers said we could breed them. Thus in due course our own worlds can become illuminated with the undying love of man's best friend."

"Nuts!" said Haraka.

Morfad gave back, "You're obsessed with the old, out-of-date idea that conquest must be preceded by aggression. Can't you understand that a wholly alien species just naturally uses wholly alien methods? Dogs employ their own tactics, not ours. It isn't within their nature or abilities to take us over with the aid of ships, guns and a great hullabaloo. It *is* within their nature and abilities to creep in upon us, their eyes shining with hero-worship. If we don't watch out, we'll be mastered by a horde of loving creepers."

"I can invent a word for your mental condition," said Haraka. "You're suffering from caniphobia."

"With good reasons."

"Imaginary ones."

"Yesterday I looked into a dogs' beauty shop. Who was doing the bathing, scenting, powdering, primping? Other dogs? Hah! Humanoid females were busy dolling 'em up. Was *that* imaginary?"

"You can call it a Terran eccentricity. It means nothing whatever. Besides, we've quite a few funny habits of our own."

"You're dead right there," Morfad agreed. "And I know one of yours. So does the entire crew."

Haraka narrowed his eyes. "You might as well name it. I am not afraid to see myself as others see me."

"All right. You've asked for it. You think a lot of Kashim. He always has your ear. You will listen to him when you'll listen to nobody else. Everything he says makes sound sense—to you."

"So you're jealous of Kashim, eh?"

"Not in the least," assured Morfad, making a disparaging gesture. "I merely despise him for the same reason that everyone else holds him in contempt. He is a professional toady. He spends most of his time fawning upon you, flattering you, pandering to your ego. He is a natural-born creeper who gives you the Terradog treatment. You like it. You bask in it. It affects you like an irresistible drug. It works—and don't tell me that it doesn't because all of us know that it *does.*"

"I am not a fool. I have Kashim sized up. He does not influence me to the extent you believe."

"Three thousand million Terrans have four hundred million dogs sized up and are equally convinced that no dog has a say in anything worth a hoot."

"I don't believe it."

"Of course you don't. I had little hope that you would. Morfad is telling you these things and Morfad is either crazy or a liar. But if Kashim were to tell you while prostrate at the foot of your throne you would swallow his story hook, line and sinker. Kashim has a Terradog mind and uses Terradog logic, see?"

"My disbelief has better basis than that."

"For instance?" Morfad invited.

"Some Terrans are telepathic. Therefore if this myth of subtle mastery by dogs were a fact, they'd know of it. Not a dog would be left alive on this world." Haraka paused, finished pointedly, "They don't know of it."

"Terran telepaths hear the minds of their own kind but not those of dogs. I hear the minds of dogs but not those of any other kind. As said before, I don't know why this should be. I know only that it *is.*"

"It seems nonsensical to me."

"It would. I suppose you can't be blamed for taking that viewpoint. My position is difficult; I'm like the only one with ears in a world that is stone-deaf."

Haraka thought it over, said after a while, "Suppose I were to accept everything you've said at face value—what do you think I should do about it?"

"Refuse to take the dogs," responded Morfad, promptly.

"That's more easily said than done. Good relations with the Terrans are vitally important. How can I reject a warm-hearted gift without offending the givers?"

"All right, don't reject it. Modify it instead. Ask for two male or two female dogs. Make it plausible by quoting an Altairan law against the importation of alien animals that are capable of natural increase."

"I can't do that. It's far too late. We've already accepted the animals and expressed our gratitude for them. Besides, their ability to breed is an essential part of the gift, the basic intention of the givers. They've presented us with a new species, an entire race of dogs."

"You said it!" confirmed Morfad.

"For the same reason we can't very well prevent them from breeding when we get back home," Haraka pointed out. "From now on we and the Terrans are going to do a lot of visiting. Immediately they discover that our dogs have failed to multiply they'll become generous and sentimental and dump another dozen on us. Or maybe a hundred. We'll then be worse off than we were before."

"All right, all right." Morfad shrugged with weary resignation. "If you're going to concoct a major objection to every possible solution we may as well surrender without a fight. Let's abandon ourselves to becoming yet another dog-dominated species. Requote: to rule successfully the ruled must be unconscious of it." He gave Haraka the sour eye. "If I had my way, I'd wait until we were far out in free space and then give those two dogs the hearty heave-ho out the hatch."

Haraka grinned in the manner of one about to nail down a cockeyed tale once and for all. "And if you did that it would be proof positive beyond all argument that you're afflicted with a delusion."

Emitting a deep sigh, Morfad asked, "Why should it?"

"You'd be slinging out two prime members of the master race. Some domination, eh?" Haraka grinned again. "Listen, Morfad, according to your own story you know something never before known or suspected and you're the only one who does know it. That should make you a mighty menace to the entire species of dogs. They wouldn't let you live long enough to thwart them or even to go round advertising the truth. You'd soon

302

be deader than a low-strata fossil.'' He walked to the door, held it open while he made his parting shot. ''You look healthy enough to me.''

Morfad shouted at the closing door, ''Doesn't follow that because I can hear their thoughts they must necessarily hear mine. I doubt that they can because it's just a freakish—''

The door clicked shut. He scowled at it, walked twenty times up and down the cabin, finally resumed his chair and sat in silence while he beat his brains around in search of a satisfactory solution.

''The sharpest, most subtle, most effective weapon in the cosmos is flattery.''

Yes, he was seeking a means of coping with four-footed warriors incredibly skilled in the use of Creation's sharpest weapon. Professional fawners, creepers, worshipers, man-lovers, ego-boosters, trained to near-perfection through countless generations in an art against which there seemed no decisive defense.

How to beat off the coming attack, contain it, counter it?

''Yes, God!''

''Certainly, God!''

''Anything you say, God!''

How to protect oneself against this insidious technique, how to quarantine it or—

By the stars! that was it—*quarantine* them! On Pladamine, the useless world, the planet nobody wanted. They could breed there to their limits and meanwhile dominate the herbs and bugs. And a soothing reply would be ready for any nosey Terran tourist.

''The dogs? Oh, sure, we've still got them, lots of them. They're doing fine. Got a nice world of their very own. Place called Pladamine. If you wish to go see them, it can be arranged.''

A wonderful idea. It would solve the problem while creating no hard feelings among the Terrans. It would prove useful in the future and to the end of time. Once planted on Pladamine no dog could ever escape by its own efforts. Any tourists from Terra who brought dogs along could be persuaded to leave them in the canine heaven specially created by Altair. There the dogs would find themselves unable to boss anything higher than other dogs, and, if they didn't like it, they could lump it.

No use putting the scheme to Haraka who was obviously prejudiced. He'd save it for the authorities back home. Even if they found it hard to credit his story, they'd still take the necessary action on the principle that it is better to be sure than sorry. Yes, they'd play safe and give Pladamine to the dogs.

303

Standing on a cabin seat, he gazed out and down through the port. A great mob of Terrans, far below, waited to witness the coming take-off and cheer them on their way. He noticed beyond the back of the crowd a small, absurdly groomed dog dragging a Terran female at the end of a thin, light chain. Poor girl, he thought. The dog leads, she follows yet believes *she* is taking *it* some place.

Finding his color-camera, he checked its controls, walked along the corridor and into the open air lock. It would be nice to have a picture of the big send-off audience. Reaching the rim of the lock he tripped headlong over something four-legged and stubby-tailed, that suddenly intruded itself between his feet. He dived outward, the camera still in his grip, and went down fast through the whistling wind while shrill feminine screams came from among the watching crowd.

Haraka said, ''The funeral has delayed us two days. We'll have to make up the time as best we can.'' He brooded a moment, added, ''I am very sorry about Morfad. He had a brilliant mind but it was breaking up toward the end. Oh well, it's a comfort that the expedition has suffered only one fatality.''

''It could have been worse, sir,'' responded Kashim. ''It could have been you. Praise the heavens that it was not.''

''Yes, it could have been me.'' Haraka regarded him curiously. ''And would it have grieved you, Kashim?''

''Very much indeed, sir. I don't think anyone aboard would feel the loss more deeply. My respect and admiration are such that—''

He ceased as something padded softly into the cabin, laid its head in Haraka's lap, gazed soulfully up at the captain. Kashim frowned with annoyance.

''Good boy!'' approved Haraka, scratching the newcomer's ears.

''My respect and admiration,'' repeated Kashim in louder tones, ''are such that—''

''Good boy!'' said Haraka again. He gently pulled one ear, then the other, observed with pleasure the vibrating tail.

''As I was saying, sir, my respect—''

''Good boy!'' Deaf to all else, Haraka slid a hand down from the ears and massaged under the jaw.

Kashim favored Good Boy with a glare of unutterable hatred. The dog rolled a brown eye sidewise and looked at him without expression. From that moment Kashim's fate was sealed.

304

49

ITSELF!

A. E. van Vogt

ITSELF, KING OF the Philippine Deep—that awesome canyon where the sea goes down six miles—woke from his recharge period and looked around suspiciously.

His Alter Ego said, "Well, how is it with Itself today?"

The Alter Ego was a booster, a goader, a stimulant to action, and, in his limited way, a companion.

Itself did not answer. During the sleep period, he had drifted over a ravine, the walls of which dropped steeply another thousand feet. Suspiciously, Itself glared along the canyon rim.

. . . Not a visual observation. No light ever penetrated from above into the eternal night here at the deepest bottom of the ocean. Itself perceived the black world which surrounded him with high frequency sounds which he broadcast continuously in all directions. Like a bat in a pitch dark cave, he analyzed the structure of all things in his watery universe by interpreting the returning echoes. And the accompanying emotion of suspicion was a device which impelled Itself to record changing pressures, temperatures and current flows. Unknown to him, what he observed became part of the immense total of data by which faraway computers estimated the interrelationship of ocean and atmosphere, and thus predicted water and air conditions everywhere with uncanny exactness.

His was almost perfect perception. Clearly and unmistakably, Itself made out the intruder in the far distance of that twisting ravine. A ship! Anchored to rock at the very edge of the canyon.

The Alter Ego goaded, "You're not going to let somebody invade your territory, are you?"

Instantly, Itself was furious. He activated the jet mechanism in the underslung belly of his almost solid metal body. A nuclear reactor immediately heated the plates of the explosion chamber. The seawater which flowed through the chamber burst into hissing clouds of steam, and he jetted forward like a missile.

Arriving at the ship, Itself attacked the nearest of four anchor lines with the nuclear-powered heat beam in his head. When he had severed it, he turned to the second cable, and burned through it. Then he moved for the third cable.

But the startled beings aboard the alien ship had spotted the twenty-foot monster in the black waters below.

"Analyze its echo pattern!" came the command. That was done, with total skill.

"Feed the pattern back through the infinite altering system till the recorders register a response."

The significant response was: Itself forgot what he was doing. He was drifting blankly away, when his Alter Ego goaded, "Wake up! You're not going to let them get away with that, are you?"

The defeat had galvanized Itself to a more intense level of rage. He became multiples more sensitive. Now, he simply turned out the alien echo copies.

The new greater anger triggered a second weapon.

Itself's echo system of perception, normally monitered to be safe for all living things in the sea, suddenly strengthened. It became a supersonic beam. Purposefully, Itself started toward the ship.

Watching his aproach, the enemy decided to take no chances. "Pull the remaining anchors in!"

Itself headed straight for the nearest part of the vessel. Instantly, those ultrasonic waves started a rhythmic vibration on the hard wall, weakening it.

The metal groaned under a weight of water that at these depths amounted to thousands of tons per square inch. The outer wall buckled with a metallic scream.

The inner wall trembled, but held.

At that point, the appalled defenders got a counter-vibration started, nullified the rhythm of Itself's projections, and were safe.

But it was a sorely wounded ship that now drifted helplessly in a slow current. The aliens had thus far used no energy that might be detected from the surface. But they had come to Earth to establish a base for invasion. Their instructions were to accumulate enough data about underwater currents to enable them to leave the Deep, and eventually to be able to drift near land, launch atom bombs and drift away again. For this purpose they were mightily armed, and they refused to die in these black waters without a fight.

"What can we do about that deamon?"

"Blast it!" someone urged.

"That's dangerous." The alien commander hesitated.

"We can't be in greater danger than we already are."

"True," said the commander, "but frankly I don't know why he's armed at all, and I can't believe he has anything more. Set up a response system. If he does attack with anything new, it will automatically fire back. We'll take that much of a chance."

The second setback had driven Itself completely berserk. He aimed his nuclear pellet gun, firing twice. In the next split-second a blast from the invader pierced his brain.

The Alter Ego yelled, "You're not going to let them get away with that, are you?"

But the king of the Philippine Deep was dead, and could no longer be goaded.

In due course, a report was given to weather headquarters: "Computer Center shows no recent data from Itself. It therefore seems as if another of the wartime antisubmarine water-weather robots has worn out. You may recall that these electronic monsters were programmed to suspicion, anger, and the idea that they owned part of the ocean. After the war, we could never get these creatures to surface; they were too suspicious of us."

The ocean of water, like the ocean of air far above, flowed and rolled and moved in a ceaseless, dynamic, driving motion many, many times more powerful, however, than any comparable air current. Yet, in essence, the quadrillions of water movements solely and only balanced each other out.

Through the Philippine Deep there began presently to flow an enormous balancing river. It carried the aliens' invasion vessel in a long, slanting, upward direction. But several weeks passed before the drifting ship actually broke surface, and another day or two before it was seen.

A naval patrol boarded it, found the aliens dead more than a month from concussion, and—after examining the damage—correctly analyzed what had happened.

And so—a new king "woke" to the first "day" of his reign, and heard *his* Alter Ego say, "Well, Itself, what's the program?"

Itself glared with a royal suspicion.

50

JOB OFFER

Henry Slesar

THEY SAT AT the kitchen table and talked, Birnham and his wife; not that the living room wasn't more comfortable, but since the end of War Four they had somehow begun to regard the kitchen as their meeting room, where the peeling linoleum surface served as a council table.

And besides, Wally wouldn't hear them from the kitchen, from behind the locked door of his small bedroom. They could talk freely here, without their words hurting him any more than he was injured now.

"This is what I hate," Birnham said. "Him loafin' around his bedroom all day, never going out, not a peep outa him."

"He's brooding," his wife said. "You know how he feels, Joe. Sort of mixed up and everything, about this offer. He's thinking it over."

"What's there to think over? Say, you know how many jobs the videopaper listed this morning, in the whole goddamn cityzone? Fifteen!"

"But you *know* how he feels about it. He'll have to do just what he hated all his life. Let people *stare* at him."

"He should be used to it by now. Aw, listen, Sheila, I know what the kid's going through. Hell, of course I do. But he's over twenty-one; he knows the score. He ain't never gonna be drafted, not the way he is, all funny like that, so we can't depend on the Army feeding and housing him. You know I ain't earned more than fifty stamps since the War. He should be grateful Mr. Metelkopf made him the offer."

"He's such a nice man," Sheila said, smoothing her skirt. "He talks so respectable. I thought people like that were—well, you know. Not so educated."

"Metelkopf's the biggest man in the circus business. He knows his stuff, don't worry about that. I mean, it won't be like any old freak show Wally would be in. It would be more like a—well, like a scientific curiosity."

309

"But the staring," his wife sighed. "Wally always hated the staring. He hated being so different from everybody."

"But he *is* different. He should see a mirror once in a while. He should go out into the Shelters and see people. He should FACE FACTS."

"Don't shout, Joe. Nothing wrong with his ears."

Birnham looked contrite. "I'm sorry, Sheila. But it's tough on me, too. They're talking about another stampcut at the plankton plant. And all this talk about War Five—"

"No," Sheila said, going white. "Don't say that, Joe. I mean, the President told us—"

"So maybe it was just talk. Things are rough, Sheila. We got no excuse not to look facts in the face. Wally, too."

"Shush," his wife said, looking at the doorway of the kitchen where their son stood watching.

"I made up my mind," Wally said.

"That's good," his mother crooned. "Anything you want to do is all right with us, Wally. You know that."

"Sure," the boy said bitterly, and went to the telephone. He looked up before he dialed, and said: "I'm telling Metelkopf yes. In case you want to know."

Birnham and his wife watched their son complete the call. They watched with pain in their eyes, the pain that never eased when his tall slim figure was in their sight, the strange balance of his weird body, the arms equidistant and uniform, the head neatly at midpoint of his square shoulders, the two legs growing straight from his torso to the ground. They sighed, and Birnham put his arms abot his wife's shoulders, and the third arm reached up and gently wiped the tear that was squeezing its way from the single eye set into her wrinkled brow.

51

JUST DESSERTS

Irving Fang

THE OBA OF Benin Province in central Nigeria disliked making these secretive trips.

He would be much more comfortable, he reminded himself, if he had remained in his palace among his four wives. He should let the petty chiefs or the British courts hand out justice, especially during the season of the Harmattan, when the winds from the Sahara brought fine grains of sand over the jungle, stinging the eyes and filling the nostrils.

But there was Mr. Ruggs to think about. The British District Officer of Benin Province had not been pleased at finding that two of the Oba's tax collectors had taken bribes. And the Oba's political enemies would love to discover more proof that he was not fit to reign. The Oba, who had ceremoniously eaten a portion of the heart of the Oba before him, would live to see his enemies crawling in the dust before him.

So he had taken of late to touring away from the capital whenever he learned of a wrongdoing. If he administered justice on the spot, he would show his interest in the public welfare. Also, the crime would not be listed on the public records.

Now he sat on a camp chair in a clearing in the center of the village of Ikgenge, a portly man in his fifties, his white hair a sharp contrast to his deep brown skin. His bright blue robe was getting gray with sand, despite the wide palm fronds held above his head by two of the palace royal guard.

Three accused thieves, flanked by files of constables, marched up and prostrated themselves fully before him in the proper manner, sprawling with fingertips outstretched, their foreheads in the dust.

The Oba languidly motioned twice with his thick hand. The first wave permitted the men to rise. The second informed the chief constable of Ikgenge that he could proceed with the reading of the charges.

311

The chief constable was proud of his opportunity, obviously, to demonstrate before the Oba himself that here was a man of intelligence and learning—the type of chief constable who was able not only to write, but to read what he had written. He puffed out his barrel of a chest, pulled in his equally large barrel of a stomach, and bowed low. Then he straightened and proceeded to the business at hand, first looking severely at the accused trio.

He opened his notebook and began: "Musa Adetunji, Ayo Badaru and Oseni Ishola stand accused on the crime of thievery."

At this the crowd of villagers around the clearing murmured a low, prolonged "Ohhh!"

The chief constable looked around sternly, then pulled a pair of gold-rimmed spectacles from his pocket and clamped them firmly on his nose. He proceeded:

"It was noted by me, Chief Constable Adenekan Akanni, that the accused men were adding new roofing to their houses. It was also noted by me, Chief Constable Adenekan Akkani, that the substance used by the accused to roof their houses was not of tins from gasoline containers, but was of metal of the best quality.

"Upon questioning the accused as to the nature of how they came into the possession of this roofing, I learned from the accused that they had not purchased it."

Another drawn out "Ohhh!" from the crowd produced another stern look, this time from over the tops of the gold-rimmed spectacles. The Oba of Benin, meanwhile, brushed at a mosquito.

"When the accused by the chief constable were asked from where the new roofing came, the accused all declared that they had found it in the bush, at a time when they engaged themselves in the pursuit of hunting.

"The accused further stated that they were unable to recall the exact place they came upon the roofing metal.

"As chief constable of Ikgenge, I examined the evidence upon the roof and concluded they had come upon it by means of thievery. They are therefore so charged," he concluded, closing his notebook and carefully replacing his glasses in his pocket.

The Oba shifted his weight in the camp chair. "Bring me a piece of the roofing," he said.

A young constable stepped forward bearing a jagged chunk of dull, bluish-gray metal that had been flattened with a rock. The Oba took it, studied it closely, then handed it to one of his aides.

"How do you plead?" the Oba asked the trembling trio.

"I am innocent, Your Highness," Musa Adetunji said fervently.

"I, too, am innocent, Your Highness," Ayo Badaru said. "No matter how my belly cried for food, I would not take the property of another man."

Oseni Ishola's knees shook violently and all he could manage was a wide-eyed nod of his head.

"Are you innocent also?"

"Y-Yes, Your Highness," Oseni stammered.

The Oba frowned, brushing at another mosquito. "Where did you find the metal?"

Ayo, the tallest of the three, replied. "Your Highness, we were hunting for small animals in the bush two days from here. We had found none and we were hungry. The day was hot and the Harmattan sand was blowing on us. Suddenly we heard a noise."

"Your Highness," Musa interrupted, "from the sky came a great round piece of metal and it fell almost on top of us."

Gasps went up from the crowd.

"Why did you not tell this to the chief constable?" the Oba asked.

"We were afraid he would laugh at us," Musa said.

The crowd laughed.

"We were afraid he would not believe us," Ayo added.

The crowd gave a disbelieving set of sniggers.

"Why do you tell this story now?" the Oba asked.

"We know the Oba will believe us," Ayo answered.

"It is the truth," Musa declared.

Oseni Ishola nodded vigorously.

The crowd murmured acceptance of the story.

"Proceed," said the Oba.

"We were afraid to approach the metal," Musa said. "We were also afraid to run. We waited. Nothing happened. I said to my friends that the metal had been sent to us from Ogun."

At the mention of Ogun, the powerful god of iron, a great "Ohhh!" went up from the assembled villagers. Even the Oba sucked in his breath.

Ogun, the most potent of all the gods, the god who had given such strength to the British, Ogun had favored three of their fellows. Surely, their village was smiled upon and would be lucky.

"But," the chief constable protested to the accused men, "you did not tell me that Ogun had presented you with the new roofing."

The crowd jeered at the chief constable.

The Oba held up his hand and the crowd fell silent. After his initial surprise, he realized there must be more to the story than a gift from Ogun. He had seen airplanes on his visits to Lagos, the capital city of Nigeria. He reasoned this was an airplane and further reasoned that airplanes do not fly by themselves.

He turned to the three accused before him.

"What else did you see?"

"Nothing, Your Highness," Musa said nervously. "We carried away as much of the metal as we could. We made new roofs for our houses."

'We were very hot and hungry," Ayo added, "but Ogun gave us strength to bear away a great portion of his gift."

The Oba frowned again. "What became of the man inside the metal?"

The three men fell back a step as if they had been struck. Their bodies shook and sweat poured from their brows. Then, one by one, they again prostrated themselves before their ruler.

The Oba grew angry. "Stand up," he said, "and tell me of the man."

The accused rose to their feet.

"They were not men," Ayo said sincerely.

"How many were there?"

"Two," said Ayo. "They were small, about so high," he indicated, holding his hand to the level of his waist. "And they were the color of fresh plantain."

Yellow-green men, three feet high, the Oba thought. He had not known there were such men.

"Ayo speaks the truth," Musa said. "Your Highness, they were the color of plantain, very small, and they stood and walked on three legs."

The assembled villagers "Ohhhed" very loudly.

"They had very long ears which stuck from the tops of their heads," Ayo recalled.

The Oba of Benin turned to the third accused.

"Oseni Ishola," he said, "the men who stand accused with you have described the two in the metal as small, the color of fresh plantain, with three legs and long ears on top of their heads. Yet you say nothing."

Oseni gulped. "Your Highness, they speak true."

"Can you tell any more about them?" the Oba asked.

Oseni Ishola thought a long while. Then he smiled bashfully and said, "They tasted like chickens."

52

THE LAST BRAVE INVADER

Charles L. Fontenay

LAURIA SWEPT DOWN the spiral staircase in regal dignity, and wished there were someone there to witness her entrance. She walked across the parlor to the gunrack and strapped a holstered pistol to her hip, just above the rustling flare of the full skirt of her evening dress.

The green sun's slanting rays in the parlor window told her it was late afternoon, nearly time to get started. She went to the full-length mirror. Beside the mirror hung the framed copy of the Constitution of Pamplin, hand-lettered on parchment. In bold red letters it proclaimed:

> We, the people of Pamplin, hold that:
> 1. No government is the best government.
> 2. A man's home is his castle.
> 3. A woman's rights are equal to a man's rights.
> 4. Only the brave deserve the fair.

Lauria looked in the mirror, almost fearfully.

She saw with approval the breadth of her hips, the erectness of her shoulders. With more reluctance, her eyes rose to her face. There was still beauty there, she told herself, to the discerning eye. That touch of slackness to the jaw, that faint hollowness of cheek: those were no doubt exaggerated by the dimness of the room.

In a table drawer, Lauria found jars and tubes. From them she carefully filled in a fuller form for her mouth, dabbed heavily at her cheeks, touched up her eyes, smeared over her jawline. She fluffed out the thinning blond hair and donned a light scarf, then she removed the heavy bars from the front door. She went out, and locked its triple locks behind her. She gazed around cautiously and stepped lightly down the gravelled path. Around the house, the grounds were a solid mass of blooming flowers. Lauria had plenty of

315

time to spend in the garden. The baskets and other handicraft articles that were her means of income left her a good deal of leisure, and cooking and household chores were routine and brief.

Farther from the house, the grounds looked better kept than they were. It was fortunate that the blue grass of the planet Pamplin grew short and neat, for Lauria never would have been able to keep the ten acres of her property trimmed. But the big trees that shaded the grounds had dropped twigs and leaves that she wouldn't clear away until the big effort of the fall clean-up.

The path curved down past a small cleared area in which a dozen upright wooden markers were spaced in rows. This was the cemetery.

She paused to look out across the neat rows of markers. There were men buried there. Twelve young men. They had died by her hand, in accordance with the Constitution and the law.

At one end of the cemetery stood a large wooden plaque on which she had carved the Constitution of Pamplin. Many times had her mother explained the meaning of the Constitution to Lauria, when Lauria was a little girl and still intruding on her mother's privacy.

"The people who colonized Pamplin left Earth many years ago because there they always had to sacrifice some of their individual rights to some government," her mother had said. "There are many kinds of governments, but all of them try to regulate people. And to regulate people, they have to invade people's privacy.

"The people of Pamplin came to this world because we don't want any government. We believe that every man and woman should have his individual right to do as he pleases, without other people bothering him."

"But what does No. 4 mean, Mother?" Lauria had asked.

" *'Only the brave deserve the fair?'* "

"That means," replied her mother, for Lauria was fourteen and deserved to know these things, "that a woman on Pamplin is not subservient to the whims of men. No man may approach her and take her in his arms unless he has fought his way through the defenses of her home. Then they may agree to share the home, if they wish, but no woman of any character will permit a man to do this until he has proved his valor by fighting his way to her."

"Then my father must have been a brave man, wasn't he, Mother?"

"Yes, he was, my dear," said her mother, smiling tenderly. "He was very persuasive, too."

Lauria never saw her father, and no other man invaded the privacy of her mother's home while she lived there. Two men tried, and Lauria remembered the tense stirrings about the darkened house in the dead of night, the flash and roar of the guns, and her frightened glimpses of the men her mother had shot down as they tried to break in.

Her father must have been very courageous, Lauria thought. She constructed a handsome picture of her father in her mind, and dreamed of the day a handsome man like him would conquer her, when she lived in her own home.

Lauria's mother had some property on which she wanted Lauria to build a house, but Lauria was impatient. Even though her mother would hire men from town, Lauria would have to do much of the work herself and it would take years. So at sixteen, Lauria got her a house, ready-built.

She crept past the defenses of one of the best homes in the area. She broke into the house at night and killed the defender, a tired old man, in a blazing gun battle. The house became her home, and she improved its defenses.

Her ownership of the house, and her manner of taking it, gave her an immediate social standing far above that of her mother. She knew that she was envied: the bright-haired, beautiful young woman who held the ramparts of the big house and challenged all comers to conquer her.

There were men who tried, and the first nearly succeeded. Even now, after many years, she could remember Poll's youthful, arrogant face, his lazy smile. They had met in the market place.

"An attractive spitfire, if ever I saw one," he had said to her. "Would you surrender to my arms, pretty one?"

"If you're strong enough to come and take me," she challenged, fire singing in her blood.

And that night he had come. In the starlight she fired from her windows at the shadowy figure that flitted among the bushes and trees, and powder smoke hung heavy in the air. It was after several hours and a long silence, when she thought he had given up and gone away, that he almost surprised her.

She was crouching in the parlor, waiting for the dawn, when there was a slight noise behind her. She whirled, whipping up her gun, and he was coming toward her swiftly and silently from the hall, a smile of triumph on his handsome face.

He was holding out his arms for her and there was no weapon in his hand when she shot him down.

She wept for a long time over his fair body, and knew to her shame that she had wanted him to conquer. Then she took him out and buried him beneath the grass. His grave was the first one, and behind it later she erected the wooden plaque bearing the words of the Constitution of Pamplin.

Others had tried, and their graves were here, with Poll's. And the years had passed, and no man had overrun the defenses of Lauria's house.

The frost of autumn was in her veins now as she looked at the graves of twelve young men, who had been young and eager in the years when she had been young. Slowly she turned away, went out the barred front gate of her property and waited for the crowd of merrymakers she would accompany to the party in town.

The music reverberated gaily amid the rafters of the huge community hall. At one end a fire blazed merrily in a big fireplace. Young couples, and their elders, danced variations of the steps that had been brought from earth generations ago.

No one wore weapons here, although every person in the hall had worn or carried a gun on the way here. The guns were checked at the entrance, and the doors were barred against any lawless raider.

Here, as in the market daily, people congregated. Here they were people and not individuals.

Outside, between here and their homes, they were individuals again, but still friendly, if wary. They carried their arms, they were careful of their language, they watched the people around them for signs of aggression. Outside was a code of conduct that was different from the sociable code inside, a code that condoned a duel over an insult, that recognized robbery, rape and even death if one were caught unarmed and alone.

And in their homes . . . well, there was Cholli Rikkard. He was one-armed because of a wound he had suffered conquering Fanni in her home. Cholli had been a gay fellow who had stormed house after house of pretty women before, but after that he settled down with Fanni and they now had five children. They shared their privacy, but half a dozen times Cholli had stayed up all night fighting off those who would invade it.

The strange thing was that one or more of those who had sought to invade Cholli's home and take his wife and house from him might be dancing here tonight, perhaps chatting amiably with Cholli. Cholli might even know them for the attackers. Here they were all friends, suspending their cherished privacy for weekly companionship.

Lauria was one of those who sat among the oldest, and talked unhappily with those on either side of her. It was not that she was that old, for she wasn't. It was that Lauria's home now had the reputation of a deadly, unassailable fortress, and few men cared even to dance with her. It was that they feared her, she told herself as she sat there after only two dances.

"Care to dance this one, Miss Lauria?"

She looked up, startled. It was Cholli Rikkard, smiling at her, holding out his one arm apologetically.

She arose, gratefully, and took his hand. She and Cholli were old friends. Perhaps it was the sympathy of the handicapped for the handicapped: the man with only one arm for the woman with (perhaps?) too much stern pride.

"Tell me something, Cholli," said Lauria as they danced. "Is it true that many women deliberately allow men to invade their privacy?"

He looked at her blandly.

"That would be a violation of the Constitution, Lauria," he said.

"I know it would," she said impatiently. "But do they?"

"I've heard rumors."

"I've heard rumors, too, but I want the truth. You know the truth, Cholli. You conquered quite a few women before Fanni shot you in the arm."

He grinned.

"Fanni always was a poor shot," he said. "Or maybe she's a better shot than I think. Yes, Lauria, it's true. The Constitution is the law, and it's right in principle, but you have to face facts. If men and women adhered to the letter of the law in . . . well, sex . . . Pamplin would be depopulated by now. I thought everybody knew that."

"I didn't," said Lauria miserably. "I suspected . . . I'd heard a lot of talk. But . . . well, tell me, Cholli, how is it done? How do men know, I mean, when a woman is going to wink at the Constitution and let a man enter her home without fighting his way in?"

"It depends, Lauria. I suppose most often a woman has an understanding with a certain man and he gives some sort of signal when he comes to her house, so he won't be shot. Some women—quite a few, it is—just sort of let it be known around that they won't shoot if a man comes around. That's more dangerous, though, and they have to be on guard."

"I'd think so," said Lauria indignantly. "Another woman could take advantage of something like that and make a good haul."

There was a silence. Then Cholli said slyly:

"Did you want to get a message to some man—or get the word around that . . . ?"

"Certainly not!" she retorted firmly. "I abide by the Constitution, and I value my privacy."

"Okay, Lauria. I just thought I could get the word passed for you." He grinned. "If it weren't for this bum arm, I might have tried for you myself before now."

The music stopped and they parted.

"Wait, Cholli!" cried Lauria in a low intense voice. He turned and came back to her, looking at her quizzically.

"Cholli," she said, almost in a whisper, "pass the word around tonight that no young man will find my home defended!"

She turned her back quickly, her face flaming, and left the hall, picking up her scarf and gun at the door. She walked home alone, swiftly, holding up the hem of her skirt with her left hand and hoping savagely that someone would try to waylay her.

It was midnight when the alarm bell sounded.

Lauria had been sitting in the parlor, with no light but that of the fire, a hot drink in her hand, lost in turbulent thoughts.

Her thoughts twisted slightly. Had she made it plain to Cholli that only young men would be welcome?

But how could she toss aside everything in which she had believed for so long, on an impulse? Would she not redeem herself by shooting down any invader?

Shame was upon her now, for having told Cholli what she did. It was not the perverse shame that had run hot in her that night when she had fought Poll and wanted to be defeated, but the shame of having done what she scorned other women for doing.

But Lauria was lonely now, and the fire was not as warm as it once had been. How many years had it been—ten? fifteen?—since the last young man had won her outer wall, only to fall beneath her bullets in the moon-shadows?

Could she turn now to the ways of other women, to dissemble, to shoot wide of the mark and put up a false defense? Could she now betray the weapons that had served her so well and true?

Or would there be a thirteenth grave in the little cemetery on the morrow?

The bell chattered nervously.

She arose and threw ashes on the fire. A weariness was in her bones. She took a gun from the rack and made the rounds of the house, checking the locks of doors and windows.

All was secure. More lithely, like a pantheress, she went from window to window, looking out, her gun ready. Some of the old wine of battle quickened in her blood.

The moon was bright, and the trees stood in great pools of shadow on the grounds. The bushes stood like dark, bulky sentinels.

At last she saw him, a moving shadow against the still shadows, creeping closer to the house. Her gun came up and she took aim, carefully, through the barred window. Her hands were as cold as ice on the gunstock.

For a moment he was still, and she lost him against the shadows. Then he moved again.

Her gun blossomed roaring flame and its stock kicked against her shoulder.

The shadow leaped, became a man as it fled across a path of moonlight. He was young, and he was smiling toward the window. Then he was swallowed up in the deeper shadows.

For a moment she was aghast, unbelieving. She had missed! Then, like a frigid hand clutching her heart, came the realization: deliberately, without conscious volition, she had pulled the gun muzzle aside when she fired.

She leaned against the wall, weak and perspiring. It was true, then. She yearned so deeply for a man, she so feared the age that crept up on her, that the principles of the Constitution no longer held real meaning for her.

She did not seek to fire again. She knelt on the floor by the window and waited, looking listlessly into the embers of the fire across the room. She felt suspended in a nightmare.

She heard the crack as the lock was broken on a window in the rear of the house, and still she did not stir. But her heart began beating faster, a cold beating that did not warm her body. She began to shiver uncontrollably.

She heard the soft, wary footsteps as he came through the house. In the dimness, she saw his bulk come through the parlor door. A black veil passed momentarily before her eyes, and her gun slipped from lax fingers and fell to the floor with a clatter.

He leaped to one side, and the glow of the dying fire glinted from his weapon.

But she stood up against the window, in the moonlight, and spread her hands so he could see she was no longer armed.

"I am helpless," she said in a voice that nearly choked her. "I cannot resist your taking me for your love."

His laugh boomed out in the rich darkness, and she could see that he did not lower his weapon.

"Have no fear of that, old woman," he said. "I'm only going to put you out and take your house."

53

THE LAST MEN

Frank Belknap Long

MALJOC HAD COME of age. On a bright, cold evening in the fall of the year, fifty million years after the last perishing remnant of his race had surrendered its sovereignty to the swarming masters, he awoke proud and happy and not ashamed of his heritage. He knew, and the masters knew, that his kind had once held undisputed sway over the planet. Down through dim eons the tradition—it was more than a legend—had persisted, and not all the humiliations of the intervening millenniums could erase its splendor.

Maljoc awoke and gazed up at the great moon. It shone down resplendently through the health-prison at the summit of the hormorium. Its rays, passing through the prism, strengthened his muscles, his internal organs, and the soft parts of his body.

Arising from his bed, he stood proudly erect in the silver light and beat a rhythmic tattoo with his fists on his naked chest. He was of age, and among the clustering homoriums of the females of his race which hung suspended in the maturing nurseries of Agrahan was a woman who would share his pride of race and rejoice with him under the moon.

As the massive metallic portals of the homorium swung inward, a great happiness came upon him. The swarming masters had instructed him wisely as he lay maturing under the modified lunar rays in the nursery homorium.

He knew that he was a man and that the swarming masters were the decendants of the chitin-armored, segmented creatures called insects, which his ancestors had once ruthlessly despised and trampled under foot. At the front of his mind was this primary awareness of origins; at the back a storehouse of geologic data.

He knew when and why his race had succumbed to the swarming

masters. In imagination he had frequently returned across the wide wastes of the years, visualizing with scientific accuracy the post-Pleistocene glacial inundations as they streamed equatorward from the poles.

He knew that four of the earth's remaining continents had once lain beneath ice sheets a half mile thick, and that the last pitiful and cold-weakened remnants of his race had succumbed to the superior sense-endowments of the swarming masters in the central core of a great land mass called Africa, now submerged beneath the waters of the southern ocean.

The swarming masters were almost godlike in their endowments. With their complex and prodigious brains, which seemed to Maljoc as all-embracing as the unfathomable forces which governed the constellations, they instructed their servitors in the rudiments of earth history.

In hanging nursery homoriums thousands of men and women were yearly grown and instructed. The process of growth was unbelievably rapid. The growth-span of the human race had once embraced a number of years, but the swarming masters could transform a tiny infant into a gangling youth in six months, and into a bearded adult, strong-limbed and robust, in twelve or fourteen. Gland injections and prism-ray baths were the chief causal agents of this extraordinary metamorphosis, but the growth process was further speeded up by the judicious administration of a care-fully selected diet.

The swarming masters were both benevolent and merciless. They de-spised men, but they wished them to be reasonably happy. With a kind of grim, sardonic toleration they even allowed them to choose their own mates, and it was the novelty and splendor of that great privilege which caused Maljoc's little body to vibrate with intense happiness.

The great metallic portal swung open, and Maljoc emerged into the starlight and looked up at the swinging constellations. Five hundred feet below, the massive domed dwellings of Agrahan glistened resplendently in the silvery radiance, but only the white, glittering immensity of the Milky Way was in harmony with his mood.

A droning assailed his ears as he walked along the narrow metal terrace toward the swinging nurseries of the women of his race. Several of the swarming masters were hovering in the air above him, but he smiled up at them without fear, for his heart was warm with the splendor of his mission.

The homoriums, sky promenades, and air terraces were suspended above the dwellings of Agrahan by great swinging cables attached to gas-inflated, billowing air floats perpetually at anchor. As Maljoc trod the terrace, one of the swarming masters flew swiftly between the cables and swooped down upon him.

Maljoc recoiled in terror. The swarming masters obeyed a strange, inhuman ethic. They reared their servitors with care, but they believed also that the life of a servitor was simply a little puff of useful energy. Sometimes when in sportive mood, they crushed the little puffs out between their claws.

A chitin-clad extremity gripped Maljoc about his middle and lifted him into the air. Calmly then, and without reversing its direction, the swarming master flew with him toward the clouds.

Up and up they went, till the air grew rarefied. Then the swarming master laid the cool tips of its antennae on Maljoc's forehead and conversed with him in a friendly tone.

"Your nuptial night, my little friend?" it asked.

"Yes," replied Maljoc. "Yes—yes—it is."

He was so relieved that he stammered. The master was pleased. The warmth of its pleasure communicated itself to Maljoc through the vibrations of its antennae.

"It is well," it said. "Even you little ones are born to be happy. Only a cruel and thoughtless insect would crush a man under its claw in wanton pleasure."

Maljoc knew, then, that he was to be spared. He smiled up into the great luminous compound-eyes of his benefactor.

"It amused me to lift you into the air," conveyed the master. "I could see that you wanted to soar above the earth, that your little wingless body was vibrant with happiness and desire for expansion."

"That is true," said Maljoc.

He was grateful and—awed. He had never before been carried so high. Almost the immense soaring wings of the master brushed the stratosphere.

For a moment the benevolent creature winged its way above the clouds, in rhythmic glee. Then, slowly, its body tilted, and it swept downward in a slow curve toward the sky terrace.

"You must not pick a too-beautiful mate," cautioned the master. "You know what happens sometimes to the too-beautiful."

Maljoc knew. He knew that his own ancestors had once pierced the ancestors of the swarming masters with cruel blades of steel and had set them in decorative rows in square boxes because they were too beautiful. His instructors had not neglected to dwell with fervor on the grim expiation which the swarming masters were in the habit of exacting. He knew that certain men and women who were too beautiful were frequently lifted from the little slave world of routine duties in the dwellings of the masters and anesthetized, embalmed, and preserved under glass in the museum mausoleums of Agrahan.

The master set Maljoc gently down on the edge of the sky terrace and patted him benevolently on the shoulder with the tip of its hindermost leg. Then it soared swiftly upward and vanished from sight.

Maljoc began to chant again. The Galaxy glimmered majestically in the heavens above him, and as he progressed along the sky promenade he feasted his gaze on the glowing misty fringes of stupendous island universes lying far beyond the milky nebulae to which his little race and the swarming master belonged.

Nearer at hand, as though loosely enmeshed in the supporting cables, the pole star winked and glittered ruddily, while Sirius vied with Betelgeuse in outshining the giant, cloud-obscured Antares, and the wheeling fire chariot of the planet Mars.

Above him great wings droned, and careening shapes usurped his vision. He quickened his stride and drew nearer, and ever nearer, to the object of his desire.

The nursery homorium of the women of his race was a towering vault of copper on the edge of the cable-suspended walk. As he came abreast of it he began to tremble, and the color ebbed from his face. The women of his race were unfathomable, dark enigmas to him—bewildering shapes of loveliness that utterly eluded his comprehension.

He had glimpsed them evanescently in pictures—the swarming masters had shown him animated pictures in colors—but why the pictures enraptured and disturbed him so he did not know.

For a moment he stood gazing fearfully up at the massive metal portal of the homorium. Awe and a kind of panicky terror contended with exultation in his bosom. Then, resolutely, he threw out his chest and began to sing.

The door of the homorium swung slowly open, and a dim blue light engirded him as he stood limned in the aperture. The illumination came from deep within the homorium. Maljoc did not hesitate. Shouting and singing exultantly, he passed quickly through the luminous portal, down a long, dim corridor, and into a vast, rectangular chamber.

. The women of his race were standing about in little groups. Having reached maturity, they were discussing such grave and solemn topics as the past history of their kind and their future duties as obedient servants of the swarming master. Without hesitation, Maljoc moved into the center of the chamber.

The women uttered little gasping cries of delight when they beheld him. Clustering boldly about him, they ran their slim white hands over his glistening tunic and caressed with fervor his beard and hair. They even gazed exultantly into his boyish gray eyes, and when he flushed they tittered.

Maljoc was disturbed and frightened. Ceasing to sing, he backed away precipitously toward the rear of the chamber.

"Do not be afraid," said a tall, flaxen-haired virago at his elbow. "We will not harm you."

Maljoc looked at her. She was attractive in a bold, flamboyant way, but he did not like her. He tried to move away from her, but she linked her arm in his and pulled him back toward the center of the chamber.

He cried out in protest. "I do not like you!" he exclaimed. "You are not the kind of woman—"

The amazon's lips set in hard lines. "You are far too young to know your own mind," she said. "I will be a good wife to you."

As she spoke, she thrust out a powerful right arm and sent three of her rivals sprawling.

Maljoc was panic-stricken. He pleaded and struggled. The woman was pulling him toward the center of the chamber, and two of the other women were contending with her.

The struggle terminated suddenly. Maljoc reeled, lost his balance, and went down with a thud on the hard metallic floor. The metal bruised his skull, stunning him.

For several seconds a wavering twilight engulfed Maljoc's faculties. Needles pierced his temples, and the relentless eyes of the amazon burned into his brain. Then, slowly and painfully, his senses cleared, and his eyelids flickered open in confused bewilderment.

Two compassionate blue eyes were gazing steadily down at him. Dazedly, Maljoc became aware of a lithely slim form, and a clear, lovely face. As he stared up in wonderment, the apparition moved closer and spoke in accents of assurance.

"I will not let them harm you," she said.

Maljoc groaned, and his hand went out in helpless appeal. Slim, firm fingers encircled his palm, and a gentle caress eased the pain in his forehead.

Gently he drew his comforter close and whispered: "Let us escape from these devils."

The woman beside him hesitated. She seemed both frightened and eager. "I am only eight months old," she told him in a furtive whisper. "I am

327

really too young to go forth. They say, too, that it would be dangerous, for I am—'' A blush suffused her cheeks.

''She is dangerously beautiful,'' said a harsh voice behind her. ''The instructors here are indifferent to beauty, but when she goes forth she will be seized and impaled. You had better take me.''

Maljoc raised himself defiantly on his elbow. ''It is my privilege to choose,'' he said. ''And I take this woman. Will you go forth with me, my little one?''

The woman's eyes opened widely. She looked slowly up at the amazon, who was standing in the shadows behind her, and said in a voice which did not tremble: ''I will take this man. I will go forth with him.''

The amazon's features were convulsed with wrath. But she was powerless to intervene. Maljoc was privileged to choose, and the woman was privileged to accept. With an infuriated shrug she retreated farther into the shadows.

Maljoc arose from the floor and gazed rapturously at his chosen mate. She did not evade his scrutiny. As Maljoc continued to stare at her, the strained look vanished from his face and mighty energies were released within him.

He stepped to her and lifted her with impassioned chantings into the air. Her long hair descended and enmeshed his shoulders, and as he pressed her to his heart her arms tightened clingingly about him.

The other women clustered quickly about the exultant couple. Laughing and nudging one another, they examined the strong biceps of the bridegroom and ran their fingers enviously through the woman's dark hair.

Maljoc ignored them. Holding his precious burden very firmly in his muscular arms, he walked across the chamber, down the long outer corridor, and out through the massive door. Above him in another moment the Cyclopean luminous cables loomed beneath far-glimmering stars. He walked joyfully along the sky promenade, chanting, singing, unquenchably happy in his little hour of triumph and rapture.

The woman in his arms was unbelievably beautiful. She lay limply and calmly in his embrace, her eyes luminous with tenderness. Orion gleamed more brightly now, and the great horned moon was a silver fire weaving fantastically in and out of the nebulae-laced firmament.

As Maljoc sang and chanted, the enormous droning shapes above him seemed mere alien intruders in a world of imperishable loveliness. He thought of himself now as lord of the earth and the sky, and the burden in his arms was more important in his sight than his destiny as a servitor and the benefits which the swarming masters had promised to bestow upon him if he served them diligently and well.

He no longer coveted slave joys and gratifications. He wished to be forever his own master under the stars. It was a daring and impious wish, and as if aware of his insurgent yearnings a great form came sweeping down upon him out of the sky. For an instant it hovered with sonorously vibrating wings in the air above him. But Maljoc was so obsessed with joy that he ignored the chill menace of its presence. He walked on, and the woman in his arms shared his momentary forgetfulness.

The end of the pathetic and insane dream came with a sickening abruptness. A great claw descended and gripped the woman's slim body, tearing her with brutal violence from Maljoc's clasp.

The woman screamed twice shrilly. With a harsh cry, Maljoc leaped back. As he shook with horror, a quivering feeler brushed his forehead and spoke to him in accents of contempt:

"She is too beautiful for you, little one. Return to the homorium and choose another mate."

Fear and awe of the swarming masters were instinctive in all men, but as the words vibrated through Maljoc's brain he experienced a blind agony which transcended instinct. With a scream he leaped into the air and entwined his little hands about the enormous bulbous hairs on the master's abdomen.

The master made no attempt to brush him off. It spread its gigantic lacy wings and soared swiftly into the sky. Maljoc tore and pulled at the hairs in a fury of defiance. The swiftness of the flight choked the breath in his lungs, and his eyes were blinded by swirling motes of dust. But though his vision was obscured, he could still glimpse dimly the figure of the woman as she swung limply in the clasp of the great claw a few yards above him.

Grimly, he pulled himself along the master's abdomen toward the claw. He pulled himself forward by transferring his fingers from hair to hair. The master's flat, broad stinger swung slowly toward him in a menacing arc, but he was sustained in his struggle by a sacrificial courage which transcended fear.

Yet the stinger moved so swiftly that it thwarted his daring purpose. In a fraction of time his brain grew poignantly aware that the stinger would sear his flesh before he could get to his dear one, and the realization was like a knife in his vitals. In despair and rage, he thrust out his puny jaw and sank his teeth deep into the soft flesh beneath him. The flesh quivered.

At the same instant the master swooped and turned over. Maljoc hit again. It screeched with pain and turned over and over, and suddenly, as it careened in pain, a white shape fell from its claw.

Maljoc caught the shape as it fell. With one hand clinging to the hair of

329

the master's palpitating abdomen, and the other supporting the woman of his choice, he gazed downward into the abyss.

A mile below him the unfriendly earth loomed obscurely through riven tiers of cirrus clouds. But Maljoc did not hesitate. With a proud, exultant cry he tightened his hold on the woman and released his fingers from the hair.

The two lovers fell swiftly to the earth. But in that moment of swooning flight that could end only in destruction, Maljoc knew that he was mightier than the masters, and having recaptured for an imperishable instant the lost glory of his race, he went without fear into darkness.

54

LAST WARNING

Mack Reynolds

DESPITE THE WIDELY publicized radar posts encircling our nation and the continuously alerted jet squadrons at its borders, the space ship was about to land before it was detected.

It settled gracefully, quietly, onto an empty field in northern New Jersey. And so unexpected was the event, so unbelievable the fact that man was being visited by aliens from space, that it was a full half hour before the first extra was on the streets in New York, and forty minutes before the news buzzed through the Kremlin.

It might have taken considerably longer for man in Earth's more isolated areas to hear of the event had not the alien taken a hand at this point. Approximately an hour after the landing, into the mind of every human on Earth, irrespective of nation, language, age, or intellect, came the thought telepathically:

We come in Peace. Prepare to receive our message.

It was a month before the message came.

During that period, more than ninety-nine percent of the Earth's population became aware of the visitor from space. Radio, television, newsreel, telegraph, and newspapers reached the greater number; but word of mouth and even throbbing drums played their part. In four weeks, savages along the Amazon and shepherds in Sinkiang knew that visitors had arrived with a message for man.

And all awaited the message: scientist and soldier, politician and re-volutionist, millionaire and vagrant, bishop and whirling dervish, banker and pickpocket, society matron and street walker. And each was hoping for one thing, and afraid he'd hear another.

All efforts at communication with the alien ship had failed. The various welcoming delegations from the State of New Jersey, from the United

331

States, and even from the United Nations, were ignored. No sign of life aboard was evident, and there seemed no means of entrance to the spacecraft. It sat there impassively; its tremendous, saucer-like shape seemed almost like a beautiful monument.

At the end of a month, when world-wide interest in the visitor from space was at its height, the message came. And once again it was impressed upon the mind of every human being on Earth:

Man, know this: Your world is fated to complete destruction. Ordinarily, we of the Galactic Union would not have contacted man until he had progressed much further and was ready to take his place among us. But this emergency makes necessary that we take immediate steps if your kind is to be saved from complete obliteration.

In order to preserve your race, we are making efforts to prepare another planet, an uninhabited one, to receive your colonists. Unfortunately, our means for transporting you to your new world are limited; only a handful can be taken. You are safe for another five of your Earth years. At the end of that period we will return. Have a thousand of your people ready for their escape.

The President of the United States lifted an eyebrow wearily and rapped again for order.

"Gentlemen, please! . . . Let us get back to the fundamental question. Summed up, it amounts to this: only one thousand persons, out of a world population of approximately two billion, are going to be able to escape the Earth's destruction. In other words, one out of every two million. It is going to be most difficult to choose."

Herr Ernst Oberfeld tapped his glasses fretfully on the conference table. "Mr. President, it need not be quite as bad as all that. After all, we must choose the Earth's best specimens to carry on our race. I believe we will find that the combined populations of Europe and North America total somewhat less than a billion. If we go still further and eliminate all inferior. . . ."

Monsieur Pierre Duclos flushed. "Herr Oberfeld should keep in mind that his presence at this meeting at all was opposed vigorously by some of the delegates. Isn't it somewhat too soon after his country's debacle to again broadcast its super-race theories?"

The British representative spoke up. "My dear Duclos, although I agree with you completely in essence, still it must be pointed out that if we were to handle this allocation on a strictly numerical basis, then our Chinese friends would be allotted something like 200 colonists, while Great Britain would have perhaps twenty.''

Maxim Gregoroff grunted. ''Hardly enough for the Royal Family, eh?''

Lord Harriman was on his feet. ''Sir, I might echo what Monsieur Duclos has said to Herr Oberfeld. It was in spite of the protest from a considerable number of delegates to this conference that your nation is represented at all.''

Gregoroff's fist thumped on the table and his face went beet red. ''It is as expected! You plan to monopolize the escape ship for the imperialistic nations! The atom bomb will probably be used to destroy all other countries!''

The President of the United States held up his hand. This whole thing was getting more chaotic by the minute. As a matter of fact, instructions from Congress were that he explain that the United States expected to have at least one third of the total. This, in view of the fact that the aliens had landed in New Jersey, obviously seeing the United States was the foremost nation of the world, and, further, in view of the fact that this country was a melting pot of all nations and consequently produced what might be called the ''average'' member of the human race.

However, that would have to wait. Order had to be brought to this conference if anything was to be accomplished.

''Gentlemen, gentlemen, please!'' he called. ''These accusations. We are getting nowhere. I have taken the liberty to make arrangements to have the representative of the newly formed Congress of American Sciences address you. Are you agreeable?'' He raised his eyebrows inquiringly, and meeting no objection, pressed the button on the table before him.

Professor Manklethorp was ushered in, bobbed his head to the assembled delegates and came to the point immediately. ''The problem which you are discussing has many ramifications. I would like to bring to your attention a few which should be examined with care.

''First, the choice of colonists must not be on a national basis, nor on one based on political or monetary prominence. If it is, we, as a race, are doomed. This new planet, no matter how well prepared for us by the Galactic Union, is going to be a challenge such as man has never faced before. This challenge cannot be met by politicians, no matter how glib, nor by wealthy men, no matter how many dollars they possess, nor by titled ones, no matter how old and honored their names. We must pick trained specialists who will be able to meet the problems that arise in the new world.

333

"Our congress recommends that all persons, of all nations, who have college degrees be given thorough tests both for I.Q. and for accumulated knowledge, and that the highest thousand be chosen irrespective of nation or race."

Pandit Hari Kuanai smiled quietly. "May I ask the learned professor a question?"

"Of course. That is why I am here. We want only to have this matter decided on a strictly scientific basis."

"My poverty-stricken country has a population of possibly one fifth of the world total, but fewer university men than one of your large cities might boast. Your desire to choose men by the I.Q. has its merits, but I have no doubt that in my country we have men of tremendous intelligence who cannot read or write, aside from having a university degree. Must my widely illiterate people go unrepresented in the new world?"

A muscle twitched in the professor's face. "Needless to say, the Congress of American Sciences has considered that. However, we must view this matter in a spirit of sacrifice. The best of the world's population must go to the new world. Possibly whole nations will go without representation. It is too bad . . . but, unfortunately, necessary."

Sven Carlesen put up his finger for recognition. "It seems to me there is another serious loophole in the professor's recommendation. He wants the thousand to be made up of university graduates of high I.Q. and considerable accumulated knowledge. I am afraid I foresee the new world being populated with elderly scholars." He smiled. "Like the professor himself, who, I understand, has a phenomenal I.Q."

Monsieur Duclos nodded. "He is right. We must consider the need to send perfect physical specimens." He looked down at his own small and bent body. "Gentlemen," he said wryly, "has it occurred to you that none of us here at this conference are suitable to be represented among the thousands?"

They ignored him.

A pale-faced delegate in black, who had thus far said nothing, spoke up softly, "I have been instructed to inform you that our organization demands that all of the colonists be of the true faith."

His words were drowned by the shouting of half a dozen of the conference delegates. Loud above them all could be heard the bellow of Maxim Gregoroff.

"Our Union now includes the population of approximately half the world. Our allotment, consequently, will be five hundred colonists, of the thousand. We will choose them by our own methods."

Lord Harriman murmured, "Undoubtedly, by starting at the top of the party membership list and taking the first five hundred names beginning with your leader."

The President of the United States ran his hand through his hair and then roughly down the side of his face. A messenger handed him a slip of paper. He read it and intensified his pounding on the table.

"Gentlemen," he shouted, "If Professor Manklethorp is through, we have here a request from the International Physical Culture Society to have their representative heard."

"I know," Sven Carleson said. "He wants all of the colonists to be able to chin themselves twenty-five times as the first requisite."

At the end of the five-year period the space ship came again, settling into the identical field where it had first landed. This time a delegation awaited it, and a multitude that stretched as far as the eye could see.

A telepathic message came from the visitor from space almost immediately.

Choose from your number three representatives to discuss the situation with us.

Within ten minutes, three advanced and entered the ship by way of a port that opened before them as they approached. Among their number was Pierre Duclos. A passage stretched before them, and, seeing no one, they hesitated a moment before following it to its further end. Monsieur Duclos led the way, depending only slightly on his cane to aid his bent body.

A door opened and they were confronted by the figure of a man seated at a desk. It was several moments before they realized that the entity before them was masked so cleverly that they had been led to believe him human.

He said in faultless English, "I note that you have penetrated my disguise. I thought it would be easier for you if I hid my true appearance. Until your people are used to alien life forms, I must use this measure."

Monsiuer Duclos bowed. "We appreciate your consideration, but I assure you that our. . . ."

The alien waved a gloved hand. "Please, no argument. My appearance would probably nauseate you. But it is of no importance. Pray be seated." He noted the cane, and nodded to the little Frenchman. "You, sir, must be highly thought of to rate being chosen one of the thousand in view of your age and health."

Although he was not at ease in the presence of the representative of the Galactic Union, Monsieur Duclos allowed himself a wry smile. "You misunderstand. I am not one of the colonists. My presence here at this

335

meeting is an honor that has been awarded me in return for some small services in aiding in the selection of the favored ones.''

''And what were these services?''

''Of no real importance. I suppose you might say that the most important was that I was the first to refuse to be a colonist.''

Bently, one of the other Earthmen, spoke up, ''Had it not been for Pierre Duclos, it is doubtful if the thousand would have been chosen, and even possible that there would be no Earth to which to return for your colonists.''

Behind the mask the eyes of the alien gleamed. ''Enlighten me further, please.''

Duclos demurred. ''You honor me overmuch. Mr. Bently. Let us approach the problem of the colonists and their transportation.''

But John Bently went on. ''For more than two years after your ship's departure, complete confusion reigned in regard to selection of the thousand. Happily, all-out warfare between nations had been avoided, although conditions were rapidly coming to a point where it was momentarily expected.

''Each race, each nation, each religion, even each sex thought they should have the greater representation. And each of these groups in turn were divided into subgroups by wealth, age, class, education, and others. Almost everyone on Earth knew of some reason why he should be one of the colonists. And most of us were willing to take any steps to make our desire come true.''

The alien said, ''That was to be expected. And then?''

''And then Pierre Duclos formed his Society for Racial Preservation whose first requisite for membership was a refusal to become one of the colonists. The purpose of the organization was to find the thousand most suitable colonists without regard to race, nationality, creed, color, education, class, wealth, or any other grouping.

''At first, the growth of membership was slow, but, after a time, man saw that his chance of survival as an individual was practically nil, that his chance of being chosen was at best less than one in two million. When he realized this, his next desire was to make sure that, even though he as an individual was doomed, the race survived. Membership in the society grew rapidly and internationally. The members, you might say, were fanatical. Why not? They knew that they had less than five years to live. Why not sacrifice those last years of life to such a noble cause?

''As the society grew in strength, nothing could stand before it. Governments that stood in the way were overthrown, social systems abolished, prejudices and institutions that had stood for centuries were wiped out. It became necessary to institute world government, to guarantee to all equal opportunity. Step by step, the society took the measures necessary to insure the selection of the best specimens Earth had to offer.

"And scientific development was pushed to the utmost. We wished to send our colonists off with as much as Earth could possibly give them. We eliminated a dozen diseases that have plagued us for centuries; we devised a thousand new tools and techniques."

"In short," said the alien, "because of this stimulus, man has progressed as much in these past few years as he could have expected in the next fifty."

"That is correct," Pierre Duclos said. "It is unfortunate that now we have on our threshold a world really worth living in, that it is fated to be destroyed."

"I see," said the alien, while what would have been a human smile on a human face flickered on his. "I am glad to report that the danger which confronted the Earth has been removed and the need to populate the new planet with colonists in order to preserve your race is now eliminated.

"Gentlemen, the Earth is safe. Man may go on with his plans without fear of destruction."

Monsieur Duclos fingered his cane thoughtfully while the other two Earthmen jumped to their feet, thumped each other's backs, shouted, and otherwise demonstrated their joy. They finally dashed from the room and from the spacecraft to give the news to the world.

The alien eyed the little Frenchman. "And why have you remained?"

"I do not believe the world was faced with destruction, monsieur. I have come to the concluson that you have perpetrated a farce upon mankind."

The alien sat himself down at the desk again. "I see you will need an explanation. But you are wrong, you know. Faced with destruction you were. The destruction, however, was not a matter of collision with some other body, or whatever you might have imagined. The destruction would have come from within. Man was on the verge of destroying himself. One more conflict or, at most, two would have done it.

"The Galactic Union has long been aware of man, who has developed mechanicallly in a phenomenal manner but has not been able to develop socially to the point where his science is less than a danger. This ship was sent to you in hopes of accomplishing exactly what has been accomplished. We believed your racial instinct would be strong enough to unite you when the race as a whole thought it was threatened with extinction."

The alien got to his feet. "I am afraid we must leave now. Let me say that I hope that man will soon be able to take his place in the Galactic Union."

Monsieur Duclos winced. "The Galactic Union," he said. "The League of Nations and the United Nations were bad enough." He smiled wryly. "And I thought that with the establishment of a world government, we had abolished such conferences forever. I can just see myself as the first delegate from Earth. Heaven forbid!"

55

LIGHT OF OTHER DAYS

Bob Shaw

LEAVING THE VILLAGE behind, we followed the heady sweeps of the road up into a land of slow glass.

I had never seen one of the farms before and at first found them slightly eerie—an effect heightened by imagination and circumstance. The car's turbine was pulling smoothly and quietly in the damp air so that we seemed to be carried over the convolutions of the road in a kind of supernatural silence. On our right the mountain sifted down into an incredibly perfect valley of timeless pine, and everywhere stood the great frames of slow glass, drinking light. An occasional flash of afternoon sunlight on their wind bracing created an illusion of movement, but in fact the frames were deserted. The rows of windows had been standing on the hillside for years, staring into the valley, and men only cleaned them in the middle of the night when their human presence would not matter to the thirsty glass.

They were fascinating, but Selina and I didn't mention the windows. I think we hated each other so much we both were reluctant to sully anything new by drawing it into the nexus of our emotions. The holiday, I had begun to realize, was a stupid idea in the first place. I had thought it would cure everything, but, of course, it didn't stop Selina being pregnant and, worse still, it didn't even stop her being angry about being pregnant.

Rationalizing our dismay over her condition, we had circulated the usual statements to the effect that we would have *liked* having children—but later on, at the proper time. Selina's pregnancy had cost us her well-paid job and with it the new house we had been negotiating and which was far beyond the reach of my income from poetry. But the real source of our annoyance was that we were face to face with the realization that people who say they want children later always mean they want children never. Our nerves were thrumming with the knowledge that we, who had thought ourselves so

339

unique, had fallen into the same biological trap as every mindless rutting creature which ever existed.

The road took us along the southern slopes of Ben Cruachan until we began to catch glimpses of the gray Atlantic far ahead. I had just cut our speed to absorb the view better when I noticed the sign spiked to a gatepost. It said: "SLOW GLASS—Quality High, Prices Low—J.R. Hagan." On an impulse I stopped the car on the verge, wincing slightly as tough grasses whipped noisily at the bodywork.

"Why have we stopped?" Selina's neat, smoke-silver head turned in surprise.

"Look at that sign. Let's go up and see what there is. The stuff might be reasonably priced out here."

Selina's voice was pitched high with scorn as she refused, but I was too taken with my idea to listen. I had an illogical conviction that doing something extravagant and crazy would set us right again.

"Come on," I said, "the exercise might do us some good. We've been driving too long anyway."

She shrugged in a way that hurt me and got out of the car. We walked up a path made of irregular, packed clay steps nosed with short lengths of sapling. The path curved through trees which clothed the edge of the hill and at its end we found a low farmhouse. Beyond the little stone building tall frames of slow glass gazed out toward the voice-stilling sight of Cruachan's ponderous descent toward the waters of Loch Linnhe. Most of the panes were perfectly transparent but a few were dark, like panels of polished ebony.

As we approached the house through a neat cobbled yard a tall middle-aged man in ash-colored tweeds arose and waved to us. He had been sitting on the low rubble wall which bounded the yard, smoking a pipe and staring toward the house. At the front window of the cottage a young woman in a tangerine dress stood with a small boy in her arms, but she turned disinterestedly and moved out of sight as we drew near.

"Mr. Hagan?" I guessed.

"Correct. Come to see some glass, have you? Well, you've come to the right place." Hagan spoke crisply, with traces of the pure highland which sounds so much like Irish to the unaccustomed ear. He had one of those calmly dismayed faces one finds on elderly road-menders and philosophers.

"Yes," I said. "We're on holiday. We saw your sign."

Selina, who usually has a natural fluency with strangers, said nothing.

She was looking toward the now empty window with what I thought was a slightly puzzled expression.

"Up from London, are you? Well, as I said, you've come to the right place—and at the right time, too. My wife and I don't see many people this early in the season."

I laughed. "Does that mean we might be able to buy a little glass without mortgaging our home?"

"Look at that now," Hagan said, smiling helplessly. "I've thrown away any advantage I might have had in the transaction. Rose, that's my wife, says I never learn. Still, let's sit down and talk it over." He pointed at the rubble wall then glanced doubtfully at Selina's immaculate blue skirt. "Wait till I fetch a rug from the house." Hagan limped quickly into the cottage, closing the door behind him.

"Perhaps it wasn't such a marvelous idea to come up here," I whispered to Selina, "but you might at least be pleasant to the man. I think I can smell a bargain."

"Some hope," she said with deliberate coarseness. "Surely even you must have noticed that ancient dress his wife is wearing? He won't give much away to strangers."

"Was that his wife?"

"Of course that was his wife."

"Well, well," I said, surprised. "Anyway, try to be civil with him. I don't want to be embarrassed."

Selina snorted, but she smiled whitely when Hagan reappeared and I relaxed a little. Strange how a man can love a woman and yet at the same time pray for her to fall under a train.

Hagan spread a tartan blanket on the wall and we sat down, feeling slightly self-conscious at having been translated from our city-oriented lives into a rural tableau. On the distant slate of the Loch, beyond the watchful frames of slow glass, a slow-moving steamer drew a white line toward the south. The boisterous mountain air seemed almost to invade our lungs, giving us more oxygen than we required.

"Some of the glass farmers around here," Hagan began, "give strangers, such as yourselves, a sales talk about how beautiful the autumn is in this part of Argyll. Or it might be the spring, or the winter. I don't do that—any fool knows that a place which doesn't look right in summer never looks right. What do you say?"

I nodded compliantly.

"I want you just to take a gook look out toward Mull, Mr. . . ."

"Garland."

". . . Garland. That's what you're buying if you buy my glass, and it never looks better than it does at this minute. The glass is in perfect phase, none of it is less than ten years thick—and a four-foot window will cost you two hundred pounds."

"*Two hundred!*" Selina was shocked. "That's as much as they charge at the Scenedow shop in Bond Street."

Hagan smiled patiently, then looked closely at me to see if I knew enough about slow glass to appreciate what he had been saying. His price had been much higher than I had hoped—but *ten years thick!* The cheap glass one found in places like the Vistaplex and Pane-o-rama stores usually consisted of a quarter of an inch of ordinary glass faced with a veneer of slow glass perhaps only ten or twelve months thick.

"You don't understand, darling," I said, already determined to buy. "This glass will last ten years and it's in phase."

"Doesn't that only mean it keeps time?"

Hagan smiled at her again, realizing he had no further necessity to bother with me. "Only, you say! Pardon me, Mrs. Garland, but you don't seem to appreciate the miracle, the genuine honest-to-goodness miracle, of engineering precision needed to produce a piece of glass in phase. When I say the glass is ten years thick it means it takes light ten years to pass through it. In effect, each one of those panes is ten light-years thick—more than twice the distance to the nearest star—so a variation in actual thickness of only a millionth of an inch would . . . ."

He stopped talking for a moment and sat quietly looking toward the house. I turned my head from the view of the Loch and saw the young woman standing at the window again. Hagan's eyes were filled with a kind of greedy reverence which made me feel uncomfortable and at the same time convinced me Selina had been wrong. In my experience husbands never looked at wives that way, at least, not at their own.

The girl remained in view for a few seconds, dress glowing warmly, then moved back into the room. Suddenly I received a distinct, though inexplicable, impression she was blind. My feeling was that Selina and I were perhaps blundering through an emotional interplay as violent as our own.

"I'm sorry," Hagan continued, "I thought Rose was going to call me for something. Now, where was I, Mrs. Garland? Ten light-years compressed into a quarter of an inch means. . . ."

* * * *

342

I ceased to listen, partly because I was already sold, partly because I had heard the story of slow glass many times before and had never yet understood the principles involved. An acquaintance with scientific training had once tried to be helpful by telling me to visualize a pane of slow glass as a hologram which did not need coherent light from a laser for the reconstitution of its visual information, and in which every photon of ordinary light passed through a spiral tunnel coiled outside the radius of capture of each atom in the glass. This gem of, to me, incomprehensibility not only told me nothing, it convinced me once again that a mind as nontechnical as mine should concern itself less with causes than effects.

The most important effect, in the eyes of the average individual, was that light took a long time to pass through a sheet of slow glass. A new piece was always jet black because nothing had yet come through, but one could stand the glass beside say, a woodland lake until the scene emerged, perhaps a year later. If the glass was then removed and installed in a dismal city flat, the flat would—for that year—appear to overlook the woodland lake. During the year it wouldn't be merely a very realistic but still picture—the water would ripple in sunlight, silent animals would come to drink, birds would cross the sky, night would follow day, season would follow season. Until one day, a year later, the beauty held in the subatomic pipelines would be exhausted and the familiar gray cityscape would reappear.

Apart from its stupendous novelty value, the commercial success of slow glass was founded on the fact that having a scenedow was the exact emotional equivalent of owning land. The meanest cave dweller could look out on misty parks—and who was to say they weren't his? A man who really owns tailored gardens and estates doesn't spend his time proving his ownership by crawling on his ground, feeling, smelling, tasting it. All he receives from the land are light patterns, and with scenedows those patterns could be taken into coal mines, submarines, prison cells.

On several occasions I have tried to write short pieces about the enchanted crystal but, to me, the theme is so ineffably poetic as to be, paradoxically, beyond the reach of poetry—mine at any rate. Besides, the best songs and verse had already been written, with prescient inspiration, by men who had died long before slow glass was discovered. I had no hope of equaling, for example, Moore with his:

> Oft in the stilly night,
> Ere slumber's chain has bound me,
> Fond Memory brings the light,
> Of other days around me . . .

343

It took only a few years for slow glass to develop from a scientific curiosity to a sizable industry. And much to the astonishment of we poets—those of us who remain convinced that beauty lives though lilies die—the trappings of that industry were no different from those of any other. There were good scenedows which cost a lot of money, and there were inferior scenedows which cost rather less. The thickness, measured in years, was an important factor in the cost but there was also the question of *actual* thickness, or phase.

Even with the most sophisticated engineering techniques available thickness control was something of a hit-and-miss affair. A coarse discrepancy could mean that a pane intended to be five years thick might be five and a half, so that light which entered in summer emerged in winter; a fine discrepancy could mean that noon sunshine emerged at midnight. These incompatibilities had their peculiar charm—many night workers, for example, liked having their own private time zones—but, in general, it cost more to buy scenedows which kept closely in step with real time.

Selina still looked unconvinced when Hagan had finished speaking. She shook her head almost imperceptibly and I knew he had been using the wrong approach. Quite suddenly the pewter helmet of her hair was disturbed by a cool gust of wind, and huge clean tumbling drops of rain began to spang round us from an almost cloudless sky.

"I'll give you a check now," I said abruptly, and saw Selina's green eyes triangulate angrily on my face. "You can arrange delivery?"

"Aye, delivery's no problem," Hagan said, getting to his feet. "But wouldn't you rather take the glass with you?"

"Well, yes—if you don't mind." I was shamed by his readiness to trust my scrip.

"I'll unclip a pane for you. Wait here. It won't take long to slip it into a carrying frame." Hagan limped down the slope toward the seriate windows, through some of which the view toward Linnhe was sunny, while others were cloudy and a few pure black.

Selina drew the collar of her blouse closed at her throat. "The least he could have done was invite us inside. There can't be so many fools passing through that he can afford to neglect them."

I tried to ignore the insult and concentrated on writing the check. One of the outsize drops broke across my knuckles, splattering the pink paper.

"All right," I said, "let's move in under the eaves till he gets back." You worm, I thought as I felt the whole thing go completely wrong. I just had to be a fool to marry you. A prize fool, a fool's fool—and now that

344

you've trapped part of me inside you I'll never ever, never ever, *never ever* get away.

Feeling my stomach clench itself painfully, I ran behind Selina to the side of the cottage. Beyond the window the neat living room, with its coal fire, was empty but the child's toys were scattered on the floor. Alphabet blocks and a wheelbarrow the exact color of freshly pared carrots. As I stared in, the boy came running from the other room and began kicking the blocks. He didn't notice me. A few moments later the young woman entered the room and lifted him, laughing easily and whole-heartedly as she swung the boy under her arm. She came to the window as she had done earlier. I smiled self-consciously, but neither she nor the child responded.

My forehead prickled icily. *Could they both be blind?* I sidled away.

Selina gave a little scream and I spun towards her.

"The rug!" she said. "It's getting soaked."

She ran across the yard in the rain, snatched the reddish square from the dappling wall and ran back, toward the cottage door. Something heaved convulsively in my subconscious.

"Selina," I shouted. "Don't open it!"

But I was too late. She had pushed open the latched wooden door and was standing, hand over mouth, looking into the cottage. I moved close to her and took the rug from her unresisting fingers.

As I was closing the door I let my eyes traverse the cottage's interior. The neat living room in which I had just seen the woman and child was, in reality, a sickening clutter of shabby furniture, old newspapers, cast-off clothing and smeared dishes. It was damp, stinking, and utterly deserted. The only object I recognized from my view through the window was the little wheelbarrow, paintless and broken.

I latched the door firmly and ordered myself to forget what I had seen. Some men who live alone are good housekeepers; others just don't know how.

Selina's face was white. "I don't understand. I don't understand it."

"Slow glass works both ways," I said gently. "Light passes out of a house, as well as in."

"You mean . . . .?"

"I don't know. It isn't our business. Now steady up—Hagan's coming back with our glass." The churning in my stomach was beginning to subside.

Hagan came into the yard carrying an oblong, plastic-covered frame. I held the check out to him but he was staring at Selina's face. He seemed to know immediately that our uncomprehending fingers had rummaged through his soul. Selina avoided his gaze. She was old and ill-looking, and her eyes stared determinedly toward the nearing horizon.

"I'll take the rug from you, Mr. Garland," Hagan finally said. "You shouldn't have troubled yourself over it."

"No trouble. Here's the check."

"Thank you." He was still looking at Selina with a strange kind of supplication. "It's been a pleasure to do business with you."

"The pleasure was mine," I said with equal, senseless formality. I picked up the heavy frame and guided Selina toward the path which led to the road. Just as we reached the head of the now slippery steps Hagan spoke again.

"Mr. Garland!"

I turned unwillingly.

"It wasn't my fault," he said steadily. "A hit-and-run driver got them both, down on the Oban road six years ago. My boy was only seven when it happened. I'm entitled to keep something."

I nodded wordlessly and moved down the path, holding my wife close to me, treasuriug the feel of her arms locked around me. At the bend I looked back through the rain and saw Hagan sitting with squared shoulders on the wall where we had first seen him.

He was looking at the house, but I was unable to tell if there was anyone at the window.

56

LONG WAY HOME

Charles G. Waugh

WAVES OF SUNLIGHT spilled through the eastern window, and in them golden specks of dust whirled to and fro. But now Jack stuffed his duffel bag, delighting in these microcosmic worlds no longer. So I blew upon my steaming coffee, saying nothing as he made his final choices.

After one more pair of socks, he clicked the lock. Then straightening, he raked his right hand through thick, blond hair—so much like Ann's—while elevating his left to check the time.

He turned and fixed me with her eyes. "Five minutes, Dad."

I looked away and nodded.

Pivoting back, he squatted to muscle the bag to his chest. He rose, then locked the burden under an arm, and trucked it through the house and down the gently sloping lawn.

I followed, pausing to place my empty drink upon the kitchen table and to scrutinize his progress. "Jack." It wasn't terribly far from "Jackie," from a football being carried, or Ann, or kindergarten—and yet it was. I wiped the moisture from my eyes.

Where had it begun? With the telescope Ann and I had given him for his eighth birthday four years before her death? Or later in the back yard that warm autumn evening as we all took turns drinking bottled cider and squinting through the telescope at the stars? Is that when they began enticing him onward, with their siren whispers: "Here we are, Jack. We are waiting for you. Come to us."

Reaching them became his obsession. Through high school and the Space Academy, whenever he became discouraged, he went out into the night, and drew strength from their incandescence. To him, they burned like diamonds set on rich, black velvet. And no offer of mine, no matter how generous, could ever change my insurance sign to "Hanson and Son."

So I strolled into morning, to the last few minutes with the man who had been my son. I tried to avoid the unseemly and the desperate, but it was hard. I knew he would really go, and desperation raged within. My heart was hammering its way out of my chest. I was sweating and trembling with anxiety. Yet, in the end, I was swept along silently because I couldn't think of anything else to do. If only Ann had been with me. She was clever; she might have known. But she was gone. And in just a little while he would be, too.

Marriage had been forbidden, so even grandchildren would escape me.

"Dad," he had said, "we don't have faster-than-light drive yet; maybe someday we will, but for now we're trying to make the jump by modifying present models. These ships should take about thirty years to complete the first expedition to the stars. But that's subjective time and time slows when approaching the speed of light. On Earth the corresponding period will be several hundred years. If we were to marry, our wives would be widows when we left; they would wait all their lives, die, and be dead for at least two hundred years before we returned. For us to expect them to raise children who would never see us, who would die without ever knowing their fathers. . . . " He stopped, smiled, and put his hands upon my shoulders. "That's why only single men can go."

"Several hundred years," I said. That's when I first realized how much my loss would be.

Jack dumped his bag into the cab, glanced again at his watch, then gently turned to me: "Dad, it's time to go."

"Goodbye, son," I said, looking away, and choking back the bile.

My voice broke, but he shook my hand, pretending not to notice. Giving me a half salute, he stepped away, and climbed into the car.

The engine hummed and he was gone.

I stood planted in that dirt road, ten years ago, straining to see the cab as it diminished into infinity; straining until the dusty curtain drifted down, until my hopes had finally fallen. Then I returned to the house to tidy up his things and shut the room.

Today, I have opened his room once more. "Hanson and Son" still leans against a wall, but I realize now, as I should have then, that I was right to let him go.

This house is my home as it was for my father. But a man's home isn't always where he lives. It's where his heart is. To Jack this house was just a way station—a place to grow in strength and knowledge before embarking on his pilgrimage to the stars.

I shall always miss him, and, for me, the hurt may never heal. But at least there are my precious memories. There the towheaded child still scampers round his telescope, genuflecting now and then, to magnify the heavens. And late at night, when wrestling with the emptiness of my life, I have found comfort walking out onto my porch, gazing upward at our host of stars, and waving to my son—on his long way home.

57

THE LOOKING GLASS OF THE LAW

Kevin O'Donnell, Jr.

THEY STOPPED THE bus at the corner of Sherman and Whalley. A burly patrolman wearing the helmet and jodhpurs of a motorcycle cop was first on. With impartial interest, he studied the forty-seven passengers, who, after bored nods, returned to the conversations they'd suspended. The driver muttered something about his schedule and the cop said, "Sure, buddy. Sorry."

He walked down the aisle, scanning the faces that reflected the frail light. "You, ma'am," he said, pointing to a white-haired woman with three shopping bags. She smiled cheerfully and bustled to the front, where two more policemen chatted on the steps. One led her away. "You." A friendly wino blinked through his personal fog. Helping him to his feet, the cop faced him in the right direction and patted him on the shoulder. "And you." He stood above a middle-aged man with shaggy hair and an air of nervous good-fellowship.

"Officer," said George Hennesy, speaking rapidly, "I'm on my way to work. I'm a night watchman, and if I don't get there by—"

"We'll write you an excuse, sir. Please come along."

Praying that he wouldn't have to leave the soft foam seat, Hennesy stared up into patient blue eyes. "Please get somebody else, huh?"

"Sir, I'd hate to have to use this on you." Big-knuckled fingers plucked a dart gun from its leather holster. With a glance at Hennesy, the cop spun the dial to "Obedience." "Sir?"

"You win." When he raised his hands, the sleeves of his ragged blue jacket slid down, baring bony wrists.

"No need for that, sir." Chuckling, he let Hennesy precede him; when he got to the door, he laid an engaging grin upon the remaining passengers. His hearty voice caromed off the rear windows: "I'm sorry we had to delay

351

you. We appreciate your cooperation and your good will—we couldn't do it without you. Thanks, and good night.''

As they swung down onto the crowded sidewalk, somebody stuck his head through a window and hollered, ''Way to be , offsir—keep up the good work, y'hear?'' The bus moved away to a rumble of agreement.

''Jesus,'' said Hennesy, bitter at having been singled out, ''they really love you guys.''

''They got reason to, sir.'' A group of old men swirled past them and he held Hennesy's arm so they wouldn't be separated. ''Ten years ago, that bus—and these sidewalks—woulda been deserted. All the people woulda been home, hiding under their beds. They ain't afraid no more, which is how come they love us.'' Shy astonishment crept over his windburned face as he added. ''It's sort of a nice feeling, y'know? Now, c'mon, you got a date with The Machine.''

Just my fucking luck, thought Hennesy as his thin soles scraped on the *broken asphalt. Twenty-eight more hours and I'd've been golden. Now Helen's gonna be unhappy, and disappointed, when I get home. Again.* His stomach full of weary hopelessness, he walked toward the Police Department van. There was no line before the entrance, but an inset light burned redly. Resigned to his fate, he fell into an at-ease stance and waited for the minutes to pass. When the old lady came out of the darkness to stand behind him, he turned to the cop in puzzled anger. ''Hey, what is this? I was the last one off; I oughta be the last one through.''

''Sorry,'' His silver helmet shimmered in the sodium light. The leather gloves in his hand were black and thick. He slapped them idly against the side of his leg. ''She had to check her bags, sir—and anyway, you gotta get to work, right?''

''Yeah, I suppose so.'' The red glow shifted to emerald green and a figure stumbled out the van's side door.

''In you go, sir,'' ordered the cop, gesturing with his chin.

''Ah, Christ.'' He went up three dirt-encrusted steps and pushed on the aluminum door. It swung open at his touch, as had those of the other Machines through which he'd passed. Stepping in, he looked for differences. None. The Machines were all alike, right down to the scuffed green paint on the metal floor. A wall of heavy blue rubber blocked his path. While he glared at it, an amplified voice blasted: ''Please insert your arms into the holes.''

''All right, already!'' Six times he'd gone through the routine; six times the same neutral voice had directed him. The least the cops could do was have a different tape at each Machine. He sighed, and thrust his hands into the holes in the rubber. Velvet-covered steel bands contracted on his wrists and sucked them inward. The previous subject had been taller than Hennesy, so the holes were high, but The Machine made a smooth adjustment and softened his discomfort. Behind him, another wall rose out of the floor. Inching up to his back, it leaned against him with an even, immobilizing pressure. The forewall retreated from his face, leaving him a pocket of greasy air to breathe and depthless darkness to probe.

As he had six times before, Hennesy made a solemn vow to visit the Hall of Records and register to vote. The machines were killing him—that one was squeezing his head harder than any of the others had—and to his way of thinking, it was all the fault of those lunatics in Congress who'd repealed the Fourth and Fifth Amendments. Them and their cronies in state legislatures around the country who'd decided that overkill was the answer to the crime problem. *I'm gonna register, and I'm gonna vote, and I'm gonna vote for anybody who runs against any of those bastards. Even if it's a chimpanzee, I'll vote for him.*

Two hundred and forty-nine sensors had wormed their way through his clothing to take up listening posts next to his skin. Their metal ears were cold, and he shivered. He felt the needles jab into his forearms and cursed. *Whatthehell does New Haven need* ten *of these monsters for?* A Machine processed an average subject in ten minutes. Allowing for delays, balks, and the occasional individual who had to be manhandled into place, it could interrogate five people an hour. One hundred twenty a day. Forty-three thousand, eight hundred a year. Ten Machines upped that last number to four hundred thirty-eight thousand, or one hundred thousand more than the population of New Haven County. *Jesus God,* he thought, *they won't even leave 'em in one place and give a sucker an even chance. Naw, they gotta keep moving 'em around, so you never know where you shouldn't oughta go.*

His knees buckled as the truth serums hit him; the manacles held him upright. The ebony before his eyes acquired a texture, deep and soft. It separated into patterns and shapes, became three-dimensional, whirled and twirled. In matching time pulsed the paternal voice he'd learned to despise: HAVE YOU DONE ANYTHING WRONG IN THE LAST THIRTY DAYS?

Took him right back to third grade, when the nuns used to drag them down to the church on Friday afternoons and make them stand in long shadowed lines, shuffling in and out of confessionals where hoarse-tongued priests gave them advice and penance, and sent them out to sin no more. Dimly, he watched himself say, "Yes." The sensor soaked up physiological data and relayed it to the computer. A jury of semiconductors confirmed his honesty.

ON MORE THAN ONE OCCASION?

"No."

WAS THAT ONE OCCASION ILLEGAL AS WELL AS WRONG?

Hah, hah, he could beat the rap, all he had to do was say *No* so loudly and clearly that The Machine would have to know he believed it himself, and then it would let him free, because it wasn't allowed to fuck around with morality, only with legality. And Helen wouldn't know anything about it, and he wouldn't have to hurt her. Again. He lifted his head, cleared his throat, smiled at the thought of fooling the Machine, and said, "Yes."

DESCRIBE THE CIRCUMSTANCES—*whadIsay?* Jet black sculptures jeered him.

—AS FULLY AND AS COMPLETELY—*ohmydeargod, that stuff really does loosen your tongue*. He giggled.

—AS POSSIBLE..

"It was Wednesday, March 19, and it was raining cats and dogs and I was waiting for a bus that wouldn't come for another thrity-three minutes, so I went into Macy's to get out of the rain and the cold. It was really crowded and all the salesgirls were busy, they weren't paying any attention to me, and the aisles were dense with shoppers—I held my wallet 'cause I was afraid somebody'd try to steal it—and I looked at my watch. Had thirty-one minutes to go. I walked around, looking at all the things on display, wishing that I had the money to buy something for my wife Helen just 'cause it was pretty and not 'cause she needed it. There was this ashtray, from Taiwan, carved out of black and white marble, so thin that if you held it up to the light you could look through it and see the shadows of your fingers. I knew she'd love it. It was small enough to go into my pocket. It fit very nice, no bulges, no sags. I left the store and didn't pay for it." Night figures paused in their dance to applaud his recital; he felt himself grin and bow repeatedly.

WHAT WAS THE PRICE OF THE ASHTRAY?

He wanted to protest that he couldn't possibly remember the exact number of dollars and cents that an unaffordable luxury would have cost if he had paid for it, but the serum opened the shell of his memory and pulled out the pearl: "Twenty-nine ninety-eight."

THANK YOU.

"You're welcome." He heard clicks and hums in the area behind the wall and he knew what they meant, but he didn't care because the people in the shadows had taken up their ballet again.

HAVE YOU DONE ANYTHING ELSE IN THE LAST THIRTY DAYS WHICH MIGHT QUALIFY AS ILLEGAL? DESCRIBE ANY INSTANCE OF WHICH YOU ARE DOUBTFUL. THE COMPUTER WILL JUDGE.

Did the dancers pause? He opened his mouth to scoff but words trickled out. "Well, the other day, April 7, that was Monday, I was walking along and I found this wallet. No ID's or nothing. I thought about turning it in to the police, but my own wallet was pretty decrepit, so I decided to keep it."

THAT IS NEITHER WRONG NOR ILLEGAL. YOU MAY KEEP IT. IS THERE ANYTHING ELSE.

He swooped through the long halls of his memories. In niches along the walls glowed abstract designs. His eyes tasted their colors, reveled in the brightness. Only two were scarlet, and he'd recounted them already. "No."

VERY GOOD. THE RECORDS INDICATE THAT YOU HAVE NOT PREVIOUSLY CONFESSED THIS CRIME. THEREFORE, YOU HAVE BEEN FINED ACCORDING TO THE USUAL FORMULA. IN ONE MOMENT YOU WILL BE PUNISHED, WHEN YOU ARE YOURSELF AGAIN, REMEMBER THIS MACHINE. YOU CAN NEVER ESCAPE FROM IT; YOU CAN NEVER HIDE FROM IT. ONLY OBSERVANCE OF THE LAW CAN SAVE YOU.

He hummed a little tune to himself, pleased that it was almost over. His first session had been much longer. The portion of his mind that wasn't watching the ballerinas wondered what form his punishment would take.

SHOPLIFT! His hands were gloved with frost; froze; crystallized; erupted with agonizing needles of ice. Whimpering, he hung from the manacles.

SHOPLIFT! The ice melted; the skin raced from white to red. Hot! Blisters bubbled and burst; baked flesh disintegrated; the bones themselves began to char.

SHOPLIFT! The gloom grew whiskery and beady-eyed with rats that scurried to his fingers and nibbled at the living flesh. Blood oozed, then dripped, then spurted. Sharp teeth ripped his hands apart and absconded with the pieces.

THAT IS ALL. SHOULD YOU WISH TO APPEAL THIS COURT'S DECISION, A TRANSCRIPT WILL BE PROVIDED UPON REQUEST. GO NOW. AND BREAK THE LAW NO MORE.

The restraining pressure eased; cool air washed over his back and began to dry the shirt that stuck to sweaty skin. The manacles opened and the weight of his arms dragged them free. He staggered to the exit door, but couldn't operate the knob. A policeman outside heard his fumbling and opened it for him.

"This way, sir." He took him by the arm and led him to a row of cots. The colors of the street corner night were heightened to an alien intensity. Hennesy sank down with numb relief. A gentle wind took chatter from the sidewalk and offered it to him, but he couldn't understand it. The cop paused for a moment before asking, "You were on the bus, sir?"

"Right." Before the Machine he would have been voluble in his outrage; after it, he could only attempt to repeat the word. "Ri . . . "

"Well, sir," said the officer as he ripped a ticket from a booklet, "HERE'S A PASS ENTITLING YOU TO ONE FREE BUS RIDE. And this is your excuse, for your employer."

"Thanks." He tucked them into his jacket pocket, and stared up at the sky. It showed stars, which he hadn't seen often. He watched them wink at each other across the great space they defined. He envied them their freedom.

The serums had spent themselves, and their effects were fading. He grew aware of a black man on the cot next to his. Short and thin, thirtyish and ugly, he was bent double. His tender hands cupped his balls; he moaned sporadic intervals. When he felt Hennesy's gaze, he looked up. "Hey, dude—what'd they get you for? What'd they do?"

Hennesy shrugged. "Shoplifting. They fined me, and gave me a dose of aversion therapy."

"Hunh! Me, too. But, shit, she's my own wife, man! Caught her stepping out with my for-mer best friend . . . whupped her some, then strapped her to the bed and showed her who her man *is*. Man's got a right, don't he?" He rubbed himself gently. "That muhfucking therapy felt like a gahdamn *mule* kicked me—sheeyit, they say I won't be able to use this for another six weeks. Now I ask you, what the hell am I going to *do* with myself, man? I mean, this here is worse than the fucking *slam*mer. Can you dig it?"

"Yeah, it's a bitch." He opened his hands to his eyes and his body was amazed at their wholeness. His mind had expected nothing else, but his body *knew* they had been destroyed. Three times. "Don't know how I'm gonna pay off that fine, though."

"They already hit your bank account?"

"Two milliseconds after the fine came down."

"How much?"

"Hell . . . four times twenty-nine ninety-eight. What's that, a hundred something? I ain't got it."

"So mug somebody, deposit the bread, and lie low for thirty days."

"Uh-uh. I got a job. Besides, they caught me once, for beating on somebody who was bugging my wife—don't plan to face an assault rap ever again." A shudder raced the memory through his body. He'd never screamed so loud in his life. Being skinned alive had not been pleasant. "That therapy is bad shit."

"Don't I know it." The black man groaned as he sat up. "Hey, looky there."

"Where?"

"The Machine, dude. Who went in after you?"

"Some old lady, don't know who she is. Looks like a grandmother. Why?"

"Well look and see for yourself."

He squinted through the yellow light. The van squatted on the aspalt like a blue beetle. A wisp of greasy brown smoke rose through a vent in its roof.

"Damn!" The black voice trembled with anger and fear. "Wonder what the hell *she* did."

Hennesy shook his head and looked away. He'd go register to vote in the morning. He *would* Unless. . . .

58

LOST LOVE

Algis Budrys

SOMEWHERE JUST OUTSIDE Hammonton, Doc Bennett first noticed the boy in the next seat. Doc woke up a little—probably because the bus had just taken a bad bounce—grunted sleepily, opened his eyes, and looked across the aisle. He saw a thin, lank-haired boy sitting with his chin cupped in his palm, staring out into the darkness, and Doc felt a brief flicker of curiosity.

The boy was about fifteen or sixteen, he judged, and thinner than he should be. Shabbier, too, Doc thought, looking at the patched jeans and threadbare jacket, and the shapeless old farm shoes on his feet.

It gave Doc a turn to notice that the boy wasn't even wearing any socks. The jeans were too short for his long legs, and his dusty ankles were bare and knobby above the shoetops.

Bennett started to take a closer look. Maybe the boy didn't have a shirt on under his jacket, either. But the way the bus was swaying made him sleepy, and he was barely awake anyhow, so even while he was leaning forward, his eyes nodded shut.

In Elwood, the bus stopped for a passenger, and Doc Bennett woke up again. He rubbed his eyes, shifted around on the stiff seat, and scratched his side. Then he noticed the boy across the aisle, who was sitting, looking down at his hands folded in his lap, and Doc thought no boy that age ought to have anything to feel as sad and lost about as this one did. The look on his face was a thousand miles away.

Doc took a better look. The boy was thin—a lot thinner than he should be; and his clothes were in pretty bad repair. He was wearing a pair of old blue jeans with fuzzy-edged patches over the knees, and his shins stuck out of the bottom of the almost white legs. Lord knew how often the jeans'd been washed to bleach the color so much. And no socks. Doc stared at his

359

knobby, grimy ankles; no socks in November—and a pair of cracked farm brogans with knotted laces.

"S a y—young fellow . . . . "

The boy raised his head and looked across the aisle. "Yes, sir?" he asked in a soft, polite voice.

Doc didn't know how to go on for a minute. He thought about a way to make the boy understand he wasn't just a snoop—he guessed the youngster must have run into his share of well-meaning old ladies.

The boy was looking at him with the lost look just behind the politeness in his eyes, waiting patiently.

"Youngster—well, look my name's Doctor Samuel Bennett. This isn't any of my business, bu—where're you headed for, dressed like that this time of year?" That wasn't very good, but it was the best he could think of. And he winced and cursed himself for a stumble-tongued old busybody when the boy gave him the answer he'd been afraid of: "I don't have any other clothes, sir."

The boy said it without any trace of embarrassment or bitterness, and that surprised Doc. The youngster was just at the age when it ought to matter very much.

Doc fumbled for the next thing to say. "Well—well, is there anybody waiting for you, where you're going?"

"I don't know, sir."

Just like that. "I don't know, sir." Doc Bennett shook his head and frowned, trying to concentrate. He ought to ask the boy's name; maybe he was running away from somewhere. Maybe he had a good reason, too—a reason that ought to be looked into. The boy looked as though nobody'd ever taken any decent care of him.

But the bus was swaying, and buses always made Bennett sleepy. He tried to keep himself awake, but it was a losing battle. He felt his head droop, and caught a glimpse of a sad, disappointed, but resigned look on the boy's face. And then he fell alseep.

Doc Bennett woke up in Egg Harbor City, a little surprised because he usually woke up for every stop whenever he traveled anywhere. He must have been more tired than he thought.

He looked around as the bus started to pull out. There weren't very many other passengers on the bus, and most of them were clutstered up front. There was nobody sitting toward the back except himself a boy across the aisle, who was looking at him hopefully.

Doc looked back at the boy, wondering what he wanted.

He was an awfully thin youngster, and dressed in shabby, worn-out clothes that were a lot too small for him and a lot too thin for this kind of weather. Doc frowned at the bare wristbones sticking out of the boy's windbreaker. No shirt collar showed at his neck, and Doc wondered if the jacket could be all he had on except for his hand-patched jeans.

Doc took a look at the boy's feet. His broken and shapeless shoes were a lot too big for his feet—and he didn't have any socks on.

"Hello, young fellow," he said, hoping the boy wouldn't shy away. He looked sadder and lonelier than any boy Doc had ever seen; he looked as though he was used to more meanness than kindness from people. He looked as though he'd never known a day without a disappointment. In some ways, he looked as though he'd found out what sixty-year-old men, sitting on park benches in the wintertime with newspapers stuffed into their shirts, had found out.

And no boy should ever have found that out—or even guessed it might be waiting for him.

"Hello, Doctor Bennett," the boy answered politely.

Doc peered at his face. "Well . . . I'm sorry, son, but I don't remember your name. Most of my friends call me Doc."

He couldn't remember the boy for the life of him. He felt ashamed of that—if there was ever anybody he should have remembered, it was this youngster.

"We only met a very short time . . . once," the boy said in a sad, haunted voice; "I didn't really think you'd remember me."

Doc shook his head. "I'm sorry, youngster; a doctor sees a lot of people. But I'm not usually this forgetful," he apologized.

The boy nodded.

That was a strange reaction. Doc hitched himself up farther in his seat, and looked more carefully at the boy.

"That's not such practical clothing for this kind of weather," he said awkwardly. "Is somebody meeting you? Where're you bound for?"

"I don't know, Doc."

"You don't know!" Doc sat up straight. Maybe he had an amnesia case here. No—that didn't jibe with the rest of it. What was it? He looked at the boy's cheeks and eyes for traces of fever.

"Don't you have anyplace to go, son?" he asked gently.

The boy shook his head. "No, Doc; not ever. I just travel. Sometimes I have somebody to talk to. Most times I don't. Most times I don't even have that."

"Lord, boy, how long's that been going on?"

The boy shrugged, and all the loneliness in the world was in his eyes. "Three years. Ever since I realized."

"Realized what, son?"

"That I had to find somebody."

"Who?"

The boy shook his head and looked down at the floor.

Too important, Doc thought. It's too important to talk about. He remembered what it had been like when he was this boy's age.

"Doc?"

"Yes, son?"

"Doc, why don't you remember me?"

Bennett couldn't make sense out of the queston. He shook his head. "There's no answer, son; why does anybody forget anything? It just happens, I guess. Can't explain it."

"Haven't you ever seen me before?"

The boy was looking down at the floor, but Doc noticed how tightly his frail hands were knotted together. "No, son," he said gently.

"Are you *sure*, Doc?"

Bennett didn't know what to do. The boy was strung up as tight as a drawn wire. He felt helpless. "I'm sure, son."

The boy looked up. "Doc—in your practice, do you know of any kids whose parents don't take any care of them?"

Doc thought he'd found his answer. He cursed silently. "No, son, I can't say I do. But you've got to remember that sometimes people *can't* do as much for their children as they'd like to."

The boy shook his head. "I don't mean that," he said in a lost whisper.

Doc hadn't thought he did. He cursed again.

"Listen, son—" He stopped. It was a big step, but he made up his mind. "Son, how'd you like to stay with me for a while, until we can get you straightened out? We'd find you a job after school—I don't suppose you've got any relatives you care for?"

The boy bit his lips. He looked down again. "Thanks, Doc," he whispered, "but it wouldn't work. Nobody's going to pay me for work they don't think I did—and, besides, Doc you can't afford it."

Doc nodded unconsciously. Then he asked: "What makes you think so, son?"

The boy smiled in embarrassment. "You're on a bus. If you were younger, that wouldn't mean anything. But they're two kinds of old doctors that ride buses—the no-good ones and the ones who never charged much."

Bennett flushed uncomfortably; there wasn't any mistaking which kind the boy thought he was. It wasn't really true—he'd pulled down some big fees in his time.

Not enough, though, he sighed to himself. Not nearly enough. Well, if he had it to do over . . . No, not then, either, he admitted.

He flushed again, and in his mind he squinted at himself suspiciously. He didn't like noble people. "You're a pretty quick judge of people," he grunted crankily.

"I've studied them, sir."

Yes, by God, I suppose you have, Doc thought. I suppose you had to. "Listen, son—what're you going to do? How're you going to live?"

"I get by, Doc. I shine shoes or I work in a lunchroom—anyplace where I can get tips. It doesn't last very long, any job doesn't, but even with less tips than somebody else would get, I make out."

"My gosh, son, the only place this bus goes to of any size is Atlantic City! And this is November. You won't find much work there."

"I know. But I haven't been up this way before. And I saved up enough in Camden for the ticket."

"Well—you must have learned some trade by now. Don't you have any special skill? Something you could get a regular salary for?"

The boy shook his head.

"You only get paid if the boss remembers you." An odd look came over his face. "I've got some . . . skills. But they wouldn't be fair."

Bennett didn't know what to make of him; he felt completely bewildered. He couldn't make head or tail of what the boy meant by some of the things he was saying.

"Doc, I've got to keep moving around; I've got to keep looking. I don't know what else to do."

"Looking for what?" Doc asked again.

"For—for somebody else. For somebody else who's looking for some-body else. For somebody people don't notice. Doc, you know those movies about invisible people? That's who I'm looking for. Invisible people. People who get on buses and have to remind the driver to take their ticket, people who get forgotten. I figure that's the way it's got to be. We're all out—all looking for each other. There can't be very many of us, but there's *got* to be more than just me!" The boy's mouth was trembling, and Bennett felt himself growing frightened for him.

I'm a doctor, he thought. A healer. Something's terribly wrong with this boy.

But he sat there helplessly, because he didn't know what to do. The best he could think of was taking the boy off the bus and getting him to a psychologist. But how was he going to manage that? He had to think of a way that wouldn't frighten the youngster.

"Sooner or later, Doc, I'm going to find somebody. I don't care what they look like, or who they are, or what they are—they've got to be somewhere in this world!" He slumped down in his seat and whispered: "But suppose we forget each other?"

He looked up. "It would be different if you hadn't set up the rules of this world. If there weren't so many of you—if it hadn't been organized so only you could live in it. But there's no place—nothing—unless we want to fight—unless *I* want to fight—and I don't want to fight—I just want to live—and be happy—I'm one of you—I was—until just a few years ago—and then you all started to forget me—

"Doc, I tried my best. I *tried* to stay one of you. I did. I tried to fit in. But I can't help it. I can't stop it. You forget me. You all forget me—"

But Bennett was falling asleep. He felt his head nodding forward.

The boy's hand clenched tightly over his arm, and for just a moment Doc felt the beat of a pulse like he'd never met before. But he couldn't keep his eyes open.

"Doc! Remember me! Remember me . . . "

"Ab—secon!" the driver called back. "Absecon, Mac."

Doc Bennett woke up with a nervous grunt. "Huh?"

"Your stop, Mister."

"O h—o h, thanks," Doc said, climbing out of the seat hastily and reaching up into the rack for his hat. He shook his head to clear it.

He was grumpy with himself as he made his way quickly toward the front of the bus. He usually woke up for every stop whenever he was traveling. Especially on buses.

He banged his hip into the steel corner of a seat and winced. Dammit! he thought crankily, people ought to have armor-plated hides. But then Evolution probably hadn't heard about human society yet.

"Thanks," he said again as he climbed down the high step and out of the bus, feeling his muscles strain to make the distance. We ought to have non-rigid skeletons, too, he added, while we're at it.

He waited for the bus to pull away so he could cross the street. Well, he thought with a slight smile, we're a pretty tough lot in our own way. The next thing that comes along better have something pretty fancy in the way of protection.

He looked up and a palefaced, thin-looking boy was watching him from a window as the bus pulled away.

Doc's smile turned a little sad. The kid looked as though he needed somebody to take care of him.

He crossed the street and walked quickly down the sidestreet toward his home, because the November wind was cold. He climbed up the stairs to the apartment over the grocery and unlocked the door with stiff fingers.

"Sam?"

He closed the door behind him. "Yes, Ruth, I'm home." He felt the ache rising up in his throat again. That young doctor in Camden had asked just a little too much for his practice. It was worth it, but it was more than they had.

Ruth came out of the kitchen, and he shook his head slowly. "It didn't work out."

She smiled. "So what?"

But he felt the ache grow stronger. He wanted to have things better for her, he always had. But it didn't seem to work out—and he supposed somebody had to take care of the people who couldn't quite work it out when it came to paying medical bills.

Like calling to like, he thought with a twist to his mouth.

"Supper's ready, darling. I hope you weren't too cold."

He shook his head. " Didn't feel a thing." He followed her into the kitchen and sat down.

"Sam, I—" Ruth stopped and looked over his shoulder. He turned around.

There was a thin, worn-looking girl of about fourteen standing in the other doorway. "You didn't set a place for me, again," she said in a lost, trembing voice.

Doc looked at her in complete bewilderment. And he thought it was odd he didn't recognize her. Despite everything, she was very pretty, and he thought he should—she looked a great deal like Ruth.

59

LUCIFER

Roger Zelazny

CARLSON STOOD ON the hill in the silent center of the city whose people had died.

He stared up at the Building—the one structure that dwarfed every hotel-grid, skyscraper-needle, or apartment-cheesebox packed into all the miles that lay about him. Tall as a mountain, it caught the rays of the bloody sun. Somehow it turned their red into golden halfway up its height.

Carlson suddenly felt that he should not have come back.

It had been over two years, as he figured it, since last he had been here. He wanted to return to the mountains now. One look was enough. Yet still he stood before it, transfixed by the huge Building, by the long shadow that bridged the entire valley. He shrugged his thick shoulders then, in an unsuccessful attempt to shake off memories of the days, five (or was it six?) years ago, when he had worked within the giant unit.

Then he climbed the rest of the way up the hill and entered the high, wide doorway.

His fiber sandals cast a variety of echoes as he passed through the deserted offices and into the long hallway that led to the belts.

The belts, of course, were still. There were no thousands riding them. There was no one alive to ride. Their deep belly-rumble was only a noisy phantom in his mind as he climbed onto the one nearest him and walked ahead into the pitchy insides of the place.

It was like a mausoleum. There seemed no ceiling, no walls, only the soft *pat-pat* of his soles on the flexible fabric of the belt.

He reached a junction and mounted a cross-belt, instinctively standing still for a moment and waiting for the forward lurch as it sensed his weight.

Then he chuckled silently and began walking again.

When he reached the lift, he set off to the right of it until his memory led

367

him to the maintenance stairs. Shouldering his bundle, he began the long, groping ascent.

He blinked at the light when he came into the Power Room. Filtered through its hundred high windows, the sunlight trickled across the dusty acres of machinery.

Carlson sagged against the wall, breathing heavily from the climb. After awhile he wiped a workbench clean and set down his parcel.

Then he removed his faded shirt, for the place would soon be stifling. He brushed his hair from his eyes and advanced down the narrow metal stair to where the generators stood, row on row, like an army of dead, black beetles. It took him six hours to give them all a cursory check.

He selected three in the second row and systematically began tearing them down, cleaning them, soldering their loose connections with the auto-iron, greasing them, oiling them and sweeping away all the dust, cobwebs, and pieces of cracked insulation that lay at their bases.

Great rivulets of perspiration ran into his eyes and down along his sides and thighs, spilling in little droplets onto the hot flooring and vanishing quickly.

Finally, he put down his broom, remounted the stair and returned to his parcel. He removed one of the water bottles and drank off half its contents. He ate a piece of dried meat and finished the bottle. He allowed himself one cigarette then, and returned to work.

He was forced to stop when it grew dark. He had planned on sleeping right there, but the room was too oppressive. So he departed the way he had come and slept beneath the stars, on the roof of a low building at the foot of the hill.

It took him two more days to get the generators ready. Then he began work on the huge Broadcast Panel. It was in better condition than the generators, because it had last been used two years ago. Whereas the generators, save for the three he had burned out last time, had slept for over five (or was it six?) years.

He soldered and wiped and inspected until he was satisfied. Then only one task remained.

All the maintenance robots stood frozen in mid-gesture. Carlson would have to wrestle a three hundred pound power cube without assistance. If he could get one down from the rack and onto a cart without breaking a wrist he would probably be able to convey it to the Igniter without much difficulty. Then he would have to place it within the oven. He had almost ruptured himself when he did it two years ago, but he hoped that he was somewhat stronger—and luckier—this time.

It took him ten minutes to clean the Igniter oven. Then he located a cart and pushed it back to the rack.

One cube was resting at just the right height, approximately eight inches above the level of the cart's bed. He kicked down the anchor chocks and moved around to study the rack. The cube lay on a downward-slanting shelf, restrained by a two-inch metal guard. He pushed at the guard. It was bolted to the shelf.

Returning to the work area, he searched the tool boxes for a wrench. Then he moved back to the rack and set to work on the nuts.

The guard came loose as he was working on the fourth nut. He heard a dangerous creak and threw himself back out of the way, dropping the wrench on his toes.

The cube slid forward, crushed the loosened rail, teetered a bare moment, then dropped with a resounding crash onto the heavy bed of the cart. The bed surface bent and began to crease beneath its weight; the cart swayed toward the outside. The cube continued to slide until over half a foot projected beyond the edge. Then the cart righted itself and shivered into steadiness.

Carlson sighed and kicked loose the chocks, ready to jump back should it suddenly give way in his direction. It held.

Gingerly, he guided it up the aisle and between the rows of generators, until he stood before the Igniter. He anchored the cart again, stopped for water and a cigarette, then searched up a pinch bar, a small jack and a long, flat metal plate.

He laid the plate to bridge the front end of the cart and the opening to the oven. He wedged the far end in beneath the Igniter's doorframe.

Unlocking the rear chocks, he inserted the jack and began to raise the back end of the wagon, slowly, working with one hand and holding the bar ready in the other.

The cart groaned as it moved higher. Then a sliding, grating sound began and he raised it faster.

With a sound like the stroke of a cracked bell the cube tumbled onto the bridgeway; it slid forward and to the left. He struck at it with the bar, bearing to the right with all his strength. About half an inch of it caught against the left edge of the oven frame. The gap between the cube and the frame was widest at the bottom.

He inserted the bar and heaved his weight against it—three times.

Then it moved forward and came to rest within the Igniter.

He began to laugh. He laughed until he felt weak. He sat on the broken cart, swinging his legs and chuckling to himself, until the sounds coming from his throat seemed alien and out of place. He stopped abruptly and slammed the door.

The Broadcast Panel had a thousand eyes, but none of them winked back at him. He made the final adjustments for Transmit, then gave the generators their last check-out.

After that, he mounted a catwalk and moved to a window.

There was still some daylight to spend, so he moved from window to window pressing the "Open" button set below each sill.

He ate the rest of his food then, and drank a whole bottle of water and smoked two cigarettes. Sitting on the stair, he thought of the days when he had worked with Kelly and Murchison and Djizinsky, twisting the tails of electrons until they wailed and leapt out over the walls and fled down into the city.

The clock! He remembered it suddenly—set high on the wall, to the left of the doorway, frozen at 9:33 (and forty-eight seconds).

He moved a ladder through the twilight and mounted it to the clock. He wiped the dust from its greasy face with a sweeping, circular movement. Then he was ready.

He crossed to the Igniter and turned it on. Somewhere the ever-batteries came alive, and he heard a click as a thin, sharp shaft was driven into the wall of the cube. He raced back up the stairs and sped hand-over-hand up to the catwalk. He moved to a window and waited.

"God," he murmured, "don't let them blow! Please don't—"

Across an eternity of darkness the generators began humming. He heard a crackle of static from the Broadcast Panel and he closed his eyes. The sound died.

He opened his eyes as he heard the window slide upward. All around him the hundred high windows opened. A small light came on above the bench in the work area below him, but he did not see it.

He was staring out beyond the wide drop of the acropolis and down into the city. His city.

The lights were not like the stars. They beat the stars all to hell. They were the gay, regularized constellation of a city where men made their homes: even rows of streetlamps, advertisements, lighted windows in the cheesebox-apartments, a random solitaire of bright squares running up the sides of skyscraper-needles, a searchlight swivelling its luminous antenna through cloudbanks that hung over the city.

He dashed to another window, feeling the high night breezes comb at his beard. Belts were humming below; he heard their wry monologues rattling through the city's deepest canyons. He pictured the people in their homes, in theaters, in bars—talking to each other, sharing a common amusement, playing clarinets, holding hands, eating an evening snack. Sleeping ro-cars awakened and rushed past each other on the levels above the belts; the backgrond hum of the city told him its story of production, of function, of movement and service to its inhabitants. The sky seemed to wheel overhead, as though the city were its turning hub and the universe its outer rim.

Then the lights dimmed from white to yellow and he hurried, with desperate steps, to another window.

"No! Not so soon! Don't leave me yet!" he sobbed.

The windows closed themselves and the lights went out. He stood on the walk for a long time, staring at the dead embers. A smell of ozone reached his nostrils. He was aware of a blue halo about the dying generators.

He descended and crossed the work area to the ladder he had set against the wall.

Pressing his face against the glass and squinting for a long time he could make out the position of the hands.

"Nine thirty-five, and twenty-one seconds," Carlson read.

"Do you hear that?" he called out, shaking his fist at anything. "Ninety-three seconds! I made you live for ninety-three seconds!"

Then he covered his face against the darkness and was silent.

After a long while he descended the stairway, walked the belt, and moved through the long hallway and out of the Building. As he headed back toward the mountains he promised himself—again—that he would never return.

60

MAN OF DESTINY

John Christopher

THEY CLOCK THE spaceships in from the main control tower seventeen miles southeast of Tycho. The magnesium flares blossom out against the stars and the searching telescopes find them and name them. The *Elistra* back from Procyon, the *Alte Wien* from Lumen III, the *Winston* from Sirius. Ships laden with passengers and freight from halfway across the visible universe, controlled corks bobbing up through the maelstrom of time and space to that same narrow arc of the lunar sky. They come in on time—solar time. There's no danger to life or goods or schedule.

It wasn't always so. When the slip process was first being developed, there were both danger and uncertainty for those isolated men, strapped in their bubbles of metal and plastic, who voyaged out across an alien dimension to the far reaches of the sky. Their job was to take routine star pictures and then come back on the reverse. But the reverse did not always work. They were stranded then, hundreds of thousands of light-years from the planet they had known as home.

From the moment the reverse failed, Theodore Pike concentrated on the lucky side of his situation. He might have been lost in the remotenesses of interstellar space, condemned to suffocation when his meager oxygen supply gave out—a week of waiting for death unless he had the courage to seek it out first.

As it was, he was slap in the middle of a solar system, a matter of three hundred million miles from a blue giant. The system, as he had planned it for the report that would not now be made, was not of any notable size. There were only three planets. One was very large and impossibly distant from the sun. But there was some hope in the other two. In size they were reasonable enough. He arrowed down toward the first of them three days

373

later; and at once set the coracle climbing up again, through a methane atmosphere, from a barren and unrewarding surface.

That left one planet. Only one.

When he released the hood and the planet's air came in, it was like the first time he had tasted wine, in the late spring at Heidelberg, under the gaudy cherry blossoms. He lifted his body clear and slid down the still warm metal of the spheroid to the mossy ground. The moss was dark green, and deep and springy. His feet went down two or three inches, but there was resilience even beneath that.

He looked up at the sky. It had a strange and strangely warm green tinge; the sun was hidden behind tufted blue-green clouds. He looked toward where it should be with contemptuous, good-humored acknowledgment. It had done its job; he was all right now. Then he stood easily erect beside the spheroid, watching the natives hesitantly approaching from the village fifty yards away.

They were humanoid bipeds, with a natural green-tinged fur, but wearing artificial decorations and the beginnings of clothing. He stood quite still as they approached. Ten yards away, with a slow and somehow graceful ceremony, they all knelt. They rested their heads on the green moss. When he spoke, they looked up. He beckoned and they came closer. Their leader knelt again at his feet. Quite casually Theo put one foot on the prostrate head.

It was accomplished. The natives had found their god.

The first few months passed very quickly. He had set himself one task—to learn the language. After that, the life of Reilly. Things were already very pleasant. The bed made of something like swansdown, the spiced and delicate foods, the sweet yellow wine which, by a dispensation of Providence, had a far less intoxicating effect on him than on the natives. They got drunk on it; a cheerful, happy drunk every seventh or eighth day. He was able to preside over their revels benignly enough, mellowed and happy enough himself in—as he reflected sardonically—his divine way.

He had been figuring on a week of seven days and only later discovered that the natives had a ten month year. The four months thus far had been rather less than one of them, but at the end of that time he could communicate well enough.

He called the chief, Pernar, into the hut that he had once owned and gave the preliminary directions for the building of his palace. The natives already had fire, but had not applied it to the working of metals. He gave them that, and the spoked wheel. They were enough to be going on with, in addition to the supreme, never-ending boon of his own personal godhead. He had found an outcrop of good granite, tinged with rosy green in the prevailing light of the planet, less than three miles from the village.

The palace went up fast. He took it over with due ceremony. The natives were puzzled but respectful.

That was where the settling down began. At one time, at the beginning, he had held vague hopes of being rescued through the slip. He had even planned great beacon towers spaced across the planet. But more sober reflection proved them futile. Even with every imaginable success, the Mendola process could not be studding the universe with ships enough to make the possibility of this planet's discovery more than fantastically remote. This was a life sentence.

He had something bigger to do now. He would leave something for the exploring slip-ships to find: a civilization founded on a manifest divinity. At its heart a shrine, and in its shirne the memory of what Theodore Pike had made of his exile.

In the eighth month of the planet's year, he provided the steam engine.

The natives stood around with their usual impeccable gravity; Pernar surrounded by his men, and even the bolder of the women and children. The tiny model hissed; the small piston began to work the wheel.

"In this, my people, is your future," Theo told them. "With this your labor will be lightened, your fields made fruitful. Your ships and wagons will cross the wide spaces of the world. All this your lord brings to his people."

They nodded solemnly and bowed. The sun was at its zenith, where its light concentrated into an astonishing blueness. Every day at this time the green became blue for an hour; by now, an ordinary miracle. He looked over their heads toward the dazzling sapphire of his palace. At its threshold stood the two gigantic replicas of his own image. The small white jet of steam climbed unwaveringly. Eventually there would have to be a larger palace, he reflected. But still here, in this spot, still enshrining the spheroid and the spot where it had landed.

Who would be in it? he wondered to himself. He had thought of it before; it was his most sustaining fantasy. The great slip-ship settling down into this blue-green world, being taken (as the tradition would demand) to the shrine of the great palace-temple, looking with astonishment—and respect? pride?—on the first interstellar coracle, the tomb of Theodore Pike. What would the visitors be like? They would be respectful, anyway. They would be proud of the memory of the first of their line. His name would leap through the vast gulfs that now cut him off from all his youth might have enjoyed. That made up for everything.

But everything was quite a lot.

Following Theo's demonstration, the natives seemed in no hurry to adopt the steam engine. Every now and then the elders would come to watch the little model puffing away. Theo explained it to them several times, and they nodded their heads in respectful approval. But all their working time now was being devoted to the harvest. The whole tribe—men, women, children—toiled in the fields through the long hot days.

Even in his natural indolence he was aware of a sense of urgency about their labor; they worked on their holiday now, only getting drunk when the green twilight had darkened into night. He had the shrewd sense not to interfere. A natural rhythm of the tribe, he guessed, best modified by the fundamental change in environment which his technology would inevitably create.

He went out into the fields one day to watch them. Pernar, the chief, was sweating with the rest. Theo lay back in the springy moss and watched them. He noticed idly that the wagons carrying produce—mounted now on his wheels, the old crude wooden skids having been discarded—did not go back to the village, but away up the slope, in the opposite direction. He asked Pernar why.

Pernar explained, "Against the Time, Lord."

"The time?"

Pernar paused for a moment, fumbling. At last he used a word Theo had not heard before.

"What's that?"

Pernar said awkwardly, "The wild air . . . the water."

A rainy season! Theo understood. It was reasonable enough that the harvest had to be in before the rains came. But that didn't explain the wagons trekking away uphill. He asked Pernar again.

"At the Time, we retreat. It is necessary."

"Necessary" was a common and useful word in the vocabulary of the natives; it stood for anything they were in the habit of doing. Eventually he would do something about it himself. But now it was pleasant enough to lie back in the green moss and watch his people going about their business. Let this coming rainy season pass in the usual way; next year he would really get down to pouring them into his mold—into the necessary mold for the empire that he would build and leave as his record to those ships a thousand years in the future.

The sky thickened into cloud over a period of several days; from thin twists and strands low on the horizon to ropes and bunched masses, and, finally, a universal, paralyzing gray. Two days after this unbroken canopy had settled over them, Pernar came to him in the palace.

"Lord, it is the Time."

Theo said, "How long will your people be gone?"

Pernar was startled. "You are not coming with us, Lord?"

"For you in your huts, the retreat may be necessary; these granite walls are protection enough against the wild air. In other years, you, too, will have refuges like this. Go in peace now."

Pernar nodded reluctantly. "Your other servants, Lord. . . ."

He was referring to the personal servants who attended the god-king in his palace.

"They will be safe here," Theo said.

"They will not stay, Lord. They dare not stay."

The best argument, Theo realized, was acquiescence. When they returned to find the palace still standing beside the storm-blasted huts of the village, that would be the real conviction. He said simply, "Let food and drink be made ready. For how long?"

"Two weeks."

"Two weeks, then."

He was aware of loneliness when the last of them had gone, up the rising ground to whatever ritual refuge they used against the storms. Now once more he was conscious of his isolation, cut off from his own people by uncountable galactic miles, by the long sweep of time itself. Only the realization of destiny made the future seem worth while. He was pleased, in a way, when the rising wind began to howl about the village. The savageness of the elements gave him something to measure himself against.

But he was not prepared for the fury that developed. The storm rose from climax to climax; rain belted down torrentially from the raging skies. On the third day it rose to hurricane force.

From an embrasure slit, he watched the pitiful native huts torn from their moorings and flung like tattered leaves about the swirling sky. It seemed impossible that there could be more violence, but more came. The air shrieked in protest, a high-pitched wail under the constant lash. Theo watched it in amazement.

He was more amazed still when Pernar came to him, drenched and battered from his voyage through the storm.

"You must come, Lord."

"Into that?" He pointed out into the storm. "You'd better stay here yourself now."

"The water . . . the water that rises."

"Floods? This place is high enough. We're all right here."

"You must come, Lord."

The argument between them went on as the late afternoon passed into night. And with nightfall, astonishingly, the rain stopped and the gale dropped. Theo said to Pernar triumphantly, "You see?"

For answer Pernar insisted on dragging him outside into the open. The ground was soggy underfoot; the mashed remains of the huts lay before them. Pernar pointed. On the far horizon a glow became increasingly brilliant against the thinning clouds. The cloud strands twisted and broke, and, in the interval of clear sky, he saw it.

A moon. A giant, gibbous moon poised above the skyline like a grinning skull.

But how? He knew this planet had no satellite.

When he considered things, it was obvious enough. One of the other two planets in the system, almost certainly the nearer one, with the methane atmosphere, was eccentrically orbited. It was this the natives measured their year by—the regular approach and the attendant pertubations. All their life, inevitably, must be regulated by it.

Pernar said, "The rising water, Lord. . . ."

He understood that, too. With one last glance at his sand-castle palace, he said, "Let's go."

The refuge was under the rocky knob of the hill's carapace, a natural cave hollowed out and improved by the work of generations. They arrived there with less than an hour to spare. Theo watched, with Pernar and the others, the brilliant globe that put out the light of the usual stars in a sky now clear and unclouded again. And he watched the tidal wave surge like a moving mountain of water to within twenty feet of where they crouched.

Watching it lap the land, almost at their feet, he considered the kind of courage that could have made Pernar go down into that doomed valley to rescue him. Nor was it any easily dismissed compulsion of religion. He had been fooling himself about that. You did not rescue a god from the consequences of his folly.

They were a peaceable and docile people. They had accepted his commands and they had given him service; if he wanted to be a god, they were willing to let him. But they weren't his subjects or his disciples. More important than those things, they were his friends.

There was still much he could give them, but more, he suspected, that they would give him.

Finding himself not a god was a relief, somehow. It was less of a strain to be human and fallible.

The floods receded, and the tribe moved again into the valley. As the great blue sun burned the water out of the steaming soil, they set to work to plant the seeds again and to rebuild the vanished huts.

Theo worked with them. He found an unexpected satisfaction in these labors, and an increasingly deeper realization of the nobility of these creatures who seemed to be without even the slightest trace of mutual hostility or anger. They accepted his working with them in the fields as casually as they had previously accepted his overlordship; the difference was that now he was one of them and wanted no more than the awareness of that oneness.

Sometimes, especially when he passed the broken and scattered stone of what had been his palace, he remembered the world he had come from, and that great ship that—in a hundred years, a thousand, a hundred thousand— might drop through the green glow of the sky.

But the memory and the thought were tinged with *fear*. Fear of anything that might come to disrupt the beauty and peace of this undemanding life.

When the planting was over, there was the season of recreation. They danced, supple, graceful, unhurried dances, to the music of flutelike instruments; and chanted poems whose tenderness he understood more clearly as his mind grew more at home in their liquid but sinewy tongue.

Day after day, week after week. Work and rest and laughter and song. Where he had once asked for worship, he found himself almost reverent.

He had not guessed there could be such joy in humility.

When he died, twenty of the planet's years later, he had been their loved and respected chief for nearly fifteen years. Only you couldn't call it chief, nor had he done so.

They buried him in his former palace, which had gradually become a mausoleum. His last request was to have the steam engine buried with him.

61

MAN OF DISTINCTION

Michael Shaara

THE REMARKABLE DISTINCTION of Thatcher Blitt did not come to the attention of a bemused world until late in the year 2180. Although Thatcher Blitt was, by the standards of his time, an extremely successful man financially, this was not considered *real* distinction. Unfortunately for Blitt, it never has been.

The history books do not record the names of the most successful merchants of the past unless they happened by chance to have been connected with famous men of the time. Thus Croesus is remembered largely for his contributions to famous Romans and successful armies. And Haym Solomon, a similarly wealthy man, would have been long forgotten had he not also been a financial mainstay of the American Revolution and consorted with famous, if impoverished, statesmen.

So if Thatcher Blitt was distinct among men, the distinction was not immediately apparent. He was a small, gaunt, fragile man who had the kind of face and bearing that are perfect for movie crowd scenes. Absolutley forgettable. Yet Thatcher Blitt was one of the foremost businessmen of his time. For he was president and founder of that noble instituton, Genealogy, Inc.

Thatcher Blitt was not yet twenty-five when he made the discovery which was to make him among the richest men of his time. His discovery was, like all great ones, obvious yet profound. He observed that every person had a father.

Carrying on with this thought, it followed inevitably that every father had a father, and so on. In fact, thought Blitt, when you considered the matter rightly, everyone alive was the direct descendant of untold numbers of fathers, down through the ages, all descending, one after another, father to son. And so backward, unquestionably, into the unrecognizable and perhaps simian fathers of the past.

This thought, on the face of it not particularly profound, struck young Blitt like a blow. He saw that since each man had a father, and so on and so on, it ought to be possible to construct the genealogy of every person now alive. In short, it should be possible to trace your family back, father by father, to the beginning of time.

And of course it was. For that was the era of the time scanner. And with a time scanner, it would be possible to document your family tree with perfect accuracy. You could find out exactly from whom you had sprung.

And so Thatcher Blitt made his fortune. He saw clearly at the beginning what most of us see only now, and he patented it. He was aware not only of the deep-rooted sense of snobbishness that exists in many people, but also of the simple yet profound force of curiosity. Who exactly, one says to oneself, *was* my forty-times-great-great-grandfather? A Roman Legionary? A Viking? A pyramid builder? One of Xenophon's Ten Thousand? Or was he, perhaps (for it is always possible), Alexander the Great?

Thatcher Blitt had a product to sell. And sell he did, for other reasons that he alone had noted at the beginning. The races of mankind have twisted and turned with incredible complexity over the years; the numbers of people have been enormous.

With thirty thousand years in which to work, it was impossible that there was not, somewhere along the line, a famous ancestor for everybody. A minor king would often suffice, or even a general in some forgotten army. And if these direct ancestors were not enough, it was fairly simple to establish close blood kinship with famous men. The blood lines of Man, you see, begin with a very few people. In all of ancient Greece, in the time of Pericles, there were only a few thousand families.

Seeing all this, Thatcher Blitt became a busy man. It was necessary not only to patent his idea, but to produce the enormous capital needed to found a large organization. The cost of the time scanner was at first prohibitive, but gradually that obstacle was overcome, only for Thatcher to find that the government for many years prevented him from using it. Yet Blitt was indomitable. And eventually, after years of heart-rending waiting, Genealogy, Inc., began operations.

It was a tremendous success. Within months, the very name of the company and its taut slogan, "An Ancestor for Everybody," became household words. There was but one immediate drawback. It soon became apparent that, without going back very far into the past, it was sometimes impossible to tell who was really the next father in line. The mothers were certain, but the fathers were something else again. This was a ponderable point.

Thatcher Blitt refused to be discouraged. He set various electronic engineers to work on the impasse and a solution was found. An ingenious device which tested blood electronically through the scanner—based on the different sine waves of the blood groups—saved the day. That invention was the last push Genealogy, Inc., was ever to need. It rolled on to become one of the richest and, for a long while, most exclusive corporations in the world.

Yet it was still many years before Thatcher Blitt himself had time to rest. There were patent infringements to be fought, new developments in the labs to be watched, new ways to be found to make the long and arduous task of father-tracing easier and more economical. Hence he was well past sixty when he at last had time to begin considering himself.

He had become by this time a moderately offensive man. Surrounded as he had been all these years by pomp and luxury, by impressive names and extraordinary family trees, he had succumbed at last. He became unbearably name-conscious.

He began by regrouping his friends according to their ancestries. His infrequent parties were characterized by his almost Parliamentarian system of seating. No doubt, all this had been in Thatcher Blitt to begin with—it may well be, in perhaps varying quantities, in all of us—but it grew with him, prospered with him. Yet in all those years he never once inspected his own forebears.

You may well ask, was he afraid? One answers, one does not know. But at any rate the fact remains that Thatcher Blitt, at the age of sixty-seven, was one of the few rich men in the world who did not know who exactly their ancestors had been.

And so, at last, we come to the day when Thatcher Blitt was sitting alone in his office, one languid hand draped vacantly over his brow, listening with deep satisfaction to the hum and click of the enormous operations which were going on in the building around him.

What moved him that day remains uncertain. Perhaps it was that, from where he was sitting, he could see row upon row of action pictures of famous men which had been taken from his time scanners. Or perhaps it was simply that this profound question had been gnawing at him all these years, deeper and deeper, and on this day broke out into the light.

But whatever the reason, at 11:02 that morning, he leaped vitally from his chair. He summoned Cathcart, his chief assistant, and gave him the immortal command.

"Cathcart!" he grated, stung to the core of his being. "Who am I?"

Cathcart rushed off to find out.

There followed some of the most taut and fateful days in the brilliant history of Genealogy, Inc. Father-tracing is, of course, a painstaking business. But it was not long before word had begun to filter out to interested people.

The first interesting discovery made was a man called Blott, in eighteenth century England. (No explanaton was ever given for the name's alteration from Blott to Blitt. Certain snide individuals took this to mean that the name had been changed as a means to avoid prosecution or some such, and immediately began making light remarks about the Blotts on old Blitt's escutcheon.) This Blott had the distinction of having been a wineseller of considerable funds.

This reputedly did not sit well with Thatcher Blitt. Merchants, he snapped, however successful, are not worthy of note. He wanted empire builders. He wanted, at the very least, a name he had heard about. A name that appeared in the histories.

His workers furiously scanned back into the past.

Months went by before the next name appeared. In 9th century England, there was a wandering minstrel named John (last name unprintable) who achieved considerable notoriety as a ballad singer, before dying an unnatural death in the boudoir of a lady of high fashion. Although the details of this man's life were of extreme interest, they did not impress the old man. He was, on the contrary, rather shaken. A minstrel. And a rogue to boot.

There were shakeups in Genealogy, Inc. Cathcart was replaced by a man named Jukes, a highly competent man despite his interesting family name. Jukes forged ahead full steam past the birth of Christ (no relation). But he was well into ancient Egypt before the search began to take on the nature of a crisis.

Up until then, there was simply nobody. Or to be more precise, nobody but *nobodies*. It was incredible, all the laws of chance were against it, but there was, actually, not a single ancestor of note. And no way of faking one, for Thatcher Blitt couldn't be fooled by his own methods. What there was was simply an unending line of peasants, serfs, an occasional foot soldier or leather worker. Past John the ballad-singer, there was no one at all worth reporting to the old man.

This situation would not continue, of course. There were so few families for men to spring from. The entire Gallic nation, for example, a great section of present-day France, sprang from the family of one lone man in the north of France in the days before Christ. Every native Frenchman, therefore, was at least the son of a king. It was impossible for Thatcher Blitt to be less.

So the hunt went on from day to day, past ancient Greece, past Jarmo, past the wheel and metals and farming and on even past all civilization, outward and backward into the cold primordial wastes of northern Germany.

And still there was nothing. Though Jukes lived in daily fear of losing his job, there was nothing to do but press on. In Germany, he reduced Blitt's ancestor to a slovenly little man who was one of only three men in the entire tribe, or family, one of three in an area which now contains millions. But Blitt's ancestor, true to form, was simply a member of the tribe. As was his father before him.

Yet onward it went. Westward back into the French caves, southward into Spain and across the unrecognizable Meditteranean into a verdant North Africa, backward in time past even the Cro-Magnons, and yet ever backward, 30,000 years, 35,000, with old Blitt reduced now practically to gibbering and still never an exceptional forebear.

There came a time when Jukes had at last, inevitably, to face the old man. He had scanned back as far as he could. The latest ancestor he had unearthed for Blitt was a hairy creature who did not walk erect. And yet, even here Blitt refused to concede.

"It may be," he howled, "it *must* be that my ancestor *was* the first man to walk erect or light a fire—to do *something*."

It was not until Jukes pointed out that all those things had been already examined and found hopeless that Blitt finally gave in. Blitt was a relative, of course, of the first man to stand erect, the man with the first human brain. But so was everybody else on the face of the Earth. There was truly nowhere else to explore. What would be found now would be only the common history of mankind.

Blitt retired to his chambers and refused to be seen.

The story went the rounds, as such stories will. And it was then at last, after 40,000 years of insignificance, that the name of Blitt found everlasting distinction. The story was picked up, fully documented, by psychologists and geneticists of the time, and inserted into textbooks as a profound commentary on the forces of heredity. The name of Thatcher Blitt in particular has become famous, has persisted until this day. For he is the only man yet discovered, or ever likely to be discovered, with this particular distinction.

In 40,000 years of scanner-recorded history, the blood line of Blitt (or Blott) never once produced an exceptional man.

That record is unsurpassed.

62

THE MAN WHO ALWAYS KNEW

Algis Budrys

THE SMALL, THIN, stoop-shouldered man sat down on the stool nearest the wall, took a dollar bill out of his wallet, and laid it on the bar. Behind their rimless glasses, his watery blue eyes fastened vacantly on a space somewhere between the end of his nose and the bottles standing on the backbar tiers. An old porkpie hat was squashed down over the few sandy hairs that covered his bony skull. His head was buried deep in the collar of his old, baggy tweed overcoat, and a yellow muffler trailed down from around his neck. His knobby-knuckled hands played with the dollar bill.

Harry, the barkeep, was busy mixing three martinis for a table in the dining room, but as soon as the small man came in he looked up and smiled. And as soon as he had the three filled glasses lined up on a tray for the waiter to pick up, he hurried up to the end of the bar.

"Afternoon, Mr. McMahon! And what'll it be for you today?"

The small man looked up with a wan sigh. "Nothing, yet, Harry. Mind if I just sit and wait a minute?"

"Not at all, Mr. McMahon, not at all." He looked around at the empty stools. "Quiet as the grave in here this afternoon. Same thing over at the lab?"

The small man nodded slowly, looking down at his fingers creasing the dollar bill. "Just a quiet afternoon, I guess," he said in a tired voice. "Nothing's due to come to a head over there until some time next week."

Harry nodded to show he understood. It was that kind of a day. "Haven't seen you for a while, Mr. McMahon—been away again?"

The small man pleated the dollar bill, held one end between thumb and forefinger, and spread the bill like a fan. "That's right. I went down to Baltimore for a few days." He smoothed out the bill and touched the top of the bar. "You know, Harry, it wouldn't surprise me if next year we could

387

give you a bar varnish you could let absolute alcohol stand on overnight.''

Harry shook his head slowly. ''Beats me, Mr. McMahon. I never know what's coming out of your lab next. One week it's steam engines, the next it's bar varnish. What gets me is where you find the time. Doing all that traveling and still being the biggest inventor in the world—bigger than Edison, even. Why, just the other day the wife and I went out and bought two of those pocket transceiver sets of yours, and Emma said she didn't see how I could know you. 'A man as busy as Mr. McMahon must be,' she said, 'wouldn't be coming into the bar all the time like you say he does.' Well, that's a wife for you. But she's right. Beats me, too, like I said.''

The small man shrugged uncomfortably, and didn't say anything. Then he got a suddenly determined look on his face and started to say something, but just then the waiter stepped up to the bar.

''Two Gibson, one whiskey sour, Harry.''

''Coming up. Excuse me, Mr. McMahon. Mix you something while I'm down there?''

The small man shook his head. ''Not just yet, Harry.''

''Right, Mr. McMahon.''

Harry shook up the cocktails briskly. From the sound of it, Mr. McMahon had been about to say something important, and anything Mr. McMahon thought was important would be something you shouldn't miss.

He bumped the shaker, dropped the strainer in, and poured the Gibsons. He just hoped Mr. McMahon hadn't decided it wasn't worth talking about. Let's see what Emma would have to say if he came home and told her what Mr. McMahon had told him, and a year or two later something new— maybe a new kind of home permanent or something—came out. She'd use it. She'd have to use it, because it would just naturally be the best thing on the market. And every time she did, she'd have to remember that Harry had told her first. Let's see her say Mr. McMahon wasn't a steady customer of his then! Bar varnish wasn't in the same league.

The small man was looking into space again, with a sad little smile, when Harry got back to him. He was pushing the dollar bill back and forth with his index fingers. A bunch of people came in the door and Harry muttered under his breath, but they didn't stop at the bar. They went straight from the coat rack to the dining room, and Harry breathed easier. Maybe he'd have time to hear what Mr. McMahon had to say.

''Well, here I am again, Mr. McMahon.''

The small man looked up with a sharp gleam in his eyes. ''Think I'm pretty hot stuff, eh, Harry?''

''Yes, sir,'' Harry said, not knowing what to make of it.

"Think I'm the Edison of the age, huh?"

"Well—gosh, Mr. McMahon, you are *better* than Edison!"

The small man's fingers crumpled up the dollar bill and rolled it into a tight ball.

"The Perfect Cumbustion Engine, the Condensing Steam Jet, the Voice-Operated Typewriter, and Discontinuous Airfoil—things like that, eh?" the small man asked sharply.

"Yes, sir. And the Arc House, and the Minute Meal, and the Lintless Dustcloth—well, gosh, Mr. McMahon, I could go on all day, I guess."

"Didn't invent a one of them," the small man snapped. His shoulders seemed to straighten out from under a heavy load. He looked Harry in the eye. "I never invented anything in my life."

"Two Gibson and another whiskey sour, Harry," the waiter interrupted.

"Yeah—sure," Harry moved uneasily down the bar. He tilted the gin bottle slowly, busy turning things over in his mind. He sneaked a look at Mr. McMahon. The small man was looking down at his hands, curling them up into fists and smiling. He looked happy. That wasn't like him at all.

Harry set the drinks up on the waiter's tray and got back up to the end of the bar.

"Mr. McMahon?"

The small man looked up again.

"Yes, Harry?" He *did* look happy—happy all the way through, like a man with insomnia who suddenly feels himself drifting off to sleep.

"You were just saying about that varnish—

"Fellow in Baltimore. Paints signs for a living. Not very good ones; they weather too fast. I noticed him working, the last time I was down that way."

"I don't follow you, Mr. McMahon."

The small man bounced the balled-up dollar bill on the bar and watched it roll around. "Well, I knew he was a conscientious young fellow, even if he didn't know much about paint. So, yesterday I went back down there, and, sure enough, he'd been fooling around—just taking a little of this and a little of that, stirring it up by guess and by gosh—and he had something he could paint over a sign that would stand up to a blowtorch."

"Golly, Mr. McMahon. I thought you said he didn't know much about paint."

The small man scooped up the bill and smoothed it out. "He didn't. He was just fooling around. Anybody else would have just come up with a gallon of useless goo. But he *looked* like the kind of man who'd happen to hit it right. And he looked like the kind of man who'd hit it sometime about yesterday. So I went down there, made him an offer, and came back with a gallon of what's going to be the best varnish anybody ever put on the market.''

Harry twisted his hands uncomfortably in his pockets. "Gee, Mr. Mc-Mahon—you mean you do the same thing with everything else?''

"That's right, Harry.'' The small man pinched the two ends of the dollar bill, brought them together, and then snapped the bill flat with a satisfied *pop!* "Exactly the same thing. I was on a train passing an open field once, and saw a boy flying model airplanes. Two years later, I went back and sure enough, he'd just finished his first drawings on the discontinuous airfoil. I offered him a licensing fee and a good cash advance, and came home with the airfoil.'' The small man looked down sadly and reminiscently. "He used the money to finance himself through aeronautical engineering school. Never turned out anything new again.''

"Gosh, Mr. McMahon. I don't know what to say. You mean you travel around the country just looking for people that are working on something new?''

The small man shook his head. "No. I travel around the country, and I stumble across people who're going to accidentally stumble across something good. I've got secondhand luck.'' The small man rolled the bill up between his fingers, and smiled with a hurt twist in his sensitive mouth. "It's even better than that. I know more or less *what* they're going to stumble across, and *when* they're going to.'' He bent the tube he'd made out of the bill. "But I can't develop it myself. I just have to wait. I've only got one talent.''

"Well, gee, Mr. McMahon, that's a fine thing to have.''

The small man crushed the dollar bill. "Is it, Harry? How do you use it directly? How do you define it? Do you set up shop as McMahon and Company—Secondhand Luck Bought and Sold? Do you get a Nobel Prize for Outstanding Achievement in Luck?''

"You've got a Nobel Prize, Mr. McMahon.''

"For a cold cure discovered by a pharmacist who mis-labeled a couple of prescriptions.''

"Well, look, Mr. McMahon—that's better than no Nobel Prize at all.''

The small man's sensitive mouth twisted again. "Yes, it is, Harry. A little bit.'' He almost tore the dollar bill. "Just a little bit.'' He stared into space.

"Mr. McMahon, I wouldn't feel so bad about it if I was you. There's no sense to taking it out on yourself,'' Harry said worriedly.

The small man shrugged.

Harry shuffled his feet. "I wish there was something I could do for you."
It felt funny, being sorry for the luckiest man in the world.

The small man smoothed the dollar out again.

"Two whiskey sour, and another Gibson," the waiter said. Harry moved unhappily down the bar and began to mix, thinking about Mr. McMahon. Then he heard Mr. McMahon get off his stool and come down the bar.

He looked up. The small man was standing opposite him and looking down at the bar. Harry looked down too, and realized he'd been trying to make a whiskey sour with Gibson liquor. It looked like nothing he'd ever seen before.

Mr. McMahon pushed the dollar bill across the bar. He reached out and took the funny-looking drink. There was a sad-happy smile on his face.

"That's the one I wanted, Harry," he said.

63

THE MAN WITH ENGLISH

H. L. Gold

LYING IN THE hospital, Edgar Stone added up his misfortunes as another might count blessings. There were enough to infuriate the most temperate man, which Stone notoriously was not. He smashed his fist down, accidentally hitting the metal side of the bed, and was astonished by the pleasant feeling. It enraged him even more. The really maddening thing was how simply he had goaded himself into the hospital.

He'd locked up his drygoods store and driven home for lunch. Nothing unusual about that; he did it every day. With his miserable digestion, he couldn't stand the restaurant food in town. He pulled into the driveway, rode over a collection of metal shapes his son Arnold had left lying around, and punctured a tire.

"Rita!" he yelled. "This is going too damned far! Where is that brat?"

"In here," she called truculently from the kitchen.

He kicked open the screen door. His foot went through the mesh.

"A ripped tire and a torn screen!" he shouted at Arnold, who was sprawled in angular adolescence over a blueprint on the kitchen talble. "You'll pay for them, by God! They're coming out of your allowance!"

"I'm sorry, Pop," the boy said.

"Sorry, my left foot," Mrs. Stone shrieked. She whirled on her husband. "You could have watched where you were going. He promised to clean up his things from the driveway right after lunch. And it's about time you stopped kicking open the door every time you're mad."

"Mad? Who wouldn't be mad? Me hoping he'd get out of school and come into the store, and he wants to be an engineer. An engineer—and he can't even make change when he—hah!—helps me out in the store!"

"He'll be whatever he wants to be," she screamed in the conversational tone of the Stone household.

"Please," said Arnold. "I can't concentrate on this plan."

Edgar Stone was never one to restrain an angry impulse. He tore up the blueprint and flung the pieces down on the table.

"Aw, Pop!" Arnold protested.

"Don't say 'Aw, Pop' to me. You're not going to waste a summer vacation on junk like this. You'll eat your lunch and come down to the store. And you'll do it every day for the rest of the summer!"

"Oh, he will, will he?" demanded Mrs. Stone. "He'll catch up on his studies. And as for you, you can go back and eat in a restaurant."

"You know I can't stand that slop!"

"You'll eat it because you're not having lunch here any more. I've got enough to do without making three meals a day."

"But I can't drive back with that tire—"

He did, though not with the tire—he took a cab. It cost a dollar plus tip, lunch was a dollar and a half plus tip, bicarb at Rite Drug Store a few doors away and in a great hurry came to another fifteen cents—only it didn't work.

And then Miss Ellis came in for some material. Miss Ellis could round out any miserable day. She was fifty, tall, skinny and had thin, disapproving lips. She had a sliver of cloth clipped very meagerly off a hem that she intended to use as a sample.

"The arms of the slipcover on my reading chair wore through," she informed him. "I bought the material here, if you remember."

Stone didn't have to look at the fragmentary swatch. "That was about seven years ago—"

"Six-and-a-half," she corrected. "I paid enough for it. You'd expect anything that expensive to last."

"The style was discontinued. I have something here that—"

"I do not want to make an entire slipcover, Mr. Stone. All I want is enough to make new panels for the arms. Two yards should do very nicely."

Stone smothered a bilious hiccup. "Two yards, Miss Ellis?"

"At the most."

"I sold the last of that material years ago." He pulled a bolt off a shelf and partly unrolled it for her. "Why not use a different pattern as a kind of contrast?"

"I want this same pattern," she said, her thin lips getting even thinner and more obstinate."

"Then I'll have to order it and hope one of my wholesalers still has some of it in stock."

"Not without looking for it first right here, you won't order it for me. You can't know *all* these materials you have on these shelves."

Stone felt all the familiar symptoms of fury—the sudden pulsing of the temples, the lurch and bump of his heart as adrenalin came surging in like the tide at the Firth of Forth, the quivering of his hands, the angry shout pulsing at his vocal cords from below.

"I'll take a look, Miss Ellis," he said.

She was president of the Ladies' Cultural Society and dominated it so thoroughly that the members would go clear to the next town for their dry goods, rather than deal with him, if he offended this sour stick of stubbornness.

If Stone's life insurance salesman had been there, he would have tried to keep Stone from climbing the ladder that ran around the three walls of the store. He probably wouldn't have been in time. Stone stamped up the ladder to reach the highest shelves, where there were scraps of bolts. One of them might have been the remnant of the material Miss Ellis had bought six-and-a-half years ago. But Stone never found out.

He snatched one, glaring down meanwhile at the top of Miss Ellis's head, and the ladder skidded out from under him. He felt his skull collide with the counter. He didn't feel it hit the floor.

"God damn it!" Stone yelled. "You could at least turn on the lights."

"There, there, Edgar. Everything's fine, just fine."

It was his wife's voice and the tone was so uncommonly soft and soothing that it scared him into panic.

"What's wrong with me?" he asked piteously. "Am I blind?"

"How many fingers am I holding up?" a man wanted to know.

Stone was peering into the blackness. All he could see before his eyes was a vague blot against a darker blot.

"None," he bleated. "Who are you?"

"Dr. Rankin. That was a nasty fall you had, Mr. Stone—concussion of course, and a splinter of bone driven into the brain. I had to operate to remove it."

"Then you cut out a nerve!" Stone said. "You did something to my eyes!"

The doctor's voice sounded puzzled. "There doesn't seem to be anything wrong with them. I'll take a look, though, and see."

"You'll be all right, dear," Mrs. Stone said reassuringly, but she didn't sound as if she believed it.

"Sure you will, Pop," said Arnold.

"Is that young stinker here?" Stone demanded. "He's the cause of all this!"

"Temper, temper," the doctor said. "Accidents happen."

Stone heard him lower the venetian blinds. As if they had been a switch, light sprang up and everything in the hospital became brightly visible.

"Well!" said Stone. "That's more like it. It's night and you're trying to save electricity, hey?"

"It's broad daylight, Edgar dear," his wife protested. "All Dr. Rankin did was lower the blinds and—"

"Please," the doctor said. "If you don't mind, I'd rather take care of any explanations that have to be made."

He came at Stone with an ophthalmoscope. When he flashed it into Stone's eyes, everything went black and Stone let him know it vociferously.

"Black?" Dr. Rankin repeated blankly. "Are you positive? Not a sudden glare?"

"Black," insisted Stone. "And what's the idea of putting me in a bed filled with bread crumbs?

"It was freshly made—"

"Crumbs. You heard me. And the pillow has rocks in it."

"What else is bothering you?" asked the doctor worriedly.

"It's freezing in here." Stone felt the terror rise in him again. "It was summer when I fell off the ladder. Don't tell me I've become unconcious clear through till winter!"

"No, Pop," said Arnold. "That was yesterday—"

"I'll take care of this," Dr. Rankin said firmly. "I'm afraid you and your son will have to leave, Mrs. Stone. I have to do a few tests on your husband."

"Will he be all right?" she appealed.

"Of course, of course," he said inattentively, peering with a frown at the shivering patient. "Shock, you know," he added vaguely.

"Gosh, Pop," said Arnold. "I'm sorry this happened. I got the driveway all cleaned up."

"And we'll take care of the store till you're better," Mrs. Stone promised.

"Don't you dare!" yelled Stone. "You'll put me out of business!"

The doctor hastily shut the door on them and came back to the bed. Stone was clutching the light summer blanket around himself. He felt colder than he'd ever been in his life.

"Can't you get me more blankets?" he begged. "You don't want me to die of pneumonia, do you?"

Dr. Rankin opened the blinds and asked, "What's this like?"

"Night," chattered Stone. "A new idea to save electricity—hooking up the blinds to the light switch?"

The doctor closed the blinds and sat down beside the bed. He was sweating as he reached for the signal button and pressed it. A nurse came in, blinking in their direction.

"Why don't you turn on the light?" she asked.

"Huh?" said Stone. "They are."

"Nurse, I'm Dr. Rankin. Get me a piece of sandpaper, some cotton swabs, an ice cube and Mr. Stone's lunch."

"Is there anything he shouldn't eat?"

"That's what I want to find out. Hurry, please."

"And some blankets," Stone put in, shaking with the chill.

"Blankets, Doctor?" she asked, startled.

"Half a dozen will do," he said. "I think."

It took her ten minutes to return with all the items. Stone wanted them to keep adding blankets until all seven were on him. He still felt cold.

"Maybe some hot coffee?" he suggested.

The doctor nodded and the nurse poured a cup, added the spoon and a half of sugar he requested, and he took a mouthful. He sprayed it out violently.

"Ice cold!" he yelped. "And who put salt in it?"

"Salt?" She fumbled around on the tray. "It's so dark here—"

"I'll attend to it," Dr. Rankin said hurriedly. "Thank you."

She walked cautiously to the door and went out.

"Try this," said the doctor, after filling another cup.

"Well, that's better!" Stone exclaimed. "Damned practical joker. They shouldn't be allowed to work in hospitals."

"And now, if you don't mind," said the doctor, "I'd like to try several tests."

Stone was still angry at the trick played on him, but he cooperated willingly.

Dr. Rankin finally sagged back in the chair. The sweat ran down his face and into his collar, and his expression was so dazed that Stone was alarmed.

"What's wrong, Doctor? Am I going to—going to—"

"No, no. It's not that. No danger. At least, I don't believe there is. But I can't even be sure of that any more."

397

"You can't be sure if I'll live or die?"

"Look." Dr. Rankin grimly pulled the chair closer. "It's broad daylight and yet you can't see until I darken the room. The coffee was hot and sweet, but it was cold and salty to you, so I added an ice cube and a spoonful of salt and it tasted fine, you said. This is one of the hottest days on record and you're freezing. You told me the sandpaper felt smooth and satiny, then yelled that somebody had put pins in the cotton swabs, when there weren't any, of course. I've tried you out with different colors around the room and you saw violet when you should have seen yellow, green for red, orange for blue, and so on. Now do you understand?"

"No," said Stone frightenedly. "What's wrong?"

"All I can do is guess. I had to remove that sliver of bone from your brain. It apparently shorted your sensory nerves."

"And what happened?"

"Every one of your senses has been reversed. You feel cold for heat, heat for cold, smooth for rough, rough for smooth, sour for sweet, sweet for sour, and so forth. And you see colors backward."

Stone sat up. "Murderer! Thief! You've ruined me!"

The doctor sprang for a hypodermic and sedative. Just in time, he changed his mind and took a bottle of stimulant instead. It worked fine, though injecting it into his screaming, thrashing patient took more strength than he'd known he owned. Stone fell asleep immediately.

There were nine blankets on Stone and he had a bag of cement for a pillow when he had his lawyer, Manny Lubin, in to hear the charges he wanted brought against Dr. Rankin. The doctor was there to defend himself. Mrs. Stone was present in spite of her husband's objections—"She always takes everybody's side against me," he explained in a roar.

"I'll be honest with you, Mr. Lubin," the doctor said, after Stone had finished on a note of shrill frustration. "I've hunted for cases like this in medical history and this is the first one ever to be reported. Except," he amended quickly, "that I haven't reported it yet. I'm hoping it reverses itself. That sometimes happens, you know."

"And what am I supposed to do in the meantime?" raged Stone. "I'll have to go out wearing an overcoat in the summer and shorts in the winter—people will think I'm a maniac. And they'll be *sure* of it because I'll have to keep the store closed during the day and open at night—I can't see except in the dark. And matching materials! I can't stand the feel of smooth cloth and I see colors backward!" He glared at the doctor before turning back to Lubin. "How would you like to have to put sugar on your food and salt in your coffee?"

"But we'll work it out, Edgar dear," his wife soothed. "Arnold and I can take care of the store. You always wanted him to come into the business, so that ought to please you—"

"As long as I'm there to watch him!"

"And Dr. Rankin said maybe things will straighten out."

"What about that, Doctor?" asked Lubin. "What are the chances?"

Dr. Rankin looked uncomfortable. "I don't know. This has never happened before. All we can do is hope."

"Hope, nothing!" Stone stormed. "I want to sue him. He had no right to go meddling around and turn me upside down. Any jury would give me a quarter of a million!"

"I'm no millionaire, Mr. Stone," said the doctor.

"But the hospital has money. We'll sue him and the trustees."

There was a pause while the attorney thought. "I'm afraid we wouldn't have a case, Mr. Stone." He went on more rapidly as Stone sat up, shivering, to argue loudly. "It was an emergency operation. Any surgeon would have had to operate. Am I right, Dr. Rankin?"

The doctor explained what would have happened if he had not removed the pressure on the brain, resulting from the concussion, and the danger that the bone splinter, if not extracted, might have gone on traveling and caused possible paralysis or death.

"That would be better than this," said Stone.

"But medical ethics couldn't allow him to let you die," Lubin objected. "He was doing his duty. That's point one."

"Mr. Lubin is absolutely right, Edgar," said Mrs. Stone.

"There, you see?" screamed her husband. "Everybody's right but me! Will you get her out of here before I have a stroke?"

"Her interests are also involved," Lubin pointed out. "Point two is that the emergency came first, the after-effects couldn't be known or considered."

Dr. Rankin brightened. "Any operation involves risk, even the excising of a corn. I had to take those risks."

"*You* had to take them?" Stone scoffed. "All right, what are you leading up to Lubin?"

"We'd lose," said the attorney.

Stone subsided, but only for a moment. "So we'll lose. But if we sue, the publicity would ruin him. I want to sue!"

"For what, Edgar dear?" his wife persisted. "We'll have a hard enough time managing. Why throw good money after bad?"

"Why didn't I marry a woman who'd take my side, even when I'm wrong?" moaned Stone. "Revenge, that's what. And he won't be able to practice, so he'll have time to find out if there's a cure . . . and at no charge, either! I won't pay him another cent!''

The doctor stood up eagerly. ''But I'm willing to see what can be done right now. And it wouldn't cost you anything, naturally.''

''What do you mean?'' Stone challenged suspiciously.

''If I were to perform another operation, I'll be able to see which nerves were involved. There's no need to go into the technical side right now, but it is possible to connect nerves. Of course, there are a good many, which complicates matters, especially since the splinter went through several layers—''

Lubin pointed a lawyer's impaling finger at him. ''Are you offering to attempt to correct the injury—gratis?''

''Certainly. I mean to say, I'll do my absolute best. But keep in mind, please, that there is no medical precedent.''

The attorney, however, was already questioning Stone and his wife. ''In view of the fact that we have no legal grounds whatever for suit, does this offer of settlement satisfy your claim against him?''

''Oh, yes!'' Mrs. Stone cried.

Her husband hesitated for a while, clearly tempted to take the opposite position out of habit. ''I guess so,'' he reluctantly agreed.

''Well, then it's in your hands, Doctor,'' said Lubin.

Dr. Rankin buzzed excitedly for the nurse. ''I'll have him prepared for surgery right away.''

''It better work this time,'' warned Stone, clutching a handful of ice cubes to warm his fingers.

Stone came to foggily. He didn't know it, but he had given the anesthetist a bewildering problem, which finally had been solved by using fumes of aromatic spirits of ammonia. The four blurred figures around the bed seemed to be leaning precariously toward him.

''Pop!'' said Arnold. ''Look, he's coming out of it! Pop!''

''Speak to me, Edgar dear,'' Mrs. Stone beseeched.

Lubin said, ''See how he is, Doctor.''

''He's fine,'' the doctor insisted heartily, his usual bedside manner evidently having returned. ''He must be—the blinds are open and he's not complaining that it's dark or that he's cold.'' He leaned over the bed. ''How are we feeling, Mr. Stone?''

It took a minute or two for Stone to move his swollen tongue enough to answer. He wrinkled his nose in disgust.

''What smells purple?'' he demanded.

64

THE MANSION OF FORGETFULNESS

Don Mark Lemon

FOUR MONTHS AFTER the salt waves had laid at his feet the cold form of his Love, came the news that Herbert Munson was the possessor of a startling secret. He had, it was stated, discovered a Purple Ray that would wither and destroy certain human cells of memory without injury or danger to neighboring cells. This rumor was followed by the still more amazing report that Munson had erected the Mansion of Forgetfulness, to which all who would free their minds of a hopeless passion might repair, and in one brief hour, *forget*.

And, sure enough, here they came—those who loved not wisely but too well, those who loved deeply but hopelessly, and those who loved the Dead and could endure their grief no longer—and the Purple Ray "plucked from the memory its rooted sorrow", and they went forth from the Mansion of Forgetfulness unscarred and fancy-free.

Yet he who showed others how to forget would not himself forget. It was agony to know that she was dead, and he would never see her face again, yet he shrank from forgetfulness as the soul shrinks from oblivion. Try as he would, he could not drag himself from the haunted halls of memory, though he remembered that the world without was wonderfully fair, and other women, perhaps as lovely as she, were waiting there to love and be loved. No! Let others forget, he would not! Not that he lived in hope, for had he not kissed the salt foam from her dead face? But that memory was all that remained of a Love who was no more.

He watched them come and go—watched the many, ah, too many, pilgrims arrive with sorrowful, love-haunted faces, but depart with unconcerned, care-free looks, and at times he feared that his philanthropy was a sacrilege. There seemed something unholy in this sudden transmutation of grief into gladness—this swift thrusting aside of the tragic presence of sorrow—yet they had chosen of their own free will to forget a hopeless passion, and they could now return whence they came and love again, more wisely if less deeply.

Some came, thinking to blot out other memories than that of a hopeless love—memories of sin and crime—but the Purple Ray would not be thwarted to such base purposes, and they left, abashed and disappointed.

It was in winter, when the snow was changed to crystal as it fell upon the walls and cornices of the beautiful marble edifice, or piled itself in drifts of sifted diamonds against the stained glass windows, when a lady came alone across the vales and entered the broad gateway of the Mansion of Forgetfulness.

Something in her manner—perhaps her agitated hesitation at the portals—moved the master to accost her.

"Kind friend," he said, "were it not better to remember what you now seek to forget?" As he spoke he drew closer about his face the cowl he wore to conceal his identity from the merely curious.

A sigh was the only immediate answer, as the pilgrim leaned wearily against a marble pillar. Then came the low spoken words:

"Perhaps I may only half-forget. I would remember, yet not remember so acutely."

"No, you will wholly forget. The Purple Ray is oblivion itself."

"Ah, well, better I kill these painful memories than break my heart!"

"Then, if it must be so, enter and forget."

"Show me the way and let me go quickly," was the plea of the veiled lady. "I have come far, and the worst is only a few steps farther on."

"Come, then!" and the master led the way to the room of the Purple Ray.

An hour passed, when the door was opened and the veiled visitor came forth and descended the broad stairway. She moved quickly and lightly, and at the foot of the stairs she laughed musically as she again met the master.

"Have you forgotten?" he asked.

"Forgotten! I know that I have forgotten something, else why am I here, yet I do not know what I have forgotten."

"So they all say!"

A flush of rosy light shone from a slender window overhead, haloing the pilgrim like a saint.

"How beautiful everything is!" she exclaimed. "Why do I wear this veil? I will no longer!"

So saying, she loosened it, disclosing a face young and exquisitely fair. The man shrank back as if pierced by a bolt.

"My God, it is her spirit!" he gasped.

"No, no!" protested the visitor. "I am not a spirit, and I fear I am too, too human."

"You are Morella!" whispered the man, staring before him like one peering through intense darkness.

"I am. Who are you that you ask?"

"Morella! I thought you dead! I kissed you for dead and then the waves swept me away and I saw you no more."

"Some fishermen once found me on a sandy beach, where they said I fainted. Who are you?"

The man drew back his cowl. "Look!" There was no light of recognition in the other's eyes. "My God! the Ray has blotted out all memory!"

"Pray tell me what you mean, and let me go," came the passionless words.

A groan was the only reply, and the man hid his face in his hands.

"You seem to know what I have forgotten. Has it aught to do with you?"

"O Morella, it were better that I thought you dead than to know that you have forgotten! Do you not recall our betrothal? See, you have the ring upon your hand! Does it not awaken one recollection of other days?"

The girl gazed blankly at the ring on her hand, and shook her head.

"Has the Ray blotted out every fair memory! Have you returned to life only to forget! Try to think, dearest: Do you not remember that day in Naples when we pledged eternal love for one another?"

"I remember no betrothal." A deep look of pity came into the speaker's eyes when she saw the pain her words had caused. "If remembrance is so sad, why do you not also forget?"

"My love!" he groaned, "you are making the world darker to me than to dying eyes! You ask me to forget! You!"

"You forget that I have forgotten."

The man groaned in utter anguish.

As she turned to go he stayed her by a gentle touch. *"Wait here while I, too, go and kill that memory!"*

He dragged himself up the broad stairway, looking back once when he had reached the landing, then turned and staggered toward the room of the Purple Ray.

65

MY OBJECT ALL SUBLIME

Poul Anderson

WE MET IN line of business. Michael's firm wanted to start a subdivision on the far side of Evanston and discovered that I held title to some of the most promising acreage. They made me a good offer, but I was stubborn; they raised it and I stayed stubborn; finally the boss himself looked me up. He wasn't entirely what I'd expected. Aggressive, of course, but in so polite a way that it didn't offend, his manners so urbane you rarely noticed his lack of formal education. Which lack he was remedying quite fast, anyhow, via night classes and extension courses as well as omnivorous reading.

We went out for a drink while we talked the matter over. He led me to a bar that had little of Chicago about it: quiet, shabby, no jukebox, no television, a bookshelf and several chess sets, but none of the freaks and phonies who usually infest such places. Besides ourselves, there were only half a dozen customers—a professor-emeritus type among the books, some people arguing politics with a degree of factual relevancy, a young man debating with the bartender whether Bartok was more original than Schoenberg or vice versa. Michaels and I found a corner table and some Danish beer.

I explained that I didn't care about money one way or another, but objected to bulldozing some rather good-looking countryside in order to erect still another chrome-plated slum. Michaels stuffed his pipe before answering. He was a lean, erect man, long-chinned and Roman-nosed, his hair grizzled, his eyes dark and luminous. "Didn't my representative explain?" he said. "We aren't planning a row of identical split-level sties. We have six basic designs in mind, with variations, to be located in a pattern . . . so."

He took out pencil and paper and began to sketch. As he talked, his accent thickened, but the fluency remained. And he made his own case

405

better than anyone had done for him. Like it or not, he said, this was the middle of the twentieth century and mass production was here to stay. A community need not be less attractive for being ready-made, could in fact gain an artistic unity. He proceeded to show me how.

He didn't press me too hard, and conversation wandered.

"Delightful spot, this," I remarked. "How'd you find it?"

He shrugged. "I often prowl about, especially at night. Exploring."

"Isn't that rather dangerous?"

"Not in comparison," he said with a touch of grimness.

"Uh . . . I gather you weren't born over here?"

"No. I didn't arrive in the United States until 1946. What they called a DP, a displaced person. I became Thad Michaels because I got tired of spelling out Tadeusz Michalowski. Nor did I want any part of old-country sentimentalism; I'm a zealous assimilationist."

Otherwise he seldom talked much about himself. Later I got some details of his early rise in business, from admiring and envious competitors. Some of them didn't yet believe it was possible to sell a house with radiant heating for less than twenty thousand dollars and show a profit. Michaels had found ways to make it possible. Not bad for a penniless immigrant.

I checked up and found he'd been admitted on a special visa, in consideration of services rendered the U.S. Army in the last stages of the European war. Those services had taken nerve as well as quick-wittedness.

Meanwhile our acquaintance developed. I sold him the land he wanted, but we continued to see each other, sometimes in the tavern, sometimes at my bachelor apartment, most often in his lakeshore penthouse. He had a stunning blonde wife and a couple of bright, well-mannered boys. Nonetheless he was a lonely man, and I fulfilled his need for friendship.

A year or so after we first met, he told me the story.

I'd been invited over for Thanksgiving dinner. Afterward we sat around and talked. And talked. And talked. When we had ranged from the chances of an upset in the next city election to the chances of other planets following the same general course of history as our own, Amalie excused herself and went to bed. This was long past midnight. Michaels and I kept on talking. I had not seen him so excited before. It was as if that last subject, or some particular word, had opened a door for him. Finally he got up, refilled our whisky glasses with a motion not altogether steady, and walked across the living room (noiseless on that deep green carpet) to the picture window.

The night was clear and sharp. We overlooked the city, streaks and webs and coils of glittering color, ruby, amethyst, emerald, topaz, and the dark sheet of Lake Michigan; almost it seemed we could glimpse endless white plains beyond. But overhead arched the sky, crystal black, where the Great Bear stood on his tail and Orion went striding along the Milky Way. I had not often seen so big and frosty a view.

"After all," he said, "I know what I'm talking about."

I stirred, deep in my armchair. The fire on the hearth spat tiny blue flames. Besides this, only one shaded lamp lit the room, so that the star swarms had also been visible to me when I passed by the window earlier. I gibed a little. "Personally?"

He glanced back toward me. His face was stiff. "What would you say if I answered yes?"

I sipped my drink. King's Ransom is a noble and comforting brew, most especially when the Earth itself seems to tone with a deepening chill. "I'd suppose you had your reasons and wait to see what they were."

He grinned one-sidedly. "Oh, well, I'm from this planet too," he said. "And yet—yet the sky is so wide and strange, don't you think the strangeness would affect men who went there? Wouldn't it seep into them, so they carried it back in their bones, and Earth was never quite the same afterward?"

"Go on. You know I like fantasies."

He stared outward, and then back again, and suddenly he tossed off his drink. The violent gesture was unlike him. But so had his hesitation been.

He said in a harsh tone, with all the former accent: "Okay, then, I shall tell you a fantasy. It is a story for winter, though, a cold story, that you are best advised not to take so serious."

I drew on the excellent cigar he had given me and waited in the silence he needed.

He paced a few times back and forth before the window, eyes to the floor, until he filled his glass anew and sat down near me. He didn't look at me but at a picture on the wall, a somber, unintelligible thing which no one else liked. He seemed to get strength from it, for he began talking, fast and softly.

"Once upon a time, a very, very long time in the future, there was a civilization. I shall not describe it to you, for that would not be possible. Could you go back to the time of the Egyptian pyramid builders and tell them about this city below us? I don't mean they wouldn't believe you; of course they wouldn't, but that hardly matters. I mean they would not understand. Nothing you said could make sense to them. And the way people work and think and believe would be less comprehensible than those lights and towers and machines. Not so? If I spoke to you of people in the future living among great blinding energies, and of genetic changelings, and imaginary wars, and talking stones, and a certain blind hunter, you might feel anything at all, but you would not understand.

"So I ask you only to imagine how many thousands of times this planet has circled the sun, how deeply buried and forgotten we are; and then also to imagine that this other civilization thinks in patterns so foreign that it has ignored every limitation of logic and natural law, to discover means of traveling in time. So, while the ordinary dweller in that age (I can't exactly call him a citizen, or anything else for which we have a word, because it would be too misleading)—the average educated dweller knows in a vague, uninterested way that millennia ago some semi-savages were the first to split the atom-only one or two men have actually been here, walked among us, studied and mapped us, and returned with a file of information for the central brain, if I may call it by such a name. No one else is concerned with us, any more than you are concerned with early Mesopotamian archaeology. You see?"

He dropped his gaze to the tumbler in his hand and held it there, as if the whisky were an oracular pool. The silence grew. At last I said, "Very well. For the sake of the story, I'll accept the premise. I imagine time travelers would be unnoticeable. They'd have techniques of disguise and so on. Wouldn't want to change their own past."

"Oh, no danger of that," he said. "It's only that they couldn't learn much if they went around insisting they were from the future. Just imagine."

I chuckled.

Michaels gave me a shadowed look. "Apart from the scientific," he said, "can you guess what use there might be for time travel?"

"Well," I suggested, "trade in objects of art or natural resources. Go back to the dinosaur age and dig up iron before man appeared to strip the richest mines."

He shook his head. "Think again. They'd only want a limited number of Minoan statuettes, Ming vases, or Third World Hegemony dwarfs, chiefly for their museums. If 'museum' isn't too inaccurate a word. I tell you, they are *not* like us. As for natural resources, they're beyond the point of needing any; they make their own."

He paused, as if before a final plunge. Then: "What was this penal colony the French abandoned?"

"Devil's Island?"

"Yes, that was it. Can you imagine a better revenge on a condemned criminal than to maroon him in the past?"

"Why, I should think they'd be above any concept of revenge, or even of deterrence by horrible examples. Even in this century, we're aware that that doesn't work."

"Are you sure?" he asked quietly. "Side by side with the growth of today's enlightened penology, haven't we a corresponding growth of crime itself? You were wondering, some time ago, how I dared walk the night streets alone. Furthermore, punishment is a catharsis of society as a whole. Up in the future they'd tell you that public hangings did reduce the crime rate, which would otherwise have been still higher. Somewhat more important, these spectacles made possible the eighteenth century birth of real humanitariansim." He raised a sardonic brow. "Or so they claim in the future. It doesn't matter whether they are right, or merely rationalizing a degraded element in their own civilization. All you need assume is that they do send their very worst criminals back into the past."

"Rather rough on the past," I said.

"No, not really. For a number of reasons, including the fact that everything they cause to happen has already happened . . . Damn! English isn't built for talking about these paradoxes. Mainly, though, you must remember that they don't waste all this effort on ordinary miscreants. One has to be a very rare criminal to deserve exile in time. And the worst crime in the world depends on the particular year of the world's history. Murder, brigandage, treason, heresy, narcotics peddling, slaving, patriotism, the whole catalogue, all have rated capital punishment in some epochs, and been lightly regarded in others, and positively commended in still others. Think back and see if I'm not right."

I regarded him for a while, observing how deep the lines were in his face and recalling that at his age he shouldn't be so gray. "Very well," I said. "Agreed. But would not a man from the future, possessing all its knowledge—"

He set his glass down with audible force. "*What* knowledge?" he rapped. "Use your brains! Imagine yourself left naked and alone in Babylon. How much Babylonian language or history do you know? Who's the present king, how much longer will he reign, who'll succeed him? What are the laws and customs you must obey? You remember that eventually the Assyrians or the Persians or someone will conquer Babylon and there'll be hell to pay. But when? How? Is the current war a mere border skirmish or an all-out struggle? If the latter, is Babylon going to win? If not, what peace terms will be imposed? Why, there wouldn't be twenty men today who could answer those questions without looking up the answers in a book. And you're not one of them; nor have you been given a book."

"I think," I said slowly, "I'd head for the nearest temple, once I'd picked up enough of the language. I'd tell the priest I could make . . . oh . . . fireworks—"

He laughed, with small merriment. "How? You're in Babylon, remember. Where do you find sulfur and saltpeter? If you can get across to the priest what you want, and somehow persuade him to obtain the stuff for you, how do you compound a powder that'll actually go off instead of just fizzing? For your information, that's quite an art. Hell, you couldn't even get a berth as a deckhand. You'd be lucky if you ended up scrubbing floors. A slave in the fields is a likelier career. Isn't it?"

The fire sank low.

"All right," I conceded. "True."

"They pick the era with care, you know." He looked back toward the window. Seen from our chairs, reflection on the glass blotted out the stars, so that we were only aware of the night itself.

"When a man is sentenced to banishment," he said, "all the experts confer, pointing out what the periods of their specialties would be like for this particular individual. You can see how a squeamish, intellectual type, dropped into Homeric Greece, would find it a living nightmare, whereas a rowdy type might get along fairly well—might even end up as a respected warrior. If the rowdy was not the blackest of criminals, they might actually leave him near the hall of Agamemnon, condemning him to no more than danger, discomfort, and homesickness.

"Oh, God," he whispered. "The homesickness!"

So much darkness rose in him as he spoke that I sought to steady him with a dry remark: "They must immunize the convict to every ancient disease. Otherwise this'd only be an elaborate death sentence."

His eyes focused on me again. "Yes," he said. "And of course the longevity serum is still active in his veins. That's all, however. He's dropped in an unfrequented spot after dark, the machine vanishes, he's cut off for the rest of his life. All he knows is that they've chosen an era for him with . . . such characteristics . . . that they expect the punishment will fit his crime."

Stillness fell once more upon us, until the clock on the mantel became the loudest thing in the world, as if all other sound had frozen to death outside. I glanced at its dial. The night was old; soon the east would be turning pale.

When I looked back, he was still watching me, disconcertingly intent. "What was your crime?" I asked.

He didn't seem taken aback, only said wearily, "What does it matter? I told you the crimes of one age are the heroisms of another. If my attempt had succeeded, the centuries to come would have adored my name. But I failed.''

''A lot of people must have got hurt,'' I said. ''A whole world must have hated you.''

''Well, yes,'' he said. And after a minute: ''This is a fantasy I'm telling you, of course. To pass the time.''

''I'm playing along with you,'' I smiled.

His tension eased a trifle. He leaned back, his legs stretched across that glorious carpet. ''So. Given as much of the fantasy as I've related, how did you deduce the extent of my alleged guilt?''

''Your past life. When and where were you left?''

He said, in as bleak a voice as I've ever heard, ''Near Warsaw, in August, 1939.''

''I don't imagine you care to talk about the war years.''

''No, I don't.''

However, he went on when enough defiance had accumulated: ''My enemies blundered. The confusion following the German attack gave me a chance to escape from police custody before I could be stuck in a concentration camp. Gradually I learned what the situation was. Of course, I couldn't predict anything. I still can't; only specialists know, or care, what happened in the twentieth century. But by the time I'd become a Polish conscript in the German forces, I realized this was the losing side. So I slipped across to the Americans, told them what I'd observed, became a scout for them. Risky— but if I'd stopped a bullet, what the hell? I didn't; and I ended up with plenty of sponsors to get me over here; and the rest of the story is conventional.''

My cigar had gone out. I relit it, for Michaels' cigars were not to be taken casually. He had them especially flown from Amsterdam.

''The alien corn,'' I said.

''What?''

''You know. Ruth in exile. She wasn't badly treated, but she stood weeping for her homeland.''

''No, I don't know that story.''

''It's in the Bible.''

''Ah, yes. I really must read the Bible sometime.'' His mood was changing by the moment, toward the assurance I had first encountered. He swallowed his whisky with a gesture almost debonair. His expression was alert and confident.

''Yes,'' he said, ''that aspect was pretty bad. Not so much the physical conditions of life. You've doubtless gone camping and noticed how soon you stop missing hot running water, electric lights, all the gadgets that their manufacturers assure us are absolute necessities. I'd be glad of a gravity reducer or a cell stimulater if I had one, but I get along fine without. The homesickness, though, that's what eats you. Little things you never noticed, some particular food, the way people walk, the games played, the small-talk topics. Even the constellations. They're different in the future. The sun has traveled that far in its galactic orbit.

"But, voluntary or forced, people have always been emigrating. We're all descended from those who could stand the shock. I adapted."

A scowl crossed his brows. "I wouldn't go back now even if I were given a free pardon," he said, "the way those traitors are running things."

I finished my own drink, tasting it with my whole tongue and palate, for it was a marvelous whisky, and listened to him with only half an ear. "You like it here?"

"Yes," he said. "By now I do. I'm over the emotional hump. Being so busy the first few years just staying alive, and then so busy establishing myself after I came to this country, that helped. I never had much time for self-pity. Now my business interests me more and more, a fascinating game, and pleasantly free of extreme penalties for wrong moves. I've discovered qualities here that the future has lost . . . I'll bet you have no idea how exotic this city is. Think. At this moment, within five miles of us, there's a soldier on guard at an atomic laboratory, a bum freezing in a doorway, an orgy in a millionaire's apartment, a priest making ready for sunrise rites, a merchant from Araby, a spy from Muscovy, a ship from the Indies. . . ."

His excitement softened. He looked from the window and the night, inward, toward the bedrooms. "And my wife and kids," he finished, most gently. "No, I wouldn't go back, no matter what happened."

I took a final breath of my cigar. "You *have* done rather well."

Liberated from his gray mood, he grinned at me. "You know, I think you believe that yarn."

"Oh, I do." I stubbed out the cigar, rose, and stretched. "The hour is late. We'd better be going."

He didn't notice at once. When he did, he came out of his chair like a big cat. *"We?"*

"Of course," I drew a nerve gun from my pocket. He stopped in his tracks. "This sort of thing isn't left to chance. We check up. Come along, now."

The blood drained from his face. "No." he mouthed, "no, no, no, you can't, it isn't fair, not to Amalie, the children—"

"That," I told him, "is part of the punishment."

I left him in Damascus, the year before Tamerlane sacked it.

66

NO HARM DONE

Jack Sharkey

THE BOY WAS a good-looking youth, with shiny—if over-long—blond hair, and bright white teeth. But his eyes were cloudy with the emptiness that lay behind them, and the blue circles of their irises hinted at no more mental activity than do the opaque black dots on a rag doll. He sat with vacuous docility upon the small metal stool the guards had provided, and let his arms dangle limp as broken clothesline at his sides, not even crossing them in his lap. He had been led to the chair, told to sit, and left. If he were not told to arise, he would remain there until the dissolution of his muscle cells following death by starvation caused him to topple from his low perch.

"Total schizophrenia," said Dr. Manton. "For all practical purposes, he is an ambulant—when instructed to move, of course—vegetable."

"How terrible," said Lisa, albeit perfunctorily. Lisa Nugent, for all her lovely twenty-seven years, was a trained psychologist, and rarely allowed emotion to take her mind from its well-ordered paths of analysis. To be unfeeling was heartless—But to become emotional about a patient was pointless.

"Yes, it's intolerable," nodded Dr. Jeff Manton, keeping his mind strictly on Lisa's scientific qualifications, and deliberately blocking out any other information sent to his brain by his alert senses. The warmth of her smile, the flash of sunlight in her auburn hair, the companionable lilt she could not keep out of her "on-duty" voice—All these were observed, noted, and filed for future reference. At the moment, nothing must go wrong with their capacity for observation of the patient. Emotion had a way of befuddling even the most dedicated minds.

"But why out here?" Lisa said suddenly, returning the conversation to the prior topic. "I should think conditions would be easier to control in the lab."

"Simply because," said Jeff, patting the small metal camera-like device on its rigid tripod, "I as yet have no experimental knowledge of the range of my machine. It may simply be absorbed by the plaster in the walls, back inside the sanitarium. Then again, it may penetrate, likely or not, even the steel beams of the building, with roentgenic ease. There are too many other people in the building, Li—Dr. Nugent. Until I can be certain just what effect the rays have upon a human brain, I dare not use it any place where there might be leakage, possible synaptic damage."

"I understand," said Lisa, nodding after a brief smile at his near-slip with her name. "You assume the earth will absorb any rays that pass beyond this boy's brain, and render them—if not harmless—at least beyond the contamination point with another human being."

"Precisely," said Jeff Manton, moving the tripod a short distance closer to the seated boy. "Now, I want you to assist me in watching him, and if you note in him any change—either in his expression or posture—tell me at once. Then we can turn off the machine and test him for results. For positive results, at any rate."

Lisa could not repress a slight tremor. The trouble with schizophrenia in its most advanced stage was the inability of contacting the patient. The boy, although readily capable of executing simple commands, could not be counted on to aid Dr. Manton nor herself in even the most basic test of his mental abilities. If the machine made him any worse—there would hardly be a way for them to discover it. If better—then new hope was born for others similarly afflicted.

"Steady, now," said Jeff, turning the tiny knob at the side of the metal box a quarter turn. "Keep your eye on him. I'm going to turn it on."

Lisa felt the sweat prickling along her back as Jeff flicked the toggle switch atop the box. Her eyes began to burn, and she realized she wasn't even blinking as she locked her gaze upon the figure of the boy through whose brain was now coursing a ray of relatively unknown effect. Rabbits and rats and monkeys in the lab were one thing. This, now, was a human being. Whether the effect upon him would be similar to that of the ray upon test-animals (scientifically driven crazy before exposure) remained to be seen.

"Anything?" muttered Jeff, sighting anxiously along the side of the box. "Anything at *all?*"

"He—No. He just sits there, Doctor. So far as I can see, there is no appreciable effect." She sighed resignedly. "He doesn't even flicker a muscle."

"Damn," said Jeff. He kept his finger lightly atop the sun-glinting toggle switch. "I'm going to give it one more minute before I give up. This thing *should* be vitalizing his brain by *now!*"

"But he's not even—" Lisa began, discouraged.

"Keep your eyes on *him,* damn it!" snapped Jeff, catching the turn of her head from the corner of his eye. "This *must* work! We daren't miss the least sign that it has!"

Man and woman stood side by side in the hot light of the afternoon sun, staring, staring at the immobile form of the patient, the patient whose disrupted mind they were attempting to reunite into an intelligent whole. . . .

My name, he thought. *Funny, I should know my own name. I've heard it often enough . . . It's . . . Is it—is it Garret? That sounds like it, but—I can't seem to recall. . . .*

He thought about the man who tended and took care of him. He had called him by name, hadn't he? And it was most certainly Garret. Yes, of course it was Garret. . . . Or was it Curt?

His mind, like badly exposed film, refused to give him an accurate sensation, from any of his senses. All he got for strenuous mental gymnastics was vague, blurry reception and muddled thought. And yet, there was a warm sensation that had never been in his mind before—Before what? Try as he might, he could not recall anything coherent before this moment in time. Just vague feelings of being alive, and simply growing up . . . .

The warmth of the sun was beginning to penetrate. He could feel it, coursing down upon him, soaking into him, revitalizing him . . . But it was unlike this other warmth, this *penetrating* warmth, that tingled through his mind. With the awareness of the sunlight came a slow awareness of shades of light, then of color, then of figures. And, for the first time, he made a strong effort, and—and *looked*.

He saw a man and woman standing in the sunlight a few feet from himself, saw the harsh glitter of that sunlight upon the strange object on three legs that rested on the ground before them. He tried to speak to them, but something restrained him.

If I can move . . . If I can just move a little bit, he realized, *they'll see me, and they'll know I'm alive and well and aware.*

He tried. He tried desperately to move. His body felt rigid, imprisoned. Just a little frantic, he thought of blinking at them, of moving his eyes toward them for sharp definite focus, so that they would *know*. . . .

Nothing happened.

I'm paralyzed! he thought for a terrifying moment. Then—*No, I'm just not used to directing myself. I haven't the necessary coordination or experience, that must be it. Take it easy, now. Slow and easy. Don't panic.*

He strained desperately, and felt just the slightest hint of movement. Had they seen? he wondered. He was certain he had moved. What was the *matter* with the two of them?!

He watched them there in the sunlight, this man and woman who stood so intensely still, the man's hand upon that metallic thing on three legs. Then he knew that that thing was the source of the warmth in his mind. It had brought him to awareness.

But what good *is it!* his mind screamed. *To be alive and aware, and unable to let them know it!* The coldly frantic feeling was growing within him, now, taking hold of his brain with the frightening fingers of raw panic.

"Look!" he cried out, then knew with crushing despair that the word had gone no farther than his brain. *Please,* he begged silently, *see me here, see that I am alive, that I am not what I was!*

Desperately, he strove to rise, felt the strange sensation of bondage that restrained his body, fought it . . . and won. It hurt. The sensation was unbearable. Yet he had moved. Perhaps only a quarter of an inch, but he had moved. The woman—Had she seen?

Then he saw the man straighten up, heave his shoulders in a great sigh, and cut off the machine with a finger-flick. The tingling warmth died within his brain, and for an icy moment, he expected to plunge back to semi-comatic nothingness. But, after a giddy scintilla of dizziness, his mind remained strong and intelligent and alive.

Ignoring the blaze of pain that racked his entire being, he tensed himself, pushed, with strangled cries bursting inside his brain at the self-torture, and made himself move another quarter of an inch.

Did they see? Did they? Did they know? Would they free his mind, and leave his body imprisoned to his innermost pleas for release?

No, he thought, giddy with joy. *They . . . They're coming nearer!* . . .

It's no use, Lisa,'' said Jeff, looking down upon the motionless figure on the stool. ''The machine is a flop. Rabbits and lesser creatures, fine, but for the mind of man, no use at all.''

''I'm sorry, Jeff,'' said Lisa, knowing that his calling her by her first name meant that work was done for that day. ''Maybe, with some adjustments—''

''Yeah,'' he grunted bitterly, as two white-jacketed guards led the boy back to his cell, *''maybe!''*

''At least,'' said Lisa, taking him gently by the arm, ''he's no worse off. The experiment just didn't work out, that's all. But there's no harm done, at any rate.''

"Nope. I suppose you're right," Jeff said bitterly, reaching to lift the stool from its patch of sunlight. Then, with a brief surge of anger at the futility he felt, he lashed out with his foot and kicked the green parsley-like top clean off a carrot that jutted just a bit higher than its fellows in the garden bed behind the stool. "No harm done," he muttered angrily, and went back with Lisa toward the sanitarium.

While a silent, agony-filled voice behind him kept shrieking, over and over, *"My eyes! He kicked out my eyes! I'm blind! Help me! Help me!"*

67

NOBODY LIVES ON BURTON STREET

Greg Benford

I WAS STANDING by one of our temporary command posts, picking my teeth after breakfast and talking to Joe Murphy when the first part of the Domestic Disturbance hit us.

Spring had lost its bloom a month back and it was summer now—hot, sticky, the kind of weather that leaves you with a half-moon of sweat around your armpits before you've had time to finish your morning coffee. A summer like that is always more trouble. This one looked like the worst I'd seen since I got on the Force.

We knew they were in the area, working toward us. Our communications link had been humming for the last half hour, getting fixes on their direction and asking the computers for advice on how to handle them when they got here.

I looked down. At the end of the street was a lot of semi-permanent shops and the mailbox. The mailbox bothers me—it shouldn't be there.

From the other end of Burton Street I could hear the random dull bass of the mob.

So while we were getting ready Joe was moaning about the payments on the Snocar he'd been suckered into. I was listening with one ear to him and the other to the crowd noises.

"And it's not just that," Joe said. "It's the neighbohood and the school and everybody around me."

"Everybody's wrong but Murphy, huh?" I said, and grinned.

"Hell no, you know me better than that. It's just that nobody's *going* anyplace. Sure, we've all got jobs, but they're most of them just make-work stuff the unions have gotten away with."

"To get a real job you gotta have training," I said, but I wasn't chuffing him up. I like my job, and it's better than most, but we weren't gonna kid each other that it was some big technical deal. Joe and I are just regular guys.

"What're you griping about this now for, anyway?" I said. "You didn't used to be bothered by anything."

Joe shurgged. "I dunno. Wife's been getting after me to move out of the place we're in and make more money. Gets into fights with the neighbors." He looked a little sheepish about it.

"More money? Hell, y'got everything you need, we all do. Lot of people worse off than you. Look at all those lousy Africans, living on nothing."

I was going to say more, maybe rib him about how he's married and I'm not, but then I stopped. Like I said, all this time I was half-listening to the crowd. I can always tell when a bunch has changed its direction like a pack of wolves off on a chase, and when that funny quiet came and lasted about five seconds I knew they were heading our way.

"Scott!" I yelled at our communicatons man. "Close it down. Get a final printout."

Murphy broke off telling me about his troubles and listened to the crowd for a minute, like he hadn't heard them before, and then took off on a trot to the AnCops we had stashed in the truck below. They were all warmed up and ready to go, but Joe likes to make a final check and maybe have a chance to read in any new instructions Scott gets at the last minute.

I threw away the toothpick and had a last look at my constant-volume joints, to be sure the bulletproof plastiform was matching properly and wouldn't let anything through. Scott came doubletiming over with the diagnostics from HQ. The computer compilation was neat and confusing, like it always is. I could make out the rough indices they'd picked up on the crowd heading our way. The best guess—and that's all you ever get, friends, is a guess—was a lot of Psych Disorders and Race Prejudice. There was a fairly high number of Unemployeds, too. We're getting more and more Unemployeds in the city now, and they're hard for the Force to deal with. Usually mad enough to spit. Smash up everything.

I penciled an ok in the margin and tossed it Scott's way. I'd taken too long reading it; I could hear individual shouts now and the tinkling of glass. I flipped the visor down from my helmet and turned on my external audio. It was going to get hot as hell in there, but I'm not chump enough to drag around an air conditioning unit on top of the rest of my stuff.

I took a look at the street just as a gang of about a hundred people came around the corner two blocks down, spreading out like a dirty gray wave. I ducked over to the edge of the building and waved to Murphy to start off with three AnCops. I had to hold up three fingers for him to see because the noise was already getting high. I looked at my watch. Hell, it wasn't A.M. yet.

Scott went down the stairs we'd tracted up the side of the building. I was right behind him. It wasn't a good location for observation now; you made too good a target up there. We picked up Murphy, who was carrying our control boards. All three of us angled down the alley and dropped down behind a short fence to have a look at the street.

Most of them were still screaming at the top of their lungs like they'd never run out of air, waving whatever they had handy and gradually breaking up into smaller units. The faster ones had made it to the first few buildings.

A tall Negro came trotting toward us, moving like he had all the time in the world. He stopped in front of a wooden barber shop, tossed something quickly through the front window and *whump!* Flames licked out at the upper edges of the window, spreading fast.

An older man picked up some rocks and began methodically pitching them through the smaller windows in the shops next door. A housewife clumped by awkwardly in high heels, looking like she was out on a shopping trip except for the hammer she swung like a pocketbook. She dodged into the barbershop for a second, didn't find anything and came out. The Negro grinned and pointed at the barber pole on the sidewalk, still revolving, and she caught it in the side with a swipe that threw shattered glass for ten yards.

I turned and looked at Murphy. ''All ready?''

He nodded. ''Just give the word.''

The travel agency next door to the barber shop was concrete-based, so they couldn't burn that. Five men were lunging at the door and on the third try they knocked it in. A moment later a big travel poster sailed out the front window, followed by a chair leg. They were probably doing as much as they could, but without tools they couldn't take much of the furniture apart.

''Okay,'' I said. ''Let's have the first AnCops.''

The thick acrid smell from the smoke was drifting down Burton Street to us, but my air filters would take care of most of it. They don't do much about human sweat, though, and I was going to be inside the rest of the day.

Our first prowl car rounded the next corner, going too fast. I looked over at Murphy, who was controlling the car, but he was too busy trying to miss the people who were standing around in the street. Must have gotten a little overanxious on that one. Something was bothering his work.

I thought sure the car was going to take a tumble and mess us up, but the wheels caught and it righted itself long enough for the driver to stop a skid.

The screech turned the heads of almost everybody in the crowd and they'd started to move in on it almost before the car stopped laying down rubber and came to a full stop. Murphy punched in another instruction and the AnCop next to the driver started firing at a guy on the sidewalk who was trying to light a Molotov cocktail. The AnCop was using something that sounded like a repeating shotgun. The guy with the cocktail just turned around and looked at him a second before scurrying off into a hardware store.

By this time the car was getting everything—bricks, broken pieces of furniture, merchandise from the stores. Something heavy shattered the windshield and the driver ducked back too late to avoid getting his left hand smashed with a bottle. A figure appeared on the top of the hardware shop—it looked like the guy from the sidewalk—and took a long windup before throwing something into the street.

There was a tinkling of glass and a red circle of flame slid across the pavement where it hit just in front of the car, sending smoke curling up over the hood and obscuring the inside. Murphy was going to have to play it by feel now; you couldn't see a thing in the car.

A teenager with a stubby rifle stepped out of a doorway, crouched down low like in a western. He fired twice, very accurately and very fast, at the window of the car. A patrolman was halfway out the door when it hit him full in the face, sprawling the body back over the roof and then pitching it forward into the street.

A red blotch formed around his head, grew rapidly and ran into the gutter. There was ragged cheering and the teenager ran over to the body, tore off its badge and backed away. "Souvenir!" he called out, and a few of the others laughed.

I looked at Murphy again and he looked at me and I gave him the nod for the firemen, switching control over to my board. Scott was busy talking into his recorder, taking notes for the writeup later. When Murphy nudged him he stopped and punched in the link for radio control to the firefightng units.

By this time most of Burton Street was on fire. Everything you saw had a kind of orange look to it. The crowd was moving toward us once they'd lost interest in the cops, but we'd planned it that way. The firemen came running out in that jerky way they have, just a little in front of us. They were carrying just a regular hose this time because it was a medium-sized group and we couldn't use up a fire engine and all the extras. But they were wearing the usual red uniforms. From a distance you can't tell them from the real thing.

Their subroutine tapes were fouled up again. Instead of heading for the barber shop or any of the the other stuff that was burning, like I'd programmed, they turned the hose on a stationery store that nobody had touched yet. There were three of them, holding onto that hose and getting it set up. The crowd had backed off a minute to see what was going on.

When the water came through it knocked in the front window of the store, making the firemen look like real chumps. I could hear the water running around inside, pushing over things and flooding out the building. The crowd laughed, what there was of it—I noticed some of them had moved off in the other direction, over into somebody else's area.

In a minute or so the laughing stopped, though. One guy who looked like he had been born mad grabbed an ax from somewhere and took a swing at the hose. He didn't get it the first time but people were sticking around to see what would happen and I guess he felt some kind of obligaton to go through with it. Even under pressure, a thick hose isn't easy to cut into. He kept at it and on the fourth try a seam split—looked like a bad repair job to me—and a stream of water gushed out and almost hit this guy in the face.

The crowd laughed at that too, because he backed off real quick then, scared for a little bit. A face full of high-velocity water is no joke, not at that pressure.

The fireman who was holding the hose just a little down from there hadn't paid any attention to this because he wasn't programmed to, so when this guy thought about it he just stepped over and chopped the fireman across the back with the ax.

It was getting hot. I didn't feel like overriding the stock program, so it wasn't long before all the firemen were out of commission, just about the same way. A little old lady—probably with a welfare gripe—borrowed the ax for a minute to separate all of a fireman's arms and legs from the trunk. Looking satisfied, she waddled away after the rest of the mob.

I stood up, lifted my faceplate and looked at them as they milled back down the street. I took out my grenade launcher and got off a tear gas cartridge on low charge, to hurry them along. The wind was going crosswise so the gas got carried off to the side and down the alleys. Good; wouldn't have complaints from somebody who got caught in it too long.

Scott was busy sending orders for the afternoon shift to get more replacement firemen and cops, but we wouldn't have any trouble getting them in time. There hadn't been much damage, when you think how much they could've done.

"Okay for the reclaim crew?" Murphy said.

"Sure. This bunch won't be back. They look tired out already." They were moving toward Horton's area, three blocks over.

A truck pulled out of the alley and two guys in coveralls jumped out and began picking up the androids, dousing fires as they went. In an hour they'd have everything back in place, even the prefab barber shop.

"Hellava note," Murphy said.

"Huh?"

"All this stuff," he waved a hand down Burton Street. "Seems like a waste to build all this just so these jerks can tear it down again."

"Waste?" I said. "It's the best investment you ever saw. How many people were in the last bunch—two hundred? Every one of them is going to sit around for weeks bragging about how he got him a cop or burned a building."

"Okay, okay. If it does any good, I guess it's cheap at the price."

"If, hell! You know it is. If it wasn't they wouldn't be here. You got to be cleared by a psycher before you even get in. The computer works out just what you'll need, just the kind of action that'll work off the aggressions you've got. Then shoots it to us in the profile from HQ before we start. It's foolproof."

"I dunno. You know what the Consies say—the psychers and the probes and drugs are an in—"

"Invasion of privacy?"

"Yeah," Murphy said sullenly.

"Privacy? Man, the psychers are public health! It's part of the welfare! You don't have to go around to some expensive guy who'll have you lay on a couch and talk to him. You can get better stuff right from the government. It's free!"

Murphy looked at me kind of funny. "Sure. Have to go in for a checkup sometime soon. Maybe that's what I need."

I frowned just the right amount. "Well, I dunno, Joe. Man lets his troubles get him down every once in a while, doesn't mean he needs professional help. Don't let it bother you. Forget it."

Joe was okay, but even a guy like me who's never been married could tell he wasn't thinking up this stuff himself. His woman was pushing him. Not satisfied with what she had.

Now, *that* was wrong. Guy like Joe doesn't have anywhere to go. Doesn't know computers, automation. Can't get a career rating in the Army. So the pressure was backing up on him.

Supers like me are supposed to check out their people and leave it at that, and I go by the book like everybody else. But Joe wasn't the problem.

I made a mental note to have a psycher look at his wife.

"Okay," he said, taking off his helmet. "I got to go set up the AnCops for the next one."

I watched him walk off down the alley. He was a good man. Hate to lose him.

I started back toward our permanent operations center to check in. After a minute I decided maybe I'd better put Joe's name in too, just in case. Didn't want anybody blowing up on me.

He'd be happier, work better. I've sure felt a lot better since I had it. It's a good job I got, working in public affairs like this, keeping people straight with themselves.

I went around the corner at the end of the street, thinking about getting something to drink, and noticed the mailbox. I check on it every time because it sure looks like a mistake.

Everything's supposed to be pretty realistic on Burton Street, but putting in a mailbox seems like a goofy idea.

Who's going to try to burn up a box like that, made out of cast iron and bolted down? A guy couldn't take out any aggressions on it.

And it sure can't be for real use. Not on Burton Street.

Nobody lives around there.

68

NOW I'M WATCHING ROGER

Alexei Panshin

NOW I'M WATCHING Roger. Roger is hanging facedown in his ropes overhead and looking at me. He isn't saying anything and I'm not speaking.

I wish I had the time to spare in relaxation that he does, but I'm kept constantly busy. There are a million things here to do. If I had Roger's free time, I'd know how to put it to good use. I wouldn't idle.

I wonder about Roger's experiments. The only time he ever seems to work on them is during our regular telecast to Earth. I asked him about his experiments once, but he didn't take notice. He jumped up into his ropes. He's very well practiced at it now. If I had more time, perhaps I could make flying leaps to the top of the dome, too.

Roger is too silent. He never speaks up when Jack does something to annoy me, and this encourages Jack to take more advantage. Roger will never settle anything, and I've saved him from Jack I don't know how many times. But how do you ask a man to back you? He either sees the need or he doesn't. It isn't proper to ask, so I don't.

On the other hand, if he's going to play the silent game, there's no reason why I shouldn't play it, too. The only time I'll speak is when I stir from my silent work to drag Jack off his back. But I don't expect he will notice.

To taunt me Jack takes off his black hat during our telecasts. He's charming and plausible. If you believe him, we would be happy to stay another eight months on the moon. I'm not sure I could juggle things that long, though I'll grant that Jack might.

When it is my turn, I nod and wave to Earth. I tell them we're keeping busy. Roger works away at his experiments in the background. He waves to the camera but he doesn't say anything.

When the telecast is over, Jack puts his black hat back on again. He spent an entire evening making it out of paper and coloring it black with ink. I didn't watch because I was busy working. Jack knows the black hat annoys me, but I'm not saying anything or taking any notice.

He may be plausible in public, but Roger and I know him better. He only eats the good parts of things and leaves the rest. I imagine he was indulged. And he's a glutton. I pointed it out when he left the rind from the Christmas fruitcake and his antics lasted for a month. He started by leaving crusts and bits of cracker on my plate and grew even more blatant when I refused to take any notice. At the end he was gobbling with both hands and flinging food about.

I do have an audio of several episodes but it isn't easy to tell what is happening.

I have a number of recordings of Jack. None of Roger except for background.

In one recording I say, "Jack, you haven't been sterilizing." It is a point I am particular about.

"It's true, Clarence 'Clancy' Ballou, I haven't been. I've decided to give it up. I'll take my chances with the moon. Let the moon take its chances with me. I wouldn't mind giving it a dose of something."

"That's against policy," I say.

"Screw policy, Clarence. Maybe you're too nice for this work. There's the universe, as regular as a clock. Then there's us, life, an out-of-place accident. We're anarchy, disorder. No matter how tough the universe makes the rules, life will survive and spread. The moon is only the first step. Someday we'll spread to the stars and take over everything. We'll rip the guts out of the universe. We'll stripmine the stars. Life will prevail. It's our destiny to crap up the works."

"You make us sound evil. That's what the regulations are for, to ensure that we don't contaminate other worlds."

"You don't understand, Clarence. We are evil. And it's up to us to make the most of it."

"But I'm good. I've always been good."

"Learn better."

It was after that that he made his black paper hat. It's supposed to be a reminder to me, but it isn't really necessary. I know which of us is which.

Jack is ouside. I've been counting our sacks of garbage. I believe that two are missing. I fear the worst.

Was it sterilized? Not if he didn't sterilize it.

I fear the worst.

Just before the telecast I say to Jack, "What about the garbage?"

"What garbage?"

"I know about the garbage. Unless you stop burying it outside, I'm going to have to tell them back home."

He takes off his black hat. He combs his hair and practices his smile.

"I've been counting," I say.

On the telecast I'm cautious. I say that some garbage is missing.

They ask Jack about it. Jack is in charge of accounting for the garbage. He says that it is all there.

I call on Roger. Roger smiles and waves from the background for the camera.

Jack smiles and tells the audience about garbage accounting procedures. He is very plausible. He thanks me for raising the question.

After the telecast he says, "I have a higher loyalty." And he puts his black hat back on.

What can I do?

Another sack of garbage is missing.

I don't know what to do.

Roger just fell off the bench. Since I enforced safety regulations and made him stop sleeping in his ropes, he has taken to biting his fingernails and falling off the bench.

I've been thinking about Jack. I've been thinking about the moon infected with life. I've been thinking about people like Jack overcrawling the universe.

Jack is larger than I am.

I've just made myself a white hat.

Another sack of garbage is missing. Sometimes I think Jack is not completely sane.

I have taken charge of garbage accounting. I think I'll rest easier now that it is in my hands.

In future I think that the answer must lie in unbreachable refuse containers. And a tight check system to see that everything gets deposited. But even these cannot be enough if the irresponsible aren't weeded out beforehand. The power of life must rest in hands that respect it. I'm not sure how that can be ensured, but I will think about it until the rotation changes.

This new job means one more intrustion on my time, but it's necessary.

Those who can do are condemned to do to the limit of their strength.

I explained on the telecast to Earth tonight as best I could. I told them the problem and how I had solved it. I'm sure I didn't tell it well—Jack was always the raconteur—but they seemed to understand. Roger looked up from his work long enough to nod and wave to the people back home.

I think things are under control.

Things are much smoother now. The change in Roger has been amazing. He is more active now. He works with greater concentration. He listens to my advice and nods. He has even been outside the dome for the first time in months.

That is the good side. On the negative side he has taken to his ropes again. I haven't the time or the heart to speak to him about it.

I'm very busy.

I just counted and counted again to be sure. One of Jack's fourteen sacks is missing; I believe a foot. I don't know how it could have happened. The right foot, I think. We must get unbreachable refuse containers.

Now I'm watching Roger. Roger is hanging in his ropes and watching me.

69

ON ACCOUNT OF DARKNESS

Barry N. Malzberg and Bill Pronzini

SO I TOOK the Holographic Magnifier and the stick figures over to the Agency, talked myself past three secretaries, paid my one hour of humiliation waiting in the outside offices, and finally got into Evers' office. "I've got some terrific stuff here," I said, pulling it out of the case and laying it in front of him. "Jackie Robinson, the Duke, the Babe, the Splendid Splinter, a hundred more. A veritable Cooperstown of the mind."

"What's a Cooperstown?" he said.

"It was a famous museum where the uniforms and memorabilia of the greats were kept," I said. "Not that it matters. What matters is this: I can let you have the holographic stuff at a very reasonable price. Very reasonable."

"Football," Evers said. "There's no market for football anymore."

"This isn't football, it's baseball. Football was a contact sport of the twentieth century; baseball, purely of American origin, was played with a small round ball and a long thin piece of timber called a bat—"

"I'm not interested," Evers said. "Nothing personal, it's just that we have lots of problems here. The whole question of entertainment . . . ." He shrugged.

"Well, I can appreciate the range of your problems," I said. "But what I've got here is really something special. Suppose I just give you a little demonstration?"

Evers yawned.

"Oh, come on," I said. "You let me in here, you let me get this far, you know you're a little interested already." I gave him an ingratiating smile. "Did you know there was a baseball player called Evers who was very famous in the early part of the twentieth century? A second baseman for the

433

Chicago Cubs. Tinkers to Evers to Chance—that was this legendary double-play combination—''

''What's a Chicago Cub?'' Evers said.

The trouble with the people at the Agency is that they are efficient but they have little historical sense. Historicity? Historicalness? They are extremely good on details, and they certainly know what will sell along the range of available techniques, but their grasp of specifics is limited. Not that I hold this against them, of course. They're only trying to do a job.

I began to set up the Magnifier, working with it until it hummed and glowed and vibrated on Evers' desk. He looked at it in a bored way and didn't look at me at all. So I said, ''For that matter, there was a Hoot Evers who played for the Detroit Tigers, an outfielder in the 1950s. Hoot wasn't his real name, but that was what they called him. I think his real name was Charles.

''What's a Detroit?'' Evers asked.

I concealed a sigh, setting up certain figures which I had preselected. Then I set the Magnifier for one-tenth life-size and hit the button, and the room was suddenly filled with heat and light and those strange smells that are supposed to be grass and peanuts and hot dogs. The ballplayers in their uniforms darting all over the office, like energetic little animals.

''Look at this,'' I said. ''National League All-Stars of the middle twentieth century versus the greatest single team in baseball history, the 1927 New York Yankees. Yankees are the home team, so they're in the field first. The pitcher is Herb Pennock, Lou Gehrig is on first, Tony Lazzeri is at second . . .''

I went on to give him the line-ups. He didn't seem to be listening, but he had one eye cocked on Jackie Robinson striding up to the plate to lead off the game. ''What's the object of all this, anyway?'' he said.

''Well, the batter has to use the stick in his hands to hit the ball out of range of the fielders. If he does that, or if the pitcher misses that plate-shaped target, the batter is allowed to take one or more bases. Four bases constitute a run, and the team with the most runs at the end of the game—''

Evers raised a hand. ''That's enough,' he said, but he still had the one eye cocked on Robinson.

So I launched into a play-by-play, a technique which I have developed in the classic sense. Robinson hit Pennock's third pitch and grounded out to Koenig at short, and then Bobby Thompson took a called third strike. The next batter was Ted Kluzewski.

''This is pretty clever stuff,'' Evers said in a grudging way. He had both eyes on the game now. ''I've got to admit that.''

"Oh, it's very clever," I said. "You can really get absorbed in it, you know. One thing you should keep in mind is that this is only a one-tenth magnification here; you can imagine what the game is like when you lay it out in a conventionally sized stadium."

"I suppose so. But I still don't see the point of it all."

"Entertainment," I said. "Abstraction. Hundreds of years ago people used to obtain amusement watching these baseball games."

"But *why*?"

"Aesthetics," I said vaguely.

"How come you're so familiar with the subject?"

"I have a background. My great-great-grandfather worked for the last commissioner's office, and all of this was passed down through the family. A kind of heritage. And a hobby too."

"A strange hobby."

"Each to his own."

"Mmm," Evers said.

Kluzewski hit a ground ball between first and second for a single; Ruth tossed the ball back in to Lazzeri. "Next batter is Stan Musial," I said. "He might have been the best batter in his division during his time. Note the very unusual position he takes; that's the famous Musial Crouch. He's virtually batting on his knees as you can see."

Evers didn't say anything.

Musial, a first-ball hitter if ever there was one, sent a towering fly ball to right center that Earle Combs couldn't quite reach. The translucent ball bounced off the wall, rolled back to the infield; Lazzeri scooped it up and fired it to the catcher, Benny Bengough, holding Kluzewski at third and Musial at second.

"That was a typical Musial double," I said.

Evers said, "I think I'm losing interest. This may be clever stuff, but it doesn't entertain or amuse me at all."

"You haven't seen enough of it yet," I said as Willie Mays came up and popped the first pitch up to Koenig at short. "Now the teams switch places and the Yankees come to bat—"

"I'm just not interested," Evers said. "Turn it off."

I hesitated, but I could see that it was hopeless; sometimes you can press the point and sometimes you dare not. So much in this business is a matter of timing. I turned off the Magnifier, began to gather it and the stick figures together.

"The thing is," Evers said, "there's no real audience for it. I can see the elements of diversion, of course, but there just aren't enough of them."

435

I said nothing. There is a time to talk and then there ia time not to talk, and off this great balance wheel are conducted all relationships and dealings.

"I suppose," Evers said, "that we might be able to do a little something with it in the Outlying Districts. But then again, it would hardly repay our investment. Visuals are a tricky commodity, you know."

A certain feeling of revulsion and pain began to work in me then. I had held it well down throughout this meeting, but it comes at odd moments, in little layers and surges of feeling. I seemed to see myself in ten other offices like Evers', past and present, at the mercy of people like him who understood very little and yet, somehow, controlled everything; I seemed to see myself getting older, beginning to die in stages, while the batteries in the Holographic Magnifier lost power and the figures of the great baseball layers lost definition and finally faded altogether. . . .

I had to say something then. So I said, "All right, I'll be going now; if you don't understand, I can't make you understand. You'll just never know, that's all, what a beautiful game it was." I turned and started for the door.

"Wait a minute now," Evers said.

I pivoted back toward him. "What?"

Evers cleared his throat. "I said there was very little in it, but, still and all, there might be *something* worthwhile. We might be able to convert it into an amusement for the juveniles, for example. Or there's the possiblity of an exhibit over in the Central District of minor artifacts that we're planning to open." He fixed me with shrewd, veiled eyes. "We might be able to make a small bid, after all."

"How small?"

"Fifteen," he said.

"That's ridiculous. This is baseball, all of *baseball*."

"Nobody knows what baseball is. I didn't; I still don't."

"It's something beautiful, something irreplaceable. . . . "

"Seventeen," Evers said. "That's my final offer."

"I've got to have twenty-five."

"Not from us."

"Twenty-two then. I have expenses to cover."

"Eighteen,—but that's it. Yes or no? I'll have to put it on the Terminals right away."

"Eighteen," I said. "Listen, you're talking about an entire way of life for hundreds of thousands of people—"

"Good-by," Evers said.

436

"Now wait—"

"Eighteen, or good-by."

The pain and revulsion deepened within me, but I said, "All right. All right. But I'm giving you my whole life here; I'm giving you hundreds of thousands of lives."

"We'll program the eighteen in," he said. "You can get a Verificatory from my secretary." He stood up. "It's been a pleasure having you and your quaint little pastime here, but now, if you don't mind. . . . "

He didn't offer his hand; he just looked away, dismissing me. So I took one last look at the Magnifier and the stick figures, and then I went out of there and took a railcab to my cubicle. Outside, the sky was just beginning to darken; night was coming on.

And the game is over, I thought. But then, if you wanted to look at it another way, they'd have called it anyway in the old days. On account of darkness. Called on account of darkness.

Then, still filled with pain, I sat down and went through my materials and tried to figure out the best places to unload hockey, basketball, and horse racing.

70

ONE MAN'S AMBITION

Bertrand Chandler

THE ROOM WAS quiet, save for the murmur of light music from the radio. The room was quiet with that quietness possible only when there are two people together. It was not the stillness of affectionate companionship, however; it was the deceptive serenity that should have as its background music the ticking of the time fuse, the sputtering of the slow match.

They were reading—she sitting in her armchair, he in his. He put his book down on his lap, filled and lit his pipe. She coughed as the cloud of acrid smoke reached her.

"Must you," she demanded, "smoke that foul thing?"

"*I* like it," he said.

"Other men," she complained, "smoke *good* tobacco."

"I smoke what I can afford," he told her.

"Cheapness!" she flared. "Cheapness! Cheapness! Ever since I was fool enough to marry you there's been nothing but cheapness! A cheap flat in a cheap town. Cheap food. Cheap drinks. Cheap clothes. A cheap car . . . ."

"We cut our coat according to our cloth."

"Oh, if the cheapness were confined to material things I shouldn't mind so much. But you're such a cheap person in all ways. Your taste in films is cheap, your taste in music. And as for your taste in books. . . ."

"*That's* not cheap," he said sullenly.

"Oh, isn't it? Cheap *and* adolescent, I'd say. Let me see." She got up from her chair, snatched the book from his lap. She read, scornfully, "*Rocket To Tomorrow*. And you say *that's* not cheap!"

"It's not. Its a very good anthology."

"Cheap escapism."

"It's not escapism. How many times must I tell you that good science

439

fiction is not escapist—a thing that could never be said about the historical novels that you're so fond of.''

"Not escapist, you say? Rockets to the moon, little green men from Mars, flying saucers . . . . ''

"Good science fiction,'' he said, "deals with problems that men and women will have to face someday. Someday soon, perhaps.''

"All right,'' she said. "I'll take you up on that. You seem to be halfway through a story called *Judgment Eve*. What's it about?''

"You should read it,'' he said. "It's rather good.''

"Read that trash! You tell me what it's about, that's all I want to know.''

"All right. The author assumes that the sun is about to become a Nova— which means, of course, that Earth and all its inhabitants will be incinerated. The people have been told what is going to happen. The story tells how various men and women spend their last hours of life.''

"*Very* helpful,'' she sneered. "I suppose that after reading it you'll be well equipped to face such an emergency. Now, just tell me what *you* would do if you learned that the world was going to come to an end tomorrow.''

He refilled his pipe. Over the little flame of the match he glared at his wife.

"Let me have my book back,'' he said.

"Oh, no. Not until you've answered my quesion. What would *you* do?''

"It all depends. . . .'' he muttered.

"It all depends on *what?* A typical, evasive answer. It all depends, I suppose, on whether or not you had the skill and the knowledge to build a spaceship to escape to Mars or Jupiter or wherever it is that people *do* escape to in these silly stories. (And did you have the nerve to say that they weren't escapist?) Come on, answer me.''

"Given enough time,'' he said, "a ship could be built.''

"But not by you.''

"No.''

"Then what would *you* do?''

"Give it a rest, will you?'' he snarled.

"Why should I? You've often said that we have no conversation these days, and now that I've gone out of my way to cater to your juvenile interests you dry up.''

"It's impossible to talk about anything,'' he said, "so long as you insist on making everything so damned personal. If we can't discuss a thing objectively we can't discuss it at all.''

"And why not?''

"Because you make everything so damned personal. The next thing will be that you'll be telling me that at least three of the marvelous men you knew in the past could have built spaceships out of two oil drums and a kerosene heater and whisked you off to the Asteroid Belt with hours to spare.''

''Perhaps they could, at that. But you haven't answered my question. What would *you* do?''

''I don't know.''

He got up from his chair.

''Where are you going?''

''Into the kitchen to pour myself a beer. Do you mind?''

''You might ask me if *I* want one.''

''Do you?''

''No.''

He walked through into the kitchen. He got a glass out of the cupboard. He opened the refrigerator, took out a bottle of beer. He had the opener poised over the cap when he was startled by a loud, brief crackle from the radio.

''You might look at the set,'' called his wife. ''It seems to have gone wrong.''

''It can wait,'' he replied.

Then, instead of the music, there was a voice—frightened, speaking hastily, fading for seconds at a time.

''Emergency transmitter . . . intercontinental missiles . . . hydrogen . . . New York has been . . . London . . . Washington destroyed . . . Moscow . . . it is believed that . . . cobalt . . . . ''

''Did you hear?'' she cried. ''What does it mean?''

''It means,'' he said, putting down the bottle and going to a drawer, ''the end of the world.''

''What shall we do?''

He opened the drawer.

''What shall we do?'' she called again.

He walked through into the living room, the carving knife gleaming in his hand.

''Reverting to your original question, my dear,'' he said, ''here is the answer.''

71

OPTICAL ILLUSION

Mack Reynolds

MOLLY BROUGHT MY plate, silver and side dishes and placed them before me without fuss or comment. I was an old customer and one of the things I like about Molly was that she never fussed over me.

I usually make a practice of eating after the rush hour but today I was early and the restaurant crowded. It was only a matter of time before someone would want to share my table.

I didn't look up when he asked, "Is this seat taken?" His voice was high, almost to the point of shrillness in spite of his attempt to control it.

"No," I told him, "go right ahead."

He hung his cane, or umbrella, whatever it was, over the back of his chair and fumbled his hat underneath it before climbing to his seat. Then he picked up the menu from where it stood between the catsup and napkins.

"Nothing fit to eat," he muttered finally.

I said, "The pot pie is quite good today."

Molly came up and he said to her, "I'll have the swiss steak, Miss. Green peas, french fries. I'll decide on the dessert later."

"Coffee?"

"Milk."

I don't know what it was that first gave me the idea that the person seated across the table from me wasn't a midget at all. Not a midget or dwarf, but a child pretending adulthood and doing a fantastically good job of it. As I say, I don't know what it was that gave me the hint, possibly I'm more susceptible to such intuitiveness than the next man.

But whatever it was, he knew almost as soon as I did.

That is, he knew that I'd caught on to him and somehow it frightened me. The whole idea was so bizarre—a child, not yet in his teens, passing himself off for some reason of his own as a mature, if stunted, adult.

443

"So," he said, his shrill voice almost a hiss. He put down his fork. "So . . . ."

How can I describe that cold voice? The voice of a child . . . but not a child. Not a child as we know one.

I reached for the sugar which was there where it always is at the end of the table next to the salt and pepper and the mustard jar. I measured out a spoonful very carefully without looking up at him. As I have said, somehow I was afraid.

He said, still softly, "So at last a stupid human has penetrated my disguise."

A *human*, he had said.

His voice was a child's but his words dug into me viciously. "Ah, so that surprises you, my curious friend. You wonder, eh?" There was a sneering quality now, a contemptuous overtone.

I cleared my throat, tried to cover my confusion by taking a gulp of the coffee. "I don't know what you mean . . . sir."

He chuckled and mimicked, "I don't know what you mean . . . sir." Then his voice snapped over at me, even as he kept his tone low. "Why did you hesitate before adding the *sir*, eh? Why?" He didn't wait for an answer. "I'll tell you why. Because somehow you've discovered that my age is less than I would have it known."

He was boiling with rage, and in spite of his size and the public nature of our whereabouts, I was afraid of him. Why, I didn't know. Somehow I sensed that—impossibly—he could destroy me at will.

I fumbled my cup back into its saucer, kept my face averted.

"You're terrified," he snapped again. "You recognize your master even as you wonder about him."

"My master?" I said. Who did he think . . . .

"Your master," he repeated. "Mankind's master. The new race. The super race, *Homo Superior*, if you will. He is here, my snooping friend and you, you and your stupid nation-divided, race-divided, class-divided, religion-divided humanity will never stand before him."

It was hard for me to assimilate. I had come into my favorite restaurant for my mid-day meal. It had been a routine day and I had expected it to continue as one. Now, I had been startled so many times in the past few minutes that I felt I was in a state of shock.

"Oh, it's been suggested before," he went on, seemingly welcoming this opportunity to explain to me, to gloat over me. "The possibility that mutations would develop, a super-race, a super-humanity as far above man as man is above the ape."

"How . . . what . . ."

He cut me off. "What difference if it was the atomic bomb, laboratory experiments, or only nature's continual plodding advance? The fact remains, we are here, a considerable number of us and in a few years, when we have developed our full capacities, man will hear from us. Ah, how he will hear!"

Long ago an icy hand had gripped my heart. Now it squeezed.

"Why," I stumbled. "Why tell me all this? Surely you wouldn't disguise yourself if you didn't wish to keep it all a secret."

He laughed mockingly. There was still much of the immature in him, super-race or nay.

"Because it doesn't make any difference," he whispered. "None at all. Ten minutes from now, you will remember nothing of this conversation. Hypnotism, my stupid *homo sapiens* can be a developed art when practiced on the lower orders."

His voice went hard and incisive. "Look up into my eyes," he ordered.

I had no power to resist. Slowly my face came up. I could *feel* his eyes drill into mine.

"This you will forget," he ordered. "All of this conversation, all of this experience, you will forget."

He came to his feet, took his time about securing his things, and then left.

Molly came over later. "Gee, she said, "that little midget was just here, he sure tips good."

"I would imagine," I told her. I was still shaken. "He probably has a substantial source of income."

"Oh." Molly said, making conversation as she cleaned up. "You been talking to him?"

"Yes," I told her, "we had quite a discussion." I added thoughtfully, "and as a result I have duties to perform."

I came to my own feet and reached up for my hat and cane where they hung on their usual hook.

I thought: *possibly man has more of a chance than these hidden enemies realize. Mental powers beyond us they may have, although they would seem lacking in the more kindly qualities. But this one hadn't been as sharp as he liked to think himself. Hypnotic powers he might possess beyond our understanding, but that didn't prevent him from making a very foolish error. He hadn't caught on to the fact that I'm blind.*

72

THE PAIR

Joe L. Hensley

THEY TELL THE story differently in the history stereos and maybe they are right. But for me the way the great peace came about, the thing that started us on our way to understanding, was a small thing—a human thing—and also a Knau thing.

In the late days of the hundred year war that engulfed two galaxies we took a planet that lay on the fringe of the Knau empire. In the many years of the war this particular planet had passed into our hands twice before, had been colonized, and the colonies wiped out when the Knau empire retook the spot—as we, in turn, wiped out the colonies they had planted there— for it was a war of horror with no quarter asked, expected, or given. The last attempt to negotiate a peace had been made ten years after the war began and for the past forty years neither side had even bothered to take prisoners, except a few for the purposes of information. We were too far apart, too ideologically different, and yet we each wanted the same things, and we were each growing and spreading through the galaxies in the pattern of empire.

The name of this particular planet was Pasman and, as usual, disabled veterans had first choice of the land there. One of the men who was granted a patent to a large tract of land was Michael Dargan.

Dargan stood on a slight rise and looked with some small pride at the curved furrow lines in the dark earth. All of his tillable land had been plowed and made ready for the planting. The feeling of pride was something he had not experienced for a long time and he savored it until it soured within him. Even then he continued to stare out over his land for a long time, for when he was standing motionless he could almost forget.

The mechanical legs worked very well. At first they had been tiring to use, but in the four years since his ship had been hit he had learned to use them adequately. The scars on his body had been cut away by the plastic surgeons and his face looked almost human now, if he could trust his mirror. But any disablement leaves deeper scars than the physical ones.

He sighed and began to move toward the house in his awkward yet powerful way. Martha would have lunch ready.

The house was in sight when it happened. Some sixth sense, acquired in battle, warned him that someone was following and he turned as quickly as possible and surveyed the land behind him. He caught the glint of sunlight on metal. He let himself fall to the earth as the air flamed red around him and for a long time he lay still. His clothes smoldered in a few spots and he beat the flames out with cautious hands.

Twice more, nearby, the ground flamed red and he lay crowded into the furrow which hid him.

Martha must have heard or seen what was happening from the house for she began shooting his heavy projectile "varmint" gun from one of the windows and, by raising his head, Dargan could see the projectiles picking at the top of a small rise a hundred yards or so from him. He hoped then that she would not kill the thing that had attacked, for if it was what he thought, he wanted the pleasure for himself.

There was silence for a little while and then Martha began to shoot again from the window. He raised his head again and caught a glimpse of his attacker as it scuttled up a hill. *It was a Knau*. He felt the blood begin to race in him, the wild hate.

"Martha!" he yelled. "Stop shooting."

He got his mechanical legs underneath him and went on down to the house. She was standing in the doorway, crying.

"I thought it had gotten you."

He smiled at her, feeling a small exhilaration. "I'm all right," he said. "Give me the pro gun." He took it from her and went to the small window, but it was too late. The Knau had vanished over the hill.

"Fix me some food," he said to her. "I'm going after it."

"It was a Knau, wasn't it?" She closed her eyes and shuddered, not waiting for his answer. "I've never seen one before—only the pictures. It was horrible. I think I hit it."

Dargan stared at her. "Fix me some food, I said. I'm going after it."

She opened her eyes. "Not by yourself. I'll call the village. They'll send some men up."

"By that time it will be long gone." He watched her silently for a moment, knowing she was trying to read something in him. He kept his face impassive. "Fix me some food or I will go without it," he said softly.

"You want to kill it for yourself, don't you? You don't want anyone to help you. That's why you yelled at me to stop shooting."

"Yes," he admitted. "I want to kill it myself. I don't want you to call the village after I am gone." He made his voice heavy with emphasis. "If you call the village I won't come back to you, Martha." He closed his eyes and stood swaying softly as the tension built within him. "Those things killed my parents and they have killed me. This is the first chance I've ever had to get close to one." He smiled without humor and looked down at his ruined legs. "It will be a long time dying."

The trail was easy to follow at first. She had wounded it, but he doubted if the wound were serious after he had trailed awhile. Occasionally on the bushes it had crashed through were droplets of bright, orange-red blood.

Away from the cleared area of the farm the land was heavily rolling, timbered with great trees that shut away the light of the distant, double blue suns. There was growth under the trees, plants that struggled for breathing room. The earth was soft and took tracks well.

Dargan followed slowly, with time for thought.

He remembered when his ship had been hit. He had been standing in a passageway and the space battle had flamed all around him. A young officer in his first engagement. It was a small battle—known only by the co-ordinates where it had happened and worth only a line or two in the official reports of the day. But it would always be etched in Dargan's brain. His ship had taken the first hit.

If he had been a little further out in the passageway he would surely have died. As it was he only half died.

He remembered catching at the bulkhead with his hands and falling sideways. There was a feeling of horrible burning and then there was nothing for a long time.

But now there was something.

He felt anticipation take hold of his mind and he breathed strongly of the warm air.

He came to a tree where it had rested, holding on with its arms. A few drops of bright blood had begun to dry on the tree and he estimated from their height on the tree that the Knau had been wounded in the shoulder. The ground underneath the tree was wrong somehow. There should be four deep indentations where its legs had dug in, but there were only three, and one of the three was shaped wrong and shallower than the others.

Though he had followed for the better part of half the day, Dargan estimated that he was not far from his farm. The Knau seemed to be following some great curving path that bordered Dargan's land.

It was beginning to grow dark enough to make the trail difficult to read. He would have to make cold camp, for to start a fire might draw the Knau back on him.

He ate the sandwiches that Martha had fixed for him and washed them down with warm, brackish water from his canteen. For a long time he was uanable to go to sleep because of the excitement that still gripped him. But finally sleep came and with it—dreams. . . .

He was back on the ship again and he relived the time of fire and terror. He heard the screams around him. His father and mother were there too and the flames burned them while he watched. Then a pair of cruel, mechanical legs chased him through metal corridors, always only a step behind. He tore the mechanical legs to bits finally and threw them at Knau ships. The Knau ships fired back and there was flame again, burning, burning . . . .

Then he was in the hospital and they were bringing the others in. And he cried unashamedly when they brought in another man whose legs were gone. And he felt a pity for the man, and a pity for himself . . . .

He awoke and it was early morning. A light, misty rain had begun to fall and his face was damp and he was cold. He got up and began to move sluggishly down the trail that the Knau had left, fearing that the mist would wash it out. But it was still readable. After awhile he came to a stream and drank there and refilled his canteen.

For a time he lost the trail and had to search frantically until he found it again.

By mid-suns he had located the Knau's cave hideaway and he lay below it, hidden in a clump of tall vegetation. The hideaway lay on the hill above him, a small black opening, which was shielded at all angles except directly in front. The cave in the hillside was less than a mile from Dargan's home.

Several times he thought he could detect movement in the blackness that marked the cave opening. He knew that the Knau must be lying up there watching to see if it had been followed and he intended to give it ample time to think it had gotten away without pursuit or had thrown that pursuit off.

The heat of the day passed after a long, bitter time filled with itches that could not be scratched and non-existent insects that crawled all over Dargan's motionless body. He consoled himself with thoughts of what he would do when he had the upper hand. He hoped, with all hope, that the

Knau would not resist and that he could take it unawares. That would make it even better.

He saw it for certain at the moment when dusk became night. It came out of the cave, partially hidden by the outcropping of rock that formed the shelf of the cave. Dargan lay, his body unmoving, his half-seeing eyes fascinated, while the Knau inspected the surrounding terrain for what seemed a very long time.

They're not so ugly, he told himself. *They told us in training that they were the ugliest things alive—but they have a kind of grace to them. I wonder what makes them move so stiffly?*

He watched the Knau move about the ledge of the cave. A crude bandage bound its shoulder and two of the four arms hung limply.

Now. You think you're safe.

He waited for a good hour after it had gone back inside the cave. Then he checked his projectile weapon and began the crawl up the hillside. He went slowly. Time had lost its meaning. *After this is done you have lost the best thing.*

He could see the light when he got around the first bend of the cave. It flickered on the rock walls of the cave. Dargan edged forward very carefully, clearing the way of tiny rocks, so that his progress would be noiseless. The mechanical legs dragged soundlessly behind him, muffled in the trousers that covered them.

There was a fire and the Knau lay next to it. Dargan could see its chest move up and down as it gulped for air, its face tightened with pain. Another Knau, a female, was tending the wound, and Dargan felt exultation.

Two!

He swung the gun on target and it made a small noise against the cave floor. Both of the Knau turned to face him and there was a moment of no movement as they stared at him and he stared back. His hands were wet with perspiration. He knew, in that instant that they were not going to try to do anything—to fight. They were only waiting for him to pull the trigger.

The fire flickered and his eyes became more used to the light. For the first time he saw the male Knau's legs and knew the reason for the strangeness of the tracks. The legs were twisted, and two of the four were missing. A steel aid was belted around the Knau's body, to give it balance, making a tripod for walking. The two legs that were left were cross hatched with the scars of imperfect plastic surgery.

Dargan pulled himself to his feet, still not taking the gun off the two by the fire. He saw the male glance at the metallic limbs revealed beneath his

451

pants cuff. And he saw the same look come into the Knau's eyes that he knew was in his own.

Then carefully Dargan let the safety down on the pro gun and went to help the female in treating the male.

It should have ended there of course. For what does one single act, a single forgiveness by two, mean in a war of a hundred years? And it would have ended if the Knau empire had not taken that particular small planet back again and if the particular Knau that Dargan had tracked and spared had not been one of the mighty ones—who make decisions, or at least influence them.

But that Knau was.

But before the Knau empire retook Pasman it meant something too. It meant a small offering of flowers on Dargan's doorstep the morning following the tracking and, in the year before they came again, a friendship. It meant waking without hate in the mornings and it meant the light that came into Martha's eyes.

And Dargan's peace became our peace.

/S/Samuel Cardings,
Gen. (Ret.) TA
Ambassador to Knau Empire

73

THE PATIENT

E. M. Hull

CANCER CURE AT LAST

London, Aug. 23, 1943—Reports reaching this capital state that a universal cancer cure has been perfected at the Midland-West Coast Hospital for Cancer Patients. Since the war, this hospital has been largely converted to military purposes, but one wing is still under the charge of the brilliant cancer research scientist, Dr. Lyall Brett, who is to make a public statement shortly.

IN THE GATHERING dusk the plane was little more than a blur; and it must have been coasting, for Bill Dobbs, guard at the Midland Cancer Hospital, heard no sound. Beside him, his companion stirred, then stood up.

"Blimey," his voice came to Bill. "A bloomin' parachute. Look!"

Bill strained into the dark, but after a moment he said tautly: "You're the one with the eyes, Pikes. Get the searchlight on 'em."

The beam blazed into the night, and abruptly had the white thing in its glaring embrace.

"Gor, it's empty."

"Some Nazi trick," Bill said swiftly. "Keep your eyes peeled, while I go hunt for it."

The parachute sank out of sight behind a low hill, fifty yards away. Bill raced across the moor and reached the top of the hill just as the moon came from behind clouds and bathed the shallow valley below him in a bright light.

There was nothing. Wait! He saw the dog, plainly. It ran past him at top speed, soundlessly, and was gone along a gully shielded by brush.

No parachute, no other movement. "Guess we dreamed it," Bill reported on the field phone to the seageant, ''because there ain't nothin' there but dog tracks.''

It was ten minutes later that the shadowy shape of a dog showed on the hard pavement of the hospital courtyard, strained its elements—and became a man, clothes and all; a big man who walked boldly into the hospital, said quietly to the girl at the information desk:

''I am Peter Grainger. May I speak to Dr. Brett's assistant, Dr. Carstairs?''

Dr. Lyall Brett looked up wearily as Dr. Carstairs opened the door of his office and came in.

''Lyall,'' Carstairs breathed. ''It's happened. He's here.''

Brett stared at him wanly. ''Who's here? Say, I thought you were in bed.''

''Heading that way, but I wouldn't have missed this for a million dollar gift to Cancer Research. I don't think I'll be able to sleep tonight! Lyall, you've got to talk to him now, this minute.''

''Harry,'' said Brett, ''what are you talking about? Who's here?''

''I've just admitted Peter Grainger as a patient.''

''I'm still blind,'' Brett began, then he stopped: ''Another patient? Are you crazy? We haven't room for a sardine, let alone another patient. Where did you put him?''

''I doubled up the day and night head nurses. If looks could kill, I'd be dead now. But I tell you, Brett, we couldn't miss this man.

''Remember my telling you of a patient who came to Carl Hamber's New York Cancer Institute last year—the fellow who'd been to every cancer institute as well as to every quack in the world? He's the perpetual cancer patient. He has an operation practically every year. They've cut cancer out of his throat, his chest, his head—and he's still alive. He's *the* cancer patient, known all over the world. If you can cure him—''

Brett was frowning. ''Come to think of it, I remember hearing of him. Do you mean to tell me Hamber couldn't do anything with him? From what you told me of Hamber's process, he and I were on the same track, though he was first. And if he hadn't been killed so tragically—''

''There you have the answer to your question, Lyall,'' Carstairs spoke quietly. ''The explosion that killed him and wrecked the laboratory took place on the night that Grainger arrived there; the same night that I left New York to come to work with you. I met Grainger at the time, and as a matter of fact, he asked for me when he arrived tonight.

"He probably knows more about cancer and the men working on it than any person now alive." He laughed grimly, finished curtly: "After all, he's got a bigger stake in finding the cure even than you. Shall I send him in?"

Brett hesitated, said finally: "I suppose so. But you get to bed."

The man was different, utterly different from what Brett expected. He loomed in the doorway. In the dim light of the desk lamp, he glowed with vitality; he said in a voice that was alive with vibrant power:

"Dr. Brett, is your system based on diet?"

"It is."

"Ah! A combination of vitamins. May I ask what proportions of A, B, C, and D you use? What is your key number?"

The curious feeling came to Brett that it was he who was being interviewed. He felt no annoyance, but he had met patients before who talked in just such a glib manner, if not so forcefully. He smiled a tight, tired little smile, and said:

"Won't you sit down, Mr. Grainger: I shall be pleased to give you a brief explanation of my system."

He watched in a developing wonder, as the man came forward with a catlike grace. Abruptly, in spite of weariness, Brett was conscious of admiraton; he said:

"Mr. Grainger, you astound me. Most cancer patients droop with pain; their spirit is worn to tatters—"

"I have other surprises for you," said the man coolly; and Brett looked at him sharply, conscious of hidden meaning. The impression faded, and Brett began slowly:

"I decided shortly after I left medical college that I wanted the broadest possible base for attacking the problem of cancer. Let other men, I thought, build expensive apparatus to cure people in whom cancer had become too far advanced for surgery.

"What I wanted was something that would check the disease at any stage, and about which any doctor, whatever his knowledge, could say: 'Now, you just do so and so, and you'll be all right in no time.'

"What do all humans do that has a vital effect on their health?—that was the question I asked myself. And the answer, of course, was as simple and straightforward as the question: They eat. Tons and tons of food. The entire world is geared to satisfy that basic need."

In his gathering excitement, he stood up, stared down at Grainger. "What was needed was a rough and ready system of measuring the daily vitamin ration that anybody, anywhere, could follow, something that would destroy the cancer potentiality of every cell in the body. Cancer, as you know, is simply cell growth run wild and—''

"I see," came the steel-toned interruption, "that you are on the right track. Accordingly, you must die, you, and all those who know your secret."

"Eh?" said Brett. And then, as the man's words penetrated, he stood and stared.

There was silence. Very carefully, Brett went to his chair and sank into it. He was not afraid, but he felt oppressed, hopeless.

Brett sighed and said: "Why do you want to kill me? On the entire earth, I am probably the only man who can make you well."

The stranger shook his head. In the half-light, his eyes gleamed: "I am not a madman, Dr. Brett; and unfortunately for you, the very extent of your success makes it necessary for me to kill you. Let me ask you a question: Can you imagine a perfect physical being?"

It struck Brett sharply that if only he could keep the fellow talking . . . He said cautiously: "Universal adaptation would be a required ability for such a being. That means . . . amorphism . . . changing shape at will . . . which would require radical cell and tissue growth like—''

He stopped, his eyes wide. Before he could speak, the man Grainger said softly: "Yes, Dr. Brett, like cancer; and you would destory the free-growth potentiality of the cell, *man's hope for biological perfection, for adaptive power so complete that he can swim and fly and live in airless space, live anywhere, under any conditions.*"

Brett gasped: "You're crazy, man! It's impossible! Don't you see what's happened to you? For years you've been under the threat of death by cancer. And it's become an obsession in reverse. You—''

The strangers' voice, strong and resonant, cut him off: "Man is on the verge of his tremendous destiny. Never has there been so much cancer in the world. The amazing thing is that no one suspected, for of all the diseases I do not include organic weaknesses—it is the only one not of germ.

"You are beginning to understand why you must be destroyed. Must! There is no promise you could make which would satisfy me. For a dozen reasons, you will be opposed to amorphism. The very idea is hideous, it is against religion—so you will think. Or you will decide that this meeting was the dream of a tired brain. Or that any promise you make under coercion is not binding.

"You must die as Hamber died and others before him, because you did not confine your research to alleviation of pain, to the development of

456

apparatus which will destroy specific cases of cancer. War has made it difficult for me to keep track of research. At one time I used to fly with my own wings, but that is too slow in a world of delayed news. Today, to reach you, I took the swiftest plane ever built, transformed briefly into a parachute, then into a dog. It took me only three hours to reach here from—where I was.

"But you can see now why I am on Earth—to protect the human race from one phase of its scientific genius."

"*On* Earth?" Brett croaked.

"Do not fear, Dr. Brett; you have an immortal soul. You will live again, your great, questing spirit undimmed; only—soon—your body, too, will be everlasting."

Brett was thinking numbly: there were buzzer buttons on his desk. But they would only bring nurses. And he couldn't drag women into this—

His mind wrenched from its hopeless thought. For the man was changing. *Changing*. His face was transforming, shining. Abruptly, there was a glistening steel-like bomb standing upended on the floor.

"Beware," Brett was thinking piercingly, "doctors, beware this patient, beware—"

The world ended in a shattering violence of explosion.

It took an hour for the dymanic cells of the man, in their blind will to cohesion, to come together. Slowly, in the darkness, Peter Grainger took form. He stood for a while, staring at the wreckage of the hospital wing; then he turned off into the night.

Next morning, the following communique was issued by the Ministry of Home Security:

—slight enemy air activity over the west coast. A hospital was damaged with some casualities among patients and personnel, including two doctors killed. No military damage.

74

THE PEOPLE'S CHOICE

William Jon Watkins

FROM: H.H. WEBER, PRESIDENT:
WEBER, FINLEY, & OSGOOD
TO: COLFAX,
ADVERTISING CONSULTANT
DATE: September 25

While I am sure that this ''advertising genius nodoby ever sees'' posture is a necessary part of your image, I still do not care very much for your way of doing business. I like to meet a man face to face, and I must say I find this corresponding rather ecentric. Nevertheless, you have given us such brilliant advice on campaigns in the past that I am sure you are the only one who can handle this problem if it can be handled at all. To be brief; given unlimited funds, could you make a short, fat, ugly woman President of the United States?

FROM: COLFAX
TO: H.H. WEBER, PRESIDENT
WEBER, FINLEY, & OSGOOD
DATE: September 25

With unlimited funds, I could get her elected God. The fee will be two million. Has she any other liabilities?

FROM: H. H. WEBER
TO: COLFAX
DATE: September 26

She has innumerable liabilities, not the least of which is that we can't type her. She's not homey enough for Golda Meir, nor flamboyant enough for Bella Abzug—and the way she looks precludes just about anything else.

Besides that she's very shy, totally unphotogenic and has a disconcerting habit of telling the truth. Six agencies turned her down before we got her—even when offered unlimited funds. Two of them literally laughed in her face!

Something of a recluse, but very personable in small groups. Extremely intelligent, but wants to be President out of some stange sense of moral duty. Not a Women's Libber or anything, just a sort of anachronism who thinks she's best suited for the job and therefore duty-bound to take it. Very sophisticated outside of this sixteenth century notion of moral responsibility.

FROM: COLFAX
TO: WEBER
DATE: September 27
Her shyness may work to our advantage. All we have to do is keep the public from seeing her until she's been elected. Ask her if she'll run anonymously.

FROM: WEBER
TO: COLFAX
DATE: September 27
ANONYMOUSLY?????!!!! Are you sure you can handle this?

FROM: COLFAX
TO: WEBER
DATE: September
$4,000,000 if she wins, nothing if she loses.

FROM: WEBER
TO: COLFAX
DATE: September 29
Agreed. She says she'll do whatever she has to do—unless it involves joining one of the political parties or is blatantly dishonest. She doesn't seem to be politically naive, but she's adamant on the point of not joining one of the parties—not that it matters much since neither of them would have her anyway.

FROM: COLFAX
TO: WEBER
DATE: September 30
Good. We'll run the entire campaign through television. Nothing until next September 12; then, I want two minutes out of every half hour until Election Day. In the meantime, get me the following:

1. About twenty Types—the kind you use in the potato chip and shaving commercials—housewives, football players, policemen, little old ladies, doctors, etc. None of them too good looking. Have the women a little on the plain side, something she can blend in with.
2. One athletic, intelligent, articulate Black male.
3. One white male, about sixty. The Grand-Old-Man-type, white hair, moustache and goatee, robust. The kind you use in the Impeccable Taste ads, but more sagacious.
4. One white female who can look like she has a Ph.D. in Political Science without losing anything as a sex symbol.
5. One white male about thirty-five who looks as much as possible like the Virile-Young-Man without looking too much like a Kennedy. All of the Four must be physically and mentally superior.
6. An estate outside New York, secluded, one where we can maintain absolute security. NO ONE who works on this project can be attached in any way. We are going to hide them away until after the election. NONE of the actors is ever to be seen in public unless I order it.

I must have ABSOLUTE authority in this thing. No one is to know for certain who the Candidate is so your client will have to agree to act like everyone else. That means she'll have to take orders just like any other actor; if word of her identity gets out prematurely or she wants to pull out part way through, you forfeit $200,000 a month for my time—from Sept. 25 to date of forfeiture. Agreed?

Contact me again when you've secured everything on the list. We have over a year to go so be very selective. Take only those who are willing to cooperate completely and only the very best of those. PCS will handle the initial screening. We'll need about three months for indoctrination before filming begins.

FROM: WEBER
TO: COLFAX
DATE: April 25
Agreed.

Files on the final selections will be sent to your office tomorrow. We have secured an estate in New Jersey about fifty miles outside the city. Two buses have been purchased and dummy buses have been rented to confuse anyone who might try to follow us.

FROM: COLFAX
TO: WEBER
DATE: May 1

I am finished studying the files. The final selections are excellent. It's surprising that Ms. Cavil has never entered a beauty contest—but very

461

fortunate for us. Williams is very good for the Grand Old Man; very genteel. I don't think Saxon's Boston accent will hurt us and I'm very pleased with Brown. I was afraid they would come up with a white man's Black man, but this one is excellent.

Begin filming the Gold-Edge Beer commercial and the Bright Detergent commercial Tuesday. We'll need these shown as soon and as often as possible. They'll give our real commercials something familiar to parallel. Begin the indoctrination tomorrow.

FROM: WEBER
TO: COLFAX
DATE: August 25

I hope these things are being forwarded to you. This is a hell of a time to take a vacation. The actors are very enthused now that they know their mission. There is none of the jealousy you might expect with this many actors cooped up together for so long. The screening must have been exceptionally good.

I think most of them—certainly the Four—know who the Candidate is but it doesn't matter; she's made converts of all of them. They seem sincerely attached to her; her influence on them is truly amazing. She has one of them studying Ecology; another Economics. One is becoming her expert on Education; another on Foreign Policy. It's like she's selected her cabinet already.

I treated the whole thing like a game but she seems quite serious—and so do they. When do we start the first commercial? We're about ready.

FROM: COLFAX
TO: WEBER
DATE: September 1

The idea for the first commercial is enclosed. Make it parallel the Gold Edge Beer commercial as closly as possible; shoot the same camera angles, etc. Most of this is the same action; read it anyway.

Open with tight shot of huddle. Close-up of Ms. Cavil in her sweatshirt, cap, whistle, etc., calling the play. Wide angle for snap from center. Cut to Saxon running his pattern; long pass to him on run; circus catch. (Shoot this one until you get something spectacular. The files indicate that both Saxon and Brown played football in college).

Follow Saxon down sideline to where he gets hemmed in by the last defensive man. Brown comes from off-camera left to block the defensive man. (Again, something that crunches. This will be shown during a lot of professional football games, and we don't want it to look pale by comparison.) Cut to Saxon as he scores.

Close-up of Saxon and Brown congratulating each other. Cut to close-up of Grand Old Man nodding approvingly from the sidelines. Close-up of button on his lapel reading: TEAMWORK COUNTS. (Distribute 5,000,000 of these buttons around the country the same week.)

Wide angle shot of crowd running up to congratulate Saxon and Brown. Keep the Candidate in front, but a little out of focus. Cut to American flag. Dub in "Hail to the Chief." Superimpose words and narrator: "Ladies and gentlemen, the next president of the United States has appeared in this commercial."

FROM: WEBER
TO: COLFAX
DATE: September 9

Very effective. A lot like the "Camels-Are-Coming!" campaign and the car commercials we did with the new models under a drape. We're ready for number-two. By the way, our client has them all meeting an hour a day for what she calls consciousness raising. You don't suppose she's a Libbie after all?

FROM: COLFAX
TO: WEBER
DATE: September 9

I don't really care what she is. My job is to get her elected. Enclosed is the second script. Shoot the same opening as the Bright commercial except that instead of having Cavil explain how the detergent works have her talk about how detergents and industrial wastes are fouling our water supply.

As she's talking, four men come into the laundromat and attack her (have them wear ski masks so we don't offend any ethnic groups). She fights, one of them tears open her blouse (tiniest flash of nipple). Saxon and Brown enter dressed as washer repairmen, come to her aid.

Series of rapid cuts; knives, feet, faces, different camera angles, mostly low. Each disables one opponent; Cavil finishes hers with a Karate chop. Fourth assailant runs for the door where the Grand Old Man, entering, jabs him with his walking stick (have the old man take a good impact on the stick and grab his shoulder in pain).

Pan around laundromat: clothes all over the floor, an old woman hysterical in the corner with the Candidate comforting her. Cavil trying to hold her blouse closed, Saxon and Brown both cut over the right eye, the old man rubbing his shoulder, the four toughs sprawled about on the floor. Dolly back out through the window to wide angle shot of laundromat.

Superimpose and voice-over: "When a crime is committed, everyone suffers. We must fight crime in the streets and the conditions that cause it. Vote for THE CANDIDATE." Both Right and Left will interpret that one to our advantage.

TO: COLFAX
FROM: WEBER
DATE: September 10

Cavil and our client both refuse to do the commercial. They say it exploits women. The men agree with them. She's turning them all into revolutionaries!

TO: WEBER
FROM: COLFAX
DATE: September 11

Of course it exploits women! How many commercials have they seen that don't? Ask Cavil this: If she had to break into a prison to free her sisters would she refuse to do it because she'd have to dress up as a male guard? And tell your client that when she's President she can appoint Kate Millett head of the FCC and change all the commercials she wants, but this one must stay as is. Causes require sacrifices.

TO: COLFAX
FROM: WEBER
DATE: September 11

She says to tell you you must mean "The end justifies the means." Anyway, they had a meeting and decided that tactics takes precedence over ideology. They'll do the script as written.

You've opened a fine can of worms with that crack about the FCC. Now they're drawing up a list of government agencies that can be controlled by appointment. And making a list of appointees!

FROM: WEBER
TO: COLFAX
DATE: September 20

Things have settled down a bit and the filming is going very well. The Karate stuff looks authentic. Brown is familiar with it and acted as technical director. I don't think they're really serious about that list. Williams told me they have Angela Davis down for Supreme Court Justice. He had such a straight face I almost thought he was serious. Anyway, it helps them pass the time between takes.

FROM: COLFAX
TO: WEBER
DATE: September 23
Release the first commercial and the buttons simultaneously in ten days.

FROM: WEBER
TO: COLFAX
DATE: October 3
Introductory commercial released yesterday as directed. Good intiital response. Five million TEAMWORK COUNTS buttons distributed. Our client has her "cabinet" out proselytizing among the other actors. Not much else to do now that the shooting's over for a while, and it keeps them busy so I encourage it.

FROM: WEBER
TO: COFLAX
DATE: October 12
Crime commercial released yesterday on schedule. Requests received for 2,000,000 more buttons. Between the five of them, they've even begun to make converts among the technical and security people. I think Cavil's trying to raise *my* level of consciousness. Are we creating a Frankenstein here?

FROM: COLFAX
TO: WEBER
DATE: October 13
Release group picture for the "$5,000 1,000-winner Who-Is-THE CANDIDATE? Contest". Follow each of our one-minute commercials with a thirty-second spot about the contest. Place hints in appropriate newspaper columns and have your Gold Edge Beer Salesmen casually pass on similar information to bar tenders. We want everybody in the country to have an opinion of THE CANDIDATE'S identity. The contest should have the effect of encouraging betting. All major radio stations will carry telephone contests with similar clues.

Dummy voting booths will be set up near every large polling place. Procedures for voting must be identical to those used in the real election. It will cost us another million in persuasion money to get "THE CANDIDATE" printed on the real ballot and to have anything written in counted as a vote for us, but it will be well worth it. Also she will have to secretly change her name to THE CANDIDATE to make it hold up in court (the Supreme Court). We have less than a month to make voting for THE CANDIDATE a conditioned response.

FROM: WEBER
TO: COLFAX
DATE: October 14

What are we going to do?! The President has just accepted a challenge to debate! What if they include us?!

FROM: COLFAX
TO: WEBER
DATE: October 15

And admit we're a legitimate alternative? Not likely. Here's the next commercial; release it the day *after* the debate.

Wide angle shot of auditorium; pan slowly to platform where the President and the Democratic nominee are debating. They cannot be heard because the crowd is booing too loudly. Both men ignore the crowd entirely. The crowd grows violent and begins to throw things. Secret Service men draw their guns. Cut to series of other weapons in the audience.

Brown jumps up on the left side of the stage, Cavil on the right. They gesture for order and the crowd quiets. Brown speaks.

"Everyone has the right to say what he wants, even the people who barred us from this platform! Even the people who denied us the opportunity to confront them on the real issues of the campaign. Even the people who have been trying to keep us from talking to you, the people, by putting pressure on television station owners to drop our commercials!"

Cavil speaks. "These men have a right to speak! Even though every word they say is put into their mouths by the rich and powerful men who are paying for their campaigns. Even though they won't tell you about the deals they've already made they have the right to speak! Everybody has that right! Not just those who agree with us! Everybody!" Saxon shouts, "Right!" Wild applause.

Pan slowly past the Candidate to Williams, smiling his approval. Superimpose words and voice-over: "It's not who you are but what you believe in that's important. Vote for the candidate nobody owns. Vote for THE CANDIDATE."

FROM: WEBER
TO: COLFAX
DATE: October 23

Latest commercial released on schedule. Over 50 million votes already in the ''Who-Is-THE CANDIDATE Contest''. People are tuning in our commercials just to study them. Papers in all major cities are carrying schedules of our commercials on the front page. This thing is really beginning to boom—I'm worried.

FROM: COLFAX
TO: WEBER
DATE: October 30

Start filming the thirty second spot. Assemble the whole group, in costumes and masks. Have the Candidate and the Four in the center of the group but not conspicuously so. Then all remove their masks and shout, ''See you at the victory celebration!'' You have two days to do this one. Plant hints in the columns that there'll be no unmasking unless we win the election. Hedge when the media asks you about it.

FROM: WEBER
TO: COLFAX
DATE: November 4

Over 85,000 votes in the contest and we're ahead of both of them in the polls! The networks are demanding that we either show our candidate or get out of the race. What are we going to do? I can't stall them forever.

FROM: COLFAX
TO: WEBER:
DATE: November 4

Set up a press conference for the sixth nationwide TV, prime time.

FROM: WEBER
TO: COLFAX
DATE: November 5

Are you crazy?! We can't show her! What's going to happen with all those people who guessed wrong? I've had three phone calls from people telling me that they've bet a lot of money on the Old Man and it better be him or else—and I have an unlisted number! We're liable to get killed right there at the press conference.

467

It's easy for you to say 'give a press conference' when you're off hiding somewhere on your extended vacation. But we're the ones who'll have to face the music. I knew this thing was going to blow up in our faces! When the press gets a look at her we'll be the laughing stock of the industry. When the public sees her we'll be lucky if we don't get indicted for fraud and conspiracy! Treason! You've got to get us out of this!!

FROM: COLFAX
TO: WEBER
DATE: November 6

GET YOURSELF TOGETHER!! Just go to the meeting and stand well back from the podium. The Candidate knows what to do. Everything is going according to plan. TRUST ME!!

FROM: WEBER
TO: COLFAX
DATE: November 7

WHY DIDN'T YOU TELL ME ABOUT THE BOMB!!!!I thought it was for real. How did you manage to get the television cables cut during the confusion? And what would have happened if the rest of that dynamite had gone off? And for what???!!!

So we didn't have to make the announcement? What good does it do us? What's going to happen tonight when she wins the election and has to make a victory speech? The losers are bound to call fraud. They might even get the election nullified! We could all go to jail! WHAT ARE WE GOING TO DO???!!!

FROM: COLFAX
TO: WEBER
DATE: November 7

Stop it. I repeat; everything is going according to plan. Don't come to the victory party tonight; I don't even want to see you near campaign head-quarters! Go back to the estate and watch it all on television as soon as you give these instructions to the group.

Everything is set. The group will come to the podium in a body as soon as we are mathematically assured of victory. The Four will be in the middle, the Candidate a little to the right. The house lights will go off and the assassination film will be shown. The TV people are already prepared for a film of some sort as part of the speech so they'll have no trouble carrying the whole thing. The film is pretty gruesome, even in black and white.

When the house lights come on again, the whole group will repeat the following in unison:

TIME AFTER TIME, THE WILL OF THE PEOPLE HAS BEEN CIRCUMVENTED BY AN ACT OF VIOLENCE. LAST NIGHT IT ALMOST HAPPENED AGAIN. THE COUNTRY CANNOT AFFORD THE DISLOCATION THAT OCCURS WHEN A PRESIDENT IS ASSASSINATED. AS LONG AS I AM PRESIDENT MY IDENTITY WILL REMAIN A SECRET.

THE DESIRE FOR PERSONAL GLORY DOES NOT BELONG IN THE WHITE HOUSE. THE DESIRE TO BE A PRESIDENT "HISTORY WILL REMEMBER" DOES NOT BELONG IN THE WHITE HOUSE. THEREFORE I WILL REMAIN ANONYMOUS.

BUT THIS SHOULD NOT SEEM STRANGE TO YOU: THE PRESIDENT IS, AFTER ALL, ONLY THE REPRESENTATIVE WHO STANDS IN PLACE OF THAT GREAT ANONYMOUS MASS—THE PEOPLE. WE THE PEOPLE!

Have them rehearse it thoroughly.

FROM: COLFAX
TO: WEBER
DATE: November 8

I have destroyed your memo, and the security guards I have permanently assigned to you will see to it that you do the same with this after you read it. I don't know when you figured it out and I must confess I did not anticipate your hiding the memos that passed between us. I congratulate you; it was a clever move and guarantees you your life.

You will be kept under close house-arrest until my Inauguration. Thereafter you will be free to move about—however, if you ever address me or refer to me as "Madame President" again, I will have you killed, whether I find the memos or not! You will be well taken care of. Do not try to escape.

75

PLAYING THE GAME

Gardner Dozois and Jack Dann

THE WOODS THAT edged the north side of Manningtown belonged to the cemetery, and if you looked westward toward Endicott, you could see marble mausoleums and expensive monuments atop the hills. The cemetery took up several acres of carefully mown hillside and bordered Jefferson Avenue, where well-kept woodframe houses faced the rococo painted headstones of the Italian section.

West of the cemetery there had once been a district of brownstone buildings and small shops, but for some time now there had been a shopping mall there instead; east of the cemetery, the row of dormer-windowed old mansions that Jimmy remembered had been replaced by an ugly brick school building and a fenced-in schoolyard where kids never played. The cemetery itself, though—that never changed; it had always been there, exactly the same for as far back as he could remember, and this made the cemetery a pleasant place to Jimmy Daniels, a refuge, a welcome island of stability in a rapidly changing world where change itself was often unpleasant and sometimes menacing.

Jimmy Daniels lived in Old Town most of the time, just down the hill from the cemetery, although sometimes they lived in Passdale or Southside or even Durham. Old Town was a quiet residential neighborhood of whitewashed narrow-fronted houses and steep cobbled streets that were lined with oak and maple trees. Things changed slowly there also, unlike the newer districts downtown, where it seemed that new parking garages or civic buildings popped out of the ground like mushrooms after a rain. Only rarely did a new building appear in Old Town, or an old building vanish. For this reason alone, Jimmy much preferred Old Town to Passdale or Southside, and was always relieved to be living there once again. True, he usually had no friends or school chums in the neighborhood, which consisted mostly of first- and second-generation Poles who worked for the Mannington shoe factories, which had recently begun to fail. Sometimes, when they lived in Old Town, Jimmy got to play with a lame Italian boy who was almost as much of an outcast in the neighborhood as Jimmy was, but the Italian boy had been gone for the last few days, and Jimmy was left alone again. He didn't really mind being alone all that much—most of the time anyway. He was a solitary boy by nature.

The whole Daniels family tended to be solitary, and usually had little to do with the close-knit, church-centered life of Old Town, although sometimes his mother belonged to the PTA or the Ladies' Auxiliary, and once Jimmy had been amazed to discover that his father had joined the Rotary Club. Jimmy's father usually worked for Weston Computers in Endicott, although Jimmy could remember times, unhappier times, when his father had worked as a CPA in Johnson City or even as a shoe salesman in Vestal. Jimmy's father had always been interested in history, that was another constant in Jimmy's life, and sometimes he did volunteer work for the Catholic Integration League. He never had much time to spend with Jimmy, wherever they lived, wherever he worked; that was another thing that didn't change. Jimmy's mother usually taught at the elementary school, although sometimes she worked as a typist at home, and other times—the bad times again—she stayed at home and took "medicine" and didn't work at all.

That morning when Jimmy woke up, the first thing he realized was that it was summer, a fact testified to by the brightness of the sunshine and the balminess of the air that came in through the open window, making up for his memory of yesterday, which had been gray and cold and dour. He rolled out of bed, surprised for a moment to find himself on the top tier of a bunk bed, and plumped down to the floor hard enough to make the soles of his feet tingle; at the few places they had lived, he hadn't a bunk bed, and he wasn't used to waking up that high off the ground. Sometimes he had trouble finding his clothes in the morning, but this time it seemed that he had been conscientious enough to hang them all up the night before, and he came across a blue shirt with a zigzag green stripe that he had not seen in a long time. That seemed like a good omen to him, and cheered him. He put on the blue shirt, then puzzled out the knots he could not remember leaving in his shoelaces. Still blinking sleep out of his eyes, he hunted futilely for his toothbrush; it always took a while for his mind to clear in the mornings, and he could be confused and disoriented until it did, but eventually memories began to seep back in, as they always did, and he sorted through them, trying to keep straight which house this was out of all the ones he had lived in, and where he kept things here.

Of course. But who would ever have thought that he'd keep it in an old coffee can under his desk!

Downstairs, his mother was making French toast, and he stopped in the archway to watch her as she cooked. She was a short, plump, dark-eyed, olive-complexioned woman who wore her oily black hair pulled back in a tight bun. He watched her intently as she fussed over the hot griddle, noticing her quick nervous motions, the irritable way she patted at loose strands of her hair. Her features were tightly drawn, her nose was long and straight and sharp, as though you could cut yourself on it, and she seemed all angles and edges today. Jimmy's father had been sitting sullenly over his third cup of coffee, but as Jimmy hesitated in the archway, he got to his feet and began to get ready for work. He was a thin man with a pale complexion and a shock of wiry red hair, and Jimmy bit his lip in disappointment as he watched him, keeping well back and hoping not to be noticed. He could tell from the insignia on his father's briefcase that his father was working in Endicott today, and those times when his father's job was in Endicott were among the times when both of his parents would be at their most snappish in the morning.

He slipped silently into his chair at the table as his father stalked wordlessly from the room, and his mother served him his French toast, also wordlessly, except for a slight, sullen grunt of acknowledgement. This was going to be a bad day—not as bad as those times when his father worked in Manningtown and his mother took her "medicine," not as bad as some other times that he had no intention of thinking about at all, but unpleasant enough, right on the edge of acceptability. He shouldn't have given in to tiredness and come inside yesterday, he should have kept playing the Game . . . Fortunately, he had no intention of spending much time here today.

Jimmy got through his breakfast with little real difficulty, except that his mother started in on her routine about why didn't he call Tommy Melkonian, why didn't he go swimming or bike riding, he was daydreaming his summer away, it wasn't natural for him to be by himself all the time, he needed friends, it hurt her and made her feel guilty to see him moping around by himself all the time . . . and so on. He made the appropriate noises in response, but he had no intention of calling Tommy Melkonian today, or of letting her call for him. He had only played with Tommy once or twice before, the last time being when they lived over on Clinton Street

(Tommy hadn't been around before that), but he didn't even *like* Tommy all that much, and he certainly wasn't going to waste the day on him. Sometimes Jimmy had given in to temptation and wasted whole days playing jacks or kick-the-can with other kids, or going swimming, or flipping baseball cards; sometimes he'd frittered away a week like that without once playing the Game. But in the end he always returned dutifully to playing the Game again, however tired of it all he sometimes became. And the Game had to be played alone.

Yes, he was definitely going to play the Game today; there was certainly no incentive to hang around here; and the Game seemed to be easier to play on fine, warm days anyway, for some reason.

So as soon as he could, Jimmy slipped away. For a moment he confused this place with the house they sometimes lived in on Ash Street, which was very similar in layout and where he had a different secret escape route to the outside, but at last he got his memories sraightened out. He snuck into the cellar while his mother was busy elsewhere, and through the back cellar window, under which he had placed a chair so that he could reach the cement overhang and climb out onto the lawn. He cut across the neighbors' yards to Charles Street and then over to Floral Avenue, a steep macadam deadend road. Beyond was the start of the woods that belonged to the cemetery. Sometimes the mud hills below the woods would be guarded by a mangy black and brown dog that would bark, snarl at him, and chase him. He walked faster, dreading the possibility.

But once in the woods, in the cool brown and green shade of bole and leaf, he knew he was safe, safe from everything, and his pace slowed. The first tombstone appeared, half buried in mulch and stained with green moss, and he patted it fondly, as if it were a dog. He was in the cemetery now, where it had all begun so long ago. Where he had first played the Game.

Moving easily, he climbed up toward the crown of woods, a grassy knoll that poked up above the surrounding trees, the highest point in the cemetery. Even after all he had been through, this as still a magic place for him; never had he feared spooks or ghouls while he was here, even at night, although often as he walked along, as now, he would peer up at the gum-gray sky, through branches that interlocked like the fingers of witches, and pretend that monsters and secret agents and dinosaurs were moving through the woods around him, that the stunted azalea bushes concealed pirates or orcs . . . But these were only small games, mood-setting exercises to prepare him for the playing of the Game itself, and they fell away from him like a shed skin as he came out onto the grassy knoll and the landscape opened up below.

Jimmy stood entranced, feeling the warm hand of the sun on the back of his head, hardly breathing, listening to the chirruping of birds, the scratching of katydids, the long, sighing rush of wind through oak and evergreen. The sky was blue and high and cloudless, and the Susquehanna River gleamed below like a mirror snake, burning silver as it wound through the rolling, hilly country.

Slowly, he began to play the Game. How had it been, that first time that he had played it, inadvertently, not realizing what he was doing, not understanding that he was playing the Game or what Game he was playing until after he had already started playing? How had it been? Had everything looked like this? He decided that the sun had been lower in the sky that day, that the air had been hazier, that there had been a mass of clouds on the eastern horizon, and he flicked through mental pictures of the landscape as if he were riffling through a deck of cards with his thumb, until he found one that seemed to be right. Obediently, the sky grew darker, but the shape and texture of the clouds were not right, and he searched until he found a better match. It had been somewhat colder, and there had been a slight breeze . . . .

So far it had been easy, but there were more subtle adjustments to be made. Had there been four smokestacks or five down in Southside? Four, he decided, and took one away. Had that radio tower been on the crest of that particular distant hill? Or on *that* one? Had the bridge over the Susquehanna been nearer or further away? Had that Exxon sign been there, at the corner of Cedar Road? Or had it been an Esso sign? His blue shirt had changed to a brown shirt by now, and he changed it further, to a red pinstriped shirt, trying to remember. Had that ice cream stand been there? He decided that it had not been. His skin was dark again now, although his hair was still too straight . . . Had the cemetery fence been a wrought iron fence or a hurricane fence? Had there been the sound of a factory whistle blowing? The smell of sulphur in the air? Or the smell of pine . . . ?

He worked at it until dusk; and then, drained, he came back down the hill again.

The shopping mall was still there, but the school and schoolyard had vanished this time, to be replaced by the familiar row of stately, dormer-windowed old mansions. That usually meant that he was at least close. The house was on Schubert Street this evening, several blocks over from where it had been this morning, and it was a two-story, not a three-story house, closer to his memories of how things had been before he'd started playing the Game. The car outside the house was a '78 Volvo—not what he remembered, but closer than the '73 Buick from this morning. The windshield bore an Endicott parking sticker, and there was some Weston Computer literature tucked under the eyeshade, all of which meant that it was probably safe to go in; his father wouldn't be a murderous drunk this particular evening.

Inside the parlor, Jimmy's father looked up from his armchair, where he was reading Fuller's *Decisive Battles of the Western World,* and winked. "Hi, sport," he said, and Jimmy replied, "Hi, Dad." At least his father was a black man this time, as he should be, although he was much fatter than Jimmy ever remembered him being, and still had this morning's kinky red hair, instead of the kinky black hair he should have. Jimmy's mother came out of the kitchen, and she was thin enough now, but much too tall, with a tiny upturned nose, blue eyes instead of hazel, hair more blond than auburn . . . .

"Wash up for dinner, Jimmy," his mother said, and Jimmy turned slowly for the stairs, feeling exhaustion wash through him like a bitter tide. She wasn't *really* his mother, they weren't *really* his parents. He had come a lot closer than this before, lots of other times . . . But always there was some small detail that was *wrong*, that proved that this particular probability-world out of the billions of probability-worlds was *not* the one he had started from, was not *home*.

Still, he had done much worse than this before, too. At least this wasn't a world where his father was dead, or an atomic war had happened, or his mother had cancer or was a drug addict, or his father was a brutal drunk, or a Nazi, or a child molester . . . This would do, for the night . . . He would settle for this, for tonight . . . He was so tired . . . .

In the morning, he would start searching again.

Someday, he would find them.

76

PONCE

Glen Cook

FOR ME IT started the day we got the new car. New in that we didn't have it before. It was a '62 Continental that the dude painted canary yellow (with a broom, it looked like) to get me to take it. It was our first. You got six kids, one trying to make the breakout in college, push a broom and moonlight as a watchman, and have a mama that's got to go to the kidney machine every three days and has diabetes besides, food stamps don't go very far, even if you can trade them off for something besides beans. We were proud of that car. Seven years we'd been saving pennies and nickels in a big lard can I got from the bakery. Once some kids broke in and got it, but that was early, when there was only a few dollars. We hid it good after that. Nobody ever found it.

First thing we did was go for a ride, cats and all. Sarah borrowed a camera from our downstairs neighbor, Wanda, and got some film with money she had, and we went to the zoo, then just rode around, showing it off.

People looked. That car was *ugly*. The kids all grinned and waved. The cats got sick and kept trying to get out.

We got home with some daylight and film left. Sarah wanted some pictures of the kids and car in front of the house. Blues maker. One rundown two-family flat in the middle of a block where most of the buildings had been demolished, leaving a stony, bricky, weedy desert, littered with old tires and bedsprings that appeared overnight, like magic mushrooms. The few surviving flats rose like dirty, scattered teeth in an old man's mouth.

But the high of the car, of success, kept on. When Lania, our ten-year-old daughter, came up with another cat, found only she knew where, we hardly argued.

Then our boy Arivial, our youngest, came back with a dog. I put my foot down, but not hard enough. A lot of angry words, and some tears, and the dog had a home.

It wasn't the arguments that convinced me. It was that dog's eyes.

That was the strangest dog I ever seen. One of them little hairy ones, Scottie I think, black as night, bony as death, wanting to be friendly but nervous about it, like some white dude you've been working with for years who's friendly on company time but don't know how you want he should act when you meet him outside.

It was his eyes. You ever see a dog with blue eyes? Not blue like some blond white dude. Not like a kitten. Not like the sky, or turquoise, or anything light, but none of the darks either. A blue with depth. And, if you've ever looked at a dog's eyes, you know they're all color, kind of a brownish gold outside the pupil. Not these eyes. Outside the blue, that looked kind of deep and far away like the colored things inside the marbles kids call cateyes, they were clear as glass. My first thought was that he did have marbles for eyes. They were round and a little more forward on his head than most.

That whole dog was strange, but his eyes had a life of their own. Whenever I looked straight at them I felt like I was falling in, like I was watching a space show on Wands's TV where Star Trek was coming to some planet. It scared me shitless.

I told Sarah maybe we better take him to the Humane Society, maybe something was wrong. Didn't want the kids to get bit. He didn't have no tags. She said we didn't have no money. Wouldn't till Firday, when the bakery check came, and that had to go for rent. Eighty bucks and we didn't even get hot water. Four rooms. It would have to wait. Maybe a long time. Next week was food stamps, then gas and electric, and cat and dog food, and clothes and shoes because school was starting and the younger ones were getting too big for last year's. . . . It's hard sometimes, but I never been in no trouble. Neither have my kids, which makes me proud. It's harder for them. They're growing up with people who steal and cheat all the time. Only thing any of us ever did was sometimes get Sarah a carton of Kools with the food stamps.

Maybe Arivial could find some soda bottles, but that was always a hassle. The dude at the confectionary always thinks he stole them. We never buy no soda.

If you think I'm old fashioned, saving up to buy a car and not trying to break the system and raising my kids the same, I guess you're right. That's the way I was raised. Times was different then.

Arivial named the dog Ponce. He didn't seem so spooky when you didn't look at his eyes. He settled right in, most of the time acted just like any other dog. He barked at strangers. He bounced around with happy whines any time anybody came home, especially Arivial from school. He really was Arivial's dog. He growled at me when I growled at the boy. Only three days after we picked him up, he bit a kid when some boys tried to steal Arivial's new shoes. I thought there would be some trouble, but nobody ever came around. Those boys must've been afraid of the trouble they'd get if they squawked.

Guess you get used to anything if it's around you all the time, like having less than most, or a dog with blue eyes. It's just there and, unless you trip over it, you don't much notice. Unless you're young and you've got time to look around. That's one problem for the kids today. They've got the time. We didn't when I was young. Too busy trying to stay fed. I worked all my life. Started picking cotton with my folks in Arkansas when I was barely big enough to walk. Only way I know. You get to my age, you're pretty set in your ways.

You've got to figure on what you're hungry for, too. My parents would've thought our flat a mansion. A man's big goal, them days, was to bring his wife to the city. Now Bobby, my oldest, was getting his foot on the next step up.

That Ponce was a smart pup. Wasn't a week before Arivial had him doing tricks. And there were some he figured for himself, like how to get out the screen door when it wasn't locked.

I came in from the bakery one night, to eat and get my watchman's uniform, and found Sarah all worried. Kids and cats and Ponce were all outside. The Lincoln was gone. I figured Bobby was off with his Mary Taylor again. I didn't see much of that car during the week. I hoped he wasn't wasting his book money. Sarah and Arivial was talking to Ponce. I thought, so what? Everybody does. The cats too. But she said it was like they were talking serious, only Ponce just sat there real quiet and stared with those eyes. The boy had been telling her what Ponce had told him. She was afraid he wasn't playing pretend, that he really believed it. I said, well, I'll talk to him when I get a chance.

I was starting to be sorry that I let the kids have the pets. They cost too much even when we didn't get all the shots and tags. And I was sorry about the car, too, a little bit. Bobby wasn't home much anymore. He might get in trouble, might have a wreck, you know how you think.

It was a Sunday morning before church when I finally caught Arivial talking to Ponce the way that worried Sarah. You ever listen to a kid talking to a pet? When they don't know you're there? They get real serious, telling their problems. That dog, see, he don't tell no secrets, don't brush it off, don't make fun. He sits there and listens, and knows it's important, even if he don't understand. That's why kids need pets, I guess. A pet's always got the time.

That's what Arivial was doing, only it was going like half a conversation. The boy would say something, ask a question, wait a while, then ask one or two questions about the answers he seemed to have gotten. I don't remember what his problem was. It wasn't something a grownup would think important. After I listened a while, I went and sat by Arivial. He was surprised but Ponce wasn't. Ponce always seemed to know where everybody was. I scratched his ears.

I told Arivial I understood about Ponce, but his mother didn't, that him talking to the dog all the time scared her. Especially when he told her what Ponce said back. He said Ponce *did* talk to him, with his eyes, and why should he lie? I always told him not to lie.

I said he didn't have to, just don't tell your mother, it makes her unhappy. He butted me some buts, then said okay. No more talking to Ponce where she'd hear, no more telling her what he said.

All the time Ponce sat there looking at me with those eyes, making me feel guiltier and guiltier. I got the feeling he was trying to tell me something, too, so I mostly looked away.

That took care of it for a week. Then it was Liana complaining. Don't know why she was upset. She was always talking to the cats. But I straightened that out, too. Then it was another of the kids, and another, till there was nobody left but me and Bobby, the two that was home the least. It got to be a puzzle. None of them bothered to explain, just to complain.

I finally got some time free, late in October, after Ponce had been with us two months. I took Arivial and Ponce to the park. You weren't supposed to let dogs run loose there, but I took a chance Ponce would behave like always and stay by Arivial. He did.

I had kind of a suspicion that I asked about then, and Arivial admitted that he'd known Ponce a while before he'd asked if the dog could stay with us. I nodded, smiled. Arivial told me how smart Ponce was, staying out of sight those days. I said yes. I never argued with how smart that dog was. He was the smartest I ever seen.

I asked what they talked about. School stuff, he said. Ponce could explain things better than his teacher. He made it fun. And there wasn't no dumb stuff, like history. I asked what kind of stuff. Mostly arithmetic, he said.

I was beginning to see why the others had been bothered. Arivial wasn't playing pretend at all. I asked why didn't he show me. He'd always been interested in arithmetic. Did real good at it in school. I'd played games with him before. That's what I expected then.

But what he scratched in the dirt with a stick looked like chicken tracks. I thought about Bobby's college books. This didn't look the same. But I really couldn't tell. I only went to school now and then when I was a kid, and only got my grade school equivalency now. I want to do high school, but there just isn't time.

I asked what it was. He said some fancy words I didn't know he knew, then said that Ponce didn't know our notation so he'd had to learn Ponce's. Took me a minute to figure out what he meant. Then I said, well, why didn't he use some of the older kids' books to learn? I was just going along, figuring he'd seen Bobby's books and was making up something that looked the same. He said he'd never thought about that.

There was peace around the house for a month. At least, nobody came to me complaining. Then Arivial brought home a note from his teacher.

It didn't say nothing but that Sarah should come in after school. She was so upset, so sure he was in trouble, that she wouldn't go. Arivial said he didn't know what it was about. Next day I took off early and went down.

His teacher and principal were both waiting. Liana had had that teacher last year. I didn't like her. She was the kind that thought you was against her if you taught your kid to brush his own teeth. But the principal was all right.

Wasn't no trouble, though. The principal did most of the talking. About where was Arivial learning arithmetic? The teacher just said she was awed. The principal said Arivial was doing high school work already, maybe higher. She thought he was a genius. Would I mind did they arrange for him to take some tests?

Then the teacher said that if he was a genius, he should get special training. I was surprised. I got in an unkind word when they asked did I know about Arivial's talent. Well, yes, I said, but I never said anything because of Liana last year. After that everybody told everybody how sorry they was, but by then I wasn't listening. I was thinking about Ponce.

I still didn't believe Arivial was really talking to him, but I worried that maybe he thought he was. Maybe the boy was a genius like they said, but what if he had to have Ponce to make it work? So he could believe in himself? I could fix it so he could study at home, but not so Ponce would live forever. Even if he was lucky and lasted maybe twelve years, there would be Arivial without him when he was twenty-one.

Teacher and principal were saying was it all right did they let some people from the universities see Arivial. If he studied fancy arithemetic?

Math, they said. He'd still have to study the regular stuff with the other kids. He wasn't no genius at everything. Sure, fine, I said, I'd be proud. But why were they so excited?

They said some things but I didn't listen. They weren't telling the truth. That was in their faces. They looked like old prospectors who had finally struck gold. Arivial was going to make them famous. I hedged then. Said everything was fine by me, sounded good, but I wanted to talk to Sarah and Arivial first.

I saw what could happen. Some good things could be done for Arivial, but it could be turned into a circus that would hurt him more. You hear about things like that in the news sometimes.

I just wanted to talk to Arivial. I knew what Sarah would say. She wouldn't want no part of it. She wanted her kids to be normal, as much like other kids as possible, to keep their heads down so to speak. She didn't realize that it was a new age, that some of the doors really were open a crack.

Arivial was waiting out front, scared to death. Sarah was waiting too, only upstairs, peeking out the blinds.

I told the boy what happened. At first he relaxed, then he got scared again when he realized people were going to make a fuss over him. He was always kind of quiet and private, and got embarrassed any time a stranger said something nice. He asked me did he have to take the tests and everything. I told him no, that was why I was talking to him, to see if he wanted to. I said the school wanted to get him some special teachers, and like that, until I was sure he knew what it was all about. Then I told him to make up his mind himself. Maybe he should talk to Ponce about it.

I don't know why I said that. I felt silly afterwards. He said yeah, that's what he'd do.

Later, almost bedtime, he came to the warehouse where I was watchman and whispered that he'd take the tests and things so he could study. He said Ponce thought it was a good idea, that he should learn as much as he could as fast as he could so he'd know how to say the things he really had to say, just in case something happened. I didn't understand, but I said okay, I'd come to school on my lunch hour and tell his teacher.

It went all right. After he got over being shy, Arivial liked the attention. And he got lots of it. The university people seemed like good folks, mostly, and they didn't get any newspaper or TV people coming around. His teacher and principal were disappointed about that, I think. Sarah got used to the idea, started getting proud. Only Bobby was a problem, and he wasn't a big one.

The old car kept breaking down and I wouldn't let him spend his college money to fix it. His romance died off because of that. Made him grouchy for a while, so he took it out on Arivial for getting into his books. He threatened to spank him or go join the Army, depending on who he was talking to. He got over it. By then Arivial had finished his books. He'd passed Bobby by.

The more he learned, the faster he went. Sometimes, when I could get away early, I went to school with him and talked to the university people. They used a lot of big words to do it, but what they said was that Arivial was starting to figure things out for himself. They could teach him something and he could almost, but not quite, tell them what came next.

What puzzled them was that he had his own system worked out and had to translate back and forth. They said he might be more than just a genius. The rate he was going, getting faster and faster, it wouldn't be long before they ran out of things to teach. They talked about sending away for teachers who knew more than they did. They were always all very excited.

Those nights I'd go home and stare at that blue-eyed dog and wonder. Somehow, he seemed the smaller miracle.

Summer came again. The university people wanted to take Arivial to California. He wanted to go, and to take Ponce.

Sarah said no. She wasn't letting no ten-year-old son of hers go nowhere for three months with no honkey strangers. When she talked hard and bitter like that, I didn't argue. I knew she wasn't going to change her mind.

So they brought the men from California to him. And a Dr. Conklin from back east, and even a man from Germany or someplace over there. I started getting real scared. They were spending more money than I made in a year, working two jobs, just to help my son learn math. I started thinking about things like Russian spies and the government looking Arivial up to protect him.

You can't keep secrets forever, especially when you got big-mouthed kids, a proud wife, and so many excited teachers. One day a radio man came to ask if he could interview Arivial on his station. Sarah got excited, I got more scared, the kids got jealous, and we all decided it was up to Arivial. I thought he could handle it. Being around all those college people, he'd changed. He was like a little boy with a grown man inside. When he was serious. Other times he was his own age. He loved baseball. Sometimes he complained about missing out on that when he studied.

His all-time hero was Lou Brock and he wanted to grow up and play left field for the Cardinals. He kept saying he'd be like Einstein afterwards, when he got old. That bothered me some. I thought maybe they were pushing too hard. Maybe he should take some time off. But he didn't want to. Math was fun, too.

I worried all the time, seems like.

Acting like that grown man, he did good on the radio. He talked about Ponce, but he was smart. He told his truth, but did it so everybody thought he was jiving them. He did the same thing later, on the TV. People were never sure how to take him.

I went downtown with him for the TV thing, wearing my church clothes. I was more nervous than him. He wanted to take Ponce, but I said better not.

Sarah worried too, but she was also proud. Now she really had something to brag to her friends about. Me too, except I didn't start till somebody asked. Sort of embarrassed, you know. Me so ignorant and him so smart. But everyboy kept telling me how great it was, even Mr. Kasselbaum at the bakery, who hardly ever came out of the office except to chew somebody out.

But it got to be too much, especially after, with help from this physicist, Dr. Conklin, Arivial wrote this article about hologrammatic numbers. He didn't know how to spell right or how to put the words down, but he knew the numbers. After that all kinds of people came to the house. We tried to be nice, but you couldn't get anything done. Just because my kid was smart didn't mean I should stop working, though Mr. Kasselbaum and the security company were good about me missing if I had to. And Sarah had the house and the kids had school, and Arivial was busier than anybody, trying to keep up with regular school, his special teachers, work on another article he wanted to write, Ponce, and all the people who wanted to talk to him.

It hurt some people's feelings and made some others mad, but we finally had to stop seeing anybody but family, friends, and the university people. Arivial kept telling me his new project was hard, that even Ponce had trouble explaining it because people still didn't have the concepts. Before they could really understand they would have to learn the hologrammatic notation.

Dr. Conkin tried to tell me about it. He said the new math would modify, prove, and expand some of Einstein's work. He was the translator, so to speak, the man who'd write it up so people could understand. He was having trouble, too, smart as he was. He said it was as much philosophy as physics and math, but when they got it straight it could be used to explain lots of things scientists had been having trouble with for years. I just kept nodding my head till he decided I was as smart as Arivial.

About that time Bobby found him a new girlfriend and had to have the car all the time. It was broke down more than it ran. Everytime it died we had to wait and scrimp to get it fixed, plus saving up for licenses and insurance, that I never thought about when I bought it. That old thing was more trouble than it was worth. I would've sold it except for Bobby.

This Dr. Conklin wasn't only interested in Arivial. Sometimes he'd start talking about Nobel Prizes and look greedy, but I guess that's just the way people are.

Bobby kept the car fixed and started running around. This time he was so involved that he didn't care about anything else. I found out he was getting into his school money for gas and things. He wouldn't listen when I tried to talk to him.

Arivial and Dr. Conklin kept getting more and more excited. They were getting close. Though he didn't believe Arivial was really learning from Ponce, he kept telling the boy to spend time with him. Told me he figured any way a man got his mind working was all right, even talking to dogs. Only the output counted. I agreed some and didn't agree. You could push it too far.

The way they talked, they had their paper down to the final match. I got the feeling mobs of people were waiting to grab it. More and more people came to the house, though we kept telling them to go away.

There was something about it on the radio, the TV, or in the newspapers every day. Everybody was on about the ten-year-old who was opening a whole new view of the universe. Part of the paper got pirated and printed and scientists started fighting like dogs around a bitch in heat. Some said it was another breakthrough to understanding as important as Newton's or Einstein's. Some others said it was the biggest fraud since organized politics. On the TV, right after one of these men had his say, they would show Arivial talking about Ponce.

I still think I took that dog more serious than anybody but Arivial. Sometimes I would just sit and stare at him for an hour. And sometimes he'd open one eye and sort of smile, as much as a dog can. I thought about trying to talk to him, just to convince myself he was only a dog, but I never got around to it. Maybe I was scared I'd be wrong. If I was, that meant I had to think about a whole lot of other things, like how could a dog talk, how come he was so smart, how come he had blue eyes, and so on.

Sometimes I think about that anyway. Maybe it's just because I'm too ignorant to know better.

The car broke down again. Water pump. When I came home from the bakery, there was Bobby fixing it. I got mad. Really mad. He'd been spending all his money and time on the car and his girlfriend. Sarah said he'd started cutting classes. I really gave it to him.

He took it for a while because I don't get on him that much and, anyway, he knew he was wrong. But when I started talking about his girl he blew up. We never came closer to fighting. He jerked the last bolt into place, slammed the hood, wiped his hands, jumped in, roared away. For about ten feet.

Ponce managed just one surprised yip.

My god, Bobby said, jumping out, my god. Pop, I didn't mean. . . . I'm sorry. . . .

I hadn't seen him cry since he was eleven. Didn't see him too good this time. It was hard to see through my own tears. I went to the dog. Ponce, I said, Ponce. . . . But there was nothing I could do. He was dead.

One by one the other kids turned up, and their friends, and Sarah and Wanda, and almost everybody in the neighborhood. A lot of the kids cried. They'd all liked Ponce. Nobody knew what to do.

All the time I was looking at those eyes. After a while the blue started fading. For a moment they were clear as colorless marbles, then they went dark. I thought I saw a lot of little lights swirling around in there, then they faded too. Might have been the street lights. They were just coming on. Then they were just plain dog's eyes.

Arivial was with Dr. Conklin, but he'd be coming home soon. We just kept standing around till a cop came by and asked what was going on. I told him. He remembered me and Ponce from TV. Told us not to block the street and went on. So I finally picked up Ponce and took him upstairs.

Arivial took it better than I expected, but he was hurt. Bad. He mostly stayed to himself for a few days, not doing anything but going to school and sometimes talking to Dr. Conklin. Conklin was upset too. Just another week, he kept saying, and they would've had it.

When Arivial got over it he went back to work. But he'd changed. He wasn't dumber, but he was a lot slower. It's been a year now and they're still trying to finish up. Arivial's showing the way, but without Ponce he can't get there except by inches.

The university people tried to convince him that he didn't need Ponce. It didn't work. Maybe it was all in his head, maybe it wasn't. I'm not sure. I don't think I ever will be.

A couple weeks after Ponce died Arivial said something that still makes me wonder. He said Ponce wasn't really dead, that he just went back. It was only a dog that Bobby killed. Ponce would come home if he really needed him.

And maybe that would be true even if the dog's talking was all in his imagination.

77

POOR LITTLE WARRIOR!

Brian W. Aldiss

CLAUDE FORD KNEW exactly how it was to hunt a brontosaurus. You crawled heedlessly through the mud among the willows, through the little primitive flowers with petals as green and brown as a football field, through the beauty-lotion mud. You peered out at the creature sprawling among the reeds, its body as graceful as a sock full of sand. There it lay, letting the gravity cuddle it nappy-damp to the marsh, running its big rabbit-hole nostrils a foot above the grass in a sweeping semicircle, in a snoring search for more sausagy reeds. It was beautiful: here horror had reached its limits, come full circle, and finally disappeared up its own sphincter. Its eyes gleamed with the liveliness of a week-dead corpse's big toe, and its compost breath and the fur in its crude aural cavities were particularly to be recommended to anyone who might otherwise have felt inclined to speak lovingly of the work of Mother Nature.

But as you, little mammal with opposed digit and .65 self-loading, semi-automatic, dual-barrelled, digitally computed, telescopically sighted, rustless, high-powered rifle gripped in your otherwise-defenseless paws, snide along under the bygone willows, what primarily attracts you is the thunder lizard's hide. It gives off a smell as deeply resonant as the bass note of a piano. It makes the elephant's epidermis look like a sheet of crinkled lavatory paper. It is gray as the Viking seas, daft-deep as cathedral foundations. What contact possible to bone could allay the fever of that flesh? Over it scamper—you can see them from here!—the little brown lice that live in those gray walls and canyons, gay as ghosts, cruel as crabs. If one of them jumped on you, it would very like break your back. And when one of those parasites stops to cock its leg against one of the bronto's vertebrae, you can see it carries in its turn its own crop of easy-livers, each as big as a lobster, for you're near now, oh, so near that you can hear the monster's primitive heart-organ knocking, as the ventricle keeps miraculous time with the auricle.

Time for listening to the oracle is past: you're beyond the stage for omens, you're now headed in for the kill, yours or his; superstition has had its little day for today, from now on only this windy nerve of yours, this shaky conglomeration of muscle entangled untraceably beneath the sweat-shiny carapace of skin, this bloody little urge to slay the dragon, is going to answer all your orisons.

You could shoot now. Just wait till that tiny steam-shovel head pauses once again to gulp down a quarry-load of bulrushes, and with one inexpressibly vulgar bang you can show the whole indifferent Jurassic world that it's standing looking down the business end of evolution's sex-shooter. You know why you pause, even as you pretend not to know why you pause; that old worm conscience, long as a baseball pitch, long-lived as a tortoise, is at work; through every sense it slides, more monstrous than the serpent. Through the passions: saying here is a sitting duck, O Englishman! Through the intelligence: whispering that boredom, the kite-hawk who never feeds, will settle again when the task is done. Through the nerves: sneering that when the adrenalin currents cease to flow the vomiting begins. Through the maestro behind the retina; plausibly forcing the beauty of the view upon you.

Spare us that poor old slipper-slopper of a word, *beauty*; holy mom, is this a travelogue, nor are we out of it? *"Perched now on this titanic creature's back, we see a round dozen—and, folks, let me stress that round—of gaudily plumaged birds, exhibiting between them all the color you might expect to find on lovely, fabled Copacabana Beach. They're so round because they feed from the droppings that fall from the rich man's table. Watch this lovely shot now! See the bronto's tail lift. . . . Oh, lovely, yep, a couple of hayricks-full at least emerging from his nether end. That sure was a beauty, folks, delivered straight from consumer to consumer. The birds are fighting over it now. Hey, you, there's enough to go round, and anyhow, you're round enough already. . . . And nothing to do now but hop back up onto the old rump steak and wait for the next round. And now as the sun sinks in the Jurassic West, we say 'Fare well on that diet' . . . ."*

No, you're procrastinating, and that's a life work. Shoot the beast and put it out of your agony. Taking your courage in your hands, you raise it to shoulder level and squint down its sights. There is a terrible report; you are half stunned. Shakily, you look about you. The monster still munches, relieved to have broken enough wind to unbecalm the Ancient Mariner.

Angered (or is it some subtler emotion?), you now burst from the bushes and confront it, and this exposed condition is typical of the straits into which your consideration for yourself and others continually pitches you. Consideration? Or again something subtler? Why should you be confused just because you come from a confused civilization? But that's a point to deal with later, if there is a later, as these two hog-wallow eyes pupiling you all over from spitting distance tend to dispute. Let it not be by jaws alone, O monster, but also by huge hooves and, if convenient to yourself, by mountainous rollings upon me! Let death be a saga, sagacious, Beowulfate.

Quarter of a mile distant is the sound of a dozen hippos springing boisterously in gymslips from the ancestral mud, and next second a walloping great tail as long as Sunday and as thick as Saturday night comes slicing over your head. You duck as duck you must, but the beast missed you anyway because it so happens that its coordination is no better than yours would be if you had to wave the Woolworth Building at a tarsier. This done, it seems to feel it has done its duty by itself. It forgets you. You just wish you could forget yourself as easily; that was, after all, the reason you had to come the long way here. *Get Away from It All,* said the time travel brochure, which meant for you getting away from Claude Ford, a husband-man as futile as his name with a terrible wife called Maude. Maude and Claude Ford. Who could not adjust to themselves, to each other, or to the world they were born in. It was the best reason in the as-it-is-at-present-constituted world for coming back here to shoot giant saurians—if you were fool enough to think that one hundred and fifty milion years either way made an once of difference to the muddle of thoughts in a man's cerebral vortex.

You try and stop your silly, slobbering thoughts, but they have never really stopped since the coca-collaborating days of your growing up; God, if adolescence did not exist it would be unnecessary to invent it! Slightly, it steadies you to look again on the enormous bulk of this tyrant vegetarian into whose presence you charged with such a mixed death-life wish, charged with all the emotion the human orga(ni)sm is capable of. This time the bogeyman is real, Claude, just as you wanted it to be, and this time you really have to face up to it before it turns and faces you again. And so again you lift Ole Equalizer, waiting till you can spot the vulnerable spot.

The bright birds sway, the lice scamper like dogs, the marsh groans, as bronto sways over and sends his little cranium snaking down under the bile-bright water in a forage for roughage. You watch this; you have never been so jittery before in all your jittered life, and you are counting on this catharsis wringing the last drop of acid fear out of your system for ever. OK, you keep saying to yourself insanely over and over, your million-dollar twenty-second-century education going for nothing, OK, OK. And as you say it for the umpteenth time, the crazy head comes back out of the water like a renegade express and gazes in your direction.

Grazes in your direction. For as the champing jaw with its big blunt molars like concrete posts works up and down, you see the swamp water course out over rimless lips, lipless rims, splashing your feet and sousing the ground. Reed and root, stalk and stem, leaf and loam, all are intermittently visible in that masticating maw and, struggling, straggling or tossed among them, minnows, tiny crustaceans, frogs—all destined in that awful, jaw-full movement to turn into bowel movement. And as the glump-glump-glumping takes place, above it the slime-resistant eyes again survey you.

These beasts live up to two hundred years, says the time travel brochure, and this beast has obviously tried to live up to that, for its gaze is centuries old, full of decades upon decades of wallowing in its heavyweight, thoughtlessness until it has grown wise on twitterpatedness. For you it is like looking into a disturbing misty pool; it gives you a psychic shock, you fire off both barrels at your own reflection. Bang-bang, the dum-dums, big as paw-paws, go.

With no indecision, those century-old lights, dim and sacred, go out. These cloisters are closed till Judgment Day. Your reflection is torn and bloodied from them for ever. Over their ravaged panes nictitating membranes slide slowly upwards, like dirty sheets covering a cadaver. The jaw continues to munch slowly, as slowly the head sinks down. Slowly, a squeeze of cold reptile blood toothpastes down the wrinkled flank of one cheek. Everything is slow, a creepy Secondary Era slowness like the drip of water, and you know that if you had been in charge of creation you would have found some medium less heart-breaking than Time to stage it all in.

Never mind! Quaff down your beakers, lords, Claude Ford has slain a harmless creature. Long live Claude the Clawed!

You watch breathless as the head touches the ground, the long laugh of neck touches the ground, the jaws close for good. You watch and wait for something to happen, but nothing ever does. Nothing ever would. You could stand here watching for a hundred and fifty million years, Lord Claude, and nothing would ever happen here again. Gradually your bronto's mighty carcass, picked loving clean by predators, would sink into the slime, carried by its own weight deeper; then the waters would rise, and old Conqueror Sea come in with the leisurely air of a card-sharp dealing the boys a bad hand. Silt and sediment would filter down over the mighty grave, a slow rain with centuries to rain in. Old bronto's bed might be raised up and then down again perhaps half a dozen times, gently enough not to disturb him, although by now the sedimentary rocks would be forming thick around him. Finally, when he was wrapped in a tomb finer than any Indian rajah ever boasted, the powers of the Earth would raise him high on their shoulders until, sleeping still, bronto would lie in a brow of the Rockies high above the waters of the Pacific. But little of any of that would count with you, Claude the Sword; once the midget maggot of life is dead in the creature's skull, the rest is no concern to you.

You have no emotion now. You are just faintly put out. You expected dramatic thrashing of the ground, or bellowing; on the other hand, you are glad the thing did not appear to suffer. You are like all cruel men, sentimental; you are like all sentimental men, squeamish. You tuck the gun under your arm and walk round the dinosaur to view your victory.

You prowl past the ungainly hooves, round the septic white of the cliff of belly, beyond the glistening and how-thought-provoking cavern of the cloaca, finally posing beneath the switch-back sweep of tail-to-rump. Now your disappointment is as crisp and obvious as a visiting card: the giant is not half as big as you thought it was. It is not one half as large, for example, as the image of you and Maude is in your mind. Poor little warrior, science will never invent anything to assist the titanic death you want in the contraterrene caverns of your fee-fi-fo fumblingly fearful id!

Nothing is left to you now but to slink back to your timemobile with a belly full of anticlimax. See, the bright dung-consuming birds have already cottoned on to the true state of affairs; one by one, they gather up their hunched wings and fly disconsolately off across the swamp to other hosts. They know when a good thing turns bad, and do not wait for the vultures to drive them off; all hope abandon, ye who entrail here. You also turn away.

You turn, but you pause. Nothing is left but to go back, no, but 2181 A.D. is not just the home date; it is Maude. It is Claude. It is the whole awful, hopeless, endless business of trying to adjust to an overcomplex environment, of trying to turn yourself into a cog. Your escape from it into *the Grand Simplicities of the Jurassic*, to quote the brochure again, was only a partial escape, now over.

So you pause, and as you pause, something lands socko on your back, pitching you face forward into tasty mud. You struggle and scream as lobster claws tear at your neck and throat. You try to pick up the rifle but cannot, so in agony you roll over, and next second the crab-thing is greedying it on your chest. You wrench at its shell, but it giggles and pecks your fingers off. You forgot when you killed the bronto that its parasites would leave it, and that to a little shrimp like you they would be a deal more dangerous than their host.

You do your best, kicking for at least three minutes. By the end of that

491

78

THE PROBLEM WAS LUBRICATION

David R. Bunch

I GUESS IT kept him hopping, there were so many holes. And I guess it was mostly hard work. But to me, as I watched this automation through the observation slit, it was somewhat diverting to see, among all the somber squatting machines with a fixed place in the line, one that could stand up tall and take off all around the floor. He wasn't a robot really, and actually I guess he couldn't take off and run all around the floor just wherever he wanted. But the metal track he was on carried him to all parts of the work area in order for him to reach every one of the squatty fixed machines, and there were occasional side trips up to the reload place. In comparison with the fixed ones this fellow had it good, I thought.

His official name was Lubro. Or so it said in gay red letters on a shiny metal plate rivited to his rear. The day I watched Lubro they were turning out millions of little metal disks destined for some important places in some important engines, and the machines doing the work were running hot. And here would come Lubro, smooth and docile on his track, until he reached a machine that was running hot turning out the disks. The machine would flip little lids up at Lubro's approach and Lubro in response would whang jointed sections of tubing out of himself and the ends of those tubes would find their way into the holes where the lids had flipped up. And while the machines worked on as though nothing were happening Lubro would stand there vibrating on his track and eject oil into the holes according to some clocklike mechanism in him. And as the tempo of production increased, Lubro ran faster and faster on his track and whanged metal tubing out of himself oftener and oftener and came up to the reload place time and again. But it seemed to me he was happy at his work, although that could have been merely my imagining because of the great contrast between a Lubro and a machine that squatted on the floor hour by hour and turned out the

493

quota time and again with, to console her, nothing but the small diversion of flipping her lids up for Lubro.

All in all, everything was going well here at automation it seemed to me, and Lubro was taking care of it, I thought, all right. But maybe he was running hot. At any rate, some Central Brain in the place made the decision and another upright thing with a clocklike mechanism in him and the power to eject flexible tubing out of himself came in to run on the tracks with Lubro. The Oiler, his name was. I guess the Central Brain thought The Oiler and Lubro could stay out of each other's way all right; one could be taking care of it in the south end, say, while the other was over north doing it; or one could be functioning on the west side while the other was shooting for lids in the east section of the work area maybe. But the truth is they didn't—they couldn't—stay out of each other's way for long. In the first place, I think Lubro was a little jealous, or maybe resentful is the better word, of The Oiler. For the very presence of The Oiler made it clear how the Central Brain felt. He felt that Lubro couldn't handle the job. Then too, no getting aroud it, The Oiler, big dark and cocky, was in Lubro's territory.

But as for production, there was an increase in it, no denying that. Especially was there more work done by certain of the newer machines in the central part of the work area. And it was one of these very machines that caused the flare-up. She was a new blonde machine without yet the grime of much servicing on her oil lids. And she squatted there, seemingly as innocent as a piece of the floor, and tooled her disks. But Lubro noticed it, and I noticed it too. Twice within the hour, when Lubro glided up, she kept her oil lids closed as though she were running cool as a bucket of grease. But when The Oiler came in at almost the same time from the opposite side of the work area her lids flew open as though she were filled with fire. And The Oiler ejected the tubes, according to the clocklike mechanism in him, and the tubes found the holes where the quivering lids hovered open, and he oiled the machine that indeed was not running cool; it was his job.

Lubro caught him at the top of the reload area. It was unethical. The Oiler was taking on oil, siphoning it from Central Supply into the can of his lower body. And Lubro should not have come in to the reload at the same time; there was but the one straight track in to the reload and no spur track for passing. But Lubro did come in. And the cocky Oiler stood nonchalantly siphoning oil until his can was full. Then he turned in that way he had, brazen, precise, sure, and he headed back for the work area as though it were understood that Lubro, being wrong, would retrace and let him through. Lubro would not! Lubro braced. Lubro hit him, hit him hard and middle-high and bounced him ten feet up the track. Lubro hit him again when The Oiler came within range. The Oiler closed and struck back; The Oiler hit twice in quick succession. The two oil cans stood toe-to-toe at the bottom of the reload area and exchanged blows. They rattled each other's skin sections and clobbered each other's joints. Rivets flew. Clocklike mechanisms were upset. They fought until it seemed in doubt that either one or the other would prove himself the better oil can.

Then the tide turned, as tides will, and Lubro got his chance. Because his clocklike mechanism was considerably upset by the hard blows he had taken, and possibly partly because he had just taken the reload, here at this strangest and most illogical of times one of The Oiler's tubelike sections popped out. Oil sprayed the area, and Lubro rammed in to wham the embarrassed oil can on the tube and spin him about until The Oiler was quite spun off the track. And there he lay, vanquished and bleeding oil, and presently all his other tubes flopped out and lay there limp and empty in plain sight, and The Oiler was a very sorry sight indeed. And because he had taken many hard blows himself, and partly, no doubt, in sheer exuberance over his victory, something got into Lubro's thinking and caused him to pull a very silly and shabby stunt. He ejected all his tubing sections to the very farthest limits they would go and sprayed The Oiler until he, Lubro, was quite empty of oil.

The Central Brain was jumping-mad in his clock, crazy-mad at Lubro and The Oiler. From these silly oil cans he had had quite enough, really he had. He immediately called a meeting of all the Junior Brains, and they all left their clocks and sat around a big polished disk of metal with a hole in the center of it and the Central Brain in the hole until they had all quite decided what to do. There was just one logical answer. Tear up the tracks, build a Lubro or an Oiler stationary for each squatty fixed machine and service these automatic tube ejectors from a Central Supply, using as many self-motion helicopters as would be required.

The Brains, having won again, having figured it out, resumed their clocklike places along the walls. And while they all agreed that automation had its bugs, yes it did, really it was quite the coming thing, yes it was.

79

PUBLISH AND PERISH

Paul J. Nahin

Mr. Thomas W. Starr
3613 Laguna Avenue
La Mesa, California 92041

March 17, 1977

DEAR MR. STARR,

It is with pleasure that I welcome you to the Faculty of the California Technological Institute. Dean Johnson has informed me that you have accepted the appointment of Instructor in Physics. Your title will change to Assistant Professor upon completion of your doctoral studies.

We look forward to seeing you in September.

Sincerely,

W. Alden Smith

Dr. W. Alden Smith
Office of the President

Mr. Thomas W. Starr
3613 Laguna Avenue
La Mesa, California 92041

May 3, 1977

DEAR TOM,

President Smith has asked me to write to you about an issue we wish to have clear, before you arrive on campus in September. Your appointment is for two years (renewable), but you must receive your Ph.D. by December 1, of your second academic year with us. Otherwise, because of the Institute's bylaws, we would be unable to recommend your reappointment to the Trustees.

Sincerely,

Pete

Peter V. Johnson, Ph.D.
Office of the Dean

Dr. Peter V. Johnson   May 8, 1977
Dean of Engineering and Science
California Technological Institute
Claremont, California 91711

DEAR DEAN JOHNSON,

The completion of my doctorate by December 1, 1978, will be no problem. I have talked this matter over, at some length, with my dissertation advisor Professor B. B. Abernathy at San Diego Tech. He assures me there will be no difficulty. He is even joking about there being a Nobel Prize in it for the two of us!

Cordially,

Thomas W. Sta

Thomas W. Starr

Mr. Thomas W. Starr   September 9, 1977
1713 12th Street
Claremont, California 91711

DEAR TOM,

Sorry we missed our regular meeting last week, but I couldn't skip the review briefing on my grant at the Pentagon (but the thought of the agony of the red-eye flight to DC almost made it worthwhile to cancel out). While losing my way wandering around the Puzzle Palace, I happened to mention

498

some of your most recent results toward inducing nuclear fusion in water, and it caused quite a stir. If you get tired of teaching in Claremont, give the Civil Service a thought—you can't believe some of the nitwits with GS-12 and 13 ratings they've got back there. A good man like you would get snapped right up, and it certainly beats what they pay young, new college teachers.

See you next week, and we will discuss the first draft of your thesis.

Regards,

Bert

Bertram B. Abernathy, Ph.D.
Professor of Physics

Mr. Thomas W. Starr   14 October 1977
Physics Department
California Technological Institute
Claremont, California 91711

DEAR MR. STARR,

It has recently come to our attention that you have been pursuing innovative concepts on the possibility of introducing nuclear fusion in water. Your doctoral research support is funded through an Army Office of Scientific Research grant to Professor B. B. Abernathy, and as you know, we retain the right to request periodic reviews of research supported by us.

Professor Abernathy has informed us that you are now writing a thesis for open publication, based on your work. Please send three (3) copies of your draft to:

> Colonel Andrew Bobble
> Chief, Nuclear Security Review Office
> (Army)
> The Pentagon
> Washington, DC 20310
> Sincerely,

Patricia Adams

Patricia Adams
Administrative Assistant
Nuclear Security Review Office (Army)

499

Mr. Thomas W. Starr   7 January 1978
Physics Department
California Technological Institute
Claremont, California 91711

DEAR MR. STARR,

   After a careful study of the material you recently sent to us for review, we
have classified it. Please forward all additional copies of your thesis drafts,
plus any other related documents, within ten days, by registered mail in a
sealed envelope within a sealed envelope.

Sincerely,

Andrew Bobble

Colonel Andrew Bobble
Chief, Nuclear Security Review
Office (Army)

Colonel Andrew Bobble   January 11, 1978
Chief, Nuclear Security Review Office (Army)
The Pentagon
Washington, DC 20310

DEAR COLONEL BOBBLE,

   I have read your letter to me of January 7, and I am at a loss to understand
what you mean by ''classifying'' my Ph D. dissertation. I have no security
clearance, and at no time have I had access to classified information.

   I am sure that any little details in my writing that might cause some
concern by your office will be easy for me to work around. If you will send
me a list of the particular issues in question, I will be glad to take them into
consideration as I finish up my writing.

Sincerely,

Thomas W. Starr

Thomas W. Starr

Mr. Thomas W. Starr   20 January 11, 1978
Physics Department
California Technological Institute
Claremont, California 91711

DEAR MR. STARR,

This letter is to inform you that there is no appeal from our decision to classify the draft material you recently sent to us. It is our final conclusion that there is no possible way to rewrite this material to eliminate the possibility of disclosing information vital to the national security of the United Sates. We can not transmit the list requested in your letter because such a list would be classified, and you have no clearance.

To discuss this matter further, it will be necessary for you to obtain a clearance from the Defense Industrial Security Corporation (at your personal expense), and to travel to Washington to meet with our staff. Even if you decide to do this, we must receive all information still in your possession.

Sincerely,

Andrew Bobble

Colonel Andrew Bobble
Chief, Nuclear Security Review
Office (Army)

Colonel Andrew Bobble   January 25, 1978
Chief, Nuclear Security Review Office (Army)
The Pentagon
Washington DC 20310

DEAR COLONEL BOBBLE,

I can't believe this! You are destroying my career with all this Catch-22 crap about national security leaks that you can't tell me about because I don't have a clearance.

I have looked into getting a clearance, too. The DISCO investigaton fee is $4,000! I haven't got forty bucks.

501

How did you get to be a Colonel? Thinking up stupid things like this? Well, you can go to hell! What I think up on my time, with my brain, is none of the Pentagon's damn business. I will finish my writing, publish it, and the army can go screw itself.

Sincerely,

Thomas W. Starr

Thomas W. Starr

Mr. Thomas W. Starr
Physics Department
California Technological Institute
Claremont, California 91711

February 1, 1978

DEAR MR. STARR,

In response to your letter of 25 January, enclosed is a copy of Title 18 of the United States Espionage and Sabotage Acts. Release of classified information is a felony offense, punishable by up to ten years in prison, or up to a $10,000 fine, or both.

We are instructing University Microfilms not to produce microfilm xerographic copies of any unauthorized thesis you attempt to submit. In addition we have notified all domestic and international journals of physics and/or chemistry that publication of papers by you, without any prior release, may constitute a security violation.

Please submit all documents on your research to us, as requested earlier, postmarked no later than 15 February 1978.

Sincerely,

Andrew Bobble

Colonel Andrew Bobble
Chief, Nuclear Security
Review Office (Army)

Colonel Andrew Bobble   February 10, 1978
Chief, Nuclear Security Review Office (Army)
The Pentagon
Washington, DC 20310

DEAR ANDY,

Enclosed are all of the documents you have requested from Tom Starr. I am taking care of all these details of transferring the water fusion work to secure, classified areas as Tom is in no shape, emotionally, to do it himself.

I know you understand the reason for his recent intemperate letter to you. He has even cut off his contacts with me, but I think he will come around in time. I am confident of his ultimate discretion and loyalty.

I am pretty sure I can handle the new classified work on water fusion for your office, but we should discuss contract funding levels on my trip to Washington next month. Take me to lunch at the Sans Souci and tell me how much you can give me!

                                 Regards,

                                 Bert

                                 Bert Abernathy

Mr. Thomas W. Starr   December 2, 1978
1713 12th Street
Claremont, California 91711

DEAR TOM,

I write this letter with regret. You are a talented teacher, and I believe that with time you will become an outstanding member of the academic community. Still, though the circumstances of our doctoral dissertation difficulties were beyond your control, I can not recommend the continuation of your contract with us beyond June 30, 1979. The Institute bylaws are most specific, and the failure to obtain your Ph.D. by December 1 leaves no room for an exception or waiver.

503

I will, if you wish, do what I can to aid you in seeking a new position for next year.

Sincerely,

Pete

Peter V. Johnson, Ph.D.
Office of the Dean

Dr. Peter V. Johnson   July 15, 1979
Dean of Engineering and Science
California Technological Institute
Claremont, California 91711

DEAR DEAN JOHNSON,

I am writing to thank you for your help in getting me a teaching job for the coming semester. Teaching freshmen physics and chemistry at Contra Costa J.C. is going to be a change for me, but without a doctorate I guess I am lucky to have that—at least I won't be pumping gas or hacking a cab. I hope I can find something for the second semester.

The nature of my work in water fusion is such that the lab facilities I saw on my interview at Contra Costa will let me continue. What the Army doesn't know won't hurt me!

Thanks, again, for your help.

Regards,

Thomas W. Starr

Thomas W. Starr

Mr. Thomas W. Starr   December 13, 1979
Science Department
Contra Costa Junior College
Walnut Creek, Caoifornia 94596

DEAR MR. STARR,

I am pleased to inform you of the acceptance of your paper "An interesting classroom demonstration of power from water." It will appear

504

in our issue of February 24, 1980.

Quite frankly, we were astounded when we duplicated the techniques described in your paper. We would be interested in seeing a second paper which elaborates, mathematically, on the specific chemical and physical processes of your demonstration, as we believe the present one will attract considerable attention.

We wish you well in your new post at the South Australian Boy's Military Prep School, and the galley proofs of the paper will be sent to you there.

Cordially,

Peterson S. Day

Peterson S. Day
Editor *Review of High School
Experimental Science*

80

PYTHIAS

Frederik Pohl

I AM SITTING on the edge of what passes for a bed. It is made of loosely woven strips of steel, and there is no mattress, only an extra blanket of thin olive-drab. It isn't comfortable; but of course they expect to make me more uncomfortable still. They expect to take me out of this precinct jail to the district prison, and eventually to the death house. Oh, there will be a trial first, but that is only a formality. Not only did they catch me with the smoking gun in my hand and Connaught bubbling to death through the hole in his throat, but I admitted it. I—knowing what I was doing, with, as they say, malice aforethought—deliberately shot to death Laurence Connaught.

They kill murderers. So they mean to kill me. Especially because Laurence Connaught had saved my life.

Well, there are extenuating circumstances. I do not think they would convince a jury.

Connaught and I were close friends for years. We lost touch during the war; we met again in Washington, a few years after the war was over. We had, to some extent, grown apart; he had become a man with a mission. He was working very hard on something; he did not choose to discuss his work; there was nothing else in his life on which to form a basis for communication. And—well, I had my own life, too. It wasn't scientific research in my case—I flunked out of med school, while he went on. I'm not ashamed of it; there is nothing to be ashamed of. I simply was not able to cope with the messy business of carving corpses. I didn't like it; I didn't want to do it; and when I was forced to do it, I did it badly. So I left.

So I have no string of degrees; but you don't need them in order to be a Senate guard.

Does that sound like a terribly impressive career to you? Of course not;

507

but I liked it. The senators are relaxed and friendly when the guards are around, and you learn wonderful things about what goes on behind the scenes of government. And a Senate guard is in a position to do favors: for newspapermen, who find a lead to a story useful; for government officials, who sometimes base a whole campaign on one careless, repeated remark; and for just about anyone who would like to be in the visitors' gallery during a hot debate.

Larry Connaught, for instance, was one. I ran into him on the street one day, and we chatted for a moment, and he asked if it was possible to get him in to see the upcoming foreign-relations debate. It was; I called him the next day and told him I had arranged for a pass. And he was there, watching eagerly with his moist little eyes, when the Secretary got up to speak and there was that sudden unexpected yell, and the handful of Central American fanatics dragged out their weapons and began trying to change American policy with gunpowder.

You remember the story, I suppose. There were only three of them, two with guns, one with a hand grenade. The pistol men managed to wound two senators and a guard. I was right there, talking to Connaught; I spotted the little fellow with the hand grenade and tackled him. I knocked him down, but the grenade went flying, pin pulled, seconds ticking away. I lunged for it. Larry Connaught was ahead of me.

The newspaper stories made heroes out of both of us. They said it was miraculous that Larry, who had fallen right on top of the grenade, had managed to get it away from himself and so placed that when it exploded no one was hurt.

For it did go off, and the flying steel touched nobody. The papers mentioned that Larry had been knocked unconscious by the blast. He was unconscious, all right. He didn't come to for six hours, and when he woke up he spent the whole next day in a stupor.

So I called on him the next night.

He was glad to see me. "That was a close one, Dick," he said. "Takes me back to Tarawa."

I said, "I wasn't there. I guess you saved my life, Larry."

"Ah, Dick. You know—I just jumped. Lucky, I guess."

I said, "The papers said you were terrific. They said you moved so fast nobody could see exactly what happened."

He made a deprecating gesture, but his wet little eyes were wary. "Nobody was really watching, I suppose."

I sighed. "*I* was watching."

He looked at me silently for a moment. I said, "I was between you and the grenade. You didn't go past me, over me, or through me. But you were on top of the grenade." He started to shake his head. "I said, "*Also*, Larry you fell *on* the grenade. It exploded underneath you. I know, because I was almost on top of you, and it blew you clear off the floor of the gallery. Did you have a bullet-proof vest on?"

He cleared his throat. "Well, as a matter of—"

"Cut it out, Larry," I said.

He took off his glasses and rubbed his watery eyes. He grumbled, "Don't you read the papers? It went off a yard away."

"Larry," I said gently. "I was there."

He looked sick. He slumped back in his chair, staring at me. Larry Connaught was a small man, but he never looked smaller than he did in that big chair, looking at me as though I were Mr. Nemesis himself.

Then he laughed. He surprised me; he sounded almost happy. He said, "Well, hell, Dick. I had to tell somebody about it sooner or later. Why not you?"

"I can't tell you all of what he said. I'll tell most of it. But not the part that matters.

I'll never tell *that* part to *anybody*.

Larry said "I should have known you'd remember." He smiled at me ruefully, affectionately. "Those arguments in the cafeterias, eh? Talking all night, about everything. But you remembered."

"You said that the human mind possessed powers of psychokinesis," I said. "You said that just by the mind, without moving a finger or using a machine, a man could move his body anywere, instantly. You said there was nothing impossible to the mind." I felt like an absolute fool saying those things; they were ridiculous notions. Imagine a man *thinking* himself from one place to another! But—I had been on that gallery. I licked my lips and looked to Larry Connaught for confirmation.

"I was all wet," said Larry. He laughed. "Imagine!"

I suppose I showed surprise, because he patted my shoulder. He said, becoming sober, "Sure, Dick. You're wrong, but you're right all the same. The mind alone can't do anything of the sort—that was just a silly kid notion. *But*," he said, and his eyes began to sparkle with excitement, his words began to come faster and louder, "*but* there are—well, techniques—linking the mind to physical forces—simple physical forces that we all use every day—that can do it all. Everything! Everything I ever thought of, and things I haven't found out yet. Fly across the ocean? In a second, Dick! Wall off an exploding bomb? Sure. Easily! You saw me do it.

Oh, it's work, you know. It takes energy—you can't escape natural law. It knocked me out for a whole day. But that was a hard one; it's a lot easier, for instance, to make a bullet miss its target. It's even easier to lift the cartridge out of the chamber and put it in my pocket, so that the bullet can't even be fired. Want the Crown Jewels of England? I could get them Dick!''

I asked , ''Can you see the future?''

''No.'' He frowned. ''Dick, that's silly. This isn't supersti—''

''How about reading minds?''

His expression cleared. ''Oh, you're remembering some of the things I said years ago. No, I can't do that either, Dick. Maybe, some day, if I keep working at this thing—Well, I can't right now. There are things I can do, though, that are just as good. I can listen in on anything that goes on; I can see anything I want to see, anywhere in the world. Or elsewhere, Dick! It's hard, but I've done it. Mars! I've seen it—it looks like a rock slide.''

I cleared my throat. ''Show me something you can do,'' I asked.

He smiled. Larry was enjoying himself; I didn't begrudge it to him. He had hugged this to himself for years, from the day he found his first clue, through the decade of proving and experimenting, and almost always being wrong but always getting closer. . . . He *needed* to talk about it. I think he was really glad that, at last, someone had found him out.

He said, ''Show you something? Why, let's see, Dick. He looked around the room, then winked at me. ''See that window?''

I looked. It opened, with a slither of wood and a rumble of sashweights. It closed again. ''The radio,'' said Larry. There was a *click*, and his little set turned itself on. ''Watch it.'' It disappeared, and reappeared. ''It was on top of Mount Everest,'' Larry said, panting a little. The plug on the radio's electric cord picked itself up and stretched toward the baseboard socket, then dropped to the floor again. ''No,'' said Larry, and his voice was trembling, ''I'll show you a hard one. Watch the radio, Dick. I'll run it without plugging it in! The electrons themselves—''

He was staring intently at the little set. I saw the dial light go on, flicker, and hold steady; the speaker began to make scratching noises. I stood up, right behind Larry, right over him.

I used the telephone on the table beside him. I was taking an enormous chance; I knew it. It worked. I caught him right beside the ear, and he folded over without a murmur. Methodically I hit him twice more, and then I was sure he wouldn't wake up for at least an hour. I rolled him over and put the telephone back in its cradle.

I ransacked his apartment. I found it in his desk: All his notes. All the information. The secret of how to do the things he could do.

I picked up the telephone and called the Washington police. When I heard the siren outside I took out my service revolver and shot him in the throat. He was dead before they touched him.

For, you see, I knew Laurence Connaught. We were friends, and I would have trusted him with my life. But this was more than just a life.

Twenty-three words told how to do the things that Laurence Connaught did. Anyone who could read could do them. Criminals—traitors—lunatics; the formula would work for anyone.

Laurence Connaught was an honest man, and an idealist, I think. But what would happen to any man when he became God? Suppose you were told twenty-three words that would let you reach into any bank vault, peer inside any closed room, walk through any wall? Suppose pistols could not kill you? Suppose you could stand under a falling atomic bomb, and get yourself a thousand miles away between two breaths?

They say: Power corrupts; and absolute power corrupts absolutely. And there can be no more absolute power than the twenty-three words that can free a man of any jail or give him anything he wants. Larry was my friend. But I killed him in cold blood, knowing what I did. Because he could not be trusted with the secret that could make him king of the world. . . .

But I can.

81

REFUGE

Donald Wismer

THE HOLE IN the end of the pistol twitched like an animal hit by a car. Dim white light outlined the orifice, making it seem like a halo. Curtis, bolt upright in his bed, could feel the man's fear and rage coming in wave-like spasms down the shadowed arm, shaking the rigid hand, flowing out to the end of the gun and pouring toward him like effluent into the river of starlight.

"No word, no movement, no sound," the low whisper came. Curtis' mind, leaping from fear to incredulity to fear again, could see as if a computer graphic the old house around him, the corridor outside full of wide-awake agents, the walkie-talkies and equipment in the next bedroom, the antennae and dishes and scramblers, the aides in nearby bedrooms upstairs and down, and the television vans parked outside with their dozing, coffee-addled crews.

In the next room, a computer was beeping softly, not loud enough to carry through the walls. A tape machine was already recording, its microphone pressed in a suction cup against the wall. A Secret Service agent was frantically beckoning his partner over, holding out another set of earphones.

Curtis heard a joint crack.

"I lay between the walls eighteen hours," the man whispered, as if in apology. Then, abruptly shifting: "If you keep whispering, Mr. President, you will live. At the end, I will walk out that door. I don't care what happens then. All I care about is now."

Not assassination, then, the President thought. His mind, which had been in the incredulity part of the cycle, froze there. Years of habit began to take hold.

"What do you want?" the President said. The whisper sounded feeble,

513

and he flushed. No one could see it, he thought. Get ahold of yourself. Get facts. Surmise the rest. Take charge of the meeting.

"I want you to tell me something," the man hissed. The halo reappeared briefly, then drew back, then reappeared. What type of fanaticism, the President wondered. Religion? Could be Shiite then, or some more local fundamentalism. Or perhaps statehood—Palestinian, South Moluccan, Northern Irish, Basque, Sikh, or some other fragment of another nation. The man continued:

"I want you to tell me why you're hiding aliens in Maine."

Curtis recoiled as if shot. Of all the things that had been flying through his mind, this was not among them. It was too remote, too unthinkable. The danger was too great.

"The Tarim refugees? They're more human than you are," the President hissed back. He felt his composure fleeing again. This was the last subject he wanted to deal with.

The halo waggled. The President sensed that the gout of anger and fear in the man was fading. In the next room a dozen agents were gathered around headphones. Scrawled messages were being passed into the corridor, where men in stockinged feet sped down the back stairs to the weapons experts below.

"Your answer is not thought out," the man said. "You should have taken the word 'aliens' and called me crazy. But I *know*, don't you see."

"They're from Central Asia, confound it," the President hissed. He envisoned the corridors outside filled with men.

The man did not answer, and Curtis tried another tack. "How could you know I would be here?" he wondered softly. "Eighteen hours ago I didn't know myself."

The man was still silent. The halo brightened as the moon appeared, very low among the trees. Finally:

"Because I killed your sister, Mr. President. After that, you had to come here. It's where you always come, when you visit her."

Horror, rage, emptiness. The room reeled as the President tried to get hold of himself. He shook his head as if to throw something off. He tensed his body.

"Don't," the man said.

Outside, one plan after another was reviewed and rejected.

"Your family has always had a thing about cremation within twenty-four hours, Mr. President. All your biographers know about it. I'm sorry."

"Sorry!" Curtis raged, yet he kept his voice still soft. Some part of him, the controlled part, knew that he had to know just what this man knew and how he knew it. "You are a madman. You are dead. There are all kinds of ways to contact me, on anything. You'll be in the electric chair in a year, in this state. I'll see to it that . . . ."

The man cut him off. Crickets creaked rhythmically outside, peeper frogs in background chorus. June bugs committed suicide against the lit screens downstairs.

"I tried a hundred ways. That was the last one. The FBI would have taken me any day."

"Ah . . . " The President knew, now. "You are Doctor Claude Beliveau, then?" He scarcely heard the reply. His thoughts kept going back to his sister. Sis . . . !

"Yes. The one who dissected the alien. The one whose wife you hunted down and killed. The only one in the world who has seen the aliens inside, and knows what they are. They must be incredibly skilled at cosmetic surgery, Mr. President. I could find only the faintest traces of their work. But they hadn't bothered with their insides, or maybe hadn't gotten to it yet."

"They threw you out of CBS and *Time* magazine and CNN and every other news outlet," said the President.

"And congressmen laughed at me, after I sneaked in and saw every one I could, even with the tapes. Who wouldn't laugh at a man showing a home movie of alien dissection? That's when I realized that you are probably the only elected official who really knew. *If* you knew. So I had to get to you, Mr. President, to find out if you knew and, if so, why you didn't tell the world." Curtis felt a chill as the breeze stirred; his bedclothes were soaked with sweat, and it was still coming.

The whispered voice began again. The world must know this thing, Mr. President. You must tell them. I do not understand why you haven't. Their science is obviously far ahead of ours. That science means a culture beyond ours, utopia itself perhaps. Riches of knowledge, art, philosophy . . . maybe even religion. We're close to nuclear war, and there's panic spreading everywhere. Please . . . the world *must know*!"

"You are an idiot," the President hissed through his rage, drawn-out sound of venom and spleen. "You must have known there was a reason. Why couldn't you have left it alone?"

He paused, his mind still on his sister, hating this man. "Utopia, you said. Utopia is in the eye of the beholder. When they came, they showed us what they had come from."

The President shuddered. Behind the wall to the President's back, a high powered assault rifle was positioned carefully, heat sensors probing for the two bodies in the bedroom, guiding the rifle toward the one and away from the other.

The President's whisper was quavering now, with hatred for the man, and fear for something else.

"What they had come from . . . Doctor, compared to that, *this* is utopia. To them, Doctor, our miserable, torn-up little world is Paradise itself."

Behind and to the President's left, the plaster exploded in a long burst of sound. The killer was thrown back against the wall.

"They really *are* refugees," the President said out loud. He watched the man die. He couldn't seem to stop sweating.

82

THE RESCUER

Arthur Porges

IT WAS BY far the largest, most intricate machine ever built.

It's great complex of auxiliary components covered two square blocks, and extended hundreds of feet beneath the earth. There were fifty huge electronic computers at the heart of it. They had to be capable of solving up to thirty thousand simultaneous partial differential equations in as many variables in any particular millisecond. The energy which the machine required to operate successfully on a mass of M pounds was given by a familar formula: $E = MK^2$. The K was not, as in Einstein's equation, the velocity of light; but it was large enough so that only one type of power could be used: the thermonuclear reaction called hydrogen fusion.

Designing the machine and developing the theory of its operation had taken thirty years; building it, another ten. It had cost three billion dollars, an amount to be amortized over roughly one hundred years, and supplied by fifteen countries.

Like the atomic bomb, the machine could not be tested piecemeal; only the final, complete assembly would be able to settle the question of success or failure. So far, no such trial of its capabilities had been made. When the time came, a one-milligram sample of pure platinum would be used.

It was the largest, most intricate, expensive, fascinating, and dangerous machine ever built. And two men were about to destroy it. They would have to release a large amount of thermonuclear energy in order to wreck the machine. It was the only way in the circumstance.

It was a heartbreaking decision to have to make. Perhaps they should have contacted higher authorities in Washington, since the machine, although quite international in scope, was located in California; but that was too dangerous with time so short. Bureaucratic timidity might very well cause a fatal delay. So, knowing the consequences to them, the two scientists did what they believed had to be done. The machine, together with several blocks of supporting equipment, including the irreplaceable computers, was vaporized. They escaped in a fast air car.

PRELIMINARY HEARING—
A TRANSCRIPT
THE UNITED STATES
versus DR. CARNOT
THE UNITED STATES versus DR. KENT
April 14, 2015

JUDGE CLARK: How did the man know the operation, when the machine had never even been tested?

DR. CARNOT: The theory had been widely discussed in many scientific papers—even popular magazines. And the man was a technician of sorts. Besides, it wasn't necessary to understand the theory; not more than forty or fifty men in this country could. He must have seen numerous pictures of the controls. The settings are simple; any engineer can use a vernier.

JUDGE CLARK: I think you'd better tell this court just what happened from the beginning. Your strange reticence has caused a great deal of speculation. You understand that if found guilty, you must be turned over to the U.N. Criminal Court for prosecution.

DR. CARNOT: Yes, Your Honor; I know that.

JUDGE CLARK: Very well. Go ahead.

DR. CARNOT: Dr. Kent and myself were the only ones in the area that night. It was a matter of chance that we decided to check some minor point about the bus bars. To our astonishment, when we arrived at the control room, the machine was in operation.

JUDGE CLARK: How did you know the machine was being used?

DR. CARNOT: In many ways; all the indicators were reacting; but primarily the mass-chamber itself, which had dislimned and assumed the appearance of a misty, rainbow-colored sphere.

JUDGE CLARK: I see. go on.

DR. CARNOT: Dr. Kent and I were shocked beyond expression. We saw from the readings that the person, whoever he was, had entered for a really fantastic number of ergs—that is, energy. Far more than any of us would have dared to use for many months, if at all. (At this point Senator King interposed a question.)

SENATOR KING: How did the fellow get into the area? What about the Security?

518

DR. CARNOT: As you know, the machine is international, and sponsored by the U.N. Since there is no longer any military rivalry among the members, the work is purely scientific, and no country can be excluded. Naturally, the complex is protected against crackpots; but this man worked on the project as a Class 5 technician, and must have known how to avoid the infrared and other warning systems.

JUDGE CLARK: We had better not confuse the issue with such digressions. How the man got in is no longer important. But your sudden knowledge of his background is, Dr. Carnot. In an earlier statement you claimed to have no information about his identity. How do you explain that?

DR. CARNOT: I had to lie.

JUDGE CLARK: Had to?

DR. CARNOT: Yes, Your Honor. All of that will become clear, I hope, later in my testimony. Right now, let me clarify our dilemma. The machine was definitely in operation, and had been for about eight minutes. We couldn't be certain that it would work—I mean to the extent of completing the job as programmed by the intruder; but the theory had been carefully investigated, and all the computations, which as you know, took many years, checked out. It is a peculiarity of the machine, related to the solution of thousands of the most complicated differential equations, that there can be neither a cessation nor a reversal of its operation without grave danger to the entire state—perhaps even a larger area. The combination of vast energies and the warping of spacetime that would result according to theory, might vaporize hundreds of square miles. For this reason, and others, our plans had not gone beyond trying masses less than one gram.

JUDGE CLARK: Let me understand your point. It was impossible merely to shut off the machine? Stop the power?

DR. CARNOT: If the theory is sound, yes. I can only suggest the analogy of breaking an electrical circuit involving millions of amperes—the current jumps the gap, forming an arc which is very difficult to stop. Well, in this case, it was not merely millions of amps, but energies comparable only to those emitted by a large mass of the sun itself. In short, the only way to prevent completion of this particular operation was to bleed off enough of that energy to destroy most of the complex. That, at least, would save the populated areas. Remember, we had only about twelve minutes in which to choose a course of action.

JUDGE CLARK: But you weren't even sure the machine would work; that is, that the man would really survive. Yet you deliberately wiped out a three billion dollar project.

DR. CARNOT: We simply couldn't risk it, Your Honor. If the man did survive, and succeeded in his mission, the dangers were almost inconceivable. Even philosophically they are more than the human mind can grasp.

JUDGE CLARK: But neither of you has been willing so far to explain that point. This court is still completely in the dark. Who was the man, and what did he attempt to do?

DR. CARNOT: Up to now, we weren't ready to speak. But if you will clear the court except for yourself, the President, and a few high, responsible officials, I'll try to satisfy this tribunal. The fact is, as you will see, that a large part of the public, in this country, at least, might approve of what that man tried to do. It may not be possible to convince laymen—people not used to the abstractions of philosophy or science—of the great risk involved. I can only hope that this court will appreciate the implications. I should add that Dr. Kent and myself have seriously considered refusing any further information, but merely pleading guilty to willful destruction of the machine. As it is, if you decide to release us to the U.N. for criminal proceedings, we still might have to do just that—which means your records would have to be suppressed. Our only reason for testifying is not to save our own lives, but the hope that we can contribute to the design of a new machine. And to better understanding of the problems involved in the operation. Among the public, that is.

JUDGE CLARK: I must take your attitude seriously; that is very plain. Do you persist in maintaining that this room should be cleared, and all broadcasting suspended? Press, distinguished scientists, senator- -all these are not qualified to hear the testimony?

DR. CARNOT: I only mean that the fewer who hear me, the fewer mouths to be guarded. And I'm sure this court will feel the same way when all my evidence is in.

JUDGE CLARK: Very well, then. The bailiffs will clear the room, except for the President, the National Security Council, and the Chairman of the Research Committee of the Congress. All electronic equipment will be disconnected; a complete spy curtain will be put on this room. Court will adjourn for two hours, reconvening at 1500.

PRELIMINARY HEARING
(Continued)

JUDGE CLARK: We are ready to hear your testimony now, Dr. Carnot.

DR. CARNOT: Do I have Your Honor's absolute assurance that nobody outside this room can hear us?

JUDGE CLARK: You do. The spy curtain, which your own colleagues in science claim bars all wave lengths, is on at full strength.

DR. CARNOT: If I seem too cautious, there is a reason, as you will see.

JUDGE CLARK: I certainly hope so. Now, will you please give the real point of this testimony? What was the man—and incidentally, has any identification come in on him yet? No? Well, what was he doing that seems to have scared you so?

DR. CARNOT: His name doesn't matter; it was on the note he left.

JUDGE CLARK: What note? Nothing was said about a note. Here this court has been trying to identify the man, and all the time—

DR. CARNOT: I'm sorry, Your Honor; that is part of the testimony we thought had better be withheld until now. The man did leave a note, explaining just what he meant to do with the time machine.

JUDGE CLARK: And what was that?

DR. CARNOT: He had set the dial for a two thousand year trip into the past. That accounted for the vast amount of energy required. You see, it varies not only with the mass transported, but the time as well.

JUDGE CLARK: Two thousand years!

DR. CARNOT: That's right, Your Honor. In itself, that's bad enough. It is one thing to send a small mass or a sterile insect back in time; even then, there are dangers we can hardly predict. The present is intricately involved with the past—stems from it, in fact. It's like altering the origin of a river; a little change at the source can make a tremendous difference at the mouth. Even move it fifty miles away. Now a modern man in the world of two thousand years ago—frankly, Your Honor, we just don't know what that might do. It seems fantastic to believe that he could change the here-and-now, and yet the theory implies that this whole universe might change completley, or even vanish. Don't ask me where or how.

(At this point, Professor Pirenian, of the National Security Council broke in with a question.)

PIRENIAN: Why didn't you and Dr. Kent merely send another man to intercept this one? Yours, by the machine, could obviously set the dials to get there first, thus snatching the first one back before he could do any harm.

DR. CARNOT: We thought of that, even in the few minutes we had. But suppose before we could cut in ahead of him that this world vanished? Believe me, the paradoxes are maddening; no amount of mathematical wrangling can settle them; only experiment. We couldn't chance it; that's all.

PIRENIAN: You're right, of course. Maybe we should be glad, gentlemen, that Dr. Carnot—and Dr. Kent—were there instead of the rest of us!

DR. CARNOT: You still don't know the real danger. What I've said so far applies to an impulsive, random trip to the distant past, where the man had no specific intentions. But Michael Nauss did have a particular plan—a wild, crazy, and yet, in a way, magnificent conception. One that the public, or much of it, might foolishly support without realizing the consequences. I speak of this country, and people in Europe; not in Asia, for the most part. And he had set the vernier with perfect precision, which made his plan even more feasible.

JUDGE CLARK: What was he going to do?

DR. CARNOT: According to his note, this man had taken with him a repeating rifle and five thousand rounds of exploding ammunition. His intention was nothing less than to arrive at Golgotha in time to rescue Jesus Christ from the Roman soldiers. In short, to prevent the crucifixion. And with a modern rifle, who can say he wouldn't succeed? And then what? Then what? The implications are staggering. Disregarding the Christian dogma, which asserts Jesus *had* to die for our sins, what of the effect on the future, the entire stream of history, secular as well as religious. Maybe Jesus Himself would have prevented this madman from saving Him—but who can be sure. Yet, if you ask the man in the street, now, in this year 2015: Shall we save Jesus Christ from the cross?—what would he answer? Whose side would he take? Ours, or Michael Nauss'. That is why Dr. Kent and I destroyed the machine; and why we face this court now. We believe the proceedings should not be released. The decision is yours. We made ours that night.

83

RIPPLES

Ray Russell

AN INVISIBLE STARSHIP stood at rest near a canal. If the eye could have seen it, the sight would have been one of immense beauty, for it was a thing of harmonious circles: an outer rim, hollow and transparent, in which the crew of four lived and worked and looked out upon space and suns and exotic worlds; contained in this circle, another, the core of powerful engines whose surging, flaming energy propelled the ship across galactic distances. And all of this unseen.

Inside, the captain spoke briefly to his specialist, first class. "Your report is finished, then? We can embark?"

"Yes sir,."

"That was fast work."

"These rudimentary cultures are all very much alike. The report is simple—planet's inhabitants too primitive to comprehend our presence here; therefore suggest a return in a few millennia when the species may be more advanced and we can set up cultural and scientific exchange, trade, and so on."

The first mate drew near them. "Do you really think they're too primitive? They already have language, laws, religion. . . . "

"But no technology," said the specialist. "They couldn't possibly understand that we come from another planet; the very concept 'planet' is beyond them. . . . No, no, to try to establish contact now would be traumatic for them. If we revealed ourselves—flicked off the invisiblity shield—there would be . . . ramifications . . . repercussions . . . "

"Ripples?" said the captain.

"Ripples," replied the specialist with a nod. "An apt word. Like a pebble dropped in a pond, spawning ever larger and larger and more grandiose images of its own smallness, so even an instantaneous glimpse of us and our ship could, with time and retellings, become magnified and elaborated and distorted—into something far beyond anything we could dream.''

"Then, let us head for home and a well-earned leave," said the captain.

The first mate added, "And a well-shaped young lady I *hope* has been pining away in solitude!"

"Ah, youth—" began the captain, but broke off as his navigator approached with a worried air. "Trouble?" the captain asked.

"Yes, sir, I'm afraid so," said the navigator.

"Serious?"

"A little. The main engine is inoperable—just as I feared."

The first mate said, "That rough landing damaged more than our pride."

"What about the auxiliary?" asked the captain.

"It will get us home, just barely, but it won't hold up under the strain of lift-off—"

"What?"

"—unless we conserve all other energy. That means switching off lights, chart banks, communications, sensors, air, invisibility shield, everything—but only for those first few vital seconds of lift-off, of course."

"Then, do it."

"Yes sir,"

The specialist, alarmed, said, "Captain! Not the invisibility shield! We must not turn that off!"

"You heard the navigator. It's our only chance—and it will just be for a few seconds." He nodded to the navigator, saying, "Lift off." Then he looked out through the transparent hull at the world they would soon depart. "Primitive, you say. Well, you're the expert. But it's too bad we can't contact them now. It might have been interesting. They're so much like us, they're almost *human*."

"Well, hardly that," said the specialist as the starship moved. "They're monofaced, and their feet are different, and they completely lack wings. But I know what you mean. . . . "

Outside, a bearded denizen of the primitive planet blinked, stared, pointed.

"Behold!" he cried to a companion. "A whirlwind! A great cloud! A fire! Men with wings and many faces! A wheel . . . in the middle of a wheel!"

"Where? What?" said his companion, turning a second too late. "I saw nothing, Ezekiel."

But, roiled by that whirlwind, the waters of the Chebar canal were a dancing spiderwork of ripples.

84

THE SAGA OF DMM

Larry Eisenberg

THE ANNOUNCEMENT OF Duckworth's discovery caused hardly more than a raised eyebrow in the scientific community. Even Duckworth underestimated what he had done.

"It's not much," he said to me, apologetically. "I was working with this long macromolecule and suddenly it split into a doule helix. But any kid with a chemistry set could duplicate my results in an hour."

"What are its properties?" I said.

"It's the most delicious substance in the world. The taste is exquisite, delicate in flavor yet vibrant, subtle yet so overpowering that whoever eats it is hooked for life."

"Incredible," I said. "Then I take it you've tasted the stuff yourself?"

"No," said Duckworth. "You see it has 100,000 calories to the ounce. That's fifty times what an average man eats in a day. Pembroke, my lab assistant, ate about a tenth of an ounce. His gall bladder almost disintegrated."

"No wonder," I said. "It's the richest food in the world."

And there the matter rested. Or so we all thought. But then someone discovered that DMM (short for Duckworth's Macro Molecule) was also an aphrodisiac. A Sunday supplement ran a lurid article on the properties of DMM, and tons of letters began to pour in on poor Duckworth. Hundreds of people came in person to his laboratory; the congestion was terrible. It made work impossible.

I ran into Duckworth just outside the University or, at least, it seemed to me that it was Duckworth. A long black beard covered his tiny, receding chin, but the great beak-like nose still jutted out proudly. I grabbed at his sleeve as he went by.

"Don't stop me," he said quickly. "I've got to get away. They've made my life a howling lunacy."

"But where will you go?" I said.

"I've received an offer of refuge from the Nazir of Waddam, an obscure but wealthy potentate in the Middle East who worships science. He wants me to set up a chemistry department in his new University."

I silently pressed his hand and watched him scurry into a cab. I was not to see Duckworth again for many months. But the crowds still seemed to surround his old laboratory buildings. Signs, some crudely scrawled in crayon, others neatly lettered in poster paint, blossomed like spring flowers. They were carried by hippies and by middle class types, too. The most popular message was

"DMM Beats POT."

And then it happened. Duckworth himself had indicated that a home chemistry set was all one needed. Somebody caught on to that fact, and DMM began to pour out of high school and college chem labs. Even the faculties joined in. The campuses became a sanctuary of happy, entwined, grotesquely ballooning bodies.

The housewifes succumbed next. When the sale of diet products plunged disastrously, delegations of angry manufacturers descended on Congress. Smiling but enormously fat Congressmen were unable to rise to greet them. Even the President lost interest in pursuing a war which, only weeks earlier, he had considered to be a matter of life and death.

The Soviet Union tried to quarantine this horror, but somehow DMM slipped through. Almost overnight, the collectives and State Farms were immobilized, and, as in America, factories became ghost buildings filled with rusting machines.

The Chinese held out somewhat longer. But when Mao, unable to control his curiosity, took a tiny taste, they were undone. The posters denouncing DMM as revisionist are still on the city walls. But the colors are faded, the lettering is cracked, and the paper peels badly.

Only one country remained untouched: the tiny nation the United States had all but bombed into the Stone Age did not have even the most common of refined chemicals. Thin and on the edge of perpetual hunger, they drove the occupying troops, sated and monstrously bloated, into the sea.

I was lying down on my divan, languidly caressing the spherical belly of my mistress, one day, when the angular frame of Duckworth materialized right before me. I beamed at him.

"How is the Nazir?" I said.

Duckworth snorted.

"A fraud like all the rest. He tricked me into coming solely for the aphrodisiac powers of DMM. He had no university. Only the biggest harem in the world."

"Duckworth," I said. "You're a fool. You should have stayed there and eaten all the DMM you could make. You were right, you know. It is the greatest stuff in the world."

"No," said Duckworth. "You see, I've continued my research into the properties of DMM, even with the meager facilities furnished by the Nazir."

"Does it do anything else?" I said. I really wasn't *that* interested, but I thought I ought to be polite.

Duckworth leaned forward and I saw the great nose looming over me like a fleshy sword of Damocles.

"DMM is inherently unstable stuff. As I told you long ago, the macro-molecule splits into a double helix. In a sufficiently long period, say a year or two after digestion, the helix itself breaks down once again into an even more unstable compond, not unlike nitroglycerin in its properties."

I looked up at him, unbelieving, and slowly withdrew my hand from my mistress.

"Are you implying that we will all become living bombs?" I cried.

"Are," said Duckworth solemnly. "*Are*. And in six months or so, even the slightest movement will set you off like an enormous firecracker. Personally, I'm headed for the tallest peak of the Himalayas."

I didn't really believe Duckworth. He was always a bluenosed moralist, and I felt he was simply trying to frighten me. Nevertheless, I did send a message to the head of the University. He in turn, without believing a word of what I said, notified the State and Federal authorities. Someone was impressed because a directive was issued, recommending that we move about as little as possible, even to the extent of remaining celibate. But when the following spring came, along with a windborne burst of ragweed pollen grains, somebody sneezed.

85

SEGREGATIONIST

Isaac Asimov

THE SURGEON LOOKED up without expression. "Is he ready?"

"Ready is a relative term," said the med-eng. *"We*'re ready. He's restless."

"They always are . . . Well, it's a serious operation."

"Serious or not, he should be thankful. He's been chosen for it over an enormous number of possibles and frankly, I don't think. . . . "

"Don't say it," said the surgeon. "The decision is not ours to make."

"We accept it. But do we have to agree?"

"Yes," said the surgeon, crisply. "We agree. Completely and whole-heartedly. The operation is entirely too intricate to approach with mental reservations. This man has proven his worth in a number of ways and his profile is suitable for the Board of Mortality."

"All right," said the med-eng, unmollified.

The surgeon said, "I'll see him right in here, I think. It is small enough and personal enough to be comforting."

"It won't help. He's nervous, and he's made up his mind."

"Has he indeed?"

"Yes. He wants metal; they always do."

The surgeon's face did not change expression. He stared at his hands. "Sometimes one can talk them out of it."

"Why bother?" said the med-eng, indifferently. "If he wants metal, let it be metal."

"You don't care?"

"Why should I?" The med-eng said it almost brutally. "Either way it's a medical engineering problem and I'm a medical engineer. Either way, I can handle it. Why should I go beyond that?"

The surgeon said stolidly, "To me, it is a matter of the fitness of things."

531

"Fitness! You can't use that as an argument. What does the patient care about the fitness of things?"

"I care."

"You care in a minority. The trend is against you. You have no chance."

"I have to try." The surgeon waved the med-eng into silence with a quick wave of his hand—no impatience to it, merely quickness. He had already informed the nurse and he had already been signaled concerning her approach. He pressed a small button and the double-door pulled swiftly apart. The patient moved inward in his motorchair, the nurse stepping briskly along beside him.

"You may go, nurse," said the surgeon, "but wait outside. I will be calling you." He nodded to the med-eng, who left with the nurse, and the door closed behind them.

The man in the chair looked over his shoulder and watched them go. His neck was scrawny and there were fine wrinkles about his eyes. He was freshly shaven and the fingers of his hands, as they gripped the arms of the chair tightly, showed manicured nails. He was a high-priority patient and he was being taken care of . . . But there was a look of settled peevishness on his face.

He said, "Will we be starting today?"

The surgeon nodded. "This afternoon, Senator."

"I understand it will take weeks."

"Not for the operation itself, Senator. But there are a number of subsidiary points to be taken care of. There are some circulatory renovations that must be carried through, and hormonal adjustments. These are tricky things."

"Are they dangerous?" Then, as though feeling the need for establishing a friendly relationship, but patently against his will, he added, " . . . doctor?"

The surgeon paid no attention to the nuances of expression. He said, flatly, "Everything is dangerous. We take our time in order that it be less dangerous. It is the time required, the skill of many individuals united, the equipment, that makes such operations available to so few. . . . "

"I know that," said the patient, restlessly. "I refuse fo feel guilty about that. Or are you implying improper pressure?"

"Not at all, Senator. The decisions of the Board have never been questioned. I mention the difficulty and intricacy of the operation merely to explain my desire to have it conducted in the best fashion possible."

"Well, do so, then. That is my desire, also."

"Then I must ask you to make a decision. It is possible to supply you with either of two types of cyber-hearts, metal or . . . . "

"Plastic!" said the patient, irritably. "Isn't that the alternative you were going to offer, doctor? Cheap plastic. I don't want that. I've made my choice. I want the metal."

"But . . . . "

"See here. I've been told the choice rests with me. Isn't that so?"

The surgeon nodded. "Where two alternate procedures are of equal value from a medical standpoint, the choice rests with the patient. In actual practice, the choice rests with the patient even when the alternate procedures are *not* of equal value, as in this case."

The patient's eyes narrowed. "Are you trying to tell me the plastic heart is superior?"

"It depends on the patient. In my opinion, in your individual case, it is. And we prefer not to use the term, plastic. It is a fibrous cyberheart."

"It's plastic as far as I am concerned."

"Senator," said the surgeon, infinitely patient, "the material is not plastic in the ordinary sense of the word. It is a polymeric material true, but one that is far more complex than ordinary plastic. It is a complex protein-like fibre designed to imitate, as closely as possible, the natural structure of the human heart you now have within your chest."

"Exactly, and the human heart I now have within my chest is worn out although I am not yet sixty years old. I don't want another one like it, thank you. I want something better."

"We all want something better for you, Senator. The fibrous cyberheart will be better. It has a potential life of centuries. It is absolutely non-allergenic. . . ."

"Isn't that so for the metallic heart, too?"

"Yes, it is," said the surgeon. "The metallic cyber is of titanium alloy that . . . ."

"And it doesn't wear out? And it is stronger than plastic? Or fibre or whatever you want to call it?"

"The metal is physically stronger, yes, but mechanical strength is not a point at issue. Its mechanical strength does you no particular good since the heart is well protected. Anything capable of reaching the heart will kill you for other reasons even if the heart stands up under manhandling."

The patient shrugged. "If I ever break a rib, I'll have that replaced by titanium, also. Replacing bones is easy. Anyone can have that done anytime. I'll be as metallic as I want to be, doctor."

"That is your right, if you so choose. However it is only fair to tell you that although no metallic cyber-heart has ever broken down mechanically, a number have broken down electronically."

"What does that mean?"

"It means that every cyber-heart contains a pacemaker as part of its structure. In the case of the metallic variety, this is an electronic device that keeps the cyber in rhythm. It means an entire battery of miniaturized equipment must be included to alter the heart's rhythm to suit an individual's emotional and physical state. Occasionally something goes wrong there and people have died before that wrong could be corrected."

"I never heard of such a thing."

"I assure you it happens."

"Are you telling me it happens often?"

"Not at all. It happens very rarely."

"Well, then, I'll take my chance. What about the plastic heart? Doesn't that contain a pacemaker?"

"Of course it does, Senator. But the chemical structure of a fibrous cyber-heart is quite close to that of human tissue. It can respond to the ionic and hormonal controls of the body itself. The total compelx that need be inserted is far simpler than in the case of the metal cyber."

"But doesn't the plastic heart ever pop out of hormonal control?"

"None has ever yet done so."

"Because you haven't been working with them long enough. Isn't that so?"

The surgeon hesitated. "It is true that the fibrous cybers have not been used nearly as long as the metallic."

"There you are. What is it anyway, doctor? Are you afraid I'm making myself into a robot . . . into a Metallo, as they call them since citizenship went through?"

"There is nothing wrong with a Metallo as a Metallo. As you say, they are citizens. But you're *not* a Metallo. You're a human being. Why not stay a human being?"

"Because I want the best and that's a metallic heart. You see to that."

The surgeon nodded. "Very well. You will be asked to sign the necessary permissions and you will then be fitted with a metal heart."

"And you'll be the surgeon in charge? They tell me you're the best."

"I will do what I can to make the changeover an easy one."

The door opened and the chair moved the patient out to the waiting nurse.

* * * *

The med-eng came in, looking over his shoulder at the receding patient until the doors had closed again.

He turned to the surgeon. "Well, I can't tell what happened just by looking at you. What was his decision?"

The surgeon bent over his desk, punching out the final items for his records. "What you predicted. He insists on the metallic cyber-heart."

"After all, they are better."

"Not significantly. They've been around longer; no more than that. It's this mania that's been plaguing humanity ever since Metallos have become citizens. Men have this odd desire to make Metallos out of themselves. They yearn for the physical strength and endurance one associates with them."

"It isn't one-sided, doc. You don't work with Metallos but I do; so I know. The last two who came in for repairs have asked for fibrous elements."

"Did they get them?"

"In one case, it was just a matter of supplying tendons; it didn't make much difference there, metal or fibre. The other wanted a blood system or its equivalent. I told him I couldn't; not without a complete rebuilding of the structure of his body in fibrous material. . . . I suppose it will come to that some day. Metallos that aren't really Metallos at all, but a kind of flesh and blood."

"You don't mind that thought?"

"Why not? And metallized human beings, too. We have two varieties of intelligence on Earth now and why bother with two. Let them approach each other and eventually we won't be able to tell the difference. Why should we want to? We'd have the best of both worlds; the advantages of man combined with those of robot."

"You'd get a hybrid," said the surgeon, with something that approached fierceness. "You'd get something that is not both, but neither. Isn't it logical to suppose an individual would be too proud of his structure and identity to want to dilute it with something alien? Would he *want* mongrelization?"

"That's segregationist talk."

"Then let it be that." The surgeon said with calm emphasis, "I believe in being what one is. I wouldn't change a bit of my own structure for any reason. If some of it absolutely required replacement, I would have that replacement as close to the original in nature as could possibly be managed.

I am *myself*; well pleased to be myself; and would not be anything else.''

He had finished now and had to prepare for the operation. He placed his strong hands into the heating oven and let them reach the dull red-hot glow that would sterilize them completely. For all his impassioned words, his voice had never risen, and on his burnished metal face there was (as always) no sign of expression.

86

THE SPY

Theodore L. Thomas

JEHN DOFAN WAS a very human-looking and highly intelligent young man, but sometimes he did not show good sense. Any young man might meet a girl night after night in an apple orchard, but Dofan had to do it in time of war, behind enemy lines, with the daughter of the mayor. On top of that he had to try to pry information out of her.

Even this might have been all right if Dofan had used a little more sense. After four consecutive nights of pressings and squeezings and heavy breathings, one does not maintain a stony silence when a girl like Betty Fuller nestles up closer and says, "We will be so happy together." The situations swiftly deteriorated after that. He wound up under arrest.

Flung into a root cellar, Jehn Dofan underwent a short but intense period of questioning by three burly soldiers, aided by the butt end of their flintlock rifles and directed by a second lieutenant bent on promotion. Dofan told them nothing. But it did not matter. As the soldiers left, the second lieutenant said, drawing himself to attention, "You hang at dawn, scum. We know how to treat spies."

For the first time Dofan saw that he was in trouble.

Betty Fuller rushed in as the soldiers went out. She flung herself on Dofan and covered his bloodied face with kisses and wept into the hollow of his neck. "My darling," she wailed, "what have I done to you?"

With this to work on, Dofan might have extricated himself even then, for Betty Fuller's father was the mayor, and a friendly mayor wields much influence even with the military if he puts his mind to it. But Dofan, although very human-looking and highly intelligent, did not show good sense for the second time in the same night.

He looked at Betty Fuller coldly and said, "You've done enough. Why don't you let me alone?"

Her eyes widened in disbelief and then flashed in hatred. She turned and tapped calmly on the door, and the soldiers let her out.

Dawn was close, and Dofan had no time to lose. He went to a corner of the root cellar and listened to make certain no one was coming. With his right thumb he probed deep up under his right jaw. He found the tiny button imbedded there, and he pushed it and held it.

He said softly, "Jehn Dofan calling Base. Jehn Dofan calling . . . ."

"We have you, Dofan. Talk."

"I'm captured, heavily guarded. They plan to hang me at dawn, less than an hour. Condition appears desperate. I need help."

"Will this rescue constitute a major interference with the natives? And, if so, are you willing to stand court-martial?"

"Yes," said Dofan. "I believe it will require major interference, and I am willing to stand court-martial."

'Stand by for instructions."

Dofan removed his thumb and paced back and forth in the root cellar in the candlelight.

Now that he had committed himself, he was a little sorry. But there seemed no other way out. This would spoil a perfect record here on the planet Earth. Betty Fuller had succeeded in ruining him. He would be drummed out of the Controllers, and she and the other Earth people did not even know such an organization existed. There would come a time when he could . . . .

A series of sharp buzzes echoed inside his head. It startled him; he had not expected his instructions so soon. He went to the corner and pressed the switch under his jaw and said, "Jehn Dofan."

"This is Charn Dofan. How are you, brother?"

Dofan felt his breath catch in his throat, and for a moment he could not speak. A real feeling of relief swept over him. Charn Dofan was here, his older brother, come to him in a time of trouble as always.

He said, "Charn, it is good to hear your voice. Where are you calling from, brother?"

"About a mile away. I command a troop of cavalry stationed in Brooklyn. I heard your call to Base and came out. Are you well?"

"Very well, brother. And you?"

"Very well."

A silence fell. The silence rested uncomfortably and strangely with Jehn Dofan. There had never been any strained silences between him and his brother. Something was wrong. He asked, "Is all well at home?"

There was a perceptible pause before the answer came. "Our parents and our family are all in good health." Again the silence.

Jehn Dofan said, "Tell me what is wrong, Charn. Base will call soon to tell me of the rescue procedure. What is it?"

A pause, then Charn Dofan began to speak. "Our Islands at home are ready to demand full statehood. The Mainlanders are trying to find some way to keep us out. A vote will be taken next week. As things stand now, we can just about muster the necessary strength, but it wont't take much to change things. We won't get another chance for a long while. We'll have to keep paying the taxes, letting them bleed us white, controlling our production."

Jehn Dofan nodded in understanding. "Yes, our people have worked toward statehood for a long time. I hope we make it."

Again the silence. Jehn Dofan was puzzled.

He said, "What is wrong? What can we do about it from here?"

This time his brother's words poured out, wrenched from the heart. "Base commander is a Mainlander! He will have to interfere openly with the natives to rescue you, and this will reflect on all the Islanders. No question about it, Jehn. It will tip the vote the wrong way. Your rescue will be an international incident back home."

Jehn Dofan shook his head regretfully and said, "I suppose you are right. But I don't know how we can stop him from here. We are . . . . ." And then he understood.

He felt sick to his stomach and he began to perspire. His breath caught in his throat. His heart pounded. He refused to accept the full realization—kept thrusting it out of his mind—but it kept intruding.

His brother continued, "Base will be calling in a few moment. I will be nearby, no matter what happens. Call on me for anything. I will abide by your decision. Good-by." The radio fell silent before Jehn Dofan could speak.

He was alone in the cellar. He slumped to the dirt, too weak to pace.

He was frightened. He had not seriously considered the possibility of dying on this planet. Yet here he was, in a position where his own brother had to point out the desirability of letting himself be executed instead of rescued. The Islands needed a hero now, not a goat. He needed time to think this out.

But there was no time. The buzzer sounded inside his head. He jumped. He went to the corner and pushed the switch and spoke.

"Base commander," was the response, and without further preamble the commander launched into a description of the rescue plans. In spite of the turmoil that raged in his mind, Dofan recognized that the plans were more violent and complex than they needed to be. It was apparent that the commander was seizing the opportuntiy to make trouble. The recognition steeled his mind.

"There will be no rescue, Commander. I have decided that I do not want to be the cause of such open interference."

The commander started to speak, but then fell silent, recognizing the impropriety of arguing with Dofan about such a matter. But his fury was apparent. Feeling it, Dofan said, "There is no need to talk further, Commander. I sign off now. Do not risk open interference by contacting me again. Good-by, sir."

They came for him shortly. They marched him between two columns of red-coated soldiers to the slow beat of muffled drums. He climbed the gallows steps in the bright morning sunshine and looked out over the Long Island countryside. As they adjusted the noose around his neck, his eyes swept the assembled crowd. There to the left, among the others, stood a tall, black-haired figure in a red coat. The eyes and nose were the same as his eyes and nose, and he looked at his brother and smiled.

A few feet from his brother, all unknowing, stood Betty Fuller, and for a wild moment he considered calling out to her for help. He saw the sneer on her face, and he was immediately ashamed of his momentary weakness. He gritted his teeth and tried to think of a way to die well.

He looked up to the sky, in a westerly direction. He could not see it, for it was light-years away, but he knew it was there. A lovely island on another planet, bathed in warm breezes, the place where his people were.

His executioners asked him, "Do you have anything to say, school-master?"

Then he knew what to do to swing the vote; it came to him all of a sudden. With his face raised toward home, he said, "I only regret that I have but one life to lose for my country."

87

STRAW

Gene Wolfe

YES, I REMEMBER killing my first man very well; I was just seventeen. A flock of snow geese flew under us that day about noon. I remember looking over the side of the basket, and seeing them; and thinking that they looked like a pike-head. That was an omen, of course, but I did not pay any attention.

It was clear, fall weather—a trifle chilly. I remember that. It must have been about the mid-part of October. Good weather for the balloon. Clow would reach up every quarter hour or so with a few double handsful of straw for the brazier, and that was all it required. We cruised, usually, at about twice the height of a steeple.

You have never been in one? Well, that shows how things have changed. Before the Fire-wights came, there was hardly any fighting at all, and free swords had to travel all over the continent looking for what there was. A balloon was better than walking, believe me. Miles—he was our captain in those days—said that where there were three soldiers together, one was certain to put a shaft through a balloon; it was too big a target to resist, and that would show you where the armies were.

No, we would not have been killed. You would have had to slit the thing wide open before it would fall fast, and a little hole like the business end of a pike would just barely let you know it was there. The baskets do not swing, either, as people think. Why should they? They feel no wind— they are traveling with it. A man just seems to hang there, when he is up in one of them, and the world turns under him. He can hear everything—pigs and chickens, and the squeak the windlass makes drawing water from a well.

"Good flying weather," Clow said to me.

541

I nodded. Solemnly, I suppose.

"All the lift you want, in weather like this. The colder it is, the better she pulls. The heat from the fire doesn't like the chill, and tries to escape from it. That's what they say."

Blond Bracata spat over the side. "Nothing in our bellies," she said, "that's what makes it lift. If we don't eat today you won't have to light the fire tomorrow—I'll take us up myself."

She was taller than any of us except Miles, and the heaviest of us all; but Miles would not allow for size when the food was passed out, so I suppose she was the hungriest too.

Derek said, "We should have stretched one of that last bunch over the fire. That would have fetched a pot of stew, at the least."

Miles shook his head. "There were too many."

"They would have run like rabbits."

"And if they hadn't?"

"They had no armor."

Unexpectantly, Bracata came in for the captain. "They had twenty-two men, and fourteen women. I counted them."

"The women wouldn't fight."

"I used to be one of them. I would have fought."

Clow's soft voice added, "Nearly any woman will fight if she can get behind you."

Bracata stared at him, not sure whether he was supporting her or not. She had her mitts on—she was as good with them as anyone I have ever seen—and I remember that I thought for an instant that she would go for Clow right there in the basket. We were packed in like fledgings in the nest, and fighting, it would have taken at least three of us to throw her out—by which time she would have killed us all, I suppose. But she was afraid of Clow. I found out why later. She respected Miles, I think, for his judgment and courage, without being afraid of him. She did not care much for Derek either way, and of course I was hardly there at all as far as she was concerned. But she was just a little frightened by Clow.

Clow was the only one I was not frightened by—but that is another story too.

"Give it more straw," Miles said.

"We're nearly out."

"We can't land in this forest."

Clow shook his head and added straw to the fire in the brazier—about half as much as he usually did. We were sinking toward what looked like a red and gold carpet.

"We got straw out of them anyway," I said, just to let the others know I was there.

"You can always get straw," Clow told me. he had drawn a throwing spike, and was feigning to clean his nails with it. "Even from swineherds, who you'd think wouldn't have it. They'll get it to be rid of us."

"Bracata's right," Miles said. He gave the impression that he had not heard Clow and me. "We have to have food today."

Derek snorted. "What if there are twenty?"

"We stretch one over the fire. Isn't that what you suggested? And if it takes fighting, we fight. But we have to eat today." He looked at me. "What did I tell you when you joined us, Jerr? High pay or nothing? This is the nothing. Want to quit?"

I said, "Not if you don't want me to."

Clow was scraping the last of the straw from the bag. It was hardly a handful. As he threw it in the brazier Bracata asked, "Are we going to set down in the trees?"

Clow shook his head and pointed. Away in the distance I could see a speck of white on a hill. It looked too far, but the wind was taking us there, and it grew and grew until we could see that it was a big house, all built of white brick, with gardens and outbuildings, and a road that ran up to the door. There are none like that left now, I suppose.

Landings are the most exciting part of traveling by balloon, and sometimes the most unpleasant. If you are lucky, the basket stays upright. We were not. Our basket snagged and tipped over and was dragged along by the envelope, which fought the wind and did not want to go down, cold though it was by then. If there had been a fire in the brazier still, I suppose we would have set the meadow ablaze. As it was, we were tumbled about like toys. Bracata fell on top of me, as heavy as stone: and she had the claws of her mitts out, trying to dig them into the turf to stop herself, so that for a moment I thought I was going to be killed. Derek's pike had been charged, and the ratchet released in the confusion; the head went flying across the field, just missing a cow.

By the time I recovered my breath and got to my feet, Clow had the envelope under control and was treading it down. Miles was up too, straightening his hauberk and sword-belt. "Look like a soldier," he called to me. "Where are your weapons?"

A pincer-mace and my pike were all I had, and the pincer-mace had fallen out of the basket. After five minutes of looking, I found it in the tall grass, and went over to help Clow fold the envelope.

When we were finished, we stuffed it in the basket and put our pikes through the rings on each side so we could carry it. By that time we could see men on horseback coming down from the gib house. Derek said, "We won't be able to stand against horsemen in this field."

For an instant I saw Miles smile. Then he looked very serious. "We'll have one of those fellows over a fire in half an hour."

Derek was counting, and so was I. Eight horsemen, with a cart following them. Several of the horsemen had lances, and I could see the sunlight winking on helmets and breastplates. Derek began pounding the butt of his pike on the ground to charge it.

I suggested to Clow that it might look more friendly if we picked up the balloon and went to meet the horsemen, but he shook his head. "Why bother?"

The first of them had reached the fence around the field. He was sitting a roan stallion that took it at a clean jump and came thundering up to us looking as big as a donjon on wheels.

"Greetings," Miles called. "If this be your land, lord, we give thanks for your hospitality. We'd not have intruded, but our conveyance has exhausted its fuel."

"You are welcome," the horseman called. He was as tall as Miles or taller, as well as I could judge, and as wide as Bracata. "Needs must, as they say, and no harm done." Three of the others had jumped their mounts over the fence behind him. The rest were taking down the rails so the cart could get through.

"Have you straw, lord?" Miles asked. I thought it would have been better if he had asked for food. "If we could have a few bundles of straw, we'd not trouble you more."

"None here," the horseman said, waving a mail-clad arm at the fields around us, "yet I feel sure my bailiff could find you some. Come up to the hall for a taste of meat and a glass of wine, and you can make your ascension from the terrace; the ladies would be delighted to see it, I'm certain. You're floating swords, I take it?"

"We are that," our captain affirmed, "but persons of good character nonetheless. We're called the Faithful Five—perhaps you've heard of us? High-hearted, fierce-fighting wind-warriors all, as it says on the balloon."

A younger man, who had reined up next to the one Miles called "lord," snorted. "If that boy is high-hearted, or a fierce figher either, I'll eat his breeks."

Of course, I should not have done it. I have been too mettlesome all my life, and it has gotten me in more trouble than I could tell you of if I talked till sunset, though it has been good to me too—I would have spent my days following the plow, I suppose, if I had not knocked down Derek for what he called our goose. But you see how it was. Here I had been thinking of myself as a hard-bitten balloon soldier, and then to hear something like that. Anyway, I swung the pincer-mace overhand once I had a good grip on his stirrup. I had been afraid the extension spring was a bit weak, never having used one before, but it worked well; the pliers got him under the left arm and between the ear and the right shoulder, and would have cracked his neck for him properly if he had not been wearing a gorget. As it was, I jerked him off his horse pretty handily, and got out the little aniace that screwed into the mace handle. A couple of the other horsemen couched their lances, and Derek had a finger on the dogcatch of his pike; so all in all it looked as if there could be a proper fight, but "lord" (I learned afterwards that he was the Baron Ascolot) yelled at the young man I had pulled out of his saddle, and Miles yelled at me and grabbed my left wrist, and thus it all blew over.

When we had tripped the release and gotten the mace open and retracted again, Miles said: "He will be punished, lord. Leave him to me. It will be severe, I assure you."

"No, upon my oath," the baron declared. "It will teach my son to be less free with his tongue in the company of armed men. He has been raised at the hall, Captain, where everyone bends the knee to him. He must learn not to expect that of strangers."

The cart rolled up just then, drawn by two fine mules—either of them would have been worth my father's holding, I judged—and at the baron's urging we loaded our balloon into it and climbed in after it ourselves, sitting on fabric. The horsemen galloped off, and the cart driver cracked his lash over the mules' backs.

"Quite a place," Miles remarked. He was looking up at the big house toward which we were making.

I whispered to Clow, " A palace, I should say," and Miles overheard me, and said: "It's a villa, Jerr—the unfortified country property of a gentleman. If there were a wall and a tower, it would be a castle, or at least a castellet."

There were gardens in front, very beautiful as I remember, and a fountain. The road looped up before the door, and we got out and trooped into the hall, while the baron's man—he was richer-dressed than anybody I had ever seen up till then, a fat man with white hair—set two of the hostlers to watch our balloon while it was taken back to the stableyard.

Venison and beef were on the table, and even a pheasant with all his feathers put back; and the baron and his sons sat with us and drank some wine and ate a bit of bread each for hospitality's sake. Then the baron said, "Surely you don't fly in the dark, captain?"

"Not unless we must, lord."

"Then with the day drawing to a close it's just as well for you that we've no straw. You can pass the night with us, and in the morning I'll send my bailiff to the village with the cart. You'll be able to ascend at mid-morning, when the ladies can have a clear view of you as you go up."

"No straw?" our captain asked.

"None, I fear, here. But they'll have aplenty in the village, never doubt it. They lay it in the road to silence the horses' hoofs when a woman's with child, as I've seen many a time. You'll have a cartload as a gift from me, if you can use that much." The baron smiled as he said that; he had a friendly face, round and red as an apple. "Now tell me," (he went on) "how it is to be a floating sword. I always find other men's trades of interest, and it seems to me you follow one of the most fascinating of all. For example, how do you gauge the charge you will make your employer?"

"We have two scales, lord," Miles began. I had heard all of that before, so I stopped listening. Bracata was next to me at table, so I had all I could do to get something to eat for myself, and I doubt I ever got a taste of the pheasant. By good luck, a couple of lasses—the baron's daughters—had come in, and one of them started curling a lock of Derek's hair around her finger, so that distracted him while he was helping himself to the venison, and Bracata put an arm around the other and warned her of Men. If it had not been for that I would not have had a thing; as it was, I stuffed myself on deer's meat until I had to loose my waistband. Flesh of any sort had been a rarity where I came from.

I had thought that the baron might give us beds in the house, but when we had eaten and drunk all we could hold, the white-haired fat man led us out a side door and over to a wattle-walled building full of bunks—I suppose it was kept for the extra laborers needed at harvest. It was not the palace bedroom I had been dreaming of; but it was cleaner than home, and there was a big fireplace down at one end with logs stacked ready by, so it was probably more comfortable for me than a bed in the big house itself would have been.

Clow took out a piece of cherry wood, and started carving a woman in it, and Bracata and Derek lay down to sleep. I made shift to talk to Miles, but he was full of thoughts, sitting on a bench near the hearth and chinking the purse (just like this one, it was) he had gotten from the baron; so I tried to sleep too. But I had had too much to eat to sleep so soon, and since it was still light out, I decided to walk around the villa and try to find somebody to chat with. The front looked too grand for me; I went to the back, thinking to make sure our balloon had suffered no hurt, and perhaps have another look at those mules.

There were three barns behind the house, built of stone up to the height of my waist, and wood above that, and whitewashed. I walked into the nearest of them, not thinking about anything much besides my full belly until a big war horse with a white star on his forehead reached his head out of his stall and nuzzled at my cheek. I reached out and stroked his neck for him the way they like. He nickered, and I turned to have a better look at him. That was when I saw what was in his stall. He was standing on a span or more of the cleanest, yellowest straw I had ever seen. I looked up over my head then, and there was a loft full of it up there.

In a minute or so, I suppose it was, I was back in the building where we were to sleep, shaking Miles by the shoulder and telling him I had found all the straw anyone could ask for.

He did not seem to understand at first. "Wagon loads of straw, Captain," I told him. "Why every horse in the place has as much to lay him on as would carry us a hundred leagues."

"All right," Miles told me.

"Captain—"

'There's no straw here, Jerr. Not for us. Now be a sensible lad and get some rest."

"But there is, Captain, I saw it. I can bring you back a helmetful."

"Come here, Jerr," he said, and got up and led me outside. I thought he was going to ask me to show him the straw; but instead of going back to where the barns were, he took me away from the house to the top of a grassy knoll. "Look out there, Jerr. Far off. What do you see?"

"Trees," I said. "There might be a river at the bottom of the valley; then more trees on the other side."

"Beyond that."

I looked to the horizon, where he seemed to be pointing. There were little threads of black smoke rising there, looking as thin as spider web at that distance.

"What do you see?"

"Smoke."

"That's straw burning, Jerr. House-thatch. That's why there's no straw here. Gold, but no straw, because a soldier gets straw only where he isn't welcome. They'll reach the river there by sundown, and I'm told it can be forded at this season. Now do you understand?"

They came that night at moonrise.

88

SUPERIORITY COMPLEX

Thomas N. Scortia

FOR THE FIRST time in a week Dalton felt the frustration of the search, the utter pointlessness of what they were doing. He turned from the elaborate charts of the presentation, the intricate DNA structures with the statistical gene-sorting arrays and slammed the pointer to his desk.

"It's no use," he said. "It's absolutely no use."

"Of course it is," Les Caldweil said. "We've spent half a decade on this project and more money than I'd like to remember."

"Do you honestly believe in it?" Dalton demanded.

"Complex 'X'?" Caldweil shrugged. "It's an article of faith with me. I've backed you and the survey team on this for five years. You tell me that somewhere in the gene structure of what's left of the human race there is the seed of an unknown genius and I have to believe it."

Dalton sat on the edge of the polymorph desk feeling the soft flowing corner bite into the flesh of his leg. Five years ago it had seemed so certain.

"The Secretary'll never buy it, Les. You know how tight funds are this year. There's no room in the budget for anything so wildly speculative."

"We've got to have the money," Caldweil said. "What do we do with all this?" He gestured widely at the room with its functional furniture and its too-neat charts glowing from softly lighted walls. Beyond this were the offices, the laboratories, the banked computerized files of the bureau of what Caldweil called "the search."

"I'm tempted to scrap it all," Dalton said. "More than once I've told Trudy that I'd be better off back at the university. Perhaps I could get something done there."

"I hope Trudy had sense enough to talk you out of that," Caldweil said.

"My wife is the sensible member of the team," Dalton said wryly.

"But you think you'd be closer to finding and defining 'Complex X' if you weren't part of this structure."

"I'd be working instead of preparing pretty charts for the Secretary of Human Resources to demonstrate a concept that he should be able to get from our reports."

"It's the personal touch, you know," Caldweil said. "Besides, your job is conceptual and administrative. We can find a hundred bench men to do the research. We can't find a dozen like you. You conceived of the project, deduced the existence of Phil Jason—"

"I wish I'd never heard the name of Phil Jason, whoever that misshapen devil was," Dalton said.

"You found him," Caldweil said wryly. "You're stuck with him."

"Phil Jason blew out his brains a centry ago," Dalton said. "Perhaps he knew what he was doing."

After Caldweil had left, Dalton screened his wife. "Trudy, sweetheart," he said. "I can't make it home for lunch."

"Oh," her voice said. She looked small and very disappointed in the viewscreen. He marveled at her youthful features. Why, she would be forty-five in another week. He reminded himself to send flowers and book the seats for the mime show.

"Oh, that's too bad," she said. "I was planning something special for lunch."

"It's this presentation for the Secretary of Human Resources. Budget time, you know, and we've got to dance for our supper."

"Don't worry," she said, smiling brightly. "He knows how important your work is."

"I wish I had your confidence," Dalton said.

"You'll see. Everything will turn out just right. I'll witch it for you."

"Do that," he said, laughing at the private joke. "I'll see you tonight. I'll be late."

"Never mind," she said. "Supper will keep." She blew him a kiss as the image faded.

For a moment he felt young and coltish. After fifteen years she still made him feel like that. Very masculine and assured beside her, very much the captain of their lives and destinies. That was her special appeal, that she did not try to gobble a man up like many of the amazons his friends had married. If it hadn't been for her and his need to be something for her, he might have ended up his life in some obscure university lab working on a penny-pinching government grant. Instead there was Phil Jason . . . .

Phil Jason who had lived a hundred years before in the middle of that fantastic jungle they had called Hollywood and had wasted his tortured life in dribbles of talent and insane flashes of insight. Phil Jason who had killed himself after siring two illegitimate childen, who had stumbled into the world and diluted his precious germ plasm in a hopelessly profligate manner.

There was incredible genius stuff in the race. Call it "Complex X." Call it Phil Jason. It was there, wildly diffuse, waiting segregation and recombination, if indeed the task had not already been accomplished naturally.

He lowered himself into the foam chair at the desk and stared at the illuminated charts with their too-pretty reductions of complex patterns. Just like Jason's Hollywood. Too simple, too elegant, too unreal.

"Damn Phil Jason," he thought bitterly. "Why couldn't he have led a normal life, been more sane, more—"

Sanity for a superman?

In that madhouse?

It was a wonder, Dalton thought, that he had lasted long enough to have two children before he shattered that not-to-be-duplicated brain with a lead slug.

The Secretary arrived at two o'clock, almost an hour late. By that time the staff was restless and the work of the day had become completely disorganized.

"I'm sorry," the Secretary said with his widest smile. "One tries to fit one's life to a schedule, but—"

He waved his hand indecisively and Adler, his aide, said, "Of course, we'll have to amend the agenda somewhat."

Caldweil smiled and said, "We had planned a tour of the facility, but—"

"To be sure," the Secretary said, "but let's get to business first."

In the board room, they seated themselves and coffee was served. Caldweil made opening remarks and turned the briefing over to Dalton. After some moments of explaining the concept, Dalton was interrupted.

"What are you implying," the Secretary said, "is that this Phil Jason was something unusual, that his germ plasm, if it survived the Great War, is of special interest to us."

"That is exactly it," Dalton said. "Jason was unique, completely unusual in a number of striking ways."

"But how can you say this ? Records are incomplete from that period."

"Our extrapolative methods are very subtle," Caldweil volunteered.

Dalton tired to silence him with a stare.

"We have the original clues. Our studies started some years ago, oddly enough as a result of a twentieth-century cultural analysis in the Federal University Humanities Department.''

''Oh, come now,'' the Secretary said.

''It is hard to believe,'' Dalton admitted. ''Jorgenson and his students were attempting a psychosympathetic analysis of some surviving films and cartoons when they happened across this single animated cartoon. It's really rather simple and naïve—you can see it later in the projection room—a simple plot revolving around a black sheep ejected from the flock under the shepherd's eyes . . . a little comic character named Trippy who was featured in these releases . . . and the revenge wrought on the flock, and the ram heading the flock by the ousted black sheep. It has a rather weird flavor, totally unlike anything being produced in the period.''

''And from this you deduce the structure you call 'Complex X'?''

''Well, that was only the start, the first clue. Jorgenson and his people brought it to me and I began to check out several other pieces associated with Jason. It became rather obvious. The man thought in a different way. Subtly but definitely his thought processes, his creative processes were quite alien. We began to check into his life. It was a raging terror. Divorces, scandals, two periods in a sanitorium.''

''He sounds like the least likely superman I've ever heard of,'' the Secretary said.

''But there are documented instances in which we found references to X rays. He was different physically. We know his circulatory system was abnormal. We have a biopsy report showing his cell structure was abnormal, polynuclear. But the most striking thing was his mental potentiality. The man was clearly a genius, and our computer program deduces . . . well, talents like emotional empathy bordering on telepathy, other traits less well defined that suggest he might have seen physical reality in a way we do not. Surely that alone would have made them think he was insane.''

''The whole purpose of the Department of Human Resources,'' the Secretary interrupted, ''is to identify the genetic resources remaining to the race after the war and to try and segregate and propagate the desirable racial traits that may be lost. I fail to see that you have proved that there is any genetic material that may be lost to the race.''

''We know Phil Jason had a son and a daughter, both illegitimate,'' Dalton said. ''We know they had children, and we know the genetic traits that made up Jason's uniqueness have been spread through the race. Perhaps they have recombined to produce another unique individual. If not, it's up to us to identify and assemble the complex, to recreate Phil Jason.''

''Well, surely if these traits existed and were segregating themselves,'' the Secretary said, "we should have no trouble identifying them."

"You would think not," Caldweil said, "but where would you look?"

"Why, in the cultural leaders of the world, in the political and scientific leaders—"

"We've tried that," Caldweil said. "We've examined most of the genetic charts of the leading men of the past three generations and then—"

"Nothing," the Secretary said. "I'm well aware that you've found nothing. However, I have not been completely out of touch with your work. I've had my own staff looking into the project."

Here it comes, Dalton thought. Here it comes. He was not prepared for the next statement.

"You know," the Secretary said, "you haven't really done your homework well. Are you aware that Phil Jason wasn't Phil Jason?"

"I don't understand what you mean," Dalton said.

"The old script can be misleading," the Secretary said. "Your superman's name was not Phillip but Phyllis. You know, Phyl with a 'y,' not an 'i.' "

"You can't be serious," Caldweil said, half-rising to his feet.

"I am indeed," the Secretary said laughing. "My staff has definitely established that your 'Complex X' was a woman script writer in Hollywood. Indeed, she did have two children and indeed did end as you say, but . . . well, it is a rather silly mistake, isn't it?"

"Yes," Dalton said tiredly, "yes, it is a silly mistake."

After it was over and the Secretary's party had gone, Caldweil said, "That tears it."

"No more money?" Dalton asked.

"No more money."

"Well, at least I can get back to some serious work," Dalton said.

"I'd better start scouting for a job," Caldweil said. "I don't have your research talent."

"Still, this explains a number of elusive problems in our inability to identify certain dominant genes—"

"I don't understand."

"What if they're sex-linked?"

"Well, perhaps you hve the chance to find out now."

On the way home, Dalton realized that he felt relieved. He had never been really happy as a government scientist supervisor. Now he could do some work again, perhaps follow up this clue. Of course, if the major characteristics of the complex were linked with two X chromosomes, if the trait could only appear dominant in a female . . . .

He was silent through most of dinner.

"Is it that bad?" Trudy finally said.

"No, sweetheart," he said. "Actually things are working out very well."

"I had lunch with Betty Adler today."

"That's good," he said.

"She's going to be living in this area now. Her husband's in government."

"That's fine," he said.

"You haven't heard a word I've said, nutty."

"I heard every word," he said kissing her.

She brought coffee into the study where he had retired to work after dinner. He had brought home several of the monographs he and other members of the staff had published in the early days of the project. It was strange, he thought, that the idea had never occurred to them. Well, why shouldn't superman have been a woman . . . poor harassed creature. He wondered what she had looked like. The appearance of Phillip Jason had never been of great interest to him. The appearance of Phyllis Jason was another matter.

His musing was interrupted by the crackling of the intercom. "I'm sorry," Trudy's voice said. "I know you didn't want to be interrupted, but it's Les Caldweil."

"Tell him I've gone to bed," he said sourly. Then, "No, never mind. I'll talk to him."

"You'll never guess," Caldweil said. His voice was filled with gloating.

"Don't play games, Les," Dalton said.

"Don't ask me how it happened, but we're in the chips."

"Damn it!" Dalton exploded.

"No, it's no joke," Caldweil said. "The Secretary called me himself. Just fifteen minutes ago. They're renewing and expanding the project."

"I don't believe it," Dalton said with a sinking feeling.

"We're all safe for another four years," Caldweil gloated. "The Secretary mumbled something about Adler convincing him we needed more time—"

"Adler? Who's Adler?" Dalton demanded.

"His aide. You remember his aide, the thin chap with the built-in sneer. That doesn't sound like what I'd expect from him."

"No," Dalton said. "Perhaps someone got to him."

"Celebration's tomorrow. Lunch on me," Caldweil said. "Good night."

As he prepared for bed, Dalton thought, another four years. Endless papers, all the time-consuming meetings, the forms, the endless paper of bureaucracy with no time to think, to work . . . It was almost as if . . . .

The thought crossed his mind. Trudy and her luncheon date with a school friend. Adler had she said?

It would be curious, Dalton thought. After they had darkened the room he lay awake thinking. Well, where would a superman hide if not at the center of power?

Look for the power centers of the world and there you find superman, making over the world in a new image, a safe image, only . . . .

Superman wasn't a man.

"Trudy," he called out in the dark.

"Yes, honey," she said—bright, alert, waiting.

"I . . ." he thought for a moment. "I don't remember."

"You're sleepy," she said. "It probably wasn't important."

"No," he said. "It probably wasn't important at all."

89

TEACHING PRIME

Leo P. Kelley

TWO OF THE children failed to make it to the eduarena. One fell in a flooded gully that had been caused by careless, not to mention illegal, strip mining and drowned within minutes. The other child ate berries that had been chemically corrupted and died almost instantly.

The others, more than a little bit proud of themselves for having survived the daily journey, scampered into the eduarena and slid into their assigned seats. As the force field sprang up outside, they finally relaxed.

The Roboteach swiveled back and forth on the oiled stage as it checked attendance and erased the names of the two dead children from its roster tapes.

"Comparative Galactic Ecosystems," it announced in its neutral, neutered voice. "Notes must be taken. Nuances must be noted. Parallels are to be drawn. Conclusions can be reached and reported at session's end. Are we ready?"

"We are ready!" chanted the children in their young voices.

"I'm not," a student whispered to his companion beside him. "This stuff is a waste of time."

"Well, we got to pass it anyway or we won't get into Highered later on," his friend whispered with resignation.

"It won't help me earn a living," the first student persisted.

"It might," his friend speculated. "Who knows?"

"Silence," spat the Roboteach. "Silence, please, while your attention is paid to the holographic simulation of forthcoming comparative galactic ecosystems. The Level has been adjusted for students who have seen but seven sets of seasons pass."

The lights dimmed and the eduarena seemed to expand as the holographic screens began to project their vividly dimensional lesson for the day.

Moving out among the children, the figures began to act out their programmed dramas.

The children watched the multicellular inhabitants of the Planet Saurus as they went about their daily tasks in the misty mountains and thin air. The Saurians slid and billowed about, their many eyes alert, their tails held high in their nervous signaling to one another.

"Heat kills," grunted one Saurian as several of his cells atrophied under the onslaught of the sun beaming down through the magnification lens above the fields of sprouting seeds the workers were harvesting.

"Heat's hell," moaned another mournfully as the mists were vanquished by the yellow eye glaring down through the smooth glass.

"Sweet water, sweet water," sang one of the workers hours later as it fought for space in the small cool mud wallow at the edge of the raped fields.

The watching children in the eduarena giggled at the grotesque rhythm of the creature's words.

A child impulsively raised her hand and told the Roboteach that her best friend had been drowned earlier on the way to class. Why couldn't some of their rainwater, she asked, be shipped to the Planet Saurus since the Saurians sure did seem to need it pretty bad. She said there was too much water outside anyway. It was always raining, she complained, since the Agroeconomists ruined the atmospheric balance.

The Roboteach told her she was perceptive but instructed her to please keep quiet until the entire sequence was properly completed.

The Saurian's flesh steamed in the relentless sun which caused the mud wallow to dry up. The child whose best friend had drowned began to cry and had to be led away lest her wailing disrupt the lesson.

The holographc screens shifted and the Saurians slid slugglishly into the empty shadows and out of sight.

Words danced gaily among the children.

DICK AND JANE. SEQUENCE TWO. COMPARATIVE GALACTIC ECOSYSTEMS. PAY YOUR ATTENTION.

"Ooohhh!" sighed the children as Dick and Jane bounced happily out among them.

Dick was tall and blond and he had blue eyes above a very nice nose. His lips were the right size but he couldn't seem to close them. His smile kept getting in the way.

Jane stood beside him, gazing fondly up into his blue eyes with her chocolate colored ones. Her hair gleamed with setspray and her dress, which glittered with green sequins, reached as far as her upper thighs and then gave up and vanished. It avoided her pert breasts, leaving them bare. She ran slim and unringed fingers through her stiff discolored hair and continued gazing contentedly into Dick's eyes.

Dick flexed the many muscles in his arms for no apparent purpose. They bulged and rippled beneath the sheer sleeves of his yellow tunic. He looked all around him, turning first this way, then that way.

"Where is Spot?" he asked Jane. "Spot is not here."

"No, Spot is not here," Jane said. "Where is Spot?"

Billy and Betty came bounding holographically and happily into the middle of the eduarena.

"Hello, Mother," Billy said.

"Hello, Father," Betty said.

"Hello, Billy," Jane said.

"Hello, Betty," Dick said. "Where is Spot?"

"Here comes Spot," Billy said. "See Spot run."

"Spot runs fast," Betty said.

She picked up a bright red rubber ball and threw it very high into the air. Spot barked and ran after it. The ball rolled across the macadam outside the box of their house and into the middle of the superhighway that ran beside it.

The monocars streamed past and over the dog's body without stopping or caring.

"Spot is not here," Billy said.

"Is Grandmother here?" Betty asked.

"Yes," said Dick. "Grandmother is in the house. Go into the house and see Grandmother, Betty."

Betty went obediently up the path to the house. She walked past the gun turrets growing up out of the grassless ground and she waded through the strewn garbage. She entered the small square structure and called out to Grandmother.

The others followed her, coughing from the fumes that spewed forth from the monocar mechanisms.

"Happy Birthday, Grandmother," Betty said as she kissed her Grandmother.

"Thank you, Betty. Thank you very much. I am going now."

"Goodby," Betty said.

"You have had a good life, Mother," Jane said. "The Euthanasia Exit is down the block. It is next door to the Crime Corps Complex."

"I have had a good life," Grandmother said. "Forty years is a good long time."

Grandmother picked up her knapsack and her pistol and went to the front door of the one-room house. She turned and waved goodbye to Dick and Jane. She bent and kissed Billy and Betty.

"The Brentwoods who live next door," said Jane, "have bought new guns with telescopic sights."

"The bounty on Grandmothers was raised again this month," Dick said.

Grandmother hurried out of the house, glancing furtively across the mounds of garbage at the Brentwood house where steel turrets gleamed now and then amid the clouds of carbon monoxide.

Betty clapped her hands. "See Grandmother run!"

"Grandmother runs fast!" Billy cried.

They all watched Grandmother run through the fusillade of Brentwood bullets, firing back grimly.

"Hurrah!" Billy cried. "They missed her!"

Jane smiled. "Grandmother runs very fast. Now it is time to sleep."

Billy took a peyote button out of his pocket and began to chew it.

Betty went and got the spoons and the glassine envelopes and the hypodermic needles and the little Bunsen burner.

They heated the heroin in the spoons and then injected it expertly into their veins.

"Sweet dreams, Billy," Jane said.

"Sweet dreams, Betty," Dick said.

They sat down on the dirty floor and began to nod.

In the eduarena, the lights changed and deepened to indicate the passage of time.

"Good morning," Jane said to everyone.

They all wished her a good morning as Betty put the needles and the spoons and the little Bunsen burner away until later.

Outside the house, the garbage mounds, they discovered, had become miniature mountains during the long night. The sound of monocars streaming past was an endless technology lullaby. Bullets zinged familiarly in the air instead of the forgotten songs of birds.

They all huddled against the protection of the house while they watched the neighborhood's usual morning melee. Betty scurried down into a gun turret and began firing at the Grandfather loping hopelessly along the edge of the superhighway toward the Euthanasia Exit to celebrate his fortieth birthday. She dropped him on the second shot and skipped to where he lay. She removed his identification disk and went away to collect her bounty.

"I feel sick," Dick said. "My head hurts. I am nauseous. I cannot see straight."

Jane touched his damp forehead and took his pulse. She pulled down the lower lids of his eyes. "You have botulism, Dick. It must have been in the uninspected cans of contraband string beans they shipped up from Mexico."

"I was very hungry," Dick said. "We had so little food all last week." He closed his eyes and fell to the macadam.

"Father is dead," Jane said.

"I am thirsty," Billy said.

"The government promised to send us some water next week," Jane said. "Wait, Billy. Wait for the unpolluted water."

"Who is that?" Billy asked, pointing to the young woman who was zigzagging up the macadam in order to avoid the bursting bullets that the neighbors were firing at her in case she turned out to be a Grandmother.

"That is Jane," Jane said. "The other lady behind her is also Jane."

The two Janes scurried past Billy and Jane and on into the house Billy and Jane followed them inside.

"We have come for Dick," the Janes said. "It is our turn with Dick this week."

"Dick is dead," Jane told them. "He is lying outside near the uncollected garbage."

"Who is he?" the Janes asked, pointing at Billy.

"He is Billy," Jane said. "But he is only nine."

"We don't care," the woman said. "There aren't many men left since Census Control succeeded. Or women either, for that matter."

They seized Billy and dragged him from the house.

Jane was left alone. "Spot ran fast," she said to herself. "Dick had a very nice nose. Betty shoots true. Billy is gone away. I—"

The Crime Corps burst into the house without bothering to knock and arrested Jane for littering.

"I am innocent," Jane said.

"You let Dick lie on the public macadam outside where he fell," the Crime Corps Commander accused. "You littered."

"I am—" Jane began.

"Dead," said the Commander as he shot her and she fell. "The punishment must fit the crime."

The eduarena environment altered suddenly. The light shifted. The bodies of Dick and Jane disappeared. The Roboteach tapped his baton to attract the children's attention.

"What happened to Dick and Jane?" he asked.

"They died," the children responded.

"More than that, much more," the Roboteach insisted with a show of almost impish impatience. "I will show you cue cards to help you think of the right answer. Look up at the overhead screen, please, and pay your attention."

A multicelled and many-eyed figure appeared on the screen.

"Name?" inquired the Roboteach.

"Saurian," a student called out.

"Correct."

Click: a bird.

"Peregrine falcon," someone volunteered.

"Correct."

Click: a striped animal.

"Sabre-tooth tiger," the children chorused.

Click: another bird.

"Passenger pigeon."

Click: a picture of Dick, Jane, Jane, Jane, Billy and Betty.

"What have all these species in common?" inquired the Roboteach.

"They are all extinct," a student announced with young pomp.

"True," said the Roboteach.

"But Betty didn't die," someone protested. "Neither did Billy. The two Janes took Billy away. Betty went to get her bounty."

"You are in error," the Roboteach announced solemnly. "You were not paying your full attention. I shall reinstate the environment. Now watch closely this time."

The scene in which Betty leaned over to remove the Grandfather's identification disk reappeared in the eduarena. The children watched closely as Betty ran along the edge of the superhighway. They ignored all other details in the scene this time. They saw the monocar glide to a halt and the driver reach out and drag Betty into the car where he strangled her and tore from her hand the identification disk. They saw him mark another X on the broad dashboard of his monocar and speed away in the direction of the Bounty Collection Center.

"But what about the two Janes and Billy?" the children cried, eager now to be right in their answers.

They were shown what had happened—what they had failed to notice the first time. The Janes fought one another for possession of Billy. He fought both of them. But the Brentwood bullets cut them all down just in case they might turn out to be Grandmothers and a Grandfather.

"Extinct species, locus Earth," the Roboteach intoned. "What then is the point of today's lesson?"

"Who says there is one?" snickered one bored student under his breath.

"The point is," said the Roboteach patiently, "that we must not let the fate of the Saurians whom you saw earlier nor that of the residents of Earth become ours here on the Planet Vorno. We must protect and preserve our environment and one another if we are to survive."

"What does *it* know?" muttered the same student who had snickered earlier. "That old Roboteach isn't even alive like us!"

He received no answer as the class was dismissed and the children of Vorno slithered out past the deactivated force field on their multiple limbs and clawed and pawed their way through the dangers surrounding them.

Two of the children did not make it home alive from the eduarena. One was caught in the crossfire between enemy soldiers from Vorno North and Vorno South. The second was struck by the landing gear of a low flying helicab.

When the survivors arrived home, their fond parents asked them what they had learned in the eduarena that day. They shrugged their scales and muttered their vague answers:

"Nothing much."

"The same old stuff."

"About Dick and Jane."

90

THAT ONLY A MOTHER

Judith Merril

MARGARET REACHED OVER to the other side of the bed where Hank should have been. Her hand patted the empty pillow, and then she came altogether awake, wondering that the old habit should remain after so many months. She tried to curl up, cat-style, to hoard her own warmth, found she couldn't do it any more, and climbed out of bed with a pleased awareness of her increasingly clumsy bulkiness.

Morning motions were automatic. On the way through the kitchenette, she pressed the button that would start breakfast cooking—the doctor had said to eat as much breakfast as she could—and tore the paper out of the facsimile machine. She folded the long sheet carefully to the "National News" section, and propped it on the bathroom shelf to scan while she brushed her teeth.

No accidents. No direct hits. At least none that had been officially released for publication. *Now, Maggie, don't get started on that. No accidents. No hits. Take the nice newspaper's word for it.*

The three clear chimes from the kitchen announced that breakfast was ready. She set a bright napkin and cheerful colored dishes on the table in a futile attempt to appeal to a faulty morning appetite. Then, when there was nothing more to prepare, she went for the mail, allowing herself the full pleasure of prolonged anticipation, because today there would *surely* be a letter.

There was. There were. Two bills and a worried note from her mother: "Darling, why didn't you write and tell me sooner? I'm thrilled of course, but, well one hates to mention these things, but are you *certain* the doctor was right? Hank's been around all that uranium or thorium or whatever it is all these years, and I know you say he's a designer, not a technician, and he doesn't get near anything that might be dangerous, but you know he used to,

565

back at Oak Ridge. Don't you think . . . well, of course, I'm just being a foolish old woman, and I don't want you to get upset. You know much more abot it than I do, and I'm sure your doctor was right. He *should* know . . . ."

Margaret made a face over the excellent coffee, and caught herself refolding the paper to the medical news.

Stop it, Maggie, stop it! The radiologist said Hank's job couldn't have exposed him. And the bombed area we drove past . . . No, no. Stop it, now! Read the social notes or the recipes, Maggie girl.

A well-known geneticist, in the medical news, said that it was possible to tell with absolute certainty, at five months, whether the child would be normal, or at least whether the mutation was likely to produce anything freakish. The worst cases, at any rate, could be prevented. Minor mutations, of course, displacements in facial features, or changes in brain structure could not be detected. And there had been some cases recently, of normal embryos with atrophied limbs that did not develop beyond the seventh or eight month. But, the doctor concluded cheerfully, the *worst* cases could now predicted and prevented.

"Predicted and prevented." We predicted it, didn't we? Hank and the others, they predicted it. But we didn't prevent it. We could have stopped it in '46 and '47. Now . . . .

Margaret decided against the breakfast. Coffee had been enough for her in the morning for ten years; it would have to do for today. She buttoned herself into interminable folds of materials that, the salesgirl had assured her, was the *only* comfortable thing to wear during the last few months. With a surge of pure pleasure, the letter and newspaper forgotten, she realized she was on the next to the last button. It wouldn't be long now.

The city in the early morning had always been a special kind of excitement for her. Last night it had rained, and the sidewalks were still damp-gray instead of dusty. The air smelled the fresher, to a city-bred woman, for the occasional pungency of acrid factory smoke. She walked the six blocks to work, watching the lights go out in the all-night hamburger joints, where the plate-glass walls were already catching the sun, and the lights go on in the dim interiors of cigar stores and dry-cleaning establishments.

The office was in a new Government building. In the rolovator, on the way up, she felt, as always, like a frankfurther roll in the ascending half of an old-style rotary toasting machine. She abandoned the air-foam cushioning gratefully at the fourteenth floor, and settled down behind her desk at the rear of a long row of identical desks.

Each morning the pile of papers that greeted her was a little higher. These were, as everyone knew, the decisive months. The war might be won or lost on these calculations as well as any others. The manpower office had switched her here when her old expediter's job got to be too strenuous. The computer was easy to operate, and the work was absorbing, if not as exciting as the old job. But you didn't just stop working these days. Everyone who could do anything at all was needed.

And—she remembered the interview with the psychologist—*I'm probably the unstable type. Wonder what sort of neurosis I'd get sitting home reading that sensational paper* . . . .

She plunged into the work without pursuing the thought.

February 18.

Hank darling,

Just a note—from the hospital, no less. I had a dizzy spell at work, and the doctor took it to heart. Blessed if I know what I'll do with myself lying in bed for weeks, just waiting—but Dr. Boyer seems to think it may not be so long.

There are too many newspapers around here. More infanticides all the time, and they can't seem to get a jury to convict any of them. It's the fathers who do it. Lucky thing you're not around, in case—

Oh, darling that wasn't a very *funny* joke, was it? Write as often as you can, will you? I have too much time to think. But there really isn't anything wrong, and nothing to worry about.

Write often, and remember I love you.

Maggie.

SPECIAL SERVICE TELEGRAM

February 21, 1953
22:04 LK37G

From: Tech. Lieut. H. Marvell
X47–016 GCNY
To: Mrs. H. Marvell
Women's Hospital New York City
HAD DOCTOR'S GRAM STOP WILL ARRIVE FOUR OH TEN STOP
SHORT LEAVE STOP YOU DID IT MAGGIE STOP LOVE HANK

February 25.

Hank dear,

So you didn't see the baby either? You'd think a place this size would at least have visiplates on the incubators, so the fathers could

567

get a look, even if the poor benighted mommas can't. They tell me I won't see her for another week, or maybe more—but of course, mother always warned me if I didn't slow my pace, I'd probably even have my babies too fast. Why must she *always* be right?

Did you meet that battle-ax of a nurse they put on here? I imagine they save her for people who've already had theirs, and don't let her get too near the prospectives—but a woman like that simply shouldn't be allowed in a maternity ward. She's obsessed with mutations, can't seem to talk about anything else. Oh, well, *ours* is all right, even if it was in an unholy hurry.

I'm tired. They warned me not to sit up too soon, but I *had* to write you. All my love, darling,

Maggie.

February 29.
Darling,

I finally got to see her! It's all true, what they say about new babies and the face that only a mother could love—but it's all there, darling, eyes, ears, and noses—no, only one!—all in the right places. We're so *lucky,* Hank.

I'm afraid I've been a rambunctious patient. I kept telling that hatchet-faced female with the mutation mania that I wanted to *see* the baby. Finally the doctor came in to "explain" everything to me, and talked a lot of nonsense, most of which I'm sure no one could have understood, any more than I did. The only thing I got out of it was that she didn't actually *have* to stay in the incubator; they just thought it was "wiser."

I think I got a little hysterical at that point. Guess I was more worried than I was willing to admit, but I threw a small fit about it. The whole business wound up with one of those hushed medical conferences outside the door, and finally the Woman in White said: "Well, we might as well. Maybe it'll work out better that way."

I'd heard about the way doctors and nurses in these places develop a God complex, and believe me it is as true figuratively as it is literally that a mother hasn't got a leg to stand on around here.

I *am* awfully weak, still. I'll write again soon. Love,

Maggie.

March 8.
Dearest Hank,

Well the nurse was wrong if she told you that. She's an idiot anyhow. It's a girl. It's easier to tell with babies than with cats, and *I know*. How about Henrietta?

I'm home again, and busier than a betatron. They got *everything* mixed up at the hospital, and I had to teach myself how to bathe her and do just about everything else. She's getting prettier, too. When can you get a leave, a *real* leave?

Love,
Maggie.

May 26.

Hank dear,

You should see her now—and you shall. I'm sending along a reel of color movie. My mother sent her those nighties with drawstrings all over. I put one on, and right now she looks like a snow-white potato sack with that beautiful, beautiful flower-face blooming on top. Is that *me* talking? Am I a doting mother? But wait till you *see* her!

July 10.

. . . Believe it or not, as you like, but your daughter can talk, and I don't mean baby talk. Alice discovered it—she's a dental assistant in the WACs, you know—and when she heard the baby giving out what I thought was a string of gibberish, she said the kid knew words and sentences, but couldn't say them clearly because she has no teeth yet. I'm taking her to a speech specialist.

September 13.

. . . We have a prodigy for real! Now that all her front teeth are in, her speech is perfectly clear and—a new talent now—she can sing! I mean really carry a tune! At seven months! Darling my world would be perfect if you could only get home.

November 19.

. . . at last. The little goon was so busy being clever, it took her all this time to learn to crawl. The doctor says development in these cases is always erratic . . . .

SPECIAL SERVICE TELEGRAM

December 1, 1953
08:47 LK59F

From: Tech. Lieut. H. Marvell
X47—016 GCNY
To: Mrs. H. Marvell
Apt. K-17
504 E. 19 St.
N.Y.N.Y.
WEEK'S LEAVE STARTS TOMORROW STOP WILL ARRIVE AIRPORT TEN OH FIVE STOP DON'T MEET ME STOP LOVE LOVE LOVE HANK

Margaret let the water run out of the bathinette until only a few inches were left, and then loosened her hold on the wriggling baby.

"I think it was better when you were retarded, young woman," she informed her daughter happily. "You *can't* crawl in a bathinette, you know."

"Then why can't I go in the bathtub?" Margaret was used to her child's volubility by now, but every now and then it caught her unaware. She swooped the resistant mass of pink flesh into a towel, and began to rub.

"Because you're too little, and your head is very soft, and bathtubs are very hard."

"Oh. Then when can I go in the bathtub?"

"When the outside of your head is as hard as the inside, brainchild." She reached toward a pile of fresh clothing. "I cannot understand," she added, pinning a square cloth through the nightgown, "why a child of your intelligence can't learn to keep a diaper on the way other babies do. They've been used for centuries, you know, with perfectly satisfactory results."

The child disdained to reply; she had heard it too often. She waited patiently until she had been tucked, clean and sweet-smelling, into a white-painted crib. Then she favored her mother with a smile that inevitably made Margaret think of the first golden edge of the sun bursting into a rosy pre-dawn. She remembered Hank's reaction to the color pictures of his beautiful daughter, and with the thought, realized how late it was.

"Go to sleep, puss. When you wake you, you know, your *Daddy* will be here."

"Why?" aksed the four-year-old mind, waging a losing battle to keep the ten-month-old body awake.

Margaret went into the kitchenette and set the timer for the roast. She examined the table, and got her clothes from the closet, new dress, new shoes, new slip, new everything, bought weeks before and saved for the day Hank's telegram came. She stopped to pull a paper from the facsimile, and, with clothes and news, went into the bathroom, and lowered herself gingerly into the steaming luxury of a scented tub.

She glanced through the paper with indifferent interest. Today at least there was no need to read the national news. There was an article by a geneticist. The same geneticist. Mutations, he said, were increasing disproportionately. It was too soon for recessives; even the first mutants, born near Hiroshima and Nagasaki in 1946 and 1947 were not old enough yet to breed. *But my baby's all right*. Apparently, there was some degree of free radiation from atomic explosions causing the trouble. *My baby's fine. Precocious, but normal*. If more attention had been paid to the first Japanese mutations, he said . . . .

There was that little notice in the paper in the spring of '47. That was when Hank quit at Oak Ridge. "Only two or three per cent of those guilty of infanticide are being caught and punished in Japan today . . . . .'' *But* MY BABY'S *all right.*

She was dressed, combed, and ready to the last light brush-on of lip paste, when the door chime sounded. She dashed for the door, and heard, for the first time in eighteen months the almost-forgotten sound of a key turning in the lock before the chime had quite died away.

"Hank!"

"Maggie!"

And then there was nothing to say. So many days, so many months, of small news piling up, so many things to tell him, and now she just stood there, staring at a khaki uniform and a stranger's pale face. She traced the features with the finger of memory. The same high-bridged nose, wide-set eyes, fine feathery brows; the same long jaw, the hair a little farther back now on the high forehead, the same tilted curve to his mouth. Pale . . . Of course, he'd been underground all this time. And strange, stranger because of lost familiarity than any newcomer's face could be.

She had time to think all that before his hand reached out to touch her, and spanned the gap of eighteen months. Now, again, there was nothing to say, because there was no need. They were together, and for the moment that was enough.

"Where's the baby?"

"Sleeping, She'll be up any minute."

No urgency. Their voices were as casual as though it were a daily exchange, as though war and separation did not exist. Margaret picked up the coat he'd thrown on the chair near to the door, and hung it carefully in the hall closet. She went to check the roast, leaving him to wander through the rooms by himself, remembering and coming back. She found him finally, standing over the baby's crib.

She couldn't see his face, but she had no need to.

"I think we can wake her just this once." Margaret pulled the covers down, and lifted the white bundle from the bed. Sleepy lids pulled back heavily from smoky brown eyes.

"Hello." Hank's voice was tentative.

"Hello." The baby's assurance was more pronounced.

He had heard about it, of course, but that wasn't the same as hearing it. He turned eagerly to Margaret. "She really can—?"

"Of course she can, darling. But what's more important, she can even do nice normal things like other babies do, even stupid ones. Watch her crawl!" Margaret set the baby on the big bed.

For a moment young Henrietta lay and eyed her parents dubiously.

"'Crawl?'' she asked.

''That's the idea. You Daddy is new around here, you know. He wants to see you show off.''

''Then put me on my tummy.''

''Oh, of course.'' Margaret obligingly rolled the baby over.

''What's the matter?'' Hank's voice was still casual, but an undercurrent in it began to charge the air of the room. ''I thought they turned over first.''

''This baby,'' Margaret would not notice the tension, ''*This* baby does things when she wants to.''

This baby's father watched with softening eyes while the head advanced and the body hunched up propelling itself across the bed.

''Why the little rascal,'' he burst into relieved laughter. ''She looks like one of those potato-sack racers they used to have on picnics. Got her arms pulled out of the sleeves already.'' He reached over and grabbed the knot at the bottom of the long nightie.

''I'll do it, darling.'' Margaret tried to get there first.

''Don't be silly, Maggie. This may be *your* first baby, but *I* had five kid brothers.'' He laughed her away, and reached with his other hand for the string that closed one sleeve. He opened the sleeve bow, and groped for an arm.

''The way you wriggle,'' he addressed his child sternly, as his hand touched a moving knob of flesh at the shoulder, ''anyone might think you are a worm, using your tummy to crawl on, instead of your hands and feet.''

Margaret stood and watched, smiling. ''Wait till you hear her sing, darling—''

His right hand traveled down from the shoulder to where he thought an arm would be, traveled down, and straight down, over firm small muscles that writhed in an attempt to move against the pressure of his hand. He let his fingers drift up again to the shoulder. With infinite care, he opened the knot at the bottom of the nightgown. His wife was standing by the bed, saying: ''She can do 'Jingle Bells,' and—''

His left hand felt along the soft knitted fabric of the gown, up towards the diaper that folded, flat and smooth, across the bottom end of his child. No wrinkles. No kicking. *No . . . .*

''Maggie.'' He tried to pull his hands from the neat fold in the diaper, from the wriggling body. ''Maggie.'' His throat was dry; words came hard, low and grating. He spoke very slowly, thinking the sound of each word to make himself say it. His head was spinning, but he had to *know* before he let it go. ''Maggie, why . . . didn't you . . . tell me?''

''Tell you what, darling?'' Margaret's poise was the immemorial patience of woman confronted with man's childish impetuosity. Her sudden laugh sounded fantastically easy and natural in that room; it was all clear to her now. ''Is she wet? I didn't know.''

She didn't know. His hands, beyond control, ran up and down the soft-skinned baby body, the sinuous, limbless body. *Oh God, dear God—* his head shook and his muscles contracted, in a bitter spasm of hysteria. His fingers tightened on his child—*Oh God, she didn't know . . . .*

91

THEY LIVE FOREVER

Lloyd Biggle, Jr.

BEFORE HE STEPPED out of his hut into the clear morning air, Mathews repeated his calculations of the night before. The result was the same. In Earth-time, this was the Day. And if it were not, if an error had crept into his records down through the years, this particular day was close enough. It would do.

He stood looking at the village below him, at the laboriously-cultivated fields on the lower slope, at the peacefully grazing *zawyi*, some of which were still being milked. From the village street the little chief saw him, and raised both hands. Mathews returned the greeting, and took the down path.

The chief approached him humbly. "Is your Day of Days satisfactory?"

Mathews looked down at the breath-taking panorama this strange planet served him each morning with his breakfast. The haze of ground mist was shot through with riotous colors that drifted and spread and changed before his unbelieving eyes. Without warning the jungle would suddenly flip into the sky and hang above itself in a dazzling, inverted mirage. In the distance the broad surface of a mighty river mirrored the pink-tinted clouds of early morning. The sight awed and stirred Mathews as it had on thousands of other mornings, and as it would each morning as long as his eyes served him.

"The Day is satisfactory," he told the chief.

The chief gave a little grunt of satisfaction, and shouted a command.

From nearby huts came warriors, eight, ten, a dozen. They carried an odd miscellany of weapons, and Mathews was responsible for many of them—spears, blowpipes, a boomerang, bows and arrows, and odd items that Mathews had invented. They were a resourceful people, these *Rualis*—quick, intelligent and brave. They reacted with rare enthusiasm to a new idea.

Women came forth to approach Mathews with shy respect. They bowed before him with their gifts. He accepted a skin of sweet wine, bread cakes, and pieces of dried meta. A whispered request, and a small boy scurried into a hut and returned with a hoe.

"The Day waits," Mathews said. He took the downward trail, and the *Rualis* marched behind him, singing lustily.

They moved quickly down the cool, sunny mountain slope, and the torrid heat of the jungle rolled up in waves to meet them. The natives moved ahead of him when they reached the jungle path. It was a custom, almost a ritual, that they should precede him into the jungle, to protect him from the nameless terrors that lurked there. Mathews had never seen these terrors, and frankly doubted their existence, but he never protested. His ability to yield graciously on matters that were really unimportant was one reason for his success with these people.

The Tree was their objective. It had been a forest giant when Mathews first saw it—fifty-eight years before, by his calculations. The Tree held some mysterious significance for the natives which he had never fathomed. They conducted ceremonies there, and their dancing kept a broad, circular track cleared. But they never invited his presence, and he never attempted to intrude.

The *Rualis* seated themselves in a circle about the tree. They had removed their clothing, and perspiration glistened on their sun-tanned bodies. Insects swarmed around them. Mathews waved his hand in a friendly salute, and turned off the jungle trail. The path he followed was faint, overgrown, almost obliterated. The *Rualis* never used it, and it had been ten days since his last visit.

He moved a dozen yards into the jungle, slashing at the undergrowth with his hoe, and reached a small clearing. He seated himself on the ground, and drank deeply from the wine skin. Insects droned incessantly overhead, colossal insects, but they did not bother him. That was one of the many mysteries of this strange planet. The insects plagued the *Rualis*, but ignored the Earthman.

Back at the Tree, the *Rualis* continued their singing. The song tossed swingingly on the breeze, backed up by intricate thumping on a dried *liayu* fruit. Mathews suspected that they were a highly musical people, though he knew too little about music himself to share their extreme pleasure in it.

He pushed the wine skin aside, and chewed solemnly on a piece of meat, feeling a deep, relaxing peace within himself. It was his Day—his birthday, by Earth-time, as well as he had been able to keep it. It was also, by a coincidence he had often pondered down through the years, the anniversary of the tragedy that had placed him on this planet.

The ship had crashed on his sixteenth birthday. It rested somewhere in front of him, hidden by the impenetrable curtain of green. Long years before the roaring jungle had swallowed it up in its clinging, rusting embrace. It had been years—decades, even—since Mathews had last hacked his way through to visit it. Now he was content to leave it undisturbed. There was nothing entombed there except memories, and the clearing had memories enough to satisfy him.

On the other side of the clearing were the graves—six of them, side by side. At one end Mathews had buried his grandfather. At the other end rested the mortal remains of old Wurr, the immortal man who was not immune to accidents. Between them lay the four-man crew of the *Fountain of Youth*.

"Seven is a lucky number," his grandfather had said. "Come along, and bring us luck." So Mathews had come, and brought luck only for himself. Of the seven, he alone had survived the crash.

At the time the *Fountain of Youth* set forth bravely for the far reaches of the galaxy, he'd had little understanding of his grandfather's quest. The adventure, the excitement was enough. He hadn't particularly cared whether they reached their objective or not.

Now he was an old man, and he understood—too well. It was not an idle whim that led his grandfather to name the new star ship *Fountain of Youth*. Grandfather Mathews quite literally sought the source of eternal life, but his objective was a planet of youth, rather than a fountain. He sought the home of old Wurr.

Wurr, the kindly old immortal! Mathews' memory could still search back over the years and bring him vividly to life. Bushy hair, black, twinkling eyes, low, husky voice, he never seemed anything but ordinary.

And the known facts about him were nothing less than staggering.

Wurr had survived a precipitous arrival on Earth when the space ship on which he was a passenger plunged into the Pacific Ocean. Wurr was found bobbing on the surface in a space suit, the only survivor. He was a mature man then, and from that day until he left Earth on the *Fountain of Youth*, three hundred and seventy-two years had elapsed. That much was documented history.

During those centuries he had not aged perceptibly. Doctors examined him, and x-rayed him, and studied him repeatedly, and their only comment was a rather frustrating shrug of the shoulders. He was an ordinary man, with a single difference.

He lived forever.

Ordinary man and immortal man, man of simple, unaffected habits, man of mystery. He was a sly and candid observer of the human scene. Historians sought him out—an eye-witness of more than three centuries of Earth's history. He submitted willingly to examinations, but he balked at answering questions. He was no different, he said, from anyone else— where he came from.

Grandfather Mathews became acquainted with him, and reached a conclusion on a subject that had been giving rise to much speculation ever since Wurr had completed his first hundred years on Earth. Wurr's home was a planet of immortality, a planet of perpetual youth.

Supposing an alien, a native of Earth, were to visit that Planet. Would he receive the gift of immortality? Grandfather Mathews conferred with Wurr. The immortal man was reluctant. He liked Earth. Eventually Grandfather Mathews convinced him, and the *Fountain of Youth* expedition was born. Earth had lately developed star travel, and Wurr knew with the exactitude of a skilled navigator the stellar location of his home planet in the Constellation Scorpio. Grandfather Mathews was confident.

Mathews understood, now, that the old man had not taken him along as a whim. He had frankly sought immortal life for himself, but he was a practical old fellow. He admitted the possibility that he might already be too old, too near to death, to be redeemed by the powers of that miraculous planet. But his grandson, only a boy in his teens—surely the planet could work the miracle for him!

That was the legacy the old man had sought for Mathews. Not wealth, not prestige, but immortality. Mathews gazed at the six graves with a searing pang of regret. Perhaps the bones had already dissolved in the moist jungle soil, but he carefully tended the graves as a lasting monument to his own loss, to a loss that seemed more tragic with each passing year as his life drew to a close, to the loss of life itself. But for the stupid accident, he might have achieved that which men of Earth had dreamed of for as long as there had been dreams.

And life was good. Even on this savage planet it was good. He had been too young when he arrived to feel deeply the loss of the civilized splendors of Earth. His very youth had given him much in common with the child-like *Rualis*. He had enjoyed love and laughter, the hunt, the occasional, half-coming tribal war. He had helped the *Rualis* to become strong, and they gave him lasting honor.

Life was good, and it was beating its measured way to the inevitable end, to the damp soil of the jungle. And it might have been otherwise.

Mathews got wearily to his feet, and went to work with the clumsy, stone-bladed hoe. He cleared the green shoots from around the headstones he had carved with such care so many years ago. The mounds had to be reshaped after every rainy season. The jungle was perennially encroaching upon the clearing. The open ground had been much larger in his younger days, but as he grew older he allowed the jungle to creep back. Now it seemed a struggle to hold the space remaining.

There were times when he thought he should remove the graves to a high, dry place on the mountain side. But this place seemed to belong to them, and they to it—here, where their quest had ended, hundreds of light-years from Wurr's planet of immortality, wherever it might be.

He could not work long in the savage jungle heat. He gathered up his things, and followed the faint trail back to the Tree. Still singing, the *Rualis* took their places behind him, and he led them out of the jungle.

The climb up the slope seemed harder with each trip. When he reached the village he was quite content to sit down and rest, and watch the children play, before he attempted the steep path to his own hut. He held a special affection for the village children, and they for him. Perhaps, he thought, it was because none of his wives had been able to bear him children, though when he gave them to men of their own race they always proved fertile. It was as though fate were not content with denying him physical immortality, and must also cut him off from the perpetuity that children could have secured for him. In his more bitter moments he believed that the six who died had been dealt with more kindly.

But he had to admit that life was good. The *Rualis* were an attractive, graceful, light-skinned people—small of stature, much smaller than he, but sturdy and strong. The shildren matured with astonishing rapidity. It was only three Earth years from birth to adolescence, and then, alas, perhaps another seven or eight years from maturity to death. The *Rualis* who reached the age of fifteen, by Earth standards, were rare. Mathews had watched many generations come and go, and he'd had wives from every generation, but no children. He had long since given up the thought of children.

When he had rested, he got to his feet and walked slowly down the village street. A child caught his attention, a girl, and even among the charming *Rualis* children her beauty was exceptional. With a smile, he stopped to admire her.

The mother appeared in the doorway of the hut, and turned aside shyly when he saw him. "You have a beautiful child," Mathews said to her. "She is the image of her great-great grandmother. Or perhaps it was her great-great-great grandmother—I do not recall exactly. But she, too was a beautiful child."

The mother was pleased, but held herself apart with proper good manners. The child prattled excitedly. "Today is my birth festival," she told Mathews.

He said gravely, "Today is also my birth festival."

The child seemed startled. "What is your age, Earthman?"

Mathews smiled wistfully. How was he to explain seventy-four Earth years to this child? And the *Rualis* had no number large enough to embrace the quantity of the fifty-seven day months they called years that Mathews' life had spanned.

"I do not know," he said. "I cannot remember."

He turned, and sought the path to his hut . . . .

The child watched him until he disappeared. "Mother," she said, "Why does the Earthman not know his age?"

"Hush," the mother said soothingly. "Age does not matter to the Earthman. Like the Tree, his kind lives forever."

92

THEY'RE PLAYING OUR SONG

Harry Harrison

LOVE, LOVE, LOVE-LEE love—my love's forgotten me-eee . . . !!''
stomp-stomp-stomp—
STOMP - STOMP - STOMP!! echoed through the cavernous Paramount
as the thousands of teenagers stamped their feet in hysterical unison,
drowning out the amplified efforts of the quartet on the stage, writhing and
tearing at their guitars unheard but not unappreciated. Squealings and
stampings shattered the air and more than one flat-chested thin-flanked and
orgiastic young thing leaped in frenzy and collapsed unconscious in the
aisle. The bored ushers—with ear plugs—dragged them onto the waiting
stretchers and carried them out.

The closing number was the Spiders' top-hit-favorite, ''Were My Pitying
Heart To Break From Pitying You'' and they hurled themselves into it with
reckless abandon, black hair falling low over their foreheads, arms thrashing and hips rotating like epileptic marionettes. They ended with a flourish
and their enamored audience had one last sight of them bowing as the
curtains closed, and with love swelling their hearts hurled after them a final
hoarse chorus of cries of worship. There had never been anything like it in
the history of show business—well, there had been things like it—but The
Spiders were surely the latest and best.

They were ushered down a back stairway and through an unmarked exit
to avoid the press of autograph hounds at the stage door.

Their yellow Rolls-Royce spun them back to their hotel and the bowing
manager personally showed them into the service elevator and up to their
suite.

''Quickly!'' he cozened. ''Screams approach—they are coming down
the hall.'' They pushed in hurriedly and Bingo locked the door just in time.

''That was close,'' Wango said, throwing his guitar onto the couch.

Then the door to one of the bedrooms burst open and at once four lank-haired, autograph-book clutching girls rushed out: they had bribed a chambermaid and lain there in concealment the entire day.

"Shall we?" Bingo asked.

"Sure," Lingo said and unbuttoned his coat.

The girls screamed even louder when they saw the many, hairy arms concealed there, and tried to flee. But the black suited figures leapt with strange agility and arrow-sharp egg-laying ovipositors penetrated the quivering flesh.

Their heightened screams were drowned in the other screams from beyond the door:

"The Spiders! The Spiders!! We want THE SPIDERS!!"

93

A THOUSAND DEATHS

Jack London

I HAD BEEN in the water about an hour, and cold, exhausted, with a terrible cramp in my right calf, it seemed as though my hour had come. Fruitlessly struggling against the strong ebb tide, I had beheld the maddening procession of the waterfront lights slip by; but now I gave up attempting to breast the stream and contended myself with the bitter thoughts of a wasted career, now drawing to a close.

It had been my luck to come of good, English stock, but of parents whose account with the bankers far exceeded their knowledge of child-nature and the rearing of children. While born with a silver spoon in my mouth, the blessed atmosphere of the home circle was to me unknown. My father, a very learned man and a celebrated antiquarian, gave no thought to his family, being constantly lost in the abstractions of his study; while my mother, noted far more for her good looks than her good sense, sated herself with the adulation of the society in which she was perpetually plunged. I went through the regular school and college routine of a boy of the English bourgeoisie, and as the years brought me increasing strength and passions, my parents, suddenly became aware that I was possessed of an immortal soul, and endeavored to draw the curb. But it was too late; I perpetrated the wildest and most audacious folly, and was disowned by my people; ostracized by the society I had so long outraged, and with the thousand pounds my father gave me, with the declaration that he would neither see me again nor give me more, I took a first-class passage to Australia.

Since then my life had been one long peregrination—from the Orient to the Occident, from the Arctic to the Antarctic—to find myself at last, able seaman at thirty, in the full vigor of my manhood, drowning in San Francisco Bay because of a disastrously successful attempt to desert my ship.

My right leg was drawn up by the cramp, and I was suffering the keenest agony. A slight breeze stirred up a choppy sea, which washed into my mouth and down my throat, nor could I prevent it. Though I still contrived to keep afloat, it was merely mechanical, for I was rapidly becoming unconscious. I have a dim recollection of drifting past the seawall, and of catching a glimpse of an upriver steamer's starboard light; then everything became a blank.

I heard the low hum of insect life, and felt the balmy air of a spring morning fanning my cheek. Gradually it assumed a rhythmic flow, to whose soft pulsations my body seemed to respond. I floated on the gentle bosom of a summer's sea, rising and falling with dreamy pleasure on each crooning wave. But the pulsations grew stronger; the humming, louder; the waves, larger, fiercer—I was dashed about on a stormy sea. A great agony fastened upon me. Brilliant, intermittent sparks of light flashed athwart my inner consciousness; in my ears there was the sound of many waters; then a sudden snapping of an intangible something, and I awoke.

The scene, of which I was a protagonist, was a curious one. A glance sufficed to inform me that I lay on the cabin floor of some gentleman's yacht, in amost uncomfortable posture. On either side, grasping my arms and working them up and down like pump handles, were two peculiarly clad, dark-skinned creatures. Though conversant with most aboriginal types, I could not conjecture their nationality. Some attachment had been fastened about my head, which connected my respiratory organs with the machine I shall next describe. My nostrils, however, had been closed, forcing me to breathe through the mouth. Foreshortened by the obliquity of my line of vision, I beheld two tubes, similar to small hosing but of different composition, which emerged from my mouth and went off at an acute angle from each other. The first came to an abrupt termination and lay on the floor beside me; the second traversed the floor in numerous coils, connecting with the apparatus I have promised to describe.

In the days before my life became tangential, I had dabbled not a little in science, and conversant with the appurtenances and general paraphernalia of the laboratory, I appreciated the machine I now beheld. It was composed chiefly of glass, the construction being of that crude sort which is employed for experimentative purposes. A vessel of water was surrounded by an air chamber, to which was fixed a vertical tube, surmounted by a globe. In the center of this was a vacuum gauge. The water of the tube moved upwards and downwards, creating alternate inhalations and exhalations, which were in turn communicated to me through the hose. With this, and the aid of the men who pumped my arms so vigorously, had the process of breathing been artificially carried on, my chest rising and falling and my lungs expanding and contracting, till nature could be persuaded to again take up her wonted labor.

As I opened my eyes the appliance about my head, nostrils and mouth was removed. Draining a stiff three fingers of brandy, I staggered to my feet to thank my preserver, and confronted—my father. But long years of fellowship with danger had taught me self-control, and I waited to see if he would recognize me. Not so; he saw in me no more than a runaway sailor and treated my accordingly.

Leaving me to the care of the blackies, he fell to revising the notes he had made on my resuscitation. As I ate of the handsome fare served up to me, confusion began on deck, and from the chanteys of the sailors and the rattling of blacks and tackles I surmised that we were getting under way. What a lark! Off on a cruise with my recluse father into the wide Pacific! Little did I realize, as I laughed to myself, which side the joke was to be on. Aye, had I known, I would have plunged overboard and welcomed the dirty fo'c'sle from which I had just escaped.

I was not allowed on deck till we had sunk the Farallones and the last pilot boat. I appreciated this forethought on the part of my father and made it a point to thank him heartily, in my bluff seaman's manner. I could not suspect that he had his own ends in view, in thus keeping my presence secret to all save the crew. He told me briefly of my rescue by his sailors, assuring me that the obligation was on his side, as my appearance had been most opportune. He had constructed the appartus for the vindication of a theory concerning certain biological phenomena, and had been waiting for an opportunity to use it.

"You have proved it beyond all doubt," he said; then added with a sigh, "But only in the small matter of drowning."

But, to take a reef in my yarn—he offered me an advance of two pounds on my previous wages to sail with him, and this I considered handsome, for he really did not need me. Contrary to my expectations, I did not join the sailors; mess, for'ard, being assigned to a comfortable stateroom and eating at the captain's table. He had perceived that I was no common sailor, and I resolved to take this chance for reinstating myself in his good graces. I wove a fictitious past to account for my education and present position, and did my best to come in touch with him. I was not long in disclosing a predilection for scientific pursuits, nor he in appreciating my aptitude. I became his assistant, with a corresponding increase in wages, and before long, as he grew confidential and expounded his theories, I was as enthusiastic as himself.

The days flew quickly by, for I was deeply interested in my new studies, passing my waking hours in his well-stocked library, or listening to his plans and aiding him in his laboratory work. But we were forced to forego many enticing experiments, a rolling ship not being exactly the proper place for delicate or intricate work. He promised me, however, many delightful hours in the magnificent laboratory for which we were bound. He had taken possession of an uncharted South Sea island, as he said, and turned it into a scientific paradise.

We had not been on the island long, before I discovered the horrible mare's nest I had fallen into. But before I describe the strange things which came to pass, I must briefly outline the causes which culminated in as startling an experience as ever fell to the lot of man.

Late in life, my father had abandoned the musty charms of antiquity and succumbed to the more fascinating ones embraced under the general head of biology. Having been thoroughly grounded during his youth in the fundamentals, he rapidly explored all the higher branches as far as the scientific world had gone, and found himself on the no-man's land of the unknowable. It was his intention to preempt some of this unclaimed territory, and it was at this stage of his investigations that we had been thrown together. Having a good brain, though I say it myself, I had mastered his speculations and methods of reasoning, becoming almost as mad as himself. But I should not say this. The marvelous results we afterwards obtained can only go to prove this sanity. I can but say that he was the most abnormal specimen of cold-blooded cruelty I have ever seen.

After having penetrated the dual mysteries of pathology and psychology, his thought had led him to the verge of a great field, for which, the better to explore, he began studies in higher organic chemistry, pathology, toxicology, and other sciences and subsciences rendered kindred as accessories to his speculative hypotheses. Starting from the proposition that the direct cause of the temporary and permanent array of vitality was due to the coagulation of certain elements and compounds in the protoplasm, he had isolated and subjected these various substances to innumerable experiments. Since the temporary arrest of vitality in an organism brought coma, and a permanent arrest death, he held that by artificial means this coagulation of the protoplasm could be retarded, prevented, and even overcome in the extreme states of solidification. Or, to do away with the technical nomenclature, he argued that death, when not violent and in which none of the organs had suffered injury, was merely suspended vitality; and that, in such instances, life could be induced to resume its functions by the use of proper methods. This, then, was his idea: To discover the method—and by practical experimentation prove the possibility—of renewing vitality in a structure from which life had seemingly fled. Of course, he recognized the futility of such endeavor after decomposition had set in; he must have organisms which but the moment, the hour, or the day before, had been quick with life. With me, in a crude way, he had proved this theory. I was really drowned, really dead, when picked from the water of San Francisco Bay—but the vital spark had been renewed by means of his aerotherapeutical apparatus, as he called it.

Now to his dark purpose concerning me. He first showed me how completely I was in his power. He had sent the yacht away for a year, retaining only his two blackies, who were utterly devoted to him. He then made an exhaustive review of his theory and outlined the method of proof he had adopted, concluding with the startling announcement that I was to be his subject.

I had faced death and weighed my chances in many a desperate venture, but never in one of this nature. I can swear I am no coward, yet this proposition of journeying back and forth across the borderland of death put the yellow fear in me. I asked for time, which he granted at the same time assuring me that but the one course was open—I must submit. Escape from the island was out of the question; escape by suicide was not to be entertained, though really preferable to what it seemed I must undergo; my only hope was to destroy my captors. But his latter was frustrated through the precautions taken by my father. I was subjected to a constant surveillance, even in my sleep being guarded by one or the other of the blacks.

Having pleaded in vain, I announced and proved that I was his son. It was my last card, and I had placed all my hopes upon it. But he was inexorable; he was not a father but a scientific machine. I wonder yet how it ever came to pass that he married my mother or begat me, for there was not the slightest grain of emotion in his makeup. Reason was all in all to him, nor could he understand such things as love or sympathy in others, except as petty weaknesses which should be overcome. So he informed me that in the beginning he had given me life, and who had better right to take it away than he? Such, he said, was not his desire, however; he merely wished to borrow it occasionally, promising to return it punctually at that appointed time. Of course, there was a liability of mishaps, but I could do no more than take the chances, since the affairs of men were full of such.

The better to insure success, he wished me to be in the best possible condition, so I was dieted and trained like a great athlete before a decisive contest. What could I do? If I had to undergo the peril, it were best to be in good shape. In my intervals of relaxation he allowed me to assist in the arranging of the apparatus and in the various subsidary experiments. The interest I took in all such operations can be imagined. I mastered the work as thoroughly as he, and often had the pleasure of seeing some of my suggestions of alterations put into effect. After such events I would smile grimly, conscious of officiating at my own funeral.

He began by inaugurating a series of experiments in toxicology. When all was ready, I was killed by a stiff dose of strychnine and allowed to lie dead for some twenty hours. During that period my body was dead, absolutely dead. All respiration and circulation ceased; but the frightful part of it was, that while the protoplasmic coagulation proceeded, I retained consciousness and was enabled to study it in all its ghastly details.

The apparatus to bring me back to life was an airtight chamber, fitted to receive my body. The mechanism was simple—a few valves, a rotary shaft and crank, and an electric motor. When in operation, the interior atmosphere was alternately condensed and rarified, thus communicating to my lungs an artificial respiration without the agency of the hosing previously used. Though my body was inert, and, for all I knew, in the first stages of decomposition, I was cognizant of everything that transpired. I knew when they placed me in the chamber, and though all my senses were quiescent, I was aware of hypodermic injections of a compound to react upon the coagulatory process. Then the chamber was closed and the machinery started. My anxiety was terrible; but the circulation became gradually restored, the different organs began to carry on their respective functions, and in an hour's time I was eating a hearty dinner.

It cannot be said that I participated in this series, nor in the subsequent ones, with much verve; but after two ineffectual attempts at escape, I began to take quite an interest. Besides, I was becoming accustomed. My father was beside himself in success, and as the months rolled by his speculations took wilder and yet wilder flights. We ranged through the three great classes of poisons, the neurotics, the gaseous and the irritants, but carefully avoided some of the mineral irritants and passed up the whole group of corrosives. During the poison regime I became quite accustomed to dying, and had but one mishap to shake my growing confidence. Scarifying a number of lesser blood vessels in my arm, he introduced a minute quantity of that most frightful of poisons, the arrow poison, or curare. I lost consciousness at the start, quickly followed by the cessation of respiration and circulation, and so far had the solidification of the protoplasm advanced, that he gave up all hope. But at the last moment he applied a discovery he had been working upon, receiving such encouragement as to redouble his efforts.

In a glass vacuum, similar but not exactly like a Crookes' tube was placed a magnetic field. When penetrated by polarized light, it gave no phenomena of phosphorescence nor of rectilinear projection of atoms, but emitted nonluminous rays, similar to the X ray. While the X ray could reveal opaque objects hidden in dense mediums, this was possessed of far subtler penetration. By this he photographed my body, and found on the negative an infinite number of blurred shadows, due to the chemical and electric motions still going on. This was infalliable proof that the rigor mortis in which I lay was not genuine; that is, those mysterious forces, those delicate bonds which held my soul to my body were still in action. The resultants of all other poisons were unapparent, save those of mercurial compounds, which usually left me languid for several days.

Another series of delightful experiments was with electricity. We verified Tesla's assertion that high currents were utterly harmless by passing 100,000 volts through my body. As this did not affect me, the current was reduced to 2,500, and I was quickly electrocuted. This time he ventured so far as to allow me to remain dead, or in a state of suspended vitality, for three days. It fook four hours to bring me back.

Once, he superinduced lockjaw; but the agony of dying was so great that I positively refused to undergo similar experiments. The easiest deaths were by asphyxiation, such as drowning, strangling, and suffocation by gas; while those by morphine, opium, cocaine, and chloroform, were not at all hard.

Another time, after being suffocated, he kept me in cold storage for three months, not permitting me to freeze or decay. This was without my knowledge, and I was in a great fright on discovering the lapse of time. I became afraid of what he might do with me when I lay dead, my alarm being increased by the predilection he was beginning to betray towards vivisection. The last time I was resurrected, I discovered that he had been tampering with my breast. Though he had carefully dressed and sewed the incisions up, they were so severe that I had to take to my bed for some time. It was during my convalescence that I evolved the plan by which I ultimately escaped.

While feigning unbounded enthusiasm in the work, I asked and received a vacation from my moribund occupation. During this period I devoted myself to laboratory work, while he was too deep in the vivisection of the many animals captured by the blacks to take notice of my work.

It was on these two propositions that I constructed my theory: First, electrolysis, or the decomposition of water into its constituent gases by means of electricity; and, second, by the hypothetical existence of a force, the converse of gravitation, which Astor has named "apergy." Terrestrial attraction, for instance, merely draws objects together but does not combine them; hence apergy is merely repulsion. Now, atomic or molecular attraction not only draws objects together but intergrates them; and it was the converse of this, or a disintegrative force, which I wished to not only discover and produce, but to direct at will. Thus, the molecules of hydrogen and oxygen reacting on each other, separate and create new molecules, containing both elements and forming water. Electrolysis causes these molecules to split up and resume their original condition, producing the two gases separately. The force I wished to find must not only do this with two, but with all elements, no matter in what compounds they exist. If I could then entice my father within its radius, he would be instantly disintegrated and set flying to the four quarters, a mass of isolated elements.

It must not be understood that this force, which I finally came to control, annihilated matter; it merely annihilated form. Nor, as I soon discovered, had it any effect on inorganic structure; but to all organic form it was absolutely fatal. This partiality puzzled me at first, though had I stopped to think deeper I would have seen through it. Since the number of atoms in organic molecules is far greater than in the most complex mineral molecules, organic compounds are characterized by their instability and the ease with which they are split up by physical forces and chemical reagents.

By two powerful batteries, connected with magnets constructed specially for this purpose, two tremendous forces were projected. Considered apart from each other, they were perfectly harmless; but they accomplished their purpose by focusing at an invisible point in midair. After practically demonstrating its success, besides narrowly escaping being blown into nothingness, I laid my trap. Concealing the magnets, so that their force made the whole space of my chamber doorway a field of death, and placing by my couch a button by which I could throw the current from the storage batteries, I climbed into bed.

The blackies still guarded my sleeping quarters, one relieving the other at midnight. I turned on the current as soon as the first man arrived. Hardly had I begun to doze, when I was aroused by a sharp, metallic tinkle. There, on the mid-threshold, lay the collar of Dan, my father's St. Bernard. My keeper ran to pick it up. He disappeared like a gust of wind, his clothes falling to the floor in a heap. There was a slight whiff of ozone in the air, but since the principal gaseous components of his body were hydrogen, oxygen and nitrogen, which are equally colorless and odorless, there was no other manifestation of his departure. Yet when I shut off the current and removed the garments, I found a deposit of carbon in the form of animal charcoal; also other powders, the isolated, solid elements of his organism, such as sulphur, potassium and iron. Resetting the trap, I crawled back to bed. At midnight I got up and removed the remains of the second black, and then slept peacefully till morning.

I was awakened by the strident voice of my father, who was calling to me from across the laboratory. I laughed to myself. There had been no one to call him and he overslept. I could hear him as he approached my room with the intention of rousing me, and so I sat up in bed, the better to observe his translation—perhaps apotheosis were a better term. He paused a moment at the threshold, then took the fatal step. Puff! It was like the wind sighing among the pines. He was gone. His clothes fell in a fantastic heap on the floor. Besides ozone, I noticed the faint, garlic-like odor of phosphorous. A little pile of elementary solids lay among his garments. That was all. The wide world lay before me. My captors were no more.

94

THRESHOLD

Sharon Webb

Me not hurt rabbit. Me not. Kodi love rabbit

WHEN THE PHONE rang, she knew it was her mother. It wasn't telepathy; it was her mother's unerring sense of timing. Sighing, she plopped the "who-dunnit" face down on its red herring, reached for her glass of sherry with one hand and the telephone with the other.

"Jean?" chirped the voice on the other end.

Who else? "Hello, Mother." She slid her toes a tad closer to the fire. "I thought it was you."

"You always say that, dear. Doesn't anyone else ever call?"

"Not much."

"What were you doing?"

"Reading."

A faint sigh blew over the receiver. "Why don't you try and get out more, dear? See some young men. Go to a dance."

"I'll think about it, Mother." A swallow of the Olorosos rolled warmly down her throat. "I really will."

Another sigh with a slight increase in volume—"Your father and I worry about you so. I never know what to say to my friends. Just today Hannah asked about you. 'How's your darling Jean?' she said. Her Martha is pregnant with her second, you know. So what can I say to her? 'She's fine. Just fine. Who could ask for more? All day long she trains monkeys. At night she reads.' "

"Kodi isn't a monkey, Mother."

"Monkeys, apes—What's the difference?"

"Quite a bit, Mother." But it wasn't any use. Her mother had a convenient mind with its own unique logic. Mrs. Greenfield was incapable

593

of imagining her daughter working in a primate center with a gorilla. "This is what you went to college for? To be torn limb-from-limb? By a King Kong?" After the initial trauma, she'd totally repressed the idea. The "slavering, breast-beating beast" disappeared into a little crease in Mrs. Greenfield's brain to be forever replaced by a small brown rhesus with long tail and dirty habits.

Her mother's voice went on, "God permitting, if you should ever have a child of your own, if you ever give me a grandchild, you'll know what worry is."

But she did have a child: Kodi.

You dirty bad stink. Me not hurt rabbit. Me not.

A chill gust of wind whipped the rickety door out of Jean's hand as she tried to close it. Groaning hinges tugged at their fastenings.

A cheery voice said, "If that grant doesn't come through, we may have to hang up animal skins to keep out the weather."

Jean pushed the door shut and looked up to see Marian Whitmore who worked with the newest addition at the center, Tic Toc, who was eight months old. "I'm afraid you're right. How's Tic Toc?"

"Adorable. He sits around all day with his thumb in his mouth, but I have high hopes." Marian breezed off down the hall, then turned and said over her shoulder, "The boss is off to an early start. He's working with your Kodi now."

"I wonder why?" But Marian was gone. Jean walked down the wide, shabby hall past the communal room where the apes were allowed to gather and play together occasionally, and entered the large high-ceilinged room partially filled with sturdy second-hand furniture that doubled as Kodi's enclosure and Jean's office.

David Copeland, all angles and bones inside his clothes, sat cross-legged on the floor. His hands moved rapidly in sign. Kodi answered in Ameslan, leathery fingers moving through the words. Then she turned her face away and offered the back of her hand in a conciliatory gesture.

"She's lying again," he said to Jean.

Jean hung her coat in her locker, replacing it with a lab jacket. "What about?"

"Look over there."

She followed his gaze to the rabbit cage, bars bent in a neat parenthesis. "Oh no." The white rabbit lay motionless, its neck at an acute angle. "Kodi?"

He nodded. "I think she pulled the rabbit out to play with it. After she broke its neck, she stuffed it back in the cage."

Kodi was listening intently to the conversation, trying to piece its meaning together.

David turned to the young gorilla and signed, "You hurt the rabbit. You made the rabbit die."

Kodi sat back on her heels, confused. *Me not hurt rabbit. Rabbit not cry*.

"She doesn't understand 'die.'" Jean felt a quick flash of pity for the confused animal. "She hasn't learned that word."

"She's going to now. I can't miss this opportunity."

"Opportunity?"

"Of course. We're going to find out what the concept of death means to a primate. How she reacts to it."

Jean watched him manipulate Kodi's fingers into the position for "die." He repated the word over and over, emphasizing the sign, shaping Kodi's motions.

Die. Die. Die.

Poor mutt. Let's teach her what death is. And guilt. And all the other nasty things that humans wallow in.

Kodi's brow furrowed in concentration lines as she listened and watched intently.

Jean felt a slow fire of resentment smoulder. Damn David anyway. Damn him and his miserable rabbit experiment. Suspicion rose. Maybe he'd never been that interested at all in the reactions of the isolated apes to other species. If that scheme were only a way to beef up interest in the project and generate extra funding, how much more lucrative might this wrinkle be? The more she thought about it, the more convinced she was. When he'd ensconced the rabbit cage in Kodi's room, what had he expected? Really? Surely he had common sense enough to know that Kodi would want to touch the rabbit like any kid with a new toy.

Like any kid—And there she was, anthropomorphizing again. The cardinal sin in Copeland's Breviary. But dammit, where was the line anyway? Where had the prehuman crossed over the line into humanity? Use of tools? Nonsense. Lots of animals used tools; all the primates did. Language? Symbols? Abstract reasoning? Kodi used them all. All the Ameslaners did, and Kodi was second generation, the smartest of the lot. And yet, anthropomorphic fantasies aside, Kodi was beast—and her baby.

Ever since that day when David handed her a little wooly infant who grasped her hair with one hand and her blouse with another and snuggled to her breast with lonesome whimpers, she'd been hooked. She had coped with Kodi and with David for nearly eleven years. And in a strange way they were a family.

She'd nearly blown it too. Even today she couldn't forget her first meeting with David. She had breezed into his office for her interview, fresh BS in hand and visions of research grants and advanced degrees dancing in her head. "Hi, You Tarzan. Me Jean." She cringed at the memory. But how could she have known then that David Copeland was the most serious contender for the Humorless Man Award since Cotton Mather?

There he sat, single-mindedly manipulating Kodi's fingers, ignoring the confusion in the big beast's eyes.

Die. Die. Die.

Rabbit die.

"I'm only thinking of you, Jean," said the chirping telephone voice. "You know how I worry."

"I know, Mother."

"If I didn't love you, Jean, I wouldn't say these things to you."

"I know." And she did know. Her mother was trying to protect her, trying to shelter her from Bleak Old Age. She was trying to surround her with a husband and a flock of children because she saw it as better so. Hadn't it always been better so? Her mother was holding a set of values up that reflected like a carnival mirror onto her own, turning them into grotesques.

She knew her mother loved her. But why, God, why did it have to hurt so damned much?

Rabbit not eat. Rabbit not move. Rabbit die. Bad.

"Kodi?"

Kodi sat facing the corner in the traditional place for punishment. She stared at the blank wall and absently passed her woolly hand over her face in the Ameslan sign for "bad."

Poor beastie. All she needed was a dunce cap to make the picture complete. "Kodi? Why are you sitting in the corner?" Jean knelt beside the animal and touched her on the shoulder. Kodi's eyes did not meet hers.

"Kodi?"

Slowly, Kodi's hands moved in sign: *Rabbit die. Kodi make rabbit die. Kodi bad.*

596

So David has suceeded. Blast his soul. Jean rubbed the nape of a wooly neck. "It's all right, Kodi. It's all right. I'll make it all right," she said, knowing that the ape caught only a few of the whispered words, knowing too that the sound of her voice was soothing. She took Kodi's face in both hands and turned it toward her. "Want Jean to tickle Kodi?" It was an irresistible invitation.

The big sad eyes searched her face, the long fingers moved; *Please, Jean, tickle Kodi*.

And for awhile, it helped.

"I'm worried about Kodi."

"Who? Oh, that monkey of yours," said the voice on the line with a mixture of exasperation and amusement. Her mother neatly bent the conversation into a U-turn. "I wish you'd show a little concern for some of the important things, Jean."

"Like what, Mother?"

"Do you know what your poor father said to me last night? He said, 'Jean is the last, Momma. The last Greenfield. She's the end of the line.' "

"Well, I guess you should have had a boy, Mother." She knew before the words were out that it was the wrong thing to say.

"A boy! God forbid I should have another one driving nails into my coffin."

"I'm not driving nails, Mother. Listen, I really have to go. I have a lot of work to do, a paper to write—"

"Monkey business. Always the monkey business—"

There was more, but Jean turned if off as neatly as a tap. After a minute she quietly said, "Goodbye, Mother," and hung up the receiver.

She had never understood why people put such great store on the survival of the family name. She couldn't carry on that family name unless she married and refused to take her husband's name. Or, while she was thinking about defying convention, she could entertain the notion of having a bastard. And wouldn't Mother love that?

What did the family name represent anyway except a diluted gene pool that got more watered down with each passing generation? Did it really matter whether or not the pool dried up with her? "Of course not," she said aloud, startling herself with the intensity of her voice, startling herself even more with the knowledge that what she said had all the trappings of a lie. Because, somehow, put that way, it did seem to matter—as if the saying of it made her living and her dying more final.

Final. And when it was all over and done with, what would be left to show she'd made the trip? A half-dozen articles. Sixteen-going-on-seventeen loose-leaf notebooks crammed with compact notes and the written Ameslan notation she and David had developed for Kodi and the other apes.

Her work had always seemed important before.

She reached for her bottle of sherry, found it empty, and lit a cigarette. Wasn't that what mothers were for? To make you hold up your life and find it a little frayed at the seams? Ready for the rag bag. To make you ask, "why?" and "is that all?" To boil everything you are down to sixteen-going-on-seventeen notebooks?

When you got right down to it, Kodi had nearly as much to show for her simian existence. Jean had a notebook nearly full of the ape's typings: pages of the curls and squiggles that were the type-written mimics of Ameslan signs that she had so painstakingly developed and taught to Kodi.

She thumbed through the collection of Kodi's typings, reading the curls and hooks as easily as English. *Me Kodi.* said the first page, the fifth, the tenth. *Me Kodi.*

"You Kodi, me Jean," she said to herself, reflecting, wondering how she could define herself without Kodi, without that notebook. She slipped slowly through the pages. Page twenty-nine: *Me hungry. Me eat now.* Page forty-two: *Me hurt here.* Neither written Ameslan nor dry English notes could express the pain in Kodi's eyes that day, nor the anguish in hers as they waited for the vet's hurried visit. Page seventy-eight: A change here. Kodi was older, better able to use language. *Sweet. Eat. Eat sweet. Sweet eat.* She remembered the delight over that page, the amazement that the ape had translated sound to sign. "Kodi. You made a rhyme." And on the following pages, the repetitions of that rhyme and others—Kodi's delight over language as a toy. She turned the pages—a fib here, a game there. Fears, hurts, wants.

There's your life, Kodi," she said closing the noteobok, laying it beside the stack of her notes and articles. "And there's mine."

She had done it in kindness, she told herself in retrospect. She had tried to spare Kodi the guilt over the rabbit, tried to ease the hurt. She had said it out of kindness—and ignorance and stupidity. She had said: "You're not bad, Kodi. Not bad. Everything dies, Kodi. Everything."

And she had gone to great lengths to explain it.

Chair die.

Only living things, Kodi. Rabbits and trees and people. Everything.

Me think Tic Toc die.
"Tic Toc, too. But not for a long time."

Kodi didn't greet her with the usual deep throaty purr. She lay on the floor, neck at an odd angle, in a caricature of the rabbit.
"Kodi?"
Kodi's hand passed slowly over her face and made the sign for "bad."
There was a single sentence on the Ameslan typer: *Me think Kodi die.*

She had done it in kindness . . . the kindness of a meddling mother. All night, unable to sleep, she lashed herself with the guilt of it. Finally she got up dressed and went back to the center.

Kodi lay sleeping on the jumbled nest she had made in the corner, and there was something written on the Ameslan typer. The woods kept blurring until Jean had to wipe her eyes with a wadded Kleenex. She stood there a long time, holding the note, watching the sleeping animal. The guilt was still there, but there was something else, something growing—a feeling of wonder.

She looked at the paper again. Had some prehuman in man's distant past stood on the threshold of humanity, thrust there by the knowledge of his own mortality. Did he ask then those questions that grew into the beginnings of philosophy and religion and science? Did he think these same thoughts:

Me think me die.
Me cry.
Why die?
Why?

599

95

TO BE CONTINUED

Robert Silverberg

GAIUS TITUS MENENIUS sat thoughtfully in his oddly decorated apartment on Park Avenue, staring at the envelope that had just arrived. He contemplated it for a moment, noting with amusement that he was actually somewhat perturbed over the possible nature of its contents.

After a moment he elbowed up from the red contour-chair and crossed the room in three bounds. Still holding the envelope, he eased himself down on the long green couch near the wall, and, extending himself full-length, slit the envelope open with a neat flick of his fingernail. The medical report was within, as he had expected.

"Dear Mr. Riswell," it read. "I am herewith enclosing a copy of the laboratory report concerning your examination last week. I am pleased to report that our findings are positive—emphatically so. In view of our conversation, I am sure this finding will be extremely pleasing to you, and, of course, to your wife. Sincerely, F. D. Rowcliff, M.D."

Menenius read the letter through once again, examined the enclosed report, and allowed his face to open in a wide grin. It was almost an anticlimax after all these centuries. He couldn't bring himself to become very excited over it—not any more.

He stood up and stretched happily. "Well, Mr. Riswell," he said to himself, "I think this calls for a drink. In fact, a night on the town."

He chose a smart dinner jacket from his wardrobe and moved toward the door. Its swung open at his approach. He went out into the corridor and disappeared into the elevator, whistling gayly, his mind full of new plans and new thoughts.

It was a fine feeling. After two thousand years of waiting, he had finally achieved his maturity. He could have a son. At last!

601

"Good afternoon, Mr. Schuyler," said the barman. "Will it be the usual, sir?"

"Martini, of course," said W. M. Schuyler IV, seating himself casually on the padded stool in front of the bar.

Behind the projected personality of W. M. Schuyler IV, Gaius Titus smiled, mentally. W. M. Schuyler *always* drank Martinis. And they had pretty well better be dry—very dry.

The baroque strains of a Vivaldi violin concerto sang softly in the background. Schuyler watched the TV accompaniment—a dancing swirl of colors that moved with the music.

"Good afternoon, Miss Vanderpool," he heard the barman say. "An Old Fashioned?"

Schuyler took another sip of his Martini and looked up. The girl had appeared suddenly and had taken the seat next to him, looking her usual cool self.

"Sharon!" he said, putting just the right amount of exclamation point after it.

She turned to look at him and smiled, disclosing a brilliantly white array of perfect teeth. "Bill! I didn't notice you! How long have you been here?"

"Just arrived," Schuyler told her. "Just about a minute ago."

The barman put her drink down in front of her. She took a long sip without removing her eyes from him. Schuyler met her glance, and behind his eyes Gaius Titus was coldly appraising her in a new light.

He had met her in Kavanaugh's a month before, and he had readily enough added her to the string. Why not? She was young, pretty, intelligent, and made a pleasant companion. There had been others like her—a thousand others, two thousand, five thousand. One gets to meet quite a few in two millennia.

Only now Gaius Titus was finally mature, and had different needs. The string of girls to which Sharon belonged was going to be cut.

He wanted a wife.

"How's the lackey of Wall Street?" Sharon asked. "Still coining money faster than you know how to spend it?"

"I'll leave that for you to decide," he said. He signaled for two more drinks. "Care to take in a concert tonight, perchance? The Bach Group's giving a benefit this evening, you know, and I'm told there still are a few hundred-dollar seats left—"

There, Gaius Titus thought. The bait has been cast. She ought to respond.

She whistled, a long low, sophisticated whistle. "I'd venture that business is fairly good, then,'' she said. Her eyes fell. ''But I don't want to let you go to all that expense on my account, Bill.''

''It's nothing,'' Schuyler insisted, while Gaius Titus continued to weigh her in the balance. ''They're doing the Fourth Brandenburg, and Renoli's playing the Goldberg Variarions. How about?''

She met his gaze evenly. ''Sorry, Bill. I have something else on for the evening.'' Her tone left no doubt in Schuyler's mind that there was little point pressing the discussion any further. Gaius Titus felt a sharp pang of disappointment.

Schuyler lifted his hand, palm forward. ''Say no more! I should have known you'd be booked up for tonight already.'' He paused. ''What about tomorrow?''he said, after a moment. ''There's a reading of Webster's 'Duchess of Malfi' down at the Dramatist's League. It's been one of my favorite plays for a long time.''

Silently smiling, he waited for her reply. The Webster was indeed, a long-time favorite. Gaius Titus recalled having attended one of its first performances, during his short employ in the court of James I. During the next three and a half centuries, he had formed a sentimental attachment for the creaky old melodrama.

''Not tomorrow either,'' Sharon said. ''Some other night, Bill.''

''All right,'' he said. ''Some other night.''

He reached out a hand and put it over hers, and they fell silent, listening to the Vivaldi in the background. He contemplated her high, sharp cheekbones in the purple halflight, wondering if she could be the one to bear the child he had waited for so long.

She had parried all his thrusts in a fashion that surprised him. She was not at all impressed by his display of wealth and culture. Titus reflected sadly that, perhaps, his Schuyler facet had been inadequate for her.

No, he thought, rejecting the idea. The haunting slow movement of the Vivaldi faded to its end and a lively allegro took its place. No; he had had too much experience in calculating personality-facets to fit the individual to have erred. He was certain that W. M. Schuyler IV was capable of handling Sharon.

For the first few hundred years of his unexpectedly long life, Gaius Titus had been forced to adopt the practice of turning on and off different personalities as a matter of mere survival. Things had been easy for a while after the fall of Rome, but with the coming of the Middle Ages he had needed all his skill to keep from runnning afoul of the superstitious. He had carefully built up a series of masks, of false fronts, as a survival mechanism.

How many times had he heard someone tell him, in jest, "You ought to be on the stage?" It struck home. He *was* on the stage. He *was* a man of many roles. Somewhere, beneath it all was the unalterable personality of Gaius Titus Menenius, *cives Romanus,* casting the shadows that were his many masks. But Gaius Titus was far below the surface—the surface which at the moment, was W. M. Schuyler IV; which had been Preston Riswell the week before, when he had visited the doctor for that fateful examination; which could be Leslie MacGregor or Sam Spielman or Phil Carlson tomorrow, depending on where Gaius Titus was, in what circumstances, and talking to whom. There was only one person he did not dare to be, and that was himself.

He wasn't immortal; he knew that. But he was *relatively* immortal. His life-span was tremendously decelerated, and it had taken him two thousand years to become, physically, a fertile adult. His span was roughly a hundred times that of a normal man's. And, according to what he had learned in the last century, his longevity should be transmittable genetically. All he needed now was someone to transmit it to.

Was it dominant? That he didn't know. That was the gamble he'd be making. He wondered what it would be like to watch his children and his children's children shrivel with age. Not pleasant, he thought.

The conversation with Sharon lagged; it was obvious that something was wrong with his Schuyler facet, at least so far as she was concerned, though he was unable to see where the trouble lay. After a few more minutes of disjointed chatter, she excused herself and left the bar. He watched her go. She had eluded him neatly. Where to next?

He thought he knew.

The East End bar was far downtown and not very reputable. Gaius Titus pushed through the revolving door and headed for the counter.

"Hi, Sam. Howsa boy?" the bartender said.

"Let's have a beer, Jerry." The bartender shoved a beer out toward the short, swarthy man in the leather jacket.

"Things all right?"

"Can't complain, Jerry. How's business?" Sam Spielman asked, as he lifted the beer to his mouth.

"It's lousy."

"It figures," Sam said. "Why don't you put in automatics? They're getting all the business now."

"Sure, Sam, sure. And where do I get the dough? That's twenty." He took the coins Sam dropped on the bar and grinned. "At least you can afford beer."

"You know me, Jerry," Sam said. "My credit's good."

Jerry nodded. "Good enough." He punched the coins into the register. "Ginger was looking for you, by the way. What you got against the gal?"

"Against her? Nothin'. What do y'mean?" Sam pushed out his beer shell for a refill.

"She's got a hooker out for you—you know that, don't you?" Jerry was grinning.

Gaius Titus thought: *She's not very bright, but she might very well serve my purpose. She has other characteristics worth transmitting.*

"Hi, Sammy."

He turned to look at her. "Hi, Ginger," he said. "How's the gal?"

"Not bad, honey." But she didn't look it. She looked as though she'd been dragged through the mill. Her blond hair was disarranged, her blouse was wrinkled, and, as usual, her teeth were discolored by the lipstick that had rubbed off on them.

"I love you, Sammy," she said softly.

"I love you, too," Sam said. He meant it.

Gaius Titus thought sourly: *But how many of her characteristics would I want to transmit. Still, she'll do, I guess. She's a solid girl.*

"Sam," she said, interrupting the flow of his thoughts, "why don't you come around more often? I miss you."

"Look, Ginger baby," Sam said. "Remember, I've got a long haul to pull. If I marry you, you gotta understand that I don't get home often. I gotta drive a truck. You might not see me more than once or twice a week."

Titus rubbed his forehead. He wasn't quite sure, after all, that the girl was worthwhile. She had spunk, all right, but was she worthy of fostering a race of immortals?

He didn't get a chance to find out. "Married?" the blonde's voice sounded incredulous. "Who the devil wants to get married. You've got me on the wrong track, Sam. I don't want to get myself tied down."

"Sure, honey, sure," he said. "But I thought—"

Ginger stood up. "You think anything you please, Sam. Anything you please. But not marriage."

She stared at him hard for a moment, and walked off. Sam looked after her morosely.

Gaius Titus grinned behind the Sam Spielman mask. She wasn't the girl either. Two thousand years of life had taught him that women were unpredictable, and he wasn't altogether surprised at her reacton to his proposal.

But he was disturbed over this second failure of the evening nevertheless. Was his judgment that far off? Perhaps, he though, he was losing the vital ability of personality-projection. He didn't like that idea.

For hours, Gaius Titus walked the streets of New York.

New York. Sure it was new. So was Old York, in England. Menenius had seen both of them grow from tiny villages to towns to cities to metropoli.

Metropoli. That was Greek. It had taken him twelve years to learn Greek. He hadn't rushed it.

Twelve years. And he still wasn't an adult. He could remember when the Emperor had seen the sign in the sky: *In hoc signo vinces*. And, at the age of four hundred and sixty-two, he'd still been too young to enter the service of the Empire.

Gaius Titus Menenius, Citizen of Rome. When he had been a child, he had thought Rome would last forever. But it hadn't; Rome had fallen. Egypt, which he had long thought of as an empire which would last forever, had gone even more quickly. It had died and putrified and sloughed off into the Great River which carries all life off into death.

Over the years and the centuries, races and peoples and nations had come and gone. And their passing had had no effect at all on Gaius Titus.

He was walking north. He turned left on Market Street, away from the Manhattan Bridge. Suddenly, he was tired of walking. He hailed a passing taxi.

He gave the cabby his address on Park Avenue and leaned back against the cushions to relax.

The first few centuries had been hard. He hadn't grown up, in the first place. By the time he was twenty, he had attained his full height—five feet nine. But he still looked like a seventeen-year-old.

And he had still looked that way nineteen hundred years later. It had been a long, hard drive to make enough money to live on during that time. Kids don't get well-paying jobs.

Actually, he'd lived a miserable hand-to-mouth existence for centuries. But the gradual collapse of the Christian ban on usury had opened the way for him to make some real money. Money makes more money, in a capitalistic system, if you have patience. Titus had time on his side.

It wasn't until the free-enterprise system had evolved that he started to get anywhere. But a deposit of several hundred pounds in the proper firm back in 1735 had netted a little extra money. The British East India

Company had brought his financial standing up a great deal, and judicious investments ever since left him comfortably fixed. He derived considerable amusement from the extraordinary effects compound interest exerted on a bank account a century old.

"Here you are, buddy," said the cab driver.

Gaius Titus climbed out and gave the driver a five note without asking for change.

Zeus, he thought. *I might as well make a night of it.*

He hadn't been really drunk since the stock market collapse back in 1929.

Leslie MacGregor pushed open the door of the San Marino bar in Greenwich Village and walked to the customary table in the back corner. Three people were already there, and the conversation was going well. Leslie waved a hand and the two men waved back. The girl grinned and beckoned.

"Come on over, Les," she yelled across the noisy room. "Mack has just sold a story!" Her deep voice was clear and firm.

Mack, the heavy-set man next to the wall, grinned self-consciously and picked up his beer.

Leslie strolled quietly over to the booth and sat down beside Corwyn, the odd man of the trio.

"Sold a story?" Leslie repeated archly.

Mack nodded. *"Chimerical Review,"* he said. "A little thing I called 'Pluck Up the Torch.' Not much, but it's a sale, you know."

"If one wants to prostitute one's art," said Corwyn.

Leslie frowned at him. "Don't be snide. After all, Mack has to pay his rent." Then he turned toward the girl. "Lorraine, could I talk to you a moment?"

She brushed the blonde hair back from the shoulders of her black turtleneck sweater and widened the grin on her face.

"Sure, Les," she said in her oddly deep, almost masculine voice. "What's all the big secret?"

No secret, thought Gaius Titus. What I want is simple enough.

For a long time, he had thought that near-immortality carried with it the curse of sterility. Now he knew it was simply a matter of time—of growing up.

As he stood up to walk to the bar with Lorraine, he caught a glimpse of himself in the dusty mirror behind the bar. He didn't look much over twenty-five. But things had been changing in the past fifty years. He had never had a heavy beard before; he had not developed his husky baritone voice until a year before the outbreak of the First World War.

It had been difficult, at first, to hide his immortality. Changing names, changing residences, changing, changing, changing. Until he had found that he didn't have to change—not deep inside.

People don't recognize faces. Faces are essentially all alike. Two eyes, two ears, a nose, a mouth. What more is there to a face? Only the personality behind it.

A personality is something that is projected—something put on display for others to see. And Gaius Titus Menenius had found that two thousand years of experience had given him enough internal psychological reality to be able to project any personality he wanted to. All he needed was a change of dress and a change of personality to be a different person. His face changed subtly to fit the person who was wearing it; no one had ever caught on.

Lorraine sat down on the bar stool. "Beer," she said to the bartender. "What's the matter, Les? What's eating you?"

He studied her firm, strong features, her deep, mocking eyes. "Lorraine," he said softly, "will you marry me?"

She blinked. "Marry you? You? Marry?" She grinned again. "Who'd ever think it? A bourgeois conformist, like all the rest." Then she shook her head. "No, Les. Even if you're kidding, you ought to know better than that. What's the gag?"

"No gag," said Leslie, and Gaius Titus fought his surprise and shock at his third failure. "I see your point," Leslie said. "Forget it. Give my best to everyone." He got up without drinking his beer and walked out the door.

Leslie stepped out into the street and started heading for the subway. Then Gaius Titus Menenius, withdrawing the mask, checked himself and hailed a cab.

He got into the cab and gave the driver his home address. He didn't see any reason for further pursuing his adventures that evening.

He was mystified. How could *three* personality-facets fail so completely? He had been handling these three girls well ever since he had met them, but tonight, going from one to the next, as soon as he made any serious ventures toward any of them the whole thing folded. Why?

"It's a lousy world," he told the driver, assuming for the moment the mask of Phil Carlson, cynical newsman. "Damn lousy." His voice was a biting rasp.

"What's wrong, buddy?"

"Had a fight with all three of my girls. It's a lousy world."

"I'll buy that," the driver said. The cab swung up into Park. "But look at it this way, pal: who needs them?"

For a moment the mask blurred and fell aside, and it was Gaius Titus, not Phil Carlson, who said, "That's exactly right! Who needs them?" He gave the driver a bill and got out of the cab.

Who needs them? It was a good question. There were plenty of girls. Why should he saddle himself with Sharon, or Ginger, or Lorraine? They all had their good qualities—Sharon's social grace, Ginger's vigor and drive, Lorraine's rugged intellectualism. They were all three good-looking girls, tall, attractive, well put together. But yet each one, he realized, lacked something that the other had. None of them was really *worthy* by herself, he thought, apologizing to himself for what another man might call conceit, or sour grapes.

None of them would really do. But if somehow, some way, he could manage to combine those three leggy girls, those three personalities into one body, *there* would be a girl—

He gasped.

He whirled and caught sight of the cab he had just vacated.

"Hey, cabby!" Titus called. "Come back here! Take me back to the San Marino!"

She wasn't there. As Leslie burst in, he caught sight of Corwyn, sitting alone and grinning twistedly over a beer.

"Where'd they go? Where's Lorraine?"

The little man lifted his shoulders and eyebrows in an elaborate shrug. "They left about a minute ago. No, it was closer to ten, wasn't it? They went in separate directions. They left me here."

"Thanks," Leslie said.

Scratch number One, Titus thought. He ran to the phone booth in the back, dialed Information, and demanded the number of the East End Bar. After some fumbling, the operator found it.

He dialed. The bartender's tired face appeared in the screeen.

"Hello, Sam," the barkeep said. "What's doing?"

"Do me a favor, Jerry," Sam said. "Look around your place for Ginger."

"She ain't here, Sam," the bartender said. "Haven't seen her since you two blew out of here a while back." Jerry's eyes narrowed. "I ain't never seen you dressed up like that before, Sam, you know?"

Gaius Titus crouched down suddenly to get out of range of the screen.

"I'm celebrating tonight, Jerry," he said, and broke the connection.

Ginger wasn't to be found either, eh? That left only Sharon. He couldn't call Kavanaugh's—they wouldn't give a caller any information about their patrons. Grabbing another taxi, he shot across town to Kavanaugh's.

Sharon wasn't there when Schuyler entered. She hadn't been in since the afternoon, a waiter informed him, after receiving a small gratuity. Schuyler had a drink and left. Gaius Titus returned to his apartment, tingling with an excitement he hadn't known for centuries.

He returned to Kavanaugh's the next night, and the next. Still no sign of her.

The following evening, though, when he entered the bar, she was sitting there, nursing an Old Fashioned. He slid onto the seat next to her. She looked up in surprise.

"Bill! Good to see you again."

"The same here," Gaius Titus said. "It's good to see you again—Ginger. Or is it Lorraine?"

She paled and put her hand to her mouth. Then, covering, she said, "what do you mean, Bill? Have you had too many drinks tonight?"

"Possibly," Titus said. "I stopped off in the San Marino before I came up. You weren't there, Lorraine. That deep voice is quite a trick, I have to admit. I had a drink with Mack and Corwyn. Then I went over to the East End, Ginger. You weren't there, either. So," he said, "there was only one place left to find you, Sharon."

She stared at him for a long moment. Finally she said, simply, "Who are you?"

"Leslie MacGregor," Titus said. "Also Sam Spielman. And W. M. Schuyler. Plus two or three other people. The name is Gaius Titus Menenius, at your service."

"I still don't understand—"

"Yes, you do," Titus said. "You are clever—but not clever enough. Your little game had me going for almost a month, you know? And it's not easy to fool a man my age."

"When did you find out?" the girl asked weakly.

"Monday night, when I saw all three of you within a couple of hours."

"You're—"

"Yes. I'm like you," he said. "But I'll give you credit: I didn't see through it until I was on my way home. You were using my own camouflage technique against me, and I didn't spot it for what it was. What's your real name?"

610

"Mary Bradford," she said. "I was English, originally. Of fine Plantagenet stock. I'm really a Puritan at heart, you see." She was grinning slyly.

"Oh? Mayflower descendant?" Titus asked teasingly.

"No," Mary replied. "Not a descendant. A passenger. And I'll tell you—I was awfully happy to get out of England and over here to Plymouth Colony."

He toyed with her empty glass. "You didn't like England? Probably my fault. I was a minor functionary in King James' court in the early seventeenth century."

They giggled together over it. Titus stared at her, his pulse pounding harder and harder. She stared back. Her eyes were smiling.

"I didn't think there was another one," she said after a while. "It was so strange, never growing old. I was afraid they'd burn me as a witch. I had to keep changing, moving all the time. It wasn't a pleasant life. It's better lately—I enjoy these little poses. But I'm glad you caught on to me," she said. She reached out and took his hand. "I guess I would never had been smart enough to connect you and Lesie and Sam, the way you did Sharon and Ginger and Lorraine. You play the game too well for me."

"In two thousand years," Titus said, not caring if the waiter overheard him, "I never found another one like me. Believe me, Mary, I looked. I looked hard, and I've had plenty of time to search. And then to find you, hiding behind the faces of three girls I knew!"

He squeezed her hand. The next statement followed logically for him. "Now that we've found each other," he said softly, "we can have a child. A third immortal."

Her face showed radiant enthusiasm. "Wonderful!" she cried. "When can we get married?"

"How about tomor-" he started to say. Then a thought struck him. "Mary?"

"What . . . Titus?"

"How old did you say you were? When were you born?" he asked.

She thought for a moment. "1597," she said. "I'm nearly four hundred."

He nodded, dumb with growing frustration. Only four hundred? That meant—that meant she was now the equivalent of a three-year old child!

"When can we get married?" she repeated.

"There's no hurry," Titus said dully, letting her hand drop. "We have eleven hundred years."

611

96

TOO MANY EGGS

Kris Neville

COXE, AN UNUSUALLY phlegmatic citizen, came to buy the new refrigerator in the usual fashion. He was looking for a bargain. It was the latest model, fresh from the new production line in Los Angeles, and was marked down considerably below standard. The freezing compartment held 245 lbs. of meat.

"How come so cheap?" Coxe wanted to know.

"Frankly," the salesman said, "I asked myself that. Usually there's a dent in them or something, when they have that factory tag on them. But I checked it over and I can't find anything wrong with it. However, she goes as is."

"At that price," Coxe said, "I'll take it."

It arrived, refinished in a copper color to his specifications, the following Tuesday. It was plugged in and operated perfectly. He checked it out by freezing ice cubes.

Wednesday evening, when he opened the door to chill some beer, there was a package in the freezing compartment. He took out the package.

It was some sort of plastic and appeared to contain fish eggs.

Coxe had not seen fresh fish eggs, considered by some a delicacy, for a number of years.

He chilled the beer and fried the eggs.

Both tasted about right.

The following Friday, his girlfriend came over to fix dinner for him, and when she looked in the freezing compartment, she said, "What's this?"

"Fish eggs," Coxe said. "How many of them?"

"Two packages."

"We'll fry them up for breakfast," he said.

613

Saturday morning, there were three packages of eggs in the refrigerator.

"Where do they come from?" his girlfriend wanted to know.

"They just appear. I ate some and they're very good."

She was reluctant, but he talked her into preparing a package.

She agreed they were very good.

"What are you going to do about it?" she asked.

"I don't think there's anything to do about it," he said. "I like fish eggs."

On Sunday, the package they had eaten Saturday had been replaced. They were coming at a steady rate of one a day. Coxe cooked a package for breakfast and took the other two to his parents.

By Tuesday, he was getting tired of the eggs, and by the end of the week, he had four more packages. He succeeded in giving two packages to the neighbors.

At the end of another week, he had eight packages.

He explained to his girlfriend. She suggested they visit all their friends, leaving a package with each of them.

At the end of another two weeks, this method for disposing of the eggs had worn thin. They finally managed to give the last two packages to the landlady.

At the end of still another week, there were seven more packages. Otherwise, the refrigerator was a good buy.

Coxe calculated that, at the present rate, had he left the packages in the compartment, it would have been filled by the end of the month. He felt that once that point was reached, the eggs would stop coming. Should this prove to be incorrect, he was prepared to arrange for some method of commercial distribution for the product.

On schedule, the eggs stopped coming.

He waited two days. No more came. It was over.

He ate the last package.

The refrigerator worked perfectly, and he began to stock it with things freezers are conventionally stocked with.

It was almost two weeks after the last package had appeared, early one Sunday morning, when the doorbell rang.

At the door was a small, nondescript man with a vaguely—and really indefinably—unpleasant aspect. His head was bandaged.

"Mr. Coxe?" he asked.

"That's me."

"May I come in?"

"Come on."

The man seated himself. "Something terrible has happened," he said. "A horrible mistake has been made."

"I'm sorry to hear that. You look as if you were in an accident."

"I was. I've been in the . . . hospital . . . for nearly two months. But to come to the point, Mr. Coxe. I've come about the refrigerator you recently purchased. It was a special refrigerator that was erroneously shipped out of the plant as a second. When I didn't come in, it got shipped out and sold."

"Good refrigerator," Coxe said.

"Perhaps you've noticed . . . ah . . . something unusual about it?"

"It runs okay. For a while there were a bunch of packages of fish eggs in it."

"Fish eggs!" the little man cried in horror. After he had recovered sufficiently, he asked, "You do, of course you do, I'm sure you still have all the . . . little packages?"

"Oh, no," said Coxe.

"NO? Oh, my God. What did you do with them, Mr. Coxe?"

"Ate them."

"You . . . ate . . . them? Ate—? No. You didn't. Not all of them. You couldn't have done that, Mr. Coxe. Please tell me that you could not have done that."

"I had to give a lot of them away, and everybody said they were delicious. And really . . . Uh, Mr.—? Mr., uh . . . ."

The little man got unsteadily to his feet. His face was ashen. "This is horrible, horrible." He stumbled to the door. "You are a fiend. All our work . . . all our plans . . . and you, you . . . " He turned to Coxe. "I hate you. Oh, I hate you."

"Now, see here."

" . . . Mr. Coxe, you'll never realize the enormity of your crime. *You've eaten all of us!*" With that, he slammed the door and was gone.

Coxe went back to the other room.

"Who was it, honey?"

"Ah, some nut. Seems he had first claim on the refrigerator."

"I'll bet it was about the fish eggs."

"Yeah, he wanted them."

"Oh, dear. Do you think he can do anything to us?"

"I don't think so, not now. It's too late," Coxe concluded. "We ate them all."

97

TRY AND CHANGE THE PAST

Fritz Leiber

NO, I WOULDN'T advise anyone to try to change the past, at least not his *personal* past, although changing the *general* past is my business, my fighting business. You see, I'm a Snake in the Change War. Don't back off—human beings, even Resurrected ones engaged in time-fighting, aren't built for outward wriggling and their poison is mostly psychological. "Snake" is slang for the soldiers on our side, like Hun or Reb or Ghibbelin. In the Change War we're trying to alter the past—and it's tricky, brutal work, believe me—at points all over the cosmos, anywhere and anywhen, so that history will be warped to make our side defeat the Spiders. But that's a much bigger story, the biggest in fact, and I'll leave it occupying several planets of microfilm and two asteroids of coded molecules in the files of the High Command.

Change one event in the past and you get a brand new future? Erase the conquests of Alexander by nudging a Neolithic pebble? Extirpate America by pulling up a shoot of Sumerian grain? Brother, that isn't the way it works at all! The space-time continuum's built of stubborn stuff and change is anything but a chain-reaction. Change the past and you start a wave of changes moving futurewards, but it damps out mighty fast. Haven't you ever heard of temporal reluctance, or of the Law of the Conservation of Reality?

Here's a little story that will illustrate my point: This guy was fresh recruited, the Resurrection sweat still wet in his armpits, when he got the idea he'd use the time-traveling power to go back and make a couple of little changes in his past so that his life would take a happier course and maybe, he thought, he wouldn't have to die and get mixed up with Snakes and Spiders at all. It was as if a new-enlisted feuding hillbilly soldier should light out with the high-power rifle they issued him to go back to his mountains and pick off his pet enemies.

Normally, it couldn't ever have happened. Normally, to avoid just this sort of thing, he'd have been shipped straight off to some place a few thousand or million years distant from his point of enlistment and maybe a few light-years, too. But there was a local crisis in the Change War and a lot of routine operations got held up and one new recruit was simply forgotten.

Normally, too, he'd never have been left alone a moment in the Dispatching Room, never even have glimpsed the place except to be rushed through it on arrival and reshipment. But, as I say, there happened to be a crisis, the Snakes were shorthanded, and several soldiers were careless. Afterwards two N.C.'s were busted because of what happened and a First Looey not only lost his commission but was transferred outside the galaxy and the era. But during the crisis this recruit I'm telling you about had opportunity and more to fool around with forbidden things and try out his schemes.

He also had all the details on the last part of his life back in the real world, on his death and its consequences, to mull over and be tempted to change. This wasn't anybody's carelessness. The Snakes give every candidate that information as part of the recruiting pitch. They spot a death coming and the Resurrection Men go back and recruit the person from a point a few minutes or at most a few hours earlier. They explain in uncomfortable detail what's going to happen and wouldn't he rather take the oath and put on scales? I never heard of anybody turning down that offer. Then they lift him from his lifeline in the form of a Doubleganger and from then on, brother, he's a Snake.

So this guy had a clearer picture of his death than of the day he bought his first car, and a masterpiece of morbid irony it was. He was living in a classy penthouse that had belonged to a crazy uncle of his—it even had a midget astronomical observatory, unused for years—but he was stony broke, up to the top of his hair in debt, and due to be dispossessed the next day. He'd never had a real job, always lived off his rich relatives and his wife's, but now he was getting a little too mature for his stern dedication to a life of sponging to be cute. His charming personality, which had been his only asset, was deader from overuse and abuse then he himself would be in a few hours. His crazy uncle would not have anything to do with him any more. His wife was responsible for a lot of the wear and tear on his social-butterfly wings; she had hated him for years, had screamed at him morning to night the way you can only get away with in a penthouse, and was going batty herself. He'd been playing around with another woman, who'd just given him the gate, though he knew his wife would never believe that and would only add a scornful note to her screaming if she did.

It was a lousy evening, smack in the middle of an August heat wave. The Giants were playing a night game with Brooklyn. Two long-run musicals had closed. Wheat had hit a new high. There was a brush fire in California and a war scare in Iran. And tonight a meteor shower was due, according to an astronomical bulletin that had arrived in the morning mail addressed to his uncle—he generally dumped such stuff in the fireplace unopened, but today he had looked at it because he had nothing else to do, either more useful or more intersting.

The phone rang. It was a lawyer. His crazy uncle was dead and in the will there wasn't a word about an Asteroid Search Foundation. Every penny of the fortune went to the no-good nephew.

This same character finally hung up the phone, fighting off a tendency for his heart to spring giddily out of his chest and through the ceiling. Just then his wife came screeching out of the bedroom. She'd received a cute, commiserating, tell-all note from the other woman; she had a gun and announced that she was going to finish him off.

The sweltering atmosphere provided a good background for sardonic catastrophe. The French doors to the roof were open behind him but the air that drifted through was muggy as death. Unnoticed, a couple of meteors streaked faintly across the night sky.

Figuring it would sure dissuade her, he told her about the inheritance. She screamed that he'd just use the money to buy more other women—not an unreasonable prediction—and pulled the trigger.

The danger was minimal. She was at the other end of a big living room, her hand wasn't just shaking, she was waving the nickle-plated revolver as if it were a fan.

The bullet took him right between the eyes. He flopped down, deader than his hopes were before he got the phone call. He saw it happen because as a clincher the Resurrection Men brought him forward as a Doubleganger to witness it invisibly—also standard Snake procedure and not productive of time-complications, incidentally, since Doublegangers don't imprint on reality unless they want to.

They stuck around a bit. His wife looked at the body for a couple of seconds, went to her bedroom, blonded her graying hair by dousing it with two bottles of undiluted peroxide, put on a tarnished gold-lamé evening gown and a bucket of make-up, went back to the living room, sat down at the piano, played ''Country Gardens'' and then shot herself, too.

So that was the little skit, the little double blackout, he had to mull over outside the empty and unguarded Dispatching Room, quite forgotten by its twice-depleted skeleton crew while every available Snake in the sector was helping deal with the local crisis, which centered around the planet Alpha Centauri Four, two million years minus.

Naturally it didn't take him long to figure out that if he went back and gimmicked things so that the first blackout didn't occur, but the second still did, he would be sitting pretty back in the real world and able to devote his inheritance to fulfilling his wife's prediction and other pastimes. He didn't know much about Doublegangers yet and had it figured out that if he didn't die in the real world he'd have no trouble resuming his existence there—maybe it'd even happen automatically.

So this Snake—name kind of fits him, doesn't it?—crossed his fingers and slipped into the Dispatching Room. Dispatching is so simple a child could learn it in five minutes from studying the board. He went back to a point a couple of hours before the tragedy, carefully avoiding the spot where the Resurrection Men had lifted him from his lifeline. He found the revolver in a dresser drawer, unloaded it, checked to make sure there weren't any more cartridges around, and then went ahead a couple of hours, arriving just in time to see himself get the slug between the eyes same as before.

As soon as he got over his disappointment, he realized he'd learned something about Doublegangers he should have known all along, if his mind had been clicking. The bullets he'd lifted were Doublegangers, too; they had disappeared from the real world only at the point in space-time where he'd lifted them, and they had continued to exist, as real as ever, in the earlier and later sections of their lifelines—with the result that the gun was loaded again by the time his wife had grabbed it up.

So this time he set the board so he'd arrive just a few minutes before the tragedy. He lifted the gun, bullets and all, and waited around to make sure it stayed lifted. He figured—rightly—that if he left this space-time sector the gun would reappear in the dresser drawer, and he didn't want his wife getting hold of any gun, even one with a broken lifeline. Afterwards—after his own death was averted, that is—he figured he'd put the gun back in his wife's hand.

Two things reassured him a lot, although he'd been expecting the one and hoping for the other: his wife didn't notice his presence as a Doubleganger and when she went to grab the gun she acted as if it weren't gone and held her right hand just as if there were a gun in it. If he'd studied philosophy, he'd have realized he was witnessing a proof of Leibniz's theory of

Pre-established harmony: that neither atoms nor human beings really affect each other, they just look as if they did.

But anyway he had no time for theories. Still holding the gun, he drifted out into the living room to get a box seat right next to Himself for the big act. Himself didn't notice him any more than his wife had.

His wife came out and spoke her piece same as ever, Himself cringed as if she still had the gun and started to babble about the inheritance, his wife sneered and made as if she were shooting Himself.

Sure enough, there was no shot this time, *and* no mysteriously appearing bullet hole—which was something he'd been afraid of. Himself just stood there dully while his wife made as if she were looking down at a dead body and went back to her bedroom.

He was pretty pleased: this time he actually *had* changed the past. Then Himself slowly glanced around at him, still with that dull look, and slowly came toward him. He was more pleased than ever because he figured now they'd melt together into one man and one lifeline again, and he'd be able to hurry out somewhere and establish an alibi, just to be on the safe side, while his wife suicided.

But it didn't happen quite that way. Himself's look changed from dull to desperate, he came up close . . . and suddenly grabbed the gun and quick as a wink put a thumb to the trigger and shot himself between the eyes. And flopped, same as ever.

Right there he was starting to learn a little—and it was an unpleasant shivery sort of learning—about the Law of the Conservation of Reality. The four-dimensional space-time universe doesn't *like* to be changed, any more than it likes to lose or gain energy or matter. If it *has* to be changed, it'll adjust itself just enough to accept that change and no more. The Conservation of Reality is a sort of Law of Least Action, too. It doesn't matter how improbable the events involved in the adjustment are, just so long as they're possible at all and can be used to patch the established pattern. His death, at this point, was part of the established pattern. If he lived on instead of dying, billions of other compensatory changes would have to be made, covering many years, perhaps centuries, before the old pattern could be re-established, the snarled lifelines woven back into it—and the universe finally go on the same as if his wife had shot him on schedule.

This way the pattern was hardly effected at all. There were powder burns on his forehead that weren't there before, but there weren't any witnesses to the shooting in the first place, so the presence or absence of powder burns didn't matter. The gun way lying on the floor instead of being in his wife's hands, but he had the feeling that when the time came for her to die, she'd wake enough from the pre-established Harmony trance to find it, just as Himself did.

So he'd learned a little about the Conservation of Reality. He also had learned a little about his own character, especially from Himself's last look and act. He'd got a hint that he had been trying to destroy himself for years by the way he'd lived, so that inherited fortune or accidental success couldn't save him, and if his wife hadn't shot him he'd have done it himself in any case. He'd got a hint that Himself hadn't merely been acting as an agent for a self-correcting universe when he grabbed the gun, he'd been acting on his own account, too—the universe, you know, operates by getting people to co-operate.

But, although these ideas occurred to him, he didn't dwell on them, for he figured he'd had a partial success the second time, and the third time if he kept the gun away from Himself, if he dominated himself, as it were, the melting-together would take place and everything else go forward as planned.

He had the dim realization that the universe, like a huge sleepy animal, knew what he was trying to do and was trying to thwart him. This feeling of opposition made him determined to outmaneuver the universe—not the first guy to yield to such a temptation, of course.

And up to a point his tactic worked. The third time he gimmicked the past, everything started to happen just as it did the second time. Himself dragged miserably over to him, looking for the gun, but he had it tucked away and was prepared to hold onto it. Encouragingly, Himself didn't grapple, the look of desperation changed to one of utter hopelessness, and Himself turned away from him and very slowly walked to the French doors and stood looking out into the sweating night. He figured Himself was just getting used to the idea of not dying. There wasn't a breath of air. A couple of meteors streaked across the sky. Then, mixed with the upseeping night sounds of the city, there was a low whirring whistle.

Himself shook a bit, as if he'd had a sudden chill. Then Himself turned around and slumped to the floor in one movement. Between his eyes was a black hole.

Then and there this Snake I'm telling you about decided never again to try and change the past, at least not his personal past. He'd had it, and he'd also acquired a healthy respect for a High Command able to change the past, albeit with difficulty. He scooted back to the Dispatching Room, where a sleepy and surprised Snake gave him a terrific chewing-out and confined him to quarters. The chewing-out didn't bother him too much—he'd acquired a certain fatalism about things. A person's got to learn to accept reality as it is, you know—just as you'd best not be surprised at the way I disappear in a moment or two—I'm a Snake too, remember.

If a statistician is looking for an example of a highly improbable event, he can hardly pick a more vivid one than the chance of a man being hit by a meteorite. And, if he adds the condition that the meteorite hit him between the eyes so as to counterfeit the wound made by a 32-caliber bullet, the improbability becomes astronomical cubed. So how's a person going to outmaneuver a universe that finds it easier to drill a man through the head that way rather than postpone the date of his death?

98

TURNING POINT

Arthur Porges

IT WAS THAT unhappy time when Earth was ruled by the Empire of the Rats. From pole to pole, the word of the Rat Emperor was law, neither to be questioned nor evaded by any rodent nor by any man.

Throughout man's early history, the rat had been one of his chief rivals for dominance, along with the insects. Lacking both the intelligence of such near-men such as the higher apes, and the blind, irresistible fertility of the insects, the rats began with a fair share of the two advantages. Their forepaws were not as dexterous as a monkey's fingers, but distinctly better than hoofs or talons; and their litters, while no match for aphid eggs, were large and viable all over the globe.

Originally small in size—from an inch or two in the case of mice, to a foot or more in some tropical species of cane-rats, and even larger in related species, like the capybara—the rats had profited from man's own belliger-ence and ruthlessness. And his perverted science. The Atomic War that began in 1992 exterminated roughly ninety per cent of all life on earth. Humanity was back to its primitive beginnings, with small, scattered, barbaric tribes surviving in odd corners of the globe. The insects came out best, numerically, but hadn't the genetic stuff to take full advantage of their temporary dominance. The rats, decimated, but much more resistant to hard radiation than man, were favored by nature, inscrutable and capricious as ever in her workings.

The rodents mutated to an unusual degree, becoming not only much bigger, but greatly improved mentally, with a new power of abstraction. When some rat-genius was able to note and understand the connection between two burrows and the idea of a pair, the handwriting was on the wall for anybody to read; but there were few prophets among the remnants of human civilization to interpret the omens.

With their frequent litters, and generations that came and went in hundreds before a man grew old, the rats maintained their vital lead. Before long they were reading, and using, man's own written records, a fair proportion of which had survived the war. Those few communities that still had retained technical competence, fought hard, using rifles, poison, flame, and gas; but were overwhelmed by the enemy, which was willing to die in his thousands to kill or capture a single human.

There was a great deal of irony in the resulting situation. The rats, because of their racial memories of man, were oddly ambivalent towards the species. On the other hand, they remembered, with fury, the traps, ferrets, and agonizing chemicals of the past. But they also recalled, in some queer emotional way, that no brown rat was ever happy living in the wilds away from man—and it was not merely a matter of food and shelter. The rats actually liked to have people around; and even now, when man was subordinate—a conquered race—the rats felt the same way.

Naturally, the humans had no such tolerance; they had always hated and feared rats; and that hadn't changed. An added irony could be found in the relatively merciful treatment afforded man by the Empire of the Rats. People were allowed to live in their own communities, provided the rats had full access to them at all times. A close watch was kept to see that no dangerous weapons were invented or re-built; and above all, reproduction was sternly controlled—the human population was kept absolutely and irrevocably fixed at ten thousand. The rats knew very well that if man was ever allowed unchecked breeding, he would, in his fierceness and intelligence, regain the ascendancy just lost by the Atomic War.

Wise in their reading of history; the rats even had a safety valve for the release of social pressure—the sort built up by fanatical and ingenious malcontents; the Garrisons, Hitlers, Toussaints, and Ghandis of the time. Anybody who so desired, was permitted to emigrate beyond the control of the Emperor. There was one place on earth—a region of South America— where no rat could survive. In those thousands of square miles of steaming jungle, a virus disease had developed that was quickly fatal to rats, but had no effect on man. It is possible that with enough time and trouble—and the doubtful help of human scientists, who were often necessary to rat-technology, and so coddled at need—the rats could have solved the problem, and made the region habitable. But it wasn't worth the effort; there was still plenty of space, since the earth was starting again from scratch, so to speak.

Their tolerance was remarkable. Instead of killing such malcontents, as many human tyrants have done, and unwisely, as it turned out, the rats allowed them to emigrate to the Amazon. But the rodents were not stupid. Anybody who wished to leave had to submit to sterilization; there would be no hidden population explosion in the jungle. Unable to breed, the colony of humans was not a danger to the Empire. Sterilization was accomplished by x-rays and drugs, and great care was taken to make sure it was irreversible by surgery; it was not just a matter of cutting cords in the male, but a thorough operation just short of emasculation, done, of course, in a hospital under the best, most painless, and aseptic conditions. With a woman, the ovaries were removed. A human surgeon could be used, under the supervision of a rat, equally well qualified, but slightly less dextrous, as both species knew.

The mutated rats, it should be pointed out, were still not as big as men, but stood about four feet tall on their hindpaws, the front ones having become very much like hands, but not quite as flexible, lacking a completely opposable thumb. Communication between the two species, strangely, was in English plus an admixture of other human languages. The rats, after all, had learned reading and writing from documents, books, records, and films of their ancient enemy. A rat's voice was still squeaky, but no less lucid than that of a hoarse and excited girl soprano, for example; and people soon learned to catch every nuance of the conversation—or orders.

The rat species had always been community-centered; the rodents liked to live together, and were quick to respond to the calls of any member of the group that was in trouble. So it was natural for the mutants to live in huge rat-cities, built to their own specifications, and above ground, but more than faintly mirroring human areas long since destroyed by nuclear fire.

Unknown to the rats—otherwise it could not have happened—the turning point came on August 20, 2067. A young scientist and his wife had applied for an emigration permit. The rats did not like to see trained humans leave their control but the Emperor's policy was fixed; he and his council believed, as students of history, that it was best to allow malcontents to go away from the community—the farther the better—as long as they were made harmless first.

The Rat-Commissioner of Emigration, who issued the final papers, was a grey-brown rodent slightly smaller than the average, but with very keen, beady eyes, too undersized for his great forehead. His stiff, white whiskers were neatly trimmed. He wore no clothes, not belonging to that tiny, anti-social group of his kind that affected human garb, and spoke of the barbarity of nakedness. There were armed guards, but more as matter of honor and prestige than need. Mankind had no power-weapons, and none

627

could be smuggled into the South American colony: there were too many rats on guard, and they were equipped with keener senses than man, able to see, smell, and whisker-feel in the worst light. Besides, in their immense bureaucracy, patterned after man's own, there were records of everybody's movements, papers to be filled out, and serial numbers for every artifact that might be turned against the Empire. If so much as an ancient revolver was moved from one house to another, the fact was instantly known and evaluated by a computer. Tight control, the rats knew, was their only chance—short of exterminating man—to stay on top. It is to their credit that they never seriously considered genocide.

"Walter Nolan," the Commissioner squeaked. "And wife, Gloria, born Gloria Bandini. Why do you want to leave, Mr. Nolan?"

"It's all down there," was the cold reply. "Why make me repeat it?"

"It says you can't breathe," the rat said. "Have we been so hard on you? You went to a good university; became a fine engineer. We have given you many advantages in pay and privileges."

"I want to be free," Nolan said stubbornly. "You wouldn't understand that."

"I'm afraid not," the Commissioner said, with a note of genuine regret in his voice. His beady eyes twinkled. "You see, when my people were slaves—or at least, not free—we didn't have the intelligence, consciousness, or civilization to know it. We died from poison, terriers, gas, and such horrors as dumb animals, without comprehension."

"I make no excuses," the man said. "Rats—the primitive, early kind, if I have the facts straight—were a great menace to my species. They destroyed more food than they actually ate; they carried dangerous diseases; and even killed or injured children."

"As to that last," was the dry retort, "your slum landlords and thieving politicians were more to blame than my kind, who knew no better, being only insentient brutes at that stage of their evolution." He sighed. "However, I see your mind is made up. But let me point out that we know what many of you are hoping for. You think that once out of our control you can mount a successful revolt against the Empire. Now we understand that a group of intelligent and dedicated men—fanatics—can produce, in spite of our safeguards, a core army, with excellent weapons. But because you can't multiply, and emigration is to be kept at reasonble levels in addition, you can always be overwhelmed if you leave your own country—and it is your own; we never trespass."

"Because you can't, and live."

"That's true; but we could find a suicide squad or two to penetrate the jungle and report before dying of the virus. But our controls make such a sacrifice pointless. Even with a new and potent weapon for each of you, a million rats with automatic arms, artillery, and even tanks, would crush you easily; that's obvious.''

''But no planes,'' Nolan said.

''I admit that we rats have a racial horror of flight, perhaps because of hawks and owls; but neither can you make planes in the jungle villages— not now. If and when you do, a few hundred men can't pilot enough of them to destroy thousands of our communities. And there would be ample warnings; your borders are always watched, as you will learn.''

He picked up the dossier. ''The papers are in order. Your wife has had an ovariotomy, and you are completely sterile—or so it says. But,'' he added, looking at them keenly, ''we never accept mere papers. I'll call the hospital and check with the surgical chief.''

He pressed a lever on his intercom, and was soon through to the hospital listed on the form. After requesting a check, he listened to the squeaky sounds for some moments.

''I see,'' he said. ''She aborted some days earlier. Then you operated. Yes, I understand.'' He turned off the intercom, and again faced the couple. ''The surgeon tells me your wife had a miscarriage a day or two before coming for the required operation.''

''If you must know,'' Nolan said in a hard voice, ''she lost our baby because she so resented having one brought up a slave to rats. It was my idea to have it, anyhow. Now we're going away where if there are no babies, there is freedom from rats.''

''All right,'' the Commissioner said. ''Believe me, I'm sorry—about the baby.'' He stamped the essential passport, handed it to Nolan, and said: ''You know the routine. You and your wife will be escorted to the boundary of the colony, and turned over to a man of your own future community. Good luck, and if you ever want to come back—''

''If I do,'' Nolan said grimly, ''it won't be as a pliant subject of the Emperor, I assure you, but as an armed invader. I give you fair warning. You can search my baggage, and make me sterile, but nobody can ransack or neutralize this.'' He tapped his head.

The Commissioner gave him a grave and steady scrutiny for some seconds, his whiskers bristling. But when he spoke, his voice was level. ''Goodbye, both of you,'' he said. ''Next case, please.'

Once outside the office, Gloria looked anxiously at the guards accompanying them to the bus, but they were well beyond earshot.

''Why so belligerent, for Heaven's sake?'' she asked her husband.

"Were you deliberately trying to make him angry? Did you see his whiskers? He could have canceled us out, you know; then where would we be?"

"I was scared stiff—that call to the hospital. I know they check, but for a minute. I thought he was on to us. So I tried to play the bitter, but planless, malcontent—a guy burned up, but with only generalities to threaten. And it seemed to work—at least, he didn't go into the abortion."

"They don't care about that; I'm not carrying a baby; that's enough for them. And I can't have any more," she added, her voice quivering briefly. "And you—never to be a father."

Once past the borders of the free territory, and heading for the largest community, deep in the jungle, called *Voltaire,* Nolan was quick to reassure their guide.

"It worked," he said, exultation in his voice. "They were completely fooled. Gloria—poor kid—has no ovaries; and me; I'm as sterile as any old mule; but our son is alive, and safe. Not in a little jar—that didn't work out; and anyway, they go through the luggage too thoroughly; even x-rays, which would be fatal. No, Doctor Soburu just implanted the fertile egg in my own peritoneum, where it will be quite all right for several days, at least. As soon as we reach *Voltaire,* one of your surgeons can put it back on the wall of Gloria's womb."

"Right," the guide said. "It should work. And if it does, you two are only the first. Others are coming soon; and even if the rats cut off all emigration later, we need only a few children—they won't be sterile! It took only Adam and Eve to give us 2,000,000,000 people, remember! We're on the way back."

At the Royal Palace, the Emperor of the Rats stirred uneasily in his sleep. As well he might.

99

THE TWERLIK

Jack Sharkey

IT LAY LIKE a blanket over the cool gray sands, its fibrous substance extended to ultimate length in all directions, like a multi-spoked umbrella shorn of its fabric.

From each of its radiated arms—or legs; the Twerlik could employ them as it chose—innumerable wire-like filaments stretched outward at right angles to these limbs, flat upon the gray sands. And from them in turn jutted hair-like cilia, so that the entire body—had it been suitably stained and raised against a contrasting backdrop—resembled nothing so much as an enormous multiplumed fan, opened to a full circle and laid over an area of ten square miles. Yet weighed upon Earth-scales, its entire mass would have been found to tilt the needle barely beyond the one-pound mark. And its arms and filaments and cilia clung so tightly to the sand, and were so pallid of hue, that even were a man to lie face down upon it and stare with all his might, he would not be certain he saw anything but sand beneath him.

It could not break apart, of course. In its substance lay strengths beyond its own comprehension. For the planet upon which it had been born was too distant from its star to have developed cellular life; the Twerlik was a single, indestructible molecule, formed of an uncountable number of interlinked atoms. But—like the radar-grid it resembled—it could see, by the process of subtraction. Mild waves of light from the cold, distant star bathed it eternally. And so, objects that thrust in between the Twerlik and its source of life were recorded as negations upon its sensitive cilia, and the composite blotting-out of the light was sorted and filed and classified in its elongated brain in a fractional instant, so that it knew what went on in its vicinity.

It could see. And it could think. And it could do.

What it did, over endless ages, was convert some of the energy absorbed from the distant star into power. It used the power to work upon the atoms of

631

the gray sand upon which it lay, and at a peripheral rate of about half an inch per Earth year, it turned the sand into its own substance and thus grew. The larger it became, after all, the more its surface could catch the faint light from the star. And the more light it could catch, on its planet whose rotation was equal to its period of revolution, the more sand it could transmute; and the more sand it transmuted the larger it became.

That was its entire cycle of life. The Twerlik was content with it. Absorb, transmute, grow. Absorb, transmute, grow. So long as it could do these things, the Twerlik would be happy.

Then, partway through its hundred billionth trip around the dim, distant star, the men of Earth came.

It's first awareness of their arrival was a sort of bloating sensation, not unlike a mild twinge of nausea, as the cilia far beneath the gleaming fires of the rocket-thrust began hungrily to over-absorb.

The Twerlik did not know what was occurring, exactly, but it soon got itself under control, and would not let those cilia nearest the descending fires partake overly of the unexpected banquet. It made them take a share proportionate to their relationship in size to the rest of the enormous body, and it urged the rest of itself to partake similarly. By the time the slim metal rocket had come down, midway between the outermost fringes of the Twerlik and its splayed-out central brain, the creature had been able to feed more than in the previous three periods of the planetary revolution.

"This thing which has come," it told itself, "is therefore a *good* thing."

It was pleased at this new concept. Until the ship had come, the Twerlik had simply assumed that life was being lived to its peak. Now it knew there were better things. And this necessity to parcel out absorbable energy to its limbs was new, also. It gave the Twerlik a greater awareness of its own brain, as the key motivator of this farflung empire which was itself. "I am a *me*," it realized, "and the rest of my extensions are but my parts!" It almost glowed with delight—not to mention an overload of absorbed energy—at the thought of all it had learned in a few moments. And then it realized what "moments" were, too; until the arrival of the ship, everything had been the same, and so the vast eons it had been there registered as no longer than an eyeblink would to a man, because it had had no shorter events for comparison of time. "So quickly!" the Twerlik mused. "I know what goodness and betterment are; I know that I am a *me*; I know the difference between a moment and an eon."

The Twerlik was abruptly aware, then, of yet another new sensation; gratitude. "This tall thing," it said, and at the same time filed away its first knowledge of differentiation in heights for later reference, "has done the *me* a service, in a moment, and the *me* is *bettered,* and *grateful!*"

And then it knew its first pain, as this rush of new concepts attempted to file themselves in sub-atomic synaptic structures incapable of coping with such a swift influx.

The Twerlik's brain throbbed with this cramming. To ease the pain, it used a fraction of the energy it had absorbed from the fires of the rocket, and enlarged the surface of the thinking-section. Wisely—for it was growing wiser by the moment—it over-enlarged it, that it might not again know pain should more concepts try and engrave themselves upon its consciousness. And just in time, too. For it suddenly needed room for concepts of foresight, prudence, headache, remedy, and alertness.

Being lost in its own introspections, it turned its mind once more to the New Thing on the planet as it felt another increase in the absorption of its cilia. It did some rapid subtraction from the shifts in light from its star, and then it "saw" that there were things like unto itself emerging from the tall thing.

Its brain instantly added the concept of pity to the collection.

For these like-creatures were stunted travesties of the Twerlik. Only four limbs, and a limb-stub on top. And these four fairly developed limbs had but five filaments to each, and no apparent cilia, save upon the useless limb-stub. And the five filaments upon each of the two limbs nearest the *me* were bound up in layers of something that was not part of the creatures at all.

"These magnificent creatures," mourned the Twerlik, "having so little of their own, have yet shared their largesse with me!" For the creatures were bearing bulky objects out of the tall thing, and setting them upon the gray sand and upon the Twerlik itself. And from these objects there flared a great deal of brightness and warmth, and the creatures were standing amid this brightness and warmth, and doing incomprehensible things with four-limbed objects that had no life at all . . . and the cilia of the Twerlik were absorbing all they could of this unexpected feast.

"I can grow now!" it told itself. "I can grow in a short period as I have never in my life grown before. I can spread out until I cover the entire— planet." The Twerlik puzzled over the latest addition to its increasing concepts. From where had this strange idea come, this idea of a gigantic ball of solid material swinging about a star? And it suddenly knew that those other four-limbed non-living creatures were called "chairs" and "tables," and that the poorly developed things were named "men."

The Twerlik tried to solve this puzzle. How were these concepts reaching it? It checked its subtractions, but there was nothing new blocking the starlight. It checked its absorptions, but its rate of drainage upon the spilled-over warmth and light from the "electric heaters" and the "lamps"—and it realized, again enlarging its brain to store these concepts—was just as it had been. Yet these new ideas were reaching it somehow. The ideas came from the "men," but in what manner the Twerlik could not determine.

Then it checked into yet another one of its newfound concepts, "pressure," and found that there was something incomprehensible occurring.

Its first awareness of this concept had been when the "spaceship" ("Larger, brain, larger!") had pressed down upon the limbs and filaments and cilia of the *me*. Then secondary awareness that told the Twerlik of differentiations in "pressure" came when the "men" had trodden upon it, and again when the "chairs" and "tables" and "electric heaters" and "lamps" had been "set up." ("More room, brain, more room!") But there was a new kind of "pressure" upon the *me*. It came and went. And it was sometimes very heavy, sometimes very faint, and it struck only near the "men" at its fullest, being felt elsewhere along the cilia in a "circle" ("Grow!") about them, but less powerfully, and in a larger "circle" about that one, but much less powerfully.

What was it, this thing that came and went, and rammed and fondled and stabbed and caressed, so swiftly, so differently—and all the time kept filling its increasing brain with new concepts?

The Twerlik narrowed its field of concentration, starting at the outermost "circle," moving inward to the next, and drawing closer and closer to the "men," seeking the source of this strange alternating pressure. And then it found it.

It came from the "mouths" of the men. They were "talking." The Twerlik was received "sound."

Its brain began to hurt terribly, and once again it made use of its newly absorbed energies and grew more brainpart for the *me*. Then it "listened" ("More! More!") to the "talking," and began to "learn."

These men were only the first. There would be others, now that they knew that the "air" and "gravitation" and "climate" were "okay." There would be "houses" and "streets" and "children" and "colonization" and "expansion." And—the Twerlik almost shuddered with joy— *light*!

These men-things needed light constantly. They could not "see' without light. There would be more heaters, more lamps, campfires, chandeliers, matches, flares, movies, candles, sparklers, flashlights—("Grow! *Grow!* GROW!")

Right here! On this spot they would begin! And all that spilled over from their wanton use of energy would belong to the *me*!

"Gratitude" was a poor word to express the intensity of the Twerlik's emotions toward these men-things now. It had to help them, had to repay them, had to show them how much their coming meant.

But how? The greatest thing in creation, so far as the Twerlik was concerned, was energy. And they had energy to spare, energy aplenty. It could not give them that as a gift. It had to find out what *they* valued most, and then somehow give this valued thing to them, if it could.

Desperately, it "listened," drawing in concept upon concept, seeking and prying and gleaning and wondering . . . .

It took all that they said, and filed it, cross-indexed it, sorted it, seeking the thing which meant more than anything to these men-things. And slowly, by winnowing away the oddments that cluttered the main stream of the men-things' ambitions and hopes, the Twerlik learned the answer.

And it was within its power to grant!

But it involved motion, and the Twerlik was not certain it knew how motion might be accomplished. In all the eons of adding to its feathery perimeter, it had never had occasion to shift any of its limbs from where they lay upon the sand. It was not quite certain it could do such a thing. Still, it told the *me*, if there were a way, then it was obligated to use this way, no matter what the difficulties thus entailed. Repayment of the men-things was a legitimate debt of honor. It had to be done no matter what the cost.

So it attempted various methods of locomotion.

It tried, first, to flex and wriggle its filaments as the men-things did, but nothing happened. Bewildered, it checked through its file of new concepts and discovered "leverage." On this principle did the men-things move. They had "muscle" which "contracted" and caused a "tendon" to shift the angle of a "bone." The Twerlik had none of these necessary things.

So it tried "propulsion," the force which had moved the spaceship, and discovered that it lacked "combustible fuel" and hollow channels for the energy called "firing tubes" and some built-in condition of these tubes called the "Venturi principle."

It pondered for a long time then, not even bothering with things the men knew as "pistons" and "cylinders" and "wheels"—since the use of these involved a freemoving segment and the Twerlik could not operate save as a whole.

Finally, after thousands of those intervals which it had come to think of as "moments," it came upon the concept of "magnetism." The forces involved came well within its scope.

By subtle control of the electron flow along the underside of one of its five-mile limbs, and the creation of an electronic ''differential'' flow along the top, it found that the consequent repulsion-attempts of its upper and lower surfaces resulted in the tip of the limb describing a ''curl.'' Once this basic motion had been achieved, the rest was simple, for the Twerlik learned swiftly. In a few short moments, it had evolved a thing called ''coordination'' and found to its delight that it could raise, lower or otherwise manipulate limbs, filaments and cilia with ease, in a pleasant, rippling whip-motion.

This new power being tested swiftly and found quite enough for its purposes, it set to work repaying the men for their great kindness to it.

The men, it noted as it worked, were undergoing a strange somnolence called ''sleep,'' inside the spaceship. The Twerlik realized with joy that it could indulge in what men-things called a ''surprise'' if it worked with sufficient rapidity.

Draining its energies with uncaring profligacy, it coiled and swirled and contracted itself until its cilia and filaments and limbs lay all about the spaceship and everywhere within it save upon the men-things. The Twerlik found that it was greatly weakened by this unwonted output, but it was a dedicated Twerlik now, and did not stop its continuation to the task at hand. It worked, and molded, and rearranged. It grew dizzy with the effort, until a stray groping strand of cilum found the energy-crammed metal housed in the tank near the firing-tubes of the spaceship. Into this metal the cilium burrowed, and then began drawing upon the energies therein like an electronic siphon, feeding out the particles of raw powder to the rest of the Twerlik, that the entirety of the creature might perform this labor of love.

It took many thousands of moments for its task to be done, but it was a contented—if desperately weary—Twerlik which finally uncoiled its incredible barely-greater-than-a-pound enormous size from the spaceship.

Once again it retreated in all directions, to lie weakly in the dim light of the distant star and await the awakening of the men-things.

It noted, disinterestedly, that the shape of the spaceship was slightly altered. It was widening slowly near the base, and bulging about the middle, and losing height. The Twerlik did not care. It had shown its gratitude, and that was all that mattered.

Abruptly, men-things were leaping from the doorway of the ship, shouting empty sounds which the Twerlik could only interpret as signs of ''fear,'' though no ''words'' were used. They were—ah, that was the term—''screaming.''

It could make no sense of it. Were the men-things mad? Had it not given them what they desired most? Had it not even worked upon the "food" and "water" for them, so that every item they possessed would be vastly improved?

The Twerlik could not understand why the men were acting so strangely. It waited peacefully for them to use the now-improved heaters and lamps, that it might restore some of its deeply sapped strengths. But they made no move to do so. They were using words, now, having gotten over their "screaming." Words like "trapped" and "impossible" and "doomed."

They were, sensed the Twerlik, terribly unhappy, but it could not comprehend why.

It seemed to have to do with its gesture of repayment. But along this line of reasoning the Twerlik could not proceed without bafflement. It thought momentarily of removing the gift, and restoring things to what they had been, but then realized that it no longer possessed the necessary energies.

So it sat and pondered the ways of men, who seemed to desire nothing so much in life as the acquisition of an element called "gold," and yet acted so oddly when they were given a spaceship made of it.

The Twerlik sadly filed "screwy" in close juxtaposition to the men-concept in its brain, and when at last the men-things had laid upon the gray sand and moved no more, it transmuted their elements into that substance they loved so well with its last burst of waning strength.

Then it lay there upon the cool gray sand, sucking life from the dim, distant star of its planet, and thought and thought about men-things, and wondered if it would ever be satisfied to be nothing but a Twerlik forever, with no more creatures to be good to.

It knew one thing, however. It must not give men gold again.

The next spaceship to land upon its planet, after two revolutions about the sun, was filled with men-things, too.

But these men-things had had an accident to a thing called their "reclamation tanks." They were all thick-tongued and weak, and a quick analysis of their conversation showed the Twerlik that these men were different from the others. They desired nothing so much as a comparatively simple molecule known to them as water.

The Twerlik was only too eager to help.

And, when the transmutation of this second spaceship had been completed, right over the thirsty gray sands, the Twerlik proudly added "permeability" to its vocabulary.

100

WHAT'S YOUR EXCUSE?

Alexei Panshin

WOOLEY'S BEARD AND manner were all that you would expect of any psychology instructor, particularly one how enjoys his work. He leaned back in his swivel chair, his feet on his desk, hands folded behind his neck, and looked at the graduate student who had been sharing his partition-board office for the past two weeks.

"I'm curious about you, Holland," he said. "By my conservative estimate, ninety-five percent of degree candidates in psychology are twitches. What's your problem?"

The room was only about eight feet wide. Holland's desk faced the back of the cubicle, Wooley's faced the door, and there was a narrow aisle between the two. Holland was a teaching assistant and was busy correcting a stack of papers. He looked warily up at Wooley, who had a certain reputation, and then returned his attention to his work.

"No," Wooley said expansively. "On the face of it, I would have said that you had a very low twitch rating."

Wooley's reputation was half for being a throughgoing son of a bitch, half for being fascinating in the classroom. He had a flamboyant, student-attracting personality that was great fun for those he didn't pick for victims.

Holland finished marking the paper and tossed it on the stack he had completed. Then he said, "What is a twitch rating?"

"Don't you know that neuroses and psychoses are old hat? They need a scientific replacement, and for that purpose I have devised the twitch rating. Radiation is measured in curies, noise is measured in decibels— now psychological problems are measured in twitches. I'd rate you about five. That's very low, particularly for a psych student."

Holland flipped his red pencil to the side and leaned back. "You mean

639

you really think that psych students are more . . . disturbed . . . than
. . . .''

"They're twitches," Wooley corrected. "That's why they're psychology students. They're not twitchy *because* they're psych students. What
they want is to learn excuses for the way they act. They don't want to
change it or even, I think, understand it. They want to excuse it—you
know, 'Mama was a boozer, Daddy was a flit, so how can I possibly help
myself?' They learn all the reasons that there are for being twitchy and that
makes them happy.''

Holland cleared his throat and leaned forward to recover his pencil.
Holland was a very serious fellow and not completely sure just how serious
Wooley was, and that made him ill-at-ease.

"Isn't it possible that you are mistaking an itch for a twitch?" he asked.
"Then if somebody scratches, you think he's crazy. But what if their reason
isn't an excuse, what if there is a genuine cause and you just can't see it? If
you want a crude example, is a concentration-camp inmate a paranoid if he
thinks that people are against him?''

"No," Wooley said. "Not unless he's a graduate student in psychology.
In that case I wouldn't make any bets.''

"Well, what are you doing here?''

"I'm observing humanity, what else? Look, I'll give you an example of a
genuine, make-no-mistake-about-it, ninety-five-rating, excuse-making
twitch from right down the hall. Do you know Hector Leith?''

"No. I haven't been here long enough," Holland said. "I don't know
everybody's name yet, and I haven't observed anybody twitching in the
hall.''

Wooley shook his head. "You'd better be careful. You've got the
makings of a very sharp tongue there. Come along." He swung his feet to
the floor and led the way out into the hall.

Holland hesitated for a moment and then shrugged and followed. The
corridor ran between a double row of brown partition-board cubicles. On the
walls of the corridor were photographs, a book-display rack, notices, and
two plaques celebrating the accomplishments of the department's bowling
and softball teams. One of the photographs was of the previous year's crop
of graduate students. Wooley pointed at the shortest person in the picture.

"That's Hector Leith," he said.

"I guess I have seen him around.''

"How old would you say he is?''

Holland looked at the picture and tried to remember the person he'd seen
briefly in the hall. "Not more than eighteen," he said finally.

"He's twenty-seven."

"You're kidding."

"No," Wooley said. "He's twenty-seven, he looks eighteen or less, and he is a genuine twitch."

The person in the photograph was only a few inches more than five feet tall, smooth-cheeked, fresh-faced, elfish-looking. He might possibly have passed for a junior high school student except for his air of tart awareness, and he certainly seemed out of place with the others in the picture. Wooley was there, too, with his beard.

Back in their shared office, Holland returned to his swivel chair while Wooley sat on the edge of his desk.

"Now," Wooley said, "he was drafted by the Army and tossed out after four weeks of emotional instability. I don't hold too much with the Army, but I'd still give him thirty twitch points for that. He started out as a teaching assistant here, but he started twitching in front of the class and now he's a research assistant. You can give him another thirty points for that."

"So what's your diagnosis, Doctor?" Holland said.

Wooley shrugged. "I don't know. Manic-depressive, maybe. One day he'll overflow all over you, try to be friends—try to be buddies and ask you out for a beer. You can't imagine how funny that is between his trying to get into a bar in the first place and the fact that he can't stand beer. He'll tell you all his problems. The next day he won't talk to you at all, hide his little secrets away. And when he's unpleasant, which is more than half the time, he'll leave three-inch scars all over you. Give him fifteen points for that and the last twenty points for his excuses."

"All right. What are they?"

Wooley paused for effect. "He thinks—he says he's finally figured it out—that he's living at a slower rate than most people, and he really isn't grown up yet. He still has to get his physical and emotional growth. He's where everybody else his age was years ago."

"Why does he think that?"

Wooley smiled. "Well, he thinks he is growing. He thinks he's gaining height."

Holland said seriously, "You know, if it were so, it would really be something, wouldn't it? I can see why it would make somebody twitchy. To be that far out of step, not know why, and be incapable of doing what people expect of you would certainly be a burden. You'd be bound to think it was you and that would only make things worse."

"Perfect excuse, isn't it?" Wooley asked drily. "There's only one problem and that is it's just wishful thinking."

"Well, if he's growing . . ."

"He isn't growing. He just thinks he is. Come on and I'll show you."

He led the way down the hall to another cubicle that was similar to their‡ own except that there was only one desk. The extra space was taken up by bookshelves. Wooley flipped on the light.

"Come on in," he said to Holland, and Holland stepped inside.

Wooley pointed to the wall at a point where a wood strip connected pieces of particle board. There were a few faint pencil ticks there, the top and the bottom marks being perhaps an inch and a half apart.

"There," Wooley said. "That's the growing he thinks he's done."

"Only he hasn't?"

"No," Wooley said, chuckling. "I've been moving the marks. I add them on the bottom and erase the top mark. He just keeps putting it back and thinking he's that much taller."

Holland said, "Pardon me. I have work to do." He turned quite deliberately and walked out, his distaste evident.

Wooley said after him, "It's a psychological experiment." But Holland didn't stop.

Wooley shrugged. Then he turned back to the pencil marks and counted them. He then picked a pencil off the desk, erased the topmost mark, and carefully added a mark at the bottom.

Then he tossed the pencil back onto the desk and turned away. Just before he got to the door, Hector Leith came around the corner and into the room. They almost bumped into one another, stopped, and then carefully stepped back.

Leith looked much like his picture: tiny, boyish-looking, incongruous in tie, jacket, and black overcoat. The briefcase he carried was the last touch that made him look like a youngster playing Daddy.

He gave Wooley a bitter look and said, "What are you doing here?"

"Looking for a book."

"Whatever it is, you can't borrow it. Get out of here. Don't think I don't know the trouble you've made for me around here, Wooley. Out."

"All right, all right," Wooley said. "I couldn't find it anyway."

He beat a retreat down the corridor, relieved that Leith hadn't walked in a minute earlier. When he reached his own office, Holland was piling papers on his desk.

"What's this?" Wooley asked.

"I'm not staying," Holland said. "I don't think we're going to work well together. They've got a desk I can use in the department office until they can find me another place."

"What's the matter with you?" Wooley asked. "Why should you leave?"

"What's the matter with you?" Holland asked. "They told me that nobody would stay in an office with you, and I can't stomach you, either. And I'd advise you not to pull any of your tricks on me."

Leith, somewhat strained, closed the door behind Wooley when he left. He wondered if he should have been less harsh. He knew that all it did was make him sound petulant, and that was something he was trying to break himself of, even with Wooley. But it was hard.

He looked then at the strip of wood marked with little pencil lines, and smiled with slightly malicious delight at what he saw. He picked up the pencil that Wooley had abandoned and replaced the tick that had been erased.

The top tick was on the level of his eyes now, perhaps even a little lower, and he wondered how long it would be before Wooley finally noticed.

He said, quite softly, "I'm growing up, Wooley. What's your excuse?"

101

WHILE-YOU-WAIT

Edward Wellen

WHEN THE MULTINATIONAL conglomerate took over the firm Neil Purley had helped build into something worth taking over and told him, in effect, "Sorry, Social Security No. 129-03-7652, but there's nothing you can do that a computer can't do better and more cheaply," Purley burned with a cold flame. If man was no match for the computer's speed, the computer was no match for man's tricky mind.

He would show them. It went deeper than that. He would show himself as well. A man's insight, intelligence, intuition should not go for nothing, be of nothing worth, wither for want of use.

With his severance pay he rented a space, leased equipment, ran an ad. And waited for his first client.

The conglomerate would be his unwitting ally. He would be using the conglomerate's identifying codewords to gain illegal access to the computer. He nicened it up by thinking of it as "timesharing in an unauthorized manner." Still, the upholders of law and order would not look kindly on that. So for safety's sake he had set up his office on the cheesebox principle.

Just as bookies interpose unmanned phones, Purley interposed closed-circuit television. The office the ad directed you to held only a cathode-ray-tube screen, a TV camera, and a client's chair. Purley himself sat at a time-division multiple-access data link in another part of town. The connection would break at the first sign of trouble. The law would never catch Purley red-handed—or touch-tone-fingered.

And that was why his first client seemed slightly puzzled when an image on the screen welcomed him. Parenthetically, the image looked nothing like Purley.

"Please sit down."

The man did not sit down. He held a clipping up to the camera eye. "This mean what it says?"

It said: *WHILE-U-WAIT Computerized Detecting. One-hour maximum per case. The lost found. Fee: (includes all expenses) $500 certified check. Satisfactory job or your money refunded.* And gave the address.

The image smiled. "It means what it says. Let me add up front, though, that we're not a detective agency and don't have a license to operate as such. We don't send operatives gumshoeing around. We're purely and simply a data-processing service that specializes in retrieving information from data banks to help clients retrieve persons, places, and things. We *locate,* in other words; the physical retrieval is up to you."

The man nodded. "That's all I want you to do for me—locate someone, and fast."

"You've brought your certified check for five hundred dollars? Kindly place it in the escrow slot. That's it." Purley scanned the signature, saw the man's name was Albert Uhl. "Now, Mr. Uhl, take note of the time. If we fail to locate your someone inside one hour, you get your check back. All right, Mr. Uhl, who are you looking for?"

Uhl sat down before the visual display. He gave the image a slightly dubious smile, as though suspecting WHILE-U-WAIT relied more on theatrics than on technology. But his need appeared greater than his doubt. He wanted to believe WHILE-YOU-WAIT would help him. And if he had to pay extra for his need by submitting himself to showmanship, he was willing to do so. But he looked a man who would demand results. He leaned forward.

"I'm trying to locate a friend of mine. He's playing around with another man's wife." He paused. "This is all just between us?"

"Of course. Privileged communication. Go on, Mr. Uhl."

"My friend went abroad to meet the woman. What he doesn't know is that the husband knows about them. This husband can be violent. He has a temper—and a gun to go with it. I'm anxious to get in touch with my friend and head him off before he runs into trouble. Only my trouble is I don't know just where he is or what name he's using." He leaned back.

Purley kept the image smiling but in his own person he grimaced in dismay. "We have to have *something* to go on, Mr. Uhl. There can't be feedback without input."

"Sure, I realize that." Swiftly and smoothly Uhl produced a snapshot. "That's why I brought this. It came from somewhere abroad about a week ago. All you have to do is figure out the exact spot it shows. I'll do the rest."

The snapshot, amateurishly blurry, showed a man standing in front of a thatch-roofed cottage. Purley zoomed in on the snapshot. That gave him a bigger blur. He grimaced again, then tapped our instructions for the computer to enhance the snapshot electronically, sharpen it up to make the man's features and those of his surroundings as clear as possible. While the computer worked on the snapshot, Purley picked up on his client.

"That's all you have to go on?"

"Yes."

"Let's try it from the other angles of the triangle. I gather the husband is shadowing the wife to the rendezvous. We can trace them through plane or ship bookings and hotel reservations. You can take a fast jet there and be on the lookout for your friend to warn him. What's the husband's name?"

Uhl frowned. He shook his head. "I don't know that. If I did I wouldn't need you."

"I see." Purley did not see anything but a total blur. If all his cases were going to be like this first one, maybe he had bitten off more than he could chew. "All right, let's see if you can give me a description of your friend."

Uhl's frown deepened. "You have the snapshot."

The image smiled patiently. "It doesn't tell me his age, eye color, height, weight—a few little details like those."

Purley presented a display on the screen in place of the image. The display consisted of a list of physical and social characteristics—sex, race, age, marital status, height, build, weight, complexion, eye color, hair color, scars, and so on. He asked Uhl to take up the light pen attached to the set and tick off his friend's profile.

Something in the tigerish way Uhl moved, the man's reflexes, plus his almost willful lack of helpful input, the failure to supply the husband's name, gave Purley to think again. He did not let the light pen work.

"Sorry, Mr. Uhl. The light pen seems to be out of order. But the computer can sense it just as well if you use your finger."

Uhl hesitated a fraction of a second, then touched his finger to the screen to indicate his friend's characteristics.

"Fine." Purley winked out the display and presented his surrogate image again. "While we work on what we have, you can relax and listen to music. Do you have any preferences?"

The man stared. "No, no preferences."

"All right." Purley faded the image from the screen and let Uhl enjoy Montovani and colored lights that pulsed to the soothing strains.

Purley himself felt far from relaxed. Uhl bothered him. While working on locating Uhl's friend, it would not hurt to get a make on Uhl.

Besides recording Uhl's state of tension in his finger tremors as he touched the screen, the computer had registered Uhl's fingerprint. Uhl seemed the right age and the right physique to have served in Vietnam. Subsidiaries of the conglomerate that had found Purley redundant did national defense work. If you knew the codeword, you had access to Department of Defense files. Purley knew the codeword. He had the computer classify Uhl's fingerprint and look for the print's match among the whorls, loops, and arches of all those who had served in the armed forces.

It took two minutes. The fingerprint matched the right index finger of one Steve Kinzel.

Purley retrieved Kinzel's service record. Kinzel had received a less-than-honorable discharge from the Army—but not before winning every sharpshooting award the Army had to offer.

Using the conglomerate's plant-security contact with the FBI—another codeword—Purley patched into the National Criminal Identification Center in Washington.

Steve Kinzel's FBI yellow sheet showed that the FBI's antisyndicate task force suspected Kinzel of being a hit man with a long string of contracts to his credit. Never caught in the act.

Purley eyed Uhl-Kinzel through the camera. The man sat seemingly relaxed, sound-bathing. A sunning snake looks relaxed. Purley felt a hollow tightness in his belly.

The hit-man angle would seem to rule out the possibility Purley had been considering—that his client was the husband in the story he had fed Purley.

But the purpose in hiring WHILE-U-WAIT remained the same. Even stronger. To locate and waste the "friend."

Purley turned to the enhanced snapshot on one of his screens. The computer had made a number of identifications and deductions.

The architecture put the cottage in the British Isles. The thatched roof was not of the kind you find in Suffolk, Essex, or Cambridgeshire; there the roof cocks up at the gable end. This cottage stood rather in a western or southwestern county, where the gables droop or have hipped hoods. That narrowed it down to Cornwall, Devon, or Somersetshire.

The gentle swells of land visible in the distance further narrowed it down to Somersetshire. Purley blew up white dots on the nearest slope into grazing sheep—Southdown breed, the computer said after a nanosecond's glance at its memory banks.

A speck in the snapshot's sky blew up into a seagull. The computer gazed at its gazetteer. The hills would be the Mendip Hills, the seagull's drink would be the Mouth of the Severn.

In short, the cottage stood on property near a Southdown sheep pasturage some five miles southeast of Weston-super-Mare.

The front of the cottage had a freshly whitewashed look. The man posing in front of it had probably just recently taken possession. The foliage of the oak tree dominating the grounds told Purley the man had taken possession of it in early spring. The shape of the oak tree also showed the orientation—the northern branches reaching for light, the southern branches taking it easy. Therefore the road the cottage faced on ran east and west.

Shadows showed it to be mid-afternoon; they also helped Purley and the computer, using the man's height as a yardstick, to determine the dimensions of the cottage. Only the man's identity remained in shadow.

Purley turned to his "blue box" an electronic device for placing overseas calls without paying for them. He put through a call to Taunton, the county town of Somersetshire.

There Purley found an obliging records clerk. The important sound of "overseas call," plus Purley's tone of urgency, proved contagious. Inside of five minutes she identified the property from Purley's detailed description and came up with the name of the present owner of Oak Cottage.

Roger Nugent.

It was all over. Investigation successfully completed, fee earned. He had not bitten off more than he could chew. Purley now had all the information his client wanted. All that remained was to astonish the client by letting the image smile modestly and say, "Your man is Roger Nugent, at Oak Cottage, between Weston-super-Mare and Axbridge, in Somerset, England."

Purley stole another look at Uhl-Kinzel. He saw beneath the relaxed form the unsoothed beast. Purley glanced at the hour. He decided to stall the man another ten minutes.

Through the computer of a correspondent bank obligating and obligated to the conglomerate, Purley determined that Roger Nugent had paid for Oak Cottage with funds from a Taunton bank account. Purley backtracked the deposits, following a suspiciously complex trail.

He traced the laundered money in Nugent's account ultimately to a U.S. Justice Department special fund. The pattern of payments told him Roger Nugent's name had been Larry Shedd.

Now Purley knew why his client had been shy about telling WHILE-U-WAIT the missing man's name up front. Anyone who kept up with the news would have recognized the name Larry Shedd and have realized the phoniness of the love-triangle tale.

Larry Shedd, before disappearing and surfacing as Roger Nugent, had testified before a Senate committee looking into the activities of a leading crime-syndicate figure, Vincent Minturn. Minturn, according to ''reliable sources,'' had put an open $500,000 contract out on Larry Shedd.

Because of this contract, the Justice Department had paid for plastic surgery on Larry Shedd, spirited him out of the country, and set him up under a new identity. Away from hit men, away from front pages.

WHILE-U-WAIT's client was not a newspaperman. His reason for discovering Shedd's present identity and whereabouts was not to expand on Shedd's life story but to contract Shedd's life span.

WHILE-U-WAIT's client's client had to be Vincent Minturn.

Purley glanced again at the hour and quickly followed up the Minturn lead.

A search of the computerized morgue of the largest wire service—the conglomerate whose facilities Purley was borrowing owned newspapers and radio and TV stations—turned up that Minturn, like Shedd, was hiding out under another name somewhere overseas.

Minturn had slipped out from under FBI and Interpol surveillance to evade a grand jury investigation arising out of the Senate hearings. Minturn had often voiced his love for the American way of life and his scorn for all other ways, but he dared not risk returning as long as Shedd lived to testify against him. The $500,000 contract was a measure of that love.

Purley smiled an unlovely smile. It had hit him that Minturn and the conglomerate had a lot in common. Money was root, stem, and flower of the evil they did. He had no self-pity, but he thought *poor Shedd*.

While he was at it, he had the computer look up everything the wire-service morgue had on Shedd. The latest reference to the vanished Shedd appeared in an item about a minor burglary a week ago at a Chicago nursing home. The minor burglary had a major outcome. Larry Shedd's aging and ailing mother had died of shock shortly after the intrusion, though as far as anyone knew, nothing of any worth was missing.

Purley knew what was missing.

The snapshot.

Shedd-Nugent had mailed it to his failing and fearful mother to reassure her that he was alive and well and doing fine . . . somewhere. He must have had sense enough to arrange for the envelope to bear a misleading post-mark. Otherwise, Uhl would not have needed WHILE-U-WAIT's help.

A thought burned bright in Purley's mind. But for it to become deed required Minturn's present identity and whereabouts.

Purley had not even a blurred amateurish snapshot to help him locate Minturn. A glance at the hour told him time was running out.

He staked all on his only handle on Minturn—Minturn's yearning for America.

According to news accounts, Minturn had haunted the hangouts of the show-biz crowd. He would be homesick for these haunts, eager for some reminder or taste of them.

Again Purley twitched the conglomerate's tentacles. He traced all overseas air shipments of Lindy's cheesecake, Nathan's hot dogs, and Stage Door Delicatessen pastrami in the past month. He narrowed the field to one Frank Fratto in Rome.

Fratto's Rome bank account led back to a Stateside account of Vincent Minturn's that Minturn had cleaned out just before disappearing. Fratto's handwriting on his bank signature card matched Minturn's on his—there were distinctive *t*'s. The computer gave it as a 98.6666 percent probability that Frank Fratto was Vincent Minturn.

The man's checking account gave Purley the man's present address—a Rome hotel. The checks led Purley to invoices of places where Fratto shopped. Among the earliest purchases were a red-brown wig and prescription sunglasses. Best of all, the measurements on file at the leading Rome tailor's for Fratto's new suits reassured Purley that Fratto had roughly Nugent's build.

Purley switched off Montovani and the lights and threw his smiling surrogate image at his client.

Uhl leaned forward. "The hour's up. Do you have a name and a place?"

Purley gave him a name and—"He's not where you might think he'd be"—a place.

Uhl sat staring at the image. "Are you sure you got the right man?"

The image drew itself up. "We're 98.6666 percent sure."

Uhl smiled. "That's good enough for me." He got up to go but stopped to shake his head. "I wish I knew how you—" He shrugged. "No time. I have to catch a plane. So long."

"Good-by."

Purley watched Uhl set out toward his doom. He sat bemused awhile, then stirred himself to forge and send an IPCQ alert—Interpol Paris to all national bureaus—warning the *carabinieri* in Italy to be on the lookout for the arrival of Steve Kinzel, a.k.a. Albert Uhl, suspected hit man. The Italian police would tail him and should catch him red-handed, trigger-fingered, gunning down Frank Fratto, a.k.a. Vincent Minturn.

WHILE-U-WAIT awaited its next client.